DOWNFALL AND RISE

CHALLENGER'S CALL BOOK ONE

NATHAN THOMPSON

CONTENTS

This work is dedicated to my mother and everyone else out there battling chronic pain. Thank you for your example of never giving up.

PROLOGUE

Beep...Beep...BLARE!!

The alarm went off, scattering sleep from my brain. I rolled painfully over and swung my shaking hand at it, still missing despite years of practice. Slapping the bedside table sent new waves of pain down my arm and into my brain, and with the alarm going off it felt like the entire world was screaming in my skull. Every nerve in my body wanted to smother the sound with a pillow and go back to bed.

I fought through it anyway, and this time, all my practice helped. I pressed the off button—not snooze, because those people are crazy—and reached for my next item. Groping around, my dizziness cleared enough for me to finally find the grip of my cane. I grabbed it, then gave myself a ten count to see how bad the pain was going to be this morning.

One...three...five...eleven...twelve... okay, it was going to be bad.

But I couldn't let that stop me. It didn't mean that it would stay this bad the whole day and mornings were always the worst time anyway. And I didn't have time to wait for it to get better, not if I wanted to try treatment before school. With a deep breath and a careful heave, I pulled myself onto my unsteady feet.

The pain beginning in my skull and running throughout my entire body argued with me the whole way.

You're wasting your time, get back in bed so that you can finally hurt less.

Liar, I told my pain. I wasn't wasting my time, and we both knew it wasn't going to get any better if I laid back down.

You're still wasting your time. You hurt just as much now as you do every morning. The treatment doesn't work.

Liar, I told my pain again. The doctor's records showed improvement to my condition, improvement I didn't have before the treatment. And I didn't hurt just as much today as I did every day, I hurt *worse*. I always hurt worse on important days. That made the treatment matter even more. I went back to concentrating on walking down the hallway, using my cane to find ground every time my feet got confused.

You don't know if you'll get better permanently. Maybe it won't work this time. Maybe you'll still screw up today, just like you always have on big days.

I called my pain a liar again. I used to do great on important days before it was there, and I was going to figure out how to do so again. Using my cane and the wall, I turned the corner into another room.

You're just trying to be positive. Treatment always puts you in a good mood and you'd agree to it even if it didn't work.

That might actually be true, I admitted as I reached for the VR gaming harness. But I didn't care. I fastened the helmet onto my head.

1

FIRST TEST

The ground shook. And the air itself roared.

I lowered my helmeted head to keep the whirling dust out of my face. I shifted and bent my armored knees to deal with the cracking, rattling ground under my nailed boots. Encased in steel, I closed my eyes to the distractions around me, to let the dust ping uselessly off my armor and the ground shake impotently under my feet.

Because if I lost focus, the monster was going to kill us all.

Chevelross the Canyon Dragon, Lord of the Navrahai Crevice. I didn't need to see him to remember his appearance. Thirty yards of taut muscles rippling under mud-brown scales. Talons and teeth like rusty gray swords. A claw full of such talons had slammed into the canyon floor earlier, and the ground had been shaking ever since.

My teammates were scrambling over the uneven terrain right now, but it was preventing them from fighting properly. Those with weapons were having a nightmare of a time trying to dodge the dragon's teeth and claws over uneven ground, while those who could use magic were even more impaired. The stinging wind brought too much sound and pain to concentrate on anything but the simplest spells, and those were not enough to bring down the canyon's dread lord.

So it really was up to me. If this didn't work, we were all going to die.

Unlike most of the other adventurers, I could work magic in heavy armor.

This meant my helmet got in the way of the stinging dust and the padding inside dealt with the ringing noise. The hobnail boots I had chosen to wear under my sabatons kept me from shaking too much. So as rock and air raged about me, I spread my hands to work the one spell that could hopefully change the situation:

"Let a fair wind be at our back,
Let firm ground be beneath our feet,
As we journey on this long, long road,
Grant us this small mercy."

I brought my hands together to finish the blessing, and golden light spread out from my gauntlets. A loud *crack* tore through the rest of the noise, and then the air grew still. The rumbling below my feet also ceased, and I tore forward into a run, fingers reaching for the massive warhammer on my back.

"It worked!" I shouted. "Reposition and attack!"

Chevelross still had one monstrous claw pressed into the ground, but as the tremors ceased, it stopped roaring and pitched forward, looking down at its claw in surprise. The dragon whipped its massive head to the right, then to the left, uncertain, and flapped its giant wings twice.

But we'd never know if it was planning to escape to the air, because we weren't going to give it that chance.

Having recovered their footing, the warriors around Chevelross renewed their assault. Several leather-clad figures leaped through the air and shredded both wings with their blades, while others in heavier armor interposed themselves between the dragon's still-dangerous limbs and their more vulnerable friends.

As Chevelross reared back to deal with the many-weapon swarm, lightning bolts and flaming arrows slammed into the dragon, as the mages and archers were finally able to bring their own weapons into play. The trapped dragon rocked and swayed, unbalanced with both wings shredded and its right foreclaw still stuck deep into the ground.

In another moment of inspiration, I slammed my own hammer down onto Chevelross's trapped claw, then onto the dragon's elbow, over and over, until I could hear its bones crunch.

Chevelross howled impotently while collapsing on three legs, stubbornly trying to rise back into a standing position. As its neck fell close to the ground, a leather-clad form darted across it, spinning and whipping his short, glowing blades all across the dragon's sinuous, less-armored throat. The howl turned into a whimper as arterial spray gushed from the red dagger-lines my companion had left in his wake.

Chevelross gave a final shudder, and then its remaining appendages gave out and collapsed to the ground in a giant cloud of dust. The survivors gathered around it let out a throaty cheer.

Attention! Chevelross the Canyon Dragon has been slain by the Gray Companions and the following un-guilded players: Paladin Player Faren! This is a server first! Congratulations to the players who have unlocked this achievement!

And because we were the first people to kill this monster on *any* of the game's servers...

Attention! Chevelross the Canyon Dragon has been slain by the Gray Companions and the following un-guilded players: Paladin Player Faren! This is a world first! Congratulations to the players who have unlocked this unique achievement!

Other updates scrolled across my interface, including the fact that I had finally hit max level. I had been trying to remain cool up to this point, but the fact that I had reached 70 on a raid boss caused me to crack a smile. Raid bosses, especially ones that had never been killed before, were usually only attempted by at least twenty, usually forty, max-level players. The fact that I had not done so and still played such a factor in its death was huge news, and I pumped a fist into the air so hard I worried I might somehow break my VR gear.

The rogue that had landed the finishing blow came up behind me and slapped me hard on the shoulder. The Australian player nearly blew out my eardrum with his enthusiasm:

"Congrats, mate! Con-GRATS!" Skybladex shouted. "You are officially now one of the top twenty bad-asses in *Heroes Unbound!*"

"Thanks, Sky," I said with a wince. "Great kill-move on the boss, by the way."

"Kill-move nothing!" Sky replied, still shouting. "We beat the thing and it was because of you! You found a way to fix a freaking earthquake! How the hell did you figure that out?"

"A really good guess," I replied. "Unsteady ground and heavy wind are classified as travel debuffs, so I used the paladin travel chant to see if it would help here. It worked way better than I thought it would."

"No way!" one of the other players said. "That spell's like level 15! It never helps in raids!"

"That's because most raid bosses do things like set the ground on fire or rain lightning on you," I replied. "The idea for that is to move around or to hunker down and weather the effects. This one triggered natural environmental conditions that affected your senses and balance, and the effect lasted indefinitely. You can't dodge it or outlast it, but it's the exact sort of thing the travel spell is supposed to help with. So it worked here."

"That's still amazing, mate," Skybladex stated. "This boss has been out for over a month and none of the other raiding guilds have cleared it yet. You were the first one to figure it out, and you're not even in a raiding guild!"

"Yeah," I remembered uncomfortably. "Not these days."

Before the expansion, back when the max level was 60, I had been part of one of the more well-known raiding guilds. We had cleared up to the middle part of the Dread Citadel before my...condition... had kept me from being a consistent member. Then it was scrambling to see what could help with my pain, balance and memory issues. I had tried to keep in contact with the guild but the treatments had become too frequent for me to be involved, and since I was embarrassed at the time, I just told them I was leaving for health reasons that I preferred not to explain.

And I still didn't prefer to explain them, and Sky knew it, so he gave it an awkward smile and left it at that.

"Congrats again, mate," he repeated. "If nothing else, this sure as hell shows you've still got it!"

"Thanks man," I replied, grinning again, because I was truly grateful. "And thanks everyone, for coming to raid with me this morning. This was the only time I could make it."

"Pssht," Sky sputtered. "It's seven pm over here in Australia, silly American. The only inconvenience for us is to just not eat dinner so early."

"Well, I appreciate it all the same," I replied. "You're the only guys that play with me these days..."

"Hey this is really sweet and all but can we loot now?" the tank asked. His name was Turtlepants. He had managed to keep the dragon's attention focused almost entirely on him, for the entire fight, despite the horrible beating he had taken during the process. Great player, terrible name.

"Yeah, let's go for it," I said as Sky nodded to Turtle. I was ready for a change of conversation anyway. "This is a world first, so he's got to have some pretty special treasure, right?"

Every single monster in this game carried treasure, and raid bosses always had the best treasure. Everyone knew that. You kill things, then you take their stuff. Bad advice for real-world living, but it's how you get ahead and have fun in *Heroes Unbound*.

Aragonas, the lootmaster—the player in charge of making sure everyone got a fair shot at the treasure—knelt by the lootable corpse and began inspecting it.

"Let's see," he began. "The Canyon Dragon's Aegis, a shield with really good defensive stats—"

"I'll take it!"

"There you go Turtle. Congrats on cementing your role as the monster abuse magnet."

"Damn straight!" Turtle replied.

Everyone else just smiled and nodded uncomfortably. These days, when games were designed to actually let you feel a tiny fraction of your character's pain through the neural link in the complex VR harness, people who wanted to hold a monster's aggression were considered to be a little strange. Necessary and appreciated, but not quite understood.

"Aaaanyway," Aragonas continued. "There's also some Ancestral Foot Wraps—leg gear with a boost to intellect and mana regeneration. Do you want them, Triumph?"

"Nah," Triumph said with typical Aussie good nature. "Give 'em to Fatuzen. They'll be a bigger boost for him."

There were a few more pieces of loot—a Dragon-bone knife that Skybladex claimed, a Tribal Dream-Catcher that a shaman player was supposed to equip and use somehow, some generic Shoulderplates of the Whale that no one wanted and was marked to vendoring, and then Aragonas stopped looting for some reason.

"Well," he said. "I guess we can try and skin the corpse. Can dragons be skinned?"

"Hey wait," I interrupted. "What about the rest of the loot?"

"That's all the corpse has on him, Faren," Aragonas replied. "Sorry there wasn't anything you could use."

"Do you want the shield, Faren?" Turtlepants offered, generously but understandably uncomfortably. I had played a key role in bringing the monster down and everyone wanted me to feel like I had been treated fairly. "Technically paladins can use it."

"No-no," I said quickly. "Keep the shield. Please, keep the shield. I just asked because the boss is still showing as lootable to my character."

"That's weird," Aragonas replied. "He shows up as empty to me. Skyblade, do you want to take a look too?"

As guildmaster and raid leader, Skybladex had the game-given privilege to double-check the lootmaster.

"Shows as empty to me, too, Faren. Sorry. Is anyone else seeing the corpse as lootable?"

A chorus of "no"s and "no, sorry"s answered him back.

"Sorry," I said. "Maybe it's a bug?"

Or maybe my condition is finally affecting me inside the game. I tried not to think about that.

"Well, the mob's showing as un-skinnable right now anyway, Faren. Go ahead and check it." Skybladex offered.

"You sure?" I asked. I didn't want to make him or Aragonas look shady. *And one small piece of gear really wasn't worth making a scene over*, I admonished myself.

"Yeah, why not?" Sky replied. "It's not like you're taking something from us if no one else can touch or see the loot. Maybe you just got a unique drop."

"Seriously, go for it, Faren," Triumph said. "You figured out how to kill the thing. None of us care if the game rewards you for it."

The rest of the guild echoed Sky and Triumph, so I walked up to the corpse and activating the looting sequence—again, something only the lootmaster and raid leader should be able to do.

"You have to tell us what you get though," Turtle shouted.

"And if it's cake you have to share!" Fatuzen yelled. "Especially if it's magic cake!"

"Or beer!"

"Yes!" That started off a chant faster than I had thought possible. "Beer! Beer! Beer!"

The entire guild took up the chant. I laughed and just focused on getting through the abnormally long looting sequence.

"It's a...."

Someone began drumming. The "beer" chants faded just enough for me to be heard.

"...Ancient Weathered Handle."

Silence.

"That's not beer," someone pointed out. A couple people chuckled. But looking back, I think most of the Aussies really were half-expecting me to deliver on virtual beer.

"Congrats...?" Sky half-offered, half-asked.

"Maybe?" I half-answered. "No stats on it, and it's un-equipable. Says it's trash-level loot..."

The guild groaned in sympathy.

"But also Unique," I finished.

The groans turned from sympathetic to confused.

"Doesn't that mean you can't give it away or destroy it?" Sky asked.

"I think so," I replied, trying to move the item to a trade window, and sure enough, getting an error message. "Yeah, I'm stuck with it."

"That... doesn't make sense," Triumph said, and he was right. The game had, for all appearances, rewarded my world-first kill of a supposedly unbeatable monster with an item that I could neither use nor get rid of.

"Gotta be a quest item somehow," I decided, and most people agreed with me. "Not sure how I start the quest with it though—there's no description to it."

"Maybe you can take it to an NPC," Skybladex offered, an NPC being a Non-Player-Character.

"Yeah, maybe," I replied, though I had no idea which NPC would want it. "But I need to go get ready for school now."

"You have fun with that mate. We're all going to a local bar for some real beer, then log on the forums and brag to the Koreans that they don't have the number one raiding guild anymore."

"Hey lay off!" Turtlepants shouted. "My grandmother's Korean!"

"Well she doesn't have the number one raiding guild anymore now, does she?" Sky shot back.

"Or any Aussie beer!" Fatuzen taunted.

"Like hell she doesn't! She can out-drink all you bastards!"

Smiling, I left my Australian friends to celebrate and began to log off, reflecting off my accomplishments.

Because if I can handle a ninety-foot long dragon *here*, I can sure handle my own body out *there*.

Logging off in thirty seconds! Thank you for playing Heroes Unbound!

The world went black, and then bright again. The throbbing headache that had left me when I crawled into the harness returned, and this time it coupled with the disorientation of leaving the simulated world of the game. I waited a few moments for part of the dizziness to pass, then I began to remove my VR helmet and harness, wincing as my eyes were re-exposed to normal light.

I heard my mother shouting from across the house. She wanted me to wake up and get ready for school, unaware that I was way ahead of her. I stumbled into the bathroom to shower and freshen up for the day. As I pulled my way around the bathroom counter, I used the bathroom mirror to look over myself.

I looked a little different than I did back before my condition developed. My once vibrant red hair had faded slightly, supposedly due to pain and stress. I was still tall and lean, but my muscle tone had taken a toll and they sagged visibly—at least to me, I had no idea what other people saw. As always, my hands and feet trembled slightly. *But none of that mattered*, I told the man in the mirror.

"You have already done the impossible," I said to myself. "The rest of the day will be no different, including the exams.

"Today is going to be a good day," I added.

When I stepped out of the bathroom, I could still hear my mom shouting.

"Wes Malcolm, I've been calling you for ten minutes! Get out of the game and get ready for school!"

"I heard you Mom! I'm already out and showered!"

Ow, I said inside my head. Loud noises made everything hurt worse, and if Mom wasn't so stressed about today, she'd remember that. *I'd better try and hurry to the kitchen before she starts really freaking out,* I thought to myself.

I headed to the kitchen, keeping a hand to the wall just in case I needed it to keep from falling.

But I made it the whole way. Another huge victory.

Today was going to be a good day.

2

SECOND STEP

"Now you know how important this test is..." my mother began in the car. Sarah Malcolm was a beautiful but tired-looking woman with short blonde hair that had somehow still hadn't gone gray yet, despite being a widow and having to deal with my condition.

"Yes, Mom," I replied. She was stressed, but that was okay. I just had to deal with it until I aced my tests. "It's actually three tests. That they moved to one day for me."

"To accommodate you," she said, sounding tense. "One final time."

She will not get to me today, I said firmly in my mind. *Today is going to be a good day.*

"I know Mom," I said, trying to grin. "I get that it's a big deal. Seriously. This is my last chance to keep my scholarship. To keep the future I've worked so hard for—"

"*We've* worked for," she corrected firmly. "You haven't been alone in this. Your sister and I have been right with you. We've both sacrificed to help you make your dreams come true."

I turned to look at her. Where the hell did *that* come from?

"I know, Mother," I said, trying to keep the frustration out of my voice. "I'm grateful for the both of you. Thank you, really. I love you guys."

She was still looking forward, her hands on the steering wheel of the car.

"I just want to make sure you're taking this seriously."

"Why the h—" I caught myself from swearing. For better or for worse, I've stuck to a lot of the habits Dad ingrained in me. Even after his suicide, and finding out about his double life, I still couldn't bring myself to disappoint him by swearing at my mother like most of my eighteen-year old classmates did.

"Mom," I tried again. "Why wouldn't I be taking this seriously? This is my life."

"You know what I'm worried about," she replied tensely.

No, I honestly don't, I wanted to shout, but shouting would hurt my head and I didn't want to turn this into a fight. *Today is going to be a good day,* I reminded myself.

"Is this about the game?" I finally asked. "The game that you let me play because the doctors told us that it would help me improve my condition? The one that I use to focus better, remember more, work on my coordination? The one I was playing this morning to help me get ready for the tests?"

Mom looked uncomfortable. I had to remind myself that she was as worried about today as I was trying not to be.

"I'm just concerned about you," she finally said. "I just want to make sure you're not using this game to cope instead of using it to help you."

The way you're still using wine to cope with Dad's suicide? I didn't ask. I'd had way too much practice fighting with Mom these days—these years, actually. I knew what would happen if I said certain things to her right now, just like how I knew I'd react to her saying certain things to me. Then that would ruin my good mood, my morning, and possibly my tests and scholarship.

Today is going to be a good day, I told myself once more. *Even if I have to work to keep it that way.*

"Well Mom, I really don't know how to answer that," I finally said, and she stiffened. Being too serious, and too calm, reminded her of Dad. A lot of things I did reminded her of Dad, and thanks to what he did, that was a bad thing now. But I couldn't help it, because being calm seemed like the right idea right now.

"Look, if it helps you understand," I continued, "I tried to play in a way that would help me today. The Aussies helped me pick a spot in the game that would simulate a lot of what I normally feel when my body starts freaking out, like where it was hard to concentrate, move, and remember things. That's happened to me every time I've tested so far, so I wanted to practice against that condition. That's why I got up so early to play—and why I've been playing after studying every day this month."

"Okay," Mother answered, still focusing on driving me to school. She was obviously still worried, and probably still tense over me sounding like Dad. But she was trying to get past this too, and I had to give her some slack or we'd fight again.

"So..." she finally continued. "How did it go?"

She was trying to show interest. That was a good sign.

"The Aussies and I fought a dragon that screamed in our ears and made the ground shake under us. I was able to figure out how to counter the effect and we killed it on our first try."

"Really?" she asked, eyes widening and brightening up a little. "That's... good, right?"

I smiled. *I knew it. Today is going to be a good day.*

"Yeah, it's great, actually. World-first kill. That means no one else has been able to do so on any of the game's servers—not even the best raiding guilds, in any country. Gaming news groups and the game's company itself like to sponsor interviews for players who pull off victories like this. I was going to tell you after the test, but I checked my email on the way out and I've already gotten an interview request. Sometimes there are even small rewards—cash or other prizes, to really spice up interest in the content. It's too early to tell if I've gotten that though."

"Really?" she said, actually sounding impressed, in spite of the fact that she hated games, and hated anything else that reminded her of Dad. "That sounds incredible, honey."

I didn't like it when she called me 'honey,' but I overlooked it because it had been a while since Mom sounded this impressed with me.

"Since I logged off early," I continued, really wanting to milk this approval for all it was worth, "I tried going over all the study questions you and I have been reviewing together this month. I was able to remember the answers to fifty math, fifty science, and fifty English. That's the total number of my practice questions, right?"

Mom nodded.

"Good. I've also been able to walk down all the halls in the house without stumbling. My head feels better than it's felt in months. Maybe even years."

Mom was smiling now too. Another rare victory. All in one day.

I was determined to make them count.

We finally pulled up to the school. I looked at all the other students walking outside, then began to gather my things and open the door.

"Wesley, honey?" Mom said as I put my hand on the door.

Uh-oh. My full first name usually meant trouble. But I still chose to hear her out.

"Yeah Mom?"

"Can you please do me a favor?"

I knew that look. She looked tense, as if she was preparing for another fight.

That was a bad sign.

"What do you want, Mom?" I asked carefully, not leaving the car yet. Even though I knew staying to hear her out would be a bad idea.

"I want you to wear the helmet today."

I needed to rethink that swearing stance with her.

Because, well, *shit*.

"I don't think that's a good idea, Mom."

Because it really, really, wasn't.

"Honey if you fall and hurt your head, today of all days, it could undo all your hard work."

I sighed.

"That's why it's a bad idea, Mother. We've talked about this."

My classmates were, objectively, assholes. Well, okay. Not all of them. But there were enough jocks who still hated me from my old football days and who also decided that I was different enough on top of that to be a target. Wearing the leather helmet around my head, on top of carrying the cane I walked around with, would bring every asshole's "hit or push this guy" impulse straight to the front of their little brains.

The problem was, despite the frequency of these events, no one had ever believed me. The jerks had always testified together at school and for some reason, the supervisors believed that I fell every single time on my own.

For the past two years.

My mother had begun to believe me, but she still didn't believe that the helmet made things worse.

"Wes, sweetheart, please do this for me," Mom asked.

She always talked like that when she needed me to do something and she didn't want to have to fight about it.

I sighed and reached for the helmet, knowing she'd check to make sure I wore it today. Call me a momma's boy, but having a fight with my mother right before I got to school, just when we had managed to get along the whole morning, would have ruined my mood even more than wearing the helmet would have. Shouldering my pack, I placed the helmet on my head and fastened the straps with my free hand.

And just because today was going to be a good day, I smiled.

“There you go, Mom. I am now theoretically safer and empirically more dorky. Satisfied?”

She gave me a sad smile, the kind she does when I remind her of Dad, and then she remembers he's dead and that she misses him, even though he lied to us all.

“I appreciate it, Wes,” she said. “And I'm already proud of you, no matter how today turns out.”

That might have just made it worth it, I thought as I got out of the car. A faint dizzy spell followed, but I walked right through it, cane held but not needed for an entire three steps. Several idiots shouted and jeered at me, but I ignored them.

Today was totally going to be a good day.

3

OUT-THINK, OUT-SMART, OUT-STUMBLE

"Watch your step, cripple-head," one of the football players muttered as he stuck his leg out in front of my cane.

"I'm good," I replied, waving the cane above his foot and walking right past him. "Thanks, though." I had been acting like I needed to rely on it for every step today in order to throw the bullies off. Not five minutes into the day and it had already proved necessary. A couple of the thug's friends snickered as he stumbled and nearly fell from his own trick.

"You fake lying motherfu—" I heard him begin to shout, then tuned him out with two years of practice. I had a free ticket out of this place to earn. He could keep all the curses and football he wanted if I could keep my full scholarship and go on to earn my architectural engineering degree.

And yes, that's a real degree. People would make fun of me if they knew, but I still wanted to design cities. Actual, real cities that people lived their lives and sought their dreams in. People told me that I was ridiculous, because no one thought they'd be interested in living in a completely new town these days, and no one believed an old city could really be fixed up either. But that was still my dream. Either reconstruct a city that was falling apart, making it a much better place to live, or else build a brand new place that people could find new opportunities in. Call me crazy, but I swore I'd never give up on that.

Enough, I told myself with a smile. *Gotta earn all that first.*

I walked into the room that would have my English test, still barely needing the cane. I was just a little more dizzy, my hands shaking just a little more than they were in the morning. But I was probably just imagining that because I was nervous. And if it was getting worse, screw it. I was tired of letting this condition limit me. I was going to succeed today no matter what, and no person or disability was going to stop me. Not this time.

Ms. Springsen looked up at me and smiled as I entered the room. She was in her early thirties, with curly blonde hair that she kept short like Mom did, and she dressed in a way that looked like she was trying to strike a balance between professional and relatable to students.

“Good morning, Wes,” she said with her honest smile. I don't know why, but I swear most of us students worked harder just because of the way she smiled at us. It wasn't like it was some supermodel smile, it was just something that said 'I believe in you, and I won't stop until you realize it.'

“How are you feeling today?” she asked.

I knew she meant it. And not in a pitying way. She was hoping for a good answer, that I was doing well, was still trying to succeed and grasp awesome things in life. We all loved her for it. Well, those of us that tried at all loved her for it.

“I feel really great, Ms. Springsen. I feel like overcoming my condition, rocking my English exam, and earning my scholarship back.”

“That's what I like to hear,” she said cheerfully. “In that case, why don't we go ahead and get started?”

I took a seat and began. Ms. Springsen started to read out the instructions and accommodations provided. I raised my hand to interrupt.

“Ms. Springsen,” I said. “I'm aware that I may not have access to as many accommodations in college. If it's alright, can you try giving me the time updates as if a normal student's time had passed?”

That comment got me another smile.

It turned out I was able to finish the English section without any accommodations at all. And I thought I had written a killer essay about overcoming personal challenges. But I knew for a fact now that my memory was back. That knowledge alone was enough to bring tears of joys to my eyes. But I had to hold myself together until all my tests were done, so I held the waterworks in check for now.

I walked out of the classroom, dodging a casual push from another bully on my way out. No strategy that time, just practice from being pushed as soon as I walked around a doorway. Not even bothering to acknowledge the jerk, I did a fist pump into the air. A third of my scholarship had already been saved. I just knew it. Today was going to be a good day.

As part of my accommodations, I was allowed a study hall for my next period, then lunch, then my last two tests. Again, no problems. For the study hall,I mean.

Lunch was a different story.

Wearing the leather helmet was going to be really awkward in the cafeteria. Ms. Springsen was nice enough not to comment on it, and I was used to jeers in the hallways anyway. But I didn't like having to sit there, eating lunch, with about a hundred people staring at my funny-looking helmet. So before I left my study period for lunch, I pulled out my jacket and beanie to try and hide my helmet as much as possible. People were going to still stare and snicker, but at least there wouldn't be full-blown laughter this way. As much as I tried to pretend otherwise, that still bothered me.

I went ahead and found a table where no one else was sitting and pulled up there.

Not so long ago, I had a lot more friends at this school. Don't get me wrong, I was never super popular, but with pretty good grades, some decent (not great, just decent) performance on the football team, and being generally known as a nice guy, I had been able to get along with just about anybody. In addition to the disability caused by my head injury, two things changed all that:

The first happened at a party at the end of my sophomore year. The junior quarterback was hosting the party at his parents' second home, the one they never really stayed at. So there wasn't a lot of supervision and us being teenagers, we used the excuse to get hammered. Well, not all of us. Believe it or not, not every single teenager is crazy about alcohol, and at the time, I was really worried about disappointing my parents. Especially my dad. Growing up, my dad had been my hero all my life. It's hard to explain why. Part of it was seeing a lot of people respect him, not because of his money or position, but for how he treated people. Part of it was how he showed me all the fun things in life. He played football and catch with me, and when I discovered video games he showed me how they worked, since he helped program them at his company. He and Mom read stories to me, taught me how to treat people, how to be chivalrous to girls, and to not care that holding the door open was old-fashioned to people. And whenever I did the right thing, he let me know, and told me I was making a difference in the world. I grew up all my life thinking that I couldn't ask for a better father.

And yes, this party happened before his suicide, so I was still worried about disappointing him. So I stayed sober for the whole thing. Which means I have a different memory than most of the other people there that night.

Their story is that I got between the quarterback and his girlfriend because I was an overly stuck up prude trying to ruin everyone's fun, and that I had a secret crush on her. My story is that I stopped the quarterback and at least two other guys from taking advantage of an unconscious girl. It caused a big stink, partly because I didn't know the exact best way to handle that situation, but my parents had taught me enough that I knew I actually had to try and do something. So I got between the guys and girl and started shouting at them. All things considered I was lucky, because even back when I was in shape the three of them still could have kicked my ass easily. Instead, a few of the other sober people acted after I did, and everyone went to separate corners to calm down. The party ended early, parents arrived and intervened, and the whole thing was hushed over. Eventually. A couple of parents wanted my head for spreading lies about their 'babies,' but some others argued that a parent should have been at that party to begin with, and that my intervention in whatever happened probably prevented some 'scandal-creating photos' from being released.

By the way, here's a pro-tip for parents: if your child is a two-hundred-pound linebacker and you are concerned about other kids making fun of him, don't call him a 'baby' in public.

At any rate, most people felt like I had attacked and tarnished their reputations—including the girl I had tried to defend. She got in my face over it one day in the school hallways, and shortly afterwards transferred to another school. I never talked to her again. A few weeks later, I found that I had a lot fewer friends on the football team.

But my father told me he was proud of me. So I got through that spring and summer alright and just put up with everything.

But the fall was different.

About three weeks into the new school year, we came home to my dad sitting limp in his office. There was a small red hole in the front of his head and a larger one in the back, with blood on the floor directly under both holes.

When we all had finished screaming and calling the police, we found that there was a note on his desk, typed and printed off of his computer. In it, he had apologized to us for living a double life and for the inappropriate relationships he had with three of the young girls in church—kids the church had sponsored through a new homeless ministry and that our entire family had been very close to.

When we finished reading that note, we all started screaming again. At that point we *knew* he had been murdered and framed, because there was no way in hell my father would ever have done a single thing that note said he did. We told the police as much when they finally came. We shouted and demanded that they find Dad's killer right now and find those girls so that they could prove his innocence.

They found the girls.

And every single one of them testified against my father.

The police and child protective services said they conducted a thorough investigation, and all signs pointed to Dad's death being a suicide, and to being guilty of all the crimes the note confessed to.

John Malcolm, formerly known to my mother as the most devoted husband she could have ever asked for, to my sister as "Greatest! Daddy! Everrrrrrr!!!!11one" (that was what she called him online, word for word), respected by everyone in his church and community, and also the man I had one day hoped to be like when I grew up ever since I was six, had gone to his grave labeled a liar, a coward, a hypocrite, and a child predator.

To call that the darkest year of my family's life would be an insulting understatement. But even after two years of therapy and soul-searching, we still don't have a better term.

Afterwards, though, a lot of people in the community started avoiding us. We became 'cursed' to a lot of people. Everyone wondered how Mom could have missed such blatant hypocrisy in my father. Everyone wondered if my sister had also been abused.

And, just at the edge of my hearing, people wondered if my Dad's behavior would be genetically passed down to me, if I would start displaying similar tendencies. I got cold shoulders in additions to the cold looks in the school hallways now, older people who knew me made this weird, forced smile when they had to talk to me, and the church youth group leader stopped inviting me to help out with the children's vacation bible school activities every summer.

So yeah, table to myself. No problem. No crowd of people coming up to talk to me about how things are going, no one coming up and saying, "Hey Wes, may I sit here?" No—

"Hey Wes! How are things going? Is it alright if I sit here?"

Huh?

I looked up from my lunch to see the third blonde-haired woman of the day that had decided to be nice to me.

"Oh, hi Christina. Sure you can sit here."

Christina was wearing her blue-red cheerleader's outfit for the pep rally after school today. She smiled at me as she sat down with her tray and sandwich.

"Want some chips?" I asked. Mom had kind of over-packed my lunch.

"No thanks," she said. Then, looking again at my three bags of Cheetos, she quietly sneaked a hand over and took one. Then, when I didn't say anything, she sneaked her hand over and took another.

"Just wanted to see how you were doing these days," she said as she popped a Cheeto into her mouth. "And to steal your food. But seriously, how have you been? Long time no see."

"Yeah, I haven't able to make it to church much these days..."

"Oh no, I totally understand that," Christina said quickly. "Doctor's appointments and everything. I wouldn't make it much either. Really, Wes, I just wanted to say hi and catch up."

"I believe you," I said quickly. And I did. Christina was one of the few people who kept me from writing off church—and maybe God himself—altogether. There were maybe four members of the youth group at church who didn't start avoiding me after Dad's suicide, and Christina was one of them. In fact, along with some of the other misfits in the drama class I still went to, they were just about the only people that still talked to me.

"I'm actually doing really good," I said after a quick bite of my own sandwich. "Head barely hurts today. Can walk without the cane if I have to so far, at least for a couple of steps."

"Great!" she said brightly. "Had any of your tests yet?"

"I already had Literature and Writing this morning," I said, a little surprised that Christina knew about them. "Think I aced both portions."

"That's awesome!" She pumped her fists halfway into the air. "That totally rocks! Thanks for letting me know!"

"You're welcome." I cracked a grin. "I appreciate the enthusiasm, but is there a reason you're so excited?"

"Well, yeah," she said. "A couple of us from church, and some of your friends from drama, got together to root for you today. I didn't know you were in drama, by the way."

"They just let me help with the technical stuff. Sound and lights. But how did you meet my friends in drama?"

"Davelon and I found out about your tests from your sister. We asked who else would probably be rooting for you today, so we got together and made these bracelets."

She pulled up her sleeve to reveal a bead bracelet that said 'Team Wes' in several bright colors.

"You're all wearing those?"

"Yeah," she said with a smile that was half-shy, half-proud. I had to grin back.

"That's... incredibly cheesy," I said. "And really appreciated. Thank you guys. Seriously. Thank you all."

"No problem," Christina said with a confident shrug. "But now you have to completely rock out today or you'll make us all look bad, right?"

"That's no problem," I said, still grinning. "I think I can still rock out."

"Good. I'm glad," the cheerleader said, then took another of my Cheetos. I tried not to look too happy, or too embarrassed, but it was hard.

Then the last person I expected to see today walked by.

"Hey lady," quarterback Chris Rhodes said, giving Christina a side-arm hug as he swung by our table. At well over six feet, he had to stoop low to do that. "I didn't expect to see you this lunch. What's up?"

Christina smiled shyly, but happily at him.

"This is my free period, so I thought I'd let Wes know the rest of us were pulling for him. See?" She pulled up her sleeve to show the bracelet again.

"That's awesome," he said enthusiastically, then turned to look at me with a smile that did not reach his eyes. "Right, your tests are today. I forgot man, you should have told me so I can root for you."

Like hell, I thought to myself.

In the line of people rooting for me in life, Chris Rhodes stands right behind Sauron and Adolf Hitler.

"I haven't told anyone," I lied. "I've been so swamped with trying to study and stay healthy for it. Sorry, man. Didn't mean to keep you in the dark."

Another of Dad's lessons crept into my mind: To learn how to love your enemies, read the Bible. To learn how to survive them, read the *Art of War*.

"Well, if you get a chance, swing by the football table so we can wish you good luck, alright?"

"Yeah sure," I gave him my second lie. "I'll try and do that on my way out."

"Great," he said, turning his dark-haired head back to Christina. "Are we still on for next week?"

"Yup," she said with another of her half-cheesy smiles. "As long as my parents know I'm home by ten."

"Great," he said, his gray eyes twinkling. "In that case, I'll see you at the game tonight. You should come too, Wes."

"Sure," lie number three said. "If I get a chance."

"That'd be great," he said with a smile. "We miss seeing you, Wes."

Bastard, I thought as he walked off.

Christina watched him go, then turned back to me.

"I didn't know you knew Chris so well," she said, brushing some hair out of her smile.

"Yeah, well, we don't hang as much since I left football," I said, trying not to sound too careful.

I don't even know where to begin on describing Chris Rhodes. He's tall and muscular, big enough to impress you, without seeming overly large. He has perfect dark hair, piercing gray eyes, supermodel good looks. He has led our football team to title games twice in a row already, breaking several high school records and helped us—I mean them, they're not my team anymore—win last year's state championship. This year, our school is expected to compete in the high school *national* championship, largely because of his skills as both quarterback and team captain. He already has done spreads in both sports and modeling magazines.

He's also the reason I'd never be valedictorian at this school, because even before my condition he was at the top of the class every single year. Science, math, English, you name it—it all came incredibly easy to him. Some of his science projects had already garnered notice from several technology companies. And where I had to work to try and *keep* my single scholarship, multiple schools were fighting over him, offering everything imaginable on a silver platter just to get a verbal commitment from him. And he earned these opportunities solely on effort. His father was a senior vice president at the giant corporation that gave most of the people in my town jobs. Chris could pay for college pretty much any way he wanted, and some scholarship packages offered to him were probably against the rules, because he didn't remotely qualify for needing financial aid.

Now, yes, I am jealous. I can't pretend I'm not. Most guys are jealous of him. But that's not the reason Chris and I are enemies.

We're enemies because he was the quarterback I stopped at that party three years ago. "Hey Wes, you still there?" Christina asked, tapping the table and threatening to take my last Cheeto.

"Yeah, sorry," I said, snatching the last chip into my mouth with a grin. "Just thinking."

"So..." Christina said carefully. "Why don't you talk to the football team anymore? I know you still hang out with Davelon, but he wouldn't say why we couldn't get more of the players on Team Wes."

Davelon was, in fact, my only remaining friend on the football team. And he's probably the reason I didn't get my ass kicked more often.

Apparently Christina didn't know that. And, being Christina, she wanted to know more about the boys she cheered for during football games. Especially the quarterback.

This was not going to be a fun conversation.

"Davelon's my only friend left on the football team," I said finally. "The rest of the guys I have to watch out for, or they'll knock me around."

"What?" she said in disbelief. "You're kidding. No way. The entire team?"

"The entire team won't knock me around," I replied. "About half of them will just avoid me or sneer at me in the halls. The other half though, the hardcore idiots, keep trying to push or trip me in the halls."

"You're saying that's the reason you've been falling so much all these years?" My friend was incredulous.

I shook my head.

"A lot of the times I've fallen just because I'm clumsy. They've only counted for like half of those times. And this year I've gotten better at dodging them."

"That's still terrible!" Christina shouted angrily. "Why hasn't anyone done anything about this?"

"I don't know," I said with a shrug. "Teachers can't be everywhere at once. The coach has promised to put a stop to it, but I still have to watch out for myself."

"What about Chris?" she demanded. "Does he know about this?"

Chris had never pushed or tripped me himself, because he's not stupid enough to risk his image on something he can get his friends to do on their own. But how did I say that to his new girlfriend in a way that she would believe?

"Wes," Christina demanded. "We've been friends since fifth grade. You stood up for me back when I had braces and extra weight and everyone else was making fun of me for it. Tell me the truth about this."

Here goes nothing.

"Christina, Chris is probably the reason behind it all."

"What do you mean?"

"I mean Chris and I got into it really bad at a party three years ago. As far as I could tell, it was the right thing to do, but everyone disagrees with me, including the girl I stood up for at that party. Maybe I was wrong, and maybe I should have minded my own business. But Chris and I have never gotten along since, and the players I have to watch for the most are the ones that Chris hangs out with. So, accept that I might be biased, but Chris Rhodes is the smartest, strongest, most accomplished, most careful, and most cunning slime-bag I have ever met. Please be careful around him."

I hadn't meant for that last part to sound like a pitiful beg. But it did.

Christina said nothing for a moment. The hum of students eating, talking, and laughing all around us filled my ears.

"Um, Wes?"

"Yes?" I said, dreading her response.

"I've never heard you say that about anyone. Like, ever. Not even my old body shamers."

"They were jerks too back then. But no." I shook my head. "I stand by what I said about Chris, and that you should be careful around him. I hope we still can be friends."

"Well duh!" Christina said to my eternal relief, almost smacking my arm but pulling her hand away at the last minute. "I'm not going to give up one of my friends just because he doesn't like my boyfriend! You know me, Wes. I'm not one of those idiot girls that doesn't heed the warning signs about a jerk until it's too late."

"Right, sorry," I said, still unable to hide my relief. *And thank God,* I thought to myself, meaning it literally for the first time in a while.

"Now I'm not saying I'm going to immediately break up with him,"

Christina continued. "I'm going to have to make my own decision about him. But if he's as bad a guy as you say he is, I'll find out about it. And I'll be smart about it too, I promise. Okay?"

"Okay," I said with a smile. "Thanks for hearing me out." I looked at the clock. "Hey, I gotta go get ready for my tests, but it was really good seeing you. I'll try to make it to church next weekend."

Christina smiled at me.

"Sure thing. It was good seeing you too. Keep us all posted, okay? Go Team Wes!" She flashed the bracelet at me.

I grinned back, gathered my things, and headed out of the lunchroom.

4

DOWNFALL. AGAIN

I washed my hands in the restroom sink, then grabbed my cane by the wall. I reflected on everything today so far.

One: I had pulled off a world-first in a video game. Now, sure, it was just a video game, but I had done so in a challenging fashion and in a way that would get noticed. That wasn't even my main goal for this morning, but it happened. Since my condition didn't inhibit me in the game, it proved that without it, I could still excel. My illness was not me.

Two: I'd been able to walk around today almost completely on my own power. I could even go a couple steps without using my cane if I wanted to. My dizzy spells had been almost non-existent, my limbs barely shook at all, and my headaches were the mildest they'd been in years. I'd been getting better ever since I began playing in the simulator, and I had every reason to believe I'd keep improving.

Three: I'd already aced one test. None of the material seemed unfamiliar and I felt pretty confident about all my answers. My memory was getting better. My brain was coming back. If I could make it here, I should be able to make it through college.

And finally, I had way more friends than I thought I did. I'd been too bitter, for too long. It was time to make more effort to connect with people.

I smiled as I stepped out of the restroom. *Today really is a good da—*

"'Scuse us, cripple-head!"

Two large idiots dashed down the halls, curving to run into me.

They almost caught me by surprise. I had to lean back suddenly, and the hand of the one closest to me narrowly missed me as they dashed past. The sudden movement still made my head swim for a minute. Even though they had missed, the jerks jeered at me from further down the hall.

"Made you flinch, cripple-head! Ha! Ha!"

Who says the actual word "ha" out loud? I thought as I stepped back in the hallway. Except for the idiots further down the hall, I was clear. The incident had cost me time though. I had better hurry before—

"Oops!" a voice shouted from behind a hallway locker. "My book slipped!"

Crunch.

I had tried to duck, tried to dodge as soon as I heard the voice. But it was too late. I had the brief impression of something block-ish and heavy slamming into the back of my helmet before I felt the leather padding cave in completely, and the rest of the impact went right on through.

Pain exploded behind my eyes. The ground and the hallway started spinning in two different directions at once. Someone started cheering that they had finally gotten me, and shouted 'ha' a few more times.

Then the floor reached up and punched me in the face.

My forehead landed with enough force to bounce, and then everything went black.

I don't know how long I was out. I think it was only a few seconds. When I woke up, I glanced around, looking for a clock on the wall. *Wait,* I thought. *Where are the walls now?*

I tried to used my hands to get up, but all they could find was empty air. It was as if the whole world was spinning and I had no chance of ever catching or grabbing any part of it. My legs just quivered when I tried to move them.

And everything—I mean everything—*hurt.*

There were loud noises all around me. I think someone was shouting and running. Maybe they were running towards me. The noise intensified the throbbing in my head.

"Wes! Wes!" The deep voice was familiar. That didn't make the loudness hurt any less.

"Noise... hurts," I croaked.

"Sorry, man," Davelon's voice whispered gently. I could barely make out his tall brown form over me. "Can you move?"

I tried to get back up, but still couldn't find the floor with my hand.

"Here, man." My friend slowly moved his hand to grasp mine. "I gotcha. I'm gonna try and pull you up, okay?"

"Sure." I took a deep breath, and tried to ignore all the spinning. "Ready."

Davelon carefully hauled me back to my feet. I took a step forward and nearly fell down again. Every organ inside me suddenly tried to trade places with each other.

"Wes! Wes, stay with me!" Davelon urged. "Are you okay?"

Head down, I opened my mouth to answer and vomited instead. Everything in my body was still hurting and quivering. I was lucky I hadn't lost control of any other functions.

Davelon swore—a rare thing for him.

"I can't believe they did this to you," he growled. "Don't worry man, they're not getting away with this. Not this time. Let's get you to the nurse."

"No," I gasped. He didn't know I couldn't do that. Not right now.

"Don't be crazy, man," my friend said patiently. "You're throwing up and you can't walk. How can you possibly not need to go to the nurse right now?"

"Test."

I was managing one word at a time now, so I must be recovering. Davelon seemed to disagree.

"They will let you retake the test, dude. Seriously, this is special circumstances. I saw them run off after attacking you. I saw a friggin' textbook by your head. I'll vouch for you."

"Won't... work," I said, finally getting a second word out. "Happened... before."

Because it had. I had fallen down and hit my head, the result of another push that no one did anything about, just before I took the test a second time. When it became clear that I couldn't finish the test, the program said they would allow me to retake it one more time, but they would not be able to reschedule the final retake under any circumstances, no matter how valid. They explained that they were already being more than generous, and that if I had to retake a test four times in a row despite having accommodations, then I probably wouldn't be able to handle college anyway.

Even dizzy, I knew all of this. I couldn't let my future slip away.

"Please," I begged Davelon, having trouble articulating from both the pain and the shame of being so helpless. "Test. Please."

Davelon sighed and shook his head.

"Look, man, I'll make you a compromise. I'll swing by the classroom and show the teacher how messed up you are right now, and how you were just attacked. But when he tells you that you can retake the test on account of being *knocked unconscious,* because *someone assaulted you*, then I'll take you straight to the school nurse—and possibly make sure you get to the hospital. We clear?"

I nodded.

"Yeah...clear...and...Davelon... thank you,"

My friend shook his head again.

"If you weren't all banged up right now, you'd remember that you used to take care of me back when I got hurt. Now come on."

Gradually I was able to walk with Davelon's assistance. Everything still spun, but not as fast, and I could make out hallways and doors. We finally made it to the classroom that was holding my science test. Mr. Jammers looked up from his desk. He was still a little blurry, but I still recognized him as the pale, skinny, brown-haired teacher in his mid-thirties. I also noticed he was glaring at me.

"You're late," he said. "The bell rang a minute ago. Report to the office to get a tardy slip."

"Mr. Jammers, he's hurt," Davelon said. "He got jumped in the hallway."

"So why did you bring him here?" the science teacher demanded. "Go tell the office. He's got to get a tardy slip anyway."

The world was just swimming around now, not spinning. I could tell more about what was going on. When I carefully turned my head, I saw that Davelon was still staring at Mr. Jammers. He took a deep breath and tried again.

"Mr. Jammers," Davelon said patiently, but urgently, enunciating key words very clearly. "He's *hurt*. He was *attacked in the hallway. I saw it happen.* He made me take him here because he was afraid you'd disqualify him for the test. I need you to tell him he's being irrational and that you won't fail him just for being injured against his will, so that I can take him to go to see the nurse and find out if he has a concussion or not."

"The nurse isn't here on Friday afternoons," Mr. Jammers said irritably.

"Everyone knows that. And the exam's out of my control. They've given all the accommodations they'll willing to give him."

"But Mr. Jammers, look at him..."

"I see him," Mr. Jammers said dismissively. "He looks like he does every time he takes this test and can't finish it. They're not going to care a third time." Then he waved his hand like he was shooing a fly. "But if I'm wrong and he's as banged up as you say he is, I don't have to waste time pretending he could ever pass the test to begin with. Get him to the office so that he can get a tardy slip and get picked up by his mother, and I can leave and go grade papers."

"Oh my God." Davelon was so surprised he almost dropped me. He turned his head to look at me. "You're not crazy. You were telling the truth."

"Is okay," I slurred, then repeated it more confidently. "It's okay. I'm good now. You can let go."

"But I just said you *weren't* crazy," Davelon retorted. I shook my head and transferred my weight from his arm to my cane.

"Everything's starting to clear up. I can walk now."

"Is this you or the concussion talking right now?" Davelon was still staring at me. "Because I don't think I'm supposed to listen to the concussion."

"It's not the concussion," I said, shaking my head carefully as a test. Everything still swam and hurt a little, but I told myself I could work with it. "It's me trying to keep my scholarship. You heard him. This is my last chance."

"You don't have a chance, period," Mr. Jammers retorted angrily. "You were late. You have to go to the office and get your tardy arrival reported. And I have better things to do than spend my valuable time on a test you couldn't be bothered to be lucid for."

Bewildered and seeing me starting to move on my own, Davelon let me slide off his arm and limp carefully over to a seat. I saw his jaw and fist clench though, as he stared at my teacher.

"Davelon," I said. "Don't worry. He's always like this. Can you go to the office and report on my tardy for me?"

Davelon blinked again, then nodded at me. "Yeah. Yeah, man, I can do that."

"You can't report on another student's tardy!" Mr. Jackass—my private name for the jerk—shouted.

"Maybe not, Mr. Jammers," Davelon said, hands still clenched. "But I can tell them he was jumped and hurt, and that you tried to not give him his test. I'll be going now. Wes." He turned and looked at me. "Good luck. We're rooting for you."

He raised his wrist,and for the first time I saw the 'Team Wes' bracelet on his arm. I gave him a fist bump in solidarity as he left the room, giving the teacher another glare as he walked out.

"That bracelet's against dress code!" Mr. Jackass shouted. He turned back to glare at me. "And I thought I told you to get out of my classroom."

"You did, Mr. Jammers," I replied with practiced patience and taking a No. 2 pencil out of my bag. "But with all due respect," I paused for a moment because the room tried to spin again, "I'm not leaving this classroom unless I have a shot at completing the test or you physically remove me."

"I'm calling security," he snarled, stomping over to the phone. He picked up the phone and began dialing and shouting at it.

In case it is not as wretchedly, painfully obvious to everyone else as it is to me, Mr. Jammers is a bad teacher. I have never met anyone so angry about doing their job as this man, which is ironic because he always taught classes with the fewest students and they were all advanced placement, meaning the kids always cared more about learning the material than he did about teaching it. And it showed. Every time someone asked him to re-explain something, or clarify a question that would be on a test, or, God forbid, ask to come in after school and get some help on anything at all, he'd be furious over the extra work. Half of the information he taught contradicted material we'd learned in our previous classes, and whenever anyone brought that up in the classroom, Mr. Jammers would throw a screaming fit right then and there. When enough students pointed this out to their parents, Mr. Jammers suddenly had fewer classes to teach. At one point, when I asked how Mr. Jammers was allowed to teach at all, one of the other teachers privately told me that he had gotten his certification by a program run by a school board member. Specifically, the member that was his dad. I never figured out how that worked out legally.

And yes, he didn't seem to like me. Now, I know every student says that about a teacher they have problems with, but so far, I have heard at least ten people ask "is it just me, or does Mr. Jammers friggin' hate Wes?" within my hearing.

As far as I could tell, he thought I was faking the whole "severe head injury" thing so that I could get sympathy and distraction from what my father did.

And for some reason, even though I didn't have him as a classroom teacher anymore, he was chosen to administer the Math and Science portions of the tests for me. Every single time.

Mr. Jammers finally finished shouting into the school phone and hung up. He glared at me, then stomped over to the desk holding my test paper.

"You came in late, so you've already lost time. Get started so we can get this over with."

I took my paper and began. Thinking still hurt, but I was pretty sure I was remembering my math strategies right, so I worked as quickly and carefully as possible. In the past, the longer I worked on the tests, the more likely I was to suddenly go blank and stop remembering information. After getting hit today, I was especially worried about that. So I worked as fast as I dared.

And at first, I dared to work pretty darn fast. The information still came easily, and the math problems weren't too hard. For about twenty minutes, I felt like I was at the level I was before my head injury. Halfway through, just as I feared, everything began to get hazy. I started to feel a lot less confident about some of my answers. At the last quarter of the test, I started seriously second-guessing my answers. By the very end, I was forced to guess on the final handful of questions.

"Time's up for the math portion," Mr. Jammers said. "Put down your pencil and pass your test and scantron forward."

For a second I worried that my head was acting up and there really was someone in front of me, then I realized Mr. Jammers was just being a jerk again.

Mr. Jackass took my old test and passed me the science portion. "Your science portion of the test begins now. You have an hour to complete this portion of your test. Any portion not completed will be considered incorrect—"

He got blurry for a moment and his voice sounded distant. I shook my head to try and clear it. That gave me a sharp, stabbing pain, but my vision and hearing got better.

My memory didn't.

I stared at the first question, scratching my brain to try and remember who Marie Curie was. I skipped the question and moved on. The next question I remembered: definition of an isotope. The third question I completely blanked on, as well as the question after that. And the question after that.

And the question after that.

Tears began to form in my eyes.

"No," I whispered.

"No talking during the test!" Mr. Jammers said from his desk.

I clenched my fist in frustration as material I had been studying for the past six months, had recalled perfectly for the past several weeks up until this very morning, slid away from my mind. Again and again, I asked myself the difference between the different light waves, between the strong and weak force, the formula for velocity.

Nothing, every single time.

I needed to pass all three tests today to save my scholarship—English, Math, and Science. I had passed English for sure. I *might* have passed Math. But out of the fifty science questions, I had only answered ten. And five of those were complete guesses. For I don't know how long, I just sat there trembling. My hand shook, the pencil in it bobbed all around. Then, still trying to hold back tears, I began to fill in random answers, knowing it wasn't good enough and knowing that I had just failed my science test again, for the third time in a row, and lost my scholarship for sure.

I had not even finished randomly bubbling in answers when I heard Mr. Jammers smugly call out:

"Time. Put your pencil down and pass your test forward."

I put my pencil down. Mr. Jammers must have seen my surprise, because his face grew even more smug. "Didn't you hear me call out your remaining time at the proper intervals?"

Judging by the look on his face, he probably hadn't, but I couldn't be sure and would never be able to prove it. When he finally came by and saw that I wasn't even able to finish the test, his smile was positively disgusting.

"Congratulations on finally being done with it all," Mr. Jammers gloated. "Now you can finally stop worrying about these tests. Pass or fail, we're both done with them *for good.*"

I couldn't even look at him. That's how low I felt. Too low to even look at someone like Mr. Jackass in the eye. If I could have crawled out of there, I would have—but that brought the sickening thought that if I fell again, I *would* have to crawl out of there. And I'd need someone's help to get back up.

I got out of my desk and grabbed my bag and cane. Mr. Jammers' smug voice called out to me one more time:

"I'll make sure your tests get graded and recorded as fast as possible, so don't worry. You'll know very quickly just how much your hard work paid off. And so will everyone else—after all, surely everyone's going to be *proud* of you."

5

ROCK BOTTOM

Mother was my ride to school, but her work wouldn't allow her time to pick me up afterwards. Davelon, after arguing that I should go to the hospital one more time, dropped me home.

I got home before Mom did, so when she came in, she found me sitting in the living room.

"Wes, what happened at school today?" Mom said with a concerned voice as she set down her purse. "I got a message from the school saying there was an incident. Did you fall again? Are you okay?"

How did your test go? was what she really wanted to ask me, I knew. Don't get me wrong, I knew she worried about my health, but I had fallen so many times over the years that she knew that I was fine, because I was sitting down calmly and not still spasming on the floor. It's been two years. The woman had learned to read the signs.

I shook my head slowly, wincing at the pain it caused. This was supposed to be the part of the day where everything I'd done over the year had finally paid off, and that I got to tell her about it. The part of the day where I got to tell her that I had proved everyone wrong. That no one had believed me about the bullies, but it was alright because I had figured out how to deal with them on my own, *and* managed to pass my test without any accommodations. Today was supposed to be a good day.

"Wes?" Mom repeated.

"Bad day," I whispered, still not looking at her. "It was a bad day after all."

"Wes," Mom repeated in her patient, trying-not-to-panic voice. "Honey, tell me what went wrong. Did you trip again? Did... did something happen on your test?"

"Didn't trip," I replied, which was technically true. I still couldn't look at her. I had told her I could handle today. I was wrong. But I had tried to continue anyway. Not that it still mattered.

Not that anything mattered anymore.

"Aced English," I continued. "Think I passed math. Science..." I couldn't finish.

"Oh honey," Mom said, clearly disappointed, but trying to be supportive. "Honey, please..."

She knew I was just as disappointed as she was. And the irritating thing was, even though I had still failed and lost my scholarship, this was still the best I had ever done on these tests.

"Honey, are you sure?" Mother continued kindly. "Maybe you did better than you thought you did."

Maybe. It wasn't likely, but maybe.

My phone beeped in my pocket. Without much energy, I pulled it out and checked the message.

"What is it? Mother asked.

I gave a short, dark laugh.

"It's from the gaming journalist who wanted to interview me. He says they were contacted and informed that I may have cheated this morning, and so they're postponing any interview until *Heroes Unbound* investigates." I looked at an earlier message. "There's also an email from *Heroes Unbound* itself, saying that they received an anonymous tip that I may have gotten help from one of their employees, or ex-employees, before I attempted this morning's raid on the dragon." I chuckled again, no brighter than I had before. "They want to know exactly how I know ex-employee John Malcolm, and what my exact relationship with him is. They also want to know the last time we talked, probably so that they can see if he had passed on any secrets to me."

"Are you serious?" Mom said acidly. She had good reason.

As I had mentioned earlier, John Malcolm, my father, had died over two years ago—long before work on the brand-new boss had even begun. As soon as *Heroes Unbound* finishes checking their records, they'll realize that and feel really stupid. But whoever gave them that tip won't care, because they had to be someone who had known both Dad and me and just felt like opening up an old wound.

Mom snarled, but the phone rang behind her. It was odd that the old landline rang. And yes, we still have a landline phone. I don't know why. She stomped over to pick it up.

"Yes?" she answered. "Speaking. What? Are you sure? That fast? That's unheard of. I thought it would take weeks! Because it always takes weeks! Even though it's all on the computer—oh.... well I understand you're as eager for results as we are... I'm glad to hear—what? *What?* Are you sure? *Every single one*? But I just talked to him! He seemed so—I don't care! And yes I'm going to insist I see the results! That's the only way I'll believe news like this!"

My mother slammed the landline back down onto the receiver. "That was the testing company," she said flatly. "They said they've already graded the results, with the exception of your writing essay." She was glaring. "They said you've failed all three tests."

The room spun again.

"What?" I asked.

"You heard me," she stated flatly. "All three. Including the one you said you aced."

That didn't make it any sense. I had felt completely confident about almost a hundred percent of my answers on the English portion. I could understand it if someone didn't like my essay, but they hadn't graded that portion yet. How could I have possibly been that wrong about my results?

"I don't understand," I finally said.

"I think I finally do," my mother growled. "You've mainly been doing two things these past months: study and play. We both know studying isn't the problem. So either the testers are wrong about your grades, or you're wrong about the reasons you're gaming."

That contradicted everything I knew to be true about this past year. I've already mentioned the improvements I'd felt to my balance, headaches, and memory.

But then again, I'd been wrong about everything else today too.

And either way, I had no future now. I was never leaving this town. I was never leaving this place where all but a handful of people either hated, judged,or pitied me.

"I think it's time we re-evaluated how much time you play," my mother said firmly. “Because what we thought was working clearly isn’t. I should have gone with my gut about this from the beginning.”

“No,” I said quietly.

“What do you mean, no?” my mother shouted. “And why are you getting up? I'm talking to you!”

I shook my head again. It hurt even more this time, but I limped past her to the room where I kept the VR headset and harness.

“Not working,” I replied. It was getting harder to talk in complete sentences, so I knew I was running out of time to do what needed to be done. “Not worth it if it doesn't work.”

I had apparently been wrong about my progress for the past six months. For all I knew, this was the most coherent I've ever been.

“It's just an escape after all,” I said, reaching for the headset and stumbling as I did so. My speech was slurring now. “To a place where I don't hurt. To a place I can't stay in.” I raised the helmet high. “It's not worth it.”

I smashed the helmet down on the ground.

“What are you doing?” my mother screamed. She sounded frightened. “Wes, stop! That's expensive!”

So she didn't hate my games after all. But it didn't matter anymore.

I slammed the headset down again and again, hard enough to feel like my own damaged, worthless head was hitting the ground instead. And unlike my head, the thousand-dollar helmet was proving indestructible.

Huh, I thought, finally dropping the headset and giving up. *If I had been wearing* this *today instead of a thin leather helmet, I might have shrugged off the attack earlier today. Speaking of which...*

I dropped the headset and jerked off my beanie, feeling for the back of my head. The leather felt warped, dented somehow, but I supposed that made sense.

... Or did it?

Everything was getting fuzzy. Mom was yelling about something again. She sounded even more scared than before. But I felt so sleepy it didn't bother me. I tried to lie down, but my hand slipped and I hit the ground, much faster than I intended.

For the second time in one day, everything went black.

Collecting scan results. Reviewing data below and generating report written by staff. Device is returning to internal monitoring.

New Log of Subject Anonymous, Flagged Entry:

The recent brain scans indicate a serious and unhealthy degree of brain instability, far beyond recommended and even necessary parameters. The brain patterns match the given description of the subject's self-destructive behavior, and are consistent with those considering further self-harm and even suicide. All accounts show that current containment protocol is to blame—both the primary containment and the supporting methods. Our team's official consensus is that continuation of current methods will—*not might*—will, *result in both the termination of the subject and ultimate failure of our final objective. It is urgently recommended that all containment methods be drastically reduced in both frequency and intensity, if not removed altogether. In fact, the team's unanimous consensus is that* no *containment protocol be enacted for at least a month, both to preserve the subject and to see if he finally yields relevant data when he is no longer under such high levels of duress.*

I am sending this log via the direct channel, to ensure its timely receipt and to ensure my recommendations are recorded and viewed by all parties.

Let's be frank, Rhodes. Our lives are depending on the success of this project. If it fails, and fails especially without providing any useful data, and fails entirely due to factors we caused—and by 'we,' I mean you—the boy will not die alone. You will, and possibly so will we, but at least this way there will be a log detailing exactly whose fault this is. So adjust the damn parameters before we all get killed.

Respectfully,

Brogen, Medical Lead.

Seriously, Rhodes. Don't fuck this up.

End of Report.

6

GO TUNNELING

During one of the football games my sophomore year, I had been injured in a freakishly bad collision. I was a tight end trying to catch a difficult pass. Somehow, three other players slammed into me, twisting my torso one direction, my neck another direction, and my head a third direction (if it's hard to imagine, just picture yourself trying to look as far sideways as you can, while slowly rotating your neck around in a complete circle, while being bent into a pretzel at the same time). I was knocked out instantly. When I woke up, the doctors told me that I narrowly avoided a broken neck. Instead, I had a concussion, something that would go away as long as I got plenty of rest.

I got plenty of rest.

And it never went away.

Instead, it got worse. My headaches turned into dizzy spells. My dizzy spells turned into balance problems, meaning most days I could only walk very carefully, with the aid of a cane or a hand on the wall. I started having memory problems for the simplest things. Like genuinely, honestly forgetting what my Mom had told me to do less than five minutes ago, or some trivia fact I had been quoting for years. Just imagine waking up one day and not recognizing a single Monty Python reference. If you have any friends that have heard of Monty Python at all, that *will* scare you.

Needless to say, my grades begun to suffer. Not at first. I had thrown myself into my schoolwork to distract myself from Dad's death, and had actually gotten entered into a rare scholarship program available to students before their senior year. All I had to do was pass a test at the end of the year.

After my disability, I had failed the test two years in a row. But because of my disability, my mother and therapist had both written to the scholarship program, detailing my situation, and they agreed to give me one last shot. That was this year.

I failed that shot.

There was no point in asking for a fourth chance. I had finished out secondary school trying to pass the test, with nothing to show for it. To have failed so spectacularly at the end meant that everything I knew to be true was not.

I was getting worse, not better.

The jocks were right. My head was crippled after all.

The only good thing was that it had answered the question I used to hear people whisper in church: no matter what my genes and my choices, I would never turn out to be a pervert like my father, because I would never get the chance. Heck, I could donate my brain to science and let doctors study this mysterious, incurable disease to their hearts' content.

Speaking of doctors...

Black became blurry. Blurry became a hospital room.

I must have fallen unconscious again. Davelon was right after all. I really did need to go to the hospital. My bad.

Not that it mattered. Being conscious had brightened my vision, not my thoughts.

I looked around anyway. I was in a typical hospital bed. Typical white hospital walls. Typical IV-thingie hooked up to my arm.

Pull it, a dark, painful corner of my mind whispered immediately. *Rid your family of the burden you've become.*

I looked at the cord.

"You're awake!" a voice to my right said. I turned my head and saw the haggard form of my mother.

She is aging, I finally realized. She had a young face for her age, not that she was even in her late forties yet, but for the first time, I had noticed the lines that had begun to form. Dad's suicide and everything else had been hard on her. My face flushed with shame. Leaving her and my sister would not relieve them of a burden. It would only add more lines to my mother's face. More crying into my sister's pillow.

"Mom," I said, turning my head from her. "I lost it. I'm sorry."

"Hush, dear," my mother said, leaning forward and grabbing my hand. "I lost it too. I should have believed you."

I turned my head to look back at her.

"What do you mean?" I asked.

"I mean all of it." She gave a sad but grateful, smile. "The bullying. The hazing. The gaming. The testing. Instead I pushed you and pushed you, and when you had done everything right, I pushed you more, until you finally broke." Her lip trembled for a moment. "You suffered for it, and I'm so sorry."

I swallowed. I didn't know what to say.

"Thank you," I finally settled on, then tried to change the subject. "Uh... What happened after I passed out?"

"I called the ambulance," Mother said simply. "But you probably figured that. Then I called the school and heard that you got into it with Mr. Jammers. I had trouble believing you were at fault with that, so I called Davelon—he's coming to see you later too—and found out that you were *attacked,* and that was why your helmet was dented in the back. Christ, Wes, I can't believe you didn't say anything about it. And you still tried to take the test."

"I knew they wouldn't let me retake it," I said uncomfortably. I realized it hadn't mattered in the end, but I was really tired of defending that decision.

"And normally I would have said you were being irrational. Davelon told me he said the same thing until he heard Mr. Jammers with his own ears." Mom's eyes narrowed. "So after what happened today, with you getting attacked in the middle of the hallway, with no one protecting you or at least disciplining the attackers, for lying to me about the whole thing and trying to cover it up—by pinning the blame on you, of all things—I'm going to call a lawyer, then go to the papers and tell them about what the school did. Those cretins could have killed you, never mind the scholarship. You better believe I'm suing the school for every penny they have, and letting everyone know why I'm doing it."

"But I would have failed the tests anyway," I offered, not sure why I was arguing. "The testers said I failed all three subjects."

"The testers were wrong, and called me earlier explaining their mistake. Apparently they confused your test with someone else—I don't know who, but they only admitted to it after I started screaming about what had happened to you today." Mother gave another sad smile. "But I got an idea of what your results probably were from your teachers. You excelled on your English test—both portions; the teacher loved your essay and wants to post it online—you barely passed Math, and you failed Science, like you said. I'm sorry," she added, still sounding sad, but proud. "I know you're not satisfied, but it's the best you've ever done. I'm proud of you, honey. I really am."

I turned my head away from her again. "Still lost the scholarship," I muttered.

"And that's the school's fault," Mother snarled. "If they don't make another exception for you, I'm going to make sure we get every penny out of them for it, no matter how long it takes me. I promise you that, honey."

I wasn't sure that would work out, but I was glad Mom was optimistic.

And I was glad I had her on my side.

There was a knock on the door.

"Mom?" my sister's voice called through the door. "Is he awake now?"

"Yes, honey. He just woke up. Come on in."

A slender and beautiful girl several years younger than me walked in. Her hair was a darker red than mine, cut very short, and she wore a black jacket and black skirt. She looked mad.

"You better be okay, because you fell again and didn't tell anybody. *Again*," Rachel said, her eyes practically stabbing at me as she spoke.

I sighed.

"Now that you understand, Mom, can you answer her? So that I can catch a break?"

"Wes was attacked at school, dear. And when the school found out, they wouldn't let him reschedule the test or get help."

My sister stared at my mother with her mouth open for a moment, then closed it.

"Mr. Jammers again?" she finally asked. I nodded.

"Figures," she said, taking a small notebook out of her jacket and flipping it open to a page with a lot of writing on it. The top of the page had the title "Punch List." She took out a pencil, erased a name that had a line drawn through it, then rewrote the same name.

"This is still how you write his name, right?" she asked. I nodded.

"Yeah, sis, but you can't punch a teacher."

"I respectfully disagree with your hypothesis, but will test it for you anyway," she said loftily.

"No, really," I said, a little concerned that my sister had a list like that, and that I hadn't noticed before. "You can't just punch a teacher. Even one like Mr. Jammers. You'd get expelled."

My sister gave me that pained, patient look, the one she started using back in 6th grade, then held out her hand and slowly began to count.

"One, I usually don't physically punch a person on my list, and if I do decide to, I'm not going to *just* punch them, so that entire first sentence is wrong. Two, it's Mr. Jammers. No matter how good his lawyer is, there are too many other lawyers in this town that would be willing to help me counter-sue him *for free.* You have no idea. Finally, expulsion? Really?" She snorted. "If Mom still has me enrolled in this school next year, I'm running away to go find a school on some other planet, where people are more normal and less douchey."

"That's fine, dear," Mother said. "By the time I'm done suing the school, you'll have enough money to study wherever you want."

"Really?" My sister's eyes widened. "That's great! Our school's super-rich! And you can probably sue the football program too!" My sister turned to another page and started scribbling something else.

"Sis," I warned. "I can't remember for a fact whether a football player hit me or not."

My sister snorted again.

"Gonna need you to say that online," she said, still scribbling. "I'm pretty sure there's a website where I can bet money that it was the football team, and make a lot of easy cash. Then you can use it to buy me and Mom a new car. And yes, it has to be you buying," my sister added, waving the pencil. "Studies still show that guys get better deals from car salesmen. You're the man in the house now. It's your job."

I grinned at her.

"Can I get out of the hospital first?" I asked playfully. "And how did you get here without a car? Did Mom drive you?"

"Nope," she answered, still scribbling. "Himari and Andre did. Oh, right." She suddenly looked up. She walked over to the door and stuck her head out. "Hey guys! He's up!"

Apparently my room really was that close to the waiting area, because Himari and Andre came right around the corner. Himari and Andre were two international students from Japan and Mexico, respectively, that came over for seventh grade, and then wound up staying when their families moved over. People in our town welcomed them at first. But when it became known that they liked anime and black clothing, they had a hard time finding people to get to know, despite the fact that they both spoke English pretty well. But their cultures seemed fascinating to me, and I figured they deserved a chance as much as anyone else, so I tried to show them around at school. A lot of the other kids still stayed at arm's length around them, but they really hit it off with the drama team and my sister. Since they were closer to my sister's age than mine, they wound up hanging out with her more, but they somehow started idolizing me like she did, even after my accident and the family's drama. I've never understood that, but I've always appreciated their friendship.

"Hey, man," Andre said as they both walked in. "Heard you had a bad day."

I flushed for a moment, then I realized he wasn't talking about me losing it at home; he was talking about everything else that happened.

"Yeah, well," I tried to smile. "They come and go."

"Well, if you need anyone beaten up," Andre began with a light tone. "...Himari knows karate."

"I do *not*," Himari said, punching him in the shoulder. "And you pronounced it wrong." She turned back to look at me, eyes worried.

"*Nii-san,* are you really alright?" she asked me.

"Why are you calling him *nii-san*?" Andre whispered. "You don't hear me calling him *'mano.*"

She ignored him and waited for my answer.

"Yeah, Himari, I'm fine," I said, still smiling. "Thanks for asking. And thanks for coming, both of you. And bringing my sister."

"No sweat, man," Andre said. "I mean, *de nada.*"

Himari rolled her eyes at him. "We just wanted to make sure you were alright, Wesley. We were worried about you."

"Seriously, man," Andre added, his eyes darkening. "You need anyone beaten up?"

I shook my head, but my sister saved me from answering.

"Too late," she said. "Mom's suing everybody responsible. This way you and I don't go to jail for beating anyone up, and we all get rich instead. So this time, I can drive you guys in *my* car instead."

"Well, alright," Andre said. "But you have to buy Wes some new shoes first, okay? His went out of style like five years ago."

"Oh I know," Rachel responded, rolling her eyes. "You wouldn't believe how hard he's holding onto those old things."

"I can't help it that they're so comfortable," I replied, then continued. "Don't worry guys. I'm not dying. I'll get out of here, and I'll see if I can figure out school after all of this."

I had no idea as to what that looked like. But I wasn't ready to tell anyone that yet.

And they weren't ready to hear it either.

"Well, we're not really worried, *mano*," Andre said. "You've always come out on top. We just wanted to be able to see you before the game this weekend. That's still on, right?"

As I said, Himari and Andre mostly hung out with my sister, but I still came to their role-playing tabletop games. Aside from electronic media, it was about the only thing I could do with people that didn't hurt.

That was another thing, something else I could share with people; I'd lose it if I quit on life.

"Yeah, guys. As long as the doctor clears me, I'm in."

Himari smiled.

"That's good, *nii-san*. We need our paladin back."

I smiled back at them all—Mom, Rachel, Andre, and Himari.

I decided then and there.

I didn't know what there was left for me.

But I wasn't giving up.

Not today.

7

LIGHT AT THE END

They cleared me to go home later that day. They said my head injury exacerbated my condition, and then they threw a bunch of other medical mumbo jumbo at me that I couldn't understand, no matter how many times Mom and I asked them to clarify. But since they had done a better job on me than any other doctor we visited, and were the only doctors our insurance covered anyway, we settled for just smiling and crossing our fingers that they were somehow on top of things and went home.

I went straight to bed.

And when I woke up, I knew I really hadn't.

I kept my room pitch-black at night, because any light at all will wake me up. I covered my cell phone with a baseball cap. I kept heavy blinds over my window. Even my alarm clock had a thin screen I pulled over it.

So when something bright from the window brought me to grouchy awareness, I knew in a second that something was wrong.

At first, I thought the blinds had moved or fallen. I always mess with them to try and block more light. When I felt the light hit my face, I figured they had slipped a little and that I needed to get up and adjust them again. But they hadn't slipped, or fallen.

They were wide open. So was the window.

And, even as groggy as I was, I knew I would never have forgotten to close either them or the window. I blinked rapidly, trying to adjust from all the starlight streaming in from outside. It shouldn't be this bright. Was there a moon outside?

Then I finally processed that if my window was open, someone other than me had opened it.

But who had done that?

The outside of my window was directly over some heavy shrubbery. If a burglar was still outside, I should be able to hear branches crack as he tried to hide. And if he had already gotten inside, the papers on my desk should have been disturbed.

As I tried to process this, I heard a sound from the hallway by my door. Finally thinking I was in some kind of overly-lucid dream, I took a step toward the hall, grabbing my cane as I walked past it. At that point, I wasn't sure if it was for assistance or defense.

I stepped carefully past my door into the hallway, following the thin beam of light that came from my room's window. The beam continued down the hall, turning around the corner to the living room—something the back of my mind insisted was impossible. The rest of me was too curious to ignore it, however, so I crept into the same room that I had tried to destroy my gaming harness in. Despite the presence of the beam, this room was much darker, but I could still make out much of what was in it, including my gaming harness. The sturdy headpiece was lying right where I left it, still undamaged from my recent foray into self-destruction.

The beam of moonlight led near, but not over, my harness, touching the center of the far wall. Somehow, it darkened as it got closer, until it completely disappeared at the wall. Despite that, I could still make out a small shape next to my harness. My mind's back-alley portion started screaming again, reminding me that I hadn't left anything in this room and neither would anyone else.

There shouldn't be anything at all next to my harness.

Nevertheless, still believing this was a dream and having no reason to think otherwise, I walked over to get a better view of the small, dark shape next to my gaming set. It was the handle to a larger object, the grip to a weapon or something, worn with age and missing the rest of whatever it was connected to.

It was the handle I had looted off the Canyon Dragon in *Heroes Unbound*, the video game. A virtual item was lying on my living room carpet.

The back of my mind went silent in shock and disbelief.

Now I was beginning to wonder if this was more delusion then mere dream. *If I wake up anywhere other than my bed, I'm changing my medication,* I remember thinking. But I still carefully bent down and picked up the handle. The back of my mind quietly pointed out that kneeling like this usually hurt and made me dizzy. For a brief moment, the handle felt warm, tingling my hands; then in a blink, it went cold, like a normal piece of metal or wood or leather, or whatever medieval-fantasy handles are usually made of. But the beam of light suddenly brightened, and when I looked up, I saw the beam crawling up to the middle of the wall and ending in a small dot.

I looked down and realized that the circumference of the handle matched the circumference of the glowing moon-dot.

My other hand let the cane clatter to the floor. Completely yielding to the weirdness of it all, I stepped carefully to the wall and ground the rod-shaped handle into the dot. The wall around the dot brightened, widening into a door-shaped rectangle, then completely filled out my vision.

I blinked from the brightness, and when I opened my eyes again, I was no longer in my living room. There were no walls and there was no ceiling. My floor had become damp grass, my living room had become fog and tall trees. My roof was now a black expanse filled with small jeweled lights.

I was in some kind of strange, beautiful, mist-covered forest.

And someone was crying.

I couldn't see her. But it sounded like a young woman my age. I heard shushing sounds next to her, as if two other people were trying to comfort her.

"Hush, Little Star," an older woman's voice said. "You'll find a way to handle this. You always do."

I started walking forward to the voices, stepping quietly, because it felt like I wasn't supposed to be here.

And I kept walking, because it felt like now that I was here, I wasn't supposed to leave.

"Not this time," the young woman sobbed. "I don't have any tricks for this, Guineve. There's too many people to save, in too many places, from too much all at once. I can save one world at most, if we sacrifice everything, and then everyone else dies."

"No, Stell!" a high-pitched, musical voice said next. "Guineve's right! Don't give up! We've always come through before!"

I thought I saw some kind of light flash ahead of me. It flashed so quickly, I almost thought I imagined it. But I kept walking forward.

I was walking forward, I suddenly realized. Without a cane.

And nothing hurt.

"We haven't," the crying woman said angrily. "And you both know that. Even if we do everything possible, every world is still probably going the way of the Lost Deeps."

"Maybe you could summon another—" the bright voice began again. But the sobbing woman interrupted her.

"I can't summon another Challenger, Breena! You both know I can't Call one for at least fifty more Earth years! And even if I could summon one in only twenty Earth years from now, it still wouldn't be enough time to get the Challenger strong enough to fight *this* many Trials and Tumults, in *this* many places, all at once!"

"Well, can you make us strong enough?" the bright voice began again, wilting slightly as she spoke.

"No, Breena," the teenage voice sighed. It sounded much closer now. "I wish I could. Especially you. Guineve *might* be strong enough if she could keep power when she left Avalon, but her leaving would cause just as many complications. I've been trying to get you all stronger, but since you're part of me, your growth is as slow as mine. We're going to try anyway. You, the others, and every native hero I can round up, are going to do everything we can to save the day. But it's just not going to work."

"You never know until you try, dear," the soothing, motherly voice said.

"Guineve," the grieving, frustrated voice said back. "You feel everything I do. You know that right now I am being completely objective when I say there's nothing we can do for ninety to one hundred percent of the people we've ever cared for."

"I know, Little Star," the motherly voice said, and this time I thought I heard hurt in her voice. "But comforting you is what I do."

"I know," the teenage voice said back. "And I'm sorry. I'm sorry for everything."

There was more crying then, and I felt intensely uncomfortable. I felt like the world's biggest voyeur right then, but it wasn't like I could turn around and go back home. Whatever portal I had come through had closed behind me.

It was either spend forever lost in the woods, or try to walk to the poor crying people ahead of me, who probably needed help anyway.

Or they'd just kick my ass hard enough to wake me up. Either way.

As I walked through a particularly deep patch of mist, I heard a hum thread out through the woods. The crying and shushing voices didn't seem to notice it until the motherly one suddenly let out a gasp.

"Stell," I heard her whisper urgently. "Little Star!"

"What?" the teenaged voice whispered back. "And why are we whispering?"

"Because someone's here!"

The three voices grew completely quiet.

"Are you sure?" the teenaged voice whispered back quietly, and very, very seriously.

Alrighty, I thought. Time to come forward before things escalate.

"Hello?" I called out. "Can someone help me?"

"Identify yourself!" the teenaged voice called back again. "Name and origin world!"

Origin world. Right.

They had been talking about different worlds.

That was always a bad sign. Especially in a dream this lucid.

"Wes Malcolm, of Earth. Um, where are we currently?"

"Earth?" the teenaged voice said in disbelief. "You just said you were from Earth?"

"His name sounds like it might be from Earth," the high-pitched voice offered. "One of the parts that have funny-sounding names, at least."

"But he can't be from Earth," the teenage voice muttered. "That's impossible."

"So is him coming here from anywhere else, Little Star," the mature woman's voice said. "Our world is closed except by invitation, remember?"

"Maybe one of the Icons are trying to joke around?" the musical voice said. "They're usually bad at it though."

"Well the timing is horrible right now anyway," the teenage voice growled. "If this is a practical joke," she called out, "we're going to be very, very unhappy with you. It's impossible for you to be from Earth."

"Um, okay. Why?" I asked, not knowing what else to say.

"Because I haven't Called you here," she said with a sigh.

"Huh?" I replied eloquently. "Sorry, can we back up to where I find out where I am? And maybe who I'm talking to? Since I already gave you guys my name?"

Silence greeted me for a moment.

"He's completely clueless," the teenage voice breathed. "He might really be from Earth."

"That would be awesome," the tiny voice squeaked. "But let me go ahead and make sure. Hey you! What part of Earth are you from?"

"What do you mean?" I asked. Dumb question, but I didn't want to tell them my hometown and hear 'Never heard of it, liar! Die!'

"Where do you want me to start?" I clarified.

"Which continent?" the tiny voice demanded.

"North America," I replied. "It's in the Northern and Western Hemispheres of our planet."

"Which country on that continent?" she demanded.

"America."

"America?" the little voice demanded.

"Yes. United States of America."

"Your country named itself after its own continent?"

"Um, arguably?" I said cautiously. I didn't want to get too much into that idea, because my country's education system couldn't even keep track of who discovered my continent first, let alone who named what, when, and why.

"Sounds pretty arrogant if you ask me," the little voice huffed.

"Probably," I replied carefully. "But it wasn't really my idea. And the Australians kinda did the same thing."

"Shoot," the tiny voice squeaked back. "He's totally up to speed on Earth. I think he's legit, Stell."

"What part of America do you live in?" the woman called Stell asked me. 'Which state?"

"Texas," I replied. "It's at the bottom-middle part of the country. Largest state after Alaska."

"What town or city?"

"Some podunk suburb you've never heard of outside the metroplex," I replied, losing it just a little. "Now can someone please tell me what's going on? I'm trying really hard not to freak out."

She didn't reply to me immediately.

"Earth," she breathed. "He's really from Earth."

"Maybe we should let him see us, Little Star," the mature voice said. "I think it's safe."

"Right, okay, you go first, Guineve. Then you introduce Breena. I'll... I'll be there in a minute."

"Little Star," the motherly voice argued sadly.

"Please, Guineve," the other voice begged.

Guineve sighed, and then after a moment I saw a tall, womanly figure stride through the mists and make a sweeping motion with her hand.

Instead of parting, the mist seemed to flow around her shape, as if it was curling into clothing. The mist around her legs and feet billowed out and began circling her, climbing up to create the skirt of a dress. More of it wrapped into a blouse around her torso, then billowed down to form long drapes that hung off of her shoulders and left her marble-pale arms bare.

The woman herself was tall, almost my height, and looked about twice my age, as if she were in her thirties or early forties. However old she was, she wore the age very well, with a mature, full figure that I was trying really hard not to pay too much attention to—another moment where I realized my body was back to normal, and at a level that was a first even for my dreams. Thankfully, the dress concealed her features well, save for her slender white arms and her pale face. Her hair was a dark black color, but the mist had formed jewel-like droplets that scattered light, giving her dark locks all kinds of bright colors, depending on how she turned her head.

"Welcome to Avalon, Wes Malcolm," the woman said with a kind, pearly smile on her beautiful face. "I am Lady Guineve of the Mists, Guardian of Avalon. May I know the reason for your visit?"

Take it in stride, I repeated to myself. *And try to only stare at her face.*

"Yes, you may know the reason for my visit," I decided to say. "But please let me know as well once you find out."

"Oh?" The pale woman arched a very regal dark eyebrow at me. Her face looked very, very serious, except for the tiny smile at the corner of her mouth. "Did you not intend to visit us tonight? Are you saying one of us neglected to close the gate tonight, and you just wandered in like a stray?"

"I, uh, maybe?" I said. This really wasn't fair. "I don't really know."

"And why not?" the tall beauty demanded imperiously, but I swore her dark and twinkling eyes were laughing at me.

"Because I just woke up, have no idea where I am, and frankly am very weirded out now."

"Weirded out?" the Lady of the Mist said, tilting her head further. "Is that some sort of new phrase?" She turned to look behind her. "Stell?" she called out. "Is that some new catchphrase on his planet?"

A faintly hissing rebuke suggested that Stell still didn't want to be noticed right now.

But I wasn't paying a lot of attention to that. I was recalling the words 'just woke up.'

Far too suddenly, I distinctly remembered not putting on any extra clothing before I came here.

I glanced downward, not remembering how much I had bothered to dress last night and fearing the worst.

"Oh thank God," I sighed in relief. "I'm not naked."

The Lady turned her head back to look at me. There was a short but very awkward moment where neither of us said anything.

"What did you say?" she finally asked.

"I mean..." *Screw it,* I decided. "Well, I just woke up. Do *you* wear a lot of clothing when you go to bed?"

The statuesque figure paused again, her semi-imperious expression remaining on her face for all of five more seconds. Then she burst out into rich peals of laughter, clutching her stomach as she did so. She started to say something, once, twice, thrice, but was unable to get herself under control.

"Stell," she finally gasped. "I take it back. This one is too perfect for you. You're taking over."

"What?" the teenaged voice said from beyond the mists. "No I'm not—"

Guineve, or the Lady of the Mists, or whoever the hell she was pointed out to where the other figure was probably hiding and crooked her finger. Suddenly the mist parted.

A girl that looked to be about my age was trying to hide behind some weird rocks. In many ways, her appearance was the opposite of the older, stately woman next to me. Where the lady called Guineve looked as if she was sculpted, perfected, and well-aged, this girl looked... unfinished. Her skin had a gray tone to it, and somehow it looked blurry. No matter where she stood, or even how she stood, shadows seemed to fall over her, robbing her form of a tiny bit of detail here and there. The blurring effect added just enough mystery to make it almost impossible to decide what she really looked like. It hid just enough of her cheeks to where it looked as if they would decide on being narrow or full by next week. Her nose looked a little small, and I couldn't decide whether that was because of the shadows or because it was still growing into its final shape or because it was just small, and not going to be bigger even when it was finished. Either way, it wound up looking cute, in spite of its still-growing state. Her gray skin seemed like it was changing under the blur, but I couldn't tell if it was turning pale or darkening. Her eyes were that gray some babies have, that make you keep guessing whether the final color will be brown or green or blue or just stay gray. Her hair was a color and weave that was impossible to pin down, and every drop of mist-reflected light made me swear that she was either a blonde, or a brunette, or a black-haired Asian, Latino, or Indian, or a light-skinned black girl (that might be darker tomorrow for all I knew), depending on the moment I looked at it.

All her little slightly-unfinished features made her so mysterious and exotic that for a second, I couldn't help but stare at her face, but I jerked my head away (hopefully) in time before it got creepy. Then I noticed something else.

She was wearing an ironic t-shirt.

I kid you not. Black t-shirt with a fake paper note printed on the front of it. On that note, with cut-out, ransom-note style letters, were the words: I have kidnapped myself. Give me one million dollars or you will never see me again.

I could feel the grin crack across my cheeks. Dream, magical-oz-adventure, bad meds, stroke, whatever this was, this girl just officially became one of my favorite people ever. I'd figure out why she had that shirt in this world at all later, but for now I was just going to quietly applaud her taste.

And yes, I like ironic t-shirts. Sue me and call me dirty names.

"Hi," I said, still grinning. "I'm Wes."

"Hi," she said back, still nervous but resigned to dealing with me. "I'm Stell."

"Is that short for Stella?" I asked.

"Yes," she replied with a small shrug. "But Stella is also short for something else that I don't want to try and pronounce right now, because no one really understands anything beyond the fact that it means 'star.' So you can call me Stell, or Stella. And I look like this because you caught me at a bad time and I don't normally even meet guests when I have this appearance."

"That's fine with me," I said with a shrug. "I normally don't take so long to remember that I dressed myself, and I usually know where I am and why, so I guess we both deserve a little slack. And Wes is short for Wesley, if you want to know. I don't know of any longer versions of my name, though, so you're safe with either of those."

She finally grinned back, and I wanted to sigh in relief. Without realizing it, I had sort of formed a gentleman's agreement with her, that we'd both pretend I hadn't walked in on her bawling her eyes out. There were a lot of questions we both wanted to ask each other right now but somehow we both managed to move the 'why do you look like that?' questions to the back of our minds until we both felt safer.

And she had a really nice smile, so I was happy about that too.

Smiles and ironic t-shirts. Sue me again.

"I appreciate that," she continued, then began speaking again. "Say... we really weren't expecting company at all. Can you tell me how you got here?"

That was a good question. One I'm pretty sure I had already asked at this point.

"Um, maybe?" I replied cautiously. "I either got here by dreaming, or by taking some really bad pain medication I don't remember anything about, or by reaching into my video game harness and pulling out a magic key that unlocked a portal hidden in the wall of my living room."

Huh. When I say those options out loud...

"I'd go with the magic key," Stell offered. (Huh?) "Since that's the only explanation that makes sense at all." *(Huh?)*

"Uh, what?" I said, and not as smoothly as I'd hoped. Hallucination or not, I kind of wished I was more eloquent when talking to these beautiful, exotic women. But she still smiled and began ticking off her fingers.

"First off, no medicine has ever granted access to any world. Ever. That would have been a first. And a scary one, because we don't want every person with a cold or the pox to accidentally wind up here after a visit to their healer or herbalist. Second, while most Challengers do enter here while dreaming, they can only do so in response to a Call, and I can't send one out yet. You probably heard me lose it while discussing that very fact."

"Um, sorry," I said awkwardly, raising a hand before I knew what to do with it.

"Don't be. You clearly had no idea you were intruding and it's not like we left you signs to know not to disturb us. Why we've never needed them is a whole other discussion for later. Finally, there are in fact a handful of magic keys that each let people visit one of the different worlds, so it's likely you just found one that I haven't catalogued yet. On Earth. Which is a total first, given the low level of magic on that world. And one that also leads to here—Avalon. Which is another total first. So congratulations on breaking two Expanse-wide records in one night. On a good day, I'd be upset. But this is the farthest thing possible from a good day, so I'm actually really, really glad you're here. I'm checking one last time though, before I really get hopeful and excited. You're from Earth, right?"

"Yes..." I said, suddenly feeling very creepy now that planets, *plural*, were officially part of the conversation. "Are... are we not on Earth right now? May I ask where you are from—I mean, where we are? Sorry, I thought I asked that earlier, but no one's said anything about that yet."

Stell grinned wider. I could tell she was trying not to laugh.

It was a good look on her, even though I was the reason for her humor. Whatever blurred her form from me was unable to hide the rich, healthy look her face had when she was happy. It was the final nudge that pushed the gray of her skin fully over from 'different' to 'exotic.'

"Sorry," she finally said when she saw I noticed her humor at my expense. "I just realized you're even more overwhelmed by everything than I am right now. I at least know what's going on, even if I wasn't expecting it to happen." She took another breath, finally stepping around those weird stones she was hiding behind to talk to me properly. Even closer, her appearance was still hard to pin down. The blur remained on her, although it seemed to shimmer slightly around her, like a drape that tried to keep up with her movements and wasn't always successful. I got the strange feeling that she was continuing to change before my very eyes, and faster than she was a moment ago. It was weird, but I couldn't shake the belief that the next time I'd see her, she'd look completely different.

Not that I had any business guessing much about her. We were still at the 'so, which planet are you from?' stage of the conversation.

"So," Stell continued, exhaling. "If you're from Earth, here's what's going on. You've traveled to a different world, exactly at the moment that people in every other nearby world needed you to. This is Avalon—yes, like the Avalon the last Challengers have described, though not exactly the same thing. This is where Challengers come when one of the other worlds need someone to help with a massive catastrophe. When the Challengers arrive, we train them to be heroes."

"Um, sorry to interrupt," I said. "But what's the significance behind the word 'challenger' that you keep throwing around?"

"I'm getting to that," Stell said with a smile. "I know it's a lot to take in, but just be patient with me for a second.

"Avalon shares a gateway with the other worlds. It helps ground and stabilize them, safeguarding them from certain hazards in the universe. It's also possible to view other worlds from here, and see if special occurrences called Trials are happening. Trials are events that are distinctly different than a world's usual difficulties, caused by an outside force no one's ever understood. They affect anywhere from just a local region to a large part of the world at once. If they're handled early, the world and people improve greatly from the experience, in too many ways to go into right now. But if they're not overcome, then the Trial eventually progresses into something called a Tumult. Not every time, as sometimes Tumults can occur on their own, but they always affect the world on a global scale. Failed Tumults, as the name suggests, are really, really bad. They can result in most of the people of the world being conquered or wiped out. Tumults also occur whenever a supernatural catastrophe happens, or whenever an undiscovered monster arises to cause havoc."

"Just so we're clear," I interrupted. "You just said the word 'monster?' As in scary thing that goes bump in the dark?"

"More like 'scary thing that hates sentient people groups and constantly seeks to kill, devour, or enslave them.' They grow stronger by inflicting suffering on sentients like you and me, and, for some reason, our peoples become stronger by overcoming them. Facing a single one usually creates a Challenge, which is sort of a personal version of a Trial or Tumult. The weak ones are no problem for the world's inhabitants, but when their numbers or power increase, then we're in the risk of having a severe Trial or even a Tumult. If a Tumult does occur, and enough time has passed, then I can call out for a person to come to Avalon. I usually use your planet because, for some reason everyone's still debating, Earthlings always wind up being the best candidates. When they answer the call and arrive at Avalon, they become what we call a Challenger. Challengers turn the tide during Tumults. They grow stronger faster than a normal person does from overcoming Challenges and Trials, and those that face obstacles with them grow faster as well. They also begin to manifest unique powers as well. As long as they've been given enough time, they've always been able to turn the tide in a

Tumult. Well, almost always." she looked away for a moment. "Their biggest advantage though, is that they can come back from the dead, over and over, as long their other body is still healthy and on their home planet."

"Wait," I said, interrupting again. "Other body?"

Stell smiled again. "Yes. The body you use here is a copy of the one you have on Earth, and as long as your primary body stays safe and sound, you can keep resurrecting, arriving here at Avalon. It's actually something unique to the people of your world, as all of the other races in the Expanse have to travel across worlds using their original bodies. My own race used to be able to do it too, though."

When I heard her talk about resurrecting, I thought it sounded suspiciously like bind points in video games. Then I heard her mention her own race, and wondered how I could ask her what race she was delicately...

"That trait is why I look the way I do," Stell continued awkwardly.

Never mind, then.

"My people have a long, complicated name you can't really pronounce, but it translates into most languages as 'Starsown'." She started to look uncomfortable again, as if this were an uneasy subject for her. "Our bodies are... different from yours. I don't want to go into all the details, but my appearance, my color, my bone structure, and even my shape and height, change from year to year, or even from day to day. That's why I look like this." She gestured to herself. "Usually I wait until my body completes transition before I greet a Challenger, but you caught me between phases, so that's why I look all half-finished."

"Sorry," I said, embarrassed as well. "As I said, I sorta didn't know I'd be coming."

I wanted to add that her look wasn't bad, that it made her look full of potential instead of the awkward thing she clearly felt like, but I didn't know if she'd take that as a compliment or as me being creepy. Successfully complimenting girls is hard for me, even when I'm not experiencing the weirdest moment of my life.

"Not your fault," Guineve called out from the mists and interrupting my train of thought. Stell shot her a dirty look.

"So..." I asked, trying to change the subject for the both of us. "Is Guineve your mother or something?"

The Lady of the Mists apparently heard that, because she gave a deep, rich chuckle.

"In addition to changing my primary body," Stell continued, still glaring at Guineve's direction, "parts of me will occasionally break off and form new bodies, called Satellites, to help interact with and stabilize the world I live in. It's really complicated to explain, but basically, Guineve is me, the part of me that specifically maintains Avalon."

I scratched my head. I really hoped I looked less confused than I felt.

"Are you aware of everything she experiences?" I asked, struggling to make sense of one single thing tonight.

"Yes," she affirmed. "It's not quite the same as hearing it directly, but I more or less share experiences with her."

I hope she didn't catch me staring at her other body, I thought. *Crap, I hope I'm still not staring at Stell.*

After hearing the gray-skinned girl's explanation about herself, I kinda felt like I had walked in while she was changing, and was wondering if I was about to get my ass kicked for it.

"So when I was talking to Guineve, technically, I was also talking to you?" I asked, realizing I was going to lose the battle of having tonight make sense.

"Yes..." Stell answered carefully.

"And when she outed you hiding back here, you effectively outed yourself?"

"...Yes," she said, her eyes narrowing. "Guineve has most of my confidence and poise right now." She glared at the other woman. "As well most of my *patience.*" That last part was said loudly.

"And good sense!" the 'older' woman called out cheerfully.

"So she's the part of you that's okay with all of this right now?" I asked. She nodded uncomfortably.

"Why does she look so much older than you? No offense," I added quickly.

On one hand, I really didn't like making this girl uncomfortable. This felt like the kind of thing that you don't talk about in polite company, in her culture. But on the other hand, I was trying hard not to scream *what the hell is going on* over and over. I think the only reason I wasn't further weirded out was because I still thought this was a dream, or a hallucination.

Or a stroke. Actually, scratch that possibility, because it didn't calm me down at all.

Fortunately, Stell just smirked at this question, and Guineve called out in a slightly dangerous voice:

"I don't look old. Let him know that, Stell. I don't look old at all."

Stell smirked even wider.

"He's talking to me, Guineve. Remember? You passed him over to me." She turned back to give me her full attention. "The reason Guineve looks *so old* is because I've been grounding and maintaining her body for a long time. Auxiliary bodies don't go through phases like mine, so I can keep them pretty stable. When I get too full of an idea or an emotion inside, I can pass that part of me onto her, and if it's compatible with the rest of what I've given her, she'll maintain her appearance. That's why her appearance is an *old withered maid, forever.* So that she can help ground and maintain Avalon."

Guineve snorted from the mists. Stell ignored her.

"So that's why she looks the way she does," Stell finished smugly. "But enough about that. We've gotten far too sidetracked talking about me."

"This isn't over," the stately woman called darkly from the mist. Stell ignored her and I just sat there feeling uncomfortable.

"We haven't talked about me at all yet," called out the high-pitched voice I had heard earlier.

"I'm trying, Breena!" Stell shouted. "There's a lot to cover here!" The gray-skinned girl sighed, then shrugged, as if giving up on whatever she was preparing to say, and then motioned forward. "I'll go ahead and introduce you to Breena. She's another part of myself that travels with other Challengers, offers them advice whenever they encounter a new world or phenomenon. She's—"

"Hi!"

A little pink light zipped forward and began yammering at me.

"So-nice-to-meet-you-gosh-it's-been-so-long-I-can't-believe-we-finally-have-another-Challenger-we're-going-to-have-so-much-fun-and-go-on-so-many-adventures-and-stop-so-many-bad-guys-everyone-else-is-worried-about-these-Tumults-but-I-know-we're-gonna-kick—"

"Ow," I interrupted, covering my ears and not quite able to handle the rapid-fire conversation of what appeared to be a talking, flying night-light. But when I stopped wincing, I thought I saw a tiny woman's body inside the pink glow.

The little fairy (she hadn't called herself that yet, but God help me if I could think of any other word for her) took a deep breath to continue speaking, but the t-shirt wearing girl interrupted.

"Sorry. We're usually a lot more organized with this. Breena, I think he's really overwhelmed by everything, and we're not doing a good job of preparing him. Maybe you could go prepare for when he works with you later?"

"Oh, that's a good idea!" the little light agreed cheerfully. "I'll go do that. It-was-nice-talking-to-you-we're-gonna-have-so-much-fun!"

And without another word, the little light-fairy zipped off. I turned back to look at Stell, who continued speaking.

"Anyway, what usually happens goes like this: one of the worlds suffers a Tumult, I Call out for a Challenger, a Challenger comes—from your world—and you acclimate to Avalon until you're ready to save the day. Are you following with me?"

"Sort of," I replied. "Having no trouble listening. Still having a lot of trouble believing this is real. How often do you people have these world-shaking events—or Tumults, or whatever you call them? That you need to summon a lovable nerd-slash-mighty warrior in a video game-esque plot?"

"Video game?" Stell blinked at me, then brightened. "Oh! Those! I love those! The last Challenger showed me all about those! But no, I'm pretty sure your people got the idea for video game ar-pee-gees (pretty sure she was trying to say 'RPGs') from us, not the other way around. But Tumults happen pretty rarely. In fact, we haven't had one like this well... ever."

"What do you mean?" I ask.

"Well," the gray-skinned woman hedged. "It's always just affected one, sometimes two worlds. Right now the signs are pointing to every one of our worlds experiencing a Tumult."

"Wait, all of them?" I asked. "At the same time?"

She nodded.

"How does that work?"

"It...doesn't," Stell finally said. "Without a Challenger, I scramble to find resources and raise up the native inhabitants any way I can, work with any other local powers, and maybe I can help a world or two get past its Tumult. But the people in the rest of the worlds are doomed, especially considering how every world is going to undergo more than one Tumult this time. But I can help a Challenger travel across worlds easily, and also help that Challenger raise armies, magic orders, or other organizations that can prevent each Tumult from destroying the world."

She gave me a very level look, and her voice trembled a little as she finished speaking. I realized that she was going through an emotional whiplash right now, seeing certain death for people she apparently cared a great deal about, and then suddenly seeing in me a lifeline that came out of nowhere.

"So anyway," she continued, her voice still trembling slightly. "I'm doing my best to be composed about this, but if you're not willing or able to be a Challenger, then all of these people are probably going to die. At best," she finished.

I wasn't a firm believer on the whole 'fate worse than death' thing, but with my condition I could understand why others went with that idea.

"Uh," I said once again. I know, genius of me. Absolutely genius of me.

"Please?" she said, and I thought I saw her eyes water through the blurring effect. "I can't make you do this, but if you don't, I'm going to have to start begging very, very badly."

"Don't do that. Just hold on a second," I finally replied. "I'm still trying to wrap my head around this whole thing—that's not a no! That's not a no!" She had started to bite her lip, and I really didn't want to make this girl beg.

"Just... let me think for a second," I continued. "How exactly does this work? Do I only come here when I fall asleep in the real world?"

She nodded.

"According to the other Challengers, you will. As far as anyone will be able to tell, you'll just be having some interesting dreams. It shouldn't impact your real life in any negative way."

"Not that worried about my real life," I chuckled darkly before I could stop myself. "But thanks. And what happens to me when I die?"

"You experience a great deal of pain, then you wake up in either Avalon or Earth," she replied. "But that's it. None of the other Challengers have reported side effects from dying."

"Have they reported any side effects at all?" I asked. Because that would a great way to tell whether I was going crazy or not.

On the other hand, going crazy might well be one of the side effects.

"That's part of the deal," Stell replied with a nod. "You'll get to keep a little bit of the growth you gain here. Maybe not the magic, because magic doesn't really seem to work on Earth, but you'll keep everything else you learn, and some of the growth your body goes through."

"What kind of growth?" I interrupted.

"Muscles, memory, coordination—"

"Really?" I interrupted again. "I'd get all of that?"

Stell nodded.

"I can't peer into your planet easily, but every Challenger has kept at least some of the power, gotten a little stronger, a little smarter, after stopping Tumults here."

"Sold," I said simply. "Though honestly, I was just checking to make sure my family wouldn't have to put up with any more problems with me. If everything you said is true, then I have no reason to tell you 'no.' I submit to your quest for a hero and my own desire to live out my biggest childhood fantasies—whether this is all a hallucinogenic dream or not."

She grinned at that, and the sparkling wetness in her eyes took on a much happier twinkle.

8

LIFELINE

So I was supposed to be the legendary hero that saved multiple worlds. That sounded like an *epic* video game plot, and I said as much to Stell. She just rolled her eyes at me and continued the explanation.

There were at least seven worlds. I asked how there could be 'at least' seven, and Stell hedged when she answered me. She clarified that she was *in charge* of seven, but that there could be more being under observation by other Starsown.

“Where are the other Starsown?” I had asked. She didn't answer. I got the feeling that she hadn’t seen anyone else from her race in a very long time. The subject seemed painful for her, so I decided to save the question for later. Or until I woke up from this dream. Either way.

“So,” Stell said finally, pointing to the strange stones I had seen earlier. “Since this is a lot to take in, and since people from your planet have a hard time believing they're really here when they do arrive...” *Yup,* I thought. *Sounds about right.*

“Let's go ahead and get you acclimated, then let you head back home.”

“Oh good,” I breathed. I had thought about that but hadn't asked. “So I can go back home?”

“Absolutely. This isn't one of those alien abduction things that one of the last Challengers told me about.” She shivered. “And the probes. I mean, really? Who thinks up stuff like that? Some of you guys are pretty weird. Anyway, back to what we're doing."

She touched one of the stones, and glowing symbols appeared over their upper surfaces. A screen of light appeared over the outcrop of rocks, as if it were the monitor to a nature-made computer.

As Stell peered into the screen and hit symbols, a bright light appeared directly in front of my eyes.

"This is your mind-screen," Stell informed me. "It's the easiest way to enable Earthlings to process the same information everyone else outside your planet gets."

"Wait, what?" I asked intelligently.

"Sorry, I thought I was clear earlier," Stell said. "Earth is the only place, for reasons unknown even to me, where people can't track their own growth without a lot of work. And the only place where people don't grow automatically from overcoming Challenges or Trials."

"I thought we didn't have those, or at least not the capital-letter versions I hear you emphasizing."

"No, your planet has struggles too—a *lot* of struggles, good grief—but something short-changes your people on the power you should be receiving from overcoming the obstacles of life. Maybe that's why you all grow so explosively once you leave Earth. Anyway, this will help you track things when you come here."

The screen in front of my face beeped again.

Welcome, Challenger, it said.

Assessment commencing. Please wait for the analysis of your history and abilities.

"That assessment will take a while, but you don't have to wait here for it," Stell said. "And sorry, I probably should have warned you that you're going to see text. After a while, you'll think it more than see it. But for now, go ahead and see if you can go home, so that you can go back to normal sleep."

"Is it still night?" I asked, surprised. "And how do I get back?"

"Here? No, it's no longer night," Stell answered. "But time flows much slower on your world than any place else. I have no idea why. Traveling back and forth between worlds will get easier for you, but for now, just concentrate on wherever you were sleeping before, and you should return to that exact spot. You'll still remember everything, in case that helps convince you that this wasn't just a dream."

"But you said my body's sleeping right now," I pointed out.

"Well, *yes,* but," she said, frustrated. "You're not *sleeping* sleeping. Understand?"

"No," I admitted.

"Look, just don't worry about it. Close your eyes, relax, and you'll go back to normal sleep, or at least whatever is normal sleeping behavior for you."

I think she was making fun of the *I'm not naked even though I was sleeping* line I made earlier. I shrugged, said goodbye, and marched out toward the way I came. I passed Guineve, who gave me a cool, stately nod, and bowed to her.

"Lady Guineve, it was an honor meeting you, and please know that, whatever age you are, you are easily the most beautiful woman I have met over the age of twenty, my mother potentially excluded. If you ever do meet my mother, please do not tell her I said that."

"Oh?" The woman's pale face warmed instantly. "Stell, I want you to know that I approve of your new boyfriend. Go ahead and keep this one."

"Guineve!" the younger woman called out in horror.

"What, what?" the high-pitched voice asked. Breena suddenly flew by. "Does Stell finally have a boyfriend? Is there finally going to be a boy in Avalon? Does that mean we all get a boyfriend too?"

"Bree-na!" Different name, same horror-filled tone.

Realizing that I may or may not have done more harm than good, I quickly began concentrating on returning to my earthly body back home. I ignored the temptation to click my heels together though.

As I drifted off to sleep, the weirdness of everything finally left, allowing me to focus fully on an earlier fact.

I had been walking.

Quickly.

And completely on my own power.

No help whatsoever.

Dream or not, crazy world or not, that experience alone, to be able to walk around without having to think about it, made this place worth coming back to.

9

GRASP

My sabaton twisted experimentally into the dirt, the articulated plates covering my boot bending and flexing enough to allow my foot its normal range of motion—or at least the motion I was normally allowed in *Heroes Unbound*. At its time, and even now, *Heroes Unbound* was touted as the most interactive and realistic masterpiece of virtual reality programming. That was quite a feat when you consider people were fighting orcs and fire-breathing dragons. I remembered first playing the game way back before my accident, and noticing how it was just *barely* different from moving an actual arm, from actually running, or from swinging a real sword (my parents allowed me to do that at a Renaissance fair one time. Stop looking at me like that). Combining that experience with a fantastic virtual world made it the most popular online game since the ancient World of Warcraft series that was released over fifty years ago.

It was so realistic that despite the dangers of addiction, my doctor prescribed it for virtual physical therapy after my accident. And it actually seemed to work. There was maybe a 3% difference between waving your hand in real life and waving your hand in *Heroes Unbound*. And instead of expounding on that difference, the magical aspects of the game actually served to help mask it.

Now, though, the differences seemed to jump out of me with every detail.

This world was both somehow less real and less magical than Stell's world of mist and lights.

And the irritating thing is, I couldn't even explain why.

But I could try.

As real as *Heroes Unbound* looked, everything still felt like I was watching a movie, or rather, I was part of a movie. It looked fantastic, it felt fantastic, and even though the movement almost exactly matched real life, I never mistook it for such. The colors, for one thing, were always a bit off. Maybe that was due to the technology's limitations; maybe they served to create a certain atmosphere. I asked Dad about it a long time ago, and all he said was, "It's to make sure it's a fun game."

But the world I dreamed up that night didn't have any of it.

Oh sure, I was wondering every minute whether or not it was real. But that's because it *shouldn't* have been real. There shouldn't have been a land of mist and glowing lights that somehow still looked like real mist and real lights. There shouldn't have been three exotic women (did Breena count as a woman? I'd better be careful with asking about that next time) that looked different than any women I had ever seen, and yet felt more real than a computer-generated villager in *Heroes Unbound.*

Avalon hadn't felt like I was in a movie. Avalon had felt like my normal life was the movie, and that the place outside the theater was more magical than anything I'd dreamed up.

I couldn't describe it any better than that.

But at any rate, the reason I had logged back into *Heroes Unbound* wasn't to see how fake it was or how crazy I was probably becoming.

It was because *Gamers' Digest* had finally agreed to give me an interview.

Well, sort of.

When we were accused of cheating, the Aussies took to forums in a storm. Skybladex had filmed the entire fight, and uploaded it proudly, daring people to find any way we were cheating. We weren't, it's actually really hard to hack *Heroes Unbound*, and its company monitors cheating very well. It was obvious that we had beaten the boss through some kind of normal ability, though people were still trying to figure out what I had done, and how I had known how to do it.

That was where the cheating arguments came in. Somehow, it got leaked that I had family that worked for *Heroes Unbound*. That was a violation of privacy, and not something most other players knew. So someone that knew me, knew I played this game, and apparently hated me enough, had spread a rumor that I had learned the secret of the boss from my father, who worked on the game, and that I had somehow gotten some help from him for my character.

That kind of claim seemed dubious to a lot of people, because again, hacking would have been discovered quickly, and had Dad actually done that, he would have quickly been found out and lost his job.

But again, having been dead for three years, he was quickly exonerated. For that at least.

I, on the other hand, was still being examined, but my gaming account had been reactivated, and the company had released a statement that Mr. John Malcolm had been deceased for three years—again, long before this boss fight was even a concept. So now most people apparently knew my dad was dead and thought that the rumormongers were just being major assholes.

Hopefully, that was all that they found out about my dad. But I was resigned to canceling the interview and giving up any potential prize money.

Until an ambitious journalist contacted me out of the blue with a proposition.

The magazine didn't want to risk propping up someone who turned out to be a cheater, but they also didn't want to miss out on interviewing someone who had gotten the first confirmed kill on a boss without even being max-level. Apparently, my story was so fantastic, no one could risk mistaking whether it was fake or real. So they decided to make a story of testing my claim as a compromise. The journalist would conduct the interview within the game itself, while we were playing. And they would test me in some fashion that they hadn't bothered to disclose.

That was why I was logged back in, waiting for a person to come test me, and at the same time, trying to get rid of a dream that should have left my mind two nights ago.

Looking up through the virtual dust, I saw a figure bounding its way over to me and finally crossing the imaginary boundary that began the canyon's entry zone. She—I could tell that much—was waving cheerfully at me and shouting at me to toss her an invite.

"Are you with *Gamer's Digest*?" I shouted over the virtual wind.

"Yep, I'm Veronica Mels! Wes Malcom, I presume? Nice to meet you!"

I blinked at that. *The* Veronica Mels? One of the most well-known pro gamers out there, creator of almost a thousand "Let's Play" stream videos on *Kitch*, where people actually paid money to watch her play. She also wore the "Gamer Girl" tag proudly, daring people to dispute either part of that title.

"Um, hi," I said lamely. You may have noticed by now that I'm not good at talking to women. "I uh, didn't know you worked for *Gamer's Digest.*"

"I don't," she said, having her character stick her tongue out at me. In the game, her character was an elf that came up to my paladin's shoulder, with long blonde hair running down her cheeks and neck. She was also a level thirty-four huntress, less than half my level in a zone that was near suicide for me to solo if I wasn't careful. Named *Cudiepie*. Figures. "But they do take freelancers. And they wanted someone good enough at the game to tell if you're the real thing." She smiled at me then, in a way that seemed both kind and sneaky at the same time. "So while I'm questioning you, I'm going to try and test you periodically. Maybe pull aggro here and there, to where you're fighting one extra monster than you planned to deal with, and see how you handle it? How does that sound?"

I stared at her for a moment, trying to formulate a response.

"Confusing," I finally said. "Handling monsters in small groups, or soloing in our case, since at your level you won't be able to hurt these mobs and will aggro a lot of them anyway because of your low level, is almost nothing like a raid fight. I could theoretically be an awesome solo player but still a cheater when it comes to raid fights."

"You could!" Veronica exclaimed with a wave of her finger. "But! One: it's already obvious you didn't hack the game. Your character didn't do crazy damage or any weird moves during that fight. And two: you had never battled that boss before. So the only way you could have won was with insider knowledge, or having a really good head on your shoulders even when the fight got stressful. I intend to test that head by putting you through an equally stressful experience."

Despite her avatar's cheerful smile, I was starting to suspect this would be an unpleasant experience. I started to say as much when she suddenly added "and we're paying you for your time."

"Deal," I said firmly.

"That fast?" She was still smiling.

"That fast," I affirmed. "College is expensive. Ready to go?"

"Yes!" she said happily, her avatar raising her hand to touch a button on an invisible screen. "We are officially recording and beginning this interview. Hello everyone, it's Veronica Mels, AKA Cudiepie, here with Wes Malcom AKA Faren, arguably the most skilled—or most devious—paladin player without a guild right now. I'm here to ask him some questions and test to see if he's the real thing. So Faren, or should I call you Wes?"

My avatar shrugged in his armor.

"Either's fine, I guess. And a pleasure to meet you, Ms. Mels."

"Please," she grimaced, though with a twinkle in her eye. "Either Veronica or Cudiepie. Though I'll go ahead and give you points for manners. Just how old are you?"

"Eighteen, ma'am, and sorry," I add with a smile. "Now that I'm getting over the shock, Southern upbringing is kicking in."

She laughs at that. "How quaint! I didn't even know anyone still talked like that. So you're from the South?"

"Texas," I affirmed, unsure of whether to add 'ma'am' or 'miss,' until I remembered my mother's advice that most women anywhere close to my age hate those terms. The first time is cute because it shows you know manners, but after than that it makes them feel old, weird, or both. "From New Arlington. Near Old Dallas."

"Oh okay," she says. "So why do you—*watch out!*"

Without another word, she spun away from me, her bow already in her hand. Before I could say anything, she fired three arrows into a pack of canyon orcs milling around in the distance. Her arrows didn't even come close to damaging them, but one of them let out a whoop anyway, and the gray-skinned humanoids came charging over to us.

"First test!" she shouted with a smile. She then held out both her arms, making no move to either defend herself or escape from the half-dozen, seven-foot tall, level 70 monsters bearing down on her.

"Save the lowbie!"

I bit back a frustrated curse and ran in front of her, sending her a group invite so that I could better pull the monsters' attention away from her.

I didn't have a lot of time, but I was able to cast two quick paladin blessings, one on her to make her less noticeable to monsters, and another on myself to make me look like a larger threat. Then I used one of my class's only offensive spells to channel burning light through the ground. The light seared the feet of the monsters, not harming them greatly but making them angry enough to target me instead of the helpless elf behind me. I barely had time to equip my defensive sword and large shield before all six monsters came barreling down on me.

The orcs were wielding crude stone or flint machetes that had glowing runes etched into them. Since orcs fought at least somewhat like actual people, I shifted into a player-versus-player stance for handling other weapons, and took the first blow on the side of my shield, knocking the monster's arm away to give my weapon an opening. I gave him a quick slash and then darted toward the next monster, taking his blow on my pauldron and bashing him in the face with my shield for a four-second stun. Then I turned to the next four monsters and used Justice's Snare to stun another for two seconds. I took three more blows on the back of my armor, then recast the Holy Ground spell to ensure they were still being damaged. Now that I was sure I had their attention, I returned my attacks to the first monster, constantly slashing and bashing him while stepping around him and keeping him between me and as many of his friends as I could. As I did that, I cycled between a number of minor chants that were just enough to keep healing me, enhancing me, and damaging the orcs enough for the one in front of me to finally die on my blade.

I breathed a sigh of relief at the change of odds. My stunning abilities and Holy Ground spell had all refreshed, so I locked down two more orcs quickly, burned them all with more magic, and focused on healing all the nicks and cuts I had received. The three non-stunned orcs hammered on my armor while I did this, sending my nerves tiny pinpricks of pain through the neural sensors on the VR rig, but it wasn't enough to disrupt my concentration and I healed myself back to full health. Then I charged into the middle of the five remaining monsters, using their bulk to interfere with their swings.

This might sound like a bad idea, and in some other games it probably is. But here in *Heroes Unbound*, it was the best strategy I could come up with. Since Veronica was insisting on playing 'monster jailbait,' I couldn't just run off and fight the monsters over a large distance, because they'd lose interest and come back for her. I had to constantly risk getting hit by all five of the remaining oversized goblins if I wanted my reporter 'friend' to survive, but getting hit non-stop in five different places is suicide, even in full plate armor. So I had to try and move to where their computer brains at least thought they could eventually reach me, forcing them to step around each other to hit me. The Paladin was supposed to be a tanking and healing class, so I was able to handle a number of blows from their glowing machetes and axes.

Provided I broke out every trick in my class's playbook.

I continued to hack at their unarmored arms with my sword, trying to land every critical hit I could. My shield bashed an orc in its snarling face every time they left themselves open from a wild swing. While I was doing that, I chanted every quick, cheap spell or special ability I knew. Paladin spells were weak, but they take almost no time or mana, which gave me more opportunities than people realized. A tiny heal here, a half-second stun here, a three-second snare, another critical strike, and suddenly it was four orcs against one very desperate and cranky paladin player.

Yes, I said cranky.

I was stressed, feeling tiny tingles of pain through my VR gear, and in danger of being made into an online laughingstock in one of the only things I seemed to be able to do without getting dizzy spells or headaches.

Or without being called 'cripple-head.'

More than that, I was sick of failing every time something hard or 'impossible' happened. I didn't know how to fix random dizzy spells that inexplicably emptied my head during tests. I didn't know how to fix having to deal with a hundred classmates determined to push me or hit me in the back of the head with a giant textbook. But I did know how to excel here, and I wasn't going to let this last bit of me be taken away.

So I blocked, dodged, chanted and stabbed faces until all the orcs were dead.

And I felt proud and mad at the same time when I heard clapping. I turned to face my interviewer, reminded myself that I was being both streamed and recorded right now, and gave my best, if strained, smile right now.

"There you go. Six dead orcs, and suicidal lowbie still unharmed. All for your viewers' pleasure. Well done, Wes! Great crowd control and footwork! And you did it all without the paladin's invulnerability shield! That's excellent!"

"Thank you," I replied. I pointedly didn't mention that I couldn't use my invulnerability skill because then the monsters would all turn and kill *her* in the first three minutes of her own interview. "But please tell me you have actual questions for me other than 'can you die from this?'"

"Of course," she chuckled, in a way that made me hope she really thought I was funny. She was actually pretty charming, I reflected, because if anyone else had sprung this scenario on me, in front of a live audience, I'd be really tempted to hate them forever.

"First real question," she continued, oblivious to my internal monologue. "How long have you been playing *Heroes Unbound*?"

"I came on during the open beta test, about three months before its official release. I've been playing it off and on since then, whenever school and life allowed."

"How much raiding did you do?" she asked, her eyes watching me casually.

Too casually, I thought. *She's about to pull again.*

"In these past two years? Not very much. But before that I was a member of the guild Augustus Imperium. I joined before they began clearing Black Talon Lair and stayed with them right up until after they had mastered the Soul-Scorched Citadel."

"I've heard of them. They're in the top thirty of raiding guilds these days. How involved were you with them? Did they give you any responsibilities?"

I could see her eyes scanning past me, and figured that we were two questions max away from her playing suicidal lowbie again.

"The guild leader, Kragmus, can give you the details about every member's responsibilities. Expectations in the guild were high: everyone had to find a way to contribute one resource and was required to lead one raid by their sixth month of membership. The guild's philosophy was that giving everyone a taste of responsibility helped us all work together and understand each other's role better."

Finding an excuse to turn my head, I looked around for whatever monster she'd already decided to pull. But we'd been walking while we were talking, and there wasn't anything in the immediate area for her to antagonize, even with her bow.

"How many raids did you help lead?" she asked cheerfully, no longer looking around.

"Four," I answered. "I primarily just brought crafting resources for others as my other contribution. Mostly for potions. Again, you can ask my old guildmates for more specifics."

"And why did you leave your old guild?" she asked carefully, glancing away again. "Did you have a falling out with the other members?"

"No," I answered uncomfortably, wondering how much it showed in my posture. "They're all still good people, and I miss playing with them. I'm just not able to commit as much as I used to anymore."

"And why is that?" Veronica asked, genuinely curious and looking a little more intently at me.

I figured this was coming, and was prepared to answer it. I initially had planned to pass off the question and just answer "school" or "personal reasons." But then I realized that not only would that make for a lame interview, it wouldn't stop people from being curious and nosy. The best way to avoid too much attention to my personal life would be to go ahead and come clean about how I got hurt. That way, in addition to satisfying a lot of people's suspicion and curiosity, it might help encourage someone else going through a similar situation. After all, I couldn't be the only gamer who had a serious disability. And I didn't know how many other gamers had actually managed to use their games to help their own lives.

For all I knew, this interview could make a difference in someone just as handicapped as me.

With those two motives in hand, I prepared to bare my personal life to the dangers of the internet, and answered her question.

"Several years ago I suffered a bad accident while playing football. The collision messed up my balance and memory pretty bad, and I spent a long time in recovery. The doctors have been unable to fully diagnose what I'm suffering from, so I spent most of the last two years in a lot of intensive therapy and surgeries. Because of that, I'm not able to maintain anything like the normal raiding schedule my old guild requires. I still try and keep in contact with most of the players, but these days the only people my schedule permits me to really play with are those in different time zones, like the Australian guild I took down that boss with."

"Wow," Veronica said, her fingers no longer reaching for her quiver *(yeah, lady, don't think I didn't see that)*. "I'm sorry to hear that. Wait." Her eyes narrowed slightly. "Did you say you were *still* suffering from this condition?"

"Yes, and it originally affected my ability to play just like everything else. But then one of my doctors began researching the effects of virtual immersion software on people with certain neural conditions. He wanted to see if integrating into virtual reality could help fix my brain's pathways. At the time, I was just using a basic computer interface to play the game, one that let me maintain most of my senses in the real world. But then *Heroes*

Unbound released their new virtual reality harness, so my doctor encouraged my family to try it out."

"And how did that work?" she asked, leaning forward, and seeming much more interested.

"At first, it didn't," I replied. "My family couldn't afford the new headset, and insurance wasn't going to spring for what they saw as just a video game appliance. But then my doctor wrote to a charity called Kid's Play. Kid's Play usually provides children in hospitals with electronic entertainment, but they were interested in my condition too, so they generously sprung for the headset. The neural link in my headset and rig lock down my physical body almost completely, allowing me to immerse fully in the game, without needing to move my body at all. Ever since, I've been incorporating my play time into therapy."

"Really? That's why you've been playing?" she asked.

"Yeah. And why I've been playing the hours I've been. It seems to be helping me improve in real life, as my pain has been diminishing and my grades have slowly been getting better. Recently, I've been trying to see if more extreme situations in the game enhanced the treatment."

Her eyes widened at that comment.

"So does that mean the boss fight with Chevelross..."

"Was to simulate my condition in real life," I confirmed. "For some reason, my condition is almost non-existent when I'm inside the game with the helmet, but the doctor and I wanted to see what could happen if I ran into something that reminded me of my disability in real life. Since the boss's roar simulated messing with my balance and concentration, I figured he would be the best test I could take at this point. So I asked the Australian players I sometimes group with if they wanted to take him on with me and they were kind enough to agree."

"Were you expecting to be the first group to ever beat the boss that day?"

"Honestly, no. My Australian buddies are a really good team, but I expected to at least wipe on the first try, like raids normally do. My strategy worked a lot better than I expected. That chant I used was one of the only ways I could see anyone beating the dragon with, but I didn't know it would completely knock his special attacks out of the fight. I'm glad I won and it still took a lot of hard work to take him down, but I wouldn't be surprised if the company continues to tweak that encounter."

"Do you think the fight improved your condition?"

I nodded.

"My pain and balance problems were almost non-existent for the first half of the day. I'm still waiting for the official grades on my test, and I still had trouble the rest of the day, but my English teacher said my performance was on par with or better than most of her other students. That was huge for me, because until this year English was my worst subject, especially the writing portion. My improvement there has been really incredible."

Gee, I thought. When I put it in that light, my day didn't sound that bad.

"Wow," the elf player said. "I'm... honestly impressed. When I offered to interview you, I didn't expect your personal story to be so fascinating. In light of everything, what you've done is... kinda amazing."

"Thank you," I said, surprised and a little embarrassed. Other than my English teacher and maybe my sister and her friends, this was the first time anyone had ever called me "impressive."

Most people just called me "cripple-head."

"Also," she added after a moment, "incoming pull."

And just like that, an arrow flew out into the air and into a pack of giant canyon bats I hadn't seen.

Again, I somehow kept either of us from dying to a pack of monsters that were my level or higher, which again, left the little elven journalist impressed.

This continued for the next hour or so, with Veronica asking me questions and opinions about the game in general, about my strategies, all while testing me in many different situations.

At one point, she asked the question I dreaded most:

"So, I hope I'm not talking about a too-sensitive subject, but what do you have to say about allegations that you cheated with inside help?"

"I didn't have any, and the person accused of helping me, my father, has been dead for several years," I said firmly. "Whoever knew about my father had to know that he has been dead long before that encounter was even designed. The accusation should have taken all of thirty seconds to disprove, and it's forcing me and the rest of my family to deal with his passing all over again. His death is an event my family's still trying to recover from, and I can't understand why someone would need to make it that much harder for us to move on. That's really all I want to say about it. I can't stop people from digging up the details of his death if they really want to, but I just don't like to talk about my dad's death or the circumstances surrounding it."

"Oh," she said. "That's... fair. I'm sorry I brought up so sensitive a subject."

That was surprising, I thought. She sounded sincere about not wanting to pry. And in an interview no less.

"Don't worry about it," I said uncomfortably. "But thank you for understanding."

"My pleasure," the woman smiled at me. I finally noticed that her character's smile actually matched her real smile from her videos online. It was a nice smile. "Thank you for such a wonderful interview. I wish I had more time to ask you better questions but this has actually been a lot of fun. I'm glad I got to talk to such an interesting player."

That smile was working far too well on me. Except for Ms. Springsen, this girl probably had the best smile I had ever seen.

Unless I counted Stell's. She actually beat both women. But then I probably shouldn't count girls I dream up in the middle of the night.

The interview ended then, and Veronica surprised me by actually asking to befriend me on social media. It shouldn't have. It was a good interview for her, and it was good networking. But it was still something new to me, feeling respect from a stranger, instead of pity based on my appearance, or suspicion based on my parents.

The only downside was the attraction. My condition affected me in many ways I'd not care to fully discuss, but even the most optimistic prognosis said I'd never be able to have kids. It didn't make me immune to a beautiful woman, but I'd learned to at least manage having hormones I'd never be able to do anything about. But after that weird dream, and having two different women smile at me so much, I felt myself wondering about meeting her again. It was ridiculous, because even if the injuries last Friday hadn't set my condition back, she was at least five years older than me. This was all assuming that she would be interested to begin with, and that she wouldn't be turned off by meeting me with my cane and stumbling gait.

But still, she had smiled at me. And it felt good to be smiled at.

But beyond that, I still felt good in general. Everything didn't seem quite as hopeless as it did last Friday. Yes, the test sucked, and getting hit by that asshole really messed up my physical progress (something my mother's lawyer also documented), but the final results of the tests were still being contested and if I could get better once, I could get better again.

Besides, today was a good day.

The rest of the week went by pretty well, in a sense. I was out of class, partly due to injury and partly due to Mother going on a warpath with the school administration and insisting that they had failed to keep a student safe. Having a witness to Mr. Jammers' actions, especially when she learned he never notified anyone of my injury, really helped her case. It was nice not having to spend part of the day dodging abusive idiots, but I began to wonder how often I'd see my remaining friends.

The school, for their part, promised to do a better job of guarding me in the future. The student who threw the book at me was suspended, although he wound up celebrating the event by taking a selfie online and showing off a new and suspiciously expensive phone. I could neither prove nor shake the nagging feeling that the phone had been payment for taking me out, and that Rhodes was the most likely buyer for the phone to begin with. The school had also promised that Mr. Jammers would be disciplined for his actions and that I would not have to see him any time soon. He wound up being placed on paid administrative leave, according to the local news.

I did wind up seeing my friends and having the tabletop game with them. Everyone had so much fun, we scheduled another game next weekend, and that time, Davelon came to it. I was surprised. Davelon did some gaming, especially virtual and shooters, but a lot of people at church still thought tabletop gaming was demonic, the old *Lord of the Rings* movies notwithstanding. If enough people found out, the new pastor might make things uncomfortable for him.

The old pastor, who had left around the time of Dad's suicide, wouldn't have cared, quoted certain passages to explain why he didn't care, and would have helped nip any harmful rumors in the bud. He was another person I missed.

We welcomed Davelon anyway, especially because he was one of the few people that were as welcoming to Himari and Andre as Rachel and I were, and rolled up a one-shot character for him (he liked fighter characters with high Search and Sense Motive skills. Go figure). He had fun, and we had fun having him, but when I watched him carefully, he looked just a little uncomfortable playing with us. I think he wanted to talk to me about something after the game, and I was right.

"So what's up?" I asked as he pulled me aside. "And shouldn't you still be recovering from the football game this weekend? Not that we don't enjoy having you here," I added quickly. Davelon was one of the team's defensive stars. He played well, and played hard, often going the extra mile for the team. The only reason he wasn't *the* team's defensive star was because he was really humble and really good at sharing credit.

"No, it's fine," he said awkwardly. "I... didn't play this week."

"What?" I asked loudly, wincing slightly as my own noise made my head hurt. "It was a playoff game. How would the coach not play you this late in the season?" A thought struck me. "Your leg's not flaring up again is it?"

"My leg's been fine for years," Davelon said, a little more forcefully than I could tell he intended to, judging by his wince. He took a deep breath and spoke quickly.

"I quit the team."

"*What?*" I half-shouted like an idiot, grabbing my head as I gave myself another small headache. I caught Andre's worried glance from back inside the house, then saw him duck his head and try to mind his own business. Himari didn't look up, but she nudged him as if reminding him to give us privacy.

"What?" I repeated more quietly. "Why?"

There were probably just as many football scouts looking at Davelon as there were looking at Chris. As much as I wanted to respect my friend's choices, I was really worried about his future here. A football scholarship wasn't something you should just throw away.

"...I had to," Davelon said after a moment, not meeting my eyes. "I... found out." He swallowed, then finally seemed to be able to find the words, and looked me in the eye. "I found out about Coach Biggs."

"What about Coach?" I said, still confused. Davelon used to be a lot faster about making sense.

"Coach Biggs has been asking me to keep an eye on you," Davelon said, still speaking quickly and not looking at me in the eye. "He's been asking me about what routes you take in the school's hallways, when you stop for the restroom, when and where you stay after class, everything."

"Right," I said slowly. "He promised Mom he'd try to protect me after I became a target from the old players." *Hurry up and start making sense, man.*

"He lied," Davelon said, raising his voice bitterly and repeating himself. "He lied."

Davelon took another breath, and looked me in the eye more firmly. "Every time you've been pushed or jumped, successfully at least, has been after Coach asked about you. Said he'd try and make sure someone was watching you when I wasn't. But every one of those times, the only people there were the ones who had messed you up."

Another breath, and he kept talking. This was really hard for him to say, and me to believe.

"Before last week, I had started getting suspicious. That's why I got to you so fast after you got attacked last week. I wanted to keep an eye on my friend just in case. But I still failed," he added miserably.

"C'mon, man," I said. The last thing I wanted was to have one of the only people still trying help me feel guilty about it. It was hard enough to accept their help without that nonsense. "The guys that attacked me weren't even football players. Probably just three of Rhodes' cronies."

"They've been hanging out with other players for a while," Davelon said firmly. "And I've seen them talking to both Chris and Coach on more than one occasion. So, Friday, I confronted Coach about it."

Davelon paused again, before continuing, and since I was so creeped out, I interrupted him.

"What did he say?"

"You don't want to know," my friend replied uncomfortably.

"I kinda do," I replied. "It's a little hard to believe that someone with a job and a reputation would risk both those things on hurting someone like me."

"That's right," Davelon mumbled. "That was the reason I had to bring this up anyway." He raised his head again. This still felt like a mix of slowly defusing a bomb and pulling a really stuck tooth. "You sure you want to know what he said?"

"Yeah, man. Help me hear something that's actually proof of what you're saying."

"He said, and I quote: 'Davelon, you're a good kid, and a good player, but it's time for you to make a choice. Are you going to stay loyal to the team, or are you going to throw out the team's future and your own for a pedophile's sick brat?'"

For a second I couldn't hear anything. Everything got blurry and started to spin. I felt as if someone had punched me in the stomach, and my already-poor balance shifted. I grabbed the porch's wooden rails and dug my cane down for balance.

I tried to make sense of the fact that people in my town now hated my dead father so much, hated me now, that they were willing to go after me, to put the final nail in the coffin life had thrown me into. It didn't make any sense. What did anyone have to gain, by messing with my already miserably hard life?

"I don't...what...why?" I finally choked out. Davelon, guessing what I meant, shrugged.

"I don't know. If I had to guess, it's because the coach is close to a lot of people who either hate the black eye you gave the football team all those years ago, or who were the most outraged by, well..."

He didn't want to say *outraged by my dad's crimes.*

Seeing that I was finally getting my composure back, Davelon began speaking again.

"Now, I know you're going to ask 'what about my scholarship offers?' Best I can tell, they're not going to be affected. My grades are good enough to get into college on their own, and scouts are still looking at me. Besides, when either your mom or my dad busts this thing wide open, it will be better for me to no longer be on the team."

"What do you mean about your dad?" I asked. Davelon's dad was a high-profile cop in the metropolis that treated our small town like a nearby suburb.

"I'm saying since there's a good chance criminal law, not just civil law, was broken, the cops or feds might get involved at some point. So I figured I should go ahead and tell Dad everything I knew about what was going on."

"That's still a big risk for me, man," I replied, grateful, but still worried. "I don't want anyone coming after you like they've been coming after me."

Davelon practically glared at me.

"Well, it was a pretty big risk for you and your dad to pull me and my family out of that burning car four years ago. It was a pretty big risk for you guys to take me in for those months when my parents were in the hospital and I needed a place to stay until they recovered. And it was at least something of an inconvenience for you to follow me around school and help me until my leg healed. And I shouldn't even have to mention that, while I was healing said leg and talking about how I was worried I'd never play again, you found time to help me with my physical therapy, and even spoke with Coach about how you thought I might be a great player if everyone gave me a chance. Which they did at that time, by the way, because that was before you took a hit for stopping Chris at that party, and before this nonsense started spreading about your dad."

Davelon was one of the few people who unequivocally disbelieved that my dad was guilty. He just couldn't reconcile the man that had saved his family's lives with the man that left that note and committed suicide.

He took a breath, but kept going.

"So excuse me if I don't forget all of that. Especially the part on how you took care of me back when I couldn't walk. So it doesn't make sense not to return the favor. Which I thought I was doing, but I wasn't suspicious enough. I'm sorry," he finished, the heat dying in his voice as he apologized.

I nodded dumbly, accepting an apology I never needed. My brain lurched around my skull, trying to find the response it was looking for.

"Davelon?" I asked after it finally found it. "Thank you for being my friend."

10

PULL

My room was glowing again. I rolled over in my bed, trying to blink away the light and go back to sleep, and couldn't because the bed was too uncomfortable. I rolled again, then again, then stopped, because rolling always hurt at least a little and this time I wasn't feeling in pain from the action. I just felt like I was sleeping on wet grass while still wearing my jeans. Looking down revealed that I was fully clothed, and looking under me revealed an entire floor of slightly damp grass.

I blinked a few times, to make sure I wasn't dreaming.

It didn't work, because I *was* dreaming again. I saw mist all around me. Drifting through the air. Clinging on the thick green leaves and long emerald grass all around me. Above me, the sky sparkled black with stars, matching the sparkle of the mist below.

After a while, I realized I could hear music. I followed the sound, expecting to see the same place I had visited earlier. But instead of the meadow with the outcropping of stones, I found the ruins of some Athenian-style white marble building. Steps and columns led up to a building that had crumbled from the top down, lacking a roof and a few walls. Yet the floor and remaining structure was clean, as if it had been recently and consistently swept and polished. The music seemed to be coming from the floor itself.

Standing over the floor was the pale woman called Guineve, in a long white dress that looked like it was made of clouds. She was looking up at the sky for something, but she turned her head at me and smiled when I came nearby.

"Welcome back, Challenger," she said regally. I offered an awkward nod and greeting back, carefully trying to stare at her face and not her thinly-covered chest. She smiled as if I was amusing her. "Stell is waiting for you downstairs. You should go see her."

I climbed the steps to track the sound, and found a white stone stairway leading down into a dark basement. The music seemed to drift from there, and if I looked carefully, I could see a faint blue light emitting from the room below. I descended carefully, wishing for the first time that I still had my cane, if only to defend myself.

It proved unnecessary.

The basement proved to be reasonably lit as soon as I got far enough away from the stairway, even accounting for the starlight that streamed down into it. The faint blue light came from an array of marble stones at the back of the wide room, similar to what Stell had showed me before.

Stell was also there, but she was not as she was before.

Her skin had darkened from a mysterious gray to a mid-brown hue, as if she was of mixed African-Latino descent. Braided hair draped down to her shoulders, bouncing to her current movements. Her body had also filled out considerably, completely fleshing out clothing that closely resembled a shirt and jeans. The shirt looked to have writing on it, but it was impossible to read given how much she was moving, and it honestly wasn't the most noticeable thing about her right now.

I tried not to stare at her hips as she was swaying, rocking, and stepping to what closely resembled a reggaeton dance beat that came from the glowing marble stones next to her.

After a couple of moments, I realized that I was still trying, and still failing, not to stare. I tried to blame it on the oddness of the situation itself, the fact that I was in another world, at the bottom of some faux Greek architecture, listening to early 21st century reggaeton music while a race-shifting girl danced in front of me. But the truth of it all was that Stell would have been mesmerizing all by herself. I still don't know if I can do her description justice. It wasn't just her figure. Guineve's figure was also incredibly eye-catching, but it didn't affect me nearly as much as Stell did. Stell moved as if she was *meant* to dance, and knew it, and had always known it. She seemed... relaxed? Excited?

Carefree, I realized. She seemed carefree. Like she finally had a break from a hundred thousand responsibilities for a few minutes, and was taking advantage of it in one of her favorite ways.

It seemed wrong to stare, but even more wrong to disrupt the scene by revealing my presence. I used that logic to remain where I was for a few more moments. But in hindsight, it's not like I had anywhere else to go.

Finally, her song ended, but she just scooted over and touched the glowing stone, starting up another one. I decided that hanging around until the end of the current song was fine (maybe?), but watching her for any longer would officially be creepy. I still didn't want to break up what looked like a private and restful moment for her, so I quietly walked back over to the stairs, trying to think of where else I could go to wait for her. But I couldn't come up with anything, because ruined Athenian temples don't have sitting rooms or coffee lounges.

On my way up, I glanced at her one last time. She was doing a spin-step as she danced, and her eyes met mine for that moment. She gave a friendly, confident smirk, completed her spin, and kept dancing.

I couldn't help but freeze. Part of it was relief at her not being offended, or feeling like her privacy was invaded. But most of it was that her smile was mesmerizing.

Stop, I told myself. *Don't fall for this girl. You don't even know if you're dreaming or not.*

Then I realized that falling for an exotic dream-girl was hard to avoid no matter what I told myself.

At any rate, my internal conversation ended because she immediately glanced my way again, but this time with a panicked expression on her face.

"Oh my gosh," she said quietly. "You're actually here. Again. This soon."

"Um, hi?" I offered awkwardly. "I um, tried knocking and calling out, but the... door was open, so, um..."

"You saw me," she said, in a voice that was almost a squeak.

"Um, yeah," I replied, struggling with the sinking feeling inside of myself. That second glance she did must have been a double-take. I have no idea who she thought I initially was. "Sorry. I didn't know where else to go." *Just move forward and keep talking,* I finally decided. "Where did you learn how to dance like that?"

"I, um." She hesitated, then apparently decided to just push forward as well. "The last Challenger was able to bring some of the knowledge from his world over here. He made it so that every now and then I can access some of your communication media with Avalon's stone technology. I haven't been able to access much of it though. This music was one of the first things I found, and it's stuck with me over the centuries."

"Centuries?" I asked. "Reggaeton music videos haven't been around for more than a hundred years."

"On your world, sure," she replied casually. "I don't know why time crawls so slowly there. But it's a little faster everywhere else, and a lot faster here."

"Oh," I said. "Does that get boring?"

"It used to. But these days, so much more happens that I can take part in. And when everything's still slow and stable, I have the music the last Challenger brought. Still trying to get the hang of it, as you can tell."

"Are you kidding?" I said honestly. "Your moves were incredible." I never had any talent for dancing, but Stell's technique was the most mesmerizing I had ever seen.

"Really?"

Her smile finally came back, and one of her hands reached up, as if to catch a stray braid of hair, before it suddenly jerked down. But she was still smiling. "I can never see myself dance, and Guineve says she isn't a very good judge. Wait." She suddenly shook her head. "Wait a minute. How did you get here again?"

Oh yeah. Maybe that was more relevant. How did I keep winding up here?

"Sorry," I shrugged. "Still have no idea. What did we decide before again? Stroke, magic power, or something?"

"Did it happen differently this time?"

"When I went to bed I woke up here. On the grass outside, I mean. I met Guineve outside and she said I should go down here."

"She would." Stell rolled her eyes. "Anyway, there are some things I can do to try and figure it out from here. I was actually about to try and put out a Call to see if I could summon you anyway."

"Right. You said several worlds were in danger somehow."

"Not yet, but they will be, which makes this different. On one hand, I've never seen so many warning signs for so many worlds at once, and that's terrifying. But on the other hand, I've never had a Challenger show up so much earlier than the Tumults began, and that's wonderful. It means I have more time to train you, help you discover your unique powers. You could potentially become stronger than any Challenger I've ever trained, strong enough that hopping between different worlds to help all of them overcome their Tumults at once would be just a simple exercise."

That sounded disturbingly awesome. Like I was living through every empowerment fantasy at once, as the hero of all my favorite video games, also at once. I began to worry more and more that this whole thing was some kind of delusion on my end.

"It sounds like you're really confident that I'll be able to save everyone that's everywhere. I hope that I can live up to that idea of a hero."

"Oh, I'm not worried about that at all," Stell said dismissively. "I mean I would be if you were someone else. And I have to make sure that your body and skills will keep up with your goals. But I'm not worried about your inner mettle at all."

"Why?" I asked. "No offense, but I've talked to you twice, and it's not like you've had a chance to really see me under pressure."

"Not under pressure..."

One of the eyebrows on her light-chocolate face rose a half-inch.

"You're on a foreign planet for the first time, talking to a multi-bodied girl that changed her shape and skin color since the last time you've seen her, and is telling you that you're supposed to save the world*s*—emphasis on the plural."

"Well yeah," I replied, somewhat lamely. "But that's not the same thing as being in danger. No one's holding a weapon to my head right now. And besides, you said I can't easily die."

"No, I said the opposite. Dying is *very* easy. Most Challengers do it at least several times. By glossing over that fact, you're proving my point for me."

"Okay, fine," I said. "I was trying to say that it wasn't going to be permanent, but I see your point. My point is that you're taking a lot of risks by just going with a guy who walked in on his own. It's not like I brought a list of references with me."

"But you did," Stell said with another one of her beautiful smiles. That was one thing that hadn't changed at all with her new look. "Every Challenger has two types of imprints on them, and once they enter Avalon the imprint lingers. With time and the right tools—" She gestured to the stones behind her. "I can read them." She looked up and suddenly called out.

"Lights!"

The top of the ceiling suddenly twinkled, creating an odd sparkling effect over our heads that, combined with the blue glow that sprang up from the floor tiles, somehow gave enough light to easily see by. Stell touched the large stones by her, and they slowly sank into the floor. Another, larger stone rose out from the middle of the room, as if it was replacing them.

"Even though you came into Avalon on your power somehow, you still left the same types of imprint every Challenger leaves. We call them Deeds and Renown. Deeds are the imprints left behind directly by the actions you do on another's behalf. They are by far the most important tool for measuring Challengers, because they record what you do no matter where you are or who is watching. I always try to read a Challenger's Deeds first, even though most Challengers come with only one or two. After they spend enough time here conquering Trials, that list tends to get much longer. Renown is the imprint people leave on Challengers by expressing opinions on them. If people are repeatedly talking about your exploits, or spreading the news of your exploits, then you're going to have a lot of titles from Renown. But since people tend to exaggerate a hero's deeds, a Challenger can have Renown for something he or she hasn't actually done. That's why I only examine a Challenger's Renown after I have seen his or her Deeds."

As the stone in the floor rose, I thought for a minute to make sure I understood all of that.

"So when I came here, something was able to look at me and magically record everything I've ever done?"

"Not exactly." Stell shrugged, her dark hair bouncing a little as she did so. "It's more like your soul was writing a book based on what you did or what people said about you, and then gave everyone in Avalon a copy as soon as you came over. I'm not going to be the only one who can see it, and you have to actively do things to hide them. And it's not everything you've ever done, just things that felt especially meaningful to someone. Actually, that's really important. A lot of times I've had Challengers that performed Deeds they didn't realize were meaningful to someone."

"Can Deeds be bad, too?"

"They can," Stell said darkly. "Some Challengers find that they hurt someone they didn't mean to in the past when they look at their Deeds. And some other people, or creatures, perform actions so heinous that they wind up generating Deeds and Renown as well, even though they're not Challengers."

"That...feels invasive and useful at the same time," I said to Stell. She gave me another raised eyebrow. "Well, on one hand, someone can find out things about me that I wished stayed private. On the other hand, if I actually *have* hurt someone, and didn't realize it, I'd really like to know, so that I can try and make it right somehow."

Also, could this somehow prove that this world was real and not a delusion of mine?

I hoped so.

"So you're about to show me my Deeds right now? And you've already looked at them, so you know whether or not I've hurt anyone?"

She gave me another smile. This one actually seemed bigger, and brighter than her earlier smile. With her current dark skin, it looked absolutely beautiful.

"I have. And you really should stop worrying about that. In fact, I've never been this excited about showing a Challenger their own Deeds before."

"Really?" I asked, puzzled. "Why?"

"You'll see. Just wait for the stone to finish."

The stone kept rising. It was already up to my waist, and now that I looked carefully, I could see writing all along its sides. I watched it rise for a few more moments.

"You look nice, by the way," I offered.

"What?" she asked, suddenly looking up.

"The... change? Your new...appearance?" I tried not to wince as I thought up a way to say 'I like your new skin' without sounding like a creep or something even worse. "I don't understand how it happens, but I know you said your skin and body changes, and it looks really good on you, so I thought I'd let you know. Sorry if that came out weird."

But she was still smiling. Only now it was even wider, with her cheeks moving like two rising suns.

"Thank you. That was actually really sweet. And I'm glad I get to see you today."

I must have been imagining things, because she almost sounded shy with that last sentence.

Then, after trying so hard to not make any more creepy stares, my eyes inadvertently glanced at her torso, and I could finally read the writing on her shirt.

Warning, OC it said, listing the abbreviation like it was a movie rating, such as 'R' or 'PG-13.' Then it went on to explain the rating.

Overly Caucasian. Do not put on dance floor.

She looked back up at me, and realized I was glancing at her chest.

"Ummm," she said.

"Oh! Sorry!" I said in embarrassment. "But your shirt..."

"Oh, right," she said, no longer weirded out. "I forgot I wore that one today."

"Um," I added. "You do know that Caucasian means..."

She grinned at me, and after a moment we both laughed.

We went back to silently watching the stone rise for a few moments, until it finally rumbled to a stop.

"It's done!" Stell said excitedly. She actually clapped her hands, like she was about to unwrap a present. "Finally!"

"Is it usually faster than this?"

"It's usually a *lot* faster," the woman said smugly. "Your list is really long."

"Really?" I asked. That didn't sound right.

But she didn't answer, and instead stepped forward to touch an indented part of the stone. Blue light began to form along the scribbled writing. On the stone's top, writing, the kind I could actually read, began to rise, as if it were being projected by a screen.

The Deed Records of Wes Malcolm
18 years old
Deed Level: Veteran Challenger
Deed List:
Steadfast Friend (Constant Action)
Guide for the Lost (Thrice Over)
Shield for the Harassed (Thrice Over)
Flame Fighter (Once)
Saver of Lives (Thrice Over)
Brother to the Wounded (Once, Year-Long Action)
Denier of Fear and Despair (Continuous, Daily)
Denier of Those Who Assault (Twice)
Orphan Shield (Continuous, Monthly)

Widow Shield (Continuous, Monthly)
Slaver's Bane (Continuous, Monthly)
Builder of Villages (Continuous, Monthly)
Skilled in Arts (Once)

"Umm," I said, as I looked at the writing in the air. "I've never been actually called any of these things. Ever."

"I know," Stell said, still happily. "This is Avalon's direct expression of your deeds, created by its own interpretation from your actions. The personal titles will appear in a moment. Some will be just translations of what you've already seen, but others will be new because Avalon didn't grasp their significance at first. I'll just read them out as I see them..."

Her eyes began to dart back and forth as she went across the list. She still sounded excited and began to point.

"See, at least three people call you a protector from bullies and mockers, so that explains 'Shield for the Harassed'... Some of the same ones said you were their personal welcomer when they moved into your town... two women credited you from rescuing them from someone who was going to hurt them very badly, and that matches the assault-denier title..."

"Two?" I cocked my head. "That doesn't sound right at all,"

"Oh?" Stell said. "Should it be more? Not everyone recognizes the things you do for them."

"No no," I said quickly. "I stood in front of three guys that wanted to take advantage of an unconscious girl during a party. But that only happened once, so I don't remember anything about a second girl. And for the first girl, all I did was stand in front of her and talk."

"I see," Stell said calmly. "Did that make her any less saved?"

"Huh?"

"Would something bad have happened to her if you hadn't stepped in?"

"I hope not." I shrugged. "I'm pretty sure someone else would have stepped in if I hadn't."

"Then why didn't they?" Stell asked quietly.

I didn't have an answer to that. I almost mentioned Davelon, and he would have acted, but he wasn't at that party to begin with.

"And if it wasn't at personal risk to you, wouldn't someone else have at least done what you did, if what you did was so little?"

I didn't have an answer for that either. So I just stood there for a moment looking like an idiot until Stell went back to reading.

For some reason, she seemed to be smiling even wider at me. It reminded me of the smile people sometimes make when they get to meet their favorite celebrity. But I had to be reading too much into that.

"Three people say you literally reached through fire to save them, so that explains two titles. Are you going to say you don't remember that one either?"

"No," I admitted uncomfortably. "That one was Davelon's family. Their vehicle lit up after a real bad crash. Dad and I were able to pull them all out, but his mom got burned badly on her legs and never walked after that."

That was a bad night, I remembered. One of the worst days except for Dad's death.

And my accident.

Davelon's mom kept clutching her legs, screaming for us to get her husband, get her baby. Davelon's father was half-consciously trying to help us, begging God not to punish his family for his mistake, and that he didn't mean to do it, even though the accident wasn't his fault.

"Dad and I wished we could have helped Davelon's mom faster, but yeah... I remember that one. No arguments around it."

That was one of the few things people actually did call me a hero about for a while. It went away eventually, and completely disappeared after Dad's suicide, but I remember the respect our actions used to earn us.

"That's the last one, right?" I said uncomfortably. It brought back more bad memories than good.

Aside from that, it was starting to feel like I had stumbled into a dream where someone spent the entire night telling me how I great I was. It was starting to worry me, and I was afraid if I were to admit it to a counselor, she would use it to explain how I had some other major issue. But Stell didn't seem to notice my internal drama at all.

"Of course not!" she said happily. "Look, I'm sure you usually get so much credit it embarrasses you, but Deeds and Renown are something I need to have the clearest understanding about. So just bear with me here."

She was still happy, but I was detecting an annoyed edge to her words.

"And it's clear you're bent on completely ignoring all the accolades being heaped on you," she added. "I get I'm maybe the thousandth person to be impressed with you, but we still need to go over this!"

Thousandth person...

I could only shake my head at that. There was so much wrong with that statement, I didn't even know where to begin. So, once again, I shrugged.

"Fine," I said numbly. "Let's just get through this."

Her eyes dazzled a little less when she saw me shrug and lower my head. She cocked her own head, then bit her lip.

"I'm sorry," she said. "I got excited, and I didn't consider that this would make you feel uncomfortable. Look, most of these are incredible, but I can sum them up very quickly for you. Will that work?"

"Sure," I replied. "And thank you."

"Okay." She took a breath. "Do you remember rescuing a dozen widows and orphans from slavery, feeding, protecting, and taking care of them for several years, and helping them form a community?"

"What?" I balked at that. I saw the annoyance flash back over her face like gathering thunderclouds.

"Oh, right, the scholarship." I finally remembered. I put a hand over my face at the memories came back. "Sure, I guess that makes sense. Why not, if all the other stuff counts."

"Other stuff..." she huffed. "Okay, whatever. But what do you mean about a scholarship? This Deed looks like it came at cost to yourself, not as a benefit."

"Early on," I began, taking a breath for the long explanation, "when I told my father I wanted to go to college, he made a deal with me. He explained that he already saved up enough money a long time ago for both me and my sister to attend most four-year colleges. But if we wanted to feel like we earned the money ourselves, he'd make it a game. We'd do work, either chores or actual jobs, to earn money. Then we'd work out some charities to donate that money to. The amount we'd donate, he'd match as a scholarship for us. Since my country's money was pretty valuable in certain other countries, my donations were able to do a lot of good, even though all it cost was me giving up a few songs, expensive meals, and other vanity items."

"So you got money for giving money?" She still looked confused.

"No, an... emergency came up, and Dad ... wasn't able to continue the scholarship. But again, it's not like I traveled to these countries and did those things. I just helped pay for them."

"You do realize money's actually one of the best ways, sometimes the only way, to help someone, right?" Stell said seriously. "Some of the Trials coming up wouldn't be there in the first place if there were more resources to deal with them. And if you manage to solve a world-ending Trial with finding more resources instead of bloodshed, I guarantee the inhabitants of that world will give zero complaints. Both Avalon and the people formerly in need have recognized you as playing a role in these peoples' rescue, and neither would do so if someone else had stepped up instead, or if it had cost you nothing. And I'm noticing a pattern with you and great Deeds."

"What do you mean?" I asked.

"You don't like to admit them," she said stubbornly. "It sounds like you either grew up with extremely high expectations or are just one of those super-humble hero types I've occasionally heard about in some of Earth's fairy tales."

"I wouldn't..."

"Oh hush!" she interrupted. "In fact, look right there. See what you did?"

The words over the pillar flicked again, and a new line was added:

Knight of Humility (Continuous, Annoyingly Constant)

"Wow," I said. "So um, it updates in real-time?"

"It can once it begins creating the column. Alright, I said I'd stop there and you're pretty much done as is for Deeds. If you need to find a place to sit I can call up another stone, but go ahead and decide now, because I'm about to look at your Renown."

She was still stubbornly smiling through all of this, even as she kept speaking.

"Look, I'm sorry I made you uncomfortable, but do you realize what a big deal this is for me? I have all the signs of multiple catastrophes on the horizon, each the biggest I've ever had to deal with, and no way of handling them on my own, except for finding the help I need to save lives. Then suddenly, without me even having to look, the best candidate ever for becoming a Challenger walks right into my backyard. You can believe what you want about being here, but you have to be either an extremely fortunate coincidence or a miracle from some heaven I haven't discovered yet." She pointed back to the list. "You're already ranked as a Hero, here. Do you realize that? Most Challengers don't start out with *anything* in their lists, or at least nothing like this. They don't save any lives or protect people from abuse until *after they get here.* Then they find their courage after we help them discover their powers. I don't care whether or not you know any magic or how to wield a weapon; we can teach that here, especially this early on. But I can only cross my fingers and look for people who have the potential to be heroes, and here you walk in with prior experience! I mean, look at you right now! You're treating all these accomplishments as a casual day's work! Probably because you're still doing most of them!"

I gave up on arguing at this point. Partly because I kept losing, and partly because, if I was honest, being praised by a beautiful, otherworldly woman felt nice.

"Okay, fair enough," I said with a smile. "And for what it's worth, I'm glad I make you happy."

"Pffft!" She smirked back at me. There was a twinkle in her eye that wasn't there before. "Alright. Before you get weird again, we're going to check your Renown. It's just loading up now."

"Didn't you say Renown's less accurate than my Deeds? Won't your picture of me be even less clear?"

"Normally? Sure. But since I have to work with Mr. Can't Remember How Many Damsels I Saved, this time I'm going to use what people say about you to fill in the blanks."

I flinched as I finally comprehended what I was about to see.

"Hey, I really don't think seeing what people say about me will be as helpful as you think."

This time she looked at me without reading my face.

"And I think you just don't want to be embarrassed by finding out how many teenage princesses are in love with you," she said with a smirk. "But since it's finished loading, you're out of time to get weird about it and I can finally see what other people think of your heroics."

She stopped looking at me and turned to the new letters rising from the blue stone. Her face looked like my sister's on Christmas day.

I tried to calm down. *This could just be a dream. Things are different in dreams.*

But the happy look dropped right off her face as soon as the first words rolled up.

"Cripple-head?" she stuttered. "What?"

She wore a startled expression now, like something had walked up to her and smacked her in the face, but she was too surprised to feel pain yet.

"Why... what... but that sounds..."

I sighed.

"Since this is apparently important," I said, trying to keep the bitterness out of my voice. "I'll explain. About two years ago, I was injured in a sporting event, and something in my head broke. The doctors have been unable to fix it, and now I have constant dizzy fits, headaches, and trouble maintaining my balance. Sudden movement causes me a lot of pain, and it's usually impossible for me to walk without a cane back on Earth. The only time I could walk at all without one was a few weeks ago, and I've deteriorated again since then."

"But... why?" Her head cocked to the side. "That still sounds so..."

"Derogatory? Yes. That's the idea."

Her eyes widened a little in comprehension. "You got hurt and... they make fun of you for it?"

"Yeah," I replied. "Pretty much."

The look on her face changed again. Her eyes watered and she shook her head.

"But...no," she said, her voice quivering. "No. You're a hero. Heroes get respect... even on Earth...you're a hero... so you're supposed to get respect."

"I'm not a hero to those people," I said numbly. I didn't let myself think about what she just said. I knew I'd go somewhere dark if I did.

"No," she said, half stubborn, half still-confused. "This shouldn't be at the very top. That's ridiculous. There can't be that many people that stupid, and that asinine, to disrespect you that way." Her voice grew firmer as she continued to speak. "That has to be a fluke. The next one should make more sense. Show me his other famous titles," she commanded.

She waited for a second. This next title I could recognize.

Retard.

I actually hadn't heard that one in a while.

"*Famous* titles!" the dark-skinned woman repeated with a shout. "Titles related to things he actually did!"

She looked satisfied after shouting.

"Sorry about that. I don't know why it's only showing what stupid people say about you, but I think I just filtered them all out. And don't let what idiots say get to you," Stell said fiercely. "I'm in charge of over half a dozen planets, and I can confirm that most people on every single one of them pay more attention to a person's actions than superficial things like their appearance or injuries." She lowered her head and muttered something angry under her breath, her braids dancing about as she did so. "Alright. Here we go."

*Dumbf*ck*

"Huh," I noted casually. "It censors itself."

"Six and a half hells!" Stell shrieked. Apparently she didn't. And she looked too angry to appreciate me pointing that out right now, so I refrained. "I thought I *fixed* this!"

"No, your magic glowing rock is right. I get called that because I still fail the tests I take at school."

But Stell's beautiful brown face just looked more baffled.

"They expect you to take the same tests everyone else does with an unhealed head injury? And when you fail, they just make fun of you for it? What is wrong with these people? Why are they even making you go to school? Why are you not just granted retirement, like most of the other worlds do for people who have become injured, but have saved and changed as many lives as you have?"

I shrugged. As much as I hated talking about this, it was nice to see someone react so well on my behalf.

"The tests in my country are standardized, so they can't easily change them. And everyone has to take them. That's just the law. But they do give me extra time and allow me to retake some of them."

"What good does that do?" she demanded. "You said you have trouble walking and keeping your balance. Does anyone at least make sure you don't fall and hurt your head during your world's stupid exams?"

As she finished talking, the magical glowing rock answered her question for her.

Easy Target.

Stell's face turned blank for a moment.

"Target," she said softly. "They don't just mock you, or deny you help when you need it... they actually try to hurt you or ruin your life further." She looked at me in disbelief. "That one's wrong though, right? Nobody's that wretched, right? To do something like that to an innocent person is what our worlds' monsters do."

Pervert.

"They don't think I'm innocent," I said quietly.

Stell looked back at the writing. Her eyes were so wide it looked like two pairs of starry skies on her face.

"I don't understand," she said for the hundredth time. "There's no Deed to match this with. Your Deeds say the opposite!" she said quickly. As her words became faster, her voice grew louder. "You protect women! Who lied and said you do the opposite?"

I laughed bitterly, because I couldn't help it.

"The first woman, the only one I remember 'saving?' She did." As Stell's jaw dropped, I went ahead and explained. "The guy I stood up to, the one leading the other two, was her boyfriend. When she woke up, she said that there was no way he would have done anything to hurt her, that I had overreacted, and that I had done so because I liked her and was jealous. And everyone felt like I had ruined the party anyway, so they weren't willing to give me the benefit of the doubt."

"But you didn't overreact," Stell said dumbly. She seemed almost shell-shocked. "Avalon's never been wrong about a person's Deeds. It wouldn't have noted anything if she wasn't in danger... cursed by the very person you protected... just how much stupid does your world have in it for this to happen? Just... How? *How?*"

Her voice had gotten shrill near the end, and she took a deep breath to try and work herself back under control.

"In all honesty, that particular incident probably exploded the way it did because I went up against the town hero."

"The town hero?" she asked flatly.

"Yeah, Chris Rhodes. Most popular guy in the history of the school."

"And he's literally called the town hero? And he drugs and tries to assault young girls?"

"That's right." There was no sugar-coating that fact.

"Why?" She almost screamed that word. “Why do people call him a hero?”

"He's smart, good-looking, comes from the wealthiest family in town, and is probably the best football player the town has ever seen."

"Okay," Stell said, after closing her eyes and taking a deep breath. "Has he saved more people than you? Or helped people like you have?"

I went ahead and thought about it. After a moment, I shook my head.

"No, he hasn't really done any of that. People talk about him all the time, so they would have talked about it if he did something like save someone's life, or stand up to a bully, or help a third-world village."

Stell had gotten quiet again. Her reaction had really surprised me. I hadn't seen someone this upset on my behalf in years, and normally the only people outraged at my treatment were all close friends and family.

"Okay," she finally said. "Okay. So he's famous for his looks, wealth, and...his football. Right. I don't know what that is, so that must be important. Does that last one matter the most?"

"Definitely," I replied. I couldn't pretend my little suburban town loved anything more than football.

Heck, even I used to really love football.

"Fine, okay. You can probably help me make sense of this. Describe what football is."

"Sure. It's a game where two teams of people throw a leather ball around and they try to stop each other from moving the ball in a certain direction."

Her dark face glared at me.

"That's it?"

"Pretty much."

"Does anything else happen when you play?"

"What do you mean?"

"Do your people play football to resolve a certain dispute? Does the winning team earn more food or wealth for their town?"

"No, none of that. But if you win enough games, you get a big shiny cup at the end of the season that shows you beat everyone else. And if you play extremely well, some people will give you lots of money to play football somewhere else."

"And that's all there is to it?"

"That's it."

She backed away from the glowing rock, grabbing and pulling her hair in frustration.

"Not a single part of anything about this makes sense. You come to Avalon with the longest list of Deeds any Challenger has ever started with, Deeds that would at least earn you enough resources to retire permanently and receive all the treatment your injury needed, yet you have the nastiest Renown I've ever seen. There are heroes from at least two tragic legends that aren't misunderstood this badly. If you behaved any differently at all, I'd think that Avalon had finally gotten a Challenger's Deeds wrong, after thousands and thousands of years of never making a single mistake. The only thing that I'm really sure of is that you're telling the truth, based on what you've said, how you've acted, and all the time I've spent studying Challengers. But that means the community you live in is full of the stupidest people I've ever heard of, which doesn't make sense either, because your world's technology base is so high. Do you understand that? I know of communities right now that are just beginning their Bronze Age, and they still sound less ignorant than the cretins you live with. Why are you so different? And why do they hate your being different so *much*?"

"That's because of my parents, specifically my father. He raised me to be and act a certain way. He's... also the real reason I get so much hate."

"But why would they—"

Bad Seed.

Pedophile's Son.

Suspected Pedophile (Just like his Father).

As if summoned by our conversation, those last three titles rose up to damn me all at once. Stell's eyes widened and watered at the same time, but I couldn't face them longer than a second.

“I think I'm going to try and head home,” I said, turning for the stairs. I heard Stell huffing, like she was trying not to cry, but I didn't look back. I was halfway to the base of the stairs when I heard her call out.

“Wes!”

I wanted to ignore her, but found I couldn't. I turned to look at her.

Two lines of clear water ran down her dark brown cheeks. “I'm sorry!” she called out. “I didn't mean to hurt you! Please don't leave for good!”

“Yeah, sure,” I said numbly. Coming here wasn't something I could control anyway. I wasn't even sure climbing the stairs would wake me up.

“And they're wrong about you!” she shouted fiercely, showing the most heat I’d seen from her so far. “Whatever your father did, even if it's true, it doesn't define you! Your actions do!” She pointed to the Deeds side of the rock.

“Your choices do! And you've chosen to be a hero on a daily basis! Please never change! And please come back here and keep being yourself! We won't take you for granted!”

That actually made me feel better. I hadn't ever had a stranger fight for me this hard. Especially since I had lost the ability to fight for strangers myself.

As if in answer to that thought, the ‘Deeds’ rock beeped again. Stell blinked away her tears and looked at it. Then she cocked her head.

“What does it say?” I asked, postponing the idea of leaving in a sad, hurt, huff.

“Cock...Blocker?” she said slowly. “I can't figure that expression out. It's from one person. It looks like it's your first real negative Deed. Or at least the person felt negative about you doing it." She looked back at me. "It looks the person gave it to you based on two occasions, one of which happened very recently... what happened? Did you kill two of a guy's roosters or something?"

The whole thing had gotten weird so fast I couldn't think for a moment (and yes, that was on top of all the other weirdness I was going through right now). I hadn't ruined anyone's sexual encounters in years. In fact, the only person I've ever stopped, deliberately or otherwise, was...

"Stell," I asked. "Is there a way to see what times I um, earned that title, and whether it matches with any of my other Deeds?"

"Sure," Stell said, moving her finger through the floating words. "It looks like it came around the time you rescued those two princesses... are they related somehow?"

I laughed darkly. "That means Chris Rhodes probably gave it to me. That's fine. I'll take it."

Stell looked even more confused.

"That... doesn't make sense. How can it be related... did he attack those women with a chicken, and you cut its head off or something? And then you did a second time, recently?" She cocked her head far to the side. "I know what a chicken is, but this still doesn't make sense... was it the same rooster? How were you able to cut its head off a second time? That sounds really gory," she finally said. "Am I understanding this right? Because Deeds usually aren't this complicated."

"Honestly no, but I can't help but like that last interpretation." I laughed again. I couldn't keep my former bad mood. People used to make me sad about my dad all the time. But Stell was the first person, assuming this was all real, to inadvertently turn my mood around so fast.

"It's actually a crude description for a person that prevents another type of behavior," I explained. "We do have chickens, but we also use the word to describe a lot of other things, most of which are really crude too."

"Well, okay," Stell said cautiously. She risked a smile. "At least it cheered you up. I don't think I need to pry into your past anymore, so in the future I'll try and respect when you don't want to talk about something. Next time, when you inexplicably break the rules again and arrive here on your own, we'll go over integrating you as a Challenger."

"Thanks," I replied, smiling back at her. "I appreciate that. I'm going to go ahead and try to head back now. But I look forward to seeing you again."

"Anytime." Her smile got broader.

As I walked up the stairs, I started to feel fuzzy. I thought it meant that I was about to shift out of this place. But before I could, I heard Stell mutter in a puzzled voice.

"Maybe he crushed a rooster's head with a heavy block? That sort of makes sense..."

11

HEAVE

"Well, Wes, why don't you tell me how you have been doing?" Dr. Dalfrey said as we both sat down. She crossed her legs, and I reflexively looked away. I saw her frown at me out of the corner of her eye, and then she started writing on her notepad. Even though I hadn't said anything yet.

Dr. Dalfrey was an attractive woman in her mid-thirties, with short blonde hair that was longer on one side of her head than the other. In the beginning of our sessions, my father's training on respectful eye contact made me a bit uncomfortable with how she made a women's business skirt and blouse look so revealing. Over time that discomfort took a back seat to just how much I disliked the woman personally.

I didn't know how, or why, Dr. Dalfrey became my counselor. She was a different counselor than the one we had after my father's death. She became my psychologist after my disability, when the insurance insisted that I see a therapist as part of a way to measure my progress. None of the local counselors in my area were willing to be my counselor at the time. I never found out why, no matter how much we begged.

But then, a miracle happened.

An award-winning therapist from New York had heard about my condition and wanted to take me on as a patient. She was even willing to move down to Texas just for me.

It had seemed unbelievable. Like some miracle from heaven.

Not two months later, Dr. Dalfrey had seemed like a curse from hell.

I don't want to pretend I have an excellent grasp of psychology or counseling another person. My basic understanding, though, is that you talk to a person, listen to them and observe them, *then* make a diagnosis based on what you see and hear.

You also at least try to help the person, and make them feel at least somewhat listened to.

Dr. Dalfrey, the award-winning professional, had never done any of that. I didn't know why. She spent most of the first year pulling away at the details of my father's death. During the first few sessions, she just listened with an unsatisfied expression. But then she started pulling for details about Dad that were never released to the public. She claimed she was helping me let go of secrets, but my answers only made her more and more upset. She seemed convinced that there was more my father was hiding, but she refused to elaborate about it other than to infer that it might be related to his work.

Frankly, it was suspicious as hell. And when I confronted her about it, she just asked me if I had any other paranoid thoughts. I don't know how she got away with it, but our insurance kept insisting that I use her as my therapist and that they wouldn't cover my treatments anymore if I refused to see her.

So I sucked up my frustration and answered her stupid 'hey you're in a conspiracy movie, Wes!' questions, often the same ones asked just different ways, over and over until she apparently became convinced that I wasn't hiding any secret details of either my dad's death or his work in software design. Considering that he stuck to coding and creating video games, I had no clue what she could have possibly been curious about.

But at any rate, ever since then, she seemed to just try and aggravate me, then threaten to assign a condition to me if I reacted at all. So I was going to have to deal with her questions anyway, because she could only torture me for about thirty minutes.

* * *

I sighed before answering her, inwardly glad that the action didn't cause me pain.

"My month started out incredibly well," I replied. I saw another frown flash across her face so quickly I thought I was imagining it. "And I wish it had stayed that way. My pain and dizziness had been decreasing to the point where I almost didn't need my cane to walk. My memory was getting excellent, and my grades were improving in all my classes."

"Is that what your teachers told you? Are you sure you were really progressing?" Dr. Dalfrey asked, not looking at me and still scribbling on her pad.

"Yes," I replied patiently. "All but one of my teachers noted I was improving and I was getting consistently higher grades on all of my assignments, in every class. That was a really encouraging thing to see for me." *And stop frowning every time I give you good news, witch.* "I tried to build off of it, to keep doing what worked, so that I could finally pass my scholarship exams. Everything seemed to be working until test day."

"And then you failed your tests again?" Dr. Dalfrey said without looking up. Her delivery while I was talking made me feel as if I had been slapped.

"I don't know," I replied, choosing to ignore her behavior for now. "Because my family is petitioning the conditions of the test, and the initial results they told me proved to be inaccurate."

"Do you feel the conditions truly made a difference this time?"

"Yes," I said, mentally counting to ten, reminding myself not to give her what she wanted with an outburst. "I really feel that getting hit in the back of the head with a heavy textbook is something that shouldn't happen during a test that concerns my future. That's something the school should prevent from happening, which is why my mother is currently suing the school."

"Hmph," Dr. Dalfrey said with a frown, still not looking up and scribbling in her notepad. "I suppose that makes sense. How are you feeling now?"

"Fighting discouragement," I answered, moving past how peeved she got when I didn't rise to her antagonism. "I feel like ever since I got hit in the head, all of my progress has reset. My pain is back, as well as my dizziness and trouble thinking."

"So you feel like giving up?" Dr. Dalfrey said, finally making eye contact with me.

"Well, yeah," I said bluntly. "I feel incredibly discouraged. Every time I try and do something with my life, something, or someone—usually a different person—shows up out of nowhere to slam me back down. I'm tired of having to start over from scratch."

"I see," Dr. Dalfrey said quietly, and sounding suspiciously attentive. Was she actually interested in my condition for once? "So what have you done since you felt this way?"

I shrugged.

"I've tried not to act on it," I said. "If I give up, I really do lose everything. As hard as everything is for my mother and sister, I know that life will just get even worse for them if I stop trying. I mean, I may be a drain to my family, but they still love me. I know they'd be hurt even more if I wasn't around." I took a breath. I didn't trust this woman, but talking about this still felt helpful to me. "So that means the best way to help my family is to still try and be less of a burden to them, but I have to do that by finding a way to move forward in life. I don't know what that looks like, especially if I failed my tests for good this time, but I know I have to find it, for the sake of the people I care about at the very least."

Dr. Dalfrey was staring at me curiously.

"That's an extremely positive and... mature outlook to have, given your situation," the counselor said carefully.

"Thank you?" I said, and it really was a question.

Dr. Dalfrey looked back down at her notepad. But I noticed that, unlike before, she hadn't started writing yet.

"What would you say is responsible for that outlook? Other than the reasons you gave?"

"I'm honestly not sure," I replied. "My friends and family are all I have left right now."

"And it's good that they're motivating you right now," Dr. Dalfrey said. "I want to encourage you to keep grasping that motivation. Can you think of any thoughts or events that have encouraged those motivations?"

"Not really," I said with a shrug. "Well, I have been doing well on a video game. I even got an interview with a company for it last week. It's been encouraging me, a little bit, reminding me that I can still be good at something. That not everything can be taken away from me."

A long time ago, Dad had tried to drill me into a lesson about games, that even though they're fun, they ultimately serve to link us to real life. If you can have fun in a game, you can have fun in real life, because somebody real still made those games. And if you can win in those games, then you can win in real life too.

I didn't share that with the counselor, but the thought crossed my mind again.

"I see," Dr. Dalfrey replied, writing into her notes, but more slowly than she usually did. "Is that the same game you've been playing for your treatment?" She flipped back several pages on her pad. "*Heroes Unbound?*"

"Yes," I replied. "That's the one."

She frowned again, flipping to the front of her pad again.

"If people are interviewing you, then it sounds like you are managing to excel in that game. How frequently have you been playing it?" Her eyes were narrowed as if she was concentrating, and her body was leaning forward with one ear turned more toward me.

"Just as much as the doctor recommended," I replied, wondering what had sparked the sudden change in her behavior. Her previous, peevishly disinterested attitude was completely gone. "Up until recently, I've been having a strict routine for studying, and I've still been going through all the other treatments. I've just tried to make my time in the game count, to play with people in later time zones to try and make certain accomplishments."

"I see," Dr. Dalfrey said again, looking down to write on her notepad, then looking back up at me. She paused before asking me her next question.

"What about your dreams? Have you had any unusual dreams?"

Something about that question made me feel very, very cold. And I couldn't figure out why.

"Unusual?" I asked. "Like in what way?"

"Just any that you remember standing out," Dr. Dalfrey said casually. "Sometimes our dreams either influence us or reveal what we are focusing on."

That answer made total sense. And if Dr. Dalfrey hadn't spent so much time hating these sessions as much as I did, I would have felt perfectly comfortable with telling her about my dreams of Avalon.

But then I remembered that this was the first time Dr. Dalfrey had shown interest in our sessions since she stopped asking questions about my father. I also remembered that if she wanted to, she could decide that the dreams meant I was going crazy, and needed to go to a special facility.

Was that me being paranoid? I then asked myself. Being suspicious about your counselor seemed like a bad argument for one's mental health. Even if I didn't like how my sessions were going, maybe there had been some purpose in antagonizing me. Or maybe I had been misreading her behavior all this time.

Then I remembered all the other times it felt like people were out to get me, and then finding out from Davelon last week that *they actually were*.

I was done taking stupid chances like that. *Earn back my trust,* I thought at this crappy world, *before I give you a chance to hurt me again.*

"Not that I can think of," I said, shaking my head just slowly enough to avoid more pain. But she was still watching me carefully.

"Are you sure?" Dr. Dalfrey said slowly. "Think carefully. Any dreams that seemed particularly vivid? Or with recurring themes?"

She didn't believe me. I had hesitated too long before answering her. But why would she care so much to begin with?

What was she looking for?

Could I find out, without giving it to her?

"Well, I have been dreaming about the video game," I said, pretending to be embarrassed. It wasn't hard, considering my dreams made me feel like I was in my own special eighties movie, or wish-fulfillment fantasy novel. "Like *Heroes Unbound*, where I can move around without being in pain."

"I see," Dr. Dalfrey was writing faster now, furiously even, but she was still pausing and waiting for me to talk afterwards. "How many dreams like this do you remember?"

"One, maybe two?" I said carefully. "They don't stand out that much."

"The fact that you remember them at all is good," Dr. Dalfrey said in a helpful voice. "It's a hopeful sign that your memory may be gradually improving. What else can you tell me about your dreams?"

"It goes much like *Heroes Unbound*. People ask me to slay evil monsters or recover some treasure they need."

"Who asks you?" she said, still scribbling furiously.

"The people that live there, that see me when I arrive."

"Do you remember their names? What they look like?"

"It varies," I lied, shaking my head slowly. "The names don't stick with me."

"What about their appearance? How much does it vary? Are they always beautiful women?"

I looked up at her.

"I didn't say anything about beautiful women," I said, somewhat defensively.

"No, you didn't," the doctor agreed. "But are there women who ask you for help? And are they beautiful?"

"Well," I hedged.

"It's fine if they are. It doesn't make you crazy, nor is it a sign of any sexual deviance. In fact, it's a known type of dream for boys your age," Dr. Dalfrey said in a helpful voice. If I had this side of her more, I would've started trusting her a long time ago.

Right now, though, I felt like I dodged a bullet.

"There are occasionally beautiful women who are grateful to have me there, but the dream always ends before they do anything more than express their gratitude verbally."

"I see," Dr. Dalfrey's pen blurred in her hands, then stopped as she looked up at me. "What are their names?"

You already asked me that.

"I don't remember," I repeated. "I vaguely recognize them as non-player-characters, or NPCs, from the game sometimes, but I don't feel sure about that."

"That's fine," Dr. Dalfrey answered hurriedly. "What about the place you go to? Are you absolutely sure you can't remember its name? Try very hard to remember."

Was that urgency in her voice?

I looked up at her again. She seemed perfectly relaxed as she waited for me to answer her. She wasn't even looking at me, just down at her notepad. I thought I must have imagined it.

Then I realized she was holding her breath.

"I think I went to the village outside the Navrahai Crevice, where I killed that canyon dragon. The other time it was in Gladeshadow, outside the elven forests in the early levels."

"I see," Dr. Dalfrey said in a neutral voice as she kept writing. "Well, thank you for sharing this with me, Wes. I think this has been a productive session. Keep looking for things that motivate you, and tell me about them in our next meeting. Especially your dreams."

"Thanks," I said, rising from my seat to leave our meeting.

I thought about that session for the rest of the day. Why had my counselor been so apathetic toward me in all of our meetings but this one? And why had she suddenly been interested in my dreams?

Why now, when I had just started whatever dream, or insane trip, or whatever it was, about Avalon?

And why did it scare me so much when she asked about it?

Maybe I really was going crazy. Whatever Avalon and Guineve and Stell and that little fairy were, it wasn't like telling anyone about them would change anything. True, they could possibly use it as a reason to put me in the happy farm, but they could make up any reason they wanted to for that at this point. They could have used my last hospitalization if they were just going to do that.

What did I have to lose if they found out about Avalon?

I thought again about my last visit, how Stell was insisting that I actually was some kind of special uber-hero already on Earth, and that I had helped so many people. She told me I could still do great things, that my real potential hadn't even been touched. I wanted to believe all of that, and it had felt painfully good to hear her angry on my behalf, to hear her say that I had been wronged, and that I deserved to be treated better than this town was treating me. I hadn't been able to bear it.

But now I had been thinking about how she was wrong.

For example, I wasn't some white knight to women. I had helped one, and no more than one, teenager like myself from what I thought was a bad situation, and from what she had insisted wasn't. It didn't match up with what Stell's magic rock had said about me. So it couldn't be real, right?

Just then, I felt my phone buzz.

I pulled it out and read a text from a number I hadn't had any contact from before.

You cock-blocking sack of shit, the message said. *Get in my way a third time and I swear you'll regret it.*

I read the message a second time, sure I was imagining it. Then I turned my phone off, blinked a couple of times, and turned it back on.

The message didn't go away.

The only person I could think who would send me this would be Chris. But didn't that mean that—

Bzzt.

This time the phone vibrated painfully in my hand, and began to play a ringtone, the one I had picked out that had proven to be the least painful for my nerves.

Incoming call from Christina, the screen said.

Feeling cold again, I pressed *accept* and held the phone to my ear with trembling hands.

"Hello?" I was trying to keep the numbness out of my voice. "Christina?"

"Wes?" Her voice sounded wet, as if she had just got done sobbing.

"Is everything okay?"

"You were right," she said suddenly. "I didn't want you to be, but you were right, and it saved me. I'm sorry. I shouldn't have doubted you at all. And I should have called and told you sooner."

The story spilled out of her then. Apparently Chris had taken her to one of the last parties of the semester, now that football season was almost over. He had been a perfect gentleman for the entire time they had been dating. But during this party, he had handed her a drink that she felt suspicious of. She almost drank it anyway, wanting to trust him, but then she had remembered my warning about him. She had refused to drink it, and Chris started to insist that she down it anyway. She had asked him to sip it and prove that it was safe, and then he became angry. He wounded up cursing her, calling her an uptight prude that refused to relax and have any fun, and that he was too good for her anyway. She had been heartbroken, but in the end she had been relieved to have escaped him without anything bad happening to her. Even though she was the one who had made the right decision, and under pressure no less, she was crediting me with saving her. And she refused to hear me tell her otherwise.

I gave up trying to convince her that she was the one who had saved herself, and told her that I was just glad she was okay. But then I asked her when all of this happened.

It had happened a few days ago. Almost right before my second Avalon dream.

I don't remember much of what we said after that. I was too busy trying to keep my hand from dropping the phone.

Because I knew now that I wasn't just dreaming. That I was either going crazy, and in a way that didn't make sense, or I was experiencing something that would get me labeled as crazy if anyone else ever found out about it.

Somehow, the latter was the more terrifying.

12

CLIMB

The mists were back.

I saw them when I opened my eyes. I had gone for a brief nap in my room. It hadn't even been time for bed. I had just told my mom and sister that I was going to lie down for a bit.

Next thing I knew, mist. Tree limbs. Soft grass on my back.

No pain whatsoever throughout my body.

That last fact kept my mouth shut and scream-less. No matter how crazy all of this was, it brought me an opportunity that I only experienced when I played *Heroes Unbound* in my VR harness. And in realizing that, my gratitude was able to eat up my fear. And in the absence of fear, clarity and curiosity came to the forefront of my mind.

I stood up, squared my shoulders, and headed toward the misty trees.

"One way or another," I said out loud. "I'm going to face this weirdness and figure it out. And you're not breaking or scaring me until I do at least that," I declared to the mists around me.

From deep within the woods, I heard a dull boom.

"Challenge accepted," I thought I heard something say. "*Avalon bears witness.*"

So there were deep, inhuman, scary voices coming from the trees now. *Bring it on*, I decided, and marched off into the misty woods.

I tried to look for new details as I walked. Was it still misty without feeling overly damp? Yes it was. Did it still manage to cling to trees and grass blades, forming little dewdrops, in spite of it not feeling wet to walk through? Yes it did. Was it still night, yet bright enough to walk around in?

No, that was different. The sky was lit with a hazy gray, as if the sun was hiding behind the clouds. I tried to find a bright, cloud-covered spot that would serve as the sun, but no luck. Wherever this day-like light came from would remain a mystery for now.

But that was okay, I decided. So help me, I would find a way to make progress on determining my crazy/not-crazy status.

I picked my way through the trees, stepping over the occasional tree root that was poking above the soil. Dodging intermittent rocks, I wondered if there was a way to make any of them glow blue and spit words at me, a geological supercomputer like the ones Stell used. But above all I kept picking my way forward, drawn to a specific location until I reached it. Eventually, the trees parted to form a misty clearing of some sort.

There, in the middle of the meadow, stood Guineve.

She was as beautiful as always, still looking like someone's ideal fantasy of a shapely woman in her late-thirties. Her raven-black hair hung just past her shoulders, but when I looked carefully, individual strands would occasionally rise up to wave in the same pattern that the nearby mist did.

Every now and then, a patch of her white dress would do the same, especially around the hems near her ankles. She seemed unbothered by this, still staring out into the mist, as if she was focusing on something important.

I wondered what she was looking at. Then I remembered that nothing stopped me from going up and talking with her. Maybe this time, I could get more answers from her.

She heard my steps and turned her head toward me with a smile, but I suspected she had already known I was here.

"Good afternoon, Wes," she said with a stately nod. Once again, I found myself trying not to pay too much attention to the low cut in the front of her dress. She seemed to notice, judging by the smirk creeping up one corner of her mouth. "What brings you to us this fine day?"

"I wish I knew, dear lady," I said, and then bowed slightly. I could actually bow here, and it didn't hurt. *Wild.* "But it's a pleasure to see you again."

"I'm glad to hear that," the mist-clad woman said, smirking wider as she did so. "I take it you would like to find Stell?"

"Actually, is there a way for you to let her know I'm already here?" I replied. “I feel like I'm developing a nasty habit of surprising her, and that's not something I want to keep doing.”

“Why, what a gentleman you are,” Guineve drolled. “I'll send her a message. But how on earth do you intend to pass the time while you wait?”

“That depends,” I replied, grinning back at her. “Do you have any coffee?”

She laughed at that. Just like last time, it was a surprisingly rich sound.

“No, but if you keep being such a dear, I might make some for you next time you stop by,” she finally replied.

“In that case, would you mind if I talked with you a bit?” I asked, quietly noting that she knew what coffee was. “I feel like I should get to know the woman I keep relying on for directions a little better.”

“Oh?” Guineve said with a raised eyebrow and shoulder. “You wish to spend time specifically with little me? Should I be worried about you, young lad? I'll have you know that I will not tolerate any improper behavior.”

But she was still smiling as she spoke. *What the heck,* I told myself as I decided to play along.

“Prithee, fair maiden,” I said with a mock bow. *Still able to bow without pain,* I thought. *Awesome.* “Know that mine intentions are naught but honorable, and that I hold thy chastity in the very highest of regards. Thou art safe with me.”

She tilted her head at that, suddenly confused.

“When did you learn Elven Courtspeak, and why are you speaking it so badly... oh!” she said suddenly.

“I had forgotten about Shakespeare in your world. You're making fun of how your people *used* to talk!”

“Yes,” I said uncomfortably. “I'm afraid that's about as good as my Shakespeare gets, so don't get too excited.”

“I'll take it,” Guineve said with a shrug. “But I'll expect you to take more lessons at some point. What do you wish to know, Wes?”

“Any number of things, frankly,” I replied. “I'd really love if you could prove whether or not I'm going crazy, but I'll settle for learning why I always run into you first when I come here— not a complaint,” I added with a smile. “But I'd love to be able to understand what it is you actually do here, and how you're connected to Stell.”

“Well,” Guineve replied regally, tossing her hair back from one of her shoulders. “My time is valuable, but I suppose I'll answer what I can.” She grinned at me again, and this time I couldn't help grinning back. The mist-clad woman looked for all the world like she had risen out of a lake to hand out Excalibur a thousand years ago. Yet she managed to maintain that solemn air, that gravity in her words, while having as much fun with it she possibly could. She had a confidence about her that enabled her to tease me without making her mean, and so far her semi-flirtatious remarks had just seemed playful instead of serious, or creepy.

"At any rate," she continued. "I wouldn't know if you're crazy or not, I'm afraid. I know Stell vouches for you, but... oh, you meant that coming *here* was a sign of being crazy." The raven-haired woman winked at me. "The Challengers all seemed to wonder that, for some reason. My assurances that things were perfectly normal here didn't seem to help, so I'm not sure what to do for you, young man. After all, if you're worried I'm not real then you're not going to be able to take my word for your sanity. But the other Challengers all figured it out on their own eventually, so I'm sure you'll do the same." She paused, apparently to think about my next question. "As for me, didn't Stell already explain what I do here? And our bond?"

"No, not really," I admitted. "I'm still trying to wrap my idea around how you both are sort of the same person. Am I talking to her when I'm talking to you? And if so, why does she keep getting surprised by me?"

"We're what you Earthlings would call 'complicated,'" Guineve said loftily. I suddenly realized that whatever else, she was the kind of person that had entirely too much fun being mysterious.

"That really doesn't narrow down anything," I replied. "We Earthlings call each other complicated all the time. Especially between genders."

"Hmph," the tall woman sniffed. "Amateurs. Let me start with the simpler question first: my role is Stewardess. Stell is in charge of monitoring all of the worlds at once. It's much easier to have a second pair of eyes on each world, so I make it my job to watch Avalon. I monitor the mists for unusual activity, greet incoming visitors, and guard against anything that might threaten Avalon. I've been doing all of this for as long as I've been alive."

"Okay," I said slowly. "I think I understand. Stell created you?"

"Correct," Guineve said with a nod.

"To help her watch over Avalon?"

"Incorrect," Guineve shook her head. "I volunteered for that."

"Why?" I asked, confused again.

"I knew she needed help," Guineve said simply. "So I told her I'd help."

"But..." I struggled to understand. "She did create you. She modifies you, based on what I heard the first time I came here. So she must have created you, somehow, for another, specific reason."

"She did," Guineve affirmed. "A reason I promised I'd never talk about."

That wasn't mysterious at all, I thought to myself.

"You're rather curious, aren't you?" Guineve asked after a moment. She had asked that question casually, with an appraising expression on her face.

"I... guess so?" I replied. "Have you not had to explain yourself to other Challengers before?"

Guineve shook her head.

"We're usually ready for their arrival. We control it, in fact. They don't arrive until Stell sends out a Call, and even then we have an idea of how long it takes for them to get here. And usually time is short, we have to prepare them for an upcoming Trial or Tumult, make them able to save lives, or slay hordes of not-things. So they're too busy saving worlds to ask about us. They just assume we're all a pantheon of goddesses and leave us at that. Only the last Challenger was even remotely curious. I don't know how he found the time to be. But even he didn't have time to learn everything."

"I see," I replied. "I keep catching you all off guard. Like having guests come over when you're still in your pajamas."

"Oh, she'd just kill you if you did *that*." Guineve gave another chuckle. "Try and find a way to knock on something when you come here, dear lad. It would be good for your health."

"But you're the one who keeps tricking me into surprising her," I said in my defense.

"Mmhmm," Guineve hummed simply with a smile. I was not reassured.

"You're not, though, are you?" I asked. "Not goddesses I mean. Not exactly."

"A fair question," the woman replied. "We try to avoid being discovered at all, much less worshiped. We're just observers. Until recently, I was one of the only two parts of Stell that knew how to fight at all, aside from herself. That was part of the reason we needed Challengers to begin with." Guineve paused her speech, looked around, and brushed away a thread of black hair that floated in front of her face.

"Why doesn't she keep making more of you, instead of relying on Challengers?" I asked. I was prying, I knew, but I was also possibly going crazy. I needed things to make a little more sense, or at least have a semi-logical explanation to them.

I needed things to be less weird. Fortunately, Guineve didn't mind the question.

"Stell can only make so many of us, and it always costs her to do so. A Starsown makes more bodies by investing in them. Parts of themselves go into the new body, such as their knowledge, special powers, or their maturity. They then lose access to those traits until they slowly grow back."

"All of them?" I asked, surprised. "Does she have to re-learn how to walk, or jump, or breathe?" The last one sounded particularly fatal, but then I wasn't exactly sure if people even breathed in this place.

But Guineve just smiled patronizingly at me.

"Of course not. That would be just silly. Common things like basic movement are re-learned almost instantaneously. It's the more complicated things, most of which you would probably regard as magic, that take a long time to return. And the memories," Guineve added quietly. "Those take the longest to re-form."

"Really?" I asked. "I can see re-learning something one day. But how does a memory grow back at all?"

"Very slowly," Guineve admitted. "One memory, Earth-seconds long, takes the lifetime of several Challengers to return to a Starsown's mind."

"That sounds... incredibly dangerous," I replied. "She could lose something dangerously important if she did that. Why would she ever directly share memories then, when she could just tell you what happened?"

"I promised I would not say," Guineve repeated.

But she had given me enough information to be curious, to draw partial conclusions. Was that on purpose?

I wanted to ask her, but then she curled her mouth into a smile, and somehow I knew she wouldn't tell me anything more. But that in itself was an answer for me.

Just then, a voice called out through the mists. It sounded faint, and I couldn't make out the words even though it echoed through the trees. Then it called out again.

"Guineve..."

I turned to look back at the tall woman next to me, but she just smiled and shook her head, holding a pale finger to her lips.

"Guineve...Guineve!"

The voice grew closer, and more forceful.

And more exasperated.

"Guineve! Guineve!" It was Stell's voice.

And Guineve wasn't answering her.

"Are you—" I began, but was cut off.

"Hush," the stately woman replied with a grin. "Wait for it."

Stell's voice grew closer.

"Guineve! Answer your mental link! Guineve!"

Now I could hear someone stomping through the grass. A few moments later, Stell stepped into the meadow.

She was still dark, with a faint Latino tint to her skin. Her hair was still in tight, tiny braids. She wore what looked like a plain brown shirt that said *I'm not crazy, I just listen to bands that don't exist yet*, and jeans that were thankfully not as distracting as the ones she wore last time.

Also, unlike last time, she was very, very ticked.

"Guineve!" The darker, shorter woman was still shouting, despite being only yards away. "There you are!"

She stopped in a huff about five feet from us. "I have," she began, taking a deep breath, and holding her hand out to where she could count on it, "the signs forming for *one* Chaos-type Trial in the Woadlands. Hints of *one* Famine-type Trial sweeping across the oasis of the Golden Sands. *One* Disaster-based *Tumult* possibly forming on the Sun-jeweled Sea, don't ask how, I've been yelling for you to come help me figure it out. Another Conflict-based Trial forming in the Spirit Kingdoms, this one might form before all the others, and would go on for centuries, and Earth centuries at that. Finally, there are apocalyptic warnings emerging of both Behemoth and Subjugation-based Tumults forming in three worlds: the Sun-jeweled Sea, which makes three Tumults on one world, Pangea, and the Lightborn Lands. That's only two each for the last two realms. But that's still Tumults, and not Trials, both strong enough to upheave two of the most powerful civilizations of our Expanse. So when I send you a mental link asking you to come look at something, I expect you to realize that it just *might* be important enough to help me with!"

Now that she was finished yelling, the dark-skinned shoulders slumped, and she began huffing for breath again.

"I do apologize, Stell," the raven-haired woman answered calmly. "But the mana-knots were unraveling in Avalon's southern forests, and I became absorbed in trying to figure out why."

Stell stopped huffing, and just glared at Guineve, her left eye twitching slightly as she did so.

"Mana-knots," she repeated in disbelief. "You actually said mana-knots?"

"That can happen?" I asked (probably stupidly). "I didn't cause that, did I?"

I really hope I hadn't unraveled anything. I still had no idea how this place worked, magic mist and glowing rocks and all.

"No," Stell said after a moment, eye still twitching while Guineve just stood there with a smile on her face. "It was not your fault, because there is no such thing as mana-knots. Guineve just made that term up and she knew I'd know it. Just like she knows I know there are no southern forests, that the south is the *only* part of Avalon without trees of any kind. She just gave me the worst excuse she could think of, on purpose."

Stell's fingers were starting to twitch in sync with her eyes, and I began to grow worried. But then her eye stopped twitching as both of her dark brown orbs locked on me.

"Oh, Wes," she said suddenly. "You're here again. On your own, somehow. Again. Hello. How are you?"

"Um, I'm okay," I turned to Guineve. "So, you didn't let her know I was here again, did you?"

"Oops," Guineve said sweetly. Stell began to huff again.

"Can you not do that anymore?" I asked carefully, but as firmly as I dared. "I know you know Stell better than me, since you're her clone, or daughter or something." I was still hung up on that, especially since Stell looked like she was my age, or a year older, tops. "But it makes me uncomfortable seeing her so uncomfortable. And stressed. She's got a lot on her plate and I know her training me is adding to it. Shouldn't we both be making her life easier?"

Stell suddenly looked back at me, letting go of the angry breath she had been holding. And Guineve nodded at me.

"You are absolutely right, Challenger Wes. It's my job to support Stell, who enabled me to exist, in any way possible. Thank you for having the courage to say that. Stell, I have been pulling your chain too hard these past months and I apologize. I've actually been using the mists to monitor the same warning signs you were looking at, and am as confused as you are. But fortunately, I have the time right now to study this matter for you, and this young Challenger looks more than ready to start helping you deal with our problems as well. I will tell you what I find out after you finish your time with him. And I know for a fact," she added, "that based on the memories you gave me, that there is no other who could have currently handled this nearly as well as you have."

"Thank you, Guineve," Stell said slowly, working through her emotions from anger to relief. "I've been wanting to hear that for months. And... thanks, Wes. Can you come with me for a bit?"

"Sure," I said, glad everyone was happy again and committed (hopefully) to playing nice. I turned to wave goodbye to Guineve.

"Make sure you keep taking good care of my little star," Guineve said to me cheerfully. "She's precious to all of us."

I nodded, not sure how to take the mist-clad woman's motherly devotion to another woman that had to be older than her. Then I followed the darker-skinned woman out of the clearing.

"So," I said, then realized I didn't have anything in my head to finish the sentence. "Hi."

I know. Genius, right?

"Hi," Stell said back, almost shyly. "It's good to see you again." She hesitated. "Um, I'm sorry about how last time turned out."

"Don't worry about it," I shrugged. "It wasn't anything I haven't heard before."

"Yeah, and that's kind of heartbreaking," Stell replied bitterly. "I still can't wrap my head around how people are treating you back on Earth. Any other world, and people would feel ashamed for not recognizing you as a Challenger, much less treating you with contempt." She shook her head as she spoke. "And contempt for such nonsense. I just can't believe it. Earth sounds like it's become horrible."

"I wouldn't know what Earth was like before," I admitted, then smiled. "But I'm glad you feel the way you do, Stell. And you were right, by the way. I found out who the second girl was."

"Really?" Stell said, turning her head at him.

"She was at another party just a few days ago, almost right before I came here last time. She thinks something I said saved her."

"Didn't you save the last girl with just your words also?" Stell said critically.

"I guess so," I admitted. "But I wasn't even at this party. I just warned her about the guy a couple weeks ago."

"Did anyone else warn her about him?" Stell asked calmly, effortlessly avoiding a tree root that I almost stumbled into myself.

"They should have. But probably not," I finally admitted to myself. Davelon probably hadn't gone to parties since he quit the football team, and he wasn't quite as familiar with Chris' dark side as I was.

"Well, it sounds like proper credit to me, and Avalon recognized the Deed as well. So, as usual, you're outnumbered at least three to one here," Stell said, looking at me and giving a grin.

"I'm outnumbered back home too," I replied. "But at least here, people like me more." All two or three of them.

"Then it's settled," she said firmly. "You should keep coming here."

"I guess I will." I grinned back. "So... when am I supposed to get on top of all those Tumults or whatever they're called?"

"You're already feeling okay about that?" Stell asked, tilted her head. "I thought you were still worried you were going crazy?"

"Well yeah," I replied with more conviction than I felt. "But if I'm going crazy, there's not a whole lot I can do about it but take a whole bunch of really dangerous pills. Which I shouldn't even bother with if this doesn't start affecting my personal life back home. And if I'm not crazy, then I'd better wise up and pay attention then, right?"

Stell chuckled at that. She had a nice laugh. Not rich in the same way Guineve's was, but with its own, softer charm.

"That's a proper Challenger attitude. Though this place is going to change you, even when you return."

I stumbled as she spoke.

"What?" I asked.

"Remember what I said before? You're going to grow more and more powerful as you overcome more obstacles. Slaying monsters, mastering magic, solving dangerous situations. It will all make you stronger, and some of that strength will follow you home. You won't be able to fly or lift houses or anything, but you should notice some change for the better. Would that count as proof for you?"

"Just how much would I change, exactly?" I asked with trepidation. The questions I had been afraid to ask earlier jumped to the front of my mind. Would I be able to walk again? Would my memory get better?

Could I function again as a normal person?

"I honestly don't know," Stell admitted. "I've never had this many Trials and Tumults appear so closely. Most Challengers help me with one, with a rare few handling two or even three at once, but no more than that. And we've never had this much time to train a Challenger either. And my information about the previous Challenger's time on Earth is sparse after they leave for good. But they all seemed a little stronger, a little smarter... they all get a little better at something they needed to be good at back on Earth. But that's how it's supposed to work, anyway. Saving others is supposed to benefit the rescuer as well. That's how the first Challengers were created, according to my people's legends."

But I was only half-listening to her talking about legends.

"Stell, if you had stressed that part before," I started to say, then shook my head. "You have successfully moved me from cautious worry about my sanity to hopeful excitement about my future. Please tell me how to begin, and as soon as possible."

She grinned at me, as if she was feeding off my excitement, and led me to another clearing.

13

CONDITIONING

"Got a question for you," I said as I stood in the middle of some more glowing rocks.

"Fire away," Stell said as she stood over a particularly tall outcropping of the same rocks, tapping the glowing lines on them like they were part of a keyboard on a computer.

"What do you call these stones you use to do your work? I've just been calling them magical glowing rocks, and I feel stupider, er, more stupid, I mean, sillier. Let's go with sillier. I feel sillier every time I call them that in my head."

"My people call them know-stones," the dark-skinned woman said as she pushed another rune.

"Know-stones? Really?" I asked. "That sounds... kind of dumb."

She looked up at me and grinned.

"Then go back to calling them magical glowing rocks. See which name makes you feel smarter."

I sighed.

"Do you really call them know-stones? I thought your race had its own unpronounceable language that I can't speak?"

"We do," she said with another smirk. "And you can't speak it. So we call them know-stones for your benefit. They store information, or spells that perform certain rituals. They know whatever I tell them to know, so... know-stones."

"Ugh," I said. "Honestly? Not one of your best jobs at naming things."

She just stuck her tongue out at me, and I laughed.

"Why are you so easy to talk to?" I asked, changing the subject. "You sound just like you're my age. But you get Challengers sporadically, so it's unlikely you would already know our jargon. How does that work?"

"The last Challenger wasn't that many Earth-years ago, so some of what I learned from him is still recent. And I can scry your planet occasionally, and learn snippets of news. But since your world has so many languages anyway, I use my translation magic to help me talk to your people. As soon as you start talking, it takes into account your mannerisms and figures of speech. It really helps with detailed conversations, and with all the dangerous material you'll be learning, it should prevent deadly miscommunications."

"Huh," I said in reply. "That sounds really neat. Cool, even."

"*Cool.* That last one I learned years ago," she said proudly. "Part of it could also be that you're the first Challenger I've had that's closest to my actual age."

"What do you mean?" I said. "I thought your race had a much longer life-span than mine."

"Exactly," she nodded. "My stage of growth would be on the cusp of adulthood. Just like you."

I chose not to bring up anything Guineve had told me about giving away memories. Or the fact that Guineve looked so much older. I suspected there was more to it than the original reason Stell gave me on my first visit.

"Actually," I said instead. "I won't legally be considered an adult in my country for another four years. I'm only eighteen."

"Wow, really? Four more Earth years? That's insane," she said with a snort. "I thought people in your country became adults when they were eighteen?"

"You're thinking of a century ago," I replied. "The new law says I'll get all of my rights at age 22."

Dad said a century ago people my age were considered adults at the age of eighteen, but recently the government believed that put too much pressure on developing teens, so the right to vote and everything else was pushed back to 22, and they began requiring special permission from their parents or the state to work, go to college, or enlist in the military. But the government passed a law after that, saying it reserved the right to conscript into the armed forces or to legally try as an adult anyone sixteen years old or older. Both laws were hailed as landmark accomplishments that would decrease the pressure and delinquency of late teens. But the media and government both frowned upon asking for proof on that matter.

"They must baby you guys these days," Stell replied. "I've heard of Earthlings fighting and winning battles, designing inventions, even ruling countries that were younger than you. At any rate, the know-stones have finished loading their scanning spell. This next part will really help you going forward. You'll actually be able to access your own mind-screen every time you come here from Earth."

"Access what?" I started to ask, but then a deep voice boomed from the mist again.

"The Challenger's Basic Abilities have been calculated. Imprinting the ability to measure oneself onto the Challenger directly."

The mist began to swirl violently around my feet. Suddenly my feet, and then my legs, and then the rest of my body were glowing blue. A screen appeared directly in front of my eyes. It matched the larger screen that hovered in the air in front of both me and Stell.

Initial Ability Record for Wes Malcolm
Race: Human. Origin: Earth (Challenger).
Growth level: Unrisen

Strength: 10
Dexterity: 10
Constitution: 10
Intelligence: 14
Wisdom: 22
Charisma: 12

Wow. Basic tabletop gaming stats... okay...

I'm in one of my sister's Pathwalker campaigns. Yep. Not going crazy at all. No siree. And I even have unbalanced stats to boot. Hurray.

"So," Stell said carefully. "Since you're probably not used to seeing yourself represented this way," (*Ha-ha*) "I should probably explain what each characteristic means..."

"Why do I even have these?" I asked numbly. "Why am I able at all to now look at myself in a way that will fit on a spreadsheet?"

"Because everyone else can," Stell said simply. "On every other world, people can visualize the ways that they grow. Your world is the only one where people have such a hard time tracking their own growth."

"So everywhere else people can look at these six specific traits, and figure out if they exercise and read enough?"

Stell shrugged. "They can track changes to themselves in different ways. But from what I've found, these six seem to work the best for helping Earth-born Challengers track their own growth, at least in the beginning. If you're ready, I'll go ahead and give you a basic explanation of what they mean..."

"Before you do that," I interrupted and raised my hand, "why don't I tell you what I think they mean, so that you can clear out any misconceptions first?"

"Well, okay," Stell said slowly. "But I'm not sure you'd even be familiar with most of them to have a lot of misconceptions..."

"Please just humor me while we find out," I asked. "You know what a tomato is, right?"

"Those red, squishy things on your world that taste terrible raw, but wonderful if you cook them or put them in other foods as a sauce?" Stell asked, sounding hopeful and wrinkling her nose at the same time. Good to know my dream fantasy woman had my exact same taste for tomatoes. *Forget the fact that she's a multi-bodied alien or a crazy delusion, let's go ahead and get married right now.* Anyway, back to quoting an ancient, semi-famous thread on the internet.

"So," I began. "As I understand it, Strength would help me crush a tomato. Dexterity would help me dodge a thrown tomato. Constitution would help me recover from eating a bad tomato. Intelligence helps me know that a tomato is a fruit, and not a vegetable. Wisdom helps me know not to put a tomato into a fruit salad. And Charisma helps sell a tomato-based fruit salad to someone else, probably someone I intensely dislike."

Stell blinked at me.

"That's... a pretty accurate description, at least for the very basics. How did you know that?"

"I didn't come up with it myself," I said with a shrug. I didn't know or remember the person who started that thread online.

"And," Stell added. "Isn't a tomato-based fruit salad on your world just salsa?"

"Found the bard," I grumbled under my breath.

"What?" Stell asked, cocking her head at me.

"Nothing," I replied. "Look, we've actually been using these... 'stats' for around a hundred years, probably more. These exact same six stats have been in numerous games I've played, computer and otherwise. The fact that I'm seeing them again here, of all places, is actually kind of frightening for me."

"Well, darn," Stell said in a frustrated voice. "I've been using these things for dozens of Challengers. I can try a different configuration if this really bothers you."

I shook my head.

"I get the feeling you'll just show me something else I've already seen, that will worry me just as much. And I don't think that's your fault."

Stell nodded. She looked a little sad.

"It's not your fault for feeling weirded out, either," she replied. "Nearly every Challenger has been surprised to find that they can suddenly track their own growth. You're just the first one to sound so familiar with being able to. The last Challenger seemed to have a vague idea of this system, but that was it."

"Yeah," I said slowly, and with another shake of my head. "No offense, but this is making it a lot harder for me to believe I'm not going crazy. Besides, if these are what I brought over from Earth, then they're definitely off."

"How do you know that?" Stell asked with another cock of her head.

"Ten's the average, right?" I asked calmly.

"Yes, in most of the worlds." Stell gave me a surprised nod. "For a person with no growth from Challenges, that is. For your world, a strength of 10 would be a person in decent shape, 12 or 14 would be someone who gets a lot of exercise, while a country's leading bodybuilder could be around 25."

"And what goes below ten?" I asked.

"A person who doesn't exercise much would be 9 or 8. 7 or 6 if they're completely out of shape. Below 6 are people working with physical disabilities."

"My Strength's at least five points too high, then," I stated calmly.

Stell's eyes narrowed again in confusion.

"What? No, you don't have any disabil—" her eyes widened again, and she stopped talking.

"Cripple-head," I said, repeating one of the names even Avalon knew I was called. "Back on Earth, I have trouble walking without the use of a cane, holding any kind of weight directly over my head, standing for prolonged periods even with my cane, and remembering random facts. Even shaking my head very quickly can force me to lie down for an hour. Not that I've been stupid enough to risk any rapid movement in over a year."

Stell had the same hurt and confused look she was wearing since the last time she heard that name for me. I just continued talking.

"At the very least, my Dexterity and Constitution scores should be well below average. I can barely hold my balance, which is a big part of Dexterity, right?" A faint nod from the woman. "And my threshold for being hit has dropped as well, judging by how easily a hit to the back of my head had me unconscious and throwing up. In fact, my Earth body is still recovering from the damage back home. My balance and pain has been even worse ever since."

Stell's eyes widened further, and her mouth dropped open. She looked horrified. I didn't understand how a being responsible for stopping dozens of catastrophes all over the place could seem so horrified over what had happened to little ol' me. Maybe it was because I was a Challenger?

She suddenly whispered something I couldn't hear.

"Sorry," I said calmly. "I didn't catch what you just said."

"You're not sick," she repeated, a little louder.

"Excuse me?" I asked, trying to keep the edge out of my voice. I had been hopeful before, but this current conversation was starting to get ridiculous far too fast.

"The body you're using should mirror the one you have back on Earth," Stell said in a confused but firm voice. "That's always been true. Challengers always bring their limitations with them to Avalon, where they learn to further overcome them. That's part of what makes them Challengers."

"I assure you that having constant pain, memory and balance issues is a challenge I'm constantly working to overcome," I said dryly. "Numerous doctors have pronounced me disabled, even if they have a hard time diagnosing my condition."

"I believe you," Stell said carefully. But she still seemed baffled, and began tapping the stone she was standing next to. "I mean, we've learned people back home are mocking you for it even, horrible though that is. But... I'm able to scan your body. Thoroughly. There's nothing there."

Now I was the one feeling baffled. Again.

"What do you mean?" I asked her. "Do you mean you can't find the source of the problem, like my doctors back home? That's not weird."

"No," Stell said stubbornly. "I mean *there's nothing there*. No muscle damage. Your muscles look like a person who used to exercise a lot, then suddenly stopped for two years. Nothing more. Your brain looks fine. You've probably been hit on the head before like you said, but again, no damage. No missing brain cells, weird brain shape, or broken neural pathways. And though my eyes on Earth are limited, I know I've kept up with your world's medical gains. I'm still a long way ahead of your best doctors, especially in examining the human body."

She looked a little embarrassed mentioning the last words, but she continued talking, speaking forcefully.

"Avalon and I can also see what your world *can't*. We can examine other parts of you, which is how we found out your Deeds and Renown. There is this: Your brain and body doesn't have any damage, but you've stopped making gains. You've continued exercising, right?" she said with a calculating glance.

I nodded slowly.

"Just what the muscle therapist recommends for rehabilitation. And you're saying it isn't working at all, I take it?"

Stell just shook her head.

"You are having absolutely zero gains, which should be impossible. Even the worst of your world's workouts should still make a tiny difference in you. But aside from getting bigger from growing up, it looks like your body has barely changed at all for the last couple of years."

That sounds about right, I realized. It was also supposed to be impossible.

"The same for your brain," Stell continued. She was still looking at the light from her know-stone (still hate that name, but moving on). "It looks perfectly healthy here, but from what I can tell of your body back home, it locks up perfectly healthy memory pathways at random. Almost as if something blocks you when you try and remember something." I don't know how she was able to figure that part out, but she was making a lot of wavy circles in the air with one hand while she tapped at her rock with the other. Also, that knowledge surprised me. None of my real doctors had been able to tell that.

"Is there a condition that causes that?" I asked, trying not to sound too hopeful. But even here, in this possibly made-up world, I would be grateful for an answer to what was wrong with me.

Stell shook her head.

"It's impossible for it to be a condition. It would be like a completely healthy person with no allergies or psychological conditions to suddenly start having all the classic, unmistakable symptoms of a virus, when their body was completely virus-free. Even that's a poor analogy. What I'm trying to say is that something else, not part of your body, is affecting you. Because if it was part of your body, it would follow you here."

"I don't understand," I replied.

"It's the only explanation that makes sense," she continued. "And here's why: say a Challenger gets a piece of metal—or arrow, or whatever—lodged into their leg, tearing it up so that they can't walk anymore. Say that they're never able to remove the item, that it stays in their body for years. When they'd come here, the leg would retain all signs of damage, but the splinter wouldn't come with them. The injury would be a part of them, they'd still have to deal with the damage the foreign object caused. But the foreign object would stay on Earth, where it belongs, because it's a foreign object, and not part of the Challenger itself. Clothing is the only exception, and it took forever to figure out how to get Challengers here without them being naked."

"I appreciate you figuring that last part out for us," I said dryly. "But I'm still not sure I'm following. It sounds like you're saying something else is actively screwing up both my body and life."

"That's exactly what I'm saying," Stell nodded. "I can't tell what's screwing up your body back on Earth, but if there was something actually wrong with you now, if you were recovering from a virus, or brain damage or anything else, I'd be able to see it. And I can't. So there isn't. I promise you that."

For the first time in Avalon, my head started hurting.

"I don't even know what to do with that information," I replied, clutching my forehead with one hand. "You're saying that something, or someone, back on Earth is actively screwing with my head, in a way none of my doctors can detect? That's—"

I stopped myself before I could say 'crazy.' Because then I would have said that I didn't have any enemies, and that had already been proven to be a lie. I could doubt a lot of things here. Dismiss a lot of things as paranoia. I had even been willing to mark off all the hazing at school as just people being idiots. But then my one of my best friends revealed a plot behind all of the abuse I'd received, one that made sense, and cost him in a huge way when he revealed it to me.

If I were to ignore that clear warning, then I'd be just as crazy as I was afraid of becoming.

But who could be my real enemies? How could I have such enemies? I was nobody. A kid with barely any future at all, that could barely dress himself. Heck, on bad days, I couldn't even do that. Mom or my sister had to help.

My head was spinning. I needed to sit down, but the freaky magic forest didn't have any chairs.

"Wait a minute, Wes," Stell said. "We'll figure out how to get to the bottom of this. There are things you can learn to counteract foreign influence on your body, and they carry over to Earth. We'll find a way to fix this."

I locked onto her words. On the sanity promised in them. If what she was telling me was true, not only could she prove that this place wasn't me going crazy, but she could help fix me.

When everything else had failed, that promise was an anchor to me. I wasn't going to let go of it.

"Alright, Stell," I said, swallowing as I got my nerves under control. "I'll hold you to that. What's next?"

"I'll take some more time later to see if I can figure out exactly what is going on, but for now let's continue with what we were talking about before."

"My suspiciously high stats?"

"Yeah," Stell said slowly. "If you could really call them that. A person who's Risen even once can probably make mincemeat of you. But we're moving on. I'll list the most important way these traits will affect you, then how they combine to affect you in different ways. Your Strength is going to mainly affect your carrying capacity and your ability to exert force on something, usually to damage it. Your Dexterity will affect your ability to avoid harm, be coordinated, and use tools, especially mechanical ones that aren't affected by extra muscle."

"You can just say crossbows and other ranged weapons," I replied dryly. I pictured Stell at one of my sister's Pathwalker campaigns, and smiled.

"It's not *just* those things," Stell said defensively. I didn't stop smiling. "Ugh! Fine! Moving on. You'll see soon enough. Constitution concerns your overall health, how much physical trauma and injury you can take, and how resistant your body is to disease and magic. And stop looking so smug," Stell admonished me. I did my best to wipe the smirk off my face and look innocent. She rolled her eyes and kept talking. "It *also* plays a slight role in all of your physical actions, because how healthy you are can limit how strong you can become and how easy it is for you to move. A poor Constitution will penalize your Strength or Dexterity, and a high one will make it easier for the other two to grow. So there!" Her eyes flashed suddenly. Apparently I finally looked like I didn't already know what she was talking about. She continued speaking. "Intelligence affects your ability to retain information and the speed at which you learn new skills. Most importantly it affects the power of most magic you'll perform as well as the total amount of mana—yes, I can tell you've heard that term before, stop acting smug—the total amount of mana you will have. Wisdom, your current highest trait, primarily affects the speed that you recover mana, but it also plays a role in a lot of different things. It helps you notice your surroundings and keep a clear head, and keeps your decisions from being influenced by outside sources."

"So it's also like my willpower?" I asked, paying attention since this one stat was a little different. But Stell shook her head.

"It's the primary component for your Will, but I'll get to that in a minute. The last one is Charisma, which affects your ability to relate to people and to express yourself. There are a few magical effects, and even a few magic spells, that directly depend on your force of personality to work. And it will help you win people to your side, and generally make them hesitant to kill you."

"Question, if you don't mind. Well, actually, two," I interrupted respectfully. Or at least I tried to.

"Fire away." Stell didn't seem offended this time

"I have a slightly-above-average Charisma, but everyone back home hates me. Why is that?"

"Good question," Stell deliberated before answering. "Probably because everyone's negativity at you is concerning events outside your control. Aside from 'Cock-blocker'—still trying to figure that one out, by the way—none of the other negative titles seemed to concern what you actually did. Finally," anger began to creep back into her voice, "a person who is an absolute dung-hole will continue to act like a dung-hole even if they interact with a charismatic person. And your town sounds like it's full of dung-holes. And yes, your slightly-above-average Charisma is keeping the problem from being worse. You should see it when you interact with people during your first meetings with them."

That did seem to be true, I reflected. That gaming reporter I met seemed to have had a lot of fun meeting me.

"Okay," I said. "That all sounds straightforward enough. Second question: why is my wisdom so high? You say a rating of 25 is just about the maximum for my world. Why am I so close to that?"

"You don't think you're that wise?" Stell asked calmly.

"I *know* I'm not all that wise," I replied stubbornly. "What I do know about the world could fill a thimble; what I don't know about it could fill its oceans. And I could point to a dozen decisions I still wish I had done differently. And my 'awareness of my surroundings' of things is not giving me any certainty right now. All I'm sure about is that a lot of weird and crazy things that I don't understand have been happening, a *lot*, for the past month. Or longer."

Stell nodded.

"See? There you go."

Silence stretched between us as I waited for her to say more.

She didn't.

"You're doing this on purpose, aren't you?" I finally said. "For my act of smugging my way through your explanation?"

"I have no idea what you're talking about," Stell replied, a triumphant grin flashing over her beautiful brown face. "But to more thoroughly answer your question: if Intelligence reflects an awareness of what you know, then Wisdom reflects an awareness of how much you *don't* know. That's why most wise people are not impressed with themselves."

"If that were true, then everybody with low self-esteem back home is a guru," I replied dryly. But Stell was undaunted.

"Nope!" she replied. "Awareness of what you don't know and having low self-esteem are two different things. If you had low self-esteem, you'd be easily bullied into advice you don't agree with, and wouldn't have a lot of confidence in your actions. Let's review: what advice do you usually get from people?"

"Best cases," I began. "I get told to abandon treatment that actually seems to be working, like my VR game. That's from my mother, who doesn't understand the doctor when he talks about using video games and media for treatment. Middle cases, I get told to take things easier, that I'm risking hurting myself even more by trying so hard.

"Worst cases, I get told I'm a waste of space and that I need to just fuck off and die."

"And do you listen to any of it?" Stell asked quietly, eyes flashing again.

I shook my head.

"It's all bad advice," I replied calmly. "I need a real reason to abandon treatment that I can tell is working, and if I don't try hard now, my life will just be more difficult later. And I refuse to fuck off and die; I have just as much a right to live as anyone else does. I'm not hurting anybody by breathing and trying to get a future."

Stell nodded.

"All of those are good examples. You're aware of your current limitations but still resisting a mountain of bad advice. You can observe and learn while still realizing you have much more to observe, much to learn. Wisdom combines awareness with efficiency, with success in one fashion or another. By our standards, your behavior merits the rating recorded."

"Thanks," I said dubiously. I still didn't feel that wise. But I was done arguing. "What's next?"

"What's next are your combination traits: Speed, Deftness, Wits, and Willpower. These attributes partially derive from two of the original six, thought they can be increased directly as well. Speed is how fast you move, particularly with your legs. It's dependent primarily on Dexterity, which gives you overall control over your body, and Strength, which provides muscular power. But you can also increase this trait independently, as there are plenty of weak, or clumsy, people who can move very fast. Deftness is where Strength and Dexterity meet once again to determine your ability to manipulate objects that require a strong grip."

"Didn't you say Dexterity did most of that anyway?" I asked. These new stats, excuse me, 'traits' seemed a little redundant.

"For objects that require almost no force to grip, like crossbows or other things with just a trigger, yes. But for things like a sword, or a bow, or even a surgeon's knife, both Strength and Dexterity are needed, at least in part. Deftness is useful to many weapon masters or master craftsmen."

"So," I said slowly. "This is what makes muscle-bound barbarians still fast enough with their giant swords, and slender swordsmen still able to strike powerfully with their smaller weapons."

"I guess you could say that," Stell replied. "These four traits reflect more focused behavior, while the first six each reflect a wider benefit. Moving on. The Wits trait is where your Intelligence and Wisdom meet to come to a quick decision, your Intelligence in providing the knowledge and your Wisdom in using that knowledge to react quickly. You'll find that it benefits your reaction times, as well as your speed in performing magic.

"Last is Willpower, or just Will for short, the one I briefly mentioned first. It's also potentially the scariest." Stell took a breath. "Will is where the awareness and resistance to influence that you get from Wisdom combines with your sense of self and force of personality in Charisma. It's used to resist when someone seeks to dominate instead of persuade you, when they secretly use magic to coerce or manipulate you, or to just intimidate you with sheer force of presence. But it can also be used to do the same."

"What do you mean?" I asked carefully.

"I mean most people think Willpower is used to resist being influenced, but it's also used to *project* influence. Not through words, or getting people to like or believe you, like Charisma deals with. A strong-willed person can also make others do what they want sometimes just through sheer presence. It's something a lot of people forget, even those outside of Earth. Be aware when you're raising Will, you're not just raising your ability to remain free, you're also increasing your ability to dominate."

"Holy crap," I said, eyes widening. "You're right."

I didn't remember who said it first, but I remembered the phrase "The right to swing my fist ends where another person's nose begins." If I could swing my fist wherever I wanted—or, always do whatever I wanted, regardless of what other people did to stop me—I was technically very, very free, but the people around me, getting punched in the nose or forced to tolerate me doing whatever I wanted all the time—had much less freedom than I did. "Have any Challengers become tyrants with that stat?"

"Not yet," Stell replied. "But I've noticed that a lot of villains and heroes both excel in this one trait."

"Will I need it?" I asked, swiftly and firmly.

"What do you mean?" Stell asked.

"I mean will I *need* it, will I fail in what you need me to do without increasing this ability directly? Because, full disclosure," I swallowed before continuing, "being able to be completely free, to where I didn't have to put up with the abuse of others, sounds intoxicating. To make all the idiots back home do what I wanted, whenever I wanted them to... that freedom scares me."

I wasn't exaggerating. I remembered all the crap I've put up with over the years. I still didn't like to talk about it, but part of me wanted to make those people *pay*. And pay very badly.

For shaming my family. For kicking me when I was down. If I could balance the scales through sheer force of will, make sure I'd never put up with it again...

Stell sighed.

"Wes, relax," she said. "It's not going to be a problem for you. In the first place, none of your traits will carry over back to Earth completely, and even here almost no one is strong enough to completely dominate another through Will alone. In the second place, those who do use Will to dominate usually use it to enhance their magic, and the magic you learn here won't follow you back to Earth. Finally, again, we screen Challengers to make sure we don't accidentally create any super-villains. We haven't had any yet, and I'm even less worried about you than I was about all my previous Challengers."

You're jinxing me, I wanted to say. *Have you people really not heard of all of those 'tempted over to the dark side' movies?*

"Sorry," I said after a moment. "I'd just like to be careful of abuse. My planet's full of stories about well-meaning people becoming powerful and then doing horrible things."

"Yeah, but, counterpoint?" Stell replied. "Your planet also sucks. No offense. But I know for a fact that, at some point, there were at least a handful of people who were either kings, ministers, priests, or other leaders that did their jobs without enslaving or hurting anybody. They just didn't get talked about because everyone else was either focusing on the tyrants they already had or obsessing about following someone else who had all the signs of becoming a tyrant in the future. And usually? Half the time, the people I see in your world getting oppressed by said tyrant were, in the past, either oppressing the tyrant or someone close to the tyrant."

"Well, I'm definitely being oppressed back home," I admitted. "So I have cause for concern."

"I don't," Stell said with a shrug. "You're not taking any super-powers back home with you. Just try not to be a bad person if you ever wind up in charge. You wouldn't be the first person from Earth that figured out how to do so."

"Thanks for the vote of confidence," I said, mostly because I didn't know what else to say. "What's next?"

"Well, let's configure your screen to where you can see your next four traits."

The blue light in front of me flickered once again.

Wes Malcolm
Race: Human. Origin: Earth (Challenger)
Growth: Unrisen

Strength: 10
Dexterity: 10
Constitution: 10
Intelligence: 14
Wisdom: 22
Charisma: 12

Speed: 10
Deftness: 10
Wits: 18
Will: 20

"Is that thing going to keep updating?" I asked.

"Yes," Stell admitted. "But I'll try and keep it to a minimum. You'll notice that, except for your Will, the new four stats are just an average of their two derivatives. This is because you've been taking actions that raise your Will directly, which leads to it being increased on its own. In case I haven't made it clear," Stell said, gesturing with her hand, "you'll be able to raise your traits in two ways: directly through use, or by investing in them whenever you Rise. Your skills will work the same way, especially the magic ones."

I was going to have to keep track of skills, as well. And I was beginning to suspect there would be hundreds of them. *Oh well. Bring it on.*

"Now we need to measure what you already know how to do: your skills, crafts, etc."

Called it.

"Now, every world of mine has slightly different skills and there are probably too many to easily count..."

Called that too. Stell narrowed her eyes a little when she saw my face.

"You know," she began. "For a guy doubting his sanity, you're doing a horrible job at being properly mystified and impressed with all of this."

"Sorry," I said with a grin. "I'll try and be good."

"Try hard," she warned. "Or I'll withhold cookies or something. Anyway." She looked up and raised her voice. "Avalon, measure the Challenger's knowledge and see what can be retained."

"Avalon will now appraise the Challenger," the deep voice boomed again through the mist.

Nice, I thought. She didn't even need to hit a button for that.

"So," I began. "I take it I can't bring all of my knowledge over here?"

"Some of what you know won't work the same over here," Stell said with a nod. "Particularly most of the new technological advances your people have made in the last two centuries. Our mana gives us some extra rules."

"I see. Good thing I don't know any rocket science, robotics, or advanced physics."

"Yeah, and your people should probably ease up a bit on all the splitting and fusing together of atoms. That's just my opinion though. My race was the only one other than yours that ever figured out how to do that."

Stell shuddered briefly after saying that. She began talking quickly again, as if she didn't want me to see her flinch.

"Anyway, Avalon, move it, we don't have all day."

"Can it actually hear you?" I asked, curious. "I mean, can you actually talk to it like a person? What is Avalon?"

"Good question," Stell asked. I thought she seemed grateful I wasn't asking about her race. "Avalon and the other worlds have a little bit of sentience. Think of a bunch of really sleepy giants, who occasionally wake up to serve as witnesses and scribes, then go back to bed. They won't answer any random question or hold an hour-long conversation with you though.

They just record or announce noteworthy events, and then go back to let everyone else on the planet run themselves."

"It feels like you do a really good job of telling this one what to do," I offered.

"Well, yeah," Stell said with a confident grin. "That's my job. But I can't really get it to kick people off its surface, or swallow them in a sinkhole, or whatever."

"That's a relief to know," I grinned back.

"Yeah, but it's also the reason I have magic. So don't get any ideas," she teased. Then the deep voice boomed out again.

"The Challenger has passing familiarity with the following skills..."

"Here we go," Stell said as the giant blue screen shifted from showing my Traits to a slowly forming list. "We're probably going to collapse these on your screen, so that you don't see a big giant list every time you want to examine how you grow."

General Athletics.

"Huh," I said. "It's been a while since I was physically active, but I'll take it."

Unarmed Fighting.

"Really?" I said, surprised. "I barely made it past yellow belt."

"These are just the basics," Stell offered. "It doesn't mean you're an expert by any stretch."

I nodded, satisfied with that explanation.

Archery.

"Wait, wait," I said. "That was just one brief course at one time."

Stell rolled her eyes.

"I swear Wes, it's like you have to argue about every little thing."

I went ahead and backed off. If Avalon thinks I can shoot a bow, then maybe I can shoot a bow.

Horse-riding.

"One three-day weekend, but whatever," I said. I shrugged when Stell glared at me. So I was arguing with a planetary supercomputer. Shoot me.

Sailing.

"That wasn't even one full day," I said, and this time I ignored Stell's hiss to be quiet.

Staves.

"Huh?" I completely cocked my head at this one. "Is this because I walk with a cane?"

Stell groaned. But I was getting a little worried.

Long Blades.

"No, stop!" I said forcefully. "Wait! I've never even held a sword except for one time at a Renaissance fair! I literally just picked it up and waved it around!"

Stell actually looked concerned when I said that. But Avalon did not change.

Shield Use.

"Definitely not," I argued. "Stell, I know enough about shields to know I don't even know how to hold them properly. We have a problem."

"We... shouldn't," Stell said slowly. "Avalon should just be drawing from your memories."

"Well, I don't remember ever holding a shield or learning how to," I insisted. "Stell, can Avalon be bugged?"

"Bugged?" She wrinkled her face at that. "Oh, that kind of bugged. No, it's a planet, not one of your Dane or Banana computer-thingies."

Before I could tell her she got the names wrong, Avalon boomed out again.

Light Blades.

"No, I don't," I called out. "And if I really did have that skill I'd have a criminal record to prove it!"

Seriously. Name three companies or colleges who will still accept you if you put 'knife-fighting' anywhere on your application.

Bludgeoning Weapons.

Well, okay, there are some debt collection agencies that would probably take that one.

Polearms.

At that point I turned to see if there was a medieval squire standing behind me, who also happened to share my exact same name. But Avalon just continued with fudging my resume.

Light Armor... Medium Armor... Heavy Armor.

Mass Combat.

By that point I was sputtering heavily and Stell looked really concerned.

"You're sure you've never even dabbled in any of this?" she asked carefully.

"I am absolutely positive I've never worn plate armor while stabbing people with a lance as part of a group exercise. And there's no way anyone would have let me forget about it if I had."

Speechcraft.

No. Not even debate in high school. Though I was glad to be done with all of the 'murder' skills.

First Aid.

Finally, I sighed. I did still have my old Boy Scout handbook. I could maybe take that one.

I don't even remember the rest of the list. But in the end I was just staring blankly forward while Stell was watching me carefully. When Avalon had finally finished forging me a new identity, Stell carefully began walking around her stones toward me. She reached out her left hand to grab at some low-hanging branches, doing something I couldn't see.

"So," she began. "One last time, you don't remember any of those combat skills but archery."

"Stell, I swear to you," I said. "I have no memory of using any real weapon. Most of those are illegal now in my country to begin with."

"Even staves and blunt weapons?" she asked carefully, still slowly walking around her rocks.

"They're not *as* illegal, but I know using a quarterstaff or club is different from walking around with a cane. And I've never—"

"Catch," she interrupted.

A large, but perfectly straight branch flew at my face. Surprising myself, my hands leaped up to grab it and protect my nose. I stared at it. It was maybe four feet long, and for a moment I wondered if I should grip it at the end or put one hand on the middle. But Stell helped me come to a decision about two seconds later.

"Aaaah!"

She suddenly leaped over toward me, yelling and brandishing another stick like a crazy person, gripping one end with both hands.

While still blinking in disbelief, I batted away her stick as it came high at my left shoulder. She screamed again, braids flying through the air as she spun around for another blow. This one aimed for my shins, and once more I somehow retained the presence of mind to bat it away.

What was I doing? part of me wondered. I was holding my own stick at the end with both hands, but that was a stupid stance unless I was actively trying to attack someone, and all I wanted to do was to not get hit while shouting 'what the hell?'

I shifted my grip to be closer to the middle, and began actively knocking away the weapon of the woman-turned-screaming-Pict, until I had it trapped against a branch.

"Stell," I growled. "Stop it!"

"Whew!" she said, smiling and dropping her branch. "That's a relief!"

"What is?" I demanded. "Were you trying out a violent new cardio routine on the both of us?"

"No." She grinned. "I was testing your skill with long blades and quarterstaves. You have basic proficiency, or I would have knocked you on your bum."

"Who tests people with random acts of violence?" I shot back. "And who still uses the word 'bum'?"

"The same person that has two thumbs and knows more about your own weapon skills than you do," the beautiful, but now slightly scary, woman replied casually, pointing both of her thumbs at herself.

But then she became more serious. "Wes, in all seriousness, Avalon has never been wrong about a Challenger yet. You just showed practice with at least two different types of weapons you swore up and down you were unfamiliar with. That means your memory is in the wrong, not Avalon."

"But that's impossi—" I began, but stopped myself. I ran a hand through my hair, and my thoughts began to race. I tried to think carefully, trying to figure out where I had held anything even remotely like a long sword or quarterstaff.

Suddenly, my head began buzzing. A sharp ache stabbed briefly though my head, and I winced at the pain.

When I opened my eyes a moment later, Stell was next to me. Her eyes were soft, and her hand was on my shoulder. I started to tell her I was okay, then I remembered the past five minutes, and the words died in my throat. But she just read my eyes and nodded at me.

"We'll get to the bottom of this, Wes. I swear," she promised. "My Challengers have always been there for me. So I'll be there for you, anyway I can in this."

"Thanks," I said, patting the hand on my shoulder. Her skin felt warm. I realized that there was a strength hiding in her grip, one she had suppressed in our earlier mock combat.

It was also a very gentle grip.

It had been a long time since someone had been able to touch me without hurting me. Even my mother and sister had to be careful when they hugged me.

"Thanks," I said. The moment passed and she let go of my shoulder. Her eyes still seemed to be searching me.

"Wes, I want to make sure. Is this the first time you've heard of any of this? Challengers? Avalon? Me?"

I nodded.

"Challenger is a pretty common word in my language, but it's never meant all of this." I gestured around me. "And I've never heard of a woman like you in my life. You're completely one of a kind." Her mouth twitched a little at that. "Avalon is just the name of an island in the legend of King Arthur, but I've never heard of it as a reference to anything else."

"King Arthur? What did he share about us?" Stell asked attentively. I just stared at her.

"What do you mean?" I asked.

"Arthur," she repeated. "Of the Bretons?"

"Right," I said slowly.

"What did he say about us? Most Challengers don't mention Avalon at all."

I stared at Stell for a moment longer.

"Did you just say King Arthur was a Challenger?" I asked, thinking I should have seen this sooner.

Stell nodded again.

"He was one of the first. One of the few to become a Pendragon. Did he not mention us?"

I shook my head slowly.

"If Arthur lived at all, he lived over a thousand years ago. We have little to no records of him. Many on my world have heard of him, but none know if he really existed. And we certainly didn't know Avalon was a place like this."

Stell smiled.

"I'm glad he became king. But what I'm trying to figure out is why you have so many skills relevant to being a Challenger, as well as why you don't remember most of them. It's almost as if another Challenger had trained you to prepare you for coming here."

I shrugged.

"I don't see how. No one has ever talked to me about this place and I don't remember ever learning how to even hold a stick like I just did."

"Well, we'll figure it out eventually," Stell promised. "But since we don't know how long you're staying here, we need to move on. It's time to test your magical affinities."

Magical affinities...

I was starting to suspect that a lot of writers back home owed Stell royalty fees.

"You're making that look again," Stell said with another glare.

"Sorry," I said. "Please continue with your explanation while I do my best to listen attentively and respectfully to your descriptions of the magics of earth, air, fire, and probably some other types of magic."

"Not helping," Stell said. "And I liked it better when you weren't so presumptuous."

"Tell you what," I offered. "If I'm wrong, I'll find a way to properly apologize. If I'm right, I'll find a way to get the money you're owed from a lot of people back home."

"Money?" Stell said in a baffled voice. "What? Why do people owe me money? What would I even do with it?"

"Whatever you want," I replied. "It's the principle of the matter, really."

"Good grief, you're weird," Stell finally declared. "You're worse than the Challenger that thought arguing with women proved he had a low Wisdom trait. I give up. We're moving on right now. Avalon," Stell said, raising her voice again while looking up. "Search the Challenger for the Ideals his soul is bound to."

Once again mist began to swirl around me. This time, I felt it pass through my chest. Again, I got a comfortable, cool sensation from the experience, instead of just feeling damp all over. I wasn't even aware it was entering my body, except for a small twinge I felt in my chest, and the fact that it sparkled into a rainbow of different colors when it passed out the other side. Blue, green, red, brown, pink. A host of other shades that winked in and out too quickly for me to process.

This whole thing had finally transitioned the experience away from disturbing familiarity and back to the wonder and mystery I felt when I first came here.

I grasped at the individual sparkling motes, but they just winked away from me. The blue, green, brown and red motes danced away from me and still lingered nearby, as if taunting me to work harder for them. But every other mote just evaded my hands and dashed off to merge into the rest of the mist. Finally, I gave up swiping at them and just stared at it all. The last of the mist finished passing through me and floated just out of reach, like a rainbow of tiny eyes that were still assessing me.

Assessment finished, the screen read out. *The Challenger has formed contact with no Ideals as of yet. Affinity may still be chosen. The Challenger has the current potential to have Innate understanding of two Ideals. Only the Foundational Ideals may be chosen: Fire, Water, Earth, Air.*

Even with a bunch of tropes about the four elements flashing through my head, I was still stunned by the beauty of what I just witnessed. Stell saw my gaping mouth, and smirked.

"There," she said smugly. "Are you finally impressed? No more quips about you guessing what was about to happen?"

I shook my head slowly.

"Stell..." I said slowly. "Thank you."

"You're welcome?" she asked, arching an eyebrow but still sounding pleased.

"Thank you for making this all..." I searched for the right word. "Beautiful."

She tilted her head at me.

"What are you talking about? And I didn't make Avalon myself, I just tweak it and interact with it."

"Thank you for keeping everything beautiful, then," I insisted. "Even though some of this is familiar to me, I know this didn't have to be so fantastic. And whatever else happens, thank you for letting me be part of it."

"Really?" she asked, tilting her head. "You know the name 'Challenger' means you're not going to have an easy time of things. It's a little soon to form an opinion for gratitude, isn't it?"

I shook my head. Whatever all of this was, delusion, or fantastic magic, I knew it wasn't going to be a nightmare anymore. I hadn't felt this happy in years, weirdness notwithstanding.

"Thank you," I repeated. "For everything."

"Fine," she said, the smirk becoming a small smile, then disappearing altogether. "Let's just move on. Ideals are the foundation for different concepts of magic. Your understanding of them allows you to perform spells, enchantments, and other supernatural activities. Which route taken with the magic depends on the Challenger."

"Am I going to be one of the only people who can do magic?" I asked, though I thought I remembered Stell mentioning magical orders at one point or another.

"No, but it's still very rare. Certain Ideals, and methods of using them, are much rarer than others though. All Challengers have an Innate understanding, the highest initial understanding possible, with at least one Ideal. It's rare to be able to choose your Ideal, and even rarer to be able to choose two. If you had been able to choose beyond the basics, you would have really been a special snowflake."

"Sorry to disappoint," I smiled.

"No you're not," Stell grinned back. "At any rate, you're suspiciously favored enough in all the other areas. Let's just move forward with explaining your choices, shall we?"

I nodded at her, and she tapped on a nearby know-stone for a few moments. My mind-screen changed from displaying my other information to a four-part list.

The Ideal of Fire: Fire is the domain of heat, passion, and swift bursts of intensity. An Innate understanding grants the Challenger an initial and constant increase to Strength, Dexterity, and Charisma. Over time, the Challenger will notice a further improvement to their Speed, fast-twitch muscles, and a strictly beneficial improvement to one's metabolism, in both their projected and original bodies. The Challenger further performs fire-based magic to greater effect, and also receives a significant resistance to fire-based magic, as well as a slight resistance to heat in both bodies.

The Ideal of Water: Water is the domain of gentleness, secrets, and fluidity. An Innate understanding grants the Challenger an initial and constant increase to Constitution, Intelligence, and Wisdom. Over time, the Challenger will notice a further improvement to their Deftness, regenerative speed, and blood flow, in both their projected and original bodies. The Challenger further performs water-based magic to greater effect, and also receives a significant resistance to water-based magic, as well as a slight resistance to cold in both bodies.

The Ideal of Air: Air is the domain of travel, thought, and freedom. An Innate understanding grants the Challenger an initial and constant increase to Dexterity, Intelligence, and Charisma. Over time, the Challenger will notice a further improvement to their Wits, learning speed, and mental retention in both their projected and original bodies. The Challenger further performs air-based magic to greater effect, and also receives a significant resistance to air-based magic, as well as a slight resistance to mental effects in both bodies.

The Ideal of Earth: Earth is the domain of endurance, quiet strength, and depth. An innate understanding grants the Challenger an initial and constant increase to Strength, Constitution, and Wisdom. Over time, the Challenger will notice a further improvement to their Will, slow-twitch muscles, and balance in both their projected and original bodies. The Challenger further performs earth-based magic to greater effect, and also receives a significant resistance to earth-based magic, as well as a slight resistance to physical effects in both bodies.

My eyes rolled through all of the information, stopping to read certain parts more slowly. My breathing caught when I read over the phrase 'projected and original bodies.'

"Stell," I said, containing my excitement. "Do the parts about both of my bodies mean what I think they mean?"

She nodded.

"They affect your body back home. You're wondering how to fix your body back home, aren't you?"

I nodded.

"Maybe it's selfish, but I think I can also be more useful here if I'm no longer dealing with my condition back home."

Stell shrugged.

"I can't really ask you to give up an opportunity like that. Especially since I've seen numerous Challengers save the day with just one of these Ideals. I trust my Challengers to make the best choice both for themselves and the rest of us."

Relieved with her acceptance, I went back to looking over the four Ideals. Excitement was building up all over me. There were a lot of crazy things happening that I couldn't explain. But if I could suddenly think better, and walk better, back home? That wouldn't just prove that I wasn't going crazy. That would prove that I wasn't a lost cause.

I thought back to the abilities granted by each Ideal. Muscular improvement. Metabolism. Better regeneration for my body. That last one would probably improve my overall lifespan, if it worked the way I thought it did. But would it be the right fix for me?

"Stell," I asked. "Just to be clear, you can't find any damage in my body, brain or other organs, right?"

"Right," she nodded. "Whatever's affecting you can't be fixed by regeneration, as far as I know, if that's what you're thinking."

That left the last two. Balance and mental retention. My best chances at being able to walk and think better.

"Stell," I said, swallowing. "I'm going to choose Earth and Air."

"Okay," she said, with some hesitancy. "You can do that, but I need to warn you that it's harder to control two opposing Ideals at the same time. It's been done before, but it's never easy. You'd have an easier time with Earth and Fire, or Water and Air, especially."

"It's my best shot for back home," I said firmly, shaking my head at her recommendations. "I'll just have to make it work."

"Fair enough," Stell said with a nod. "Just think out your choices and Avalon will respond. Brace yourself, though. The transition will be intense."

I nodded one more time and closed my eyes.

Avalon, I thought. *I choose Innate understanding in Earth and Air.*

Avalon acknowledges contact with the Challenger, a voice said in my mind. *Assimilating knowledge now.*

My head began to tear itself apart.

Flashes of things, pictures, concepts flew through and crashed into my mind. Soaring through the sky to look down at the ground below. Going into the ground and finding out just how far down it went. Seeing an air current move, and tracking the wind by the effects it left. Seeing a stone change over thousands of years. My body felt like it was twisting, condensing, and stretching all at once. The top half of me wanted to fly up into the sky, and see what was beyond the clouds. The other half felt like it was about burrow into the earth, until I reached the core of Avalon's magic. I felt the Ideals whisper at me, offer flashes of power, and then get in each other's way. It was impossible to focus on the concepts of one for any longer than a second before the other shoved its way to the front of my mind.

Fly up, Air said. *See every part of the world in one small passage of time.*

No, go down, Earth said. *Watch every stage of time on one small part of the world.*

I had one second to think that Stell had really under-warned about this before my mind and body began to rip again. The next second, I asked myself what I was so worried about.

My mind and body felt like they were ripping apart all the time back home.

This was nothing.

With that stubborn thought, I began to fight through the pain.

Stop getting in each other's way, I thought. *There must be something you both have in common, or one of you wouldn't be able to exist at all.*

But both Ideals continued to struggle. Each kept trying to argue its own case in my mind. I shucked off their words and tried to think of something that connected the two Ideals.

Where do Earth and Air connect? I asked in my mind. The Ideals did not answer me. I tried to think of the answer on my own.

Was it with rain? I asked myself. But I felt both Ideals tense. Rain must be where Water and Air met. That probably meant clouds were almost as much of the domain of Water as they were of Air, since they were just trapped moisture. Water did connect the two, I realized, but it was an Ideal with its own territory. It was more than the connection of two points.

Connecting two points...

That thought grasped at my brain. Air and Earth were arguing for two different things. One wanted constant travel. One wanted stillness. One wanted change to happen quickly, and often. The other wanted change to happen slowly, and seldom.

What was something that connected the two?

Instants, I thought with a smile, ignoring the pain in my body and the battle around my mind. No matter how big or small the measurements, time was composed of instants. And what symbolized instantaneous connection, and served to connect Earth and Air.

The answer sparked into my brain.

Lightning.

Lightning traveled between the sky and the earth all the time during storms. And, unlike rain, it traveled in both directions—from the clouds to the ground, and, usually immediately, from the ground back up to the sky. And, as far as I knew, there was no water in lightning. It was something both Earth and Air had at least a portion of a claim to, without Water as a third party. There were some rare accounts of it happening even without clouds at all.

Fighting against the pain in my skull, I visualized a single bolt traveling from the sky into the ground, spending part of its charge into the soil, then shooting from the ground back into the sky. *In this instant,* I thought to the two Ideals, *you are connected.*

The pain in my head and body began to settle down, and the voices from both Ideals grew less intense. They seemed to gravitate toward the picture, muttering at it in agreement. Then, slowly, both of their voices faded into the background of my thoughts. The images competing in front of my eyes also faded away, and I began to see the mind-screen Stell had originally created for me.

The words had changed again:

You have acquired Innate understanding of a Second-Tier Ideal, the Ideal of Lightning.

The Ideal of Lightning: Lightning is the domain of instantaneous connection, power, and revelation. An Innate understanding grants the Challenger an immediate and gradual increase to Strength, Dexterity, Intelligence, and Charisma. Over time the Challenger will notice an increase to their Speed, Wits, fast-twitch muscles, and an improved health for their neural pathways in both their projected and original bodies. The Challenger further performs lightning-based magic to greater effect, and also gains a significant resistance to lightning-based magic, as well as slight resistance to paralyzing effects in both bodies.

The Challenger has overcome a significant challenge facing an attack on both his body and mind, and grown stronger for it. The Challenger's Constitution and Wisdom have both improved by one degree.

My head spun for a moment, then settled down. I felt a tiny difference to my body. Like I had suddenly become healthier, more clear-headed.

"Did I just level up?" I asked. "I mean, did I just 'Rise'?"

"No," Stell said, her voice edged with relief and something else. "But it looked like you broke the rules somehow. Again." There was just a hint of bitterness in that last comment. "You gained access to an Ideal on another tier."

"What does that mean?" I asked. "And why are the benefits for this new one better than the other two?"

"Located immediately beyond the Foundational Ideals are the Secondary Ideals," Stell answered me. "They represent the places where two or more Foundational Ideals connect. Their connective nature means a broader benefit to your body, while their magics are more focused, with spells that are only useful for very specific purposes. The four Foundational Ideals seem less powerful in comparison, but their magics usually cover a broader, more flexible scope."

"Okay," I replied. "I think I follow you. Sorry I keep cheating," I offered lamely. Some part of me that had started treating this all like a game was screaming out *'Hax! Challenger is OP! Nerf Incoming!'*

"Don't apologize," Stell replied. "Your... exploits... are surprising, but it's going to help us save more lives. All things considered, I have zero problems with that. In fact, I hope you'll keep breaking the rules if it helps you solve my incoming headaches."

"I'll try and do that for you," I said with a smile.

"Good boy," my dark-skinned guide said in gentle mockery. "Now we need you to prepare you for..."

"Alert," Avalon's voice rumbled from the mist. *"Avalon bears witness to a Challenge rising in another world. Possible Trial forming."*

Stell's eyes snapped upward.

"Guineve!" she called out.

"I know, dear," the other woman's mature voice called back from the mists. "I'm sending you what I know right now."

I felt something stir in me, like I was a racehorse looking at the man holding a whistle. Or a warhound, looking at a man waving a bloody piece of meat through the air.

"When do I leave?" I asked, feeling the eagerness wanting to creep into my voice. "And where to?"

14

COMMIT

Stell turned and looked at me.

"I'm not sure you're ready. You haven't really Risen yet."

"Do I need to overcome Challenges to rise?" I asked.

"Yes, but if you die..." Her voice trailed off. "Right. You've become a Challenger now. You can't die permanently."

"Which means we have nothing to lose if I come along," I said patiently. "There are no penalties to dying, right?"

"Other than the fact that it's traumatic and extremely painful?" Stell asked. "No. But a normal person would say that's enough to avoid it."

"I understand that," I said, though part of me pointed out that I really didn't. "I mean, I'd like to avoid it if possible. But the people on the other worlds don't come back if they die, right?"

"They don't," Stell admitted, biting her lip as she thought for a moment. "I need to review what we're facing."

She tapped at her know-stones (still hated that name, by the way) for a moment, nodding and talking to herself.

"A Nest-type Challenge," she muttered. "Out in the one place where it could grow on its own, without something from the environment to destroy it while it's still weak. No villages or guardians nearby." She paused, closing her eyes. "Merada would need some time to get there. Anyone she brought with her would face a much greater threat by that time. Whereas I can transport you there now..."

"Wait," I interrupted, raising a hand. "Just so we're clear, I'm going without you?"

Stell nodded.

"I can send myself to the worlds in an emergency, but it costs a whole lot of power. One single trip can make me useless for decades, if not centuries, depending on how much power I spend. Even using my power on Avalon is difficult."

"Really?" I asked, curious. Stell nodded, looking glum for a moment.

"My race is supposed to just send projections of ourselves to other worlds. Our abilities decrease somewhat when we live away from our home world."

Something in her face steered me away from asking further questions about her background.

"But you won't go completely alone," Stell said, her voice picking up energy. "Breena's one job is to escort Challengers for me."

"Is that the fairy?" I asked.

"It's not the official name for her race," Stell nodded. "But yes. You'll have to be the one summoning her though." She rolled her eyes for a moment, without telling me why.

"How do I do that?" I asked, curious.

"You'll have to Rise first," Stell replied. "Luckily we have time for that."

"Have I grown enough to Rise yet?" I asked.

"You're not even in the first stage yet, so yes. Rising the first time is something innate. It takes the least amount of personal growth to achieve, but the trigger for every person is different."

"How do we find mine?" I asked.

"You already did," Stell replied. "You challenged Avalon itself when you came here."

"Oh, right." I remembered. I had been scared and confused by everything happening and had chosen to face it all head on. "So what do I do now?"

"Pick a good spot to stand," she said, looking over and pointing at a flat part of ground. "Probably right there."

The spot of ground was relatively free of loose rocks, roots, or other things to trip and hurt myself on. Other than that, I couldn't think of a reason for Stell to have picked this spot.

"Am I going to flail around or something?" I asked worriedly as I made my way over.

"I hope not," Stell said, still not looking up from her glowing computer-rocks. "The first Rise is always a little unpredictable. But it's low-risk, and as you keep reminding me, you come back when you die."

"Thanks," I said dryly as I moved into position. But Stell probably would have shown more concern if I really had anything to worry about.

"Alright," I said. "Ready. I think."

"Okay," Stell said, finally glancing up at me. She took a deep breath, but her eyes remained steady on me as she did so. "Find a way to look inward. Find that heavy part inside of you and *push.*"

I closed my eyes to focus on following her instructions. I had no idea how to really look into myself, I realized. Not in the way I wanted to. But then I remembered the movements inside my body when I acclimated to the Ideals. I found that spot where they rested, took a deep breath, and as I released it I felt that heaviness in my body, the part my magic had fought over, and *shoved.*

I'm not sure that was a good way to describe it. Imagine pushing a stray thought out of your mind, only instead of your head you do it in your chest. Does that make any sense?

At any rate, I pushed, not to get out of my body, but because I realized that the weight inside needed to move forward.

Then I started to rumble.

Not the ground. Not Avalon. Not the mists. Me.

I started to quake. Muscles all over my body started twitching, and I heard my bones creak. Thoughts started snapping faster inside my head, and everything felt just a little clearer, a little easier to understand. That wasn't quite it though. The things I could see and hear and smell became sharper, more noticeable, and the things I couldn't see, the shadowy parts of the mist, as well the edges of my hearing and even my sense of smell, became more glaringly obvious, like little warning signs that said I still didn't know everything. But I didn't feel troubled by all of this. Actually, I felt just a little more confident, more comfortable in my own skin. But by the time I understood all of this, everything was over but a few tremors in my limbs that gradually faded too.

And the lightning, I realized. There were still tiny little bolts of blue and white running up and down my body. Stell was watching me very carefully.

"How are you?" the dark woman asked. "Do you feel okay?"

"*Hell* yes," I answered before I could stop myself, the swear word slipping right out and for once feeling completely okay with it.

I felt amazing, like I could punch through a tree right now, that I could do anything. It was incredible.

"Not the flashiest Rise I've ever seen," Stell noted casually. "Arthur managed to get trumpets to sound, every single time. Which was cool, up until it got weird. But anyway, good job getting through your first Rise. Your three magics merged together beautifully. Take another moment to get settled, then pull up your mind-screen."

I did as she directed, pulling the screen by mentally desiring to look at it:

Wes Malcolm
Race: Human. Origin: Earth (Challenger)
Growth Level: First Rise (Spark)
Path: Unknown
Saga: Unknown
Profession: Unknown
Vital Pool: 230 points
Stamina Pool: 230 points
Mana Pool: 260 points

Strength: 14
Dexterity: 14
Constitution: 13
Intelligence: 18
Wisdom: 24
Charisma: 16

Speed: 16
Deftness: 14
Wits: 23
Will: 24

Rise Points: 6 (can increase the six primary traits at a 1:1 ratio, or the four secondary traits at a 1:2 ratio.

Insight into the Following Ideals
Earth: lvl 1
Air: lvl 1
Lightning: lvl 1

Skill List truncated.

"I get six points right off the start?" I asked incredulously. "And can increase the last four stats twice for every one point I spend? And the Ideal increased each related stat by two points right off the start?"

"Yes, yes and yes," Stell said quickly. She seemed to be very much in business mode. "But the growth from Ideals will only be half that for each stage of Rising in the future. Now, I'd normally like to take my time in explaining everything that's happened to you, but since you're somehow already annoyingly familiar with this process, and since this Challenge will slowly escalate into a Trial or Tumult even faster than the other ones already forming, I'm going to have to delegate the rest of your training for now to Breena."

"Okay, sure," I said. "Where is she?"

"You're going to have to summon her. I'll teach you how in a minute."

"Wasn't she flying around before on her own?"

"Yes," Stell said uncomfortably. "But I sorta grounded her because she's still coming down off a sugar-high."

"A what?" I said in disbelief.

"Guineve made cupcakes last evening and left them out overnight. Probably on purpose. Don't ask about it."

Stell took a deep breath and walked over to me.

"Okay," she began. "You're going to do magic by reaching into the same place you used to Rise and balance out your Ideals. You're going to pull on part of that to make your first spell. This one depends purely on your status as a Challenger and isn't connected to any of your Ideals. Reach into that same place, but this time I want you to pull down hard, and call out in your mind."

"Okay," I asked slowly. "Is all of magic just pushing and pulling?"

"Not hardly." Stell shook her head. "I'm just trying to keep things simple. If you can do those parts, I'll be able to walk you through the rest."

I made the necessary gestures and vocalizations Stell required of me. It felt weird. Mostly because my Baptist upbringing suddenly kicked in, saying any magic you didn't see in the old Lord of the Rings was completely taboo, and even that was only liked by people like my parents. I relaxed when the process began to feel like a scientific formula I was performing with my body, instead of forming a pact with Hell that exchanged my soul for dark power.

But enough of that. Subconscious hang-up conquered, I moved on from creating an arcane gateway to calling through it, reciting the phrase that Stell taught me my new familiar would respond to.

"Breena," I began in a strange, arcane tongue. *"Will you be my friend?"*

"Oh-my-gosh-yes-yes-yes! He's finally heeeeeerrrrrrrre!!!"

Something small and bright flew out of the small hole I made and fluttered all around me.

"Hi! I'm Breena! And you're really really tall! But that's okay! I'm your new familiar! We are going to have! So! Much! *Fun*!"

She buzzed by me one more time. She was still too fast, and too small, and too bright to get a good look at her.

"Breena," Stell called out. "Deep breaths and count to ten!"

"Huff, huff." The little nightlight paused long enough to do what her—mother? Maker? Older sister? Whatever Stell was—said, and began puffing and counting.

"Stell," I began in a concerned voice.

"It'll be fine," she interrupted. "Trust me."

Breena finished huffing and counting and floated up to me. She seemed to dim, and enlarge, growing from a tiny speck no bigger than my eye to a twelve-inch body that was still somehow obviously a woman. And yes, the fact that I noticed that at all worried me too. But enough of my issues. Picture a young, peppy woman, with a sparkling short dress, pink spiky hair, and softly glowing skin that couldn't decide on which color it wanted to be. She had thin, gossamer wings that sparkled with her and seemed to make her twice as large. The wings flapped slowly, too slowly to be the reason she was floating in front of my face.

"Okay, okay," the glowing little woman said with a final huff. "I'm ready now. Sorry about that. Let's try again. I'm Breena. You're still too tall. But I'm over that. I accept your conditions. If you will have me, I will be your familiar. Deal?" She stuck out a tiny hand.

"Hello Breena, I'm Wes," I said, sticking my finger out for her to shake. She gave it a vigorous pump with both hands. "I accept you as my familiar."

And I'm checking my veins for needle marks when I wake up, I added mentally.

"I hope you can teach me how to save and rescue people," I added.

"Yes!" she yelped. "That's the best part of the job! That and the pastries!"

"Wait, wha..."

"Don't get her started," Stell warned from behind me. "Just accept that people in lots of places like her and know how to bake, and leave it at that."

"Stell," I began, giving her a narrow-eyed look. "You're not lying about the whole 'come back from the dead' thing, right? Because I'm not as confident about all of this as I was a minute ago."

"Since you summoned her, she just disappears if she gets too hurt. And you can re-summon her when you revive, or whenever you get time. Oh, you were worried about *both* of you dying. Yes, you can both come back. The difference is she won't feel nearly as much pain."

"But she can actually teach me what I need out there," I tried to clarify.

"Sure," the dark-skinned woman shrugged. "Probably. Look, we actually have time for you to try and figure this out by going out there. We don't have enough time for anyone but Breena to take over your training right now. This type of nest grows quickly, fast enough to form a Trial or even a Tumult long before the other ones even emerge beyond the stage of dark rumors and warnings. I have to go warn my Satellite on the Woadlands, as well as the nearby communities, and you have to go confront these creatures. If you can destroy the nest on your own, that would be great, but at the very least, I need you to distract and slow these things until the people on that world can finish preparing to deal with them on their own."

"Okay," I decided. "Do you at least know what things I will be fighting?"

"No," Stell shook her head. "All I can tell from here is that they're going to multiply fast, and they can grow stronger with multiple generations. You can update everyone later when you finish confronting them. Okay, I'll make you a portal to the Woadlands, get ready."

"Good luck, dear," Guineve's voice called out from my left. I turned to see her wave slowly at me, her expression calm, but grave. "Take care of him, Breena. He's a good one."

"Of course!" the bright little girl bubbled, then winked at the mist-clad woman. "And I won't forget to do 'stage two' with him!"

"What?" Stell asked abruptly, but her two Satellites ignored her.

"Not in front of Stell, dear," Guineve chastised mildly. "Operational security, remember?"

"Oooh, right! Right! This won't work if she finds out before we rope him in."

"What?" I asked, totally baffled, because something about this sounded all kinds of worrisome.

"Don't worry about it," the little fairy said quickly. "And hurry! The portal's this way!"

I was barely able to make out her pointing before she zipped to where the mist was swirling and rising in a rectangular door-like pattern.

I hesitated for a brief moment before I realized that this would not be the first magic portal I had walked through, and that, as odd as it sounded, this little adventure might help me make more sense of exactly what was happening.

"Alright, Breena," I said to the little light, who had shrunk back down to less than six inches and was bouncing up and down impatiently for me. "I'm hurrying, I'm hurrying. You and Stell are probably right. No time to worry about going crazy. Let's do this."

"Crazy?" the tiny, glowing, flying, pink-haired woman asked. "Why would you worry about going cra... oh. That's right. You're from Earth."

That was the swiftest understanding anyone had shown about this whole thing.

"Don't worry," she continued as I stepped up to the misty door. "I'll set you straight. Let's go!"

I took a deep breath and stepped through the misty door.

15

COMBAT

Mist parted, then vanished.

Tall, massively wide trees greeted me, somehow taking up all of my vision while leaving me plenty of room to walk. Adorning the ground were bushes of varying sizes, and completing the scenery was a green carpet of moss that draped over part of the ground and the bases of the largest trees. Sunlight streamed down between giant leaves and even larger branches, giving everything a healthy, faintly golden color.

The beautiful sight caught me for a moment, and when I took my next breath I felt fuller, cleaner, and healthier.

"Aahhhhh," Breena sighed, apparently feeling the same. "Feels this good every time. Okay!" she finished suddenly. "Now that we're in a bit more danger, let me take a look at you."

The little fairy buzzed all over me, and I could feel her eyeing me critically.

"Hmm, solid foundation... looks like you suddenly stopped progressing at some point, weird, weird. You don't seem like the quitting type... maybe foul magic? Wait, wait, *three* Ideals?" The excitement peaked in her voice. "And such a nice mix! How did you pull that off?"

"Not sure," I admitted. "Probably all that headache practice I've been doing back home."

"Huh?" She tilted her tiny head. "That sounds darkly funny for some reason. I wish I knew why. You're weird. Anyway, this is super awesome for me, because you and I can eventually share Ideals. We're going to get so strong together!"

She bobbed again, and I got the feeling she was flexing.

"Great," I replied, trying not to grin and to pay more attention to my surroundings. "Do you mind telling me how to use them? I feel like that would be very important right now."

"Right, right!" the little fairy said with another bob. "Our bond isn't that strong yet, but I can still help you pick your first two spells for each Ideal. Let's start with Earth. Let's pick these two as signature spells."

My mind-screen suddenly opened on its own.

You have learned the Earth Spell Stoneskin (Calcite)

Stoneskin (Calcite): Creates natural armor provided by a certain mineral from the earth. Current version increases armor class by 5. Unarmed damage is also increased by 3. The caster's Intelligence Skill level increases the bonus. Spell cost 5 mana, duration 15 minutes. Casting time is 10 seconds.

You have learned the Earth Spell Earth Bones (Calcite)

Earth Bones (Calcite): The caster's bones are strengthened by adding a mineral from the earth. The caster gains one point to both stamina and strength per skill level. Vital and Stamina points gained by this increase are lost first. Spell cost 10 mana, duration 15 minutes. Casting time is 10 seconds.

"Calcite?" I asked. "Really?"

Calcite was pretty close to the bottom of the Mohs Hardness Scale.

Breena's little shoulders shrugged.

"These two will grow with you over time, becoming more powerful and easier to activate. Eventually you'll be able to leave them on permanently, with no strain on your mana."

"Great," I said. But I couldn't really feel much more optimism than that. Even though I felt different, I still wasn't sure how much the stat and armor increases counted.

Besides, calcite wasn't exactly a mineral known for protection.

"Okay," Breena declared. "Now to teach you a few basic spells I know for Earth. It's not a domain of magic I've mastered, but these will get you started."

You have learned the Earth Spell Muddy Earth

Muddy Earth: The caster turns a ten-foot-radius patch of earth to sticky mud. Movement through the area is restricted to an amount dependent on the creature's size and Dexterity, with the difficulty increased by the caster's Intelligence and skill level. The mud lasts for fifteen seconds, with the duration increased by the caster's Will. Mana Cost: 30 mana. Base duration is 15 seconds. Base casting time is 3 seconds.

You have learned the Earth Spell Tremor

Tremor: The ground under the target inexplicably and violently shifts, displacing the target. The Caster's Intelligence and skill level increase the intensity of the effect. Dexterity and the number of legs helps resist the effect. Mana Cost: 20 mana. Duration is instantaneous. Base casting time is 3 seconds.

"That should cover you for Earth," Breena declared. "Especially since that's all I can remember for now. You're going to have find the rest on your own or wait till I grow stronger."

"Looks like a lot of abilities that will either enhance me or control terrain," I noticed.

"Yep," the little fairy bobbed. "That's Earth for ya! There are a few other things it can do though. Every one of the four foundational Ideals have all of the basics, but each has their own niche. You'll find healing spells in all four, for example, but Water is generally the best, especially with us squishy folks. There are other, higher Ideals that focus almost exclusively on healing. But anyway, moving on to Air."

You have learned the Air Spell Quick Step

Quick Step: The target gains an increase to their Speed and Dexterity equal to skill level. The air movements around the caster's feet are controlled, allowing the caster's steps to adjust the force and landing of their footfalls. Spell cost 15 mana, duration 15 minutes. Casting time is 10 seconds.

"Neat," I replied, then turned to look at the next one.

You have learned the Air Spell Wind Armor

Wind Armor: The wind wraps around the caster, making it more difficult to attack or stand next to him. At this level the caster gains a moderate deflection bonus against ranged attacks and a slight deflection against close attacks. Both bonuses are increased by Intelligence and skill level. Spell cost 15 mana, duration 15 minutes. Casting time is 10 seconds.

"Those'll stick with you pretty well," Breena hummed. "Now for the back-up basics. We'll start with one of my favorites."

You have learned the Air Spell Glimmerdust

Glimmerdust: The caster creates a patch of sparkling motes that hang and travel through the air, distracting creatures caught in its radius. Creatures with low Will and Wisdom will be distracted for a longer amount of time. The difficulty to resist the effect depends on the caster's skill level and Intelligence. Spell cost 25 mana, duration 15 seconds. Casting time is 3 seconds.

You have learned the Air Spell Healing Wind

Healing Wind: The breeze brings a comforting touch carrying regenerative particles. Heals a base of 10 vital points that is further increased by the caster's Intelligence and skill level. Spell cost 25 mana. Casting time is 5 seconds.

You have learned the Air Spell Friction Slash

Friction Slash: A sharp, wide current of air slices through a three-foot space. Can damage multiple targets at once. Base damage is 30 vital points, further increased by the caster's Intelligence and skill level. Spell cost 25 mana. Casting time is 3 seconds.

"Wouldn't it make more sense to take the healing spell as a signature spell?" I asked Breena.

"Nope," the tiny woman replied. "I have the Ideal of Water in full. When you grow strong enough you can pull from it. Now, on to the last one!"

The little light buzzed around in a circle. "I'm so pumped! Lightning is one of my favorites. I can't wait to share it with you! Zap-zap!" She stopped bobbing for a few moments. "Sorry. Where were we? Oh, right. Signature spells!"

You have learned the Lightning Spell Spark Bolt

Spark Bolt: The caster fires a super-heated bolt of current into a target up to a hundred feet away, for an initial damage of 80 vital points and a chance to briefly paralyze the target. Further channeling increases the damage by 10 points per second as well as the paralyzation chance. Skill level and Intelligence increases the intensity of the spell. Spell cost 50 mana. Casting time is 6 seconds. Each second of channeling increases the cost by 10 mana.

You have learned the Lightning Spell Outer Current

Outer Current: The caster's skin and grip retain a dangerous electric charge. Enemies that come within a foot of contact with the caster, or within contact with an object gripped by the caster have a chance to take 10 extra damage and must resist a brief paralyzing shock. Skill level and Intelligence increases the intensity of the spell. Spell cost 25 mana. Casting time is 5 seconds.

"Wow," I said. "Those are some of the biggest numbers yet," I replied. The casting time for *Spark Bolt* worried me though. Six seconds didn't sound like a long time until I realized that people only wait their turn in my sister's Pathwalker games.

"Yup," Breena replied. "Lightning's one of the best Ideals for single target damage, though it can be mean to groups as well. Though you can't cast the spells quickly—not at first. Later on, you'll have access to all kinds of quick-cast damage and travel spells. Speaking of which, on to the next batch."

You have learned the Lightning Spell Sparking Flash

Sparking Flash: The caster briefly blinds the target with bright light, lasting at least three seconds. Wisdom and Will resist the effect. Skill level and Intelligence increases the intensity of the spell. Spell cost 25 mana. Casting time is 4 seconds.

. . .

You have learned the Lightning Spell Shocking Digits

Shocking Digits: Caster gains a charge in each finger. Each charge can fire a tiny bolt at one target for 5 damage each and a small chance for paralysis. All bolts can be released at once. Skill level and Intelligence increases the intensity of the spell. Spell cost 35 mana. Casting time is 15 seconds.

"That should give you a pretty good spread," Breena decided. "Now we're ready to kill things!" The tiny woman gave an enthusiastic pump into the air. "Probably and preferably gibber-kin!"

"Gibber-whats?"

"Small furry things that breed and breed and try to eat or hurt everybody. They get meaner over time."

"And I'm supposed to kill them with magic?" I asked cautiously.

"Sure, you can," Breena said with a small shrug. "Or you can use your weap—"

Tiny hands suddenly covered a tiny mouth.

"Oops," she said quietly.

I used one hand to cover my own face.

"I take it I was supposed to leave with some kind of weapon and/or protective gear?"

"That would have been a good idea," Breena bobbed in a little nod. "Although I don't think the armory was open at the time anyway."

"Armory?" I asked. "Avalon has an armory?"

"Not really," Breena shook her head. "Stell doesn't keep a whole lot of weapons around. The normal ones tend to rust and the magic ones are better served going back to someone in their respective worlds. The rest are all tied to specific Challengers and reject any other owner."

"Great," I said. "So, magic, punches, or kicks?"

"We may be able to find a weapon," Breena said hopefully. "Gibber-kin like to take shiny objects. Maybe we'll find something you can use. What are you proficient in, anyway? No, let me check," Breena flew next to me, and I saw a tiny little screen open up in front of her own face.

"Holy sparkle-coated star-balls!" she shouted. "You know the basics in just about everything! Your mommy and daddy must have been major weapon masters to train you in all of this!"

"I remember zero instances of being trained in medieval murder-tools by either of my parents," I said firmly. "Or anyone else for that matter."

"That's weird," Breena said. "Maybe you inherited skills from your genetic memory? Was your dad a great hero, or a former Challenger?" The little glowing woman suddenly looked at me critically. "Are you absolutely sure your daddy wasn't a Challenger? Because..."

"I used to think my dad was a great hero," I interrupted quietly, because I absolutely had no interest in this conversation. "But the world says I was very wrong, and he apparently did some very bad things. He has never mentioned anything about being a Challenger."

"Maybe you could ask him..." Breena began.

"He's dead," I said bluntly. "I'm not able to ask him anything."

"Oh," the little fairy said softly. "I'm sorry."

"Let's just focus on the task at hand," I said calmly. At least I hoped I sounded calm. "When should I cast any of these enhancement spells? Which direction should I go?"

"Hold off on the enhancement spells for a few more moments," Breena said thoughtfully. "And I'll try to handle the reconnaissance for you."

The fairy shrank to her smallest size and dimmed completely. She was almost invisible. The only signs of her at all were a faint *zipping* sound that sped through the air, and even that was quiet.

"Huh," she finally said after floating over to me. "I don't hear any gibber-kin."

"Should you be hearing them?" I asked. Wasn't really sure what to expect here, after all.

"Well, yeah, they're gibber-kin," the little fairy replied plainly. "Everybody hears gibber-kin. It's hard to find something more obviously into biting you than a gibber-kin. If we can't hear them out here, then Stell landed us out too far."

"Does she do that a lot?" I asked. The little fairy shook her pink-haired head.

"Nope. Never."

"Okay," I began logically. "Then, either Stell finally messed up a landing, or we're facing something else out here."

"But there isn't anything else out here," Breena said in almost a whine. "Gibber-kin are the only things that fit the profile. Nothing else starts out that weak, breeds that fast, and gets more dangerous over time. Especially out here."

"Not even goblins?" I asked, but in truth there were over a dozen fantasy tropes that disagreed with Breena's recent statement.

"Don't be racist!" she suddenly shouted, and actually lit up and kicked me with her tiny feet. I think. I actually couldn't feel anything, and at her current size that wasn't surprising. "Goblins have come a long way from their stereotype! Some of the smartest, most advanced creatures I know are goblins! And most of them don't eat *anyone* these days!"

"Sorry, sorry!" I said quickly, raising my hands. "It was just a guess! I threw it out based on my world's books. I didn't even know that was a sensitive subject!"

"Well it wasn't a nice guess," Breena huffed. "Don't be mean to any goblins, okay? Unless they earn it first!"

"Deal," I said. "I promise to be nice to every goblin, orc, gremlin or kobold we meet. Everything except gibber-kin. Especially if any of those things actually exist."

"You didn't know—oh, sorry. Forgot you were from Earth again. Anyway, we need to figure out what's going on here."

She fluttered over to my shoulder and sat down, changing to a size of about four inches tall and containing her glow until her body was merely colorful instead of bright. "Alright, new plan," the tiny woman declared. "I've got friends and family in this area..."

"Wait, what?" I interrupted again. She seemed annoyed, but I pressed on anyway. "You have family beyond Stell? How does that work? I thought you were one of her, uh..."

"Satellites," Breena said with an eye-roll. "We're called Satellites. And she put us all—except for Guineve—with people to sorta grow up with. All of the other Satellites have adopted families on their respective worlds. I travel a lot, though, so I got to know all of the other small-folk on each of these worlds. The batch near us has a lot of my cousins and nieces."

"Stell said this area was remote," I pointed out. "I thought no one lived out here."

"Humans and other big folk don't," she said with a shake of her head. "But little folk like me live in this area. So do a number of animals I can talk to. It's safe because nothing really dangerous hunts us out here, and any

Challenges or Trials that do form are ones we're able to hide from. Just keep marching until we reach one of my old hot spots."

Without much else to go on, I did as she said. I tried to keep my eyes everywhere, looking for hidden movement, listening for the snapping of branches or other forest sounds I still recognized from camping.

After about thirty seconds, I realized we had a problem.

"Breena," I said, carefully and quietly. "I'm not hearing anything. Should I be?"

She looked distracted, like she was thinking carefully.

"I already said that you should be hearing gibber-kin if they were here," she muttered, her face locked in concentration as she stared far off.

"I'm not hearing *anything*," I repeated, still quietly but more forcefully. "Should I be hearing anything at all? Birds? Some breaking branches? Anything else?"

Her tiny eyes widened even further. That was all the answer I needed.

"*Stoneskin*," I said softly. As a signature spell, I innately knew that saying its name and making a tiny gesture would begin the spell's activation process. *"Quick Step. Earth Bones."*

I held off on *Wind Armor* and the lightning spells, because I didn't want to buffet or shock Breena by accident. She still looked very pale.

"I should have noticed," the tiny woman said tensely. "I was so sure... we have to hurry. Move forward quickly until you get to a really old tree. I'll let you know when you see it."

By then, I had begun to notice the change the magic had done to me. A rumbling sensation crawled all over me, and I both heard and felt a faint creak as I took my next step. The sensations comforted me, made me feel stronger, more protected.

My footsteps seemed surer, faster, more graceful. With each step I was vaulted forward, then parachuted very softly to the ground.

Breena's behavior had also changed, and completely. Gone was her cocky, playful attitude. Her tiny mouth was set in a thin line, and her eyes darted all about. I saw her tiny, slightly pointed ears twitch hopefully every now and then, and each time they did, she seemed more frustrated afterwards.

Still utter silence.

The only noise at all in the forest was from my soft steps. In other circumstances, it would have been almost peaceful, but the fact that we both knew we should have been hearing some kind of noise made it strangely terrifying. I would have been scared out of my mind right then, except for one fact that bounced in my mind with every step.

This was still not as terrifying as becoming crippled had been.

The new power in my legs was now a motivation, a desire to be useful, a need to be the person I used to be, to do the things I once took so much pride in doing. People were in need of help. They may not count as people to those back home, but here they were both desired and missed. Even if this all was some crazy, yet completely lucid, dream, I didn't want to let people get hurt and miss my chance to be the old me, the one that could help people.

"There," Breena whispered in my ear softly. "That large gray tree just up ahead." I felt one of her tiny hands grip hard onto my shirt.

We reached the tree she was talking about, this one half again as wide as all the others, with gray, slightly warped bark. There were tiny holes all along the base of the tree, some going as high as ten feet. I stopped running, and Breena stood and floated off of my shoulder, wings fluttering softly, and silently.

"Hello?" the tiny pink woman called out quietly, glowing in one brief burst. "Beryl? Sylt? Lotus?"

Her voice had grown louder, but was still far from a shout. Nevertheless, something reacted.

I saw a brightly colored bird land on a branch some twenty or thirty feet above us. It pointed its beak right at my fairy companion and began chirping quickly, almost angrily. In fact, it chirped more angrily than any bird I'd ever heard in my life.

Breena quickly flew up to about fifteen feet away from the bird and started making chirping noises back at it. The bird just waved its wings angrily, squawking as if it were about to have a little bird-seizure, then flew off like a bullet up into the trees. Breena floated back toward me, her eyes never leaving the animal until it disappeared.

"What did it say?" I asked quietly, though my eyes were roaming all about us. Some unknown instinct was screaming at me that we were already in trouble and that I needed to *hurry up and get ready, idiot!*

"And don't land on me," I added, quietly casting *Wind Armor*.

"'Turn back, turn back,' he said," Breena replied, still in shock. "I asked him where the other fairy folk were and if there were any bad things nearby. He just said 'taken, all gone. Turn back now.'"

"Shit," I said, immediately activating *Outer Current*, then quietly began casting *Shocking Digits*. That last one would take longer since it wasn't a signature spell, and I realized I should have cast it sooner.

"And then he just flew off," Breena said dumbly. "They're all gone...where...why?"

I finished casting the last spell. My body hummed and crackled all over, and my fingers twitched, each one with a single extra bolt of electricity. For whatever reason, the Earth spells in my skin and bones didn't insulate or screw up the two lightning spells coursing through me, and they all worked together perfectly.

That was good, because we didn't have time for complications.

"Breena," I said, still searching the trees. "Get down. Or up, since you can fly. But you're a target right now."

Breena turned to look at me. I could tell she hadn't fully snapped out of it yet.

"What? No, Wes, you don't understand. This can't happen. Why would the fairies already be gone? What monster hunts fairies from the start?" She looked around wildly. "What monster hunts *everything* from the start, and leaves nothing behind? What's going on?"

I deeply resented Breena at this moment. She was supposed to be my guide. She wasn't supposed to get surprised and dazed. I didn't know anything about monsters, and I didn't know anything about all the rules these monsters were supposedly breaking. But I did know about being surprised by people who wanted to hurt me.

And this was a scene straight out of dozens of horror movies I had seen and several dozen more horror games I had played. I'm pretty sure anybody else from Earth who at least had a TV would draw the same conclusion I had just drawn.

"We're being attacked," I growled out. "That's what's happening. Get away from the trees."

"What?" she asked, and then suddenly like a string, she snapped back into focus. "Oh!" She immediately flew behind my shoulder. I thought for a half-second that it was my warning that brought her back to focus. I was immediately proven wrong.

"Heeeessshhh."

A saliva-filled mouth half-laughed, half-slurped. My eyes shot over to the ugliest thing I had ever witnessed under three feet tall. Something humanoid and unfinished stood some thirty feet away. Skinny arms and legs, with twisted muscles wrapped in oily wrinkled skin, stretched out menacingly in a wide gait. Those limbs connected to a round potbelly hanging over a sunken chest that heaved with every breath. On top of that torso was a round, wrinkled, hairless head, wrapped in that same oily-black, dripping skin. The head was too big for the tiny body, and its drooling mouth was far too wide. I could barely make out two curved ears pressed flat against the creature's oil-coated head, and its tiny eyes squinted at me and Breena. It gnashed its teeth at me and flicked an unnaturally long and disgusting tongue at my fairy companion.

"Yeeeeesshh," the creature slurred for another gross moment. "Ha!"

With that bark, its eyes suddenly popped open, sickly, yellowish orbs with black pupils that focused erratically on us after bouncing madly. Its ears flared wide as well, almost doubling the size of its head. Then it began slapping the ground, slobbering all over it as its mouth guttered in time with the slaps.

"Ha! Ha! *Heesssh*!"

The creature's raspy speech ended in a slur-filled roar, and it suddenly brandished its tiny black claws upward.

"No," Breena whispered above me, her voice catching on something in her tiny throat. "Oh no-no-no-no. Not this."

As my eyes finished taking in the creature, something clicked, and my mind-screen shimmered for a half-second. When it closed, I felt the words pressed deeply into my mind.

WARNING! WARNING!

FOREIGN CONTAMINANT DETECTED.

CONTAMINANT IS ILKLING-CLASS HORDEBEAST.

BEWARE! BEWARE! BEWARE!

Right after that, the creature leaped forward, hopping and bounding on all fours toward us, tongue lolling out of its mouth and eyes rolling about in its head.

"Nonono," Breena repeated shaking her head in my peripheral vision. "Not the Horde. Anything but the Horde."

Suddenly, she seemed to snap back to her senses, looking quickly around.

"Wes! Watch out!"

Her gaze had been to my right, away from the creature that was running toward me and being really obvious about it. Immediately grasping the nature of my familiar's warning, I pivoted, driving my fist around in a punch and cursing myself for not recognizing the attack earlier. I saw another of the frightening, disgusting little monsters sailing at me through the air, black claws outstretched, mouth opened wide. My fist pounded into its face just above the needle-filled mouth. I felt my calcite-lined knuckles crunch into its nose-slits, and a split second later I felt an electric charge leave me and course into the monster's slimy skin. The tiny head snapped backward, and its body was dragged along in a backward somersault, limbs flailing about until its head slammed with a crack into one of the nearby tree trunks. The entire body then slid downwards into a still and boneless heap. I had a brief moment of shock over the fact that I had just killed a living thing with my bare hands, and that I didn't feel any remorse at all.

"Wes!" Breena shouted as she zipped by my head. "Focus! To your left!"

Another Ilkling was leaping at my other arm from several yards away. It surprised me just how high these creatures could leap, practically doubling their height in the process. I twisted and moved my arm out of the way, but I was unable to get a good enough footing to counterattack. I felt the creature's claw tips scratch against my skin, sharp enough to mark the calcite covering my arm but lacking enough power to penetrate my skin. A small spark jumped from my arm to the monster's claw, causing the little Ilkling to yelp as it flew by.

I swung my head about then to get a clearer view of the new battlefield. Several Ilklings were within fifteen feet of me, with two of them grasping at a small pink woman that strafed by them, shooting fiery bright sparkles behind her. The third one was the Ilkling that I had noticed first, and it was rushing towards my leg, its mouth locked open to brace for a bite. Remembering how well these things could leap, I stepped quickly forward, bringing my right foot backward. I swung my calcite-toed boot forward in a football punt, connecting hard with the little monster's skull. There was another crunch, another buzz of electricity, followed by the increasingly frequent sight of another squat little monster sailing through the air to flop miserably against the bare earth.

It survived, but only barely, twitching weakly on the ground. These little monsters were frightening, extremely disgusting, and much stronger than they looked. But even disregarding my magic, I was over twice their height and outweighed them by well over a hundred pounds, therefore producing almost comically one-sided results when they came at me head-to-head. I learned a lesson in that.

Always bring a grown eighteen-year-old to a toddler fight.

"Heesh!" Interrupting my learning experience was a fourth Ilkling that I hadn't noticed. I don't know where it came from. Maybe it crawled up a tree limb and leaped at me. Maybe it just crawled up while I was celebrating the result of my absence of compromise with the last Ilklings. Whatever happened, it was able to latch onto my arm with its spindly limbs and bit down with its teeth, all while raking at me with its tiny sharp claws. My calcite skin blunted the attacks slightly, but insufficiently, and one of the little bastards finally drew blood.

I yelled out in pain.

"Son of a bitch!"

The back of my mind said I should get a handle back on my profanity. The front of my brain said I could do that after I murdered all the little shits that were trying to eat me.

My other hand reached up and grasped the slimy thing by the wrinkles on its skin. My fingers almost slipped off, but in my anger I gripped the little maggot as hard as I possibly could. The monster began writhing when my electric current spell kicked in, but afterward it had only begun to bite down harder, determined to eat its way past my spell. I yanked it off with another shout, and the damned thing took a red chunk of me with it. Shouting again in pain, I slammed it into the ground, kicking and pummeling it until something inside it snapped and the creature lay still.

Trembling with adrenaline, I barely remembered to look back up and search for Breena. The little fairy was still flying frantically about, weaving around another Ilkling's leap and turning to launch another cluster of sparkling darts into the scorched face of the next monster trailing far behind it. The creature shrieked and fell backward, writhing on the ground for a moment before it finally fell still. Then wisps of smoke were the only movement around it. But the other black gremlin was gaining on Breena, looking as if it might catch the tiring fairy in its next leap. Trying to think quickly, I charged past a low-hanging tree branch I had noticed earlier and ripped off of its limb with one pull. I then turned and made a leap of my own, meeting the little monster in the air with a powerful two-handed swing of my new club. There was a cracking sound as the stout wood connected with the tiny creature's shriveled skull, followed by another hum as the magical current somehow traveled from my grip, up my wooden weapon, and into the snarling monster's face. The creature flew through the air with a smoky hiss and did not get back up. I looked wildly around for more opponents and to check on Breena, but she looked unharmed and the only remaining monster was the one still twitching from my punt earlier.

The little woman grew slightly, back up to eight inches as she floated over to me.

"Wes!" she said hurriedly. "Are you alright?" At the end of her question her gaze latched onto my bloody arm.

My bloody forearm that no longer hurt and wasn't bleeding anymore, despite missing a chunk of muscle.

"Yes," I said in slow realization, holding up my arm. The pain was diminishing rapidly, and the wound looked to be already scabbing over. "But why am I alright? And should I be worried about infection from that creature's drool?"

"Infection? What?" The fairy tilted her head at me. "No, you're fine. As long your vital points aren't all gone, you can't bleed to death or get normal diseases. But let me fix that quickly anyway."

She muttered some words I couldn't understand, and a blue glow began to fall onto my wound, numbing it and repairing before my very eyes. A second or two later it was completely back to normal.

"My what?" I asked, exasperated with her words, even while marveling at her healing magic. "What the heck are vital points?"

"Vital points are created when the mana in your body interacts with your Constitution. They're another difference between the Unrisen and heroes like you. When your vital points run out, you're as vulnerable to injuries as you are back on Earth. But here they serve as a temporary shield, something that goes first when you get hurt, making sure you don't bleed or lose muscular function. As long as you don't run out of them or get subject to an attack specifically designed to pierce them, the only thing you'll feel from injuries is a reduced sense of pain, and you can fight or act normally. Provided you can handle the pain, that is."

"That's the weirdest thing I've ever heard o—oh," I said, catching myself.

"They're hit points. Got it. I should have realized that when I saw them on my mind-screen. What do we do about him?" I turned and pointed at the last Ilkling, that was still twitching and trying to crawl away from us. "Can you make it tell us where they took your kin?"

Breena's face flashed in memory as I mentioned the other fey.

"Right, the others." Worry writ itself all over her face, but she slowly shook her head. "Horde at this stage don't really speak. They might throw out a garbled word here and there, but we don't think they're capable of understanding conversation. He'd probably just gnash at you— and leer at me."

"Leer at you?" *The hell?* I thought. "What do you mean by that?" I was really, really not liking where this was going. My only consolation was the fact that since these creatures were completely naked, I could tell for certain that they were not equipped to do anything I was *really* worried about.

Breena shook her head.

"They're just disgusting by nature," she said. "They get something out of making females feel uncomfortable. And the other breeds of them are even worse." She glared at the oily little monster. "But no, even if you torture these things, it won't tell you anything because it won't understand you."

I wanted to ask her what she meant by 'other breeds' of Horde, but we didn't have time for another lesson. But another thought finally smacked me in the head, after watching the wretched thing crawl for far too many moments.

"Where is it going then?" I asked, hoping I knew the answer.

"Probably back...to... its lair," the little fairy said with gradually widening eyes.

I stepped forward, brandishing my heavy stick and growling at the wounded, but hateful little thing.

The Ilkling turned its wrinkled head at me for a moment, its eyes growing wide at the sight of my threatening stance. Then it hissed, and tried to scamper more quickly, one of its back legs flopping in an awkward limp.

"Do these things have vital points too?" I asked after a moment. "Or will the monster bleed out if I push it too hard?"

Breena buzzed by me, glaring impatiently at the monster. She shook her head again.

"Your kick penetrated its vital points quickly enough to cause lingering damage, but aside from its limp it will gradually recover in the next ten minutes. Faster if you give it time to rest."

"So waiting for that won't increase its speed and will just make it more dangerous," I said quietly. "Got it."

I forced the creature to crawl as fast as it could while counting to two hundred in my head. When I reached that number I fired one of my finger-bolts at it. I wanted to keep it weak enough to remain harmless but strong enough to lead us to where the other monsters and their captives were.

At least I hoped there would be captives. In a video game this would be no problem. The prisoners *always* lasted long enough for you to save them, and the few times they didn't it was either never my fault or I had a little timer on the screen to let me know just how long I had to get to them. We had to hurry, but as I thought that, I realized there was another problem.

"Breena," I said quietly, with my eyes roaming all around the massive forest. "Is this thing smart enough to lead us into a trap?"

"Not when it's afraid," she said calmly, in control of her own fear now. "At this stage the Horde is more about hunting weak prey than waging war and conquest. A Smear-sized group of Ilklings isn't going to do more than make a well-hidden lair and hunt out all the vulnerable, preferably intelligent creatures it can catch."

"Why do they care about intelligent creatures?" I asked.

"Because the Horde thrives most off of consuming the beautiful, the valuable, and the rare. My race—and especially myself, since I'm technically just a part of Stell, molded into a fairy—are all of those things. Unlike myself, however," she added with an edge, "fairies are vulnerable to anyone who can catch them and resist their little magics. They're the perfect captives to let this batch of Horde grow from a Smear to a Contagion or worse."

"That sounds bad," I said, without taking my eyes off of the nearby forest.

"It is," Breena agreed. "But I don't have time to describe why. Just know that we have to hurry because there still might be just enough time to save my friends."

That seemed a little optimistic to me, but I wanted to hope that any captive to something as disgustingly awful as these things could live long enough to be rescued.

Twigs under my feet snapped. Leaves rustled by me as I stomped on. Part of me wanted to be more careful, but the rest of me knew that the Ilkling ahead of me was making noise enough for both of us. I just kept my eyes and ears open for the sight of anything else.

My mind-screen blinked at me very quickly, and information splashed quickly into my brain.

The Icons of the Woadlands have been made aware of a new Challenge forming.

Mother Glade has been made aware of your arrival and will observe your actions.

Lady Titania has been made aware of your arrival and will observe your actions.

The Stag Lord has been made aware of your arrival and carefully welcomes you.

Great Pan has been made aware of your arrival and approves of your actions on his world.

Woad Princess Merada has also been made aware of your Challenge and will offer assistance as soon as possible.

"Who are the Icons?" I asked, after blinking rapidly. I made sure I was still watching the Ilkling ahead of us before Breena began her explanation.

"The Icons are the higher authorities of the perspective world. Some worship them as gods, while some just hold them in veneration."

"Are they Starsown, like Stell?"

"No," Breena replied. "They're usually just former inhabitants that have Risen in such a way to where they permanently reflect an Ideal or two. Guineve would be the closest thing to a member of one of their races. Stell said not to confuse them with perceptions from your world, though. Even if they sound similar, they're really not like the gods of any of your planet's religions. In fact, most of your religions wouldn't count them as gods at all, just really strong, really long-lived mortals that stick to certain roles."

I wasn't sure of that. The names made me think a little of some Celtic, Norse or even Wiccan deities, but I didn't care enough to interrupt.

"Is Merada another part of Stell?" I asked, watching the Ilkling ahead of us carefully. It was changing speed, which meant that either it was close to its nest—or Smear, or whatever they were called—or that Breena was wrong about its health and the wretched little thing was about to keel over.

"Yes, she's another Satellite." The little fairy nodded to me. "But it will take her forever to get here. Look! We're close," my companion said in a hushed voice, worry crawling back on her face. I turned my attention back to the Ilkling we were chasing. I had already zapped it once earlier, when my internal count had reached two hundred and it had tried to rest. My new count was up to a hundred and eighty. I debated whether I should use another finger-bolt on the creature or save it for when we showed up to wreck its friends' faces.

But the decision was soon made for me. The little Ilkling suddenly darted behind one of the few large rocks I had seen in this forest and disappeared. I raced forward, stick at the ready, but all I found was a tiny hole that the rock and nearby shrubbery covered up. Breena fluttered around me, her expression still worried.

"Okay," I said to my winged little companion. "Counting that one, and the four we killed earlier, and since you somehow already know the size of this Smear or whatever, how many more Horde monsters are probably down here?"

"Since only a handful of Horde attacked us earlier," Breena began, staring intently at the hole, "and since all of them were Ilklings... I'd say anywhere from one to two dozen Ilklings total, with just one larger type of Horde-being to serve as their leader. So after four casualties, you're looking at least nine, but no more than twenty total Ilklings, plus the leader. Who might know we're here now," she added worriedly.

"Right. So no time to waste." I began to refresh my personal spells, letting the rush of magic wash over me. "So how do I get under that rock?"

"Just push your way through," Breena said, peering into the hole. "It should widen out further in. The initial opening is clear from what I can see, though."

I had no choice but to take her word for it. Grabbing the ground near the edge of the two-foot hole, holding my stick close to my body, and fervently wishing I had a real weapon, I pushed, pulled, and kicked my way into the tiny opening as quickly as I dared.

I fell rather un-gloriously into a much wider room, rising quickly while sputtering dust and probably worse from my mouth. I held my stick at the ready in both hands as I looked about. The place looked like the earthy-walled den of some small animal, save that it was just large enough for me to stand up in. All of that had made sense to me, though, except for the size. What was especially weird to me was the large hallway at the other end of the barrow, with an even higher ceiling and flickering lights farther along the walls. When Breena flew down with me, I pointed at the place.

"Are those lights other fairies?" I asked.

"What?" she asked, confused and peering forward. "No, they're just lights. I forgot this is your first Challenge. The Ilklings aren't very smart, but they use the oil from their skin to make their homes. They widen and harden the walls with it and can use certain patches of it to burn slowly for light."

I cocked my head at that.

"Light? Why would they need light?" I asked.

"To see with?" Breena said slowly, as if her answer was obvious. "Everything that can't naturally do magic needs light to see with. Certain monsters and deep-folk need only very little to see with, but everyone still needs some. Isn't it the same on your world?"

"Yes," I said slowly, and with embarrassment. "Sorry, operating under some wrong impressions. But we should hurry. Stay near me so that I know what to look out for."

With that, we began a slow descent into our enemy's lair.

16

MONSTROSITY DENIED

The small den had no other openings aside from the creepy, dungeon-esque hallway. Breena briefly whispered that this was normal. This early on, the Ilklings wouldn't have had time to do anything but make a few rooms, including something she just called 'the Pit,' the hallway, and the exit. There were rooms we'd check first for the captives, rooms we'd expect to find remains or other looted items, rooms we'd expect to just find monsters, and finally, the Pit. We'd check the Pit last for some reason she didn't want to say.

I moved us forward as fast as I dared. Breena neither cautioned me nor demanded I hurry. I took her silence as approval, and examined the walls for anything suspicious, like dart traps or anything else I could think of from my movies and games. There were none, but the walls were still suspicious. I could see patches where the Ilklings had smeared the disgusting crap from their skin. The black smears seemed to warp the earth and stone into something else, with a harder, gnarled texture. Stranger even still was that both the black oil and the walls themselves seem to naturally form the most disturbing stick-figure art I had ever seen. It looked like a caveman's drawing, only creepier, more gruesome, and somehow more perverted. There were scenes of small creepy things, which I gathered to be more Ilklings, rolling in something gross and getting bigger, and thicker. Many scenes had monsters of all types cavorting around other figures of different sizes with lines drawn on them as if they were in chains. Some pictures had the captives running from the Horde figures, while in other depictions they were writhing as the figures did things to them that I really didn't want to make out clearly. But even my willful ignorance couldn't stop me from noticing that the greater the Horde-beings, the more painful and depraved the torment they inflicted on their victims.

I really didn't want to see more of these creatures, I realized. I didn't want to be anywhere near anything even half as sadistic and perverted as these pictures suggested they were. That one encounter I had with them earlier suggested that I had only seen the tip of their disgusting depravity, that whatever came next would be progressively worse and worse, until I was stuck watching the most graphic versions of one of those adult murder films a former teammate had once told me about. My foot almost stopped falling forward right then, almost locked up on the spot.

But my foot moved forward anyway. Because a tiny voice inside had suggested that seeing more of what these creatures did would not be the most scarring thing I could experience. What would be even more scarring was the possibility of spending the rest of my life knowing what these creatures were doing, and that I had done nothing to stop it from happening. So I stepped forward, again and again. The possibility of this being a dream or delusion was currently gone from my mind. That tiny voice was tugging on my inner ear, insisting that I was needed right now, that I had a purpose, that I was right where I belonged. In spite of everything else, the rest of me resonated with that, and so I kept walking forward, Breena by my side, my improvised club at the ready. We reached the spot where the oil torches began and kept walking, now with our shadows jumping all over the walls. We kept going until we reached a corner in the hallway and turned with it.

There, we found our old guide.

The Ilkling was sprawled on the ground, body twisted in an unnatural angle. The leg that had caused it to limp earlier was gone, save for a blackish, gory spurt near the joint, as if it had been violently torn off. Atop the body were two other Ilklings. One was holding the severed leg of its kin, taking small bites from it one moment and beating its fellow's corpse with it the next. The other was grabbing the corpse's head by its hands, hissing and spitting at it and then slamming it down onto the oil-warped earth.

For a moment this sight baffled me. Then I realized I was on a time crunch and that, for whatever reason, these two idiots were making it easier for me by both killing one of their own and having their backs toward me while they desecrated its corpse. I stepped forward quickly, winding up my long club for a hit and slamming it into the head of the leg-wielding Ilkling. There was a loud crack, followed by another zapping noise, then the little monster somersaulted into a hard patch on the wall and slid down. The remaining Ilkling suddenly dropped the broken head and leaped up, eyes rising just in time to see my club slamming down on its forehead. The first blow seemed to just floor the little monster, so I swung down two more times, wincing as the force traveled from my club into my hands. But the creature's head cracked and gave in, rewarding me with a gory sight of thick black mush. I heard the sparks from my lightning magic cauterize the wound, creating small spots where the monster stank of cooked meat.

I cursed and gagged as bile rose in my throat, nearly falling to my knees with nausea. The earlier kills had been pretty clean; I'd just beaten the monsters to death without them cracking open. This last kill seriously made me rethink every violent video game I'd ever played.

"Are you okay?" Breena asked, fluttering between my face and shoulder.

"Yeah," I coughed. "That was pretty gross though." After another moment, I had pulled myself together. "Why were they killing one of their own, instead of letting him raise the alarm and be ready for us?"

"At this level," Breena began, as she also eyed the body in disgust, "they're too primitive to do things like raise alarms, or to stop themselves from turning on each other at the first sign of weakness. It takes the more powerful species of Horde to keep Ilklings under control, and there should be only one of those here."

"So," I began. "Because of their catastrophically bad genetic defects, we have three more Ilklings dead and still retain the element of surprise?"

"Yeah," Breena said thoughtfully. "Pretty much."

Huh.

"Whatever," I said with a shrug. "I'll take it."

We kept walking forward. This time, I chose to hurry. It was a risk, maybe even a fatal risk, but I felt like I finally had a handle on just how perceptive these things were. Aside from their disgusting habits and creepy wall art, these creatures pretty much felt like a beginner challenge in one of my sister's campaigns. I wasn't going to start running, shouting, and banging my club to a beat, but I was choosing to err at least slightly on the side of haste rather than the side of not reaching the captives in time. I figured I would find out very quickly whether or not that was a bad idea.

I was right.

The hallway turned into another corner, leading to a hallway with even better lighting and more black stains all over it. My eyes had adjusted pretty well, and I could see that this hall had a row of two or three openings along it, probably leading to other rooms. But at the end of the hallway was a much larger room, and I could clearly see what the Ilklings were doing there.

I wish I hadn't.

Mixed in with three Ilklings were several small, brightly lit figures, either writhing on black patches of the floor or trying to crawl away from their captors, who were hissing in delight. One monster was hunched and growling over a tiny yellow spark that kept trying to crawl or flutter away. After a moment the Ilkling suddenly slammed its foot down on the tiny glowing figure's left arm and wing. There was a high-pitched, slightly masculine, and very agonized scream from the little glowing figure, and the Ilkling over it began cackling and grinding its foot onto the figure's wing, spitting on it afterwards. Another wrinkled monster was holding a blue-lit figure over its drooling mouth, and I could hear the little blue light make tiny, feminine sobs. The nasty thing lowered the sobbing little fairy into its maw, closed its mouth and made as if it were to swallow her whole, then suddenly spat her out onto a hard spot of the floor, cackling at the pained screams that tore out from the tiny sprite. The third monster held a green figure with torn gossamer wings by its feet, one that was constantly pleading in yet another high-pitched feminine voice. The Ilkling licked its captive with its disgusting tongue, smiled at her, then suddenly lifted the little green woman high up and slammed her onto the ground, cackling at her agonizing shrieks.

I got a sense that the monsters had been torturing the poor sprites for some time, and were being just careful enough to avoid killing their victims. I also got a sense of *what the hell is wrong with you things* and *kill these little shits with fire right now!*

Breena gasped by me. I was about to lose it right there, but my brain tackled my rage and held it down for two and a half seconds. In that time, I came up with a quick plan.

Then I acted.

"*HEY!*" I half-shouted, half-roared out. "*ENOUGH!*"

The Ilklings were close enough for me to see what they were doing, but just far enough to be running distance away from me. For a second the three looked at me, two still holding their fairies, while the one stomping on the male fairy had his foot raised in the air.

"I SAID ENOUGH!" And with that, I fired off three of my tiny finger bolts. The magic of each bolt made them fly true, thankfully striking in exactly the way I wanted. Each one struck the Ilkling just hard enough to knock it away from its captive. More hisses came, these in anger, and when they looked back at me their ears flared and they began charging on all fours.

"Heesh!" the one in the back half-spit, half-snarled.

"Mine!" the one in front slurred, surprising me by speaking an actual word.

"Mine!" another screeched, and soon the word was taken up as a chant.

"Mine!"

"Mine!"

The chant came from two of the other rooms as two more small Ilklings came charging out, one carrying the bloody femur of some small animal. But the chant only intensified as they stared at me and Breena. "*Mine, mine, mine.*"

Then their time was up.

The distance had been just enough for my purpose. While they had been chanting and spitting and charging, I had been working another act of Earth magic as fast as I dared. I had just finished when they were halfway to me, then I thrust my hands at the floor before me. I probably wasn't pointing to the perfect spot, but the magic apparently knew enough of my intent to turn the ground just in front of them into slippery mud.

"Breena!" I shouted quickly. "Distract them!"

The first one slipped one clawed hand on the mud and fell face-first, snarling as it fell and slid. The next slid into him, snarling angrily as its pack-mate became an obstacle. To my surprise, the two began shoving each other and wound up striking the third Ilkling who had almost picked its way past the muck. The remaining monsters tried to push their way past the brawling pile. Their shoves were violent enough to start pushing the entire ball of squabbling Ilklings out of the enchanted muck.

Breena had started casting at the same time I did, but she had apparently been holding her spell until she could see what I was doing. I would have to ask her to show me how to do that. But then she completed her spell, which proved to be one she had taught me. A thin cloud of shimmering motes flared out, dazzling one of the Ilklings completely and briefly blinding the rest. The ones almost out of the muck shrieked and fell backward, clutching their eyes and causing the whole pile to devolve into a shoving match where the nasty monsters alternated between swatting at each other and the new flecks of light.

It wouldn't last. My magic mud was about to expire, and Breena's magic glitter would end soon after that. But that was alright. The stupid things had been distracted long enough for my next spell to finish.

I completed the spell with an angry shout, slashing my right hand outward. A hot, curved current of air three feet wide blasted out just above knee-height for me. The sharp edge of my *Friction Slash* spell flew straight into the tightly packed pile of hissing, drooling idiots, taking the head right off the closest one. I heard a shriek as another one lost an arm, and a third one fell while clutching a badly damaged leg. Breena followed up my act by shooting a series of what looked like pressurized, sparkling water droplets into the monsters, and another of the closest ones fell dead.

But by then, my mud was starting to dry up or sink back into the ground, and Breena's magic sparkles were fading from the air. The remaining three Ilklings were starting to pull themselves back to their feet, disentangling from each other as they did so. They were no longer chanting or leering at Breena. Actually, they were still looking at her, but their gazes were full of terror now, which really was a better look for the disgusting things. They seemed ready to bolt at any second. But the best place to run was where their tortured captives were.

I couldn't have that.

I rushed forward, using the gusts from my *Quick Step* spell to launch me forward in rapid bursts. I was on them in seconds. Three or four loud cracks later, our enemies were reduced to a crumpled, filthy, and thankfully dead heap. As I whirled about, I saw what was in each of the rooms.

One room was empty, with just a few rocks arranged in key places. I gathered it to be a sleeping area. Another room looked to have a few random shiny objects, some small coins and other things that looked either mildly rare or valuable. I took it to be a treasure room, where the Horde-beings just dragged whatever caught their eye. The third room reeked, and was full of half-eaten animals, such several small rodents and what looked like relatives to the colorful bird that had warned us earlier.

"Breena!" I yelled. "We're clear up to here!"

But the little fairy was already darting forward. As I ran, she zipped past me, fluttering over to the wounded fairies as she sought to find the most wounded among them. Up close, I could see more of their features. They were tiny, beautiful people even after the horrible abuse they'd endured, much like my childhood movies had insisted they were. The only difference was that they all looked like tiny adults instead of young children. They also wore sparkling clothing that looked to be made out of either leaves or some gauzy film I didn't recognize. As I reached the yellow-glowing male, my mind-screen informed me that the common name for his species was *Pixie* and that he was *Badly Damaged.* I immediately began casting *Healing Wind*. I thought about trying to use first aid, but I knew absolutely nothing about fairy anatomy, and I trusted magic to work better than my half-remembered health class lessons at this point.

Besides, I would need a special tool to set a fairy's fractured hip bone anyway, and I didn't have it.

That random, impossible thought almost interrupted my casting. When I managed to pull the spell through anyway, the tiny glowing man looked a bit healthier, with his glow no longer sputtering and his breathing a little more normal. His left leg and wing still hung limply, and the tiny humanoid started sobbing again.

"It's okay, little brother," I said softly, wincing inwardly at my choice of words. But it wasn't like I could call him 'dude' or 'bro.' "Breena's a healer. She can help get this fixed."

At least I hoped she could.

My little companion actually flew by at that point, looking down at the male fairy.

"Drat. Broken bones. The one thing Water Magic isn't great at." Nevertheless, she hovered over her broken kin and began rotating her hands and singing a gentle song. A soft blue glow fell over the tiny man, then after Breena continued chanting, another glow fell over him, a green one this time. Breena's yellow-colored kinsman began moaning much more softly.

"There. His pain should be less, and his bones will mend correctly, although slowly. Can you take it from here?" She was looking anxiously behind her at the two other fairies still moaning and weeping on the floor.

I nodded, though in truth I had no idea what I was supposed to do next. I tried to speak more comforting words.

"There buddy, it's okay. You're going to get better now. Your two friends are going to be okay too."

Again, I wasn't a therapist, and my only example of one back home totally sucked.

"No," the little man squeaked softly, fighting through whatever pain-killing magic Breena had given him. "More than two...next room...sister...aunt...niece."

With that, he sighed and closed his eyes.

I panicked until I saw that his chest was still rising and falling. Then I re-panicked when I processed what the little man said.

"Breena!" I shouted. "He's unconscious. There are more captives in the next room!"

And, I remembered, we hadn't killed all of the Horde in this place. It felt like all the Ilklings had already charged us, but their leader hadn't confronted us yet.

We had at least one more foe in this place, and he was the strongest.

Breena looked up at me, then looked at the three other fairies in the room. The green and blue ones were still moaning and weeping horribly, and she bit her lip again.

"They're hurt pretty bad," she hedged. "I don't know if I can leave them... and it will take time to stabilize them..."

It didn't take a genius to tell she was torn and didn't know what to do.

Which means you have to step up and act, son, my father's voice leaped into my mind.

And just like that, before I could argue or call him a hypocrite, I was acting on it.

"Breena," I said, gently setting the little man down. "Keep an eye on him too." I picked up my slightly damaged murder-stick, pointing it to the dark doorway leading to the only part of the nest we hadn't entered yet. "I'm going in."

Her head snapped up at me.

"But you can't go alone!" she snapped, eyes wide. "You don't know what you're facing!"

"Yeah," I said, still walking toward the doorway. "You said a bigger one should be here. Is he going to be more violent to his captives than these freaks were?" I hooked a thumb to the pile of dead, toddler-sized psychopaths in the hallway behind me. Breena nodded glumly. "And can his victims come back from the dead, like I can?" This time Breena didn't answer. I think she knew that only hearing 'yes' would have changed my mind anyway.

"Right," I said. "I'm going in then."

"Wes!" Breena called out one more time. "Be careful!" She bit her lip for a moment, before speaking again. "And don't go near the pit! No matter what!"

I nodded, still not knowing what the big deal was about that pit she kept mentioning, and not having enough time to learn more about it.

I hoped that everyone was right about me coming back from the dead.

The hall behind the doorway was dark for a long stretch, but my enhanced feet traveled quickly. In less than fifteen seconds, I reached the end. The entire room was lit, and easily several times larger than any of the other rooms combined. Here all of the stone on the floor was black, as if it had been coated several times over with Horde oil. I couldn't tell if the stone was worked or natural, but it somehow reminded me of both. Probably because it rose and fell evenly, but here and there I thought I could see a line for a tile or brick. The walls were high, easily reaching over twenty feet in height, far beyond what the tiny Ilklings would either need or be able to make on their own. At fifteen feet up, more of the black oil torches flickered.

But all of that was superficial detail compared to what was in the center of the room. A large pit of *something* writhed, bubbled, slurped, and burped. It looked like someone had combined the most disgusting elements of mud, tar, and slime, then mixed them all together into a goop pile that was colored black, brown, and snot-green. I half-expected it to stink, but thankfully it didn't.

I was also thankful that the three tiny people in black cages directly in front of the pit looked to be still alive.

I took one more glance, but I still didn't see anyone or anything else hostile in the giant room. With that, I crept forward as quickly as I could.

"Hello?" I said quietly. "Do you understand me? I'm here to save you."

The tiny figures kept rocking and crying for one more moment, until one lifted her head up in disbelief. She squeaked and chirped at the other two, then flew up to the front of her cage facing me.

All three of the little creatures were women and looked to be untouched. They looked to be even more beautiful than the three in the other room, and glowed silver, white, and red respectively. They shouted excitedly at me, then started chirping again, pointing at the empty cage next to them, and at the pit behind them. I couldn't understand much of what they said, except for three words.

Hurry. Help her.

As I came closer, I thought I saw part of the pit bubble more intensely than the rest. When I came to the very edge, I could tell that something was thrashing wildly inside of it.

And I could just barely, barely hear a tiny muffled scream come from a spot about eight feet away from the edge. Too far away for me to reach from the rim of the giant hole.

Feeling my entire body grow cold with horror, I raced around the cages, feeling my wind magic suddenly surge and spur me on much faster than it should have been able to. The rush of current let me leap straight to the edge of the pit, which I caught with one hand. Dropping my stick on the ground and wishing I had a way to cover my nose, I vaulted into the disgusting sludge, hoping I was landing near, but not on top of, the tiny drowning figure in it. I didn't know how deep the pit was. I didn't know if the muddy sludge was acidic or poisonous or some other horrible property. I didn't know if I had just killed myself to save a tiny little person that couldn't be saved anyway.

I worried about all of those things. But what I hadn't expected at all was for the goop to suddenly splash away as soon as my feet touched it. The substance had only to brush against my skin for it to suddenly recoil guiltily away from me, as if it was alive, and somehow apologetic. I would have been flabbergasted if I thought I had time, but as soon as I hit the bare squishy floor I just stumbled over to where I thought the fairy was, still encased in the muck. The substance containing her pulled away with it when I came close, as if it were trying to keep her. I snarled at it and stubbornly reached for her, and then it spat her out at me. From what I could see, the little woman was pink in glow and hair color, like Breena usually was. She was coughing, sputtering, and trying to sob all at once. I covered her with my hands, then tore a corner of my sleeve off to wrap her when I realized she wasn't clothed.

“No, no!” she suddenly shrieked in a tiny voice. “I'm sorry! I'll do it! I'll do it! I'll be good now!”

Her words and condition made the whole experience that much more messed up and horrifying. “It's okay,” I tried to say, but I was still pulling my way through the nasty sludge that kept clinging at me then immediately splashing away.

Please be okay, I wound up thinking instead. *Whatever happened, please be okay. Please be well. Just hang on.*

Then, as if some just and loving god had heard my prayer, the remaining sludge immediately splashed off the tiny poor woman. I heard and felt the rest of the Pit shudder at the same time, and the remaining muck in front of me began to slowly move out of my way. Another glance at the little fairy showed that her skin suddenly looked healthier. Furthermore, she had stopped thrashing and was beginning to still completely, as if under a calming sedative.

That was yet another baffling occurrence in an already head-wrenching day, but I had to concentrate on getting the little woman to safety. I was just glad that she wasn't affected by any of my passive combat spells. I'd have to get Breena or Stell to explain that to me, but it looked like they'd only activate if I was the recipient of harm, or if I was moving in a way that projected the desire to cause harm. At any rate, I could carry her without hurting her, so I focused on just doing that. The muck parted a pathway as I climbed back out of the pit, but I stopped and looked at the remaining fairies in cages.

"Is she the last one?" I asked urgently. "Is there anyone else in there? Anyone I haven't seen yet?"

They shook their heads at me. Looking back at the muck a second time, I thought I could see a few animal bones in spots of the pit, but no other struggling mounds indicating that anything left in there was either humanoid or still alive. I finished climbing out of the pit, holding the last tiny victim to my chest and speaking softly to her, trying to tell her that she was safe here, that nothing bad would happen anymore.

I was about to kneel down and open the remaining cages, when I noticed a figure standing in the doorway.

I didn't know how I had missed him until then. I didn't know where he came from.

But I did know that the last Horde-being left in this place was standing in front of the only doorway out of this place.

And just like the first batch of Ilklings, he was making my mind-screen yell at me.

. . .

WARNING! WARNING!

FOREIGN CONTAMINANT DETECTED.

CONTAMINANT IS WRETCH-CLASS HORDEBEAST.

WARNING!

WRETCH-CLASS HORDE-BEING HAS BEEN ENHANCED.

DETECTING THE FOLLOWING KNOWN ENHANCEMENTS:

LEADER OF A SMEAR-CLASS NEST.

INCREASED SIZE MUTATION.

DARK ICON BLESSING.

BEWARE! BEWARE! BEWARE

Unlike last time, the intensity of this message was almost enough to give me a headache. Thankfully, it faded quickly from my eyes, so I could at least see what the magic of this world was screaming about. The Horde-being in question, apparently called a 'Wretch,' (really unflattering names these guys have, the deadpan corner of my mind noted) stood a bit over four and a half feet tall. That was well over a foot taller than the Ilklings had been, but it still barely came up to my chest. However, unlike the Ilklings, the Wretch stood straight-backed and upright, with slightly firmer muscles. Its skin was still black, but it was tighter, and not as wrinkled as its smaller cousins were. Furthermore, most of it was covered in coarse brown fur. Only its hands and a few channel-like patches of its skin seemed capable of dripping Horde oil. Its head was perhaps the most striking difference. The Ilklings had heads like wrinkly, over-toothed, drooling bowling balls. Their leader had a more oblong head, like a cross between a deer and a man. It was baring its toothy maw at me, and it had two large antler-horns that grew out of either side of its head and would almost reach my shoulder when it stood straight up.

The final differences were that it was clothed in a dirty loincloth, convincing me that it had a gender, unlike the Ilklings (probably male); and that it carried a silvery, leaf-shaped blade in its left hand that looked to be about two feet long.

Unlike me, it was actually armed with a real weapon. Further unlike me, its weapon was in its hands and not lying uselessly near the muck-pool. Shifting to hold the rescued fairy carefully in my left hand, I cursed both myself for not being more careful, and my luck for not providing me with a better outcome for my choices.

Then my luck seemed to redeem itself.

After staring at me for another moment, the horned monster seemed to notice the pit behind me, and it began to tremble. The short sword fell from its hand. It lowered itself to its shaking furred knees and in a quivering voice, spoke up.

"Great one," it rasped, to my comprehension and surprise. "This Wretch surrenders."

What?

That didn't make any sense. I had an injured captive in one arm. My other arm was weaponless.

My spells gave me some armor, but if an Ilkling's teeth could still pierce my skin, then there was no way that sword was letting me walk out of here without paying a pound of flesh.

But the horned monster had lowered its face to the ground in complete submission. "Surrender," it hissed, its speech still somewhat garbled and not completely articulate, but understandable enough. "This Wretch surrenders. This Wretch grieves. This Wretch repents."

Well, I thought for a moment. *What the hell do I do with that?*

My conscience had no problem letting me kill in self-defense earlier. Every single Ilkling so far, except for the two that were busy killing one of their own, had attacked me first. Furthermore, every one of them had taken part as far as I could tell in hurting or torturing another intelligent creature, and had probably killed dozens of harmless animals as well. Finally, they had been dumb as bricks, not really selling me on the "having sentience" angle. They just seemed like a pack of particularly large, four-limbed, perverted murder-cockroaches. To say I had felt peace about killing them, especially after witnessing what they were doing to those poor pixies, was an understatement.

But this last one had an intelligent gleam to his eyes, was no longer acting as a threat, and seemed to show remorse for his actions.

The tactician in me said to put a lightning bolt in his skull, while it was vulnerable and unarmed, as soon as I could put the fairy down safely. My conscience was resisting that idea. But, as usual for my conscience, it didn't have an alternative action for me. I had to figure something out, and quickly.

"Stay right there, and do not rise," I commanded, finally deciding at the very least that I needed to secure the little hostages first. I carefully put the pink pixie down, then reached over to the cages. The barred doors had no key, just a semi-complex latch on the outside that was too heavy for the fairies to move and too complicated for the stupid Ilklings to unlock on their own. I wondered how the monsters had managed to either find or make such a thing. But all three doors popped open and, after a moment, three little heads bravely peeked out. "Take her," I whispered, pointing to the pink fairy. "Stay out of the way for now."

Then I turned back to the Horde creature, quietly grabbing my club. Even with his head low, the Wretch had noticed my opening the cages. He spoke again, his head still lowered.

"Forgiveness, great one," the creature rasped. "This Wretch should not have taken those. Great one is right to take them back. Punish this Wretch as you will."

Now that was really strange. It would have been one thing if the monster had begged me to spare him. But as far as I could tell, the thing was showing genuine remorse. He was even accepting the fact that his actions had consequences. What was I was supposed to do with that?

"You understand my speech?" I asked slowly. *Probably should have checked that earlier,* I thought.

"Yes, great one. This Wretch will heed."

"Okay," I said carefully. "Do you understand that it was wrong to capture these little women? And their friends in the next room?"

"Indeed, great one." Again, he spoke without raising his head. "This Wretch has no excuse."

"And that it was wrong to hurt them, and to lock them in cages?" I pressed on. One of these questions should help either me or my conscience figure out what to do.

"This Wretch did not know such things. Now this Wretch does. This Wretch will strive to do better. This Wretch will obey."

The fawning tone in this creature's voice disgusted me. But I had to admit that it was also, beyond all else, submissive.

Should I really kill something that was trying to change its ways? Especially when he hadn't killed anyone else yet?

"And you understand now that it was wrong—extremely wrong—to throw anyone into a filthy pit where they would drown in disgusting muck?"

At this, the horned creature raised his head slightly, in confusion. "Wrong how? The pit would give us her magic, and not kill her. It would only prepare her," the monster insisted. His face was hardly human, but his head was still clearly cocked in a way that suggested I asked him something I should have already known. Out of the corner of my eye, I could see the pink fairy begin to shudder again, and the other three began to pet and comfort her. But they were all pressed against the wall, as far away from the both of us as possible, and the glances they sent my way showed just as much fear as when they looked at the monster in front of me.

That, unfortunately, made too much sense. Right now I was on speaking terms with the thing that had captured them.

“What were you preparing her for?” I asked. Some instinct in the back of my mind made me grip my club tighter, and I felt my combat spells quietly begin to reactivate on their own.

“To be this one's bride-meal,” the monster said, each word coming bluntly out. “How you not know?”

Bride-meal?

What the fu—

But the monster interrupted my inner expletive.

“Did great one not come for bride-meals?” the creature demanded, rising slightly from the floor. Suspicion was starting to color his voice. His beast-man head still tilted at me, but his hands were gripping the floor now, in case he needed to rise completely and quickly. “Did great one not come to collect? This Wretch did not know great one was coming. This Wretch would have had all four already prepared for great one, only hoping great one would leave one for this Wretch. Why has the great one come, if not for tribute? How does the great one not know Pit?” He raised a claw to point behind me. “Pit knows great one. Knows great one well.”

He must have seen me rise from the pit of crap unharmed.

That was why he had been submitting, I realized. He wasn't yielding to the righteousness of my cause. he wasn't surrendering because I had kicked the crap out of his tinier brainless kin. He was submitting to me because of the way the nasty muck had reacted when I had entered it. He took the Pit's submission to me as some kind of sign of authority on my part, that the Horde-being should recognize as well.

I had been thinking the creature was having a crisis of conscience. That hadn't been the case. What had been the case was that this horned, murderous, lustful, depraved savage saw me as kin. As a greater form of everything he aspired to be.

"No," I said out loud, firmly rejecting that possibility, even as disgust for the idea crawled all over my pores. "No way in Hell."

The monster before me brightened at that comment.

"Yes! Hell! Great one is from Earth! Welcome! Welcome new lord!"

"What?" I spat. I was deeply resenting the fact that I was still talking with this thing. *This is all your fault,* I thought angrily at my conscience.

"Pit said a great one would come!" the little monster shouted excitedly. He had pulled himself to his feet, and was holding his sword as he waved both hands around. "Said you would come ahead of many more lords! You lead us! You make us strong! We serve again!"

He stood to his full height, grabbed his sword, and pointed at the four little figures huddling behind me, drooling and leering at them.

"And this Wretch will teach the young lord all about little bride-meals!"

My bad, I finally heard my conscience say. *Go ahead and kill it with fire. Right now. Please.*

I'd have to use lightning instead, but other than that, my heart and mind were finally on the same page.

I turned my head partially to where I could see Breena's kinfolk out of the corner of my eye, not willing to fully look away from the Wretch. Their eyes had grown more and more horrified the longer I had talked to the stupid thing in front of me, but now they were looking at me in horror as well.

Even in this dire moment, the painfully familiar feeling of suspicion made me wince.

"Ladies," I began, glad they could understand me even if I couldn't always understand them. "Stay far behind me. I'm going to try and give you a break for the door. If he takes me down, or if I get him clear from the door, I want you to run to the next room and let my friend know I might have lost, and that she needs to get you all to safety. Understand?"

Three little heads nodded—the pink one was still huddling in her sisters' arms—and a little bit of trust glittered from their eyes once more. I turned my head back to the Wretch in front of me.

"What?" the monster said, sputtering drool as he cocked his head. Then his eyes fell on the pink fairy I had rescued from the Pit.

"Clean," it said, eyes growing wide. "Bride-meal is clean! Is clothed! Is *whole.*" That last word was spat out of his mouth. "Bride-meal is ruined! Why? *Why?*"

"There are a number of problems with your sick logic," I began, tightening the grip on my club. "But we'll start with the fact that the little woman you were torturing isn't anyone's meal, and isn't anyone's bride unless she joyfully consents. And she sure as hell isn't any combination of the two."

The monster's deer-like head looked at me like he had been slapped.

"No," he finally growled. It pointed a quivering finger at me, like some priest discovering an apostate in the middle of his congregation. "You not great lord! You false teacher! You false teacher! No waste prey! You traitor! You bad! You wrong!" He pointed his blade at the fairies. "Mine!" he growled, black saliva rising visibly in his mouth. "Mine! Mine! Bad-wrong traitor! Bad false teacher! Mine! Mine!"

I braced my club over my shoulder, taking a step to the left to test him and to get a better stance. In hindsight, I probably should have found a way to continue the charade until he dropped his guard long enough for me to find a way to kill him, but I saw no such opportunity. Oh well.

"Sorry, you depraved freak," I said calmly. "I don't know who you were expecting. But you're not allowed to hurt anyone else today."

"Bad-wrong traitor!" the creature snarled at me again, stepping forward and raising his silvery short sword. "Bad false teacher! I kill you! I kill you! Mine! Mine!"

He was hissing and spitting the whole time, but the antlered little monster didn't rush at me like his idiot cousins had earlier. Disappointing, but not entirely unexpected. What was unexpected was how well he seemed to be holding his weapon. His clawed hand kept a steady grip on the handle, and he advanced toward me cautiously. I watched the thing warily, trying to figure out a good tactic for this fight. I had the better reach, even if he tried to use its horns, but the monster had the better weapon. I also had four tiny people I was trying to protect, but since they could all fly, and the Horde creature was trying to keep them from escaping, maybe that hindered him more than me.

I decided to wait for him to try and get in range, since I figured I had the advantage of time. The longer the fight went on, the longer the captives had a chance to recover their strength and make a break for it. And, even better, Breena might be able to finish healing the other pixies and come join the fight.

The monster crept forward cautiously, leaning as if he was going to step into range of my swing, then darting quickly back. Then he sneered at me, more black saliva coating his teeth. *He's counting on my patience giving up and making a mistake,* I realized. The Horde wretch was a total freak, but he had been smart enough to guess my age and gather that I was inexperienced. The fact that I was just using a random stick as my weapon probably reinforced that.

Don't let him intimidate you, a quiet voice said in my head. *You have the advantage. Let him be the one to over-commit.*

I didn't know where that thought came from, but I could tell it was the right call. Getting a dash of inspiration, I smiled at the monster and relaxed. The thing hissed at me, tensing, but didn't come any closer. The wretch's eyes started roaming across my face, as if my new confidence had unnerved him. But moments passed and he still didn't take the bait. That was fine. I waited a little longer, and then, just when the creature seemed to settle into waiting, I removed one pinky from gripping the stick and pointed it at him. I had one last finger-bolt on that particular hand. I fired it quickly, replacing my grip in under a second, and the tiny little bolt smacked the Horde wretch right on the nose. The creature yelped and snapped his mouth, then he snarled and charged forward at me.

I swung my tree-bat sideways at its head.

His speed surprised me, ducking my blow almost perfectly, with only the tips of his horns scraping on my weapon. It kept low and continued his lunge forward, pulling its sword back to thrust into me.

I was off-balance, but I had a split second of inspiration and kicked out with my leg. I caught the smaller creature square in the chest. He weighed a lot more than the Ilklings, so I couldn't launch him into the air, but he still fell back several feet.

It still wasn't a perfect idea, though. The creature's sword arm had begun flailing as it sailed back, and the weapon scraped all along my leg. The calcite armor slowed it for only a second. Then a long line of pain lit up the outward side of my leg.

I screamed in pain. Getting cut with a blade was a new kind of agony for me. But I fought my way through far worse every day back home. Trusting in what Breena had said about my vital guard, I stepped forward anyway, bringing my club down in a two-handed, overhead slam. I caught the creature on the side of the skull near one of the antlers, and I heard the horn crack. The monster sank to his knees, then immediately tried to rise again. I brought my weapon over once more, cracking down on his head again, and was surprised by how much tougher than the Ilklings he was. In addition to having a tougher hide, and probably tougher bones, I figured the thing's vital guard pool was several times greater than what the Ilklings had.

My luck ran out on the third swing.

I heard another loud crack, and this time it wasn't one of the monster's horns. When I pulled my weapon back, it had gone from a makeshift three-feet-long club to a splintered six-inch handle.

Noting the change, the wretch lowered his head and charged, antlers catching me in the torso. They barely pierced my earth armor, to my relief, but then the monster pulled his sword back and started stabbing at my hip. It pumped its arm once, twice, thrice back into my upper leg in a matter of seconds, letting out another drool-filled hiss in this process.

"Die! Die! Bad-wrong traitor die!"

I heard my electrical armor fizzle on its blade, but for all intents and purposes he was able to perforate me and remain shock-free. I'd have to ask about that later, when all of my screaming and bleeding was done.

A shout tore out of my throat as soon as I completed that thought. One of my hands wrested its way forward, wrapping around one of the blasted thing's antlers. The other one, the one with all of its finger-bolts remaining, latched onto the Wretch's face, clenching and discharging all five of the tiny currents at once. I heard a muffled screech under my hand, followed by a sizzle as smoke rose from between my fingertips. A moment later my *Outer Current* spell added its own amps, and the screaming began all over again.

The monster screamed one more time, then he raised his sword arm to stab me again. But now he was suffering spasms, so I had no trouble grabbing his wrist. Then my *Outer Current* spell triggered again, and I was able to start electrocuting the beast through both hands.

I decided to modify my previous rule:

Don't bring a grown eighteen-year-old to a bloodthirsty toddler fight.

Bring a grown eighteen-year-old with a taser.

My smaller enemy writhed and struggled under my grip. He was much stronger than the Ilklings I had fought earlier. In fact, he was almost as strong as a normal grown man, despite his short height.

Which meant he was still nowhere near as strong as I was. Not on this world, where I was augmented by magic and free of whatever inhibited me back home.

I twisted to suddenly yank his wrist down onto my knee. The strike, combined with my lightning magic, was finally enough to make the monster lose his grip, and his sword fell to the ground with a clatter. Then I jerked its face close to my knee and repeated the process, the adrenaline letting me bash its face while ignoring the pain in my hip.

Then, shrieking from his burns and the blows to his head, the monster began to writhe and twist under my grip, while swiping at me with his non-shocked claw. It didn't come close to landing with his much shorter arms, but I still had to arch my back slightly, and this affected my grapple. Incidentally, so did the screaming pain in my stabbed hip. The Hordebeast finally began to jerk himself free, but at the last moment I reached up and grabbed his cracked antler. As the monster finished writhing out of my grip, I jerked down hard on his damaged horn, hearing it crack as it tore off the monster's head. The Wretch screamed again and leaped backward, putting more distance between him and myself. The monster clutched his blackened face where my finger-bolts had all gone off at once. Then he bared his claw at me and hissed, eyes growing large and bloodshot.

"Bad-wrong traitor! Kill you! Kill you! Hurt prey over your corpse!"

"I don't know what you mean by that last part, but it sounds disgusting, so no," I replied, surprising myself with how calm I had remained after getting stabbed. The vital points Breena had told me about must be working to keep me from bleeding out. But the pain still came through, and that seemed to limit my leg as much as the actual damage. "I don't know what possesses you freaks to act the way you do, and I don't know why in heaven or hell you thought I'd be on board with it. But it's not happening."

"The Pit will tell!" the short monster suddenly screeched. "False teacher! Traitor-man! The Pit will tell on you! You not hide! Tell on you to other earth-men! Tell on you to Father! You not hide! You not hide!"

The dumb little wretch suddenly leaped forward, claws outstretched.

I had wanted time to reach down and grab the sword at my feet, but with the pain in my hip I wasn't sure I'd be able to anyway. I'd have to figure out how to withstand it better, because Breena had said there shouldn't be anything else inhibiting me at the moment, and the idea of being stopped by something so petty and familiar as pain was just embarrassing. But enough introspection.

As the monster threw itself at me, I braced the broken antler in my hands and stabbed at the stupid creature's neck.

A shock ran up my arm, and I heard a tearing sound, followed by a rasping wheeze. My thrust knocked the monster off-balance, and he wound up charging past me, tearing the horn out of my hand in the process. I painfully replanted my feet, turning to face the creature as it staggered to a stop. But my attack had apparently pierced through the last of his vital points, and as he turned toward me he swayed on his feet one final time, black blood bubbling from his mouth and neck.

"Traitor-prince," the monster croaked. "Father... curse you."

With that, his eyes seemed to roll in its head, and the monster collapsed limply to the floor, stopped breathing, and became completely still, save for the occasional jerk from one of his shocked appendages.

I waited for a moment, then knelt down and picked up the short, silvery blade. Then I limped over to it as cautiously as I could and reached down to drag the sword across the monster's throat, just to be sure. There was no reaction, save for another new pool of black blood.

My conscience spoke up again, pointing out that I had just slit something's throat, and how that was a new thing; just saying, might not want to make a habit out of that. The rest of me duly noted its concern as I wiped my new blade off with the dead monster's fur.

Then I looked around and stood up, trying not to think about how much my leg was still hurting.

"Everyone okay?" I asked, finally spotting the four tiny glowing women huddled in a corner. I winced as I heard the pink one whimper, and none of them answered me. They were close enough that I could see the fear in their eyes as they stared at me. They had heard what the monster called me, I realized. Somehow, their opinion of me scared me more than the actual fight with the creature had.

"Can you move?" I asked persistently. Still no answers, except for the whimpering from the one I had pulled out of the pit earlier. "The way behind me should be clear," I said. "Unless there were more than..." A quick mental count. "Thirteen of these things. You can leave anytime you want. Breena can check you for injuries."

"You know Breena?" one of the little pixies squeaked.

"She came with me," I nodded at them. "She says she knows most of you. Tiny, with wings like yourselves? Pink spiky hair? Really excitable?"

"That's her!" the silver one shouted in a musical, chittery voice. "Let's go get her!"

"Breena's here!" another one said happily as she started to move. "I knew she'd come!"

"Yeah, she's in the other room," I said, a little miffed that someone else was making them feel better, instead of the guy who had just freed them and gotten stabbed in the process. *And why was that still hurting?* I asked myself. According to Breena, the pain should be diminishing as my vital points recovered. That made me glance back at the Horde wretch, but the monster wasn't even twitching at that point. I reflected on how much harder it was to kill than the Ilklings had been.

Focus, I told myself.

Then the muddy pit near my feet began to churn violently.

Bubbles began to form and pop quickly, and a certain spot in the muck near me began to rise, tremble for a moment, and then fall back downward, as if it couldn't hold itself together. Then, as if trying again, it rose back up into a lump.

A weird, buzzing feeling started forming in my head. The bubbles were forming more rapidly, then stopping, as if in a pattern.

As if it were trying to speak.

Come, come, I thought I heard in the belching pop of the bubbles. The form rose again, then pulled away from me, as if beckoning.

"Come," another bubble belched at me, and this time I could not mistake the disgusting noise for anything but speech. They began to pop in slow, but audible sequences. "Come...and...will... forgive."

The form broke apart once more, and tried to rise again.

"Come," the bubbles insisted.

The words were unmistakable to me, even though the bubbles weren't particularly loud. I somehow got the feeling that the fairies at the other end of the room couldn't hear it.

The fairies...

My mind snapped away from the unreal phenomenon and turned back toward the tiny people I had come to rescue in the first place. They didn't seem like they could hear the pit's words, but they had gone back to cowering against the wall as soon as the muck from the pit had started rising. The one I had already pulled out of the muck started screaming in panic.

"Why haven't you left yet? Get out of here!" I shouted. "Head for the door and don't fly over the pit! Go get Breena! And don't leave anyone behind!"

The tiny women snapped their heads toward me as I spoke. They took the screaming one in their arms and flew out the door. I turned back to the disgusting giant blob in the room that somehow thought it could tempt me over to a grosser version of the dark side.

The muck was rising again, this time growing thicker. Before the lump hadn't even been the size of one of the Ilklings. Now it was almost as big as the wretch I had just killed, antlers and all.

"Come!" the bubbles burped and insisted. "Come, and, *know*! Come, and, *feel*! Gain! Gain! What! You! *Lack*!"

I felt a presence tug at me inside, as if it was expecting to find a connection to me that wasn't there, and kept searching.

Kill it! something suddenly said from somewhere. *Kill it quickly!*

Great idea, I thought. Especially since I had zero interest in even finding out what this nasty mess was even offering. I swore I'd never be able to look at cafeteria food again after this.

But how? I wondered. It wasn't like I could punch or stab it to death.

The bubbles were starting to talk again. I tuned them out to concentrate.

The Ideal of Lightning suddenly came to the forefront of my mind. Specifically, of bolts coming out of nowhere, called 'bolts out of the blue' to fall on those who were often believed, for whatever reason, to be unrighteous, or enemies of heaven.

I felt the lightning suddenly surge at me with this thought, though I had not tapped into it since the last battle.

Destroy it! I felt something command. *It is unworthy! Unrighteous! Unjust!*

The filth in the pit was rising again. It seemed to have more success in maintaining a shape. The bubbles were belching in clearer, albeit more disgusting, sounds.

"Come," the black-green slime burped again, and more forcefully. "Will...serve...you! Come!"

I had no idea why this thing could talk. No idea why it thought I would listen. All I knew was that it repulsed me, and it disturbed me that it thought we had a connection.

And I somehow knew that it would take my rejection even more violently than the wretch had. It was already stirring angrily at my hesitation.

So I didn't argue with it, didn't try to figure out what it was offering, or why. I just started up my best chance to kill it.

Hot, bright strands flickered all along my forearms as I began my most powerful single attack spell, *Spark Bolt.* I knew this spell was still only in its early stages, but Breena had informed me that I could also channel the spell into a constant current if I wanted to. I hoped that would be enough to stop the pit from whatever it was about to do. I didn't feel confident about another fight.

My hip was still hurting far too much.

The filth in the pit was still rising, getting bigger and bigger. But it wasn't calling out to me anymore. It was rearing at me as if I were an offending heretic it wished to destroy.

"Dare," it burped angrily. "Dare... oppose..."

I stopped listening. The lightning called, and thrusting both my hands forward, I answered it.

A shocking torrent nearly as thick as my arm leaped out of me and directly into the rising angry muck. Now looking very much alive, the rising figure let out what I took to be a splattering roar of pain. My hip was screaming at me, and there was a dull ache growing in my head the longer I kept the spell going, but I didn't let up. I hadn't been expecting to be able to prolong the bolt, but I was going to take that newly discovered advantage for everything it was worth.

"Dare," the muddy slime splashed out, writhing as current sparked all over it. "Dare...refuse..."

My hip was throbbing its way into my brain. Screaming the fact that I had been stabbed over and over again, as if I hadn't noticed it happening in the first place. I tried to ignore it, to focus on keeping the sizzling blue-white light on the monstrosity in front of me. But it was getting harder to focus and my vision was growing dim.

Just when I felt everything start to go black, the pit gave a final, angry hiss, and the rising part of it collapsed back down.

"Noooo..."

The bubbles seemed to burp out a final wail.

"Traitor...prince..."

Then the muck stopped moving at all, slowly settling down, and separating to where it began to look like dirty water instead. My lightning ended not a moment later, along with the last of my adrenaline. I started to sink to my knees, but one gave out completely under me. I barely managed to stop my fall with my hands. The ground suddenly rumbled around me, and an imprint from my mind-screen quickly branded its way into my brain.

A Challenge has been overcome in the Woadlands. All Icons bear witness that the upcoming rise of the Horde has been thwarted by being destroyed at the source by Challenger Wes Malcolm. No further invasions may incur until a new Horde Pit has been constructed.

Really? I thought. *Instant messaging that I beat the final boss, with all the juicy details? Why didn't they get information like that earlier?*

Speaking of information that became useful minutes ago...

Warning, my mind-screen said. *A champion of The Bloody-Horned Huntsman, a Dark Icon, has afflicted you with the Curse of the Blood-Trailing Death. Lacerations and puncture wounds will continue to bleed even when vital points have recovered. Additional healing will be required.*

I finally glanced back at my hip. *Yep, still bleeding.* So that was why it was getting so hard to think. *And look, I really did leave a bloody trail on the floor. Made abstract art with every step.*

The fairies got away though. That was good. *I did feel good*, I realized. Even with the stab. *Warm and fuzzy... Look, one of the little fairies came back....*

"Wes! Wes!"

A really high-pitched little fairy.

"Wes! Wes! Can you hear me! Hold on! Look at me! Look at me!"

An *annoying* high-pitched little fairy.

"Blast it, Wes! You're not dying on your first Challenge! Especially not on my watch!"

That wouldn't let me sleep.

"And especially not because I was panicking too much earlier!"

And really, really liked to yell.

"Okay, *(huff)*.... Okay, a Dark Icon's curse... the bloody one...I can still handle this... *Healing Wind,* followed by *Corrected Flow,* and *Renewing Drops.* Here we go."

Great. Still talking. *And now she's poking me.*

Worst coma ever.

Wait... Do people talk to themselves in comas?

My eyelids cracked back open.

A little pink woman was flying all around me, making hand gestures and talking nonsense words that somehow made me feel better. The warm feeling left, replaced by a painful, wet coldness originating from my hip, to be replaced again by a newer, healthier warmness that made it easier to think.

"Wes! Wes!" the prettiest of the little fairies shouted at me. Which one was it again? Breena. It was Breena. Did I even learn any of the other pixies' names?

Why was I hanging around fairies anyway?

Wasn't I practically a grown man?

"Wes!" the pretty, but extremely annoying, tiny woman shouted. "Can! You! Hear me!"

"Yes," I moaned. "And ow."

"Oh thank all the lost Icons!" The little fairy buzzed over to my neck and wrapped her tiny arms around it. The feeling would have felt pleasant, if I was less self-conscious about her being a tiny fairy. Also, she was choking me. That was a problem too. But she let go after I made my first choking gurgle.

"Sorry!" she gasped. "And don't ever do that again!" she suddenly shouted, waving a tiny sparkling finger at me. "You don't face the final part of a Challenge alone and unprepared! That could've gone much worse! You could have already been killed! *Killed,* Wes!"

Good Lord, her voice could get shrill.

"Please stop yelling," I said, pushing on the ground to raise my face off the floor. "And don't I come back when I die anyway?"

"Yes! Eventually! But doesn't mean you should go around doing it! People are 'eventually' okay after stabbing themselves in the leg or setting their hair on fire! But you don't see everyone going around bald, crispy, and with bloody legs! Give me one good reason why you couldn't wait for me to finish up in the other room!"

Still shrill. Still yelling.

"Didn't I tell you?" I asked with another wince. I sat up and grasped my head. Whatever Breena had done had fixed my leg, but I had a colossal headache for some reason. "That I had to save the others? That we were short on time? And that you needed to stop yelling at me?" I let out another groan. "Because I'm pretty sure we already talked about all of that."

"Yes, but you still should have waited!" Breena insisted. In concession to my aching head, she had lowered her voice a tiny bit. It seemed like it just made her angrier. "I'm a water-and-air sprite! I can heal injuries well even at my weakest stage. I was able to fix all of the serious injuries in the other room with just a handful of spells!" She pointed out with her tiny hand. "Even when it comes to the Horde's abuses, I can save and restore any of my own kind easily! The only thing I can't fix is if they've been submerged in the

Horde Pit. And that's mostly because nothing can pull someone out of a Horde Pit!"

"What do you mean?" I asked, shifting to look at her. I probably had an angry look on my face. Because I hate it when people try to make me think hard on a headache. Especially a post-being-stabbed one. "They already put a fairy in there earlier. The pink one, the only pink one other than you. They threw her in there. That was why I hurried."

"The pink one?" Breena's eyes snapped wide. "Petal-bell? They threw her in there? Are you sure?" I nodded, and Breena covered her mouth and began heaving.

"No.... oh Icons...what have I done...what have I let them do...Petal-bell." The heaves became sobs. "What am I gonna tell your mother, your sisters?" she continued. "Petal-bell's gone.... I should have been there..."

"She's not gone," I stated angrily. "Get a hold of yourself. Stop crying and yelling at everyone. She flew away with the others. I thought you checked on her already."

My little friend's head shot back up.

"I did," she said suddenly. "That's right, I did. She was unharmed. Just really frightened." Breena buzzed directly in front of me, looking even angrier. "Why did you tell me she was in the pit then?"

"*Because I found her there*," I said, enunciating every word slowly, and in total exasperation. "And then I pulled her out. What is wrong with you? Good Lord. I need to ask Stell if they make depressants for fairies. Or pixies, or sylphs, whatever you call yourselves."

"Sprite-folk, technically," Breena answered in a distracted tone. Then she did another take. "And what do you mean you pulled her out of the Pit? That's impossible!"

"Apparently not if you use both hands," I said sarcastically. My conscience popped up and pointed out that I should be nicer to the woman who had just healed my leg. But this whole mess was my conscience's fault, so I snarled at it and told it to shut the hell up. I get cranky after I get stabbed in the leg, apparently. Sue me.

"Really?" Breena asked, tilting her head in confusion. "That's all you had to do? And it worked?"

"Yes," I said firmly. "Basic safety techniques for public swimming pools. Reach, throw, go with assistance. Except that I actually had to jump in to go pull her out on my own."

"You *what?*" Breena shrieked in a squeaky voice—the kind dog toys make right before they die. "You *went into the pit?* Are you *crazy?*"

"*I! Don't! Know!*" I replied, finally shouting back. My head hurt, my leg was numb, and I was still getting yelled at. I'd had it. "But since I'm arguing with a tiny glowing woman? Without the use of mushrooms? Probably!"

Thank God, Jesus, and Buddha, that finally shut her up.

"And I only did it because all the other little hallucinations asked me to! And it sounds like you already cut them slack, because, like me and everybody else around here, *they've had a bad day!* So please extend the same courtesy to me, since I'm just the poor guy who tried to save everyone, and all that I've gotten out of the deal is a stab wound from my very first medieval knife fight!"

Well, technically the weapon was closer to a sword, that I decided to keep. But that wasn't the point right now. And thankfully Breena finally agreed.

She flew around me, examining me all over, then started muttering again. She gestured at me, and some dusty sparkles flew over me. My headache finally started to vanish, and the numbness in my leg fled.

"Wes," she began again, much quieter. "I'm sorry. And thank you for saving all my friends. I forgot you don't know anything about the Horde."

"I don't," I admitted. "Except that they are small, have a whole lot of disgusting habits and are violently opposed to making people not want to kill them."

"Actually, Wes," Breena began carefully. "This went really, really well. Normally, when a Smear of Horde emerges, the locals struggle with them for a long time, as the best-case scenario."

That was probably because the Horde had never decided to emerge in my home state, I reflected. Seriously, even the arseholes in my crappy home town wouldn't have let these guys reach the ten-minute mark. Being that vile, and that easily punt-able, is just asking to be used as stress relief.

"As the worst-case scenario," Breena continued. "The Horde grows enough to fully conquer and corrupt several of the local countries and becomes a full-blown Trial, and quickly moves past that to become a Tumult. There are legends of what they've done in the past, legends that we've worked hard to ensure stay accurate, in case the Horde ever found a way to come back. And for over a thousand years they haven't, Wes. We worked so hard to completely stamp them out. We thought we did, but we kept records just in case. In case someone figured out how to renew one of their old Pits. And they did," Breena added, looking around. "We have to get in touch with Stell and the Icons so that they can send someone strong enough to...destroy...the...pit." Her eyes were resting on where the nasty muck had come from. The pit of dirty water was slowly evaporating. In spite of that seeming slowness, however, it had already diminished by over half of its original size. It was currently less than two feet deep and continued to shrink before my very eyes. We both continued to watch it, and in five minutes the water had completely evaporated.

Breena looked at me again, her mouth silently forming the question, *"How?"*

"I just zapped it until it died," I said with a shrug. "Was I not supposed to know how to do that?"

Seriously, I thought, *why was everyone so surprised I figured out how to do the job they gave me? Did they lose a handbook they were supposed to give me? Was there a free training seminar I forgot to stop at on the way and get coffee from?*

I heard the last drop in the pit sizzle into nothingness. When it did so, the ground rumbled again. I felt something surge within me. I suddenly felt stronger, healthier, more aware, and more confident. And I felt my inner self suddenly flex, like it wanted to push out again.

The Woadland's Icons have acknowledged Challenger Wes Malcolm's accomplishment in ridding their world of an ancient threat. Their recognition increases the power gained from overcoming a Challenge.

Wes Malcolm's muscles and reflexes have undergone trial by combat. His success has improved his Strength, Dexterity and Constitution by one point, respectively.

His repeated use of magic and resistance to dark curses have sharpened his Intelligence and Wisdom by one level, respectively.

Mother Glade approves of your actions and views you with more favor.

Lady Titania approves of your actions and views you with more favor.

The Stag Lord approves of your actions and views you with more favor.

Great Pan rejoices in your accomplishment and holds you in esteem.

The Bloody-Horned Huntsman resents your interference and now views you with disfavor.

Huh, I said to myself with another wince as my mind-screen updated. Nothing about the Woad Princess this time. And the thing about the bloody guy was new. Also, killing toddler-sized monsters in so many different ways was good for my growth. I turned to comment to Breena, when static suddenly leaped into my mind. Unlike with the mind-screen, these words were in a different font, and both phrases appeared at once, super-imposing over each other at random.

Traitor-prince. Malus will find you.

Hold fast. Invictus knows your name.

The fonts continued battling in my mind for an entire epileptic minute before dissolving away. I clutched my head in confusion. My thoughts were all scattered, and it took a moment before I could think clearly about where I was and what I was just doing. It didn't exactly hurt, but it had felt like someone had grabbed me and shaken me violently for a few moments.

Actually scratch that, because back home shaking my head really did hurt me.

The point was, it had become really hard to think, and it stayed that way for many long moments.

"Wes?" Breena asked. "Are you okay?"

"Yeah," I said after another minute. "Just a really bad upload to my mind-screen. I think I need to have Stell take a look at it."

"What?" the little fairy said with a cock of her head. "It's not supposed to be able to hurt you. All it's supposed to do is make you more aware."

"Well, in the process of making me aware of what Malus and Invictus thought of me, it almost flipped my brain over."

"What?" the little fairy shrieked. "Why would you even joke about that?"

I faced the little woman and gave her my best glare.

"Breena," I said, cutting her off before she could scream at me anymore. "I completed your Challenge, saved your friends, and made all but one of your Icons happy. Are we really gonna have another fight about something I don't even understand?"

For a moment she didn't answer me. She just hovered right there and starting huffing.

"No. But... Ugh! This is so! Frustrating!"

She clenched her fists and pumped them down, much like my sister would during fights with my mom. "You're breaking all the rules, Wes!" the little fairy griped. "*All* the rules! And it's only your *first day*!"

I gave up. We were going to be here all day if I kept trying to get my questions answered. This place was damp and cold and dark, and I didn't feel like getting yelled at anymore.

"Breena," I said. "I'm getting up. We'll work out all of this in the sunlight. I'm tired of this place. Did we get all of the Horde? And are the sprite-kin or fairies or whatever alright?"

"Fine," the pink little woman sighed. "And I'm sorry I blew up again. We'll talk about it when we get out."

All the rooms looked clear. The fairies we found turned out to be the only hostages. Well, the only living hostages. Apparently, the Horde had eaten all the animals they had captured. Their remains were both in that slaughter-room we had passed, as well as the pit. The sight of both had successfully cured my new appetite, confirming that I could get both hungry and nauseous in this projected body.

The fairies were all slowly healing, thanks to Breena's magic. The male with the broken leg seemed weak, but no longer in pain. He could now flutter slowly and gave me a tiny thumbs up. The other two that had been in the room with him also gave me a wan smile.

"They'll keep healing, right?" I asked Breena.

Watching people get hurt is hard. Even if they have wings and sparkle.

In fact, watching creatures so tiny and so helpless get hurt is even harder.

"Yes, Wes, they'll be okay," Breena said, looking at me with a smile. But her tiny eyes were watery, and I could tell how much she had been worried about her friends, and how that worry was probably the reason she had been yelling so much. But I think my own concern for her adopted family comforted her. "Lady Titania's champions are coming for them, and they'll be able to help them more than we can. They're tougher than they look, and this damage is recoverable. We got here in time for them. These three will be as good as new by the end of the week. Even the nightmares will go away in time."

"Good," I said, relieved. I waved back at the tiny creatures, and they smiled at me and chattered in some other language. We walked past them to head into the next room.

"Wait," a halting voice said.

I turned and saw the other four fairies, the ones in cages that I had rescued from the larger, freakier Horde beast.

The red-glowing one had spoken up, flying a little higher so that I could see her. I figured what was coming and braced myself for it. I remembered the last time a little kid had walked over to me in church, how all of the other adults' heads suddenly locked onto me, watching my every movement. Now another tiny person was coming near me, and although she looked like a miniature adult, I could still feel everyone's eyes watch me.

And I didn't want to believe it, but I knew what they were thinking.

That monster, that depraved thing that had terrified and tortured one of them, had found a kinship in me. It was one I didn't understand, and one I had rejected with every fiber of my being. But I wasn't stupid. People back home, who had known me for far longer than these little women did, had chosen to suspect me of the most heinous crimes imaginable—and they had done so with no evidence whatsoever. Given what these women had witnessed, they had to be terrified of me, and I dreaded what would happen as soon as Breena and Stell heard the full story.

"Thank you for saving us," she said softly. "We're sorry you were injured on our behalf. And that you had to endure that monster's awful speech."

"You're welcome," I said automatically, then processed the second half of her statement. "Wait, what?"

"Wait, what?" Breena echoed next to me.

"The monster that caged us tried to recruit the Challenger," the tiny red woman said as she turned to my friend. I saw Breena's eyes widen, and I tried to hide my wince.

Here it comes, I thought.

"That's ridiculous!" Breena shouted, even louder than she had before. "What was it thinking? It had to have known that Wes would've already killed the rest of its Smear!"

"We know," the tiny red woman sang back. "The Challenger had even rescued Petal-bell from the Pit, but it still chose to believe that he could do so because he was somehow in league with the Horde. Even the Pit itself tried to enlist him." The little red fairy shuddered, then looked at me. "That must have been horrifying for you, sir knight. For someone as kind and brave as you to deal with such wretched offers."

"You..." I started to speak, but struggled to finish my question. "You didn't believe it?"

The little red-glowing woman looked startled.

"Of course not, sir knight," she said, blinking. "That creature put me in a cage. It hurt my cousins. It put my niece in its Pit." The little sprite's voice quivered. "And you saved her, then saved the rest of us, then you battled the monster bare-handed on our behalf. Why would we ever trust a word out of its mouth? And why would we ever suspect you, of all people, after what you've done for us?"

"You... wha..." I had started to speak again, but I had no idea what to say. I had no idea what to even think. "Really?" I finally asked. I looked at Breena. "That...that's all they needed?"

"What do you mean, Wes?" Breena cocked her head at me.

"I mean all I did was..." I had started to say. But how did I say it? How did I say that none of what I did mattered back on Earth to people, in the face of what my dad had allegedly done? How did I say that the harder I worked to be better than him, the more suspicious people became of me?

I tried again.

"All I did was..."

"Save me," a quiet, but musical voice interrupted behind me.

I turned and saw the pink-glittered girl I had pulled from the pit. "Carry me," she continued. "Cover me to protect my dignity. Comfort me as I screamed and shrieked at you."

She had a pleasant, bell-like voice now. It sounded much different than when she had been shrieking and whimpering. And to my immense relief, she was wearing proper clothes now, the fairy version at least. I had no idea where they came from, and right now I didn't care.

"Thank you, Challenger," she said firmly, squaring her shoulders. "You stopped something horrible from happening to me."

Then, before I could speak or react, she flew right up to my cheek, and gave me a peck with tiny glowing lips.

"Bless the knight who risked the very worst for the very least of us," she intoned, her voice quivering slightly. "Let your body bear record of your heroism, Friend of the Small."

"Hear, hear," the red-glowing fairy spoke again. "Please accept our favor, sir knight."

To my further surprise—and slight discomfort—she kissed me as well. The other two fairies followed suit, blowing pixie dust at me and making my eyes water.

Yeah, that was probably why my eyes were watering. It couldn't have had anything to do with what I was thinking before.

I had thought these tiny women had been horrified of me. Had made the same judgments everyone else had made of me back home. But they hadn't. I had misread them. They hadn't been horrified *of* me earlier. They were horrified *for* me. Despite everything they had been through.

I had felt a tremor of power in the pink pixie's words, and now it washed over me. Some of her dust swirled over me as well, and I suddenly felt as if I had just finished a refreshing cool shower.

You have been blessed by the Small Folk of the Woadlands. They have imparted you with their favor as well as some of their grace. Your Charisma has increased as a result.

Furthermore, the sprite children of the Woadlands will recognize this blessing and mark you as an ally in the future. Your Deeds and Renown will update accordingly.

Lady Titania witnesses this blessing and approves.

All of this info flashed into my mind-screen in a matter of seconds. I blinked, and then turned to the fairy.

"Thank you," I said, at a loss for words. "I appreciate your favor."

At the time, my words sounded dumb to me. But if the little sprite agreed with me, she didn't show it at all. She just smiled at me, let out a little giggle, and flew back.

Breena flew up next to me.

"Alright now," she said with a glare. "If you're done trying to seduce my friends..."

"What?" I sputtered, old worries suddenly surfacing back. "I didn't—they're not even—"

But my companion just giggled at me.

"I'm just kidding. And yes, you earned a break. I'm sorry I kept yelling at you. Here, have another kiss."

Before I could say anything else, she fluttered up and kissed me on the nose. This time, all it made me do was sneeze pixie dust for a moment. And my nose started burning for some reason. "There. See ladies? He's taken. You're going to have to find your own Challenger."

The other sprites all giggled at that, despite everything that had happened today. I guess that was a good sign. I wish humans could figure out how to bounce back from trauma like that.

Heck, I wished *I* could figure out how to bounce back from trauma like that.

But enough melancholy thinking. We won. Everybody got saved. I needed to move on.

"Alright," I said, turning to Breena. It was time to get out of here before more tiny women tried to hit on me. Yes, they were pretty, and to be honest their kisses felt kind of nice, but they were tiny enough to make me feel like I was about to wind up on the five o'clock news if they got any more comfortable with me.

"What's next?" I asked my companion. "Do we wait here for someone to pick them up, or do we need to make sure the area's safe?"

Breena shook her head.

"You were recognized as having overcome the Challenge, so the threat has been purged. No more Horde should be alive. We'll scan the area just to be safe, but my friends will be fine. Lady Titania's envoys will make sure of it. Especially when she finds out the invaders were Horde."

"Yeah, I'm going to need you to explain everything I heard today," I said as we began walking out toward the exit. The hole had gotten larger when I forced my way through, so climbing out wasn't going to be nearly as difficult as climbing in was. "For today, though, maybe you can tell me who Invictus, Malus, and the Bloody-Horned Huntsman are? Preferably without getting mad at me for asking?"

"Yeah, sorry about that earlier," the little fairy said a little guiltily as she flew out of the hole ahead of me. I grunted, grasped at some tree roots, and pulled myself out after a couple of seconds.

"The Bloody-Horned Huntsman is a Dark Icon. He's a power that formed long ago from some unbeaten Challenges. He draws power from creatures being hunted, tortured, and sacrificed in his name. The more sentient the creature, the more power he gains. He also empowers others to do the same kind of acts. From what I could see, that wretch you killed had his Mark of Favor."

"Is that why it had antler horns?" I asked in realization.

"Yes," Breena answered with a blink. "And good guess. The Mark also made the wretch stronger and smarter than its type of species normally is. He probably had the power to curse you, as well. That's why your wound bled so much, and why you had delusions about Malus and Invictus."

"A curse can mess with my mind-screen?" I asked. That sounded really bad.

"Not really, but that's the closest explanation I can think of. If you got a concussion or something then you might have seen something that wasn't there, but I didn't see any signs of you having one."

"I didn't get hit on the head in that fight," I said firmly. I could remember that much.

"Well, then there's no reason you'd get a message about Malus or Invictus, because they're not real," Breena insisted stubbornly. "And Stell will be even firmer with you than I am on that. Malus is just a boogeyman. He's a lazy explanation for all the evil in the universe. Before the Icons came he was believed to be the source of all Challenges, Trials, and Tumults. But there was never any real evidence of him."

"Didn't you say the Horde were boogeymen?" I asked carefully.

"Yes," Breena said in a flustered tone. "But the Horde are *real.* You've seen them. A bunch just tried to hurt my friends. You killed them for it. Thank you, by the way." Her voice quivered for a moment. "But there's never been any proof of Malus existing. A long time ago, there *might* have been a Dark Icon by that name, and he may have been powerful enough to be remembered long after his destruction..."

"Wait a minute," I interrupted. "Destruction? Icons can *die*? Aren't they like gods or something?"

"Yes and no. Some people worship them, and unlike mortals, they draw power from gaining Renown. But they can die, and have done so in the past. Especially the Dark Icons. A number of the previous Challengers have had a field day with them, in fact.

"But, like with you, death is rarely permanent with them. Usually, they can slowly pull themselves back together. It just takes centuries. That's what happened with the Bloody-Horned Huntsman. Arthur killed him ages ago and he's just now recovered enough of himself to cause some minor trouble. But he's still nowhere near the strength he had over a thousand years ago. In fact, Arthur hurt him so badly that some of the Icon's strength was lost permanently.

"However, there are plenty of other Dark Icons that were so thoroughly broken that they never came back at all. Usually that happens when they die a second time, before they've recovered most of their strength. These days most Dark Icons don't even take the risk of summoning up their full power because then a Trial or Tumult kicks in and they risk Stell being able to call in a Challenger, who is then further empowered by the other Icons that want the Dark Icon gone permanently. Plenty of so-called dark lords have met their permanent destruction just like that."

"That sounds like a lot of old stories back home," I mused.

"If they're about how some evil power sweeps across the land, only to be stopped at the last moment by some noble hero coming out of who knows where, who is favored by the gods of light, then yes. That used to happen all the time." She even rolled her eyes as she said that. "We cleared out entire pantheons of evil idiots that way. Nów, though? They finally wised up. Bloody-Horns was the last to take that risk, and even he tried to be subtle about it.

"But Malus? Never seen any evidence of him. Every now then a cult pops up in his name, but they are always quickly put down and have no details about him except for some non-lucid nightmares. There's no trace of his power, no monsters unique to him, just... nothing. I don't know how his name traveled to so many worlds, but in all our centuries we've never seen any evidence of him. Just some very old, very disturbing stories that we can't even trace the origins for."

"Do they even have the same theme?" I asked. I really didn't like Breena's answer or reaction to my question. I'd have liked something more to go on than 'ignore it, the problem's not real.'

"No, not even that," Breena answered. "Wait, there is one. Supposedly in every story he's an ancient evil, older than all of the other Icons put together, older than the oldest of Stell's race, and the cause of all monsters. He wants to both destroy the world and bind it into eternal suffering at the same time. Which is impossible, because it's hard to torture people when they've been completely destroyed. But all of the stories say he wants to do just that. Destroy people utterly, down to the last speck, and yet bind them into eternal pain and shame. He wants to kill, torture, and enslave, all at once, over and over. Unrealistic goals by any standards. And it's just more proof that he isn't real."

"Okay, fine," I said, dropping the issue for now. "What about Invictus?"

"Ugh," Breena said. "I mean, sorry, no offense to you, but, *ugh!* Invictus is an even bigger myth. Bigger than your Easter Bunny."

"Don't tell me he or she's the opposite of Malus," I said dryly.

"What?" she asked, before she shook her head. "No, the stories are unrelated. Well, sort of. If Malus is the monster you tell children about to make them behave, Invictus is the one you tell them about to get them to go back to sleep. He's the mythical Icon of Challengers but again, no evidence because unlike all the other good Icons he's never actually shown up. Actually, people used to say he wasn't an Icon at all, but something older, more powerful, that predated all the monsters and Dark Icons. He was the imaginary hero that was ready for them when they came, and the reason they never destroyed us all. But there's no evidence of any of that, because if that happened nobody ever bothered to write about it. All we've got is a few random people—usually kids—that credit certain acts of salvation to him. And they never explain why."

"That actually sounds disturbingly familiar." I said carefully. Because a lot of people thought that about all the deities in my world. Especially mine —or rather, my dad's.

I wasn't a hundred percent sure what I believed at the moment.

"Yes, I heard a lot of faiths back in your world work that way, especially the monotheistic ones," Breena said, raising her hands as if to avoid offense. "And all of them have more basis for belief than Invictus. There are at least enough sightings or other circumstantial evidence of them, however contested, to form groups, churches or whatever. But Invictus only has a handful of old, extremely questionable sightings, and the last written mention of his name comes from the remains of a text that predates Stell by at least a millennium. That's all we've got."

"Okay," I said carefully. "So I'm getting messages about two people or Icons, or whatever you want to call them, that I've never heard about. So it can't be a hallucination."

"I know," Breena grumbled. "So it must have been a side effect of the curse. I'll have Stell and Guineve look at it when we get back."

"Okay," I gave up. It had been a long day. I had killed something for the first, second, third, and more times in my life, seen tiny people be horrifically and revoltingly abused, and then rejected recruitment from their abusers and a gross hell-pit. I was done trying to make sense.

"You said you wanted to look around to make sure it's safe, right?" I asked Breena. "Can you do that on your own while I guard the entrance to your friends?"

Thanks to Breena's healing, I had recovered most of my vital points, and resting had restored about half of my magic power. But I still felt all out of sorts from the experience and didn't feel like another adventure at the moment.

"That's fine," Breena said. "I'm faster than you anyway. And, Wes?" She was staring at me, looking a little concerned. "Even if a bunch of things we don't understand happened, you did *fantastic* today. Guineve and Stell are going to be really impressed. And even though I yelled a lot, I'm really impressed too."

She smiled as she said that last part, and her face glowed a little brighter than the rest of her.

"Thanks," I said, still feeling a bit numb. "I'm just... going to sit here for a bit and guard the door."

"Sure," she said with an understanding smile. "I'll be back."

She was gone in a trail of pink. I reflected that if this all was some crazy part of my brain, then I had a serious problem with fairies.

Then another part of my mind spoke up, and asked what it said about my mind if I had dreamed up the Horde, and all the things I saw them do, and their invitation to lead them to do more of those things?

I didn't like any answer I could come up with.

A twig snapped some distance away.

I figured it was just an animal and didn't get up.

Then I remembered that the Horde had eaten all the animals around here.

And that Breena and the other fairies didn't walk and weren't heavy enough to snap twigs even if they did.

I swore and leaped up, drawing my new sword. The arm holding the weapon twitched to correct its positioning, then twitched again when I asked it how it knew to do that.

I barely noticed a whirlwind of green and brown bound over to me, landing less than ten feet away. Still, somehow my weapon had tracked my new guest the whole time.

Not that it mattered. This time, I had brought a two-foot sword to a spear fight.

The woman landed in a crouch, with long, lean limbs covered in brown and green leather sleeves and leggings. *Camouflage,* my brain pointed out helpfully. *She's wearing camouflage.* She also had a stiff, studded leather chest-plate over her upper torso. Her head was bare, save for a short cloak around her neck that had her hood put away. Her nose and mouth had a tint of wild to them, reminding me something of either a hawk or wolf, and I couldn't make up my mind as to which. Her eyes and hair were both a type of rich, healthy brown that reminded me of good quality wood—dark chestnut for her eyes, and a lighter shade for the wavy locks that escaped her braids. A tattoo of blue swirls so detailed I would get lost trying to puzzle it out crawled from the side of her cheek up to her temple, just next to her hairline. In a savage, queen-of-the-wood way, she was every bit of beautiful.

She was also pointing a metal-tipped spear at my chest.

To my surprise, I was still holding my sword in a way that would have deflected her attack.

"Please don't," I found myself saying calmly. "I've already had a bad day."

She glared at me for another minute longer, looking every bit like she was going to knock my puny weapon away and pin me to the tree stump behind me. Then, after a snort and a smirk, she relaxed and lowered her weapon.

"Challengers," she grumbled. "Cocky, the whole lot of ya."

She looked around. Then she glared at me again.

"Now what's this about Horde in me Woadlands?"

Her accent gave off a distinctly Celtic feel, sounding close to Scottish or Irish, but distinct enough to where I could still tell that it wasn't either. Not that I had heard a lot of Scottish or Irish people talk.

"Breena is looking to make sure that we got them all, but all the ones in this hole are dead. Including what looked like their leader. Also, I'm Wes. May I please know your name?"

I'm doing awesome, I thought. Even after a long day, I had caught someone sneaking up on me, kept my weapon ready, talked her down from a fight, and now I was remembering my manners and trading names. Mom would be proud of that, I figured.

She cocked her head at me, waves and braids of brown fluttering as she did so.

"Ye really don't know me name?"

"No ma'am," I said, giving up on looking cool and leaning on a nearby stump. *Sorry Mom. All tapped out.* "So far I have talked to one brightly colored bird—courtesy of Breena translating, - a handful of sprite-folk too injured to really talk, and one antlered creep that needed me to kill him too much for us to have a really healthy conversation. Not a single creature I've met here has had the courtesy to update me on introductions. If I had to guess though," I leaned slightly forward. "You're either one of the two female Icons, or that Woad Princess my mind-screen told me about earlier. Merada, maybe? Can I guess Merada, the Woad Princess? Without getting stabbed?"

She blinked at me for a moment and didn't reply. Then a titter leaked out of her scowl. She clamped her mouth shut, but it leaked out again.

Then her head tilted back, and she started chuckling. Her hand moved up to cover her mouth, but then it gave up and started clutching her side while her chuckle deepened. She laughed at me for a solid thirty seconds, occasionally raising a finger as if to say she needed to get serious, and failing each time. Finally, her laughter petered off, and she looked up at me.

"Guess I needed that. Thank ye. And ye're right. I'm Merada. A part of Stell down here, in charge of this local world. So everyone here's under me watch. Now." Her voice became serious. "I was late to the party, and I'll own that. How many of me little ones did I lose?"

I sighed, and her mouth twitched in response, her hard face quivering again for a moment.

"None," I said. "And before you..."

Too late.

"What do ye mean none?" the brunette warrior princess demanded angrily. "Ye expect me to believe a wee one like ye with just one Rise to his name swooped down and saved all me little ones in one hour? From somethin' the Icons still have nightmares about, even after thousands of years? Are ye tryin' to puff yer chest up and impress me? Or spare me feelings?"

"Yeah, no," I replied, my voice sagging with fatigue. "I'm not up for a second round of this. Breena!" I called out in a hoarse voice.

"Do ye not know this is serious?" the beautiful amazon growled at me. "I knew these little ones as well as she did! Watched them grow into their own. This was supposed to be the safest part of the Woad, where we could leave them to play and not even worry about beasts. And ye tell me ye were able to swoop down and save them all, after the Horde's been here for over a day!"

"They were here that long?" I asked, then shook my head. Another thing that could be explained after a nap, a real one not brought on by blood loss. "Never mind. Breena!" I called out again. "One of Stell's aspects is here! Come talk to her!"

"Aspects?" Merada asked, momentarily forgetting her anger.

"I was afraid 'sister,' 'daughter,' or 'clone' would be more offensive."

"Good guess, though just use 'Satellite' in the future," the amazon replied with a snort. Then, after a moment, she spoke again. "Are our little ones really okay?" Her voice took on a worried tone. "Are ye really tellin' me the truth?"

"As far as I know," I said with another sigh. "Look, every sprite I talked to said there were only seven of them, and seven are all alive. They're hurt and traumatized, but Breena said they'll all make a full recovery."

"Icons," the brown-haired woman breathed. "How in the Lost Deeps did you pull that off? Usually the Horde starts puttin' people in its Pit with this much time."

"I'm not sure," I admitted, noting her use of the phrase 'Lost Deeps.' It sounded like there was a story behind that term that would have to be explained at a later time—especially since it wasn't the first time I'd heard it. "All I know is that I did something that was supposed to be impossible, and Breena won't stop yelling at me about it."

Merada tilted her head at that.

"Sounds like something yer kind would do. I got the message about the Pit when it was destroyed," she added. "That's how we found there was Horde to begin with, and that ye had a hand in their destruction. What took care of the Pit?"

"That's another thing that Breena won't stop yelling at me about, so I'm not going to be the one explaining it."

"But I was already yellin' at ye," the brunette woman pointed out.

"I know." I smiled. "Consider my silence as your punishment." There was a fiery bluntness to her personality that actually wound up being really attractive, even if I was too tired and cranky to fully appreciate it.

She narrowed her eyes at me, but the brown pupils were twinkling, and she was smiling back.

"Yer lucky I believe ye about me little ones bein' okay. Where are they?"

"They're too weak to fly long distances yet," I said, lifting my hand to point down the hole. "So I'm outside to guard the only entrance in. But they're all down there. If you want to see them for yourself, or if you can heal better than Breena, you're welcome to go down there and see them."

She looked down where I was pointing and bit her lip.

"Can they hear me if I call to them?" she asked. "And are ye sure ye got all the Horde?"

I shrugged.

"Down there, certainly. We think we got every single one up here as well, but Breena's flying around and checking to make sure. If you want to wait and help me guard up here, I'll understand."

"Good," she replied, coming to a decision. "No offense, but ye look tired and I'm a fair bit stronger than ye."

"None taken," I replied. "I get the feeling that you've been doing this a lot longer than I have."

"Damned right," she replied with another snort. "Would have gotten here faster if Stell had teleported me like she had you."

"Yeah, why didn't she?" I asked. "That seems like it would be a really good idea."

"Politics," the beautiful woman huffed. "Poppin' across the world instantly takes a lot of power and makes all the Icons nervous. That's why only Avalon is allowed to do so, and only fer a Challenger."

"Huh," I replied. I had never thought about what instantaneous travel would do for a world. Especially with one that still had people running around with spears and swords.

I was too tired to think of the idea any further though, and if Breena took too long coming back, I knew I was going to say something that would make the fiery princess next to me either laugh again or stab me. I didn't have the energy left to appreciate the first or stop the second.

Thankfully, Merada had no problem with me being too tired for any more conversation. I saw her eyes move back and forth, scanning the trees and shrubbery. She seemed to be listening intently for any more enemies and doing a much better job at it than I was doing.

Then her head suddenly whipped to the right. Her body and spear followed an eye-blink later, then both relaxed a tiny bit. A moment later, I heard a faint zipping sound.

A pink, familiar and faintly sparkling figure zipped into view, suddenly circling around Merada. The amazon princess gave a wide smile at the sight, then tilted her head toward the fairy and nuzzled the tiny figure embracing her cheek.

"Hey little me," the brown-haired woman said to the currently six-inch figure. "You okay?"

"Horde were here," the pink woman croaked, and I saw the stressed, tough exterior my tiny companion had been wearing suddenly break apart at the seams. "Horde were *here*, Merada! In our safest forest! With my most vulnerable cousins!"

"I know, I know," Merada said in a low, comforting voice. "Shh. Everyone's okay, though, right?"

"Sylt, Beryl and Elm were all hurt," Breena sobbed. "And Petal-bell was put in the pit!"

"The pit?" Merada's eyes widened. She shot me her most vicious glance yet. "Ye bastard! Ye said no one died!"

"They didn't!" I said quickly, some of my tiredness evaporating at the sight of her spear rising. "For the love of God! Breena, explain!"

"He pulled her out," my fairy companion whispered with a sniff. "He just reached in with his bare hands and yanked her out."

"What?" the Woad Princess asked. "How? That's impossible! He's human! It would have corrupted his hands! Especially an Earth-man's!" Her eyes darted to my hands, as if to confirm that they were still attached.

"I really don't know what to tell you people," I said with another sigh. "Apparently everything I did down there was impossible and I had no idea at the time. I'm sorry. I've been a very bad boy. I promise I didn't break the rules on purpose."

"Oh," Merada said. She looked down at Breena. "Ye should have told him about the Pit, Breena. We're lucky he didn't die."

"I know," the tiny woman sniffled. The cuteness of the act somehow broke through my crankiness. "But they were breaking all around me, and I just got overwhelmed. I thought we would've found gibber-kin, Mer. Gibber-kin aren't a threat to fairies at all! But they were Horde and they were breaking my cousins' legs and..."

"Shh," the brunette woman said, raising a hand to calm her tiny friend. "It's okay. Everyone's okay, right? We can fix limbs. Petal-bell survived the pit too, right? So that means she'll get better too, right?"

Breena sniffled again and nodded.

"They're already getting better," she said. "He got everyone in time. He even beat the pit's champion on his own."

"Really?" The warrior princess looked at me again, and I think I finally saw a bit of respect in that gaze.

I shrugged though, because the respect was unmerited.

"He was shorter than me by about two feet, and I think I had the better magic."

"And the better weapon, too, by the looks of it." She nodded toward the short sword still in my hand, eyes narrowing as she measured me.

"No, that was his," I admitted. "I had a stick, but it broke on his head."

"Stell said the armory was empty," Breena muttered sheepishly.

"How did ye kill it then?" Merada asked, incredulous. "Pit champions have strong vital pools! And spell-worked bodies!"

"Maybe that's why his own horn worked so well on him," I said with another shrug.

She actually blinked at that, then looked back at the little fairy floating next to her cheek.

"He was like this the whole time," Breena grumbled. "All like, 'look Breena, an ambush! But it's okay, because I know exactly what to do even though I've never done this before! I'm gonna combo a bunch of spells together and do martial arts and make you look bad the whole time! On my very first day of the job!'"

"My voice doesn't really sound like that," I protested.

And I wasn't trying to make her look bad.

"Does too," she argued.

"Wait, wait," Merada interrupted. "He's only had his first Rise, right?"

"Yep," Breena answered. "And he slapped Ilklings around like he had been beating little kids his whole life."

"I have not!" I protested. "I've never struck a child, ever! And it's not hard to fight monsters that are only half your height when you can do magic!"

"He blew up the Pit too," Breena muttered. "Without permission."

"Damn it, Breena!" I snapped. "Stop being such a little snitch!"

"Well I have to be because you're a big giant cheater that just cheats and cheats!"

"Stop, stop," Merada interrupted us. She looked at me again, and that smirk was back. "Alright Mister Big and Strong Challenger, maybe ye should just calm down and realize ye are yellin' at a little fairy the size of yer palm, and no one wins arguments like that. And Breena, why don't we just say 'thank ye' to the young man who's had just as bad a day as ye have and hasn't even been rewarded for it yet."

"I tried to reward him!" Breena protested. "But when I kissed him he got all shy!"

Just like that, my cheeks started boiling.

Probably because of the heat, I decided.

"Can I just go back?" I asked, giving up on the conversation. "The Horde's all dead, right, Breena? You didn't find any more?"

"Nope, and since Merada's here it's probably safe. Titania's guards are still coming, aren't they?"

"They'll be here in minutes," the Amazon confirmed. "As soon as we got the message about the Horde, everyone dropped everythin' else to deal with this. The Icons'll want to meet with Stell later though, to go over about the Horde. Give yer young man a rest until then." She flashed me a bright smile.

"Um, thanks," I said, numb, tired and embarrassed. "Do we walk through another portal or something?"

"I'm on it," Breena said distractedly, while moving her hands in a circle. "Just give me a second, Mister Cheater McRedCheeks."

"Hey!" I retorted, long before I came up with anything witty to say.

"Breena," Merada admonished again. "Don't tease the big strong virgin. He might get scared and not come back." The brunette amazon turned to look at me. "Speaking of which, I reckon I should apologize to ye about yer welcome, and thank ye properly myself. Since now's not a good time, I'll have to make it up to ye some other night," she said, the last part with a wink.

"Wait," I said, working through the implications of what she was offering. "What?"

A zap sounded behind me, and a swirling circle blurred into existence.

"Hey!" Breena suddenly shouted. She flew away from the portal she had just formed and flew back in front of Merada's smirking face. "Operational security, missy! And no cutting in line! You be good and wait for your turn!"

"Fine," Merada said, still smiling. "But don't take too long on getting bigger, lass."

My brain heard those last two lines, ran them through processing, then spat them back out with a loud *snap.*

"Wait," I repeated, reaching into my broken head-box to find something else to say, and failing. *"What?"*

"Time to go!" Breena said cheerfully. "Come on, Wes!"

"But," I protested as my brain began to garble. "Buh? Wha? Znuh?" That last one sounded like my best word right now, so I stuck with it. "Znuh?"

"Come on, Wes!" Breena repeated. "Stell's waiting for us! Bye, Merada!"

"Say hi to Guineve and Stell for me," the brunette woman replied, winking at me again. "Take care, Mister Big Strong Virgin!"

Before I could say anything else, tiny hands pulled hard enough on my collar to drag me through the portal.

17

HOPE UNEARTHED

For a moment, the world dissolved into a riot of bright colors. Then it passed, and I was back in Avalon's mists.

"Huh," Breena said with a frown. "That took longer than I thought. Next time, don't distract me when I'm building a bridge."

"Znuh?" I repeated again.

"Fiddlesticks," Breena sighed. "We broke the virgin. Come on, we'll find Guineve or Stell and get you something to eat."

"Food?" I asked, trying out the word and deciding I liked it. "I can have food here?"

"Duh," my bonded companion said, rolling her bright eyes. "Why couldn't you eat food here?"

Seeing my dazed look, the glowing little woman sighed again, as if to give up on talking to me altogether. She grew to just over two feet and latched onto one of my shirt sleeves. With a *"come on!"* she tugged me through Avalon's mists until I reached a glade.

As if by magic, the smell of food wafted into my nose, and Breena no longer needed to pull me.

There was a table set up nearby. I wandered over to it in a daze. I saw Guineve setting a plate of some kind of doughy bread with all kinds of savory toppings and fruit next to it. The raven-haired woman smiled at me as I approached.

"Well look who's back in time for lunch," the tall woman said cheerfully. "Did you already finish your first Challenge so fast?"

"Uh-huh," I nodded dumbly. "Why is there food?" I asked. Another full sentence. My brain was probably back.

"Because we need to eat, silly," Breena interrupted before Guineve could reply. "Guineve, is there enough food for him? He won, but he overworked himself and was bitten and stabbed and cursed and yelled at and flirted with too much. So we broke him. Food fixes guys, right?"

"As I recall, it does. Sit down, dear, and have some bread and fruit. Sorry there's no coffee yet."

My stomach took over for my brain and directed my actions here on out.

That was fortunate, because I was still working out what would happen if my projected body ate here, and my stomach was smart enough not to bother with any of that. If I could bleed, I could eat, and that was that.

Still, after a couple of bites of really, really good bread topped with all kinds of tasty sausage and cheeses, I began to wonder something.

"Guineve," I said after swallowing. "How do you cook here? And where do you get the cheese and meat?"

"They come from animals, dear," the raven-haired woman said sweetly. "And I have all kinds of methods to cook. Here, have a glass of mist-juice."

"Oooh! Can I have one too?" Breena asked with a flutter.

"Of course, darling. I already made you one."

Mist-juice somehow tasted clear like water and sweet like fruit at the same time. It was incredibly refreshing.

But was it really safe to drink? my mind wondered. *These things are made on another planet and—*

Brain, my stomach interrupted. *Shut up and let me eat.*

One light, yet incredibly refreshing, meal later, it became much easier to think coherently. I realized that I had been in this place much longer than I had the previous times I had gone to sleep. In fact, I remembered that I hadn't even gone to bed before I had come here.

"How are you feeling now, dear?" Guineve asked in a motherly tone.

"Much better, thank you," I replied, examining the goblet I had drunk from. Breena was currently inside a similar goblet, slurping loudly.

"How did your first Challenge go? Did everything turn out alright?" Guineve asked, her gray eyes studying me as she spoke.

I sighed. Now that I had food in me, it was a lot easier to go back to my earlier strategy of taking the things I couldn't understand in stride.

"It went... okay. I guess. People got hurt, so I wish I had gotten there faster, but no one died, and everyone told me they'd make a full recovery. I got bitten once, and I messed up and let another monster stab me a couple times in the thigh. Apparently, he was able to curse me as well. Breena thinks I've recovered from everything but the curse."

A hint of concern flashed in Guineve's gray eyes.

"Was Breena not able to fix your curse?"

"I was able to stop the blood-loss component," my fairy piped from her cup.

"But I'm seeing names of dead Icons, apparently," I finished. "If Malus existed at all."

Guineve flinched as she stood over me. She hid it so well, I barely noticed. If I hadn't been watching for her reaction, I would have thought she was just turning to look at something.

"I see," she said simply. "We'll take care of it. Stell's busy right now, so I'll run some magic on you while you rest."

"What's Stell doing?" I asked. I didn't comment on the fact that she probably knew I saw her reaction.

"The Icons of the Woadlands apparently found your Challenge noteworthy. They wanted to talk to Stell about it."

"It was!" Breena piped again. She actually stuck her head out of the cup for that. "It was Horde, Guineve! And Wes killed them all! I only got to help with a couple!"

"Horde," Guineve said calmly, and there was another subtle flinch. "You're sure, Breena?"

"They looked exactly like I remembered," my friend squeaked. "It was just the small ones though. We were lucky."

"Indeed," the tall woman replied quietly. "Would you like any more food, Wes?" She sounded distracted, which was abnormal for the stately woman.

"No ma'am. That was perfect, thank you." It was really filling, despite being a light meal. "I take it Stell might want to talk to me now? Should I go during her meeting or wait afterward?"

"You were right," Breena squeaked. "He's much smarter when he's not hungry."

"Quiet, you," I replied. I slid over the rest of my mist drink as a distraction. Breena made a happy chirp and took the bait immediately.

"Stell will want to see you now, Wes," Guineve replied, pointing out with one hand. "Don't worry about interrupting the meeting. The Icons will mostly just thank you for your work and will ask Stell all the hard questions. Walk through the path between the trees out in that direction, and you'll get there within thirty steps."

"Thank you," I said while standing up. I noticed that there was actually a trail this time, though it was made of tiny white pebbles. I said my goodbyes —Breena opted to stay with the mist-juice—and headed for the path up ahead.

As I walked by, Guineve took my arm in a gentle, but firm, grip.

"*Do* worry about mentioning Malus to the Icons," Guineve said quietly. "The Icons are going to be agitated enough with the reappearance of the Horde. Avoid mentioning Malus to Stell for now, also." Guineve's voice changed again, as if it was quivering. "The name is a bit of a trigger for her, and she won't want to explain why."

"...Alright," I said quietly, and carefully. "I'll keep the details to a minimum."

"Just tell them the types and numbers of Horde you found, and their local champion," Guineve whispered. "The Woadlands' Icons are a decent group, but the Horde triggers many dark memories for them. Don't make anyone over-speculate."

"I'll try," I promised, and when she loosened her grip, I nodded farewell and walked off.

Thirty steps later, I had arrived to the location Guineve mentioned.

There was another open clearing, with white marble-tiled floor covering most of the ground. Here and there were broken columns, and in the center were five giant pillars of light- green, gold, pink, brown, and in the very center, azure-blue.

I walked forward slowly, noticing that four of the pillars formed a semicircle around the blue one. As I walked closer, I could see the shapes in each.

The shortest figure was my height, while the rest were from eight to a dozen feet tall. The green light had a shapely eight-foot-tall woman dressed in leaves, with flowers blossoming in a circle around her auburn hair. The figure in the gold light was the most muscular man I had ever seen, easily twice my height, and bronze-colored, as if he was made out of that very metal. Silver chain links formed a hauberk over his chest and shoulders, and his powerful arms were crossed over his chest. Adorning his feather-like brown hair were the two most impressive antlers I had ever seen, making the Horde wretch I had fought earlier look like a cartoon mascot on a mug. Next to him, in the pink light, was what looked like that fairy godmother out of that ancient movie about Oz. She was my height, clothed in a sparkling white dress, with similarly colored gauze wings flapping slowly behind her. Her hair was a rainbow of shimmering colors adorned with a white tiara, and her face seemed to be etched in a permanent smile. She even had a tiny glass wand in her hands.

The brown light had a figure about nine feet tall, but he was floating in the air, lying down as if he were on an imaginary couch. He looked utterly relaxed, with boyish blonde hair and a rogueish grin etched onto his face. His chest was bare muscle, toned except for his belly. His legs ended in brown-furred hooves that hung in the air as if they were resting on a footstool.

They were all circled around Stell, who stood in the blue light. She still had her earlier dark-skinned appearance, but superimposed over her body was a giant blue outline that suspiciously resembled Guineve. As they talked, the outline mimicked most of Stell's gestures and movements, but did so in Guineve's composed way. I almost blurted out a question, but then realized that Stell was probably maintaining the appearance for any number of reasons.

"Here he is," Stell said, and as she did so the outline confidently pointed over to me. "I had allowed him a bit of rest to recover from the ordeal, but this is the man responsible for ending the threat on your world. Wes Malcolm, of Earth." Now the outline's head turned to acknowledge me, pointing to each light as she spoke.

"Wes Malcolm, before you are the Icons who oversee the world you just visited: Mother Glade." The woman wreathed in flowers nodded. "The Stag Lord." The massive armored man inclined his horns. "Lady Titania." The fairy queen actually stepped forward and curtsied. "And last, but not least, Great Pan."

The hooved, floating figure made a lazy wave, and then spoke.

"Lady Starsown is too kind. Prithee, Challenger, pay me no such extra respect."

"Noted," I replied with a bow. "It is an honor to meet all of you. Even you, last, definitely least, but-still-Great Pan."

The first three Icons either smiled or quietly chuckled (or tittered, in Lady Titania's case). Stell's Guineve outline just smiled, while Stell herself hissed at me with shocked eyes. But the goat-man started hooting.

"Oh, I *knew* I'd like him," the goat-man laughed.

You have gained more favor with Great Pan. He holds you in even higher esteem.

Under her calm outline, Stell sighed in relief.

"No more jokes, okay?" she begged. "That won't work every time."

"I'll move to my best behavior," I promised. But I knew I had made the right call with the guy who looked like a satyr version of Peter Pan.

The fairy queen stepped forward again, wings fluttering slightly as she glided closer to me.

"I understand I have you to thank for the rescue of my great-great-grandchildren, young Challenger. My servants have just recovered them. Though harmed, they are all whole. Had you not been successful, we would have assumed they would have still been safe, since most Challenges are not harmful to the fairy folk. Had you not been so swift and brave, some of my children would have been permanently lost, which is also rare for a sprite." The sparkling queen lowered her head, closing her eyes briefly. "We had become comfortable in our security, and had thought old foes to be gone for good. We were wrong, and but for you, it would have cost me my dearest children."

Her voice had a musical tone to it, and I couldn't help but detect a faint kinship to Breena in the queen sprite. How it existed, I had no idea.

Stell and her projection stepped forward, making a gesture with her hand.

"Indeed. I had thought the Horde to be gone for good as well. I had no idea I was sending my newly Risen Challenger into an ancient evil's nest, so he knew less of the Horde than any of us. We must all be more careful in the future."

"He knew nothing at all, and was still victorious?" the giant antlered man rumbled. "He was either very fortunate or very skilled."

I could feel his golden-brown orbs search over me, trying to measure my strength.

Sensing permission from Stell, I stepped forward to answer him, shaking my head to do so.

"I'd have to go with fortunate," I answered honestly. "Though sadistic and disgusting, the creatures I fought were the size of small children on my world and fought just as badly. Their champion barely came up to my shoulder, though he was armed."

"Whose champion was he?" The Stag Lord asked.

"After his death, I learned he was marked by the Bloody-Horned Huntsman."

"That ill-bred dog dares to surface again," the giant man growled. "And to ally with the Horde. You have done me a personal favor, Challenger. Bloody-Horns is an old enemy of mine."

"He has done us all a favor," the woman with flowers in her hair uttered. "The Horde's presence alone harms my woods like no other. In saving Titania's blood-children, preventing my domain's direct corruption, and in slaying a champion of the Stag's mortal enemy, you could say that he has personally done us each a great boon."

"Eh," Great Pan said. "I had no true stake, but I really like his style. He didn't even let any of us know he was visiting our world. By the time we found out he had arrived, he was halfway done with solving our problems for us!"

"That's... one way to put it," Mother Glade muttered.

"I must apologize," Stell said quickly. "I did not have time to instruct him on greeting a world's Icons, so I assumed it would be best that he was sent to deal with the problem directly. I then notified you all personally. But I was as surprised as you to discover the Horde's existence."

"What level of Horde would we classify this nest as?" the horned giant rumbled again.

Stell looked at me, so I answered the question.

"I identified the smallest monsters as something called Ilklings, while the champion was apparently an empowered Wretch. There were no more than thirteen monsters total, and I saw no other types."

"A Smear then," Mother Glade said simply. "At that size, the nest had been in existence for less than two days. You were right in moving so quickly, Lady Starsown."

"Thank you." Stell's projection nodded at the Icon regally. "I will now explain the names we are using to the Challenger."

She turned to look at me, and continued speaking.

"The different groups of Horde are classed by both species and population. A Smear usually consists of a dozen or so Ilklings, like the ones you have encountered, led by a Wretch who is empowered both by the Smear's Pit and by a local Dark Icon to serve as its Champion. Know that every Horde Pit will have one champion. The champion will both protect the Pit and work to make it grow, because the champion will grow in power as the Pit does.

"A Smear grows rapidly. If it stays unchecked for enough time, no more than a month but as little as a week, depending on the prey and resources available, it will grow into a Stain. A Stain consists of over a hundred Ilklings, a dozen or so normal Wretches, and one empowered Mongrel. In as little as a month, or no longer than a season, a Stain will grow into an Outbreak, consisting of thousands of Ilklings, hundreds of normal Wretches, scores of normal Mongrels, a dozen empowered Mongrels, and one empowered Spawn. An Outbreak usually requires a small army to deal with and there will always be heavy casualties, even if the Outbreak is repelled. If it is not, several population centers will be lost before the end of the year, and the outbreak will progress to a Contagion. A Contagion consists of at least ten thousand Ilklings, thousands of Wretches, several hundred Mongrels, scores of Spawn and one empowered Brute. These numbers assume the Horde have only overrun one population center. They will increase drastically for every settlement overrun, and I have seen this number increase by as much as thirteen times. At this level the local country will be considered to be suffering an invasion and usually must mobilize its entire army to deal with the threat. If it fails, then the Horde will conquer, consume, and enslave the country—in that order—and the Contagion will progress to a full-on Plague. Plagues have hundreds of thousands of both Ilklings and Wretches, thousands of Mongrels, hundreds of Spawn, dozens of Brutes, and one empowered Terror with his own dozen Dark Champions. A Plague will constantly replenish its losses and will attempt to conquer an entire continent, growing further with more conquered territory and population."

Both Stell and her projection looked at me with a steady gaze. "A Plague needs a minimum of five years to form. It is realistic for a Nightmare," she paused before mentioning that word, "the next category of Horde size, to form after claiming a continent and conquering the rest of the world, in as few as ten years. That's just what we've seen. Keep in mind that if the Horde manages to conquer territory faster, it will grow more quickly than the above projections."

"Wow," I said. "That sounds extremely bad. How often is the Horde successful at conquering territory?"

The Stag Lord, who I was quickly taking to be the military man of the bunch, spoke up.

"The largest tribe in the Woadlands is just over a hundred thousand strong, and only half of that number can serve as warriors of any sort, meaning they are able to hold a weapon and have the strength to swing it several times. Only a third of that number would be a match for the average Mongrel, and only the champions would be a match for most Spawn. The tribe's king or hero may be a match for a normal Brute, but I doubt it. Therefore, know that the largest of Contagions are easily a match for the largest nation in the Woadlands, and that a Plague would almost certainly ravage a great part of our world."

That was... brutal. Especially given the size of this world. I mean, my country back home still fielded a total army of about a million troops total.

"But an even worse aspect of the Horde is its willingness to submit to other dark powers," Mother Glade interjected. "Even at the later stages, there are many monsters far more powerful than all but the strongest species of Horde. But if something or someone appears before a Horde Pit or champion and demonstrates sufficient amounts of both strength and depravity, the Horde will submit to the creature as their new ruler. Usually this ruler winds up amplifying the Horde, unlocking powers it would not otherwise have, and employing strategies it would not otherwise have thought of. It is said that the ruling creature will also develop new power and abilities from its bond with the Pit. This is why the Dark Icons were so eager to bless the Horde in the past."

"And we make them pay for it whenever they do," The Stag Lord rumbled. "My brother will answer for this."

I remembered how both the pit and its champion had responded to me and felt very sick. But apparently no one noticed, because Stell continued talking.

"Generally, if a Plague or even a Contagion forms, several countries, or tribes, in the case of the Woadlands, will band together, supported by the Icons and hopefully a Challenger to end the threat, which is by then a Trial or even a Tumult-level challenge."

"Has every world always been able to stop the Horde?" I asked, then realized it would have been a stupid question. These things sounded like Sauron on steroids, only creepier. A world that was overcome by the Horde was probably no longer around.

"No," Stell answered simply, to my dismay and surprise. The other Icons lowered their heads. Even Pan looked somber at that moment.

"Do you have any further questions for my Challenger?" Stell asked, her projection nodding calmly at the other figures.

"The creation of a Horde Pit is disturbing," The Stag Lord rumbled again. Apparently, the other Icons were content to let him do most of the talking. But the way they stood together gave me a suspicion that Mother Glade was at least his equal, and Lady Titania wasn't that far behind.

I had no idea how Pan ranked, and I don't think he cared to find out himself.

"Did you see anything to suggest the means of its creation?" the horned man continued. "Any signs of another party involved?"

"I don't know," I answered simply. "But I'm not sure I'd know what to look for. The cavern they were resting in was natural for the first half. They had torches that looked to be lit by the oil that drips from them. The pit itself and its nearby rooms and halls were of worked stone. The stonework's quality improved the closer I got to the pit. There were many types of dead animals and the fairies were kept alive and in cages. The only equipment I saw the Horde use was this sword I took off the champion." I held the weapon up for viewing. "And a loincloth he wore, that I didn't have any interest in." Great Pan chuckled at that. "No other creature was there, save the victims. I have no idea whether the monsters can do their own stonework or not, so I don't know if they built the structure or just took it over."

The Icons seemed satisfied by my answer, or at least they didn't direct any further questions toward me.

They asked Stell a few more questions, mostly about things I didn't understand and didn't feel like finding out at that time because my brain was overloaded. But I gathered that they were concerned as to how the Horde Pit had formed in the first place, and were all committed to locate anyone with the knowledge to do so and visit upon them all sorts of unpleasantness. I couldn't find it in me to disagree with them.

"Thank you for your time, Lady Starsown," Mother Glade said formally. "Challenger Wes Malcolm, I will say again that you have done us all a great favor. After this meeting, I hope you understand the degree of the threat you have averted. Not only that, but you have both made it more difficult for a new incursion of Horde to form, and enabled us to recognize its reappearance faster. I cannot speak for the Icons on other worlds, but know that you have each of our favor. May it strengthen you as you seek to perform further heroism. With the Lady of Avalon's permission?"

The flower-wreathed woman looked to Stell, who gave a stately nod.

Some of the light surrounding each figure formed separate beams and flowed over to me. My body hummed as they touched me, and I felt a stirring in me similar to what I had felt after destroying the pit.

Challenger Wes Malcolm, my mind-screen said. *You have completed in advance the first part of a Challenge directly issued by the Four Great Icons of the Woadlands, thereby receiving the reward all creatures gain from overcoming the Challenges of Avalon's worlds. A further Challenge has been issued, to find the mortal or creature responsible for bringing the Horde back into existence, and further thwarting said creature. You will be rewarded further as you overcome each Challenge.*

Right, I forgot. In these worlds I get stronger every time I overcome an obstacle.

Mother Glade now holds you in high esteem.

The Stag Lord now holds you in high esteem.

Lady Titania now holds you in high esteem.

Great Pan's impression of you is unchanged. But he would still drink a beer with you if he could.

That last one cracked a smile out of me.

But apparently, I had done the equivalent of stopping a forest fire by putting out a spark, and everyone couldn't stop congratulating or rewarding me for it. At least I wasn't getting yelled at anymore. By now, I had figured out to avoid mentioning that I touched the Pit, and the Icons didn't ask questions about how I was able to destroy one.

The mighty lords and ladies soon said their goodbyes and took their leave, leaving me alone with Stell. Guineve's projection over her faded, and she shuddered, looking very tired. I opened my mouth to say something, and then closed it when she turned and hugged me.

"Thank you," she said as she put her face into my shoulder.

"Huh?" I asked eloquently, but returned the hug anyway. "For what?"

"For proving me right," the dark-skinned woman replied, not letting go or taking her head out of my shoulder. "This should have been the final problem that overwhelmed me. I shouldn't have even had a Challenger by now, but you showed up out of nowhere, didn't complain, and just took care of this for me. I'm sorry I didn't prepare you for fighting Horde."

"Yeah, well, punting them like footballs worked just fine," I said, trying to make a joke. It sounded a lot better in my head.

"I don't care," she mumbled. "You're getting better training. I'm not leaving you under-prepared again."

"Great," I decided to say. Stell let me hold her for almost another whole minute, then gently pulled away to be at arm's length. But she did not let go of my shoulders. I hesitated for a moment, then asked anyway:

"Stell? That comment earlier about Horde submitting to others, was it true?"

"Of course," she said, slightly startled. "It's happened in the past. Why?"

"How does the Horde know to submit to someone?" I persisted. "Is it just based on strength?"

"No, like Mother Glade said," Stell said shaking her head. "We've seen powerful figures cow them, then do something depraved to show they have the same goals. Why are you asking, Wes?"

"Has the Horde ever been wrong about someone?" I asked, still ignoring her next question. "Has it ever submitted to someone who didn't want their power or their desires? Have they ever submitted to a Challenger, Stell? Even once?"

Stell looked up at me.

"What?" she asked, clearly confused.

I was shaking now. Maybe I was shaking before and didn't realize it. Maybe I had been shaking the whole time and everyone was just pretending not to notice, trying not to judge the suspected pedophile's son who was being recruited by dark powers with even darker desires, because they saw him as a kindred spirit.

"I don't think so, Wes," Stell said calmly. "But if they have, all of the other Challengers rejected them and killed them afterwards. Isn't that what you did?"

"I told it to let Breena's friends go."

The words spilled right out of my mouth. *See me*, the intent behind them begged. *See me and find me to be good.*

"And then what did they do?" she asked slowly. She had a patient look about her face, like she had accepted something about me and had decided to just deal with it. I was scared to find out what.

"It was just the Wretch at that point," I said, looking at my memories instead of her. "Breena and I had killed all the Ilklings by then. But the Wretch bowed when he saw me near the fairies. He said he should have been expecting me. And when I said I wanted to free the little pixies, he thought I wanted to take them for myself. Thought I wanted a bride-meal, whatever the hell that was."

She nodded quietly, her eyes still looking up at me.

"Doesn't mean what you think it does," she said, thankfully sensing my disgust at the idea. "It means something far worse. I know you rejected him, though. Tell me what he did then."

I didn't answer for a second.

"Wes?" Stell continued. "I know you're horrified by this, and I know you've got something going on that makes you scared of yourself. It's okay. I'll take it as part of the package. But I know being recruited by that thing was probably a trigger for you, and you're wondering what it saw in you. But a Wretch is stupid, Wes. It probably mistook you for whoever, or whatever, brought the Pit into existence out there in the Woadlands. It was probably expecting to meet its creator, which means that we need to look for a human in that area, one that looks like you."

"Earth-man," I mumbled.

"What?" The beautiful brown woman cocked her head.

"Earth-man," I repeated. "It said it was expecting Earth-men. Just not this soon." Awareness struggled in the back of my head, and I stopped avoiding Stell's eyes. "It was expecting *many* Earth-men, Stell. And both it and the Pit spoke to me. Offered me power, and devotion. When I rejected them, they called me a traitor-prince.

"They said their father, whoever that was, would curse me. Make me pay for my treachery."

Stell blinked and sucked in a breath. Some of her calmness dissipated.

"Okay," she said slowly, after a few moments of silence. "That's supposed to be impossible, but so was the Horde coming back to begin with."

She stepped away from me for a moment, thinking.

"I don't know how people from your world can get here without being Called. You were the first, but Avalon still recognized you as a Challenger, someone who was here to help, immediately. As far as I know, no one from

Earth can get to any of the worlds without me at least knowing that they've arrived."

She started to pace in front of me.

"The Horde-being knew of a figure it called Father, which means it had some idea of meeting someone else. Since it said you were the first Earthling..." Her pace and speech were quickening. "Then 'Father' wasn't from Earth either, which means I shouldn't have to worry about anyone else from Earth crossing on their own. So something else is trying to instigate contact with your world, and the Horde was supposed to play a role in it."

"Couldn't 'Father' be that Dark Icon, the huntsman guy?" I asked, curious.

"Nope!" Stell replied with a smile and a snap of her fingers. "Ilklings and Wretches will venerate the Dark Icons, but they will never credit them with creation because the Icons cannot create Horde themselves. They need to empower a mortal to do so, and the process is complicated and not fully understood by anyone, even those that created Horde Pits in the past. I know because I've interrogated them. So someone else with knowledge of Earth is actually trying to contact Earth. Which is bad, but probably stoppable."

"Has that ever happened before?" I asked.

"No." Stell shook her head. "We get knowledge of Earth from Challengers, and I can scry the world occasionally, but your planet is regarded as the Silent Planet for a reason. Contact has been long lost. So long that any records of real contact with Earth have also been lost by all but a handful of the wisest scholars on each world."

"And would any of them try to contact my world?" I asked. Tired as I was, this still managed to fascinate me.

"Of course not," Stell said simply.

"Why?" I asked.

"Because they're not crazy," she replied. "Sorry," she added as I raised an eyebrow. "Let me explain. Despite the fact that the best Challengers come from Earth, and they have always done an incredible amount of good, your people are regarded as one of the most dangerous creatures on every single one of the other worlds, by the handful that know of you. Earthlings are just different."

"How so?" I asked.

"Well," Stell hedged. "Nobody's perfect but... you know how on Earth you will have people who do bad things, and no one can figure out why, including the culprits themselves? Like people who seem to kill for just no reason? Or at least no reason that really makes sense?"

"Yeah," I said slowly. "We call them serial killers. Because they keep doing it until you find them and stop them. We think."

"Right. Well, as far as I know, none of the other worlds have people like that."

For a moment I didn't say anything. Stell began talking again.

"Don't get me wrong," she said quickly. "People *do* murder. And steal. And such. But they always have a motive that everyone else can at least understand, even if they don't agree with it. But even then, things never seem to deteriorate to the degree compared to what I find in Earth. Even when you get away from the supposedly high-crime urban areas of your planet, people still seem to hold grudges longer, make friends outside their close networks more slowly. I can't check often, but every time I've been able to examine your world, I find it to be a place where the population has a stronger desire to cause harm than on any other world. For a final instance, take the Horde." She paused for a moment, speaking carefully. "Can you honestly say that you've never seen or heard of someone on Earth doing something just as disturbing? If not almost exactly the same thing?"

Damn, I thought. She had me there.

I shook my head reluctantly.

"Actually, I've read of even more graphic and disturbing acts being done by people with no discernible motive. And worse stuff being done during our wars."

"And how often does it happen?" she persisted. "Once or twice a decade?"

"In my neighborhood?" I asked.

"No, on the whole planet."

"I have no idea," I admitted. "Definitely more often than that, though. Probably once a day somewhere on the planet."

"Pangea is the most violent world under Avalon's influence," Stell replied. "And even there, I find a graphic torture-murder inflicted by non-monsters *maybe* once a century. People just aren't that motivated to hurt each other like that. I don't know why your planet's different," she added uncomfortably. "Maybe because you don't have other threats, like monsters?"

"I don't know either," I said. This conversation was getting uncomfortable fast. I didn't like hearing about how my place was 'full of the bad people.' "Why do you call from Challengers from Earth, if we're all so warped?"

“Wes,” Stell begged, eyes suddenly widening. “I didn't mean you—”

“Well, why didn’t you mean me?” I demanded. The back of my brain was saying to stop raising my voice. I ignored it. “Do you have some kind of tool that lets you check and see if someone is secretly very evil? Something more than a giant glowing rock that disagrees with everyone I live with back home? Are you expecting serial killers and sex criminals to leave behind warning signs before they engage in their behavior? Because on Earth, they don't, Stell. You just wake up one day, and find out someone, maybe even someone you know, started killing people, or has been hiding bodies under his house, or has been doing horrible things to little girls!”

“Wes...” she tried to beg again. I didn't let her. I didn't even realize I could stop talking.

“You just come home one day,” my words spilled out, “hoping to surprise the man you grew up wanting to be with something you did, hoping to make him proud. You grow up looking up to him, knowing that if you could be like him—heck, if you became just *half* the man he was, the world had better watch out, because you were gonna to do great things! Great things for everyone! You go straight to his office, hoping to make him proud with your news, but you can't, because now he's limp in his chair with a bloody hole in his head! He's dead, Stell! And the only thing he leaves you is a note that says he's done horrible things to little girls! That he's been living a lie his whole life, that he just woke up one day and couldn't take it anymore! And only after his death, Stell! Only after his death do his victims have the courage to come forward and out him! Only after his death! And he lied so well that, even after all of that, you just can't bring yourself to believe them! You think maybe the eight- and ten- and thirteen-year old little girls are the liars! You think maybe the victims are liars, Stell! Right when they need you to believe them the most! Do you know what that means, Stell? That means if he did it, then he hid it so well that he's still fooling you! He's still fooling you even while rotting in the ground with a hole in his head! And since you have the exact same genes—those are the things that make Earthlings do what they do, Stell—then maybe you're just the same! Maybe you'll wake up one morning and find that you've been lying to yourself too, and that you've also done all kinds of horrible things, and you can't face it, so you put a hole in your own head, just like your dad did, and you leave your family to deal with the consequences! So how do you tell, Stell? How do you tell if you've got a monster

Earth-man with you? Because we can't tell, Stell! We can't! Not even with our own family! Not even with ourselves!"

Just like that, my words became shouts, my shouts became screams, my screams became sobs. And I hadn't planned any of it. I had just wanted to ask her a simple question. Thought I was just mildly curious. I hadn't even realized she offended me. Then all of this just heaved out of me. And I must have tripped in the process, because I was on my knees bawling, hurting with every breath.

"Wes," I heard Stell say, her voice quivering. But I couldn't see her. Everything had gotten too blurry and wet. Must have been the blasted mist.

"How can you tell?" I heaved. God, breathing hurt so much right now.

Everything hurt so much.

"How can you tell?" I asked again. I couldn't stop. "How can you tell?"

"Wes, I can tell," Stell replied. My vision cleared a little. I realized I had made her cry again. "I can tell, Wes. Please listen."

She was standing over me. Her tear-stained eyes were begging me to look at her. And my ears were begging for an answer, so I turned to her. I had no idea how I must have looked right then. All I knew was my chest was still heaving, and that it hurt so very badly.

"I've tried to tell you, Wes. I told you about your Deeds, and I know you're not impressed with them. So I won't argue with you about that anymore. So I'll share a secret about me, and I'll just hope you won't tell anyone."

She knelt down next to me. When I started watching her face, she closed her eyes and hummed for a second. Her hair started to wave slightly behind her, even though there was no wind right now.

When she opened her eyes again, they were gray. Her ears had turned gray as well, and become sleeker, and slightly pointed.

"Choosing people to become Challengers isn't a job my race used to have," she said quietly. I was too mesmerized to interrupt, so she kept talking. "I don't know the whole story behind it. Maybe other Starsown used to. But I do know that we were given the responsibility by someone else, because of what we can see and hear from other races of people. When I see a person do something, Wes, I see that action... talk to them. And that person always talks back, without realizing it. They hold a conversation with their actions that no one else can see. It's not detailed, usually only one or two words that they say to each other back and forth, like their deeds and soul are agreeing with each other, or striving to do something. My ears hear it coming from the person."

She pointed to her two elf-like ears peeking out from her hair. They fluttered slightly. "And my eyes see the words written over the person."

She pointed to her gray pupils.

"Legends say that's why we were given the responsibility to anoint Challengers. I don't know who gave it to us. All I know is that we didn't appoint any Challengers until after almost a hundred generations of us.

"As soon as you came to Avalon, as soon as you accepted my request for help, something in you started talking with every step. When I invoked my power and called up your Deeds from Earth, I was able to see even more of the conversation your soul has with its surroundings. I can still see the results of the conversation you had with your actions even when you were in the Woadlands, Wes. Even when I wasn't there. Based on your actions, Wes, I've heard your heart and flesh cry out two things. Do you know what they are?"

"No." My voice was still hoarse. "What are they?"

She gave me a level gaze as she answered.

"Protect. Prevail."

Something inside my chest twitched when she said those words. I flinched as if I had heard someone call for me.

"Protect, and Prevail," she repeated, and for some reason I flinched again. She looked at me and nodded, like something had failed to surprise her.

"That's what you emanate, Wes," she continued. "That's the conversation you have with yourself when you think no one is looking. That's the obsession you have that leaks out when a Starsown watches or listens to you. You cry out inside to do those two things the most, and you cry out even more for something, or someone, to show you how to do those two things better. That's how I know you're okay, Wes. You can lie to yourself about your desires all day, you can even ignore what everyone else here sees in you. But as long as you walk and talk and do things you enjoy, you'll never hide who you are, and what you really want to be, from me or any other Starsown you come across."

"That's impossible," I muttered dumbly.

"No it's not," she retorted calmly. "And it's far less impossible than you coming to another world, and rescuing someone from an evil pit of despair, and blowing that same pit apart with lightning magic that normally doesn't work that way.

"And Wes?" Stell continued. "That's the other thing about your planet.

Even though all sorts of messed-up things happen, heroes *always* emerge. Always. No matter when I look, there's always over a hundred people on your planet standing up to some local tyrant or helping someone oppressed that they don't owe anything to. And they almost never get noticed. You're the most misrepresented one I've heard of, so much so that it surprised and outraged me, but you're not the first to not get enough credit. That's unique to your home too, Wes. If people on all my worlds stood up to evil the way some of you on Earth do, I'd never need to create Challengers. But I do, and even with all of your planet's other problems, I've always found the best champions come from Earth. And I've never been wrong about a single Challenger, Wes. I hope I can convince you," she finished. "That you can at least trust my judgment of you. Especially if you keep choosing to help me. So that you don't have to battle these fears and our own monsters at the same time. Is there a way I can help you? Or at least make you believe me?"

My breathing calmed. Her words were soothing to me. I could think again. And I began to realize that this fear really had a hold over me.

I usually kept it in the back of my mind. I didn't have an answer for it, and I was afraid I couldn't find one, so I told myself I didn't have time to pay attention to it. But ever since my dad's death, and ever since everyone else had started whispering about me, I had wondered if my fear was right. More than that, though, I wondered how to disprove it. But everything I did to try and be the person I wanted to be didn't work. Didn't remove the doubt. Instead, I began to doubt my actions, my hopes. I had started downplaying everything I did that I thought was right, so that I wouldn't put too much hope in it later, in case it failed and I turned to be a monster after all. *I can't fix me*, I realized. Or if I could, I could never know for certain. And I couldn't figure out how to stop doubting myself.

I had to find a way to believe Stell. That should have been crazy. I was asking myself to believe that I was traveling to another world, where I could talk to fairies and fight monsters and shoot lightning from my hands. No matter how real it all felt, no matter how rational and in control of my actions I felt, the very nature of this all called my sanity in question. I needed more proof. Something concrete.

Christina's phone call, and Chris' text came to mind, but that could have been some kind of coincidence. Or maybe that conversation was predicted by my subconscious. But if I could just have one more thing...

That was it, I decided to myself. If I could get one more piece of evidence, something I could take back with me, I'd be all in. No more reservations, for better or for worse. But how could that happen? I didn't think I could bring anything back from here. And honestly even if I could, owning a short sword would cause more problems back home than it solved.

I thought for a moment longer, then I had my answer.

"Stell," I asked. "You said I can keep some of the changes to my body, right? Some of this comes with me back home?"

"Yes, you will." The woman nodded. "We talked about this. That's part of the deal. You can't take any objects back, but some of the changes your Ideals cause, like balance and metabolism and such, and muscular improvement, carry over completely. So will any non-magical skills you learn. Spells never will. Your abilities, your Strength, Dexterity, Wisdom, will carry over by a fraction, usually ten percent. But the score you start out with is automatically treated as zero if it's 10 or lower. So if you raise your Strength here to a rating of 20, for example, your original's body strength will improve by two points."

"Since my original body's strength was 10, that means I'd have a rating of 12 back on Earth, right?"

"That's correct," Stell nodded.

"Would I be able to tell?" I asked carefully.

"Um," Stell hesitated. "Probably. Since it would represent an increase of muscle mass by about twenty percent. But your Constitution score also affects your appearance slightly as well. So would any Ideals that improve your slow-twitch and fast-twitch muscles."

"So if I want to be sure," I said slowly. "I need to raise both my strength and Constitution to 20."

"With the Ideals you've chosen, you should be able to see the change when you get back."

"What about Dexterity?" I asked. "Assume I find a way to increase all three ratings to 20. That would give me a twenty percent improvement to my balance as well, not counting whatever I get from the Ideal of Earth. Right?"

"You'd almost certainly feel an increase of that level, yes," the woman replied confidently.

"I," I started to say, then paused to swallow. "I think I can pull that off."

"Really?" she asked. "That should take at least sixteen points, even with the bonuses you got for performing your first Rise."

"As long as it doesn't take much more, I should be fine," I replied. "Let me check."

Wes Malcolm
Race: Human. Origin: Earth (Challenger)
Growth Level: First Rise (Spark)
Path: Unknown
Saga: Unknown
Profession: Unknown
Vital Pool: 240 points
Stamina Pool: 240 points.
Mana Pool: 290 points

Strength: 15
Dexterity: 15
Constitution: 14
Intelligence: 19
Wisdom: 25
Charisma: 17

Speed: 17
Deftness: 15
Wits: 25
Will: 25

Rise Points: 6 (can increase the six primary traits at a 1:1 ratio, or the four secondary traits at a 1:2 ratio.

Insight into the Following Ideals
Earth: lvl 1
Air: lvl 1
Lightning: lvl 1

Skill List truncated

Spell list truncated

When I looked away from my mind-screen, I could tell that Stell was glaring at me again.

"You didn't spend your extra points from your first Rise, did you?"

"No," I said, surprised she would care. "Why would I?"

"What do you mean, 'why would you?'" the woman snapped. "You could have died!"

"Exactly," I nodded. She started to open her mouth, so I hurried to explain. "See, I had no idea what would be beneficial to me, because I didn't know what habits I'd form during the Challenge. I also figured that higher ratings became harder to raise through practice. So I didn't want to make any changes until I knew what I was doing."

"That...makes sense," Stell grumbled. "But it also means you solved your first Challenge, one against *Horde*, no less, while still figuratively keeping one hand behind your back. Do you realize just how much you were making everyone else look bad?"

I shrugged again.

"All I have to say is that my opponents were two handfuls of naked, kindergarten-sized sociopaths that fought dumbly and without weapons or magic. If it makes you feel any better the boss monster was able to at least tag me before he died."

Choking on his own horn, I thought but didn't add. Huh. Being humble on purpose was hard.

"And that if one of the locals like Merada had gotten there sooner," I added. "They would have made even shorter work of the place."

There, see? Humble. But she still didn't look appeased. Did it not work?

"I'm glad you're at least feeling better," the attractive but slightly grouchy woman replied. "You're still a bit short of what you want to do."

"Yeah, that's where I need your advice," I said. "You described how to Rise before. Do I need to do that same exercise every time?"

"Mostly," Stell replied slowly, eyes widening as she considered me. "You should be able to internally figure out any differences though."

"Good. It felt like I needed to do exactly that."

"Are you about to Rise again, Wes?"

The beautiful woman's eyes were widening further.

To answer her question, I reached into myself, where I had felt some kind of heavy weight resting over my stomach. The weight had grown slowly as I had battled the Horde, then again considerably after I destroyed their Pit. Receiving the acknowledgment from the Icons for accomplishing the task earlier had swollen it even further, to where it was distracting if I allowed it to be.

I mentally grabbed at the ball, twisted it to a slightly different position, and *pushed.*

The ground under my feet rumbled. The wind whistled by my ears. And something in my nerves started crackling.

I felt everything start to expand again. Knowledge of things I had thought impossible, control over stone, wind, and storm, poured into my head. I felt the vital and magical energy in my veins thicken, then spread out. And I felt my muscles, bones, mind, and soul suddenly surge with a newfound strength.

"Yes!" I shouted as I completed my second Rise. My mind-screen surged open, listing the changes:

Wes Malcolm
Race: Human. Origin: Earth (Challenger)
Growth Level: Second Rise (Spark)
Path: Unknown
Saga: Unknown
Profession: Unknown
Vital Pool: 250 points
Stamina Pool: 250 points.
Mana Pool: 310 points

Strength: 17
Dexterity: 17
Constitution: 15
Intelligence: 21
Wisdom: 26
Charisma: 19

Speed: 20
Deftness: 17
Wits: 26
Will: 28

Rise Points: 12 (can increase the six primary traits at a 1:1 ratio, or the four secondary traits at a 1:2 ratio.

Insight into the Following Ideals
Earth: lvl 1
Air: lvl 1
Lightning: lvl 1

Skill List truncated

Spell list truncated

4 skill points available.
Signature Spells have improved.

I grinned at both the sight and feel of what I was able to do. I swung my limbs about, marveling at how they felt different. I felt sweat on my forehead—Rising was mentally and physically exhausting—but it was worth every bit.

Best of all, I could make the changes I wanted, and still have at least a point left over.

"Incredible!" Stell shouted. "You Rose twice in one visit! That's almost unheard of!"

"Thanks," I said with another grin. My confidence was returning quickly. "Now let's see how this goes... Wait, skill points?"

"Right," Stell said, nodding as if she had forgotten something. "Starting at your second Rise, you can use the power to sharpen your skills as well. Anything ranging from swordplay to magic to miscellaneous skills like wilderness survival and alchemy."

"By 'alchemy,' do you mean pretending to turn iron into gold, or do you mean making magic potions and other items?" I asked.

"The second one," Stell groaned. "The first one is just more evidence that your planet has too many dirtbags in it."

I shrugged.

"Anyway, can I spend three skill points to raise each of my three magics, and just hold on to the fourth for now? Since I don't have a favorite weapon style yet or anything?"

"Sure," Stell replied. "But you can't increase a skill too much beyond your Risen level. Not with the points you get from Rising, anyway."

"Good to know," I replied. "Alright, let's go..."

Assigning the points turned out to be intuitive. I just willed it and there they went. It was another intense experience. It felt like I had compressed a whole bunch of exercise sessions and classes all into a span of about fifteen minutes.

I was starting to realize that not everyone could handle Rising. Well, I mean they could if they wanted to. But the experience was so strenuous that it was hard to want to do it again. And it got harder each time, for each component of each Rise. That included the surge from beginning the process, followed by the increasing of my abilities, and ending with the strain of absorbing new knowledge and skills. But the euphoria afterwards was unbelievable. Much like working out, I guess. For some people, the pain and effort of exercise makes it difficult. But others live off of getting that second wind and the improvements to their body, and so they use that to push through the pain.

I hope I would wind up in the second group, at least when it came to being a Challenger.

I put three points each into Strength and Dexterity. Then I put five points into Constitution, and the last point into Charisma, giving me a score of 20 in every ability. Then I put three of my skill points into each Ideal-related magic skill. I looked at my new score afterwards:

Wes Malcolm
Race: Human. Origin: Earth (Challenger)
Growth Level: Second Rise (Spark)
Path: Unknown
Saga: Unknown
Profession: Unknown
Vital Pool: 400 points
Stamina Pool: 400 points.
Mana Pool: 310 points

Strength: 20
Dexterity: 20
Constitution: 20
Intelligence: 21
Wisdom: 26
Charisma: 20

Speed: 23
Deftness: 20
Wits: 26
Will: 29

Rise Points Remaining: 0 (can increase the six primary traits at a 1:1 ratio, or the four secondary traits at a 1:2 ratio.

Insight into the Following Ideals
Earth: lvl 2
Air: lvl 2
Lightning: lvl 2

Skill List truncated

Spell list truncated

1 skill point available.
Signature Spells have improved since last viewing.

I blinked after reading everything.

"How do you feel?" Stell asked tentatively.

"Ready," I replied. "Ready to take one good look and stop doubting. Stell." I turned to face her. "If this works, then when I come back I'm going to apologize for all the doubting, yelling and moodiness. And I'm going to thank you for the incredible opportunity you've given me and fight wholeheartedly for your people and their dreams. Give my regards to Guineve and Breena. And Merada as well. Furthermore, please make sure Merada knows she doesn't have to sleep with me as a reward for helping her with that Challenge. I don't want people to start feeling obligated to do that."

"Wait," Stell said as her eyes widened. "What?"

"I think I'm about to get pulled back," I said quickly. "Bye Stell!"

"No wait," she protested. "What do you mean she—"

But I had been right. The mists suddenly shifted around me.

I woke up to utter agony. My pain was screaming along every nerve, throwing an absolute fit with the slightest movement.

You're wasting time! it shouted. *How could you even fall asleep during the day! Everything's ruined now! Just lie back down!*

That was right, I realized. I had taken a nap during the day. I opened my eyes to look around the room. Just doing that made my pain explode again.

You screwed up! it screamed. *You slept wrong and screwed up! Just like you always do! Just stop moving!*

I wanted to scream myself, it was so bad, but I was too frightened to risk moving my throat muscles.

You screwed up! my pain kept screaming. *Everything's ruined because you screwed up! Just lie back down and give up!*

For a second my vision blurred, almost to a red color. My waking pain had never been this severe, I remembered. But I wondered what could be the cause of it. Just thinking that seemed to make my nerve endings scream at me.

Stop thinking! my pain shouted. *You always think too much! You always ruin things! You always have to meddle!*

What? I thought. I personified my pain and doubts out of habit, but this was different. I started to try and move, to fight through it and think, to focus.

Wrong! something shouted along my nerves. *Wrong! Wrong-wrong-wrong! Wrong-bad! Stop betraying your body! Stop betraying! Stop betraying!*

For a brief second, I thought I was finally going full-on crazy. Then I remembered I was done thinking that.

Focus, I told myself. Pick something and concentrate on it.

No! my pain shouted as I stared at an old movie poster on my wall. *Stop betraying! Stop betraying! Stop betra—*

It suddenly diminished.

I felt like I was exercising mental muscles I just recently gained. The screaming in my nerves settled down to a dull murmur, a complete reversal of every morning in the last two years I had before now. In a matter of a dozen or so seconds, my waking pain had gone from the most intense I had ever experienced to the most controllable I had in years. I shifted, grabbing my bedside table for support, and heaved my body to a sitting position.

My head swam briefly, but only briefly. The dizziness was gone almost instantly, not even lingering a little, like it used to. Deciding to risk it, using just the table for support, I pulled myself to my feet without my cane.

My head swam again. I felt my balance sway for a few moments. Then it settled down, to where it just felt like I was standing on a boat.

I laughed, and it barely hurt. I took a step forward, keeping my hand on the table, and my balance swayed again. Then it settled down. I'd still need my cane to walk, just to be safe. But I wasn't guaranteed to fall over instantly if I had one hand free. At least not for the first few steps.

Remembering my last visit to Avalon, I hurriedly tried to pull up my shirt with one hand. It was extremely difficult, which was also encouraging. Before it would have been impossible.

In less than five minutes, I had my chest bare. I reached for my nearby phone and activated the camera function, setting it so that I could see myself.

Muscle definition I did not have yesterday, or even this morning, was there now.

A laugh tore out of my throat, shaking my head a little and causing more pain. I didn't care. I just kept laughing, and felt myself sway all over the place. Every second I didn't fall just made me laugh harder. I felt tears start to fall down my face.

I had done it.

I had proved my pain wrong, my fears wrong, my community wrong.

I had proven them all wrong.

Whatever happened next, whatever setback they tried to set up for me, it didn't matter.

Because I wasn't going crazy. I was part of something incredible, something beyond my wildest dreams. And the best part was, it wasn't some kind of escapist fantasy.

Because it enabled me to come back here, and win.

Slowly but surely, I'd get my body back.

Then I'd find a way into college, find a way to be something, anything again. Maybe they'd let me retake the test and I could finally pass, maybe not. I didn't care. I'd just find another way in, take out a loan or something. Or I'd find a way to get a job. If I kept getting better, I could finally learn how to drive a car. Then I could go anywhere. Maybe I'd be able to achieve my dream of engineering cities. Or maybe not, maybe there was something else out there that I'd enjoy just as much. But I was the one that got to make that choice now. Not my sickness, not my psychologist, not my enemies.

I decided to make one more dare. Well, two, technically. First, I let go of the table I was holding onto.

I swayed for a few seconds, but as long as I didn't make any sudden moves, I could maintain my balance. That was a success. Before it usually took me pressing against something with at least one hand, or sitting down, to not be in danger of falling. Now?

Ten seconds. Fifteen seconds. Thirty seconds. I might even be able to do this all day.

Time to take another risk.

I lifted one leg up, without holding onto anything, and took a step forward.

It was hard. Everything felt like it was trying to turn both sideways and upside down. I wanted so badly to reach out and grab the nearby table that I hoped was still on my right. But I didn't. I kept enduring the swimming sensation and planted my foot firmly in front of the other. I almost leaned too far forward and fell right then and there. But again, I didn't. I needed to stand still for about a minute before everything stopped spinning. Then, taking a breath, I tried it again.

The same thing happened. My head swam, and I almost pitched too far forward. But I still made it, and after a wait, I found I was able to stand on my own.

Then I got really excited, and I finally lost my balance. But I grabbed the desk before I fell on the floor.

I laughed. I had lost maybe years of progress after that jerk had hit me in the back of the head. And I still hadn't recovered to the state I was at the start of test day, after I had beaten that boss back in *Heroes Unbound.* But this was definitely the biggest leap in progress I had ever made in a single day—scratch that, because it hadn't even been a whole day, just a midday nap. I started laughing again, so hard my head shook, and it hurt, but I didn't care. I heard Mom call out from the other room, asking if I was okay, if I had fallen again. I couldn't stop laughing long enough to answer her.

That got me a knock on my door, and I heard her holler for my sister. I was finally able to shout out that I was fine. I'd tell them later. And I'd probably ask them to keep it a secret too, so that some asshole didn't show up to ruin my progress again. I wanted to be ready for when they tried again. And I knew they would. But it didn't matter.

My enemies had spent all that effort, all that planning and money, just to try and keep me from taking two steps forward.

They failed.

* * *

Internal scans complete. Updated info available. Please review recent report

New Log of Subject Anonymous, Triple-Flagged Entry.

As everyone has already noticed, subject has begun to break Containment on his own, despite Containment's autonomous escalation. We have confirmation that Containment is displaying an increasing degree of autonomy as subject continues to overcome protocol. However, projections still indicate that Containment will not break its own established parameters until long after subject has completed the procedure.

Before everyone panics, please note that the new brain scans are also—at long last—proof of relevant data. Subject's improvement to his physical body, as well as the internal changes noted, are proof of outside involvement. Finally, we have confirmed that there are long periods, usually at night, where absolutely no data is collected from the subject at all. Such a thing is supposedly completely impossible, as no brain activity is supposed to be both permanent and only found in former subjects.

Recommendations are to increase surveillance on both the subject and Containment. Increasing outside pressure may be necessary; however, it is important that we no longer attempt to manipulate Containment's internal protocols. Such actions are currently classified as a needless risk and may only encourage the subject to break Containment on his own, or, even worse, somehow compel Containment to break parameters.

Further surveillance, however, will enable us to both collect more data and figure out how to finally generate said data on our own.

If we can do that, Rhodes, you and your son can go nuts on the boy for all I care. We'll deal with the consequences afterwards, when we're all gods.

Team Lead Out.

* * *

Another week began back home. I decided to show Mom and Sis a little bit of improvement so that they could get excited with me. I kept it slow and didn't show off my new muscles. That was hard, because I really wanted them to know, but I knew they'd start asking why, or how, if my progress was too rapid. Then I'd have to come up with some lie to explain it, and they'd see right through it because they're family and I'm only good at lying to people who I know are out to get me. Then they'd corner me and force me to tell the truth, and I'd have to tell them that I'd started going to a magical world of monsters and fairies and beautiful women where I was becoming this fantasy superhero who could do magic and kick ass.

Call me paranoid, but I figured that conversation wouldn't go well.

So I took it slow. I let myself walk just a little better with the cane in front of them. They still got excited even over that much. I told them it felt like the damage from the attack was wearing off.

I told them I wanted to hurry up and finish high school, preferably before the year was up. I asked Mom if there was a way I could go only to Ms. Springsen's class and maybe get the rest of my education online or at a local junior college.

That got her so excited she ran over and hugged me, before she could remember hugs usually hurt.

Apparently, she had been waiting to talk to me about trying again, but had been afraid to. She was afraid she had pushed me too hard earlier and had been criticizing me instead of just being there for me when I needed her. She hadn't expected me to want to try again so soon, and she hadn't expected me to come up with my own plan.

She didn't mention anything about how the lawsuit was currently going. I chose not to ask but I figured that the school and the football team were trying to settle with her. I didn't hear anything about the criminal investigation Davelon mentioned either. I decided to ignore both for now and began trying to read books, to see what random facts I could remember the next day.

When I tested myself, I was pleased with the results.

I tried the physical therapy exercises again, trying to see if I could do them longer. Then I actually felt my pain intensify, and it felt like something in my nerves was panicking. It hurt so bad I almost quit right at the start, but when I fought through it I found I could do everything just a little better, exert just a little more force, hold limbs just a little straighter, and for longer periods.

I hadn't been able to do any of that before, even when I was getting better playing *Heroes Unbound.* Back then, my balance had been improving and my pain tolerance had been increasing, but it was more like I was learning to work around the problem. Now, it felt like the problem itself had been solved, if only by a tiny bit.

It was still incredibly encouraging. I couldn't wait to figure out how to get back to Avalon so that I could find a way to get better again.

In fact, I realized I needed to get back to Avalon. I needed to apologize to Stell for freaking out back there, and for biting her head off, and for all those times I called everyone a hallucination.

That needed to be my focus, I realized. Get to Avalon. Save all their worlds, and whatever else they needed me to do, and find a way to keep growing in the process. If I had wanted to make a gameplay comparison, it was time to both power-level and go super-completionist. Stell had also said certain skills carried over. Could I learn something that could help me out over here?

Actually, I wondered, did that work both ways?

Could I keep exercising and learning over here, and then see if it would improve my projection in Avalon?

There was only one way to find out.

I talked to Mom again about taking an exercise break, instead of going straight back to school. The question surprised her. Apparently, the doctor hadn't wanted me to go back yet anyway. It was too risky, he said. Especially in what was currently being investigated as an unsafe environment. She hadn't known I had wanted to go right away, and now she was worried maybe I was pushing myself too hard. It was a little funny to think about how she had see-sawed so much from worrying I wasn't taking things seriously to now worrying if I was being over-committed. But then again, maybe being a single parent isn't easy, especially when your kid's had the problems I've had.

Now that I thought about it, I probably needed to give her more credit too.

Especially since I didn't find empty wine bottles in the trash anymore.

That was another reason to get better, I realized. I wasn't just improving my own future. I wasn't just ensuring I could still have goals and dreams. I was ensuring that my mother could start sleeping better at night. I was ensuring that my sister and her friends wouldn't have to keep looking out for me, even though they were all at least two years younger than me. I was ensuring that Davelon wouldn't have to give up anything because I was too weak to protect myself, and that Christina could see that her support for me mattered in the long run.

If I won, if I beat whatever this condition was, then my friends and family would too.

So I had to get back to Avalon and keep winning.

18

THREE STEPS FORWARD

I looked up at the mist. It had worked, I realized. I couldn't describe exactly how I did it, except to say that stimulating my brain, and then exhausting it right before bed seemed to be what worked best. I didn't have it down perfectly yet, but I knew that I could at least get back to Avalon pretty reliably now. That thought made me very happy.

"It worked," I muttered, looking down at myself. I was wearing some long-sleeved tunic and vest with leather pants. The back of my mind pointed out that I should probably find a way to get armor, but the rest of me was still focusing on the most important fact.

"It worked," I repeated much more loudly, and then before I knew it I was shouting. "It worked! It worked! Ha!"

I started laughing loudly. I may have even danced a bit. Or maybe I didn't. No one saw me so I don't have to admit whether or not I did.

I took off running, wanting to see how I improved for real here. My body back home had improved only slightly. Well, slightly in a sense. There is a big gulf of difference between 'one' and 'zero,' in my opinion. But here, I was theoretically just below Olympic levels of performance. Well, below Olympic levels during an event with perfect drug testing.

At any rate, I wanted to see how fast I could move, how strong I was now.

I wasn't disappointed.

It felt like the ground was leagues below me as I ran. I moved better than

I had even during the peak of my football days. I spent an uncountable amount of time running faster than I ever had, jumping farther than I ever had, and it wasn't even leaving me winded.

Eventually I did get a little fatigued, after doing a sprint that would have left even Chris and Davelon back home retching up. After a couple of deep breaths, I started laughing again.

"It worked!" I screamed. "IT WORKED! HELLO, AVALON!"

"Stell, darling," a mature woman's voice called out. "He's back. You wanted me to let you know, remember?"

"Yes, Guineve," Stell's voice called back. She sounded sarcastic. "Thank you so much for bringing that to my attention. Especially since this time I would have been *completely surprised*."

"Anytime, dear one," Guineve called back in a cheerful, motherly voice. *That was a surprisingly long conversation at this distance*, I wondered. Did they have that much practice yelling at each other?

It didn't matter.

"Hello, beautiful and wonderful women of Avalon!" I called out. "I'm back!"

"Welcome back, dear," Guineve called out. "Head on over. We're both this way."

"Hi, Wes," Stell called out. "I'll be ready for you in a few minutes."

I took off in that direction, realizing that this was even more amazing than when I had first arrived here and found out that I could move around.

"No," I whispered to myself. "Calm down. Be cool, Wes. You're about to talk to people. Quit bouncing all over the place."

It mostly worked. I slowed down to an easy jog. (*I could jog! Awesome! And I could do it for minutes without getting tired!*)

I mostly had it together by the time I reached Guineve's clearing. The raven-haired beauty was standing next to a table similar to the one they had set up for me last time.

"Good morning, Wes," Guineve said to me while setting down a white pitcher. "How are you this fine day?"

"Good morning, Guineve. I'm better than I have been in years, thank you. And might I add that you look absolutely lovely today, as usual?"

That part just slipped right out of me. I decided to blame it on the new Charisma score.

Fortunately, my comment seemed to have pleased Guineve.

"Why, thank you, dear," Guineve replied with a broad smile that stayed on her face. She lifted up a saucer that had a white cup on it. "I believe you asked for coffee last time?"

"Why, thank you, Guineve," I replied with gusto. "I actually hate coffee! And I've always been afraid to admit it! But you made it, so it must taste amazing and I can't wait to try it out! I'd love a cup!"

Once again, Guineve chuckled and gave a contented sigh.

"I have missed our little talks. Never change, Wes."

Actually, I figured I had changed a great deal. But this woman kept feeding me, so I had every inclination to keep her happy.

I took the cup and calmed myself down enough to take a careful sip. That's one of my problems with coffee, actually. It's not enough that you have to fiddle with it for several minutes until it has just enough cream or sugar. You have to drink it very carefully, give it time to cool, or it will get mad at you and bite your tongue. Soda and water are civilized drinks. They don't have that problem.

And no, I can't speak for alcohol, because religious upbringing and head injury, remember?

To my utter surprise, it tasted amazing.

The first cup of coffee with just a hint of bitterness, like what chocolate had. And the sugar and cream felt like it was inherent to the drink itself, not like they were added at the last minute, right when someone realized that they were about to drink something terrible and needed to mask the taste as best as they could.

"Guineve," I said, gulping down a mouthful. "This was the best cup of coffee I have ever had, and you may have redeemed the beverage for me."

"You're welcome, dear," Guineve replied, still wearing a broad smile. "But you may want to wipe the cream off of your face."

That's right, I realized. There was whipped cream in the coffee. How did it get there, I wondered? And why didn't I notice it before?

I tried to calm down again. I was reminding myself of Breena, and that was bad. I wondered if Breena felt like this all the time. It would probably explain a lot about her.

"How did it go back home?" Guineve asked kindly. "Have you recovered from your first Challenge?"

"Back home is fantastic," I said, finally getting myself under control, and hoping I could stay that way.

"My body is doing better than ever, and I have you all to thank for this opportunity."

"That's so good to hear," the statuesque woman said sweetly. "Stell will be ready for you in a minute. And Breena's actually out right now. Thank you for what you did on your last visit, by the way."

"You're all welcome," I replied. "Really. I'm glad to have helped. And it really wasn't that hard. Those things weren't anywhere near the stages everyone has worried about. And compared to dragons and all the other things I'm expecting Stell to eventually throw at me, those things were kind of easy."

Guineve sighed.

"I hope we never have to deal with another Horde dragon," Guineve replied sadly. "Only Stell and I really remember the last one."

"What happened?" I asked.

"We lost," the tall woman said simply. But a shadow hung in her eyes until she shook off the memory. Since she didn't elaborate, I didn't ask.

"I'm sorry," was all I said. I was relieved to see the pale woman chuckle again.

"You shouldn't be. You've probably made sure we won't have to fight one again. But since you want us all to stop congratulating you about that, I'll let it go. Would you like an omelette?"

After another inexplicably delicious meal, I was on my way to see the Starsown. Or at least her primary body. That was still weird and hard to understand for me.

When I got there, Stell had another surprise for me.

Gone was the dark skin that suggested a mix of African and Hispanic descent. The black hair remained, but now it hung straight down, shining in the misty light of Avalon. It draped around light golden skin, with slightly slanted eyes and dark pupils. Her figure had slimmed out a tiny bit, and she seemed just a little taller. She was wearing similar clothing, only this time the writing on her shirt said, 'Never trust an atom, they make up everything.'

She had lowered her head slightly when she saw me, as if she was nervous about how I'd react to her new appearance. I had no idea how to fix that, but I tried to put my best step forward.

"Good morning Stell."

"Hi, Wes." She fidgeted slightly.

"You look nice. I like your hair and shirt."

Because saying 'I like your new skin' didn't sound right to me no matter how many different ways I phrased the idea in my head.

"Thank you," she said, smiling and finally loosening up. *Phew. Right call.* "Um, how are you? How did... everything go back home?"

I spread my arms.

"Stell, I owe you both a huge thank you and a huge apology," I began. "I've been doubting you and everyone else here. I've been lashing out whenever you said something harmless that I chose to take personally, about problems you didn't really know about. I'm sorry. And thank you for your patience. Even more than that, thank you for this huge opportunity. You've provided a way to both prove this is all real and provide me with an amazing chance to escape what I've always feared to be a completely hopeless situation. I'm yours. You want me to kill monsters, fine. You want me to fight Horde and save people from them, absolutely. There's no way I can repay the opportunity you've given me, and since I don't believe you'd ever ask me to do something evil or wrong, I want you to know that I will do anything you ask, to the best of my ability. I owe you, and even repaying you just helps my body all the more."

"You mean it worked?" the now-golden-skinned woman in front of me asked. "Er, I mean, of course it worked! But you noticed the change?"

I nodded.

"Muscles, balance, everything is better, to a degree I can easily notice. I'm still a long way from being cured, but you've given me my best opportunity to get my body back. I can never repay what you've just given me. Thank you."

"Oh, you," Stell laughed. The sound hadn't changed one bit, despite everything else. "You're adorable. You're going to forget every time you save someone's life here, aren't you?"

"What do you mean?" I asked. "I haven't really saved... anyone... oh. Right."

D'oh.

"Yes, well," she continued, still chuckling. "Since you're so grateful for all the 'free help' we've given you, that totally has nothing to do with you growing on your own here, why don't we discuss how we can train you and prepare you for all those upcoming catastrophes I talked about before?"

So we did. I was still giddy from earlier, so I tried not to be too goofy. It mostly worked. At least I was able to avoid asking her how she changed to look like an extremely beautiful woman from a different part of Earth every month. She volunteered some of that info anyway, explaining that since she showed me her Starsown ability, the one that turned her eyes and ears gray, she had initiated another change. As far as she knew, the changes are completely random. She had no real control of how she looks like next and she'd never really been able to figure out the pattern.

She had volunteered all that information even though she seemed uncomfortable sharing it. At the same time, I wondered if she also was glad to have someone to talk to. The only people she saw here were either ones she had created herself, like Breena and Guineve, or god-like figures that visited from another world on business. And she had to wear a disguise to talk to those so that they would take her more seriously. I never even heard them use her real name. Just 'Lady Starsown.'

She left the subject quickly, though. That didn't bother me, even though I still wanted to know more about her. We'd already visited this matter several times in the past. I was sure we'd revisit it again.

We moved on to how I'd be saving the world, or worlds, and what I needed to know to do it. Everybody was still really, really impressed with my performance last time. I still felt like the whole thing was just handed to me on a platter, except for getting stabbed and cursed at the end. Thankfully, they had long confirmed I was no longer cursed.

Nobody could explain the warning I got about Malus and Invictus earlier, and they all got so mad every time I mentioned either name that I just gave up and let it go. That was frustrating because I *knew* doing that would come back to bite me, but I couldn't think of a better idea until everyone calmed down about those two names and actually told me something about them.

Still. If both figures were so mythical, why did everyone get so mad every time I said either name?

Oh well. Hopefully, I wasn't some minor character in a book or something, and all this obvious, ominous foreshadowing wouldn't get me killed.

My training was still combat-focused, even though every single problem that I encountered wouldn't be solved with violence. "Just *most* of them," Stell had explained. I'd still need to know how to look for clues, talk to people, and not step on buttons that triggered Temple-of-Doom-style traps.

But most of the problems of Avalon's different worlds were caused by things that go bump in the night. People outside of Earth just weren't dickish enough to backstab each other when there was an invading army of pig-monsters to deal with, or a giant flying lizard wanting to burn their houses and eat all their damsels.

The one thing that worried me more than dealing with fire-breathing, multi-headed, slathering hordes were Challenges based on diseases. Healing magic and medical knowledge were both weak areas for me, although Breena assured me that she would grow in power with both as I kept Rising. But I would probably spend most of my time finding alternative ways to cure plagues, instead of trying to cure them directly with my own skills and powers.

All of that was good thinking, Stell assured me, but my focus for now needed to be on staying alive. Sure, I could theoretically come back from the dead, even though the idea was completely untested on me so far, now that I thought about it, but I wouldn't come back right away. That meant anyone I was trying to save would be in danger until I could resurrect and return to that world.

When I asked about 'bind-points' like they had in my video games, Stell just glared at me.

Then she said, "Yes, you sort of have them, but you still won't come back right away, so don't get used to dying."

I assured her it wouldn't be a problem, and that I promised to tell her the moment I felt that dying would be addictive behavior.

The main problem with training me was that Breena hadn't spent enough time seeing me in action to gauge what combat skills I needed to focus on, or what spells I should focus on learning. During the last Challenge, we had all sprinted to help the hostages as soon as possible, and my little fairy admitted she hadn't been able to pay as much attention to me as she needed to. But, she had said when she arrived, she had a solution. One she was really excited about. The next Challenge, she was going to leave entirely up to me. One that was significantly safer than the Horde, and wouldn't feature any hostages to rush in and save. She wasn't going to give me any more details, though. Every other concern I voiced was met with "Trust me, I have a plan!"

* * *

Your skill with Short Blades has improved to Layman, rank three. Your damage and accuracy bonus with short blades have both improved to 3%. Your Vital Strike Chance bonus with all weapons has increased by 3%.

Your skill with Unarmed Fighting has improved to Layman, rank three. Your damage and accuracy bonus with fighting unarmed have both improved to 3%. Your Natural Armor bonus has increased by 3%.

Your dangerous and strenuous physical exercise has improved your Strength, Dexterity, and Constitution by one point each.

Your vital points are currently at 75%.

Your stamina points have just dropped to below 50%.

"See?" Breena called out next to me. "Look at all those increases! The training is working!"

"No!" I shouted, sucking in breath with each swing, and ignoring the pain from half a dozen bite marks. "It!" *Swing.* "Is!" *Slash.* "Not!" *Stab.*

My blow finally landed on the hairy, fanged mess trying to leap up on me. It took it right through the mouth, piercing its vital guard and shredding its throat. I pulled my short sword back quickly, barely retaining the weapon as the gibber-kin wrenched itself off my weapon and into a choking pile at my feet. I used that respite to leap onto a higher outcropping of stone, one that the other gibber-kin would have trouble climbing.

"No, look at that technique!" my fairy companion piped cheerfully. "You're doing great!"

I wanted to scream an entire sonnet of expletives at her right then and there, but the rabid angry balls of fur just below me weren't interested in giving me the opportunity. They were interested in gnawing off any part of my lower torso they could reach with their blunt, oversized teeth.

And yes, I said *blunt* teeth. These ugly, cross-between-a-second-grader-and-a-wooly-badger-looking monsters that ran about on all fours—they had no greater passion in life other than finding something bigger than them, swarming it all over and biting it to death with their *blunt* teeth. Because whatever bastard of a god that had created them had opted for painful deaths instead of quick and efficient ones.

That same god had probably been the hell-muse that sparked Breena's current concept of training.

I kicked out at a gibber-kin that had halfway climbed up the ledge to me. The damned-blasted thing happily accepted the kick for an opportunity to try and bite into my leg. The bite hurt, but with my improved earth armor activated it didn't really break the skin, much less my vital guard. Meanwhile my stone-toed boot had cracked into its jaw, and my shocking touch spell had triggered. Not weighing much more than the Ilklings, the gibber-kin was sent flopping through the air, spasming slightly as my new and improved taser magic ran its course.

Something about my posture must have told Breena I disagreed with her. That was unfortunate, and not my intent. I had actually wanted my posture to tell her to either shut the hell up, to actually help me fight these things, or to just snap a couple arcane bolts into the back of my head so that I could die painlessly, instead of having these frothing furry monsters swarm up and tetanus me to death.

“Wes,” my little fairy flew up and said firmly. “Don't get discouraged! It's perfectly normal to have days like this! Just because things aren't going as well for you as they did on the last mission doesn't mean you're doing a bad job!” *Dear God in heaven,* I thought, *she was in my face, waving a tiny finger, trying to give me a pep-talk right now.* All while three creatures, effectively were-honey-badgers, had almost finished pulling themselves onto my ledge. “I mean, think about it,” my friend—my companion—my life-linked and supposedly loyal partner—continued. “You led them away from everyone else they could have hurt, you were smart enough to head for the high ground—though it's a shame you have the wrong weapon for it, ask us for a longer one next time— and best of all, you're still alive! Most new Challengers would have already been screaming while being eaten alive by now! You're doing really, really great, Wes! Don't be so hard on yourself!”

They were all out to get me, I decided. Ilklings, gibber-kin, fairies. Everything under three or four feet tall would always try to kill me, no matter where I met them or what they had to work with. They couldn't even help it, I suddenly understood. It was just one of nature's laws.

I swore then and there that I would never either have kids or pursue a career in education, nor would I ever tolerate those others who did. Destructive behavior was destructive behavior, noble intentions or not, and I was done enabling the breeding of short, dangerous creatures of any species.

“Breena,” I growled, moving to deal with the three precariously-perched demons that were mere seconds away from continuing to pursue their macabre goals for my groin. “They,” *(Kick-bite-zap-snarl-hurtle)* “Are,” *(Bite-riposte-gurgle-zap-flop-flop).* “Trying!” *(Slash-bite-ow-ow-punch-punch-crunch-zap-throw).* “TO BITE OFF MY CROTCH!”

Breena paused in her lecture to tilt her head at me. "Yeah, but... why does that have you so upset?"

I made the rookie mistake of turning to gawk at her in outrage. Another gibber-kin seized on that opportunity to leap off of one of its pack-mates clear to the ledge. Another half-second was all it took for the thing to claw its way up my leg, gnashing its mouthful of molars at where my legs met my hip.

"I mean, they're gibber-kin," Breena continued absently. "That's what they do. Everyone knows that. Didn't I tell you? Wait, *did* I tell you?"

A shriek that I will never, ever consider unmanly hurtled out of my throat, seconds before the creature chomped into my left inner thigh, thankfully missing everything else in the region. I wanted to cry in relief but I didn't have time. I just stabbed my weapon down into its neck and let my *Outer Current* spell finish it off. My hind-brain was screaming that if I stayed on this rock for a second longer, the rest of the gibber-kin would overwhelm me, so I took the risk of leaping up to the next rocky ledge behind me.

"I mean, your vital guard will keep you from bleeding to death, so loss of that thing shouldn't affect your capabilities at all," Breena continued, flying up with me. "Even if that part of you is completely chewed off, since you're a Challenger, your vital guard will slowly repair your injury. Maybe even by the end of the month, in your case."

"A month?" I screamed. The gibber-kin had not released its grip in death and continued to hang off my inner thigh. The other gibber-kin were still trying to climb the ledge below me. Having seen the last one reach me directly by leaping off another's back, they were now all furiously trying to duplicate the act. But since they were all trying, that meant at least one of them would stay below and miss out on all the biting. None of them were willing to make that sacrifice, so they all dissolved into a massive angry pile trying to climb each other's backs and failing, while snapping at each other in frustration.

That gave me another five seconds of respite. I could use that time to suck down some more air and maybe remove the newly attached hate-ornament on my leg, or gain even higher ground using the next rocky ledge behind me. Breena's chittering actually made the decision easy for me.

"I would be without my manhood for a whole month?" I shouted as I leaped up the waist-high ledge behind me, a feat made easier in part to my enhanced body and wind magic, and in greater part to my newly acquired castration phobia.

"I know," the little pink pixie squeaked. "Isn't a Challenger's magic amazing?"

I had a long response I could give Breena. I could explain that certain parts of the human body, nay, most parts of the body will be missed even if they are not immediately necessary and even if they somehow grow back over time. I could explain to her that even though I am in constant pain back home, even though said part is effectively rendered impotent by said pain, I had no desire to experience something similar here. In fact, I had a desperate desire to not experience anything of the sort, and to escape such pain for as many moments as possible.

But all of that would take time I did not have.

Now that I was higher up and the gibber-kin were duking it out for the privilege of un-manning me, I did finally have time for some spells. *Five,* I counted down internally as my hands and mouth shaped formulas. *Three, two, one...*

Sparking Flash.

Light spat out of my hands like a bolt through the night, and just as bright. The flash did nothing but temporary sear eyeballs, but it ensured that the gibber-kin got even more tangled up as they struggled with each other. But it would only last for about three, two...

Muddy Earth.

The still-blind creatures were now slipping around in the greasy dirt. They were now actively using their claws to remain upright, but that still gave them no purchase on the slippery mud. So they clawed into each other's bodies to try and remain on their feet or to climb up on each other's back. That resulted in gibber-kin getting scratched. Normal gibber-kin were angry to begin with, and scratched gibber-kin were apparently worse. They moved from snarling and wrestling each other to full-on attacking each other with slashes and bites.

That was the key, I realized. They were looking for the closest target. Like the Ilklings had been, only these things were just pure aggression. It was as if they barely tolerated each other's company just because they hated everything else on the planet a little more. But anything that attacked them went straight to the top of their kill-list, even if it was each other. All I had to do was to make them keep hurting each other.

Strong Gust.

Breena had been having trouble deciding what new spells to teach me recently. She said it had to do with me constantly answering "everything" to her "What do you want to learn, Wes?" questions. But my increased skill in Air magic had allowed her to teach me a new Air spell. This was back before she decided she wanted to see how well I performed for herself, to figure out how I kept 'cheating,' as she called it. It did no direct damage, but that was important right now. I targeted the gibber-kin who had stayed out of the melee below the most and used the spell to push them into the ones that were fighting.

"Good job on putting your new spell to work!" Breena cheered. "I was wondering how you'd use it!"

And just like that, my enemies began to dwindle. They weren't quite willing to kill each other, like the Ilklings were, but they still tore each other up pretty badly in their attempts to display dominance. At least three gibbers were down on the ground, moaning weakly, doing all they could not to drown in the mud. Others looked like they were close to succumbing to their wounds as well. For a half-second I felt sorry for the crazy things, until I realized that this whole thing could have been avoided if they had taken any of the half-dozen opportunities I gave them to stop trying to castrate and kill me.

Also, I really needed to have a talk with Breena about that whole 'test you with castration monsters' thing, because dealing with that nonsense was really weird and not okay.

Then I remembered everything would change for the worse as soon as the mud turned back to normal ground, so I hurriedly reset the spell. Then I blinded them with another flash, to ensure they would keep running into each other.

And then I started to feel the drain of casting too many spells too quickly. My head swam, and for a moment it felt like I was dealing with my condition back on Earth. But the feeling quickly passed, even though something still felt spent inside of me. I checked my mana pool, and realized I had room for maybe one more spell left. I needed to let them fight for as long as they were willing, then finish off as many of the healthy ones as I could.

Fortunately, the two healthiest ones had found each other and began fighting as well, since they could no longer get to me and there was nothing else out here to take their frustrations out on but each other. I waited for as long I dared, because as soon as the ground firmed up under them again, they would find a way to launch themselves back at me, and so I had to act before that point. I began to count down the most conservative estimate of how much time I had left.

Three, two, one...

Friction Slash.

A three feet long blade of overheated air swept out from me into the last pack of fighting gibber-kin. The magic still wasn't powerful enough to do much more than a sword slash, but for their low pools of vital guard, plus the damage they had already done to each other, that was more than enough for my needs. Even more importantly, the blade managed to pass through every single monster in the pile.

That was the second time this strategy worked for me, I realized. Force a large group of small angry things together, make them bite and fight each other for a bit, then hit them all with my main area attack spell.

Best of all, they were now too injured to climb up to me. So I finally had time to try and remove the dead gibber-kin still clinging to my upper leg.

"Great job! But what are you doing now?" Breena wondered at me.

"Um, belatedly lowering my exposure to tetanus?" I replied.

"Hm. I guess that kind of makes sense," Breena mumbled. "But aren't you worried about the gibber-kin's fast recovery rates?"

"What?" I asked, still distracted by the act of removing the dog-sized hate-ornament under my waist.

"You know how I mentioned these things recover their vital points faster than almost any other monster their size?" She paused suddenly. "I mentioned that earlier, right? Or did I? Hold on, let me thin—"

She stopped talking as soon as the blood-rippling scream erupted from my lips. I ripped the dead gibber-kin violently off my leg, upper quadriceps be damned, let my hand form a death grip on my short blade, and leaped down into the closest gibber-kin that was slowly working itself back upright. The creature screamed its rage at me and tried to bite at my toes or anything else it could reach, but I just screamed back and stomped my foot down on its face. The little hate-beast died when it tried to swallow my foot whole and choked, but it was a near thing. I pried it off my foot and, still screaming, proceeded to hack and stomp my way through all of the remaining gibber-kin, screaming out Breena's name like it was my new favorite swear-word.

Because it was.

Five, maybe ten, or even fifteen minutes later, and they were all finally dead. I was covered in even more bites, as the Breena-blasted things had managed to catch me even in those last minutes, but I was panting and alive while they were all limp and dead, so maybe there was a God after all.

The gibber-kin threat to the native inhabitants has ended. You have completed your second Challenge, Wes Malcolm.

Your Intelligence and Wisdom have improved by one point each.

Your skill in General Magic has improved to Layman's rank 2. Spellcasting will be 1% easier to understand, and spells will cost 0.5% less in time and magical energy.

Your skill in General Melee has improved to Layman's rank 2. Weapon skills will be 1% easier to learn, and all weapons will gain 0.5% more damage and accuracy.

"Fantastic!" Breena screamed. "You passed the main test of the training! And almost perfectly!"

The fairy buzzed in front of me. "Look at you! Completely covered in blood, most of it your own, and still victorious! You really do know how to fight through pain and use your vital guard! No wonder you were able to mow through the Ilklings so easily!"

"Breena," I panted in warning.

"Now we just need to show you how to track guard-breaking attacks, so that you don't make the mistake of ignoring serious injuries! But I could tell you were already watching out for that this fight!"

"Breena," I panted again.

"Although I think you may be a little too worried about non-vital injuries," Breena mumbled distractedly. "I mean, I don't have that same part, so I'm not that familiar with it, but losing it shouldn't impact your effectiveness that much. I do know that—"

"Breena!" I yelled.

"What?" she squeaked. "I'm right next to you."

As if I didn't need to yell to get her attention.

"Do. I have. Rabies?" I asked in what I thought was a super-controlled tone. Because after today, if I got out of here without turning into a gibber-kin myself and biting someone's head off, and even managed to keep asking sensible questions, *that* would be the real victory.

"Ooh!" the little fairy suddenly piped. "Good question! Let me check."

I counted backwards from ten, trying to get myself back under control.

Breena is normally a nice person, I reminded myself. *Breena healed me last time when I got really injured. Breena is just trying to make sure I get strong enough, fast enough to save their worlds from the upcoming disasters.*

"Nope, you're all okay!" the little pixie piped cheerfully.

"That's good," I replied. At least that went well...

"But if that one gibber had hung on a second longer, you probably would have been infected with some other really creepy stuff."

"What?" I asked flatly.

"Did I forget to mention that too?" Breena wondered. "Gosh, I really got scatterbrained today. I guess I was so excited about today's adventure that I had trouble focusing. I'll have to make sure I didn't forget anything else important. But you didn't even die from it, Wes! Do you realize that?"

Twitch, my right eyebrow said. *Twitch-Twitch.*

"I mean, even when I'm on top of my game, it's normal for a Challenger, even one who's Risen twice, to die at least once in an encounter like this! But all you got was just a whole bunch of not-quite infectious bites! You didn't even lose any limbs!"

Twitch-Twitch-Twitch.

"Breena," I said slowly. "I think it's time to head back to Avalon."

"Huh? Are you sure? I mean you completed another Challenge, but we could still look around—"

"No."

"There might be some spare monsters we can stir up or I can show you some of the natural wildlife—"

"No."

"Well, what about—"

"Breena," I said, gritting my teeth. "Portal. Now."

"Ugh! Fine. I guess you earned a break," the deceptively adorable little sadist muttered.

19

STEADY NOW

"Well," she said as we reappeared into the misty world. I had no idea where we were even returning from. I remember being told at the beginning of the Challenge, but now all I remembered was rocks and trees and a dozen or so angry monsters shrieking and spitting and biting all over me.

But none of that mattered now, I decided. I had survived. Everyone else had survived, as I dimly remembered leading those monsters away from a wood-walled village that people were running into. I had even gotten stronger, though I didn't get enough power to Rise. But I gained a little improvement to every ability but Charisma, and I got an improvement to two general skills that I didn't even know I possessed.

I'd ask Stell or Breena about those. Later.

"Well that was just fantastic," my foot-tall fairy chittered. "Even if you did cut it a bit short. Still this was great research, don't you think?"

"I think I want to know if Guineve's made lunch," I said numbly. Breena muttered something else, but I didn't care. I still hurt all over and was almost castrated no less than six times. The mangy beast that had latched onto my thigh had been by no means the only attempt, just the closest to being successful.

I staggered over to where I remembered Guineve to be last time, belatedly remembering I was still holding a bloody sword and that I needed to sheathe and probably clean it. I wiped it on a shirt sleeve before jamming it back into the sheath I had taken from the Horde wretch so long ago. My bitten arms ached like crazy, but I was eventually able to get the weapon back in.

"Hey, Breena?" I interrupted the rapidly chattering fairy.

"Yes, Wes?" She cocked her tiny head. It was hard not to compare her to a curious and hyperactive puppy at the moment. It was even harder to find said idea cute.

"The Challenge is over," I said firmly. "I defeated a monster's incursion from another world. All by myself. Like you wanted me to."

"Yeah that's what I've been trying to say all along. Weren't you listening?" The little fairy put her hands on her tiny hips. "I swear, Wes. You get mad I don't tell you things and then you tune me out for like thirty seconds, no a minute, no like two minutes. And then you go and..."

"Breena," I repeated tiredly, then waved my bloody arm at her pretty face. *"Ow,"* I articulated meaningfully.

The little brat had the nerve to cock her head at me.

"Why are you waving a bitten arm in my... oh, you want me to heal your arm! Why didn't you say so?"

"Because I was—"

"And no," she said while crossing her arms. "Sorry. No can do."

Twitch.

"What?" I asked carefully.

"Think about it, Wes!" the little pixie buzzed. "This is good for you! This way you can truly appreciate how badly wounds hurt! Every minute spent healing naturally is another minute encouraging you not to get hurt again in the exact same way!"

That idea might have been true, if I didn't hate it so much. But as it currently was, pain was gaining zero traction with me as a teacher right now.

"Besides, you can heal yourself now that your mana's recharged a little, remember?"

I groaned as I realized she was right.

Two *Healing Wind* spells later, I was mostly recovered.

"See? You even got to practice your magic that way!"

I reactivated my *Quick Step* and bounded away as fast as possible.

"Huh? Why are you castin—Hey!" the little sylph shouted, just before she became a dot in the distance.

"Hey! Wes, wait up!"

"It's for your own good!" I shouted behind me.

"Wes, I can't keep up with you! Weeees!"

Five blissfully silent minutes later, I reached Guineve's table. This time, it was out by a lake, surrounded by misty woods.

"Welcome back, Challenger," Guineve said as she saw me return. She frowned. "Bad trip?"

"I think my Challenger-issued fairy has developed some serious complications and needs to be looked at by my local dealer. Is Stell around?"

"Yes. But why don't you have another bite to eat?" The woman motioned to a plate with more bread, fruit, and some braised pieces of meat that looked like beef. "I'll message Stell to expect you." The woman had a serious tone, and for once wasn't faking it. That made me wonder if I really looked that angry. I tried to lighten the tone.

"Guineve, if you are competing to become my favorite, know that you have already won," I said as I sat down tiredly. I saw that she had made coffee again, and was grateful for the first time in my life. There was even a small bowl of confectioner's sugar I could add to it if I wanted. I noticed that some of the pastry-like bread and fruit had already been sprinkled with it.

As I began to eat, I heard a familiar buzzing sound behind me.

"Why did you suddenly take off and sprint? I mean, that's a good idea to build endurance but it's a terrible idea to just do out of nowhere. People don't like surprises, Wes. I probably should make a lesson for that too. And what are you eating?" She flew over and looked at my meal. "Ooh, sugar! Wait, no! No! I'm being a bad example!" Breena shook her head furiously, muttering to herself. "Gotta be tough! Gotta be tough! Guineve, I thought we talked about this! We got to make him tough! If he isn't tough, he won't be ready! If he's not ready, he'll get hurt for real!"

"Breena," I warned.

Now that I had a working body, I found that I had developed certain habits. Mainly, a desire to fight to the death for my current meal, and especially after a hard day.

"Yes, I know, you almost got castrated, blah, blah, blah." Guineve's eyes widened upon hearing those words. The little fairy didn't seem to notice. "But you could have lost so much more!"

"Breena," Guineve's voice came out, and for the first time I heard a note of real panic come out. She seemed to be looking at me. Again, the little fairy paid no heed.

"I mean think, Wes! You use so many other parts of your body so much more! But I've never seen you use *that* part even *once*! Now I'm no expert, but if that part was really important, I'd see you use it all the time! Like your head, or your arms or your legs! What if you had lost one of those, huh? Don't you think that would hurt more?"

"No, Breena," I said in a low voice. "I don't."

"Wes, I'm so sorry," Guineve said shamefully. "I truly didn't know she had become like this. It's not her fault."

"What do you mean?" I asked as my fairy kept rambling. Concern crept back into me, despite my temper, fatigue, and hunger. "Is she okay? Did something happen to her?"

"In a sense," Guineve said, the normally composed woman looking uncomfortable for once. "Stell can give you the best explanation though. But Breena will be fine. I promise," she assured.

That was good, at least.

"You're not listening! " my little fairy yelled. "Hey! Listen! Listen! Look! Look! Hey!"

That did it.

"Guineve, can you hand me the bowl of sugar please?"

"Certainly, if it will help," the tall woman said as she passed me the little bowl.

"You're! Still! Not! Listening!" my little fairy squeaked, flying in front of me and pumping her arms up and down. "Sugar's bad right now! Hey! Look! Listen—"

Puff.

As I flicked the bowl, the tiny cloud of powdery confectioner's sugar washed over my little companion like the world's tiniest snow storm. Breena blinked quickly, looked like she was about to ask me a question, then made a little sneeze.

"Why did you—*achoo*! I can't—*achoo*!"

"Thank you, Guineve," I said calmly. "That certainly helped. Was that the last of the sugar?"

"No, dear," the raven-haired woman said calmly, not reacting at all to recent events. "I always make enough for seconds of everything."

"You are wonderful, and I promise to tell you that more often."

"Thank you, dear," she said with a smile. "Never change."

Breena was still sneezing, and still trying to get my attention. The little fairy flew right in front of me, sugar sprinkling off with every beat of her wing. She would firmly point her finger at my face, open her mouth to speak, then sneeze again. It was so cute, I started to feel bad for her. Then I remembered the last three hours of my day, and what had almost happened to me six or seven times.

Puff.

"Wes!" my snowy little enemy screamed as another sugary cloud engulfed her. "Stop-*achoo*-making-*achoo*-sneezes-*achoo*-tasty! *Achoo*!"

"Wes, dear," Guineve said gently. "Why don't you go find Stell and tell her about today?" I didn't immediately respond. "You can take your food with you," she added. "I'll have some more when you come back."

"Yes, ma'am," I replied, graciously accepting her peace offering and getting up with my plate. "I'll be back. Where do I take the plate when I'm done with it?"

"This is Avalon, dear. Just let it go and it will return to me."

"Awesome," I replied. "See you in a few."

Breena tried to protest again, but Guineve interrupted her.

"Breena, dear, Wes has to go to report to Stell about how today went. Why don't we clean you up, and I can explain why Wes is so unhappy with you?"

"But I'm—*achoo*! Wait," the little fairy squeaked, her wings suddenly drooping. "He's mad? I made him mad?"

Well, I was mad five seconds ago, I thought. *But now I feel like I just kicked a puppy.*

"It's not your fault, dear," Guineve said gently. "Stell will fix it."

"But how did I make him mad?" the pink-haired woman asked in a small voice. I winced and after exchanging a nod with Guineve, quietly began walking away.

"Sweetheart, I think it's time. You're old enough for the talk."

"Old enough?" I heard the little fairy squeak behind me. "Are you treating me like a kid again? I'm almost as old as you are!"

"I know, dear. Why don't I explain why a man like Wes would be so upset right now?"

"Oooh, *that* talk!"

Right-o, I decided. *Go find Stell. We're out of here.*

I finished my food on the way, almost getting lost in the process of savoring it. This stuff was seriously good enough to make me give up fast food cold turkey. Well, most fast food. Pizza was going to stick around.

More misty woods. More ruins of Athenian-like architecture. I started to wonder how all this had been made. Did people used to live here? Did Stell grow up here? What happened to this place?

"Hey, Wes," Stell's voice drifted lightly over my shoulder. "Um, Guineve says I need to reconfigure Breena a bit. Can you elaborate on exactly what happened today?"

I explained the encounter in great detail. Stell winced as I described the initial attack by the gibber-kin. Her wince gradually deepened as I reported everyone's actions throughout the whole fight.

"Wes, I'm so sorry," the now-golden-skinned woman said as soon as I finished talking. "This is all my fault."

"Okay, but maybe you can explain why," I started. "First off, those monsters were the most terrifying things I've ever seen. Why isn't everyone summoning the Icons over these guys?"

"Because they're not nearly as dangerous," Stell replied, and she raised her hands to quickly explain. "To *groups* of people. If a pack of gibber-kin catches you alone out in the open, you're in for a bad day. It's kind of amazing you survived your first encounter with them. But for communities? All you need is a group of people who don't lose their heads and can work together to use the creatures' own aggression against them. They'll run straight into a wall of spears, or a pit trap, or a magical effect, and die one after another. Unlike Horde and a whole lot of other bad things you haven't seen yet, gibber-kin never adapt or learn. They just get angrier and angrier. That's why they turned on each other when you did that trick with the mud."

"Yeah but the same thing worked on the Ilklings," I rebutted.

"*Everything* works on Ilklings," Stell said with an eye roll. "They're not really a fighter species of the Horde. They're the workers, scavengers, hunters of small game. That's why they were able to kill every animal in that area, snatch up every fairy, but they died by the bucket-loads to what was basically a grown man with a stick. You got the absolute tamest example of what has been a thousand years of nightmares to everyone else. And you're forgetting that the Pit's champion still almost killed you."

"Fine, fine," I said. "I am aware that I basically stumbled into early heroism by showing up at the right place at exactly the right time. I am also aware that I nearly bit off more than I could chew at the end, and was lucky

Breena was around to patch me up. I ask your forgiveness for my ignorance and arrogance. Now, why was I thrown into a pack of rabid crotch-biters?"

Stell sighed.

"That's... complicated. And all my fault. The last mission really upset Breena. Aside from myself and Guineve, the fairies that were attacked were basically her closest family. She has a scattering of what she considers to be kin across all of Avalon's worlds. But she's known the ones in the Woadlands for the longest. She calls all the elder ones Aunt or Uncle, and all the little ones are her nieces or younger siblings."

"Does she have any nephews or little brothers?" I asked, picking up her use of 'uncle' as the sole male gender noun.

"Well, no. That male pixie you rescued before was one of her uncles. Fairy gender ratios skew in a rate of ten to one, in the female's favor. It's not a problem, since they usually just procreate through the magical energy found in nature."

"Usually?" I cocked my head. "What do you mean, usually? And since when does a species have more than one means to procreate?"

Stell looked uncomfortable with that question, but she answered it anyway.

"Fairies occasionally come into contact with other races of people. If they spend enough time together, and if the relationship takes a certain direction, the fairy can change to become... compatible... with the other race."

"Wait..." I said as some of Breena's comments surfaced into my mind, now seen in a completely different light. "What?"

"Not going to happen with you," Stell insisted quickly. "Breena can't develop an interest in a Challenger like that. None of my girls can. I made it impossible, because it would complicate things way too much."

"That's good," I snorted. "Because she's usually only a foot tall. And I value my eternal soul."

"She would grow much bigger in that event," Stell said automatically. "But, again. Won't happen. With any of us. Especially me," she said firmly. "I've made sure we won't even think of the idea. Your people come here to save worlds, not hook up with your boss or coworkers."

"That's a good point," I conceded, far more reluctantly than I thought I would.

Just then, I heard a tiny little shriek erupt from the distant mists. I turned, my hand reaching for the short sword still strapped to my waist. "Are we under..." I started to ask. But Breena's next scream answered my question for me.

"THEY DO *WHAT* WITH THAT THING?"

An awkward silence descended upon the mists. Seconds stretched it out even further, until Stell finally spoke up.

"See?" she said with a nervous laugh. "The idea's already nipped in the bud. She won't ever even hint at it anym—"

"THAT'S NOT FAIR!" the tiny, but paradoxically loud. voice shouted again. "HOW AM I SUPPOSED TO—"

A shushing sound quickly followed, and I could no longer hear my fairy companion scream across the planet.

I looked back at Stell. Her new skin allowed me to see a crimson blush form across her entire face, right before she tossed her hair forward and covered it with her hands.

"I am so sorry," she muttered from behind her fingers. "This is just the result of my adjusting her too much earlier. Please let me deal with this, and forget all about it," Stell begged. "You will never have to deal with this ever again. Just pretend this never happened. *Please.*"

"Um, okay," I said, choosing to be generous. "Maybe instead you can explain why Breena took her current method of training me to the level she did?"

"Yes," Stell said quickly. "We were talking about that before. Let's get back on track.

"Breena basically had a meltdown last time you two went out. She had taken you to the Woadlands expecting a Challenge that you wouldn't even need weapons to deal with, in a specific zone safe enough for the local population to risk you handling it alone."

"I thought you said that you sent me because I could get there the fastest?"

"That's technically also true. But no," she admitted. "It was supposed to be almost beginner-proof. We just wanted you to get basic practice."

"Okay," I said, shrugging it off. I'd received worse insults. "Well, I did, so I guess it worked."

"No, it failed, because you didn't," Stell shook her head furiously.

"What are you talking about?" I asked. "I used most or all of my spells. I punched, kicked and swung improvised weapons. I practiced fighting with Breena, because that was back when she actually helped me with encounters." A growl snuck out there. I mentally reprimanded myself and kept talking. "I took damage and learned how to deal with it where I could. I got a whole day's worth of practice on the basics."

"No," Stell repeated firmly. "You didn't. You didn't die and return. You didn't have to retreat and rethink your strategy. You didn't reach your limitations because even though you ended the fight bleeding and unconscious, you still cleared the entire dungeon with nothing more than a stick and a handful of spells—including the Pit itself, for Avalon's sake. I'm still researching how you were able to do that. And don't say it," she warned.

I was about to say, "I just zapped it until it died." Apparently, she could tell and didn't want to hear it again.

"I still hit my limit," I repeated. "Bleeding, cursed and unconscious is my limit."

"Oh, yeah?" Stell asked with an arched eyebrow. "Do you really think that? Did you really think 'gee golly, I should really be more careful in the future; I should wait for Breena and Stell to train me more before I go off and fight another Dark Icon's Champion. Maybe the next time one catches me alone, I could just keep it busy until Breena shows up?' Or did you think, 'Man, I did awesome! I beat a whole dungeon of monsters that everyone else pooped their pants over, and saved and cuddled with a whole bunch of pretty women in the process, all while practically naked from a tactical standpoint!'?"

"I strongly resent both that last sentence and the context it creates," I said firmly. She just rolled her eyes at me. "And I was *not* cuddling a bunch of women that tiny, and I was *not* naked from any standpoint, tactical or otherwise! Come on Stell! They weren't even child-sized!"

"You mean they were palm-sized?" Stell replied smugly.

"Not helping! Not helping at all!" I shouted.

She chuckled at my distress.

"My point is, did you feel like the Dark Champion was too much for you, too skilled and powerful for the current you that needs to keep getting stronger, or did you feel like you could have handled him even more easily if you had any real equipment whatsoever, not counting a half-broken stick that didn't survive the fight?"

"Armor of any kind may have negated his attack entirely, judging by how well my enhanced skin resisted it," I answered confidently. "As long as my shocking magic held up, any kind of long-ranged weapon would have ended the fight in three swings tops, if I figured his vital points correctly. A spear would have been best. Can I have a spear?" I asked absently. "Spears are awesome. I mean, I'd ask you for firearms if I thought you had them, but I don't know how to use those anyway."

"Wes," Stell groaned. "That all is exactly my point. You got a terrible example of just how tough Challenges can be. They're called Challenges for a reason."

"Well, then," I argued. "Why did I have to go unarmed? Did you guys really forget to give me weapons?"

"No," Stell grumbled, looking uncomfortable again. "I was trying to make you one, then send it to you."

"What?" I asked. "Really?"

"Every Challenger gains some unique summon spells," Stell explained. "In addition to summoning Breena when she first comes."

"Right," I asked, remembering. "Can I un-summon her?"

"No," Stell said flatly.

"I can't, or I'm not allowed to?" I asked to clarify.

"Yes," was the Starsown's only response. "Moving on. After you link with your Ideals, I can begin to detect other summoning powers. Most other Challengers can summon a weapon unique to them, that grows with them as they Rise. Others can summon an animal companion that also bonds with them. The last Challenger could summon a tool that eventually let him build or make almost anything on the spot, though it was usually temporary."

"Awesome," I replied. "Did I get any of that, and when could I use it?"

"No, and probably never," Stell said. "Actually, I did find potential for a bonded weapon, and tried to unlock it for you. But it turned out to be just a handle. Which is a first," she said, annoyed. "But with you, firsts are the new normal."

"Sorry," I said lamely. And that sucked, I realized. I really wanted my own personal super-weapon.

"So am I," Stell replied sincerely. "I normally have a better idea of what to do with all of this, Wes. Normally Challenges don't catch me so off-guard that I wind up sending someone out without a weapon or other gear. I've done this sort of thing for over a thousand years. I haven't had a Challenger every single one of those years, but the number I have had cannot be counted on any of my digits, including those of my Satellites. I have a routine developed that has served me well for literally every single Challenger except yourself. And don't apologize, because it's not your fault," she continued. "Now, yes, you came here on your own and have all sorts of unique or rare abilities. You are also much more competent than most people believe. You should have been the one losing your mind when you first saw a monster, Wes. Not Breena. Not everyone else. She, and by extension me, shouldn't have been the one panicking, even though we thought the Horde to be either completely cut off from us or extinct."

"How can you tell?" I asked honestly. "It looks to me like these Challenges seemingly pop up out of nowhere."

"They can't," Stell replied. "Which is how I know how to track for Tumults and Trials and Call for a Challenger. Each monster has certain criteria for breeding or appearing. But a great many of them have also had their criteria for emerging wiped out by Challengers as well. We thought that was the case for the Horde and it's a little disturbing that someone knew how to build a Horde Pit out there. Everyone is still on high alert from that.

"But Breena was confronted with the sight of an ancient enemy among the closest members of her second family. She had to witness them being horribly abused, and it completely threw her off her game. She spent the entire Challenge worried sick over what the Horde might have done to one of her uncles, two of her aunts, and her littlest nieces and sisters."

"That sounds like a horrible experience, and her reactions were completely understandable. I really don't blame her for that."

"Well, she blames herself. Especially since she found you half-dead a few feet from a Horde Pit."

"Again, I don't blame her," I replied. "I can come back from the dead, and her adopted family doesn't have the same ability, as I understand it."

"You're more or less right. But Wes, until that day, after we all found about the crazy risks you took, we weren't sure if anyone could come back from the Pit, Challengers included."

"Wait, what?" I said once again.

"We've never had a Challenger get that close to a pit alone," Stell continued. "Even during the first Horde." She looked down. "That was back when I tried to draw Challengers from the same world a Trial or Tumult was forming in. Way back when I first started being a Stewardess. I thought people from their own world should be empowered to handled their own problems. I still believe that. I still look for ways to do that. But the Challengers from that world never came back when they went to battle the Horde Pits."

"What happened to them?" I asked.

"I don't know," Stell said quietly. "But as far as I can tell, they were lost, along with everyone else on that world. So that's why Breena's been panicking," Stell continued. "She had me draw out some of the empathy I put in her, so that she wouldn't panic much the next time you did something crazy. Because until today, Wes, you've been taking everything in stride. See magic for the first time? No problem, you just asked how to do it, then made one of the hardest Ideal combinations work like a charm. See a monster for the first time? Again, no problem. You beat it to death with your bare hands and feet, then went and grabbed a heavy stick to deal with the rest."

"In my defense," I began. "I see monsters in video games all the time. And they looked far scarier than everything back there."

"Well, we didn't know that at the time, Wes," Stell insisted. "So I told Breena to take a good hard test of your abilities, so that we could see how you do under further pressure, and make sure we were done finding all your surprises."

"Today was pretty pressuring," I said dryly. "Did you tell Breena to let those things castrate me if they had a chance?"

"No," Stell sighed. "And I'm sorry about that. She's just now getting educated about... certain things. Even as we speak."

"Right," I said, and I suddenly remembered that somewhere else in the forest, two women were basically just talking about my penis. After how the rest of the day went, I didn't know how to even begin processing that fact.

Stell seemed to guess what I was thinking about. We stared at each other for another long, awkward moment, then she cleared her throat and continued speaking as if we had heard nothing.

"So, anyway, Breena and I decided to take you on a harder, more controlled test, but before that, she asked me to take back some of the sympathy I put in her—because she didn't want to panic again when she saw people get hurt. I apparently took back more than I was expecting. And we were counting too much on the fact that you could come back from the dead and regenerate, and we paid less attention to the fact that you're still building trust with us and have had prior experience with being... incapacitated. Experience you probably didn't want and didn't really need to relive."

"I think I can understand that," I replied. "Especially since you're predicting several cataclysmic events that you need to get everyone prepared for. Just... have her tone it down a bit, okay?"

"Yes. I will do that," the woman replied, and for a second I had to get used to the fact that she had new features again. "And it will probably never happen again."

"Probably?" I zeroed in on that word like my life depended on it. Because it did.

"It won't happen again," Stell said more firmly. "But... Breena will continue to change. So will Guineve and all of my other girls. Because I am changing."

That last sentence came out in a rush, as if it was delivered under duress.

"I'm sorry, I don't understand," I replied. "Does your changing forms affect them?"

"No," she replied, uncomfortable again. "I'm going to go ahead and tell you what I normally keep secret about myself."

"Really?" I asked, feeling strangely guilty. "Are you sure you have to? I mean I don't want to force you to share things you don't want to share or anything."

"I appreciate that, Wes, but this stuff is affecting you too, so if I tell you, it might help." Stell took a deep breath. "Guineve told you a little bit about what happens when I make new aspects of myself. When you live as long and change as much as I do, my Satellites help keep me from becoming... too much. But when I make one, the separation isn't complete. I usually don't feel anything from their end, but the reverse isn't true. If I go through periods of intense change, some of that will seep over to them. If I get hurt really badly, for example, some of the trauma of the wound will transfer over to them. How much depends on the degree of the trauma, as well as the distance. So losing a limb would affect everybody to a significant degree, but it would affect Guineve more than one of my aspects on another world, like Merada in the Woadlands or Anahita in the Golden Sands."

"Please tell me that's a completely arbitrary example, and that no one's planning to hurt you," I said slowly.

"What? No. No, of course not. That was just an example," Stell said, looking at me. "Though it's sweet of you to worry, I guess. But if I start changing a lot—internally, not just my appearance—it affects the rest of us to some degree. Understand?"

"No," I admitted. "I'm sorry, Stell. All this is doing is making me more concerned for you. Can you make it clearer for me?"

"Ugh," the gold-skinned woman said in a frustrated tone. "I'm transitioning into adulthood, okay, Wes? The last bit of puberty is happening right now."

Huh?

"Huh?" I repeated, not even realizing that I didn't say it out loud the first time. "What?" Puberty?"

"Yes, Wes, puberty. When I said I was technically close to your age, this was what I meant."

"Puberty?" I repeated again. Stell rolled her eyes.

"Do you understand why I was hesitant to tell you now?" she demanded.

"No," I repeated. I dimly realized my jaw was hanging open. "Puberty? Like, real puberty? The same puberty I'm wrapping up?"

"For the third time, yes, Wes! That's exactly what I said not five seconds ago! Five Avalonian seconds!"

I dimly remembered that time traveled differently here. And that Guineve had also mentioned that Stell's emotional age was close to mine. It didn't make anything clearer in my head.

"But, but," I repeated, gesturing all around. "But, Avalon! Planets! Tumults! Challenges! Icons! You talk to gods, Stell! Are they all going through puberty too?"

"No," she grumbled. "Thank goodness. Most of them were not Icons back then, and they were even more obnoxious when they were my age. Ugh. My emotional age, I mean. Starsown are really, really long-lived, okay?"

"Okay, fine," I said, getting enough of my brain together to grasp that one fact. "But that means, even though you live practically forever by everyone's standards, you've been doing all of this while you've still been growing up? Is that...right?"

Because that made no sense to me.

"Yes," Stell sighed in relief. "I'm glad this is making sense to you now."

Damn it.

"I had to deal with it during the last Challenger too, although it wasn't as much of a problem then. I don't know why everything's so much more severe now. And I don't really want to go into a lot of details with you, no offense. But the changes in my emotions are impacting my aspects, especially Breena, since she's the least emotionally mature."

"Isn't she your second oldest aspect?" I asked.

"Yes," Stell replied. "But she's also a fairy."

Oh, well, I finally told myself. *Just roll with it like you've had to do with all the other nonsense around here.*

"Do Starsown normally start watching planets that young?" I asked after a second. "As young as you were, when you first started this?"

"No," Stell said quietly. "Normally they start right about my current age, after they've had a family member train them for a number of centuries."

"Why weren't you trained that way?" I asked.

"Because my family's gone," Stell said quietly. "We live long, but we're not immortal. Something happened and now everyone's gone. And I'm here on Avalon."

"Oh," I said. Suddenly the mists around me felt larger. And lonelier. "I'm sorry," I said, and I felt like an idiot because I knew it wasn't enough.

"It's okay," Stell mumbled, looking away for a moment. "Look, I didn't mean to drag you into all of my personal issues. Don't get the wrong idea, this wasn't something you were supposed to know," she said that last part much more quickly. I had no idea what the wrong idea was, though. "Most Challengers don't get to know too much about me. Until recently, I didn't even appear to most of them. I just borrowed Guineve to be my face for them."

"Did she ever rat you out, like she did when I came?" I asked suspiciously.

"No," she glowered. "That, along with her other pranks, is a fairly recent turn of events. Back when she woke up one morning and decided she would act like somebody's bored mom for a couple of centuries and see what she could get away with.

"The point is," she continued doggedly, "I'm used to keeping as much about myself hidden from Challengers as possible. It keeps things from being too complicated. You all have to go back to Earth at some point, and it's not like I have a way to stay in contact with you."

"You don't?" I asked suddenly.

"No, Wes," Stell sighed. "I could barely get that reggaeton music, remember? I can maintain low-level monitoring on that planet, and that's it. I'm not able to keep up with former Challengers except to make sure that they've kept some of their power, and then I have to move back to watching all of the other planets I keep track of. But back to the point," she said quickly. "Last time when you talked, it helped me understand some of the things that you were dealing with." Her voice softened as she continued. "It didn't enable me to fix what you had to deal with. I can't make the idiots back on Earth see what kind of person you are. But knowing some of your internal struggles helps me work with you as my Challenger. I shared all of this because I realized you needed the same benefit, to know that my Satellites and I have our own hang-ups, and you're going to have to deal with us working through them too."

"Fair enough," I shrug. "And... Stell? If it helps, whenever I'm here and you don't need me to go save the world or train, you can talk to me about anything you want. I won't mind."

"That's sweet, Wes," Stell said with a smile. "And also something we won't have much time for. But thank you."

That was pretty much it for today. I had to sit through a tearful apology from Breena who said she would 'super make it up to me someday.' She also gave me the exact same explanation Stell gave about me scaring everyone by running into threats they thought extinct and solving them in ways that should have killed me permanently by using powers I shouldn't have yet, all while hearing voices about long-dead gods, and pretty much turning triangles into squares wherever I went. Then she apologized again, and explained that she wouldn't resort to risks involving unnecessary mutilations, because she got most of the data she needed while I was in were-badger hell. Next mission, we'd work on wearing armor. She got frustrated when she asked if I wanted armor that focused on mobility or heavy defense, and I just said 'yes.'

Also, she said that she would be training my base abilities, but the Charisma training was going to be delayed for a while. The tiny woman refused to elaborate when I asked why, and I was too weirded out to investigate further.

I called it a day and tried to see if I could pull myself back to my own world on my own again.

It worked. That reminded me that I could now enter Avalon almost at will, and that I had also gotten stronger again. That good news was enough for me to feel happy about my time there, castrating were-badgers notwithstanding.

20

STAND TALL

That's right, I told myself as the pastor kept preaching. *This is why I don't like church anymore.*

Well, that and the way everyone here still looked at me.

Different people have had different experiences with church. I knew that, even though I spent most of my life in a small suburb that pretended it wasn't connected to a larger city whenever it felt like it. I knew that some people have had frankly shitty experiences with organized religion and had perfectly good reasons to be suspicious about it.

I *used* to not be one of those people. Church used to be a really good place for me. I'd go and hear about how God loved me and how he wanted me to love others. I'd meet people who weren't perfect but were mostly trying their best at being loving and good. We'd have a good time together, and we would all get together about twice a month to try and do something meaningful, like bring food to homeless people and try to help them find housing, or partner with businesses to raise money for charities. Or we'd find struggling families in the community to see what we could help them with. When we started running out of homeless people to find housing for and families that still needed assistance, we expanded our projects to include nearby cities and towns. There would be stories about what we did in several papers, in several different towns.

That was then. This was now.

Now, most of the people who took part in those projects moved out of town for one reason or another. My parents never talked about why. I do know we stayed because my parents' jobs wouldn't really let them move.

When we had that mass exodus of people, a lot of the fun stuff in church stopped happening. Nobody had any desire to organize anything else but Dad, and his projects ended for good after his death.

Right before he died, the old pastor left as well. I never found out why, just that it was abrupt and that a lot of the people left in church were excited about his replacement.

After hearing the new pastor preach one sermon, I would never think highly of those people again.

The old pastor kept most of his sermons short, simple, and relevant. Love God, love other people. Make them feel loved. Pray and care for the sick, help those in poverty where you can, stand up whenever you see someone being mistreated. Every sermon of his I could remember was either about that, or where the Bible talked about doing that, or constructive ways on how to do that. He made helping someone else seem less scary, made it easier to get out of my comfort zone and make a difference.

The remaining people in church got excited when that pastor was replaced, and they weren't shy about showing it. I thought that was kind of rude at the time, but I tried to give them the benefit of the doubt. Maybe the new guy would be phenomenal, I thought. Maybe he would really encourage us to love each other and our neighbors, keep the church a place where new people like Himari and Andre would still feel comfortable visiting.

Nope.

His first sermon was to beware of the Devil dragging us all straight to hell. And that would happen if we didn't pay more attention in politics, especially national politics, or the politics in communities other than our own, and that we needed to protect God's church from outside threats by never letting them in so that they could corrupt and damn the rest of us.

He wouldn't elaborate what those threats were, but he specified that they always came from elsewhere—never within—to corrupt "God's people." Again, no clarity provided. No idea on who these people were, what they said, where they came from, or who they looked like. Just that 'we'd know who they were.'

The one time he got close to specifying was after my Dad's suicide. He didn't mention my father by name, but he stated several times that our 'current trials' were proof that the Devil was already among us, and that we needed to make sure he wasn't still there.

He had looked straight at my family when he said that.

He may have been looking straight at me.

Except for that one specification, people took that term to mean whatever they wanted. Everyone got nastier with each other, new people were no longer welcome, and it pretty much became one of those churches I had always had trouble believing existed. I had no idea why Christina and Davelon kept going, but I could tell they weren't thrilled about the place now either.

Today though, as I watched him from the pulpit, he was actually talking about something specific. Instead of just saying 'be afraid' or 'be wary,' he was actually arguing for a real position. Our church needed to do more politically, he said, because the changes in the country were putting all of our souls in danger. Pretty soon God and the Bible would be thrown straight out of America. If we didn't want to get kicked out of our own country as well, we needed to start fighting for the Bible's right to exist, and the only way to do that was to campaign for the Ten Commandments to be posted in every government building, in every town.

If we didn't do that, he said, America as we knew it would be finished.

I tried to tune him out at that point. In the past, I had wanted to argue with him, tell him he was giving the rest of us a bad name, and quote a dozen or so passages from the Bible that said to be the exact opposite of paranoid. I wanted to point out that his refusing to articulate what we were supposed to be wary of was just making sure we'd be afraid of everything. But Dad's suicide and the testimony of those three girls pretty much ruined any credibility I had left in church, and my injury the next year made it a lot harder for me to call up facts in a discussion. That, and I was still just a kid in many people's eyes.

Still, I thought as I watched him rant, *maybe I should try anyway*. Dad's suicide was years ago. And maybe people weren't as suspicious of me as I thought they were. After all, I was practically crippled, Avalon notwithstanding—not yet—and it was ridiculous to think I was capable of hurting anyone, even if they were a child.

It wouldn't hurt to talk to him, I decided. My mind was working better now; it was much easier to recall facts. And maybe he wasn't like this on purpose, I thought. Maybe he'd hear me out and it would give him something to think about. Or maybe not. But shouldn't someone try anyway? Shouldn't someone at least make the effort? Sure, I was really young, but that hadn't stopped me from saving lives here or in Avalon. Why let it stop me now?

After the service, I resolved. I'd at least ask him to make more sense of his position, ask who we're supposed to be afraid of, and why, because after talking about the Ten Commandments for a bit, he went right back to talking about fear and vigilance. I'd see if having to articulate his position would at least make him more reasonable.

And if he didn't get more reasonable, I figured I owed it to the last bit of my own faith to try to stand up to him.

While I was planning that, I kept doing my best to ignore the two women sitting some distance behind me.

"Did you see who's come back," one whispered.

"In the flesh itself," the other whispered.

"Why do you think he came back?"

"Probably to try and get right with God."

"Took him a long time to want to do so," the other woman muttered. "Hasn't it been over a year?"

"Well, sometimes it takes tragedy and illness to bring a person back," the other woman said sadly. Sort of sadly that is.

"Probably hoping to get better by doing so, the poor thing."

"Well, you never know..."

Tune them out, I told myself. *It's nothing you haven't heard before. And it's not like you only run into them at church.*

The service ended. I waited for a moment for people to get up, then I got up myself.

The pastor was still at the pulpit. I took another look at him. He didn't seem that old, mid-thirties to early forties would be my guess. Head full of black hair, plain black suit.

But enough distractions, I told myself. *Just walk up and talk to him*. I grabbed my cane and pulled myself out of the aisle.

"Buddy Wes! Buddy Wes!"

A small voice several aisles ahead of me had started shouting. I barely had time to look down before a tiny black-haired shape slammed into my knees.

Ow, I thought. *Right. Small children have no brakes or air bags.*

"You're finally back! We missed you!"

"Hi, Little Gabby," I replied, seeing everything spin painfully, but thankfully at least this time I was able to brace and keep my head from hitting anything. My body was still improving. "How are you?"

"I'm gud, Buddy Wes!" the little girl said, smiling up at me. Gabriella was one of the few Hispanic girls that still went to our church. I think she turned eight this year, but she was still smaller than most kids a grade behind her. She was bilingual, but young enough that she still didn't form her words properly, giving an adorable quality to her accented English and Spanish. She was clinging to my knees tightly, the way she used to when she would beg me to carry her on my shoulders so that she could feel tall for a while.

I felt the whole service room go tense, and I didn't even dare to smile at her.

"Buddy Wes, are you coming to see us at vacashiyon bible school this year?"

"I'm sorry, Little Gabby," I said, trying not to even be seen moving toward the little girl, which was probably impossible because she was still hugging and pulling on my legs. "I don't know if I'll be better this summer." She had barely grown at all in two years, I realized. I had always wondered if little Gabby was one of those kids that were destined to be short and adorable for their whole lives. And I wanted to tell her I missed her too. But I didn't dare right now.

Do you think it will matter? a voice said inside me, and I winced in pain as it spoke. *Do you think it will matter what you dare to do?*

"But when are you coming baaaack?" she asked in a drawn-out plea. "We miss you!"

Her big brown eyes were shining and watering. I almost caved in to giving her a hug, concussion and poor balance be damned. Or at least a pat on the head. She loved those too.

But then I heard them again.

"Tsk, tsk."

"So that's why he's back."

"Poor girl. She doesn't even realize."

"Is her mother even watching her right now?"

I hate it when fear doesn't lie.

"She lives with her aunt now."

"Her aunt always was too trusting."

"Doesn't she know it's genetic? The poor boy probably can't even help himself."

"I know. His father probably couldn't help it either. Look, he's sweating."

"Buddy Wes?" Little Gabby repeated her plea.

"I," I started to say, then realized I couldn't finish the sentence. *I'm sorry? I can't see you anymore? I have to be careful or people will think I'm like Dad?*

Aren't you like your dad? Pain whispered again inside of me. *Don't you look like him, talk like him?*

My tongue stuck to the roof of my mouth, and I couldn't say another word to the little girl I had once read Bible stories to every Sunday. Her dark little face was starting to crumple, and she bit her lip.

"Now, Gabriella," a male voice said from in front of me. "Wes can't be with you little ones anymore. He's very sick."

The pastor was walking steadily towards me now. His voice sounded gentle, and firm. But I swore that I could see the relish in his eyes when he called me 'sick.'

"But when will he get better, Pastor Barnes?"

"He may never get better, Gabriella," Pastor Barnes said solemnly. "We just have to pray."

"But I pray for him all the time!" the little girl wailed. Her face was really scrunched up now, and she looked seconds away from crying. "Why doesn't he get better?"

"Gabby, don't question God," Pastor Barnes said firmly. "Now go see your grandmother."

"Bye, Buddy Wes," the little girl sniffled, before she lowered her head and stomped off.

Pastor Barnes moved his head to look back at me. He was about my height, I realized, which actually made him tall. Other than that, he was neither wide, nor skinny, nor muscular. Just the normal mix of fat and muscle most men had at his age.

"Good afternoon, Wes," the man said in a neutral voice. "Welcome back."

In a small town church, someone would not just tell you, "welcome back," if you were actually welcome. You got pulled over for a hug, or at least a handshake, and the person asked how you were doing, and if you had been well. If they knew about your family, they would ask about your family. They would invite you over some time for dinner, or some other event.

They definitely would not stand in front of you with their hands in their pockets, with no trace of a smile on their face.

Unless they wanted to put on a show in front of their whole congregation, I realized. *To make sure everyone knew they could stand up to the 'Devil's' people.*

I heard some more whispering, but I was tired of it, and I was finally able to ignore it completely.

"Hello, Pastor Barnes," I replied calmly, to my surprise. "How has everyone been?"

A frown flashed his face. Was he not expecting a reply at all? Was he really just expecting me to just slink away? With my tail between my legs? As if I actually had something left to lose?

"Everyone's been well," he replied. "It's a shame you have been gone." His voice was still neutral. "These last few years have been some of the church's best."

That last line was actually said meaningfully. I couldn't tell if he was just trying to let me know I wasn't welcome or actually trying to impress me with the church's status.

I reminded myself that I had gotten up to speak to him.

"Are you sure, Pastor Barnes?" I asked frankly. "Everyone seems so tense now. Not just at me, but at each other too. Like we're all on edge, instead of working with each other. And I haven't seen us do anything in the community like we used to. I'm just worried, Pastor Barnes."

Outrage flushed all over the man's face. I heard gasps behind me, and some more muttering.

"I'm sure it would seem that way to *you*," Pastor Barnes said, regaining control at some point near the end of that sentence. "But the facts say otherwise. Attendance in this congregation has doubled every year. Along with tithes and offerings. You don't see us out in the community because we bring the community here, son. The same with projects. People contribute by bringing their money here, directly to God."

More muttering behind me. This time it had a vindicated note to it.

"I wouldn't know anything about your numbers, Pastor Barnes," I replied carefully. My conscience had insisted I say my piece, but this conversation was becoming increasingly meaningless. "And maybe I came on a lower turnout day, so I'm not seeing the whole picture. But there are so many people I know that used to come here, that still live in this town. I saw none of them here today, and that worries me."

Maybe I was being more insolent than I thought. Maybe I was pretending the old pastor was still here, the guy who loved hearing about people's doubts and helping them work through them, or just listening to them when he didn't know what to say.

Or maybe the new pastor was just an asshole who took everything I said as a challenge to his authority, and didn't appreciate me making him look bad. But after my words, the flush went all the way down to the man's neck, and he practically bared his teeth at me when he spoke again.

"Not everyone who comes here once or twice chooses salvation in the end, *young man*. And I'm sorry, but unsurprised, to know that neither of your sister's immigrant friends or others so dear to you made the right choice with their lives. But that harms only them, because the church can do without their presence. The people who can really make a difference in the community have all made both this place and heaven their home, whatever you may say or think. And those people are going to be the ones making real change, using God's money to bring in leaders that will pass laws that honor His own rules. And when that happens, maybe the consequences of those laws will motivate others to choose salvation before it's too late."

"Amen," someone muttered behind me, and for a second I couldn't recognize anyone standing around this man.

That wasn't true, I realized. It had been far longer than a second.

It had been two years. I hadn't recognized anyone in this town, save my family and a handful of others, in two years. Everyone I had grown up with was either gone or... changed. Into what, I couldn't articulate. Maybe they were always like that, and just had stopped pretending after Dad's death. I didn't know. But this place, the place my parents brought me to learn how to love my enemies and my neighbor, had become a place of something sick and malicious. Where people who didn't even like each other whispered together about others they hated even more.

And since I had only seen what was directed at me, I just took it personally. But mentioning 'immigrant friends' in a way where the word immigrant was a slur? Mentioning that people had lost their salvation just for missing sermons?

Even at my mind's most damaged state, I could remember enough facts to know both of those ideas to be un-biblical. And really, really douchey.

There was a smug grin on the pastor's face, and I realized I had been right earlier. Even in his anger he had been relishing this, this triumph of his.

He had boasted of numbers and tithes and the prestige of his members to *me*, a half-crippled eighteen-year old kid. I was a nobody, and I was still someone he couldn't bear to be ignored by.

I shook my head. The movement hurt a little. But this was a rare case where my stomach hurt more than my head.

There was nothing more to say to the man, so I turned, slowly and carefully, to leave so that I could find a ride home. Either Christina or Davelon should be still around.

Pastor Barnes apparently felt like he hadn't already had the last word, because he called out to me again.

"You should repent and submit to authority, son. I know you take your disease and suffering as a sign of God's judgment and abandonment, but if you repent now, you may yet find some small measure of God's mercy."

"Actually, Pastor Barnes," I said as I stopped and turned my head slightly. "The first chapter of James says I should consider all my troubles as pure joy, because the testing of my faith produces perseverance, and that perseverance will make me mature and complete in time. Also, Jesus said 'blessed are those who mourn, for they shall be comforted,' in Matthew 5. So I shouldn't take my every single problem to be a sign of His judgment, and I shouldn't ever expect a 'small' amount of mercy from God, because the New Testament says over and over that God is rich in love, slow to anger and abounding in mercy. I miss hearing messages like that here, Pastor Barnes. Good day."

A gasp had swept through the room as I had started speaking, but it had vanished by the time I had said goodbye. I turned back to walk out of the room. More whispering had begun behind my back, and for once, I was able to ignore it completely.

My nerves were agonizing. But the rest of me was rejoicing. I had stood my ground, despite my balance problems, and recalled something I had read twice in a row without my brain blanking out on me. That was easily worth the newly increased pain I was feeling.

More than that, I felt...lighter. A heaviness had fallen upon me when that man had begun dumping hate out of his mouth. I felt like some vagrant ghost had taken refuge inside my conscience, and as soon as it had moved in, it began hollering about how it had been wronged and dishonored and evicted from its rightful home. When I had finished talking with that man, though, I felt it give a satisfied huff and move on.

It had the right idea. I wanted to get out of there as fast as I could, too.

When I had gotten home, I thanked Davelon and Christina for the ride, but I asked them to stop inviting me. They were hurt, but after hearing about what happened, they understood and didn't fault me for it.

I could tell they felt torn about the place. They still went because they felt obligated to, and because they didn't know where else to go. They just shook their heads when I asked about the other churches in town.

I got home, greeting my mother and sister who hadn't gone. Then I went to go wash the sweat off my face in the bathroom. The stares and whispers I noticed while little Gabby had held onto me hadn't been easy to deal with.

I looked back up at the mirror, and blinked. When I opened my eyes again, I still saw the same thing.

"Mom, Rachel," I called out. "Did either of you write anything on the bathroom mirror?"

"Rachel!" I heard my mother shout. "What did I tell you about leaving your little lipstick notes everywhere?"

"I haven't done that since I was thirteen, Mom!" my sister shouted back as stomped over to the bathroom. "Wes, what are you talking about?"

When she got to the bathroom mirror, she blinked too.

"What?" She sounded confused, and I started to feel relieved, because it meant she had seen it too.

"That was weird," she said next. "For a second it looked like there was something written on the mirror. But nothing's there. Right, Wes?"

I looked back at the mirror, still seeing the exact same words scrawled over it.

"Yeah, it's clear," I lied. "That's weird. I thought I saw writing too. What did you see?"

Rachel shook her head slowly.

"It was only there for a second. I couldn't make it out."

"Same here," I lied again.

"Do you think it was a trick of the light? Or are we both going crazy?" my sister asked jokingly.

"I think it's just been a long day," I replied tiredly. I was tired, but I hoped I wasn't still sweating.

"Already?" she asked carefully. "Church still that bad?"

I shook my head slowly. At least this time, it didn't really hurt. Or I was too busy not freaking out to not feel any pain.

"Worse," I replied. "New pastor's a jackass, and probably an evil cultist in disguise. And all the other jackasses still at church think he's great."

"Bummer. One more reason for me not to bother checking it out myself."

"Good call," I said. "I'd recommend you do exactly that. I'm going to lie down and see how many brain cells I lost in that sermon."

She muttered a goodbye and went to her own room, looking distracted. I hurried to my room as fast as my better balance allowed. I closed the door and locked it, then, to get myself under control, I closed my eyes and slowly tried to count to ten.

I didn't make it.

I limped over to my bed and lay down, closing my eyes again.

I still saw it.

The same writing I saw on the mirror stood out against the dark of my eyelids, with the exact same angry, scrawling script.

Traitor-prince. Malus is watching for you.

21

TRUDGE INSTEAD OF STUMBLE

The next day I woke up feeling especially fuzzy. A corner of my mind was screaming that I had seen something intensely disturbing right before I had fallen asleep, but I couldn't remember what it was. I had the dim memory of seeing something horrible written on a mirror, and the words following me for the rest of the day every time I closed my eyes. But I couldn't remember what they were. No one else looked like they remembered anything, so I didn't bring it up and chalked it up to just another bad dream. There just wasn't much else I could do about it.

Well, there was one thing, I realized.

I could get stronger.

I told my mother I needed more time off, that I wanted to see what I could study online, safe at home, and that I wanted more time to do exercises, both physical and in my game. She was thrilled by all of that, even if she still hadn't come around to liking my game. Didn't matter to me. As long as she let me play it and hopefully keep getting better, I'd take it.

When I wasn't gaming with my Australian friends, I was practicing the movements I had done in Avalon. The similarity between the game and that place was uncanny. I had done comparisons a long time ago, but now that I had actual combat experience from Avalon, I found it to be almost identical to combat in *Heroes Unbound.* Looking back, it was like that game had wound up being the perfect set of training wheels for actually going on adventures in Avalon or the Woadlands. Swinging a sword didn't seem that different, for instance. Neither did my punches and kicks, although those attacks weren't as supported in the game. Even the magic had a few things in common, especially the basic positioning to begin a spell.

When I realized that, I started to ask myself more questions.

Was I unique? Would other people who had played this game also have the same benefits if they became a Challenger? Were these benefits a coincidence, or by design?

Could *Heroes Unbound* have been designed by another Challenger?

That last idea seemed absurd. The game wasn't even ten years old. I know time passes more slowly on Earth, but surely Stell would have reacted more to getting a Challenger that much sooner.

But what if the Challenger had traveled to Avalon a long time ago?

Say, thirty, maybe forty years or so?

Could they have been a hero in Avalon's worlds, then, long after they came back, decided to go into game design, using their projected body's experience as a template for virtual reality?

And if so, wasn't that a waste of time? I mean sure, go ahead and make a successful video game, but in the end, a Challenger was supposed to gain a great deal of power. Like a sharper brain, a healthier body, and a bunch of minor magical benefits that somehow carried over into this world. I would hope that the kind of person who had successfully been a hero in other worlds would keep being a hero in this one and do things like save a third-world country, make a new breakthrough in medicine, or just create a really awesome charity.

At the very least, if there had been a Challenger this century, I should have heard about an awesome person who did something like that, save lives, help people in developing countries, etc.

But maybe I was presuming too much. If a lot of other people had my condition, then this game really was helping lives.

But why put so much of the rules that governed Avalon and the rest of the Expanse into it? That couldn't have been easy, and how could they have known for certain that the next Challenger would wind up playing the game?

Too many questions, too few answers, too little time.

I pulled my focus back to getting healthier on Earth and preparing to stop the coming cataclysms in Avalon's worlds.

According to Stell and Breena, the preparations were coming along very well. They were able to get some basic weapons in the armory—something they assured me they would have already had if Stell had been able to call me like a normal Challenger, but whatever. I was finally getting time to practice moving about with different types of armor. Once again, the experience was suspiciously familiar. Playing *Heroes* had made it easier to understand Breena's explanations when she described how to walk in it. I also got more practice with different weapons, eventually getting to use things like a spear and a long blade.

I had another minor Challenge come up. A large but primitive coastal village on the Sun-jeweled Sea was facing an intense storm created by rogue magic. Dealing with the rogue magic was necessary, but the Challenge would still be failed if the village was wiped out. Even after I dealt with the source of the rogue magic, I still had to deal with the storm it had summoned. This Challenge was neat because it wasn't solved by just killing things, although I did find a nest of lizard-men-things sailing around casting dangerous and unstable storm magic. It turned out that they were manipulating the air currents to make harsher seas, apparently in preparation for the upcoming Tumults and Trials. I had asked Breena if it was normal for monsters from one Challenge to help prepare for another. She said it wasn't, and the whole thing made her very nervous. Two bits of good news though. The lizard men had been easy to find and deal with. They were just a few miles off the coast, in a large, easily-seen ship that was glowing from all the rituals they were performing. When they somewhat rudely declined my request to not destroy the world and tried to attack me, I just retreated to my own vessel that Breena was helping me pilot and wrecked their ship with strategically worked lightning and air magic. It turned out that other than that ritual they were performing, they had no real weapons or offensive magic—just some claw-like fingernails and faith in their Dark Icon to grant them victory over their enemies.

Casting at sea was a little difficult, but the extra balance and concentration from my Ideals seemed to make the process much easier. Ironically, what helped me the most was a new Earth spell Breena taught me called *Stone Grip*, a spell that created a bond between myself and objects I wanted to hold onto. I was nonplussed until she explained that I could use it on my *feet*, allowing me to grip the deck of a ship or raft and not fall over easily. I thought that was the most brilliant thing she'd taught me yet. With that worked out, all it had taken to wreck their ship was a gust of wind into their sails to direct them towards some high rocks, and a few attack spells for when they tried to correct their course. Boarding the boat didn't pull up any real clues except for the diagrams they were drawing and a few religious paraphernalia that Breena said was for a Dark Icon called the Writhing One. But the real good news was that Breena was able to determine that wrecking the ritual had delayed the upcoming storm by several days.

Three days later, as the waves were finally beginning to swell and the wind was beginning to pick up, I had thrown down the last heavy rock into the water, walked away from the edge of the cliff I was on, and collapsed onto the grass with a heavy sigh.

"Wes, what are you doing?" Breena chittered at me. "The storm is coming! You need to evacuate like everyone else has!"

"I will," I panted. "In five minutes. I have that long for sure." I took a few deep breaths to fully answer her. "I have spent the last three days carting heavy rocks from Avalon and the Woadlands to here, directing people where to move them, and personally placing the ones too heavy for Unrisen people to move. Give me," I panted, "time to catch my breath."

"Number one, *no*," the little fairy said firmly and confidently. "Number two, we don't even know if this idea will work." She ticked off another finger.

"It will work," I panted back. "I just spent three days making sure it would."

"Number three, even if your big, strong, human man body can handle the storm, my petite, delicate, shapely, princess body deserves to not have to. So get up and make sure I can fly out of the rain."

"Fine," I sighed as I got up, my back aching terribly. As I walked over to the cave the villagers were using to hide from the storm, Breena stopped flying and landed on my shoulder, squirming around until she apparently got into a more comfortable position. Which was right on my sorest spot.

"Really?" I asked the little fairy in annoyance.

"Flying around all day is tiring," she yawned.

Yup. Stell definitely needs to work on her empathy some more.

"Tell you what," Breena said with another yawn. "I can respect your needs and compromise. If your shoulders really hurt that much, I can just rest in one of your pockets—"

"No."

Definitely not going that route.

"That way your shoulders can rest and—"

"No."

"I can stay completely out of the rain!" She looked proud of the idea.

"No." I was not.

"Why?" she asked, tilting her head. "Are your legs as tired as your shoulders?"

"No. And no pocket rides for tiny woman-things. The world isn't ready for that and neither am I."

"But I'm so small!" my (hopefully) naive friend protested. "And I can get even smaller! I'd hardly weigh anything in there! And if you're worried about me playing a trick, there's all these people that would be watching us!" She pointed to the nearby villagers huddling in the cave.

"And now it's so much worse," I replied with a sigh. "Great. No pocket rides and that's final. Stay out of my pants."

With a huff, she snuggled back into my shoulder and didn't say anything.

Two hours later, while we were all under the cave, the storm was in full swing, and all the villagers were muttering about how they could still see their crude houses.

"Is that really working?" Breena asked, peering at the waves crashing against the rocks I had piled up.

"It won't be a perfect fix," I admitted. "They'll still have a bit of flooding get through. But most of their stuff should survive. Best I could do." I shrugged helplessly. "Sorry."

"To be honest, we weren't even expecting you to do that much," Breena replied, looking out at the storm curiously. "We figured you'd just help people evacuate so that they could rebuild later. What did you call those piles of rocks again?"

"Depending on where I placed them, they're either called rock armor or groynes. The rock armor will deflect or absorb the wave energy while the groynes will help trap any dangerous debris the storm brings. And afterwards," I said with a tired sigh, "unlike more permanent coastal protection, the rocks can be moved elsewhere so that the drift can return to its natural cycle, to prevent any long-term damage to the beach. Not that I'm going to get started on that today."

"Wow," Breena squeaked in an awed voice. "When did you learn all of that?"

"I've tried to study erosion in the past to have a career in city-planning," I replied. "But since I was rusty on most of the stuff, I had to go over everything again online."

"What's 'online?'" Breena asked. "Is that some kind of library you can go visit?"

"Exactly," I said, rotating sore muscles. "Get Stell to tell you about it sometime. It's something you can read anywhere, anytime you want as long as you have access to a special tool called the internet."

Her little fairy eyes popped open.

"What?" she shrieked—or squeaked, because she was in super-tiny size. "That's amazing! That means anybody can learn anything!"

"I guess," I replied. "Provided they can read or hear and have access to the internet. And they go to the right places."

"But why were you going to school before if you could just use the internet?" the little woman asked with a tilt of her spiky, pink-haired head.

"That's... a good question," I realized. "I guess because not everything you learn online is necessarily true, so it's a little trickier to figure out. And school provides people who can help you learn things that are hard for you, called teachers. There's also a lot of people there, so it helps you learn to interact with others."

"Oh, okay," the little fairy said. "I guess those things are all good, too. Good thing you got all of that."

"Yeah..." I said slowly. "Sure I did."

I didn't, I realized. I had teachers like Mr. Jammers lie to me. I had a lot of other people do me harm. Except for Ms. Springsen, maybe school really had been a waste of time for me.

In the end, the village had survived with only minor damage from the rain and wind. The people were all shocked when they discovered just how little their damage was and they thanked me profusely for saving them months of rebuilding. I had wanted them to thank me by handling the boulders all by themselves, but then I remembered that most of these boulders had come from another world anyway. That had led to another back-breaking couple of days that had me feeling completely miserable until I realized that my Constitution and Strength had both risen by not one but two points.

"Breena," I asked while resting on the beach, "how fast is a Challenger supposed to Rise?"

"It depends, I guess," the little fairy mused as she hovered next to me. "How hard you work, how valuable the work you do is, how many people are affected by it."

"Do I have to do it by completing Challenges from Avalon?" I asked.

"No," the pink-haired woman snorted. "Then no one would Rise but Challengers. Plenty of people do it at least once or twice by overcoming personal goals of some type or another. It can be almost anything, as long as it's at least somewhat difficult, important in some way to someone, and makes you grow in the process."

"Grow how?"

"Grow in any way," the pretty sprite said with another shrug. "Be a better swordsman. Get more exercise. Figure out how to stop burning your bread, or what your friend needs from you when they're sick."

"Is it normal for a Challenger to grow as fast as I can?" I asked. "And could I Rise from overcoming Challenges back on Earth?"

"I don't know," the little fairy admitted. "It's much harder for us to track how you change back on Earth. And we've never needed to either. As for how fast you're growing, I don't know because you're a special case. We have a lot of extra time to train you because you came to us much sooner than most Challengers. But so far, yes. You've been within parameters. Barely. But if you were to suddenly Rise any time soon, or right now, *that* would be crazy fast. We've never... wait, why are you getting up?"

She asked, watching me suspiciously.

"No reason," I said cheerfully, standing up and stretching my arms. They felt exhausted, but with a 'good burn' feel to them. Far better than they should have felt. "By the way, 'ding,'" I said as I reached into myself, grasped that inner weight and *pushed*.

While Breena started chattering in surprise, I looked at my stats once again.

Wes Malcolm
Race: Human. Origin: Earth (Challenger)
Growth Level: Third Rise (Spark)
Path: Unknown
Saga: Unknown

Profession: Unknown
Vital Pool: 520 points
Stamina Pool: 520 points.
Mana Pool: 560 points

Strength: 26
Dexterity: 26
Constitution: 26
Intelligence: 26
Wisdom: 28
Charisma: 22

Speed: 30
Deftness: 30
Wits: 31
Will: 32

Insight into the Following Ideals
Earth: lvl 3
Air: lvl 3
Lightning: lvl 3

Skill List truncated

Spell list truncated

2 skill points available.
Signature Spells have improved since last viewing.

I took a second glance at the screen to confirm it had the changes I had wanted to make and nodded in satisfaction. I had decided to put two points into Dexterity, one point into Intelligence and Constitution, and converted the remaining two points into four points of Deftness. I also increased the spell level of my Ideals by one each, bringing them all up to third level. Then I left two skill points free for future discoveries.

"Already?" Breena squeaked. "Seven frazzled fairy gumdrops, Wes! Slow down so that the rest of us can breathe! Now I have to come up with a whole new type of training! Good grief, you'll be past the first five Rises before I run out of things to teach you!"

I shrugged.

"Sorry, not sorry."

That comment earned me a tiny, sparkling punch to the face.

22

OWNING PROGRESS

About a month had passed. On Earth, at least. Time flew much faster in Avalon. By now, I was going to Avalon almost every night.

I was scheduled for another appointment with my therapist soon. My test results were still up in the air, although my English teacher still insisted I did a marvelous job on the writing portion, and Mr. Jammers still insisted I failed both my Math and Science portions and shouldn't be allowed to take the test a fourth time. We were waiting on the scholarship program to make the final decision.

I had gone to Ms. Springsen's class a few times to say thank you and goodbye. She was just the same as I remembered, a beautiful and kind woman who brightened other people's lives and proved to me that not everyone in this town was rotten.

I still played tabletop games with my sister, Himari, Andre, and her other friends from the Drama club. Davelon had actually come a few times as well. He tried to hide it, but he was actually a lot nerdier than he cared to admit. But that was okay. It just made him more fun.

His dad was still looking into getting my attackers and the football coach prosecuted, but he had hit a stone wall in the investigation for now. And Davelon quietly confided that he had been drinking more heavily. My own dad's death had hit Davelon's father, Thomas Brown, pretty hard, and it came out whenever the man got drunk. When he was drunk, he blamed himself for Dad's death, saying that he had failed a friend that he had already owed his life to. That didn't make sense to me because Davelon's father wasn't even affiliated with the investigation into my dad's death, and Davelon didn't have any more light to shed on the matter. He was glad to see me doing better, though. He hoped that fact would help his own dad move on. I didn't begrudge him that. Davelon had watched my back for years when everyone else hadn’t, and if he hadn't shown up at school that day, I would have been even worse off.

That gaming journal still hadn't released my interview. The game admins ruled conclusively that I hadn't cheated, but someone local had gone online and leaked all the personal stuff about my father and insisted that I also was involved in those girls getting abused, even though they had no way to prove it. But online no one really needed proof, since they could say whatever they wanted, as often as they wanted, and if a few of them did get banned from a few forums, the rest would just holler all the louder.

I was thinking about all that as I sat on my bed and wiggled my toes in front of me. I had tears in my eyes.

But the tears didn't have anything to do with bad memories.

They had to do with the fact that my leg hung in the air in exactly the way I wanted to, without making my head spin. I was naming fact after random fact without my memory locking up. I probably looked like a total idiot, waving my foot in front of my face and constantly muttering to myself, but I didn't care. With a heave, I put both feet on the ground and pulled myself off the bed.

The pain rose up suddenly, like it usually did these days, and I could swear it was a living thing that I was infuriating with every degree of progress. Again, I didn't care. It's not like I owed my pain any favors.

And I was standing without my cane. After I fought through my pain, there wasn't even any dizziness. I had to shuffle a little to stand more comfortably, but that was it. So I took in a deep breath, and took a step forward.

Dizzy for half a second. No other problems.

I started to laugh and took another step forward. Dizzy for a whole second. Other than that, I was fine. The time kept increasing slightly with every additional step I took. Five steps resulted in about three seconds of dizziness and walking ten steps meant a whole five seconds of dizziness. I had to stop after that, because five whole seconds was my limit at the moment.

I'd have to wait until I stopped laughing before I could see how far I could really go. Because if I kept laughing while dizzy, I'd throw up.

"Honey?" my mother's voice called from down the hall. "Are you okay?"

"Yes!" I screamed while laughing. "Yes! Yes!"

When she opened my door to see me, I made her stop about five steps from me and wait for me to stop laughing. She had a worried, I-think-my-son-has-gone-crazy-look, but she did what I asked anyway. Her eyes went wide when I started walking toward her, having to stop for a second or two every time, but still doing it caneless, and when I was right next to her, my arms spread wide. A brief spike of pain screamed through me so hard, I thought I could hear words again, but I fought through it almost immediately, and as soon as it passed, I was able to hug my mother normally for the first time in two years.

Internal scans finished. Please review recent report.

New Log of Subject Anonymous. Triple-Flagged Entry.

As everyone as no doubt noticed, test subject had become increasingly, and dangerously, stable.

It has been acknowledged by the lab that there are signs of Containment becoming increasingly ineffective, despite its escalating—and autonomous—attempts to inhibit and control the subject.

It has also been recognized by the lab that Containment becoming strong enough to break parameters is no longer the least optimum result. The lab is aware that the subject's discovering, conquering, and harnessing of Containment would result in total failure of all long-term goals, both for the project and for the organization as a whole.

But the lab has also confirmed and, more importantly, begun to duplicate, the subject's entry into the location designated Alpha-Zeta-Avalus. Actual human visitation of the location is still impossible, but previous openings were successful enough to grant ocular access to the world resembling the description of Avalon. The openings should be stable for human passage in less than a month.

We've done it, Rhodes. Divinity is less than a season away. Then we activate Malus protocol without restraint.

Team Lead Out.

23

WIN WHILE YOU'RE AHEAD

"I've searched around your community out to ten miles," I told the man in front of me, an older man in a homespun tunic of wool. "Those were the only dens I could find."

"I believe you," the man replied, nodding his head at me. "Had there been any more of those monsters, we would have lost our entire harvest by now. Instead, you have ensured we will have a bounty for seasons to come. We are grateful, Challenger."

I smiled and shrugged at the man's praise.

"You're welcome," I replied. "It's kind of my job, though."

"No, Challenger." The old man shook his head. "The legends say your kind only saves us from great devastation, and then we find our own way afterwards. But you have taken what the heavens would consider a small devastation and turned it into a great abundance. Most of our fields have been saved, as well as all of our flocks. Not only will we have enough food for the year, but we will have additional hides for clothing, additional meat for feasts. The remainder we will sell to bring greater wealth to our village, allowing us to sow an even larger crop next year, as well as purchase better goods and build better homes for many families."

"That's really good to hear," I replied. "I had no idea those things were so valuable. I thought I was just helping delay the problem."

"No, Challenger. Again, we thank you for everything. We wish you great fortune, as great as the fortune you have provided us."

I bid my goodbyes to the village and left for a convenient place to portal back to Avalon. We probably could have done it there, but it always felt weird asking Breena to teleport me in front of other people.

"Aaaand we're done. Early. *Again*," Breena said, flying to rest on my shoulder while we walked. She landed with a *whumph* this time, crossed her arms and scowled.

See, that was why teleporting with people watching was awkward now. Because whenever I finished a Challenge in a certain way, Breena would get an attitude about it.

Apparently, that 'certain way' had happened again. For like the fifth time in the row.

"Is that really a bad thing, Breena?" I asked patiently. At least, I thought it sounded patient. But everyone's a critic these days.

"No, Wes," the little fairy grumbled. "It's great that you got to help these people so fast. It's also great that you found a way to solve a community's problems so quickly. And it's just fruitin' peachy that you bypassed a whole curriculum of teachable experiences that I worked on by turning the problem into the solution!"

"Isn't that what I was supposed to do?" I asked slowly. "You were really big on the fact that this was another Challenge with a time limit, like that one with the storm coming. That was why I tried to fix the problem as quick as I could. I wasn't even expecting my idea to work."

"Your 'time limit' was how long it takes a person to starve to death, Wes!" my fairy companion retorted. "I thought that would have been obvious! Do you know how long it takes one of you humans to starve? At least three days for the weakest, sickest child! And that's only after they run out of food! Were they out of food, Wes?"

"Well, no," I sputtered. "But..."

"But nothing, Wes! The only reason I said 'we're short on time' was so that you wouldn't spend forever teleporting between worlds to go get rocks again!"

"I wouldn't have gone to get rocks," I said tiredly. "People can't eat rocks. I would have found food, and possibly money, on another planet."

"Exactly! And I didn't want you to try and do it this time, because when the real problems start you won't be able to just teleport all over the place and ruin economies! So when I said 'we don't have time for that!' I was trying to get you to stop breaking my training sessions, Wes! And it didn't work!"

"Huh," I said. "Didn't know that. So how long does teleporting take? Because we only had like a week before the storm hit last time, and I still had enough time to move several tons of rocks."

"Don't ask me that!" Breena said, getting flustered. "Just accept that it's magic, and that it takes however long I say it does!"

Breena would have made a bad dungeon or game master, I realized. But having somehow grown wiser through my constant Rising, I didn't say that out loud.

"Ugh, I mean seriously!" the little fairy continued. "How hard is it to not break the rules? Almost every Challenger before you never broke the rules! They listened to me, followed the obvious hints about what to do or where to go, did the logical solution to the problem, and we had a nice, healthy progression for them so that they were ready for when the Trial or Tumult started. They had much less time than you, Wes! But it was still enough to follow all the rules!"

"How was I breaking the rules?" I asked. I couldn't help it. It was like I was back in my sister's game, explaining how I was able to make a building explode or how I got my paladin's armor value to be so high.

"You know how you were breaking the rules!" Breena screamed. "Don't tell me you thought I was expecting you to use the monsters you killed to feed the village! These people are literally going to eat their problems now!"

"Why not?" I asked. "They were eating the village's grain and sheep. They had the same diet as humans do. Except for the fact that they tried to eat me. Besides, people and animals that size eat each other all the time back on my world."

Granted, those animals were at least several points ahead on eating us, last time I checked. Especially the bears. Bears are pretty much the only guys who go around saying "I brought claws to a gun fight and won" on a regular basis. But I wasn't even fighting bears. I was just fighting very large moles. That came up to my shoulder. And had massive retractable bone spikes jutting out all of their bodies at strictly nightmarish angles. Dread moles, they were called. And the name fit. Fighting those things underground was barely more terrifying than fighting Ilklings, and maybe two hairs calmer than being caught by a pack of rabid gibber-kin.

I had no idea why something that terrifying and bloodthirsty had roots and grains as their favorite food. But I supposed that was just what they ate when they couldn't get Challengers.

I did learn, however, that the best way to kill a dread mole is with a long spear, at the right enclosed spot, with lots and lots of lightning magic.

And on further reflection, it was starting to feel like the only problems not solvable with lots of lightning bolts were those caused by lightning bolts in the first place.

"Really?" she asked. "That made sense to you? Not 'go to a nearby village and try and buy or beg for more food?'"

"Why would I do that?" I asked. "I don't know anyone here who sells anything, much less food, I have no idea how much food costs, and I only have a dim idea of how the local currency works. Besides, I don't carry money, because Stell and Avalon currently provide everything I need."

"That's what this quest was supposed to teach you!" Breena practically shouted. "You were supposed to be forced to learn how much things cost! And how to get money when you needed it! In case we ever had to fund an army or something and Stell didn't have any hard currency on her, because even on Avalon money doesn't grow on trees!"

"But didn't I learn all of that by doing what I did?" I countered.

"Well let's see," Breena harrumphed while crossing her arms. "How much will that leftover dread mole meat sell for?"

"I asked about that," I said proudly. "They'll make at least thirty silver pieces per pound. But their merchant says he can get fifty silver from his contacts."

Giant mole meat was apparently a delicacy. But I had already guessed that.

"And how much leftover meat do they think they'll have?" Breena continued.

"According to their butcher, even if they use techniques to preserve it, they have about a hundred pounds that will go bad before they can eat it."

"One *hundred* pounds?" Breena sputtered. "How were you even..." She trailed off, somehow looking lost and angry at the same time.

"They were big moles," I said defensively. "Those things must've weighed over five hundred pounds each, and there were a dozen of them."

"I wasn't expecting you to kill all of them, Wes! Some were almost ten miles away!"

I had learned that some of the more 'natural' monsters, those derived almost entirely from animals, only became a Challenge when they came near where people lived. That was the only time they were deemed to be a danger to the environment. Unlike Horde and the gibber-kin, which got a 'kill-with-fire-on-sight' designation as soon as we became aware of their existence.

"They seemed like they would have become a Challenge later," I said with a shrug. "And I would have left them alone if they hadn't started attacking me first. But since they acted like they were part of the problem, I treated them like it."

"That's not the point!" Breena sputtered again. "The point is that you just whisked up five thousand silvers, or fifty gold coins, practically out of nowhere! And you didn't even realize it!"

"Yes I did," I argued. "That's why I dragged every mole corpse back to the village, even if the trip was several miles. You think I did that for fun? I did that because of the way everyone kept getting excited about every corpse."

Well, it was fun at first, because I realized that I was able to move five hundred pounds now with just my muscles and a little bit of magic. But then I realized that five hundred pounds was still heavy for a miles-long trip.

"No, I thought you did that because you were crazy. And I thought they were all shouting at you because they also thought you were crazy. And you wouldn't stop doing it when I told you to. Now do you realize what you did?"

"Yeah, now I do," I said. "I didn't expect their tanners and butchers to be able to use everything I brought them. I thought more would be wasted, but the only way to make sure was to drag back every single corpse. Besides," I added. "It was free strength and stamina training."

After years back home with no idea whether or not my exercises were working, being able to automatically tell when I was making progress was amazingly addictive.

"Well yes, but... ugh!" For a moment it seemed like the little fairy would give up and just give me the silent treatment for the rest of the way back. But after a minute she battled through her frustration. She took a deep breath and continued speaking again.

"Let me try again, Wes. Let me see if I can ask you two simple questions, and clear everything up. How many bags of grain were you expecting them to need for the winter, and how much were you expecting each bag to cost?"

"Right," I said. "I was thinking about that. I couldn't get an accurate amount from the villagers. I think they were too embarrassed? But anyway, I had to estimate. I figured, worst case scenario, a hundred-pound bag of grain would cost up to a hundred silvers each, and that each family would need two, or at most three bags to get through the winter. There were several hundred people in this place, so I figured I'd need to come up with three hundred gold pieces max... wait, why are you shaking your head at me?"

"Wes..." Breena began. She was covering her tiny face with both of her palms. "I can't even.... I just can't. I give up." She shook her still-covered head slowly. "Where do I even begin? How?"

"Hey," I protested. "I did say it was a worst-case scenario. Since no one told me an exact amount, I figured I should high-ball it to be safe. That's why I was surprised that the Challenge ended when it did."

"Wes," Breena groaned. "Fifty coppers, okay? That's the current price for a bag of grain here. When times are tough, it can get up to two and a half silver pieces at the very most, during the most severe famines. And they would have made it with fifty bags. One hundred bags would have let them completely recover and have a surplus left over."

"Wow, really?" I asked. "That's good news then."

"You exceeded their needs by a hundred times over!" the little fairy shouted. The pink glow on her face was starting to deepen into an angry shade of red. Thinking back, I probably should have stopped talking then, but listening to my Wisdom score all the time proved harder than I expected.

"Really?" I said instead. "That doesn't sound quite right."

"Wes," my tiny friend grated. "Do not. Insult. My basic math."

"Your math's fine, but only if you're counting just the meat," I said. "But I saved as much as I could of the pelts too. I heard the tanner talk to the merchant and they said the village would get at least fifteen gold pieces for each one."

"Pelts," Breena repeated in a clipped voice. "That's right. I remember now. You saved the pelts."

"Well yeah," I replied. Didn't she see me drag those whole corpses back to the village? Why would I have just taken the meat?

"I couldn't get a price on the bones, fangs, and claws though," I continued. "But everyone seemed about as excited about those as they were about the pelts. I'm going to have to get someone else to explain the significance on that... Breena, are you okay?"

That got me another punch.

It didn't hurt, of course.

But Stell really needed to look at Breena's empathy again, because this behaviour was starting to become habit-forming.

Eventually, she calmed down and explained that she and Stell weren't anticipating me to strip my enemies bare for resources, because I had not done so in the past, and from what they had learned about my background, it wasn't something I did in my daily life. Breena and Stell were aware that I came from a resource-rich environment where most of my basic needs were provided for me, and that, since my people generated so much waste,they were going to have to teach me about conserving resources.

I had to explain then that my friends and I actually simulated situations like this in tabletop and video games, where you had to think of every advantage you could. Then she asked if I was a dirty rotten cheater when I played those games too, and I didn't have an answer for her.

At any rate, I had apparently reached the point where I needed to be for when the Trials and Tumults began. I looked at my status on my mind-screen once again:

Wes Malcolm
Race: Human. Origin: Earth (Challenger)
Growth Level: Fifth Rise (Spark)
Path: Unknown
Saga: Unknown
Profession: Unknown
Vital Pool: 820 points
Stamina Pool: 820 points.
Mana Pool: 840 points

Strength: 34
Dexterity: 34
Constitution: 32
Intelligence: 34
Wisdom: 34
Charisma: 29

Speed: 42
Deftness: 40
Wits: 43

Will: 42

Rise Points Remaining: 12 (can increase the six primary traits at a 1:1 ratio, or the four secondary traits at a 1:2 ratio.

Insight into the Following Ideals
Earth: lvl 5
Air: lvl 5
Lightning: lvl 5

Skill List truncated

Spell list truncated

4 skill points available.
Signature Spells have improved since last viewing.

"Wes, stop looking at that so much, or you'll go blind," Breena said tiredly between slurps, her voice echoing out of the cup of mist-juice she was hovering inside of. She seemed pretty exhausted, even after Guineve's lunch.

"You don't understand," I said excitedly. "I was beginning to walk on my own even before my last Rise. My mind and body are at the best they've ever been since the accident. If I'm not fully recovered by now, I'm at least very, very close."

"That's good, Wes," my little fairy told me. She seemed to mean it, even if she was still upset over my 'cheating' earlier. "But it's honestly hard to believe you suffer from any kind of disability back home. You seem like you were born for this place—for all of these worlds. It's hard to teach you things because you keep learning and improvising so fast. I have seriously never been this exhausted as a guide."

"Really?" I asked. That did sound difficult. Breena didn't strike me as the kind of person who was low-energy.

"She's right, Wes," Stell said. She had joined us for lunch. And she had changed again, even more quickly than last time. She had gone to a much paler skin color, with curly blonde hair that hung loosely over her head, as if she had just gotten done with a shower. Her eyes were a bright green. She had changed t-shirts once again, to a brown one with a velociraptor holding a Rubik's Cube, with the words 'Clever Girl' written over its head.

She refused to explain why she changed again. The other Satellites had said that this was faster than normal, but they wouldn't share anything more either.

"You keep insisting you weren't trained," the now-blonde woman began. "But you already have foundations that you shouldn't have. You have instincts you shouldn't have gotten in your Earth suburb, and claim you've never practiced most of these skills, but you hold a short blade like you've swung it before and brace behind a spear like you've had to stop an enemy's charge at some point in your life. If you were from the same period as Arthur or Roland, it would have made sense, but you keep insisting that all of these weapons are obsolete by now. There's a mystery about you, Wes. And it's honestly fascinating. When you're not being aggravating, that is," she huffed.

"Thanks," I replied. "I think."

"Well, at any rate, I think it's time to admit we've run out of basic skills to teach you," Stell continued. "There's always more to learn, but you think so well on the spur of the moment that I have no idea what to teach you next right now. I have no idea what Path or Saga you'll take eventually—don't ask, those are just specializations based on your skills and choices—and this is the first time it's ever taken me this long to predict. But as long as you keep growing and thinking as fast as you do, it won't matter. In fact, Breena could probably use a break for a couple of nights from trying to train you or take you on Challenges."

There was a tired burble of agreement from the cup of mist-juice Breena was currently in.

"Okay," I said. "Can I still come here and train? Do random Challenges if they show up?"

The cup made a tiny wail.

"Sure, fine, Wes," Stell said with a smile that was somehow the same, no matter how much the rest of her changed. "You can work your little muscles and mind to your heart's content. Just don't break anything the rest of us can't fix." Another wail sounded from the cup. "And Breena needs the next few nights off."

"Deal," I said. "And I'll try and make it up to her." I needed to find a way to bring snacks from back home here. That always worked on my sister when I made her mad after a game.

"You do realize you don't have to train so much," Stell added, looking a little concerned. "For our timetable, your progress is phenomenal. If you miss a Challenge here and there, someone else can handle it. Really. I mean it."

"Thanks," I said, a little uncomfortable with what I was about to admit. "But, while I like helping your people, I'm kind of doing this mostly for me. Since I started coming here, my condition has been improving phenomenally. I'm starting to walk without my cane now. And my mind doesn't freeze on me whenever I take a practice test. This change is happening quickly, and I can even track it with my mind-screen. That's a phenomenal help."

"Yeah, it's taken for granted everywhere else that people can track their own progress," Stell admitted. "I'd hate to think how the people on your world must flounder around in trying to improve something in their lives. It probably makes it easier for self-improvement scams to exist too."

"Those are both problems," I nodded. "It's been that way especially for me. I've gone from doctor to doctor, trying all kinds of treatment for over a year without being able to tell it was working, until I finally found one that let me slowly progress. And even then, my family wasn't sure the treatment was working. This has been a huge benefit to me, Stell. So much that I don't feel like I'm doing you any favors at all."

"That's sweet of you, Wes," Stell smiled again. "But it's untrue. I've said that you can skip Challenges, but if you had done so at the beginning, we would have been in a lot of trouble."

The cup near us was now snoring.

"I think I need to get her in a proper bed," Stell said, with a pitying glance at her smallest Satellite. "Or at least a large and soft flower. Also, I sort of need to completely redo my projections on the economy of the village you just saved. I think their development might suddenly advance by a generation or two. At least."

"Oops," I said, scratching the back of my head.

"Don't worry about it," Stell said while shaking her newly golden mane. "There are worse problems than people suddenly being able to feed and clothe themselves a lot better. Just be more careful when you come back next time, okay?"

"What do you mean?" I asked.

"I mean it looks like you tried to come to Avalon a whole bunch of times earlier but didn't quite make it. I still don't understand how you come here on your own, and I'm worried you'll have some kind of accident because you're trying too hard to get here."

"Um, Stell?" I replied. "It was tricky in the beginning, but I haven't had any trouble coming at all for a while now. Really. If I just close my eyes for five seconds, I can make it happen without a hitch."

For a moment she just looked at me without saying anything.

"You're sure?" she said finally.

"Yeah," I said, trying to work out the implications of what this meant, and not liking it.

"Wes," Stell said slowly. "You haven't told anyone about us or this place, have you?"

"Not a soul," I promised. "Never. I assumed you wanted to keep this place a secret, and even if you didn't, too many people would have thought I was crazy if I talked about it. They'd lock me up as soon as I said I traveled to a magical fairy land full of beautiful and incredible women that needed my help every night."

"Beautiful?" Stell blinked for a moment, then shook her head. "Never mind. Not important right now. But in the off-chance you find out anything, let me know, okay?"

"Absolutely," I affirmed. Because I'd be stupid not to protect this place.

"Guineve," Stell called out. The raven-haired woman had walked away after making us lunch. "We need to go to Vigilance Level One."

"Understood, dear," Guineve called back, her voice calm, but firm. "Just tell me the details when you're done eating."

"Thanks," Stell shouted. She turned and looked at me. "It's probably nothing, but we're going to make sure anyway. But even if someone else finds a way to come here, Guineve's powerful enough to handle anything short of an Icon. And that's on her bad day."

"Good to know," I said, getting up. "In that case, I guess I should go master the art of getting out of bed back on Earth."

"Take care, Wes," Stell said with a somewhat nervous smile. "And... stay safe, okay?"

"Of course," I replied. "And you too."

24

OLD MEMORIES, LATE DISCOVERIES

"Daddy," I asked my father, looking up to him. "Why are we doing this again?" I pointed to all the trash on the road, and the walls we had just cleaned of graffiti. "You and Mom always say to clean up our own mess. Why are we cleaning up someone else's?"

"Because we're strong," my father said simply, stuffing more trash in the garbage bag he was holding. "And you remember what I said before?"

"Service is strength," I repeated, and probably for the hundredth time.

"Exactly," my dad said, smiling despite the fact that his hands were full of smelly paper. "The people who made this mess were weak. They couldn't handle their own problems, so they made a mess in someone else's neighborhood and sprayed hate over other people's walls to feel better about themselves. And the people that live here already have a lot on their plate. They have too many other burdens to have time to deal with the fact that some idiots spew nonsense all over their neighborhood every other weekend. But cleaning up for them isn't a burden for us, because we're the strongest people in town."

He had smiled proudly at me when he said that last part. I always felt like I was king of the world when he smiled at me like that. I would try to work for it, to get that smile more, but these days he would make that smile even when I couldn't figure what I had done to deserve it.

But the back of my mind pointed out that this wasn't real anymore, that this was just a dream about a memory that took place years ago. My dad was dead now, my mind insisted. He was rotting in the ground with a bullet-hole in his skull.

I told the back of my mind to shut up. I could remember my father's death and disgrace when I was awake. But for now, I wanted this happy memory, when I was little again and he was a big, strong hero.

"And you know what that makes us, son?" my father continued, still smiling as he picked up the last of the trash. "When you're strong enough to make sure no one who lives near you is bullied? When no one's starving? Or cold? When everyone who lives near you is safe, healthy, and respected?"

"It makes us kings," I recited. "Whether anyone knows it or not. Because serving, helping, and protecting are all jobs of a king."

"That a boy," my father said proudly, tossing one more beer bottle into his bag. "That's the last of the trash. We have time to get ice cream for you and your sister, and you can help me pick out flowers for your mother after we go clean up. What do you say?"

That question was rhetorical, and even child-me knew it. But I still let out a happy yip as we walked the trash off the street.

I turned back to look at the walls and road. Clean of trash. Clean of hateful slogans that my parents had taught me to be disgusted about. Now the neighborhood block looked better than it did even before it was trashed.

The only thing that ruined it was the massive yellow eye that glared at me from the back of an alley.

"Dad," I said as we walked. "What's that?"

I pointed to where I had seen the eye, but it had moved on, as if looking away. In its place was part of a massive, scaly body, colored red with black stripes, slithering its way past the back of the alley like it was trying to stalk us.

The back of my mind had stopped insisting that this was a memory and started screaming at the sight of that thing, but the child version of me was merely curious. My father was not even that.

"That's just Mister Annoying," Dad said with a roll of his eyes. "He barks and howls around here to try and make you think he's big and tough. And he thinks he can tell you how to be strong. But he can't, because he doesn't know how to be strong himself, and he's too weak to ever learn. We don't have anywhere else to put him, so just ignore him until he goes away."

"Will he ever go away for good?" I asked.

"He'll pretend he won't. But he gets smaller every time you don't listen to him. He's gotten smaller since I was your age, and he's less than half of the size he was back during your grandfather's time. But he'll whine and lie to you whenever you do what it takes to be a king."

"Okay," I said with a shrug. Because back then I thought if Dad said something wasn't important, then it must be true.

The back of the alley let out a low growl, almost like an engine turning, but nothing came out. I just concluded my father was right, and followed him as we walked back to the car.

"How long has he been around?" I asked. "Is he older than you and Grandfather?"

My dad chuckled at that.

"He's older than even your great-great-great grandfather. But he's done less with himself than any one of us. Do me a favor and never listen to him, son. Because he's an idiot and a liar and a weakling."

"Okay," child-me promised. "I'll do that."

And just like that, we kept walking.

The back of my mind started talking again, noting that my dad had just started to look sad, and how this was also different from that day.

"Son," he said, and for the first time ever he seemed a little hesitant, and ashamed. "I'm sorry. I tried to make you ready as well as I could, and I didn't get as long I wanted to be with you. Or your mother and sister. I want you to know I miss you all terribly. And I should have been able to do more to make you ready. But I got worried for you, and then I tried to make it to where you wouldn't need to be ready at all, and I failed. And because of that, you've been on your own."

"What are you talking about, Daddy?" I said. It was still a name that slipped out of child-me often, even when I tried to act all grown-up. "You haven't gone anywhere. You're right here. You're showing me how to be strong. We're going to buy ice cream and flowers for Mommy. You just taught me how to handle Mr. Annoying."

Dad's eyes looked wet, and he just ruffled my hair without saying anything.

We were just a block or two from the car. But the windows shuddered just for a second, as if something loud had passed through nearby.

My father snapped his gaze around for a moment, and then we kept walking.

This time, the wind blew from another alley. It whispered at it flew passed us.

And I heard it.

"*Traitor-prince.*"

"Daddy?" I asked. I looked around, because everyone knew the wind couldn't talk and I wanted to see what was going on.

"*Traitor-prince,*" the windows said as they vibrated. Then they shuddered again. And the wind whispered again as it blew by, only louder.

"Traitor-prince."

"Traitor-prince."

"Daddy?" I asked again. "Is that Mr. Annoying?"

But my father had long stopped walking and dropped his garbage bags.

"No, son. Get behind me. Head to the car."

Wind and shuddering windows and clattering rocks all spoke again.

"Traitor-prince, traitor-prince. Catch and kill the traitor-prince."

"Daddy," I said, tugging on my unmoving father's sleeve. "Why aren't you coming? I don't want to walk to the car on my own."

This was scary, child-me said. And it was going to be a lot scarier without my dad.

So why wasn't he coming?

"Traitor-prince. Traitor-prince..."

The rocks and wind and windows were all getting louder.

"I can't come with you, son," my father said to child-me. "You're going to have to fight these things on your own when you wake up. I can only help you with the ones that followed you here."

"But, Dad," I protested. "I don't want to leave you!"

"Traitor-prince! Traitor-prince! Catch and kill the traitor-prince!"

"You have to!" my father shouted over the other voices. Dad never shouted before. He never needed to. "I can't come with you anymore," he added, his voice quivering. "I wish I could. And I wish I had prepared you better, done my job better, so that you'd never have to fight them at all. But you'll be okay. I know you better than anyone else, and I know you're strong. In spite of how I messed up, in spite of everything that has happened and will happen, you'll win. And you'll thrive, far beyond what anyone thinks will be possible. Remember that for me."

"Okay, Daddy," I said, and child-me sniffled, still not understanding what was going on. "I'll do that for you."

"Good," my father said, smiling and with twinkling eyes. "Now get to the car. I will see you again, but not yet. Hopefully not for a very long time."

Child-me didn't understand that last part, but I ran to the car anyway, because the voices were getting even louder now, and Daddy had always been right before.

"TRAITOR-PRINCE! TRAITOR-PRINCE! CATCH AND KILL THE TRAITOR-PRINCE!"

"MALUS FILTH!" my father roared, and suddenly I realized that Dad must have been catching and eating bears with his bare hands his whole life, somehow behind everyone's backs, to be able to sound that loud and that mean. "COME SEE IF YOU CAN TOUCH HIM HERE! COME SEE IF YOU CAN WALK RIGHT PAST ME AND STILL LIVE!"

The voices quieted immediately. For a moment they were altogether silent. Then they began again, quieter than before, as if they were trying to build themselves back up.

"Traitor-prince, traitor-prince..."

"YOU! WERE! WARNED!" my father roared again, and as I neared the car I turned back and looked at him one last time. He stood tall and straight, with flecks of stone breaking out of the asphalt to add to his muscles. The air around him began to billow and whirl quickly, giving me the impression that he was surrounded by a dozen invisible chainsaws. The skin that wasn't covered by rock was starting to glow like heated metal. His left fist was clenched and sparking with powerful electric current. His right hand was open, and some kind of massive, angry weapon was blazing into existence into his palm.

Far away, at the opposite end of the street, something black and hazy was massing together, stretching across whole blocks.

"*Traitor-prince, traitor-prince*," it chittered, like some crazy man made out of insects. "*Curse and catch and kill the traitor prince!*"

"YOU WILL DIE REGRETTING YOU EVER TRIED!" my father roared back. He stretched out both hands, holding weapon and lightning as he threw his voice out to the sky.

"VENI INVICTUS! VENI IN AUXILIUM MEUM!"

Everything near my dad began to shake. I grasped the car door, and he turned to look back at me one last time.

"Son," he said, his voice suddenly quiet again. "Whatever else happens, I love you."

I woke up in a cold sweat, back in my room on Earth. Air came into my mouth via huge gasps I couldn't stop making. My body was shaking all over. I couldn't hold either hand steady for even a second.

He was gone.

Dad was gone again.

Why did he have to leave again?

Why couldn't he just get in the car?

I bawled, still shaking all over. For how long, I don't know, but eventually my shaking died down and I could breathe without heaving.

The back of my mind, which had been quietly waiting for the dream and my little breakdown to finish, now threw its thoughts forward into the rest of my skull. Why did I dream after leaving Avalon? That had never happened before. And as far as I could remember, I never dreamed about Avalon. I either went there in my sleep or I didn't think about it at all until I woke up.

I recognized most of the magic I saw surrounding my dad at the end of the dream. At least two of the spells were ones I could use, though my versions were much, much weaker.

But that just prompted more questions.

Could my father have gone to Avalon? Someone had clearly gone there recently, at least recently enough for Stell to have been surprised by my own arrival. Could that...

No, I decided. That was absurd. My father was dead. And unlike every other visitor to Avalon that I had heard about, he had died in disgrace, with all but a handful of people believing he was an awful degenerate that had taken advantage of little girls. If he had gone to Avalon, he would have already been a legend.

But I could remember every word he had said in my dream. And he had known he was dead. And he tried to warn me about something.

And he had spoken Latin near the end.

I had never heard him speak Latin.

And I don't even know Latin, except for the word 'veni' which means 'come here.'

Whatever language he had spoken, I had never heard of, not from anyone.

So how could I have just dreamed up every word?

I couldn't, I realized.

Suddenly the past couple of years came together in a new light.

The fact that there was a typed, instead of handwritten, note on my father's desk when we found him.

My therapist's questions about my dad's work.

Her new questions about my dreams.

The fact that my injury had completely baffled doctors for years.

I had ignored all these things before because they kept making my life seem like it was part of some conspiracy movie, and I knew it wasn't.

But now I was traveling to other worlds.

What if Dad had really gone to Avalon before?

What if other people had found out, and wanted to go there as well?

And why wouldn't they?

A person could get stronger, healthier, learn to do magic. Possibly live multiple times. I had no idea if I could even age when I was there. And even if a magical wonder-world wasn't really a person's cup of tea, they could probably just come back here, stronger, faster, and more powerful. Like I was doing.

What if my dad had gone to Avalon, and had been murdered and framed by someone else?

That meant he might have been innocent. I still hedged at that thought, because the idea of my father being vindicated sent too much hope through me, and I was scared to trust it. But I could at least, very carefully, count it as a possibility.

Next question. What if those same people were suspecting that I, or another one of my family, was going to Avalon as well?

That was scary. I tried to think of who it might be, which was nearly pointless. It could have been anyone. Probably someone from out of town. But how would they find out, unless they were in constant contact with my father? Unless they could have seen him slowly gain muscle definition or change in some other way none of the rest of his family had noticed?

What if he had gone a long time ago, back when he was my age or younger, and I never had a chance to notice? But who would have noticed then? People in his high school? In his college? In his church?

Church...

That reminded me just how much my town had changed, and for the worse. Most of the people I had grown up knowing were no longer here. And except for my English teacher and a handful of my friends, they all hated me.

That couldn't be a coincidence. And I had been an idiot for not noticing that before.

My phone suddenly rang.

I nearly jumped out of bed in surprise, then looked over to the light coming from it.

An incoming call from a number I had never saved as a contact, and it was three o'clock in the morning.

For a while I just let it ring, too scared to move. Then I realized anyone who knew my number probably knew where I lived, and that avoiding the phone call wouldn't do me any good.

Looking at my phone like it was a live snake, I reached over and reluctantly picked it up.

"Hello?" I asked as bravely as I could.

"Wes?" a frightened girl's voice said into the phone.

"Yeah," I replied slowly. "Who is this? And why are you calling at this hour?" I was expecting an ominous voice, someone threatening me, even just heavy breathing noises. I was not expecting a frightened teen girl my age.

"It's Regina... and I'm sorry," the nervous girl finally said.

"Regina?" I asked, barely believing my ears.

"Yes," the girl repeated, and my brain finally connected the voice and name to a face.

"Regina from that party years ago?" I asked again, not needing her to confirm it. "You're actually calling me, and in the middle of the night?"

"Yes," she repeated, anxiety running through her voice. "And I'm sorry."

"Are you apologizing for calling this late, or are you apologizing for getting into my face and calling me a creep, or are you apologizing for spreading rumors about me after I had risked my own safety to protect you?" I couldn't keep the hard edge out of my voice.

"Yes," she said with a sniff. "All of it. I should have called years ago. And I should have believed you when you told me what had happened. I'm sorry."

"Okay," I said slowly, and suspiciously. I was already in a paranoid mood from that last dream, and this conversation was not helping. "So why are you calling right now, and at this hour?"

"I've been avoiding talking to you because I've been ashamed," Regina continued. Her voice was slightly steadier now. "It didn't take long to learn Chris' real character. But I had already lashed out at you, and my family was moving, so...." She took a breath. "No. Those are terrible reasons. I should have told you both sorry and thank you, and instead I ran away. You were a total knight to me, just like you were with everyone, and in return I was a total bitch. I'm sorry. And thank you. I would have been assaulted at the very least, and I spent forever being too ashamed over that fact, instead of acknowledging that worse things didn't happen, and that you were the reason why. Thank you," she repeated.

"I... forgive you," I found myself saying. Something heavy lifted off of my spirit as I said that. "I accept your apology. And your gratitude." I took another breath. Any other time, this phone call would have somehow been both inconvenient and appreciated. But after that last dream, I needed to know if there was more. "But why are you calling so late?"

"The same reason I can't tell anyone else about this," Regina said, her voice still catching here and there. "I figured if I talked to you at night, it would be safer."

"Safer how?" I demanded, not in the mood for puzzles.

"Wes," Regina began again. "I signed an NDA. Me and my family. Chris' father stepped in after he heard about the party, and my family made an agreement to not talk about the issue."

"How could you sign an NDA?" I asked. "You weren't even eighteen years old back then."

"Mr. Rhodes was very persuasive," Regina said quietly. "He said he knew exactly what the law said. He also 'suggested,'" I heard the emphasis on that final word, "that I take a certain amount of money as compensation for the event, and that I never talk to anyone about it, ever. He also 'suggested' that this was the most effective way to protect everyone's reputations and keep everyone safe."

"He went that far?" I asked in disbelief. "To threaten you, a teenage girl, all those years ago?"

"I think he went farther, Wes," the girl who had once hated me said. "I think he had another agreement with my parents, that they never told me about. And I'm still too scared to find out what it was."

"That all sounds crazy, and hard to believe," I said frankly. I wasn't trying to be mean, but I was still dealing with my newfound paranoia, and this conversation's new direction just wasn't helping.

"I know," Regina admitted.

"And I don't think it's the only reason you're calling at this exact time," I added.

"No," she continued. "I... heard about how you were doing. And I wanted to warn you."

"Warn me?" I said in disbelief. "Warn me, more than three years later? After I've already become disabled? After I've probably lost my scholarship, my reputation, and my future?" The harsh edge had rushed back into my voice, and I nearly hung up on the phone right then and there. "After I've probably lost all of those things? Did you think I had some favorite plant that might still be in danger?"

"Yes, Wes, I'm calling after all of that," Regina half-shouted, half-pleaded. "Because now I know, Wes! I finally took the courage to ask what happened to you, and I know they're not done! They're not done! Chris would never let you go after just crippling you! He'd only stop after he was sure he destroyed you, and there's no way he'd think that yet! And his father's even worse, Wes! Whatever monster Chris might be, his father's ten times worse!" She took a deep breath. "That's the real reason I called, Wes. You're right. I should have called earlier. I should have found a way to warn you as soon as I found out what Chris was really like, but I didn't. You have the right to blame me for all of this if you want. But whatever you do, Wes, you need to know that you're not safe yet. Because as long as you're not terrified of Chris or Mr. Rhodes, they're going to keep going after you until you are. And somebody should still warn you, because you're the closest I've ever seen anyone come to fearless, and that means they're going to keep going after you until you finally break!"

"How do you know I haven't broken yet?" I asked quietly. "You haven't seen me in years."

"No, but I talked to Christina the other day," Regina said, shame coming back into her voice. "That was another reason I should have spoken up. That would have been on me too, if you hadn't stepped in, just like how you stepped in with me. You wouldn't have dared to warn her if you were already broken, Wes. Broken people don't warn others away from danger," she added bitterly. "They let them stumble into the same danger they stumbled into themselves, all because they were stupid and trusted the wrong person!"

"Okay," I said calmly. "But you're warning me now, instead of letting me stumble into danger?"

"I..." Her voice caught again. The silence on her end of the phone seemed to struggle with itself, until she finally spoke again. "I don't know. I just had to, okay? And I gotta go. Just... you didn't hear this warning from me, okay?"

That last part was a desperate plea.

"Okay, Regina," I said, trying to remain calm. "Thanks for calling. I accept and appreciate your warning, your apology, and your gratitude. Have a good night."

"You too, Wes," she muttered. "Be careful. Goodbye."

She hung up. I sat there for a moment, alone in the middle of the night, thinking about enemies and other things in the dark that whispered curses at me, and wondering how long they had been hunting me.

How was I supposed to survive them here?

I couldn't do magic here on Earth. And knowing how to swing a sword or a spear wouldn't help me with anything but getting sent to jail. And that wasn't even considering whether I had recovered enough to fight, or even run from, my enemies.

That also wasn't considering they had all the information about me, and I knew nothing about them. Was it the Rhodes family? Were they behind all this? According to Regina, even if they weren't, they would still be out to get me, so I couldn't discount them no matter what.

I couldn't beat them, and I knew it. I could barely stop their son from drugging and hurting his girlfriends.

My phone beeped again.

I looked down at it.

There was no call or text. But the background had changed. It was just a blank screen with purple words:

Hold fast. I know you.

A split second later, I remembered that I had just woken up, and that this was the first time I had done so without feeling any pain whatsoever.

25

THREE STEPS BACK

"Hello, Wes." My therapist smiled at me. "How are you? While don't you take a seat, and we can talk about your progress?

How about we don't? I wanted to say. *How about I don't give you anything at all while I try to figure out how much you know, and why you're after me, and just how screwed I am, since even my therapist is part of the plot against me?*

But I really don't need to explain why it's a bad idea to reveal to your psychiatrist that you've figured out her evil scheme and that you know she's out to get you.

I had tried to get out of this meeting, but my mother had figured out long ago how to tell when I was faking being sick. She wouldn't let me skip the appointment without a good reason, and since I refused to share my suspicions about the massive conspiracy that was after me, here I was.

"Sure, Dr. Dalfrey," I said as I stumbled carefully to a nearby seat. And it was carefully, because this woman was now the last one I wanted to have an accurate measure of my progress. "Just give me one second."

Her eyes tracked me as I limped over to the sofa, guided myself down onto the seat and put my cane off to the side.

"You're looking so much better today," Dr. Dalfrey said brightly as she watched me. "You're stumbling a little, but it almost seems like you don't need the cane anymore."

Shit.

"That's incredible, Wes," the woman continued. "Do you realize how much progress you've made? You should feel excited about this!"

Right. I was trying to deceive a woman who read people for a living.

"Yeah, it's honestly scary," I replied. "I've been disappointed so many times that I guess I'm afraid my recovery might only be temporary again.

"Well, that's an understandable concern," Dr. Dalfrey said patiently and sweetly. "But in this case, it's unwarranted. Look at your arms. You're even getting muscle definition back."

Double-shit.

I had known going into this meeting that there was no way to hide my regenerated muscles. The weather was warm today, and no sane person would ever wear long sleeves during a warm day in Texas. Wearing long sleeves right now would have trumpeted the fact that I needed to hide my arms.

I had been forced to just hope that she wouldn't notice them. So, of course she did.

"Yeah, I'm hoping I can keep it," I said. "It feels good to look like I did back when I played football."

"I was just thinking that," the blonde doctor said, and for a moment her eyes felt creepy on me. "But given how quickly you're suddenly progressing, I dare say you might even surpass your old physique. That's truly incredible, Wes, and I'd love to help you figure out why you're recovering so well."

Yep, I thought. *I'm screwed.*

She was catching every sign of progress, I realized. It was as if she knew exactly what to look for.

"I'm honestly not sure what the cause is, Dr. Dalfrey," I said with a shrug. "I guess now that I'm taking so much time off from school, I'm in a safer environment, and I have more time to try to perform the recommended exercises. Maybe it's just the result of having no one around to push me or knock me unconscious with a book."

She gave me a sympathetic smile. One that I would have believed genuine, if this wasn't the first time she had tried to make one.

"I'm sure that is helping, Wes. And it truly is a shame you were forced to experience all of those attacks. But even taking that into account, you're still improving almost unnaturally fast. Are you sure you're not doing anything different?"

"I have no idea, Dr. Dalfrey," I replied. "I mean, I'm grateful, but I'm as baffled as you are. I just hope I keep improving until I make a complete recovery."

"So do I, Wes," the woman said with a thin smile. "So do I."

Don't sweat, I told myself. *She'll see it. Just try and make it through the meeting. Mom is coming to pick me up in less than an hour.*

"Why don't we talk about your dreams again?" the woman asked. "Have you been having any about going to another place?"

"Not that I can remember," I replied slowly. "Do you really think that there's a correlation?"

"Anything's possible, at this point," Dr. Dalfrey said calmly. "But since we talked about the subject in your last session, I felt we should briefly revisit it."

I slowly shook my head.

"I really can't remember anything," I replied. "I know we talked about this before, but I've been pretty focused on other things, like the doctor's recommendations for my body and brain exercises."

"That's fine, Wes," the therapist said, looking down at her notes. "It was a long shot anyway. And honestly, things have progressed so well that most of this is no longer necessary. I think we've already accomplished our goal for today."

"What do you mean?" I asked, disturbed. "I just got here. Are you saying we can end the session early?"

That would have been great if I could have gone home on my own, but I couldn't drive and my mother had already left for work. I'd have to call her and the fastest she could get here was in thirty minutes. Assuming she could get off work at all.

"Sure," Dr. Dalfrey said with a completely unfriendly smile. "You could say that."

I tensed, and she saw it.

"Wes, I have to apologize for underestimating you so much. At some point after our first meeting, I had assumed the rest of our meetings would never be productive,so I stopped taking them seriously."

"I noticed," I said slowly. "Why are you telling me this?"

And how many steps would it take me to make it to the door? I asked myself.

"I'm just encouraged by our progress. I only played a small role in it, but it was a necessary one," she said smugly.

"Necessary how?" I asked, inching a little closer to the edge of my seat and to my cane. She looked at me as I did so, and smirked even more.

"By noticing your commitment to stay positive," she replied. "Even after your last episode that led to you being hospitalized, you still found a way to be hopeful at your next meeting with me. There could have been any number of reasons for you choosing to do so, but the most likely one was that you had somehow discovered a new opportunity. That let me assume, and recommend to others, that you had just possibly found a way to reach Avalon."

I immediately rolled off the couch, barely noticing the small spike of pain. I started to crawl toward my walking stick lying nearby.

"Help!" I immediately shouted. "Help! I've fallen and I need help!"

She doesn't own this whole building, I reminded myself. Her office here was a rented suite. That meant someone she didn't control could possibly hear me and come in. They wouldn't get involved if I screamed I was in danger, or that my therapist was out to get me, but helping a fallen person up was much safer. All I needed was for them to be present, and to walk me out of the room to somewhere safe. If I could just have that happen, then everything would be fine. I could call my mother and get her to pick me up and never leave me alone with Dr. Dalfrey again.

All I needed was just one person, who wasn't out to get me, to hear me and care.

Dr. Dalfrey chuckled. She watched me roll on the floor, still shouting for at least fifteen more seconds.

"Wes, I'm going to give you credit for that. If I hadn't cleared the whole building today, your little trick just now might have actually worked. You're much smarter than others give you credit for. Just not smart enough to ever matter, it seems. But that's hardly your fault."

I just shouted louder. What did I have to lose? And who knew whether she was telling the truth?

"Would you like me to shout with you, Wes?" she asked with another smirk. "Would that help? I'll give you another moment or two to realize no one is coming to save you."

I finally reached my cane and grabbed it with one hand. I started crawling toward the door.

"But as I've said," she said with a sigh. "All of this is no longer necessary.

We found the way into Avalon ourselves. There's no more need to watch you flounder around."

She waited until I was almost at the door out, and then she hit a buzzer on her desk.

"I'm done," she said. "Come get him."

Heavy footsteps started coming toward me from behind the door. I rolled out of the way just as it kicked open. A slamming sound from behind me told me that the second door, the one behind Dr. Dalfrey, had flung open as well.

Two large burly men in orderly scrubs stomped through the door closest to me, and the noise behind me told me there were at least two others I couldn't see.

"You need four grown men for a disabled teen?" I shouted in disbelief. And just for the heck of it, I shouted out "Help!" one more time. Still no reason not to, at this point.

"Probably not," the witch said blandly. "But why stop stacking the odds against you now?"

"Oh for..." I started to retort, but then the thugs closest to me were next to me, and one of them reached for me.

Right, I decided.

Time to drop the act.

The stick in my hand shot up into the fake orderly's face, colliding into his nose with a red-colored crunch. He backed off, swearing and clutching his face. The second one grabbed the front of my shirt and pulled me off the ground.

"No don't pick him *up*, idiot!" Dr. Dalfrey shrieked. "Just pin him to the floor and put him under!"

As the thug lifted me to my feet and began to pull me into a sleeper hold, I threw all of my weight forward, grabbing his shoulder with all of my remaining free fingers. Since he was expecting me to resist his pull instead, he staggered backward, off balance from my sudden push. My momentum and angle of movement carried me past one of his shoulders. While still holding his shoulder, I hooked my foot and cane under his most stable leg and tripped it in a basic white-belt judo throw. The big oaf went tumbling to the ground, cursing in surprise, and I stumbled past him through the door he had opened.

Dr. Dalfrey swore in frustration.

"Bird in the web!" she suddenly shouted. "Execute! Bird in the web!"

Suddenly my brain began to scramble, like old television static. My balance problems returned tenfold, and so did the pain. I nearly fell down right then and there. I staggered, barely still on my feet, and I heard the would-be orderlies work to untangle themselves at the door behind me.

I gritted my teeth and pushed against something in my head.

To my joyful surprise, it worked. I had my balance and focus back immediately.

I was in the hallway leading to the main lobby. I took off, able to run awkwardly now, pushing on my cane and against one of the walls to propel myself faster.

I had just reached the lobby when a hairy hand grabbed my shoulder. Thinking fast, I whirled and snapped my elbow into a familiar bloody nose, then slammed my cane into my attacker's stomach to knock the wind out of him and push him off of me. It worked, though I lost my cane in the process.

But if I could just get out of the building, where there would be witnesses, then it would no longer matter.

I staggered into the lobby, noting that all of the seats and even the front desk were now empty. I could have sworn it hadn't been that way when I first came in. But no matter. The glass-door exit was less than a dozen feet away, and the hallway wasn't big enough for all four men to rush me at once.

Just treat it like you're trying to catch a pass, I told myself.

I still couldn't run in a straight line, but with my brain working again, I could remember a zig-zag passing route I used to run back when I played football. I juked and stumbled my way to the front door, dodging a tackle from another grown man who shouldn't have had nearly as much trouble catching me as he did, and made it to the front door. I pushed it open and stumbled out the door while another hand grabbed me from behind.

"Help!" I screamed out as loud as I could. "Help! Help!"

I sent a flurry of short kicks and punches behind me, then twisted my way out of another grip. My shirt tore and I lost a shoe, but it didn't matter, because I was outside now, where the whole world could see and hear what was happening.

This was a rich suburb that still treated itself like a small town. Even if no one lifted a finger to help me, they would still talk about what they had seen. The news would make it all the way through town until it reached someone who cared about me. They would contact the police. They could contact Davelon's father, who would use every connection he had to help the boy that had helped save his own son's life. Worst-case scenario, I would be kidnapped for a while until someone found me, since if they could have killed me, they would have already done so. Best-case, and most likely scenario, they would back off and run, since they couldn't risk witnesses. They'd probably try again later, but I could get more help myself, maybe find long-term safety with the police or with Davelon's family.

And I could still get stronger in Avalon, as the four idiots behind me had already found out.

I thought all of this while running out into the parking lot, screaming my head off. I could hear my attackers behind me, and knew they were less than seconds from running out as well. But that was okay. I would juke and dodge like I'd been doing. Every additional second I was free was another second I had to scream and draw attention to myself. It was a small neighborhood. People would recognize me immediately.

So I ran.

And screamed for help.

And realized that no one was outside.

But that was impossible, I told myself. There should be nearby traffic, at least. There were too many people who either had the day off, or were out running errands as a stay-at-home parent, or were just taking a lunch break right now. One of them should be driving by at any minute and witnessing the situation. Then they'd help, call the police, or just tell their neighbors or coworkers what they saw.

But there wasn't a soul out here except for the people trying to get me.

I refused to believe that. Something in my legs shifted, and I ran straight out into the middle of the street, hearing a bunch of heavy panting and cursing behind me.

I realized that both ends of the street were blocked off with flashing lights.

Police cars.

They were accompanying construction trucks working on the road.

That seemed extremely unusual. But I didn't care. The absolute best-case scenario was me finding an officer right now, and there were at least four cars of them nearby. I only had to pick a direction and run to them. Heck, all of them could probably notice me at this point if I was loud enough.

I ran to the cars on the right, screaming as loud as I could at the pair of officers I could see standing around.

"Help! I'm being attacked! Please help me!"

One of them looked at me, then clutched his radio and gave his partner a questioning glance. His partner just shook his head and apathetically and waved his hand, as if to say 'don't bother.'

I refused to believe what I had just seen. I ran toward them anyway, still screaming for help. As I ran toward them, I finally pulled out my cell phone and tried to make a call, but I had absolutely no signal at the moment. I refused to believe that as well, and kept running, screaming and dialing.

Then something heavy slammed into me from behind, driving me toward the ground and knocking the phone out of my hand. I felt the air leave my lungs and tried to roll with the tackle, but I couldn't break free.

"It's about damn time you caught him!" a rough man's voice said behind me.

"Shut the hell up," the thug wrestling with me growled. "If this was easy, you would've caught the prick yourself. Now grab his legs."

I kicked my feet away, trying to use them to push myself back up. I used another twist I had learned from fighting unarmed in Avalon to get a hand free.

"God damn it!" the brute said as he slammed his fist into my face. "Stay down!"

Stars flew all over my eyes. I tried desperately to fight past the pain.

"You got him?" I heard one of the officers ask.

"Yeah, we'll have him down in a minute," the man that had hit me said. He threw me another punch. And then another.

"Well, whatever," the officer's voice trickled into my rattling skull. "You've got thirty minutes left to wrap it up."

The beatings must be affecting my hearing, I decided. There was no way a police officer would admit to this level of corruption in a high-class office neighborhood during broad daylight hours. I chose to believe that someone was only moments away from helping me, and I somehow got my forearm in the way of the next punch. In another small victory, I put my knee into my attacker's gut.

"Son of a bitch!" the man over me swore. "I said help me hold him!"

More hands began to restrain me. I fought harder, swinging whatever appendage I could, trying to bite whoever my teeth could reach.

"Doc!" one of the fake orderlies called out. "Use the damn code!"

"I can't believe you idiots still need my help," Dr. Dalfrey's voice and footsteps sounded clearly over the tussle. I heard her sigh.

"Bird in the web, execute," she repeated tersely. The blurriness came over me again. Combined with the struggling and the blows it was almost enough to knock me unconscious. *Almost.*

"I said bird in the web, execute!" the woman snapped again. Another wave of blurriness that I had to struggle through. "Bird in the web, execute! Bird in the web, execute!"

My struggles weakened, but they still persisted.

"Use the shot while you can, idiots! Bird in the web, execute! Bird in the web execute!"

Blurriness kept coming into me like waves crashing onto a beach during a storm.

One of the fists stopped punching me and reached to grab my throat. I fought it, but my neck was still pulled into an angle, and I felt something sharp and cold poke into it.

Another second passed, and I was done. Whatever drug they put into me flooded through my body, and combined with the blows and the strange blurriness Dr. Dalfrey was somehow causing me, my muscles and consciousness were finally giving up.

With a final, silent curse directed at this town and every dirt-bag that lived in it, I closed my eyes and escaped to Avalon.

26

PARADISE UNDER SIEGE

I stumbled forward, aching all over. I felt like I had been the target of a vicious beatdown. A minute later, I remembered I *had* been the target of a vicious beatdown.

But I had made it. There were mists and trees everywhere.

I was back in Avalon. My body ached for a second longer, and then I felt the pain and damage slowly begin to heal.

"Stell!" I called out. "Guineve! Breena!"

No one answered. I limped forward, until my legs pulled forward into a walk, then a swift trot, then a full-on run.

"Stell! Guineve! Breena! Answer me! They're coming! They're coming!"

Dr. Dalfrey had said her people—whoever they were—had already found their way inside. I had to warn Stell and her Satellites that she was going to be invaded soon. Assuming the invasion hadn't already begun.

"Stell!" I repeated, shouting even louder than I had moments ago back on Earth. "Breena! Guineve!"

"Wes?" Stell's voice called out from the mist. She sounded curious, but unharmed.

"Stell!" I shouted gratefully. "They're coming! You're under attack!"

"What?" her voice called back. I heard her rapid footsteps through the mist. "Wait! Who's coming? How are we under attack?"

I stomped toward her voice, seeing her figure come out of the mist. I tripped on a tree root, one that I had almost always seen in time before, and stumbled into her arms.

She was half a foot shorter than me, but she caught me easily. "Wes! Just calm down. What happened?" She looked at me more carefully, her eyes widening slightly. "And why were you stumbling? Are you hurt?"

"Yeah," I panted, still trying to recover from the phantom pain all over me. "Just not here." My body suddenly shuddered, and I felt as if I had been dropped or slammed into a small enclosed space. It dazed me for a second, and then I could see and think clearly.

"They've kidnapped me," I said after a moment. "Back on Earth. They probably threw me into a van just now. I've been kidnapped."

"Kidnapped?" Stell asked, her eyes going wide. "By who? Slow down, Wes. Who's kidnapped you?"

"I don't know," I panted, slowly getting myself back under control. "I think they were the ones that tried to get in before, the ones behind those failed attempts you noticed. I think they've been watching me this whole time. They figured out how to get here, Stell." I looked her in the eye. "They could get here any minute."

"You're sure?" she asked seriously. "You're sure they can come here?"

"One of them was taunting me before I became unconscious," I said. "She already knew about Avalon. She had been pretending to be one of my doctors for years, just to figure out how I was coming here. She said they had finally figured out how to get to Avalon on their own, and they didn't need to be careful with me anymore."

I took another breath. "They beat and drugged me, and she said a phrase that made it hard for me to think. When they knocked me out, I came here to warn you guys."

And that was all I could do, I realized. I had no plan for getting away from these people back on Earth. Especially not since they were able to block off an entire street and put the police in their pocket to catch me. That alone was mind-boggling. I was just now processing the fact that at least one cop had casually stood by while four men nearly twice my size were beating my face in, and the only thing that officer had bothered to do was to ask my attackers if they needed a hand in kicking my ass.

It was ridiculous. I'd never be able to trust anyone back home ever again.

Could I even get back home?

Was the rest of my family in danger?

Were my friends?

I shook my head. There was too much going on to have a nervous breakdown right now. I had to focus on one thing at a time.

"Avalon," Stell intoned firmly. "Activate Vigilance Level Ten. Notify all Icons and Satellites of a possible breach. Provide full information to my Satellites." Her voice rang with authority as she continued speaking. "Designate yourself as experiencing a territory-wide Challenge and upgrade the severity of said Challenge as needed. Override any restrictions against your taking defensive measures independently, as well as any against updating Challenger Wes Malcolm with constant information."

"Acknowledged," a voiced boomed from the mists. *"Removing all restrictions concerning Challenger Wes Malcolm."*

"I have restrictions?" I asked suddenly. "Why?"

"There are a few things you don't get, to prevent information overload," Stell said distractedly, then she continued speaking in a firm, commanding tone.

"Avalon, further orders. Provide all possible restrictions against any new arrivals from Earth, as long the nature of their Deeds is different from Challenger Wes Malcolm's. Do not automatically recognize Challenger status. Do not assist in unlocking Ideals. Do not assist in resurrecting from death. Classify all new arrivals from Earth as humanoid monsters, unless they match Deed and Renown parameters established by Challenger Wes Malcolm."

"Provide confirmation of last order," the mists rumbled.

"Confirmation code is Wool-Covered Wolf. Repeat, confirmation is Wool-Covered Wolf."

"Accepted," the voice rumbled back. *"Avalon will comply."*

"You can do all that?" I asked.

"I don't know," Stell admitted, biting her lip briefly. "This has never happened before."

"Where's Guineve?" I asked, looking around. "And Breena? Do I need to summon her?"

Soft blonde hair fluttered as Stell shook her head.

"Let's wait on summoning Breena," she said. "Right now, she's only as powerful as you are, and not as durable. Keep her hidden for now. Guineve is finishing her preparation magic at the moment. Anything powerful enough to get through her is not going to be hindered by us summoning Breena. That reminds me." Stell called out again. "Avalon, release all remaining restrictions concerning Wes Malcolm's untested abilities and powers. Allow him to advance and unlock them naturally or by his own experimentation. Confirmation code Throw the Hatchling Out of the Nest."

"Confirmed," the mists rumbled back.

Before I could ask, she cut me off.

"I mentioned before about every Challenger having unique abilities. You have a whole slew of half-formed powers I can't understand, and I locked them in case they were some kind of dangerous mutations that would get you killed. I was going to unlock them if they ever finished forming and became safe for you to use. But just in case... in case something happens," she added, looking worried again. "I've unlocked them, and if they ever finish forming on their own, you can just use them at your own discretion."

"What happens if I try to use them now?" I asked.

"Nothing," Stell replied. "There isn't even enough magic in them to make you aware of them right now."

"Alright. Thanks anyway," I said, taking a breath and trying to clear my head. "So to recap, wait for Guineve, and if someone comes sooner, deal with them on our own if we can, or delay them until she's ready if we can't."

"You've got it," she said. Then she paused, giving me a slightly guilty look. "I can fight some, but I can't easily release my real power more than once here. It takes a long time for my primary body to recharge spent power. I can still hit things without magic, but you're going to have to do most of the heavy lifting until Guineve arrives. Can you manage that?"

"Yeah," I said. "They were able to get me on Earth. But if they're like I was when they just arrived..."

"They should be even worse off," Stell finished for me. "If they're just normal humans."

"Good," I said. I was sure the people after me weren't done pulling unfair tricks out of thin air, but here in Avalon, I could at least do the same.

In fact, fighting my earthly enemies in a completely whole body was something I couldn't help but look forward to.

"Are we going to know when they arrive?" I asked. "Or are they going to be able to sneak in, like I can't help doing every time?"

Probably could have phrased that better, I thought with a wince. But Stell just shook her head.

"You were able to sneak in because I had grown complacent and diverted most of Avalon's vigilance to other processes. That shouldn't happen at all this time. We'll get a warning as soon as they attempt to arrive, along with their exact location. Avalon will even try to prevent them from crossing over, although I'm not counting on that to do anything but delay them a little."

"That's great news," I replied. "I'll use this time to get ready then."

My limbs began whirling and my mouth began intoning as I brought forth my magic. My bones and skin became reinforced with minerals, while little gusts of wind buffeted around me and added momentum to my movements. Finally, electricity began coursing through my body and darting around my digits.

I rushed over to the armory Stell had finally gotten around to setting up and grabbed a spear, threw on a light coat of mail, strapped a small shield to my wrist and strapped a club to my belt.

Let them come, I thought to myself grimly. *See how well you do against me when I'm no longer crippled, unarmed, and taken by surprise.*

As I rushed back to Stell, I heard Avalon's voice boom again from the distant mists.

"Unauthorized entry detected. Avalon is resisting the attempt. The attempt is happening at the following location..."

An image of one of Avalon's glades appeared into my mind-screen, along with a yellow path that seemed to lead me to the location.

"Resistance is being overcome. Invader's ETA is currently five minutes and ten seconds. Five minutes and nine seconds..."

The countdown continued to sound off in my mind.

I made it over to the location just as the final minute was ticking down. Stell was standing further back, watching the mist constrict around a tiny purple hole in the air.

I walked in front of her.

"Are you not wanting them to see you?" I guessed as I took position. Some kind of static sparked around the purple hole, and it grew by another inch. Stell nodded calmly at my question.

"The less these people know about Avalon, the better. But I'll stay close in case you need help."

"I shouldn't," I admitted. "But then again, they shouldn't have been able to kidnap me in broad daylight either."

I made sure all my passive spells were still working, and checked over my armor and weapons one last time. I contemplated my spear, then flipped it over to the blunt end. Despite everything, I had still never killed a human being yet. Plenty of monsters, sure. But I had been killing monsters in video games all my life, and most of the ones here had looked so unnatural, it was no problem. I didn't want to risk freezing up in a fight, so I used the less lethal part of the weapon instead.

"Thirty seconds," the mists intoned. The hole had grown to almost a foot in diameter, and the mist wrapping around it seemed to struggle to hold together.

"Ten, nine..."

Just get on with it, I thought angrily. The suspense was making this worse than my experience with actual combat.

Finally, the countdown ended and the mist around the purple hole dissipated.

"Containment failed," Avalon intoned. *"Prepare for unauthorized entry."*

Purple lightning flared all around the hole as it enlarged rapidly, expanding to two feet, then four feet, then eight feet.

And Chris Rhodes stepped into Avalon.

My jaw dropped. But my high school nemesis just looked around with a frown on his face. He was wearing a durable-looking black t-shirt, and pitch-black pants made out of the same fabric military soldiers used.

"Chris?" I shouted. "What the hell? Why are you here?"

Instead of answering my question, he only scowled further. Then after another moment, he reached into one of his pockets and threw something back into the hole still hovering behind him.

Four more men, two of them ones I recognized from my kidnapping, stepped through the portal as well. They were wearing bulkier versions of the combat fatigues Chris was wearing, and I could see knives long enough to be called machetes strapped to their waists. There were also gun holsters resting on their hips, but every single one of them was empty. One of them noticed and swore in surprise.

"I told you it wouldn't work," my old nemesis said with a sneer. "We'd know by now if people could bring guns here. You're lucky all your knives and padding made it."

He finally turned to look at me.

"Cock-blocker?" he asked incredulously. "You're not supposed to be here. And when did you go all Greek hoplite?" he added, pointing to my shield and spear.

"Good question," I said with a snarl. "How about I not answer it, and instead you turn around and go back home, so that you can release my body and turn yourself over to the cops?"

"Cops?" Chris skewed his head at that. He turned and looked to one of the fake orderlies. "I thought they helped you catch him?"

"He was knocked up pretty bad, Master Rhodes," the thug said in response, having a strangely mafia-style accent. "He probably didn't realize he saw them."

"Well, whatever. Get in position to detain him again for when Dad and the others get here."

"Yes, sir," the thug said, but as he and the other three tried to walk forward, they stumbled.

"What's the problem?" Chris asked, looking down. "Is there something wrong with the ground?"

"It's hard to move here, young master Rhodes," the thug said again, shaking his head. "Everything feels off."

Chris stepped forward, waving his hand around.

"Not really," he said. "It's different, but by so little, it's barely noticeable."

"It's supposed to feel that way for you," a cold voice said from within the portal.

Three more figures walked in.

My eyes widened in surprise, but then my mind-screen began to scream words all over my vision.

WARNING! WARNING! WARNING!

FOREIGN CONTAMINANTS DETECTED!

CONTAMINANTS ARE WARLOCK-CLASS SUBJECTS WIELDING MALUS POWER.

REPEAT! WARLOCK-LEVEL MALUS POWER DETECTED! WARLOCK-LEVEL MALUS POWER DETECTED!

BEWARE! BEWARE! BEWARE!

A moment later the entire message vanished from my vision and mind. Static swept over my brain again.

And a new message crawled into it.

I found you.

Traitor-prince.

27

MY LITTLE NIGHTMARE

When my vision returned to normal, I turned my attention back to the three new figures that had walked through the dark hole in the air.

I recognized every one of them.

The one on the left was my smirking therapist, still dressed in her pencil skirt and woman's business suit. She looked around, and seemed to approve of what she saw, except for me. She frowned slightly when she saw my face. But that was normal for her.

The one on the far right was Pastor Barnes. He had changed his outfit from his usual Sunday suit to some kind of black clerical robe. He was frowning in disapproval as he looked around, and he outright scowled at me. He was holding a small pouch with a chain wrapped around it. He carried the pouch by the chain.

The middle figure was a man I hadn't met in years. He wore a matte-black business suit of a rare and exotic cut. It bulged in places, implying that it was somehow fortified. The design, color, and protection suggested to me that it was easily the most expensive set of men's clothing I had ever seen.

But then again, he could afford such a piece quite easily, because he was the richest man I had ever met.

Warren Rhodes, Chris Rhodes' father.

He stood at least a head taller than Pastor Barnes, stood even taller than I did. And unlike either of us, his body bulged with powerful muscle, making even his son and Davelon look lean. His gut was also large, but that just somehow made him look even more imposing. He was, and always has been, the most terrifying figure I had ever met, and the force of presence he generated was second only to Dad's back when he was still alive. And unlike Dad, Mr. Rhodes, whom no one ever dared to call by his first name, and with whom almost no one ever realized that they didn't dare, always seemed to be masking a deep sense of scorn for everything, even when he smiled at me. I had always thought that he had resting bitch face because of it.

Today the mask was gone, and as he strode through the portal, he cast a look around him at the world of mist, vibrant trees, and glowing rocks, a look that said this place was utterly unworthy of him, and that he was completely entitled to anything it had to give. His eyes were cold, in such a way that he could say "I hate you" just by making eye contact.

Naturally, he looked straight at me.

"Of course it feels that way for you," he said again to Chris without looking at his son. "That was why I let you play that idiot game to begin with."

"Father," Chris said with exasperated formality. "You own that game now, and you said I had to play it because Wes played it. You kept saying I shouldn't lose to him in anything."

"Yes," Warren Rhodes said, casting a loveless half-glance toward his son. "It was, in part, me not wanting the shame of having a dead pedophile's brat be better at something than my own son. It was also because we suspected John's stupid game was partially made to prepare someone else for this world. So you learned to play it as another gift from me." His eyes traveled between the two of us, noting our stances. "It's disappointing to see that he still achieved greater mastery than you."

Chris looked like he wanted to growl at his father but didn't dare. Barely.

"I'm sorry, Father," he said with careful formality. "I shouldn't have put that matter so far below my other duties in sports, modeling, and technology."

"No, you shouldn't have," his father agreed, as if his son had said something stupid and obvious. "You should have excelled at everything because you're my son, instead of failing to live up to your bloodline. Your apology is rejected. Now go take care of that pedophile's cripple-headed little shit."

Chris gave his father an incredulous look. Once again, his father did not even glance his son's way.

"You want me," Chris began, "to attack him, head on, without a weapon of my own? While he's standing there braced with a spear, having the advantage of reach, armor, and probably magic, given the weird way his skin looks right now?"

"Sorry to interrupt," I said. "But I just realized I have a better question. Why haven't I begun beating you all yet?"

They all looked up at me. Two of the thugs actually seemed to be figuring things out the quickest, because their eyes widened. But unlike me, they were still processing instead of acting.

Holding my spear high, I charged forward. I noticed Warren Rhodes turning and throwing something into the portal behind him, and then his goons were in my face. Still using the blunt end of my spear, I slammed my weapon violently into the chest of one that had leaped right in front of me. I heard a hiss of surprise as he flew back into the portal, nearly knocking over Pastor Barnes in the process. Before another of the thugs could finish moving, I swung my stick out at his feet, tripping him, then I whirled my weapon around and slammed it into him again before he even hit the ground.

"Jesus Christ, he's fast!" someone swore as body guard number two went hurtling through the portal.

"Oh, God damn it," I heard Chris growl, and before I could move onto the third thug, I saw my nemesis leap into the air and kick me in the face.

To my surprise, the kick was strong enough to knock flecks of stone from my nose. Before I could even finish processing that fact, I felt several other blows rain all over the unarmored parts of my body.

"There!" my enemy growled while snapping a couple more strikes at my face. "Happy now, Dad?"

Finally recovering, I dropped my spear, knocked his arms away with my shield-bearing limb, and threw my own punch at his chest.

My fist connected, and with a *whumph* and a *sizzle,* the superstar quarterback went flying nearly a dozen feet in the air, barely missing the portal as he crashed into a nearby tree.

"Not yet, son," his father answered. "Try winning. That might do it."

I kicked my spear back into the air and caught it with one hand. Just as I was about to use it on the nearby Father-of-the-Year candidate, the two men I had just dimensionally defenestrated came charging back through the portal.

Along with four more friends.

Who had already drawn long combat knives.

I immediately leaped backwards, bringing my spear's reach into play. I had to change my strategy, I realized. It didn't matter how many I could knock through the portal if they could just run right back in.

I might even have to kill them. But could I do that? Even if I could, what if they could somehow come back like I *theoretically* could?

New plan, I decided quickly. *Break all their limbs.*

In retrospect, I probably should have turned the ground to mud right outside the portal, because that had always worked before. But I had wanted to see what I was dealing with before casting any of my real spells, and Chris had distracted me with his sudden appearance and knowledge of kung-fu. And now I didn't have time, because Rhodes' men were rushing me.

The bodyguards staggered as they attacked, still not used to Avalon's rules. I took as much advantage as I could, jumping away from their knives and slamming the staff end of my spear into a nearby attacker's arm as hard as I dared. There was a loud crack, and the man dropped his knife with a yelp, clutching his injured arm. I twisted away as another knife scraped against my shield, then I drew the blunt end of my spear back and slammed it into my opponent's kneecap. It crunched, a little more graphically than I imagined it would, and another man went down screaming.

The next three had shaken off most of their disorientation and came at me in a group, using some kind of three-person attack formation I couldn't recognize. I leaped back once again. And since I was still using a much longer weapon than they were, I started strafing around them, knocking the blunt parts of my spear into any vulnerable limbs. Two more cracks sounded out, and all three of them went down in a tumble.

A fight against seven armed, grown men, and it was completely one-sided. I couldn't believe it, and a look at my opponents' faces told me neither could they. They were trained combat professionals, all at least my height, and with much more visible muscle, and here I was, knocking them around as if I had been a superhuman all these years instead of a disabled teen. I seemed to be at least twice as fast and strong as the best of them, and just as skilled with my weapon as they were with theirs.

Somehow, this felt like a bigger victory than coming out on top of any of my other battles. I had won every fight I ever had with gibber-kin, dread moles, and those nightmare gremlins that everyone else was so afraid of. But winning against other human beings, instead of being beaten and mocked and thwarted by them?

That was entirely new.

The last two had to be creeping up behind me, since I hadn't seen them for over a minute. I stepped forward to twist around, my spear whirling back and clunking over another man's head by total chance.

But I had given the last attacker an opening, and he rushed the distance and lunged into me. I was still able to sweep my shield up in time, but his weapon scratched off my guard to slash at my mailed shoulder. The metal rings stopped most of the blow's force, my mineral-skin got the rest, and my vital guard remained untouched.

That was right, I reminded myself. Even if these guys do land a blow on me, one that gets through my armor and spells, my enhanced vitality was guaranteed to handle anything but a stab to the brain. These idiots were from Earth; they didn't have any magic to bypass my special hit points.

I dropped my spear, snapped my head into my attacker's face a couple times, then grabbed him by the shirt and lifted him off me. I grabbed his arm with both hands, took a run with him for about ten steps, then I slammed him into a nearby tree and yanked his arm backwards until I heard it crack. He went down with another cry of pain and tried to crawl away from me.

By then, the melee was clear. Two of my attackers were getting up to their knees slowly and groggily, but the other five just writhed and moaned on the ground.

I would have felt bad for them, if they were actually experiencing one-tenth of the pain I'd had to deal with every day for the last two years. That, and they all just tried to kill me.

Warren Rhodes watched the whole scene with disgust, baring his teeth and looking as if he were about to spit on all of us. Dalfrey shrugged next to him.

“Impressive,” she said, eyeing the scene of me practically dancing around seven armed men. “That people from Earth can grow here this much, and this fast. Beyond our predictions, even.”

“That's bad news for the predictors,” Rhodes growled. “I don't pay people to fail.” As he said that, he shot a dark look at the men still writhing on the ground.

“Don't be too disappointed, Rhodes,” Barnes said next to him. “Just think, if a half-crippled thing like John Malcolm's son can become like this here, and this soon, what awaits us?"

"Everything we were already due on Earth," Rhodes said with another growl. He looked and kicked at a guard that was still crawling forward. "Get back on the other side and tell everyone they just lost their medical for a month. If they can't deal with John Malcolm's little shit in the next ten minutes, the coverage is gone for three months. If I have to take so much as a single step forward, the whole team gets downsized. The severance package will be a bullet delivered into the back of the head."

"Yes, Mr. Rhodes," the man gasped on the ground. "I'm so sorry, Mr. Rhodes. I'll be right back with the others, Mr. Rhodes."

As the man crawled his way back to the portal, Rhodes looked at the mist and called out.

"Everyone else, hold your ground! We seek parley with the Lady of the Mist!"

I held off from attacking at the moment, just in case Stell had a better plan than me laying into them some more.

She didn't answer them at all, and I loved her for it.

"Stell of Avalon!" Rhodes called out again, and I felt my skin grow cold when I realized he knew her name. "We have your Challenger's body on Earth! This is your last chance to talk!"

I heard footsteps behind me. Stell came to stand by my side, crossing her arms. She met Rhodes' glare with a glare of her own that was about ten degrees colder in Celsius. She had changed to a long-sleeved black t-shirt that said "Keep Calm and Demand Trial By Combat" on the front.

"Alright," she said calmly. "I'm here. You have about ten seconds to make sure you don't regret it."

"I called for Stell of Avalon," Warren replied with a snort. "Not some tiny-chested teenage girl. Go get your queen."

"Nine seconds," Stell replied calmly.

"I wasn't kidding when I said we have his body," Rhodes growled, casting a brief and derisive glance at me. "Your hormones are endangering his life. Now go get your queen."

"*Five* seconds," Stell replied. "Less if you keep pretending you can still give the order to hurt someone with a broken neck."

Warren cocked his head back as if he had been slapped, then he looked at Stell again. This time his gaze was as frosty as her own.

"Chris," he growled. "Get over here and talk sense into this little girl."

"Four seconds," Stell said calmly, and without missing a beat.

"Wait—ow—stop, wait," Chris said, walking away from whatever tree I had knocked him into, still clutching his side. "Everybody just stop." He shot both his dad and me a dirty look, then with another breath, he stood up straight and tried to put his winning smile back on. "Look, we're sorry. We misread the situation terribly. Wes is a criminal back home." He ignored my snort. "So we let the situation escalate out of control. We came here for him because he's dangerous. Can we talk to you about that? Are you Stell, or someone that can speak for her?"

"I'm the one who answered when you called for Stell," the lady of Avalon said. "So I'm the one you're dealing with at the moment. Wes is here, in my world, by invitation. You are not. And I don't appreciate any portion of the conversation I heard just moments ago. This is not your world. You are not getting any free power here. You are not welcome. Call off your toy soldiers and return to your own lands. And if you harm a single hair on my Challenger's head," she added with a growl. "I will make you, your organization, and possibly your entire planet pay very, very dearly. Let me know if I need to convince you of any part that message."

"No, wait, okay," Chris said surprisingly. "You win. We'll leave here, okay? We'll turn around and head right back. But consider this: people on our planet know how to come here now. Don't you want to know how? Even if we leave, future contact's unavoidable, right? Because if we can figure it out, someone else will too."

I had forgotten just how fast Chris could think, I realized. Especially how fast he could think while talking.

"You just might have a point," Stell acknowledged with a tilt of her head. "If I could trust a single word out of you."

"Come on," he said, trying that same smile that had worked on so many girls back home. "You haven't even let me introduce myself yet."

"No need," Stell replied calmly. "I know exactly who you are."

"Oh, really?" he asked, still smiling.

"Yeah," Stell nodded. "You're the guy with the crushed rooster."

"What the—" the tall dark-haired quarterback sputtered. I chuckled in spite of it all, remembering Stell's confusion over the phrase 'cock-blocker.'

"Yeah," Stell said with a confident nod. "It's happened at least twice, right?" She almost seemed sympathetic. "Poor little rooster. Was it in the exact same place both times?"

"Crushed roost—" Chris sputtered. "What are you even talking about? My rooster's fine!" He turned his head and growled at me. "You bastard, what the hell did you tell her?"

"He didn't need to tell me anything," Stell answered calmly. "It's pretty easy to recognize. People must be a lot less perceptive back on Earth. Honestly, I'm not sure how you've managed to hide it for as long as you did."

Dr. Dalfrey actually snickered at that, and Chris turned to glare at her.

"She's not going to play ball, Dad," Chris snarled. "She doesn't think we're a threat."

"Up to this point, we haven't been," his father said darkly. "Barnes, start us off."

"As you command, my lord," Barnes said formally. He reached behind him to grab at the portal.

Purple-black energy began to coil around his hand. Before Stell or I could act, he threw it forward. Three splotchy flames landed onto the ground in front of him.

"Brothers and kin from beyond the lock," the robed false-pastor intoned. "We beseech thee. Join us, that we may have fellowship in hate."

The oily flames suddenly whipped into a blaze.

"Warning," Avalon boomed. *"Foreign contaminant de—"*

Our planetary supercomputer suddenly hissed, and went silent.

Stell's blonde hair whipped through the air as she turned her head.

"Emergency systems engage!" she shouted. "Full override!"

"Attempting," the mists said after a moment, a haze of strange static accompanying the words.

"Wes!" She turned her head back toward me. "I've gotta fix this! Kick their asses!"

"Yes ma'am!" I said, charging the three people who had come from my world to ruin a second one.

This time, I didn't hesitate to use the bladed end of my spear.

In fact, I regretted not charging them earlier with it.

Chris dodged to the left, but he wasn't my target anyway. I thrust my spear directly at his dad, a man I had grown up seeing for most of my life. One the entire town had respected for the business he had brought in.

I expected something inside me to kick in, to get in the way of trying to hurt a fellow human being in a way that could easily kill him. But my muscles complied completely. Even my conscience was silent.

But my weapon still stopped inches away from the giant arrogant man.

A purple haze flickered in front my spear-blade, and it felt as if I was trying to push the weapon through a barrier made of thick jello. The man's eyes had grown wide and furious at my attack, and he seemed to be straining as hard I was at the moment.

Somehow, he won whatever contest we were performing, and I felt myself suddenly pushed away. But the effort seemed to have cost him something, because there was a trickle of sweat running down his left temple.

"Did you see that, Chris?" Warren Rhodes said in a deadpan voice. "Nothing but a cripple-headed brat made of pedophile dung, and he still had the balls to try and take my life. That took courage, son. Make sure you learn a lesson from that."

"Okay, Father," my old nemesis said dubiously, but formally. "I will do my best to model the courage it took to strike at you."

"Wrong lesson, dumbass," Warren spat. "Courage is a virtue, and virtues are for the weak."

He tilted his head back at the purple opening in the air. "Any time now."

Barnes had begun chanting again, and I whirled to try and deal with him. But before I could do so, another knife-wielding figure rushed out at me.

The reinforcements from the portal had arrived.

I was too busy knocking weapons out of my face to count how many. But I noticed the two remaining attackers from earlier had recovered enough to get back in the fight, and suddenly I was knocking weapons away on three fronts. Bones still cracked and bodies still kept tumbling down, but there were consistently more attackers in my face than there were lying on the ground.

I gritted my teeth at this. I had improved to handle half a dozen grown men on my own, and the universe's only response was to send several dozen more at me. Every time I grew stronger, every time I took one or two steps forward, my problems on Earth all hopped on a train to run out ahead of me.

I was tired of it.

No, I was angry about it.

So angry that something inside of me snapped.

I had gone back to striking with the blunt end of my spear after failing to strike Rhodes. Just out of habit. *Don't kill humans*, something inside of me said. Maybe it was my conscience, maybe it was just societal conditioning to not hurt another person if I could help it. Maybe it was just a habit.

But if it was, I decided then and there that it was a bad habit.

Something inside begged me to stop, but I ignored it as I brought the bladed end of my spear back around. Once I did that, a man began to fall with each swing as I stabbed out, catching a leg here, an arm or shoulder here, and very rarely, a side or hip of the most aggressive or least lucky attacker. The opened flesh also sizzled with a faint hint of electrical magic, making my enemies spasm, pass out, or maybe even die as they fell onto the bloody grass.

Even then, I was holding back, avoiding an enemy's center mass whenever I dared to risk it. Part of me felt that this tiny portion of mercy was costing me, that I was gambling my life and Stell's everything by still choosing to be soft. The other part of me argued that this compromise was still too much, that I was losing something irreplaceable with every drop of blood I tore out of my enemies.

Looking back, I realize that both voices were right.

And I still don't know what I should have done differently.

"Dalfrey," Warren said, still not moving from his spot. "This is taking far too long. It's time to show why we risked bringing you all the way from New York."

"Oh, really?" the blonde woman asked dryly. "Your little pack of toy soldiers isn't going to last long enough against my patient? You really want to risk using a one-time resource here?"

"Do it," Rhodes spat. "They're going to come after us anyway, if they ever find out we stole it. Unused, the relic is just a liability now."

"Fine," Dalfrey sighed, reaching into her suit and pulling a vial full of some angry liquid. Another one of Rhodes' soldiers jumped in my face, so I didn't see how she opened it, but a drop of the liquid suddenly landed onto each of the purple flames.

WARNING, Avalon boomed directly into my mind. *FOREIGN CONTAMINANT DETECTED.*

The right-most flame began to sputter and expand, as if someone had just thrown gasoline all over it.

"That was mildly impressive," Dalfrey said, blinking. "But was it really necessary to use our only spare vial, instead of just using the patient's own blood?"

"Your patient's blood was rendered useless long before he was born," Rhodes said with another sneer. "Those in the Order that told you otherwise were lying to you."

"I can see why you were so angry about your prescribed duty then," Dalfrey replied.

"Angry?" Rhodes snorted. "Why be angry when you can be vengeful?" He turned to look at the chanting pastor-turned-cultist on his right. "Don't drag it out, Barnes."

Barnes chanted a few more alien syllables, then nodded.

"That should do it."

The sputtering flame began to collapse, and in one minute, it seemed to go out completely, except for a few embers that still smoked at the burnt patch's edges.

And as I looked closely, the burnt patch suddenly bubbled. Then it rolled. Then it splashed.

"WARNING. FOREIGN CONTAMINANT DETECTED. CONTAMINANT IS HORDE PIT. PREPARE FOR ARRIVAL OF HORDE-TYPE MONSTERS.

AVALON'S CHALLENGE IS UPGRADED TO A VILE-CLASS TRIAL."

The mists themselves seemed to shudder at the pronouncement.

"Horde?" Stell screamed. "You actually dared to bring Horde to Avalon? Have you no conscience?" she kept screaming. "Have you no sanity? Have you no fear of *me*?"

"No, not particularly," Chris' bastard father answered. "And I have better things to do than to explain myself to a flat little girl pretending to be a grown woman."

"Adjusting to Starsown's assistance," the mists droned out again. *"Avalon is stabilizing. Switching from emergency power back to main source."*

"Keep both open for now," Stell shouted. "Guineve! You're out of time! We've got heads to break!"

"Yes, dear," Guineve's calm voice floated through the mist. "Preparations are done now anyway."

The mists in the distance began to churn, as if something was moving through them very quickly.

But a hiss in front of me drew my full attention back to the fight.

Rhodes' remaining men had pulled back from me, cautiously holding their combat machetes in a guarding stance. To their left, the Horde Pit continued to broil and expand.

"Faster, Barnes," the massive man in the middle intoned. "We don't have time for a normal progression."

The man in the black robes began chanting again, and the few lit patches of purple fire around the pit began to sputter and flare.

A long spindly limb, too long to belong to any of the Horde I had fought before, twisted out of the pit for a brief moment, then splashed back down. Several smaller figures seemed to roll about near the pit's edges.

"You!" Stell shouted, running forward. She swung an arm, and one of Rhodes' men was immediately blasted away with a scream and a cracking sound. "Dare!" Three more men jumped in front of her, and Stell swept her leg out in a wide kick. The result was so violent that all of the remaining men immediately tumbled away from her. I wondered if those guys would ever walk again.

Purple chains suddenly appeared in the air, writhing around the pit.

I don't know where, how, or why they came from. But they erupted along the edges of the pit and snapped at Stell, who snarled in frustration as she was forced to snap them apart one by one.

"Guineve!" Stell screamed. "Horde! Get here now!"

"Coming, dear," Guineve's voice carried calmly through the mist. The rolling section of fog came closer and closer.

Now three long limbs could be seen twisting in the center of the pit, and they were distinct enough for me to see that they were arms with long-fingered, oily brown hands. At the edge of the pit opposite Stell, I saw three Ilklings crawl out. They gave Stell a drooling glance, but they leaped toward me instead.

I snarled and cracked my spear on the neck of another member of Rhodes' security team. I could probably deal with the little ankle-biters one kick at a time, but it was going to make my current melee even harder. I needed to get free long enough to start using magic again.

"Done," Barnes said as he suddenly stopped chanting. "He'll be here any moment."

"Ugh." Dalfrey wrinkled her nose. "I was hoping to avoid meeting that gross, perverted thing."

"Perversion is just a matter of taste," Warren said in a calm and untroubled voice. "Right, Chris?"

"Yes, Dad," Chris sighed in barely hidden disgust. "You're absolutely right."

Hypocrite, I thought at my high-school rival as I slammed my shield into another man's face. *I've caught you drugging* how *many women again?*

But then the leftmost fire guttered, and I found something new to hate for the rest of my life. Smoke billowed in droves from the dying flame, and it stung my eyes when I got close.

"*WARNING,*" the planet suddenly boomed. "*UNAUTHORIZED ENTRY DETECTED. AVALON IS RESISTING THE ATTEMPT. THE ATTEMPT IS OCCURRING AT—*

"*WARNING! RESISTANCE IS BEING OVERCOME. INVADER'S ETA IS CURRENTLY FIVE MIN- INVADER'S ETA IS CURRENTLY TWO MINUTE—ETA IS IN 30 SECONDS—TEN SECONDS— CONTAINMENT FAILED. PREPARE FOR UNAUTHORIZED ENTRY.*"

Avalon's voice seemed to scramble as it spoke over itself.

"*WARNING! WARNING! AVALON HAS DETECTED THE INVADER AND WILL BE UNABLE TO ASSIST IN DEFENSE. AVALON'S TRIAL HAS BEEN UPGRADED TO AN ABOMINATION-CLASS TUMULT. EVACUATE. EVACUATE. EVACUATE.*"

Then the planetary supercomputer went silent.

Stell paused in the act of ripping chain-tendrils apart.

"Avalon?" she asked, her eyes flickering with troubled doubt.

But no answer came. On impulse, I sent a quick probe to my mind-screen. There was a one-word message that repeated, over and over.

EVACUATE. EVACUATE. EVACUATE.

"Besides," Warren said to Dalfrey. "The thing's going to ignore you, because its target is probably her." The man shrugged as he spoke. "Why, I don't know. Maybe it just likes half-flat chests." He scowled again, looking at his men. "Everyone else fall back. Your work is done here. Barnes, Dalfrey, hold your ground."

"Yes sir, Mr. Rhodes," a chorus of pained voices said as they finally gave way from my blood-covered spear. I briefly winced as I noticed my bloody weapon, and winced even more when I looked at the number of bloody bodies on the ground. I couldn't tell if I had killed any or if they were all just wounded. And I had no idea if they would even stay dead if I had killed them, or if they could come back like I supposedly could.

Were we even sure I could come back? the back of my mind asked again.

Because I knew that question was about to become very, very important.

The tiny purple spark at the bottom of the boiling smoke seemed to hiss.

And then something else hissed with it.

"Stellllll..."

And just like that every fleck of skin on my body tried to jump up and crawl off of me. The fact that the voice had directed its attention at someone I knew made it that much worse.

Everything froze for a moment. Me. My enemies. The movement in the pit. Even the mists and smoke and other magic suddenly seemed to stop as everyone took in that something *other*, and *wrong*, had come to Avalon.

"Stellll..." the voice said again. My friend finally reacted to the sound.

"No," the mighty woman said in a small voice, her body suddenly quivering. "You're gone. You were never real. You're just a bad dream I keep having in my sleep. They said that I made you up one night. They... they promised! You're not real!"

She had backed away from the pit, putting one foot behind the other and barely keeping upright in the process. The tendrils and figures in the pit had suddenly lowered, as if in worship, and in a manner horrifyingly similar to what the previous Horde-beings had tried to do with me.

Pastor Barnes stepped backwards and suddenly prostrated himself. Even Dr. Dalfrey chose to hide and carefully kneel, her face turning pale and green. Warren Rhodes just remained standing, with his usual scowl still etched on his face.

Chris Rhodes backed away from all of us. He had a look of shock and horror on his face that probably mirrored mine.

A long spindly black arm pulled its way through the new smoke, using a hand nearly the size of my head to grasp the ground. With a heave, the rest of the ten-foot figure pulled its way through. A thick, yet somehow still bony shoulder revealed itself, and then as the limb twitched, another arm came through the smog. Both hands dug long, writhing fingers into the ground, and with another heave, the rest of a very bad dream pulled itself forward.

The thing's body twitched at all sorts of odd angles. It swayed as it slowly stood, lacking even a toddler's grace at standing still. Yet it never toppled over, somehow suggesting superior balance, that its movements were either intentional or inherent. Something on the black chest pulsed, and I realized that it was covered with smog and something else, something that crawled all over it. A second later I realized the objects were grasping hands that crawled worm-like all over the creature's chest, sometimes grabbing the torso itself, sometimes grasping empty air around the thing. Two long, bony legs limped and dragged out next, and every now and then either a shadow, or a tail, or an additional leg would form out from the creature, solidifying out of smog or tar into greasy shriveled flesh, and help prop up the massive thing. At some point, after I looked away from the third or fourth limb, they would vanish. I never knew how or why.

Finally, the neck jerked forward out of the billowing smoke, revealing the creature's head.

The size of the thing's head seemed to change every time it swayed. When the monster swayed away from me, the head shrunk to be smaller than a human skull. But when the thing's balance made it twist forward, the head somehow grew as it drifted toward me and lolled, stretching outward until it was shaped almost like a pumpkin, or even wider when it grinned.

I wish I couldn't remember its grin. I wish I couldn't remember a single speck of its face.

Even when I tried not to look, the eyes drew me to the grin. They dotted the top of the face and they caught my gaze every time I tried to look away. I would think they were big, then I would realize they were just two little holes, then suddenly they would flare up and look like two giant starry points, covering half of the creature's face.

Then, because I had seen one half of the monster's head, I would instinctively look at the second. And I would realize the creature's mouth covered the entire second part of its face. That was always true, no matter what expression the monster was making with its mouth. When its mouth was just a small line, the head would shrink. When the mouth grinned, or worse, opened, the head expanded. When the mouth did open, the creature looked two-dimensional, as if its mouth were just another empty hole like its eyes that you could look right through. But then light came up from the throat, brighter and more colorful than the white light that sometimes shined from its eyes. I saw tiny, faint flashes of a dozen different colors that turned the hole into a fleshy gray tear full of bloody muscle, the only part of the creature's body that wasn't night-sky black. Sometimes, the lights would rise from the creature's throat in tiny sparks, as if they were trying to escape, only to be stopped when the monster closed its toothy lips.

"Stelllll," the giant thing repeated again, its mouth and head both growing wide. Its black eyes suddenly gleamed with starry light, and as the mouth opened again a tiny red mote desperately shot forward. The mouth stayed wide open, as if to let it escape, and then a long, worm-like brown tongue wrapped lazily around it to pull it back down its gullet.

"Stelllll... Ohhh Stellll." This time the abhorrent voice came out as a long, hungry moan, and the glowing eyes closed completely as the thing smiled.

Barnes and Dalfrey started quivering. Chris shot me a look of utter horror and denial. Stell just stood stock-still, except for her trembling shoulders. Warren Rhodes maintained his bearing, although his derisive expression was gone.

"Honored Ambassador," Warren Rhodes said formally. "We have upheld our end of the bargain. We have gained entry to this place. We have found what you seek."

Chris gave his father a wild, unbelieving look, then he went back to shivering in mind-numbing terror.

So did I.

"Yesssss," the ten-foot tall monstrosity said. It turned its head to look at the man I had grown up knowing. "Bargain honorrrrred."

One of the hands on its chest suddenly stretched out on a wiry, single-jointed arm. It opened its downward-facing palm and three black drops fell to the ground. The entire earth shuddered as they fell, and for a moment I feared that Avalon had been damaged. But the drops just sat there on the grass like black gelatin clumps.

"Knowledge, toolsss," the creature hissed. "All you neeeeed. Jussst add time. One hour. Then one day."

"My thanks, Honored Ambassador," Rhodes replied formally, watching the fallen black drops with a blank expression on his face. He motioned for Barnes to scuttle forward and put the three black drops in his chained pouch. "At the appointed time and after the appointed events, we will fulfill the other half of our bargain and acknowledge you as the Lord Umbra of this Expanse."

"Don't carrrrre," the monster said with a roll of its tongue. It turned its eyes elsewhere, and they twinkled when they found my currently-blonde friend. "Want! Stellllll!"

The thing, the Umbra, Rhodes had called it, took a jerky step toward my friend, swaying towards her, forming new legs for balance. The smile on its face nearly doubled in size, and another light tried to escape from its mouth before it was caught and re-swallowed by its tongue. Its two arms swayed slightly to help maintain balance, but the fingers on its hands constantly jerked toward the Starsown at unnatural angles. The hands on its chest also stretched out, reaching for her, and I heard faint moaning noises come from both them and the monster's chest, as if its torso and palms were dotted with hungry maws.

Stell had not stopped backing away from the nightmare in front of us. Her breaths came in hurried pants, as if she were hyperventilating. "No," she tried to say, but her voice came out in a hurried squeak. "No," she tried again, her voice stronger. She closed her eyes, and repeated her earlier chant. "You're not real. You're a nightmare I had when I was a little girl. You're a bad dream I had about losing everything." She opened her eyes again, as if she had been expecting the abomination to be no longer there, and suddenly looked disappointed. She sucked in another breath.

It was clear that she was inches away from having a total breakdown, and I couldn't find a single reason to blame her for it. Not in front of this thing. She was this creature's target, and she was still handling its appearance better than me or anyone else. I hadn't even dared to breathe yet.

The Umbra took another awkward step forward, somehow back down to two legs. Its two main hands were still raised toward my friend, and I realized that its arms were almost as long as the creature was tall. Its many-jointed fingers kept twitching towards her in impossible ways.

"Stellllll," it croaked. "*My* Stellllll. Found you. Finally."

Its voice was still all kinds of get-me-on-medication-right-now disturbing, but the thing was getting more coherent. "Missed you," it added, this time without prolonging the words.

"Stay... stay back," she said, getting a little more force into her voice. "Don't come any closer."

She finally took her eyes off the monster, and a little bit of panic left her face.

"Wes, Guineve," she called both names out, and I finally snapped out of the thing's trance.

I was still stupendously terrified, but a tiny part of my brain was screaming at me to take action.

"R-right," I finally said after a couple of tries, and I started walking towards Stell.

"What are you doing?" she asked, looking even more horrified. "No! Don't come near me! He'll see you!"

That was good advice. I wanted to follow that advice. The rational part of my mind *told* the rest of me to follow that advice.

For some horrible reason, I ignored it, and slowly tried to get my shaking body between the monster and Stell.

"Wes!" Stell hissed. "What are you doing? Get back!"

But the monster treated me as if I wasn't here at all.

"Shhhh, Stell," it hissed, its voice becoming less garbled. "Don't worry. Everything will be fine. Come to me. Be mine. Be my little Stell."

It took another step forward, on three legs this time.

"No," Stell said firmly, sucking in a breath. "I am not yours. This is not your place. Be gone!"

A chuckle tumbled out of the Umbra's throat. Little lights flared all around the inside of its mouth, and I thought I heard tiny screams from them.

"Just like your mother. Just like your sisters." Stell's eyes quaked a little wider at the comment. "They miss you, you know. Do you not miss them?"

The monster opened its mouth again, as if to show off the tiny lights writhing inside of it. Again, whenever they tried to escape, the tongue always caught them, and this time I could hear them cry out for sure.

Stell tried to reply, but whatever words she wanted to make stayed stuck in the middle of her throat.

"Do you not miss them? Please, Stell," the monster begged with a wide, toothy smile. "Come," it burbled. "Help us. Help them accept me. Show them we're all one family now."

Her whole body heaved again, and she took a jerky step backwards. She seemed like she would topple over any moment.

My brain ached as I tried to comprehend what she was experiencing, being the target of whatever horrible, mind-bleaching scheme the monster was threatening her with, and had already threatened everyone she had ever grown up with. I just couldn't process it. I didn't even know what the monster wanted to do exactly, but I knew it would destroy her, destroy the woman who had given me my legs and brain back.

My grip on my spear tightened a tiny bit at that. And I kept walking over to her.

She looked at me then, asking me for help and begging me to stay away all in one terrified glance.

"Stell," I somehow croaked out. "Are we... are we faster than it?"

It was a cowardly question. But anything strong enough to terrify Stell wasn't something I could find a way to deal with. It hadn't even deemed me as existing yet, my power was so beneath it.

For a second, she just stared at me. Then she seemed to process my words. She gave a slow, jerking nod.

"M-maybe," she stuttered, and I could see the thinking part of her come back alive bit by bit.

"Maybe?" the awful giant hissed, its glowing grin widening. "Does my little Stell want to run away again? Does she want to play another game? That's okay. Uncle Cavus doesn't mind. He can let you run a little."

Could you get any creepier? the bravest, smallest part of me growled. The slightly larger, thinking part of me realized that if it felt that confident about catching us, then we didn't really have much chance of escape.

But then the mist suddenly moved.

With a powerful boom, Guineve stood in front of us in all of her stately glory. Her mist-made dress and raven hair fluttered slightly in the faint breeze, and she held her arm toward the Umbra in a warding gesture.

"Wes," she said in a tight, but calm, voice. "Take Stell. Get her away from here."

The Umbra stopped walking forward and tilted its head at the new woman, its skull shrinking with its smile. Its eyes stopped shining as it considered her for a moment.

"Guineve, no," Stell whispered. "You're not strong enough." She spoke again, her voice much smaller. "I couldn't make you strong enough."

The holes near the top of the monster's face suddenly gleamed, probably in awareness, and it slowly cocked its head back into an upright position.

"Yes, I am, darling," Guineve replied, but I could see the lie in the way her outstretched arm shook. The woman was terrified along with us, but unlike us, she was brave enough to stare our nightmare down. "Wes, Stell's going to need help. Get her somewhere safe so I can fight freely. I'll be fine. Just take her somewhere else, far, far away, so that she and Breena will be safe."

She has just saved us both, I realized. Not because she was strong enough to fight this thing. None of us believed that at the moment. She had saved us by giving us a course of action, and a reason for it. Now our brains could plan, actually have something to do other than just sit there and be terrified.

"Satellite," the creature hissed, glow-grinning slightly. "Stell made a little mother-satellite. You look so much like her. What race did she make you from?"

Guineve stretched out her other hand. The mist began to circle around it, forming a spiral that spoke of some kind of hidden power. The other hand began to glow. I saw white flames dance around the fingers.

The Umbra's grin suddenly vanished, and its eyes became glowing slits.

"Bad Satellite," it hissed. "Bad. She belongs to me. All of her belongs to me," A third, sharp-nailed foot stomped and pulled the creature forward. "Even you belong to me."

Black smoke began to roll around the Umbra's two long arms. They spread out wide, moving the monster into a ready stance.

"Little Star," Guineve said calmly. "You have to go right now. It will be okay. I love you."

"Guineve." Stell's horrified eyes were growing wet. "Don't."

"I'll get her away, Guineve," I found myself saying. "Then I'll come back, and you and I will figure this thing out." I swallowed, then I tried to firm my voice for my next words. "Don't lose to it before I get back."

Part of her face turned to look at me, and the corner of a smile tilted out.

"Thank you, Wes. You were the bravest, the sweetest, and the best of them. I should have told you sooner."

"Thank you," I said, and the back of my mind screamed expletives at me when I flashed her a cocky grin. "But you have to tell me again when I get back. Come on, Stell."

I yanked on my friend's arm and pulled her away as white fire and walls of mist suddenly exploded behind us. I heard a grating, warbled shriek of outrage as we ran, which surprised me, because Guineve was not supposed to be that monster's match. With that knowledge, the rest of my brain began to clear. *Right,* I thought. *Since I'm the only one not currently facing the worst childhood demon ever dreamed up, I should figure out the plan.*

That's right, son, a memory of my father's voice surfaced again. *Step up and act.*

Once again, I firmed up at the sound of his words.

I would get Stell to the nearest clearing that had her stones, I decided. I had seen her both talk to Icons from there and create portals for me to travel in, so I knew she could make her escape there. Then she could call for aid, and probably bring some Icons to help us fight. Since Guineve was strong enough for the Umbra to at least take her seriously, an Icon or two should at minimum help make the match close. Best case scenario, we call in every favor every one of those demigods owed us and bury that thing under a massive pile of beatdowns.

"No," Stell moaned as I dragged her behind me. "Not Guineve. Please, not Guineve."

Her legs started to give out from under her, and I realized that she had just had it. She was dealing with some nightmare that had probably eaten her family, probably eaten her entire home world, and now she was sacrificing her closest friend, and a part of herself, to face the monster that had apparently been hunting her ever since she was a little girl.

I was the one person the monster was completely ignoring. Had that been otherwise, I doubt I would have lasted even half as long as Stell had.

I reached over and caught her with my other arm as she started to fall. I reflected on the fact that I may have been strong enough to carry her weight, but she was easily strong enough to knock my head clean off if she had a problem with the way I held her. Thankfully, she accepted my support instead of tossing me off of Avalon, and I ran while carrying her.

"My fault," she whispered. "She has to feel what I feel. She's terrified, Wes. And it's all my fault."

"It's not," I argued quietly. "And I'm going back to get her after I save you."

My friend needs me, I told myself. *I can go back to being a coward after I'm dead.*

"You can't save us," she muttered bitterly. "My parents couldn't even save me. My grandfather and uncles couldn't save me." The bitterness started to leave her voice, and it became small again. "They hid me here, with a note that said everything was just a bad dream."

Shit, I said quietly to myself. *And I had been thinking that I had it bad.*

"They *did* save you," I chose to argue. "Because that thing hasn't gotten you yet. So that means I can save you too. At least until you can finish saving yourself."

"He'll kill you," she said, giving me a horrified look. "You're nowhere near strong enough. He'll rip you right in half."

"And then I'll come back," I growled. "I'm a Challenger, Stell. Remember? You chose us Earthlings for that very reason."

I saw wheels turn behind her eyes when I said that. So I continued talking.

"I don't need to be strong enough to kill it. I don't even need to be strong enough to drive it off. I just need to be strong enough to anger it. Then I have to come back and fight it again and again, as many times as it takes, until you're able to go to one of your worlds and get some Icons to come help us fight."

"That..." She started to argue, then her eyes widened. "That could work. Maybe. Cavus is just one Umbra. Maybe we can get enough Icons to fight him. Maybe a local hero or two, or my other Satellites could help. But wait," she whispered. "The Icons have never seen me in this form before."

"Get your Satellites to vouch for you," I said, thinking quickly. I had to. I was the only one that a giant creepy demon-thing wasn't obsessing over. "They know what the real you looks like, right? And you put one on every planet specifically to help you monitor with things and communicate with them, right?"

"Yes," she said, sucking in a breath. "That could work. That could work, Wes. And...Wes?"

She said my name again, and despite everything, I suddenly brightened.

"Yes?" I found myself saying hopefully.

"You can put me down now, Wes. This is a good spot."

"Oh, right. Sorry."

I told myself to stop feeling disappointed for no reason, and I set the Starsown down on her feet. She actually flashed a quick smile at me, and I told myself it didn't help because there was nothing to help. We were just friends. Then I told myself to stop being an idiot and focus.

She walked over to the middle of the empty clearing and held out her hands.

"Engage emergency power to nearby know-stones," she said aloud, and in spite of it all, the name for those rocks still made me wince. The glowing, glyph-covered rocks slowly rose from the grass in response to her voice. "Activate emergency portal. Enable system-wide message to all Icons. Message is the following: Attention Icons of all worlds. Avalon is under attack by a Tumult-class invader. Per ancient agreement, I am invoking my request for mutual defense. I will be arriving at each of your worlds in a form my Satellites will recognize, to bring you to Avalon so that you may assist in its defense. Please prepare. Failure to maintain Avalon will result in losing access to Challengers and losing our means of surviving Tumults and Trials. End of message."

She turned and looked at me.

"There's no guarantee you can come back from fighting an Umbra," she admitted, and something in her green eyes looked like it was about to tear in half.

"Then you had better get help quickly, Stell," I said gently. "They have my Earth body. This is probably my best chance anyway."

Her eyes teared up.

"Guineve was right, Wes. You really are the best of them. I wish..."

A boom sounded far behind us, and Stell blinked the wetness from her eyes.

"You're right," she said firmly. "If we want to save Guineve, we have to hurry."

A portal formed behind her. She walked over to one of the rocks and pulled at an indented piece. It came right out, and she pressed the piece in her hands.

"Guineve won't want to leave you alone with that thing. She's gonna be needed to help the Icons fight Cavus when they get here. And she..." My friend suddenly shuddered. "Can't come back from losing like you can."

We both chose to ignore that I might not be able to come back either.

"You'll have to make her leave. I made this," she pointed to the stone, "for that purpose. In case I ever had to make her go somewhere safe. It will take her to a realm that will be difficult for that thing to find her. That's her and my best chance, at least until I can come back with help. I need you to last that long, Wes." Her eyes glittered. "I'll never forgive you if you don't."

"Deal," I said firmly. "Now hurry up and go."

She reached out and hugged me one last time, even harder than when I had come back from fighting Horde. Then she removed her face from my neck and ran to the portal without saying anything. She gave me one last look, tears filling her green eyes, and then she disappeared.

Then I was alone.

I held the stone and looked down for one moment, screwing up my nerves.

Another boom sounded out from behind me.

"Avalon," I said out loud, trying something on a dare. "Confirm if Challenger Wes Malcolm has access to your global command console."

"Access confirmed," the mists said, and for the first time, the deep voice spoke quietly. *"Evacuate, Wes Malcolm."*

"I can't, and I don't have time to explain why."

I turned and began to run back to where I heard the explosions. "Avalon, provide any additional power available for Satellite Lady Guineve of the Mists."

"Lady Guineve has been fully reinforced," Avalon rumbled back quietly. *"Satellite cannot contain any further power. Evacuate, Wes Malcolm."*

"Avalon, confirm if you have any more power available," I commanded.

"Confirmed. Leftover power available for other commands. Evacuate, Wes Malcolm."

"I already said I wasn't leaving," I huffed as I ran. "Avalon, direct maximum possible power to enhance Challenger Wes Malcolm's combat and survival capabilities."

"Challenger's command is acknowledged, but contested," Avalon rumbled. *"Additional combat not recommended. Evacuate, Wes Malcolm."*

"Avalon, override your recommendation," I growled, still running. "Enhance Challenger Wes Malcolm."

"Confirmed, removing override and enhancing Challenger Wes Malcolm to maximum possible extent. Recommendation remains. Evacuate, Wes Malcolm."

I felt mist began to slide into my body. I suddenly felt lighter, stronger, and full of adrenaline. Spurred on by this, I ran faster, hoping I wasn't too late.

Two thoughts suddenly jumped into my head.

"Avalon, confirm that you have enough power for this device to teleport Lady Guineve to a safe location, and confirm whether this stone is necessary for her to return. Then confirm whether Stell will have enough power to teleport back with Icon support." I took another breath, wrestling with voicing my next request. "Then confirm whether enough power remains or is necessary for Challenger Wes Malcolm to resurrect upon death here on Avalon."

"Confirmed that power remains to safely teleport Lady Guineve of the Mists," the mists rumbled softly. *"Confirmed that stone is unnecessary for Lady Guineve to return on her own power, though immediate return will require time or intervention of Stewardess Stell upon Starsown's return. Confirmation that Starsown has enough power to return with maximum possible assistance."*

This was seriously the best news all day.

"Confirmation that resurrection is dependent upon the inherent power of the Challenger, not Avalon. No confirmation regarding whether Challengers or any other being can resurrect after contact with Umbra species. Contact with Umbra not recommended. Evacuate, Wes Malcolm."

Well, never mind.

My body's in my enemies' hands anyway, I tried to remind myself.

I was on borrowed time no matter how I looked at it.

One last boom sounded out, and then an eerie silence settled over the mists. I ignored the cold lump forming in my stomach and ran as fast as I dared.

And then the mists parted, and I was back to where the nightmare was.

Lady Guineve was on her knees panting in exhaustion. She took deep breaths, as if she had been starved of oxygen. Mist hung in tatters from the edge of her collarbone to the tips of her knees. She held one hand over her chest, as if she was trying to hold herself together.

The ground all around her was pitted, as if it had been blasted into fine gravel and dirt. There was an empty crater where the Horde Pit had been.

I was able to let that sink in for a moment. The Umbra, the creature that we were all scared witless over facing, had been forced to call the Pit into assisting it.

This thing was not as strong as Stell thought it was. And Stell, and all of her Satellites, were probably much stronger than they realized.

This thing's going to die as soon as we have our rematch, I promised.

Speaking of the monster itself...

It was over a dozen feet away from Guineve, but it still loomed over her thanks to height and the reach of its grotesquely long arms. Smog circled around it, similar to how mist had once circled around Guineve. But the smog circled in patches, exposing the monster's midnight-black skin. Many parts of its body looked torn, and with gray, wet flesh bleeding out of the rips. The hands crawling over the creature were working to stitch the tears, but they worked slowly. The monster would need time to repair its wounds.

But it wouldn't need that time to finish Guineve.

"Bad little Stell-piece," the thing hissed, the tear of its mouth tilting, as if it had been knocked sideways. "Bad, dirty-wrong Stell-piece. To wound me. To tell me no and fight me back. Bad friend. Bad daughter. Bad wife. Bad slave."

"You are not my friend," Guineve hissed back, pain and anger whispering out through her clenched teeth. "You are not my father. And you are certainly not my husband or my master. You are a wretched and warped abuser from a wretched and warped species. You have plagued my dear Little Star with too many nightmares for too many centuries. The opportunity to protect her from you is something I will cherish forever, regardless of what is about to happen to me. The fact that I was also able to strike out and injure you is my eternal glory."

"False, unfaithful, little Stell-piece," the thing hissed. It took another step forward, and suddenly the strong, kind, beautiful woman who had welcomed, fed and cared for me was in reach of its ten-foot arms. "I kept your entire family forever, even your ugly men, and you still say such things. False, wrong, faithless Stell-piece. I will fix you. Then I will keep you. Then I will find the rest of you and fix and keep those parts as well, forever. I have been too patient! And for too long!" Its voice warbled as it left its lopsided mouth, and it raised a skull-sized hand.

I was out of time. I barreled forward, clutching Stell's stone in my right fist.

"Guineve," I shouted, pressing the indent in the middle of the stone and throwing it at her. "Catch!"

Her head whipped around at the sound of my voice, and I saw a tiny spark of hope peek out from behind her mask of steely defiance. Then she saw the rock that fell into her open hands and saw that I was alone and running towards her and the Umbra.

"No!" she suddenly shrieked. It was the first time I had ever heard her make such a noise. Maybe that was why it sounded so terrifying. "Wes, no! He'll kill you! He'll rip you apart for good! Wes, don't do this! Stell! *Stell! Stell don't let him...*"

The monster's massive hand swung down. But Guineve had gone and vanished into tiny motes of light.

"Yessssss," the night-colored creature hissed as it closed its tiny eyes and clenched its hand. "Finally. A tiny part of her. A tiny part of my little Stell. Oh, I've waited so...what?" It opened its eyes and looked down at its clenched hand. Then it opened its fist, and it realized its hand was empty. "She's not here. Where did she go?" it asked quietly. Then its eyes and mouth stretched, color bursting out. "Where did she go? She's not here! Where did she go? Where is my Stell?"

It turned and looked at me, and suddenly I didn't feel brave anymore. I didn't feel like I did at the party three years ago, when I got between an unconscious girl and three guys who were fully capable of kicking the crap out of me. It didn't feel like when I was standing between four tiny women and a four-foot tall midget who wanted to murder me for protecting them.

The horror of the gaze that Stell and Guineve had been forced to deal with descended upon me, and I felt like I was a puny tiny manling, standing where I had no business, trying to protect a host of women far stronger than me from a creature that initially didn't even fear me enough to kill me. It was all I could do not to just roll up in a ball and start crying my eyes out.

"You took her," the monster's voice boomed out from its throat. The lights in its throat all fluttered about, giving me the impression that they were flaring in agony. "You took my Stell. YOU! TOOK! MY! STELL!"

It took a step forward, on just two legs this time, and as the ground rumbled from its footfall, my mind tried to tear itself in half. A tiny part of me was desperately trying to figure out if it should try fleeing, or delay the monster somehow, or even risk striking a blow. But I couldn't do any one of those things because the greater part of my mind was demanding I fall to the floor and start blubbering.

Somehow, though, I took a tiny step backwards.

Maybe Stell would have been proud of that.

"WHERE IS SHE?" the monster roared, and my ears rang in agony. "WHERE DID YOU HIDE MY STELL?"

The tiny, sane part of me got a moment of control, and it used that moment to make me bite the inside of my mouth as hard as I could. The pain and taste of blood was enough to distract the broken part of me for a little longer. Barely.

I took another step backwards, not daring to open my mouth. I had dropped my spear a long time ago, and the club I had grabbed would do even less to this creature. Actually, I realized the whole idea of me trying to strike this thing at all was laughable. So I took another step backwards, because it felt like a slightly less stupid idea.

It is too late for smart ideas, the pain in my cheek hissed. I tried to ignore it and took a fourth step backwards.

"WHO TOLD YOU?" the giant thing growled, so loud it shook the inside of my skull again. "WHO SAID YOU CAN HIDE MY STELL?"

I had to be in reach of that thing's arms, the sane part of me said. The fact that it hadn't attacked me yet was good news. I could probably use that. Wait, no, that was wishful thinking—

Boom.

The monster's giant hand fell forward, landing past me. The grass impacted by the hand disintegrated, and the monster's worm-like claws dug deep wounds into the violated earth. The long, thin arm tensed for a moment before it pulled the rest of the massive creature forward.

The Umbra hung its body low as it pulled itself forward, bringing its face down to my level. When it bared its glowing, toothy mouth at me, I realized its head was currently half the size of my entire body and that it could be even bigger if it wanted to be. The midnight-black skull tilted at me, eyes twinkling in consideration.

"You're hiding the rest of her too, aren't you?" the creature whispered to me, as though trying to get a secret shared. "You know where every tiny piece of my little Stell is and you're hiding her from me. Because you don't know what I'll do to you if you get in my way. You've never seen me before," it hissed, made all the creepier by the monster's non-threatening tone. "I know that. I know you've never even heard of me. You should have," it suddenly growled, and the little lights inside it flared like writhing fireflies. "She should have behaved and told everyone about me! So that the other boys would know better! Know she's off-limits." The lights inside its mouth suddenly dimmed, and it seemed to get itself back under control.

"But she didn't," the creature whispered, in a horribly soothing tone. "She didn't, so you didn't know. She was an unfaithful little tease, and she tricked you, but it's not your fault. You didn't mean to get in my way, did you? *Did you*?" Its throat flared again for a moment, and then it mastered itself.

"No," it continued, still coming terrifyingly close to my face. "You didn't. You couldn't have. You just met me. And now you know better. You know what to tell me now. Tell me where every pretty piece of my little Stell went, and I'll let you go. You don't even have to go get her for me. You can go home and go back to bed. You can even pretend I was a bad dream, like she always did whenever she wanted to be coy. Everything will be okay. Everyone will be happy. If you just. Tell me. Where. She. Is."

The monster punctuated each of its last few words with a glowing hiss, less than three feet from my face.

I didn't have the strength to tell it no. I didn't even have the strength to point out how freaking creepy this thing was, and that it needed to crawl back into whatever toxin-induced nightmare birthed it and leave the rest of us alone for good. But, again, I didn't have the strength.

And I didn't have the strength to think up a good lie, either, that would send it on a false trail away from Stell. That would have been perfect. But any world I sent it to would have at least one Satellite of Stell's, and one of them had her main body right now. What lies I could think up would still give this thing far too much of what it wanted.

I also wanted to back away again. Moving even one step backwards felt like an incredible idea at the moment. *Put another few inches of distance between myself, and the Jack O'Lantern from Hell? Sure, I'll take that.*

But I couldn't find the strength.

I even wanted to do something with my hands. Get them in the way, use them to somehow move backwards, even take a risky swing at the thing's eyes. Any one of those things had to be a better idea than just letting them hang next to my sides.

Still, I couldn't find the strength.

But I wanted to keep my mouth closed, delay the thing from finding my friend for as many moments as I could, no matter how many or how few. Every second I stalled gave Stell one more moment to find help, gave Guineve one more moment to recover for her rematch with this thing.

I bit harder onto the corner of my cheek, and when I reached deep down...

I found the strength.

The creature tilted its massive head further, looking at me with its pulsing bright-then-empty eyes, and waited a heartbeat for me to answer. Then another. Then another. Then I couldn't get myself to even count anymore.

"You're. Not. Talking," the monster hissed, torturing the little lights in its throat with every word. "Not. Even. Trying." It drew the rest of its body closer, so that it could loom over me while still keeping its face close. "You're being useless! Useless on purpose!" the monster suddenly roared, eyes flaring for one bright, horrible moment. "THIEF!"

In another moment a skull-sized hand reached out and grabbed my throat, instantly shutting the door that precious air took to my lungs. The Umbra lifted my entire body into the air effortlessly, the ten-foot arm holding me high above its horrible, giant head.

"You dare?" it screamed, with such force that the nearby mist somehow shuddered. "You dare want her for yourself? In place of me?"

The arm holding me up suddenly slammed straight down into the ground. The earth appeared in front of me for a brief moment, and then with a *thud,* Avalon's ground and sky swam together for a painfully long time.

"You think you're worthy?" the monster shouted, its face enlarging to fit its angry mouth as it hoisted me back up into the air. I felt my reinforced body shudder from the earlier impact, and I knew Avalon was struggling to help me survive.

Deep down, I also knew it wasn't going to work.

"You think you're better than me? That you deserve to have her instead? Stupid! Stupid!" The Umbra shook me savagely with each insult. "Stupid! Dumb! Ugly little boy! I hate ugly, dumb boys!"

The hand holding me suddenly whipped around in a long arc. Air whistled behind me as I left its grasp. I saw Avalon turn slowly under me. Rocks and dirt flashed by far below me. If I could stop spinning long enough, I could almost pretend I was flying.

But the moment passed, and I crashed back down to the ground.

I landed painfully on top of something I'll never identify, and then I bounced back into the air. I was almost able to see where I was going to land next, but I gave up the chance at the last moment so that I wouldn't land on my neck.

Another painful bounce, and this time I only flew a few feet into the air. I realized I was about to crash into a copse of trees, but before I could do anything about it, a limb slammed into my back and I landed again.

Finally, I had stopped moving. I was looking up at the dark, cloudy sky. My limbs all ached, and my spine felt like it was trying not to weep in agony.

Warning, my mind-screen suddenly flared up and said. *Vital guard is dangerously low. Mortal injury imminent.*

No shit, I wanted to reply. But my mind-screen began to repeat its earlier warning.

Evacuate. Evacuate. Evacuate.

I would have laughed bitterly, but I didn't have the stamina or time for it. Instead I reached out and pulled myself to my feet as fast as I dared.

I had just finished getting my legs under me when I began to hear low booming noises that gradually became louder and closer. I shook off my dizziness and raised my head. A blurry mass of smog and sharp claws was seconds away from me.

"YOU'RE NOT BETTER THAN ME!" a sky-wrenching roar blasted into my ears.

I had time to raise the shield I had somehow retained right before several truckloads of force slammed into it. I felt the wooden barrier explode just before I flew through the air again, my poor ruined arm trailing feebly and painfully behind me. I landed much quicker this time, bounced much faster before I came to a full stop.

By now the rest of my body had joined my arm in screaming as loudly as possible at my brain.

Warning! my mind-screen called out. *Vital guard exhausted! Critical injuries detected! Mortal injury imminent! Evacu—*

"UGLY DUMB BOY!" the monster screamed again, and the force of its shout made air burn my face.

I was hoisted into the air again. I tried to resist with my remaining good hand, but the creature's arm was like oily steel cable.

"You're not as strong!" the creature continued, blasting bright, smelly hate into my face. "You're not as smart! You don't even have as many limbs!"

Its other long hand grasped at one of my legs, and it suddenly pulled. I screamed as I had a sharp, brief sensation of pain, and then all the feeling in my leg just below the socket went away. But the agony just above my leg remained, and the monster dropped me to the ground right in front of it.

Warning! Mortal injury detected! Evacua—

My mind-screen cut off completely after that.

"See?" it cackled, waving a fleshy new club that rained all over me. "Not as many limbs! Ha-ha! Who's better now, ugly dumb boy?"

Its laughter was an ugly, spitting sound. I don't know how it even made that spitting noise, because it looked like plenty of things tried to leave its mouth but none ever succeeded.

But I knew at the time that I didn't need to think about questions like that anymore. My vital guard was exhausted. I was going to bleed out in a minute or two at the most. And the way my leg had been removed, I couldn't have applied a tourniquet even if I had the time or two working hands.

In other words, the back of my mind pointed out, *mission accomplished.*

I had known I wouldn't have beaten this thing anyway. I just had to delay it for as long as I could. And I was bleeding to death right now while it raged over me.

Therefore, mission accomplished.

"Still got nothing to say?" the Umbra cackled over me. "Come on, ugly dumb boy! Beg! Beg to live!"

I didn't expect to feel so free right then. Yes, the monster leaning over me was still terrifying. But so was the fact that I was bleeding to death. Somehow, the terror of the one completely canceled out the terror of the other somehow. So I laughed. And the thing over me cocked its head.

"Did it break?" it asked itself. "Did the ugly little boy break already?"

"Maybe," I admitted, still laughing at it. "But I was laughing because I realized I don't know where Stell is anyway. But I know where she will be."

"What?" the creature said, its eyes lighting up brightly. It dropped its bloody new club, hissing eagerly. "You know? Where is my little Stell? Tell me where! Tell me where my little Stell goes! Cavus will let you live if you give him back his little Stell!"

Huh, I thought. *That's right. The thing's name was Cavus.*

It wasn't that important right now. I tried to remember it for later though.

"Here," I rasped. "Stell's coming right back here."

"Here?" the creature sounded confused. "Back to me? But she always hides! She runs from me!"

"Not this time," I coughed. "Just wait right here. Because she's coming back to kick your ass. You creepy freak." Another cough as I insulted it.

There. I had done it.

I had resisted to the bitter end.

"Me?" the glowing maw gaped. "Kill me? Stell won't kill me. She can't. Even if she could, she's too afraid of me. No one can scare her like I can. No one can make her feel small like I can. I am her whole world! No matter how much she tries to hide, she knows she's nothing without me! A dumb ugly boy like you would never understand us! Dumb ugly thief!"

The Umbra reached for my unbroken arm.

"Pretending to be brave? Do you think I'll spare you? You think Uncle Cavus will spare you like he always spares all the pretty little girls, even the ones that grow up? Do you think I'll spare you too, so you can stay with them? No!" it shrieked.

This time I could hear and see my limb rip right off, and the pain cut right through my apathy. I screamed and screamed, in spite of the fact that I was already marked a dead man and that all the pain in the world would be gone in two minutes max.

But before those two minutes ended, the gigantic horror took the time to punctuate his every word by clubbing me over the head with my severed arm.

"I don't!" <*Slam*> "Spare!" <*Slam*> "Ugly!" <*Slam*> "Boys!"

A snapping noise sounded over my head, and I saw the monster hurl its bloody, broken club away. What was left of me was lifted back into the air.

"She doesn't love you!" the glowing maw screamed in my face. "No one does! No one will ever love you!"

The creature started to slam me back into the ground, head-first.

But everything had gone cold and dark long before I ever landed.

28

RISE UP AND RAGE

V*ital signs detected,* a voice said in my mind. *Assessing complete report of Challenger's status. Assessment complete. Providing report now:*

Challenger's resurrection was successful. Vital guard and vital functions have returned to optimal state. No complications other than the standard trauma resulting from termination.

Challenger is advised to avoid mortal injuries for at least three days. If at all possible.

That last part came out as a sigh somehow.

Challenger has overcome a significant personal Challenge, my mind-screen reported. *Challenger has made new growth that will require further examination.*

That was right, I reminded myself. Stell had mentioned once that after five Rises a Challenger's growth changed slightly. Further Rises were just a little bit more complicated.

Also, did I get all my limbs back?

A quick check confirmed that I was whole again.

Then another, belated check confirmed that yes, I was alive. And I was back in Avalon.

I had strange, phantom-like pain all over my body. But that pain was lessening, and I was alive, so I chose not to dwell on it. Processing the fact that I had just died wouldn't help me in any way right now. In fact, contemplating my recent death and dismemberment would probably just drive me crazy.

I looked at my mind-screen to see if I could figure out what I had gained, but none of my characteristics seemed to have changed yet. I couldn't even tell how close I was to my next Rise. I realized that I had leftover points I could have used to make myself stronger and more skilled, and I wanted to kick myself for forgetting to use them earlier.

But then again, I had gotten the feeling that Avalon had more than tripled my current power during the last fight, and I had been still completely helpless. Adding those points would make me strong compared to a normal human, but the understanding Stell and Breena had given me of my Traits convinced me that there were many creatures that were much, much more powerful than I was in every category. That Umbra Cavus was probably going to be at the top of the list. I figured his traits, assuming he even had comparable ones, to be in the upper-hundreds at the very least. Those small handful of points would change nothing for this fight, and I couldn't shake my intuition's impulse to hold onto them.

I looked around. Nothing but mist, trees, and rocks all around me. No sign of the Umbra or of its human helpers.

That was another thing I could break my head on: People from my home town were helping *that thing*. Had a deal with it. Had offered up a person to it. Had even promised to recognize the creature as having authority over them somehow. All for what?

Knowledge, the Umbra had said. *Knowledge and tools.*

What knowledge? What tools?

But the fact that people I knew believed that creature had something to give them, something that was worth sacrificing a girl who looked young enough to be one of their daughters to, was head-cracking. These people knew for a fact that the monster wanted to do all sorts of horrible things to someone else. They might even have known what exactly Cavus wanted from Stell. I hoped I never found out myself, and even more so, I hoped Stell never had even the slightest chance to find out.

Her name reminded me what was at stake.

The woman was a friend and was responsible for managing over half a dozen worlds. She was constantly working to save, help or improve billions of lives on a daily basis.

The thought of all of that made my fear of the thing subside, at least for now.

Long enough to commit to getting back into the fight.

"Avalon," I said aloud. "Confirm whether you are still functional. Confirm also whether Umbra Cavus is still located on this world."

"Functional status confirmed," the mists whispered next to me.

"Abomination-class intruder's presence is also confirmed. Avalon recognizes the return of Challenger Wes Malcolm."

"Thank you, Avalon," I replied unnecessarily. "Please restore all possible augmentations. Focus on speed, durability and general survival."

"Redirecting all possible power to Challenger Wes Malcolm per given specifications. Increasing parameters to account for the recent increase of Challenger's power."

"You can do that?" I asked in confusion. "You can even tell how much I've grown? Why? I can't even figure that out right now."

"Confirmed," the mists replied dryly. *"Explanation is unavailable at this current time. Stand by for augmentation."*

As I stood there being baffled, power surged back in to me, and I felt stronger and faster again.

Further out in the distance, something hideous and familiar roared.

"Right," I decided. "Since you are done being informative, I guess it's back to work." I took a moment to re-cast my own augmentation spells.

"Confirmed," the mists whispered eerily. *"Good luck, Challenger Wes Malcolm."*

"Wait," I said as I started to run. "You're not going to tell me to evacuate again?"

"Negative," the mists rumbled. *"New directives discovered concerning Challenger Wes Malcolm. Avalon is submitting the following message per said directives: Hold fast. End of message. Sender unknown."*

I stumbled when I heard the now-familiar phrase, but I kept running. Whoever Invictus was, I could only hope he was on my side. And it wasn't like he was telling me to do something I wasn't already doing.

I ran as fast as I could, but I began to slow when I heard voices. It sounded as if my friendly neighborhood cultists were having a conversation with their freak of a patron.

"Honored Ambassador Cavus, we ask you to stand by our deal for the sake of everyone's long term goals."

Warren Rhodes' neutral voice carried over the mist.

"The little Starsown was the long-term goal, Earth-thing!" I heard the

Umbra snarl, and its voice still raised the hair on the back of my neck. "You said I would find her here!"

"And find her you did, Lord Umbra," Rhodes replied formally. "We have upheld our end of the bargain, and as an act of goodwill, we are willing to assist you in relocating the Starsown."

"If you had assisted earlier, she never would have gotten away to begin with!"

For a moment I didn't know how Rhodes was able to keep talking to the thing. Then I realized why.

Because the nightmare thing still had something he wanted.

What would happen if he got it, whatever it was?

Probably another nightmare, I decided, and I began to creep closer to the mist.

"We lack your strength, honored Umbra. Even with our magic, the three of us would not be any sort of match for the Starsown's Satellite. But with a small increase of our power, we can help you find her, and soon."

"Soon?" the monster hissed expectantly. "How? And how soon?"

I stopped moving altogether. I needed to take this chance to learn Rhodes Sr.'s goals and thwart them.

Especially since I was probably going to die again soon.

The delay was the most important thing, I reminded myself. As long as I kept coming back, I could delay this monster and its pets until Guineve recharged and Stell got back with her Icon allies.

And if I couldn't keep coming back, I reflected, then I was probably dead no matter what I did at this point anyway.

"As soon as we learn how this world's portal network works, great one," Warren Rhodes replied respectfully. "We know that you are familiar with her technology, and that it was designed to resist you if you chose to use it. But the fact that previous Earthlings could make use of it proves that it will not resist us. Teach us the intricacies of this world's runes, Lord Umbra, and we will use them to send you to that which you so desperately desire."

Cavus was silent as I crept forward. He was probably considering Rhodes' offer.

"With your help," Rhodes carefully continued after a moment. "We can master this planet's technology much more quickly. We can use it to send you to each planet as you hunt for the Starsown and her Satellites. You would not only regain the opportunity to obtain her primary body, you would gain quick transportation to her Satellites as well. It would be a net gain on both of our parts, especially in the sense of time saved. And have you already not paid enough dues to time, Lord Cavus?"

"Yesss," I heard the massive creature hiss after a moment. "Give me back my time. Teaching you this old world myself is a small thing, if it gets me my Stell faster. But you will honor your oath," the Umbra growled suddenly. "You will send me to her. You will help me make all of her mine. And then you will acknowledge me as the high lord of all the worlds you conquer. Not merely Avalon. Not merely its nearby Expanse."

"As you command, Lord Umbra," Rhodes replied calmly. "All of our flags will fly under your banner. All crowns shall be under your own. All Icons will be under your pantheon."

"Good, good," the warbled voice muttered. "Now go while I prepare your instruction. I will need to be... alone for this."

"By your command," Rhodes replied, and I could see him bowing in my mind. I waited for his footsteps to fade.

Then I realized I was being an idiot.

Why wasn't I going after Rhodes and his cronies instead?

If I took them out, and they stayed down, then Jeepers Creepers over there would be stranded. He couldn't chase after anyone. He would just have to wait here until Stell and Guineve came back. And this time they'd kick the crap out of him. Game over, final boss dead, best ending unlocked. I'd probably even be able to rescue my body on Earth.

But before I could head after them, I heard Cavus speak again.

"Now where did it go..."

My ears perked up to hear what the Umbra was after.

"Where did that rock that took my little Stell-piece go?"

Shit.

I had completely forgotten about the rock I had used to save Guineve. I had meant to break it as soon as I used it to whisk her away, but then that giant thing had turned on me, and then plans had changed to just not peeing on myself.

If he found that rock, Guineve could be in danger again.

I tried to think of what to do. Maybe I could find the rock first? I'd have to remember where it fell, but...

"Yessss," the creature hissed. "There you are."

Expletives danced entire ballrooms through my skull.

Swallowing my spit, I crept back toward the creature that had just torn me in half not more than thirty minutes ago.

"Little Stell-piece? It's just us now. Can you hear me?" the thing cackled. "You can. I know you can hear me right now. He used this old tool to keep you from me, but I have it now. I can bring you back to me."

I stepped into view, but the creature was ignoring me. It hunkered low, crouched on its long skinny legs. As before, whenever it swayed too much a new leg or tail grew out of the smog on its torso to touch the ground and re-balance it. The Umbra was clutching the talisman I had thrown earlier in one hand, while stroking it with the other, letting its many-jointed fingers crawl and writhe all over it.

"Yes, little piece of Stell, I found you. You were bad earlier. You hit me and called me names, but that's alright. I know you were tricked by that ugly dumb boy. That's why I want you to stay away from other boys, little Stell. They're dumb and ugly and when you tease them, they try and take you from me, because they think they're better than me. You're not supposed to tease anyone but Uncle Cavus, Little Stell. But it's alright now. Your Uncle Cavus killed the dumb ugly boy so that he can't trick you anymore. You're safe. I promise he'll never bother you again. I even took little pieces of him with me to prove it. Don't you want to come out and see, little Stell? Come see what I did to the dumb ugly boy, my little Stell. Just come out and see, then make that pretty wet-eyed face you make when I show you pieces of dumb ugly boys that tried to take you from me. Make that face for your Uncle Cavus, and all is forgiven."

I swore in my head. This thing had an appearance that would put any movie monster I've ever seen to shame, and the worst thing about it was still what it said.

And it was still after my friend.

I didn't have a second stone to save Guineve if that thing brought her back. I had to find a way to destroy it right now, and that meant I needed a way to break it before the monster could notice me.

But that was impossible.

My best weapons, my spear and short sword, would have been too slow and too weak. The Umbra would see me coming and knock me a couple miles away again. Then, when I had died again, it would take Guineve, and I didn't doubt for a minute that her fate would be worse than my repeated dismemberments.

All I had was...my...magic.

Use me, a quiet voice begged inside of me. *I rage.*

I knew this voice.

I'd always known this voice.

It was my lightning magic.

Use me, the quiet voice begged again. *I rage.*

It wasn't supposed to be able to talk. But then, I wasn't supposed to be able to die and come back. Who was I to judge?

Use me, it begged once more. *I rage.*

If the monster did not react to my forming the spell, then it would not have time to stop the bolt from destroying the rock. Yes, my magic should be nothing compared to Guineve's blasts of mist and white fire, but I just needed to destroy that rock. Then I'd have to die again. But Guineve would stay safe and get strong enough to fight again.

Use me. I rage.

Adjusting my stance so that I could see the Umbra and get a clear shot at the rock it was holding, I began to create the strongest, fastest bolt I could form.

No, not that. Use me. I rage.

I looked downward, and I could finally recognize that the voice was not my lightning magic. In fact, it couldn't be my lightning magic.

It was too old.

It wasn't my lightning magic that told me I could conquer the monster under my bed by checking to realize he wasn't real.

It wasn't my lightning magic that told me to stand up to that bully in Sunday School.

It wasn't my lightning magic that whispered not to give up when I found out I was disabled.

Who are you? my mind asked.

Because even though I had always listened, I had never answered it back.

You know me, it answered. *And I know you. Now use me. I rage.*

I shook my head. I was not understanding. But that was normal, I realized. I was talking to a voice in my head and I had been torn violently apart mere minutes earlier.

Show yourself, I finally said. *Show yourself that I may know I know you.*

Yes.

My right hand suddenly grew heavy. I looked down and saw the strange handle I had first seen way back before I discovered Avalon. The one I had somehow found in my old game that morning. The weight was comfortable in my hands.

You know me, and I know you, the voice inside the handle said to my mind. *And we do not have much time. Your worries are my worries, your foes are my foes, your loved ones are very much so my loved ones.*

Now use me. I rage.

I tightened my grip on the weaponless handle and raised it into the air. I let an unknown familiarity guide my next actions.

Let the lightning beget light and fire, something inside the handle said. *Then let the fire beget more light. Then let the light beget growth. Darkness becomes fuel for light, fear becomes fuel for courage, courage becomes fuel for triumph, triumph becomes fuel for more growth. Light your fires, smite your unrighteous fears, expand every joy in your defiant heart.*

It is time. Use me. I rage.

I had begun casting as it spoke. Its words were gibberish to my waking mind but perfect wisdom to every still and quiet corner of my head. My fists sparked with gray lightning that burned my knuckles and created silver fire. The flames burned and ate and somehow made me less heavy inside. My joy was back, and suddenly I knew I wasn't just a sad little orphan that had lost his future before dying horribly and far from home.

I was Wes Malcolm, Challenger and Protector of Earth and Avalon.

I was whole despite all my harms.

And I raged.

Lightning crackled between my blazing hands and I raised them over my head. A defiant cry tore out of my throat, and the Umbra finally whipped its head up to look at me. Its empty eyes suddenly blazed white at the sparks and flames dancing across my hands, and all the little lights started surging around inside its mouth, as if they were trying to boil their way to freedom.

Before it could do anything else, I threw my rage.

Gray lightning carrying silver fire whipped across the air, and instantly so, as lightning always did. The burning bolt cracked into the rock in the Umbra's hands, overloading its glyphs and shattering the stone into big, blazing chunks. The fire on the chunks burnt out rapidly, and I felt the rock's magic release harmlessly into the air.

But my own flames had ridden the lightning as it traveled over, and that fire had jumped onto the Umbra abomination. The monster's wormy claws disappeared behind a flash-fire, and the creature's new screams turned all previous noise to children's whispers. Its legs pumped it high into the air, but when it landed it fell on its back, rolling and holding its hands to itself.

"It burns!" I heard it scream. "It burns-it burns-it burns-*gurk*!"

One of the little lights had flown all the way to the front of its mouth, and looked like it was close to struggling free. But even as the creature screamed and gurgled, its worm-like tongue whipped out and wrapped around the little light.

"Stop!" my mouth roared. "Talking!"

"Let lightning beget-light-beget-fire-beget-more-light!" the quiet voice and I said together. *"I still rage!"*

I threw my next smoldering bolt at the Umbra's face.

Those are not his lights, the quiet voice urged. *Take them back!*

Smog rolled off the creature's maimed hands to protect it. My lightning struggled to make its way through the filthy cloud, but the fire riding my bolt just gouged its way through the black fog and burned all over the creature's mouth. Crackling noises came from all over the pitch-colored skin, and the tongue wrapped around the little light turned into ash.

I saw the tiny red mote leap free from the monster's mouth. A micron-sized cry of joy tumbled into my ears.

"Free! I'm free!" the tiny voice shouted into the atoms all around it. *"Stell! Stell! Wait for me! I'm coming!"*

"No!" the Umbra said in a muffled wail. "My tongue! My light! My little food-slave!"

"I told you to stop talking!" I shouted. "And leave my friend alone! Just... just leave her alone!"

The handle had remained in my hand the whole time, and when I focused it began to form a blade, until it resembled the short sword I had taken off of the Horde wretch during my first Challenge. My hands smoldered and sparked again, and though I couldn't fire another blast at the monster yet, I saw both forms of heat travel up my blade.

At my second or third shout, the monster rolled its way back to its feet. Its maimed head turned in my direction.

"You," it garbled, and for the first time the light in its eyes changed from white to bright red. Smog reformed over its body, and I saw more clawed hands dance inside of it.

But it wasn't scaring me right now.

"Yes!" I shouted back. "Me! Back for a rematch!" I tightened my grip on my weapon and brandished it. "I bring great tidings and several hundred amps' worth of ass-kicking! Come over and partake, you bastard child of cheap horror movies and cheaper children's programs!"

Something inside me felt spent and I couldn't create another gray bolt yet. Why, I didn't know. So I just braced for the thing to charge me again. But to my latest surprise, it fell backwards and scuttled away from me.

"You!" it shrieked, and for the first time, it sounded truly frightened. "You! You're you!"

"Already noted!" I growled, stepping forward. "Be more current!"

"I killed you!" it screamed madly. "I already killed you!"

"I was there for that too!" I growled. "Try the most recent episode of this season!"

"But they buried you!" the creature screamed. "They already buried you! They said you were already cold and dead and full of worms! They promised me long ago!"

Wait, what?

"Who promised?" I growled. "Who buried me?"

"Rhodes!" the Umbra screamed. "Liar Rhodes! Get over here!"

"We have not left, Master Cavus," a voice said some distance behind me. I saw Warren Rhodes step out of the mist with his two warlocks in tow. "And we kept that promise. Your old foe is dead."

"Liar Rhodes! Liar Rhodes!" The massive Umbra was backing away from me, the smog still covering it. "He lives! He comes back from the dead! He has the light that burns me! He even looks like him!"

Looks like him...

My head spun.

Save for my youth and my lighter muscle mass, I was the spitting image of my father. Everyone had told me that growing up, at least until his death. Then everyone wouldn't say it, but would give me suspicious looks.

"Rhodes," I growled, turning from facing the monster from beyond, to the monster from my home. "Why does he think he's killed me?"

"Shut up, Wes," Warren hissed, and for the first time I felt the tension in his words. Then he cleared his throat and re-addressed the cowering monster before us. "Honored ambassador, the Earth-bound body of the foe you slew in honorable combat was also slain and buried on Earth nearly three years ago. I confirmed his body was lowered into the grave. Also, this individual cannot be him, because aside from the hair and a few other features, his body is different."

"He burns with the old light!" the monster screeched. "He comes back from the dead! He denies me of my prey! He even took one of my little food-slaves! No deal! No deal!"

A drop of sweat fell from Rhodes' temple. "Honored Ambassador, you took an oath before Malus, just as we did."

"And you broke it! Kill the Malcolm or no deal! Kill him for good!"

The Umbra scuttled away from me, legs and tails rapidly forming to help it keep distant from me.

At that moment, I had no idea who to try and attack, but my mind latched onto the one name the monster had said.

"Malcolm?" I roared. This was the final piece of confirmation I needed. "Rhodes?" I turned on him. My fists and weapons suddenly flared with their two forms of heat and light. I saw the three humans in front of me rear back. "Did you kill and frame my dad, Rhodes? Did you help that thing kill my father? *Did you murder my Dad?*"

"Dalfrey!" Warren hissed. "The code! Now!"

"But if it works at all, it will fry him completely!" the blonde witch hissed back. "I thought we needed him!"

"We need our lives even more!" Rhodes hissed. "Use the main code now! Barnes, reinforce it!"

"Oh honored Aegrim," the preacher-turned cultist intoned. "Hear our supplication..."

"Kill switch!" Dalfrey screamed as I stomped forward. "Kill switch execute!"

I heard something pop inside, and it suddenly became very hard to think. The magic in my hands started to sputter out.

Warning, my mind-screen said. *Primary body taking damage from internal source.*

But I had far too much practice with putting one foot painfully in front of the other over the past few years. I kept stomping forward, slowly but surely.

"It's not working!" Dalfrey screamed again. "Kill switch execute! Kill switch execute! Kill switch execute, for Christ's sake!"

"Mighty Aegrim, tame your blood, mighty Aegrim, tame your blood," I heard Barnes chant, over and over.

My pain was increasing and my vision was getting blurrier. But I didn't need twenty/twenty vision to keep walking forward, and I could still see enough of the three blurry shapes in front of me to target them. I struggled to re-ignite my burning lightning, and felt the flare on my hands sputtering back on.

"Send a message!" Rhodes said to someone I couldn't see. "Beat him until I say to stop!"

"Kill switch execute!" Dalfrey kept screaming. "Kill switch execute!"

"Mighty Aegrim, tame your blood," the false preacher still intoned. "Mighty Aegrim, tame your blood..."

The painful buzzing in my head increased. I stubbornly took another step forward, tried to reach for my magic again, and then I felt something *whumph* into my stomach.

Warning, my mind-screen said. *Primary body is taking damage from external sources.*

Another sharp pain cracked into my right knee, followed by a boot-like impact against my back. I staggered down to my unhurt knee, then caught myself with my free hand when that gave out as well.

I growled and crawled forward.

"Kill switch execute! Kill switch execute!"

"Honored Aegrim, tame your blood..."

"Bloody hell, Malcolm," Rhodes swore. "Do you have to make everything so expensive?" He snarled and took a step near me, raising a hand that suddenly blazed with purple-black and blood-red flames.

"I call upon Malus himself to power my hands. I speak hate over his foes. I accept the cost to wield his blessing directly." And he hurled the sputtering fireball into my face.

Then it grew cold and dark once more.

I was numb, blind, deaf, and dead. But I still somehow heard it.

Hold fast.

I know you.

I know what is coming and I grieve.

But when you are ready...

Trust your rage.

29

LAST HANDHOLD

Internal scan complete. Sufficient data collected from experiment. Please read final log.

Conclusion Report Concerning Subject Anonymous.

As stated in the subject line, we have completed all possible tests regarding Subject Anonymous. We are pleased to announce total success concerning our goals. Had we chosen to present our findings to the rest of the organization, we would have no doubt achieved legendary fame and prestige before our inevitably ordered executions.

First Item: Subject Anonymous' direct study. As noted before we were able to examine the subject's bizarre ability to enter Planet Avalon on his own power, and with the help of Rhodes' <REDACTED> contact, we were able to deduce the remaining factors and form a network of our own. Unlike the subject's abilities, our own network is formed by establishing systems at key locations. This is still marked as a future field of study for other projects, but as our current project's goals have been accomplished, we are marking this entry as successful.

Second Item: Assimilation into Avalon's systems: Though an abject failure at first glance, our goals concerning this matter have been completed via indirect means. Avalon has categorically rejected all attempts to assimilate with its systems, and we have been unable to shake its designation as 'foreign contaminants.' The entity bases this designation on the supposed nature of our 'Deeds' (capitalized by the entity, not us). The entity initially demanded the release of Subject Anonymous *but has now completely rejected all attempts of communication. We further believe it to be indirectly resisting our operatives whenever we enter its planet, but if so, this resistance has failed to make any meaningful impact on our goals. This still would have resulted in a failure concerning the second phase of our operations, had we not gained alternatives from Rhodes' <REDACTED> contact.*

The first tool gave us the ability to 'link' to a system that provided information in almost exactly the same way Avalon did for Subject Anonymous. The only difference noted is the fact that operatives all report hearing a level of incoherent and uncomfortable whispering from an unknown source. As of yet, no other side effect has been reported, nor has the current side effect caused any visible harm.

Aside from the network of information, we have examined Subject Anonymous' "Challenger" status. We have confirmed that the subject has become augmented by overcoming what the different worlds' inhabitants all refer to as "Challenges." We have determined that the so-called Challenges are tasks that the natives deem both difficult to accomplish, and provide some tangible benefit to the natives themselves. Our staff has been unable to duplicate Subject Anonymous' success, but we are concluding further attempts to be unnecessary based on two arguments. The first argument is that the tools provided by Rhodes' <REDACTED> contact can easily augment our subjects at a much faster rate, and with much less difficulty. Estimates assess that most of our staff will obtain twice the amount of power that Subject Anonymous gained in half as much time. Furthermore, all signs of aging seemed to have halted in staff members that have augmented.

The second argument is that, even bringing into account the random <REDACTED> changes that our staff undergo as they augment, the process is still much safer than Subject Anonymous' so-called 'Risings.' The very nature of overcoming Challenges puts us to be dependent upon the natives themselves, effectively allowing both their problems and their gratitude to dictate all of our gains. Even the so-called personal Challenges Subject Anonymous overcame were proven to have changed his personality to be even less ambitious, even less ruthless, even more likely to regard the needs of others as more relevant than his own. This dependency has also been noted in those natives that chose to Rise themselves, though not to the same pathetic degree as Subject Anonymous. Therefore, this study recommends that Rising be avoided altogether, even if the means for our staff to do so is later discovered. It should not need to be said, but serving the natives contradicts our long-term goals of dominion, and this study does not need to prove that power *gained through force is always greater than power gained through service to lesser beings.*

Our current means of gaining power, ensuring that the natives do not overcome the Challenges, Trials, and Tumults of their worlds, has not only proven to be a rapid and reliable source of power, but also has the added benefit of restricting the growth of the natives themselves, thereby creating a dependency on their end. This solution is ideal, as it leads to a far more rapid realization of all of our long-term plans. In fact, this process has resulted in correcting our initial estimate of completing all plans by a factor of ten. We expect total resistance to crumble within one or two Earth generations, long before the deadline Rhodes' <REDACTED> contact has given us. Be advised that the shorter deadline regarding the Starsown is still in effect.

Third Item: Concerning the Challenger's ability to resurrect. Our team is pleased to announce a full realization of this power, with practically no complications whatsoever. As long as we have an available portal to either Avalon or another world, projected or original bodies can resurrect. The only difference from the Challenger's resurrecting nature is that the body resurrects on Earth, not Planet Avalon. The resurrected person can still create a projected body and send it back through the portal. Alternatively, our staff can keep our original bodies in Avalon and occasionally send a projected body to Earth.

This option has been the preferred choice of all senior management. Given the footholds we are quickly establishing, this choice also seems to be safer for our leadership, especially since the existence of the projected body can allow the original body to resurrect if deceased. Note that tests concerning the limits of our resurrected powers are not yet exhaustive. Operatives have reported the experience to be extremely traumatic, but providing said operatives can deal with the trauma, there is no apparent limit. However, it is likely most operatives will only recover from the trauma two or three times. In fact, it is suspected that most can only handle one additional death before the trauma caused would render them useless.

It should be further noted, however, that individuals can be forced to resurrect their projected bodies by simply maneuvering them to the nearest gate. This is not advisable for all operatives, as traumatized staff are unlikely to survive long in Avalon's worlds, but in the case of our trafficking resources, this item is a major windfall, and will allow us to keep our Earth-based revenue and influence for centuries to come.

We have further tested the power's limits by forcing Subject Anonymous to repeatedly resurrect. The first fact of interest is that Subject Anonymous cannot control the resurrection process. Unlike our own operatives, if SA's projected body is terminated the primary body does not become aware, effectively preventing SA from having a choice in the process. This is why we were able to test the process so thoroughly, as, given SA's meek temperament and youth, it is unlikely he would have chosen to resurrect a single time after the first death.

Furthermore, SA always resurrects at the same location, give or take a few meters. This, combining with directed blows to SA's original body, has enabled us to finally have effective parameters for restraint. This is especially fortunate due to the fact that Primary Containment proved even less effective in SA's projected body than it did in his original body.

Once new restraint parameters were established, tests were begun on SA to see if certain methods of termination yielded any useful data. The staff did their best to exhaust all possible methods, allowing us to determine that the cause of death had no bearing whatsoever on the subject's ability to resurrect. SA came back from decapitation just as fast as from being slowly bludgeoned to death, and he came back from bleeding to death just as fast as from termination by incineration or drowning. Further tests made to determine if destroying a certain part of the subject's body affected the resurrection process proved ineffective. No matter which body part was shot, dissolved or otherwise removed first, the subject resurrected in the same amount of time and in the same state.

The only difference noted was that different types of death left different types of trauma on the subject. Ironically, the traditional means of termination produced the least amount of trauma. The subject handled stabbing or slashing injuries with far less trauma than expected, probably due to the fact that said methods were done in the early stages of the termination process. The subject used some method of self-denial to avoid processing the trauma of dismemberment deaths, but both drowning and slow-burning incineration proved to be significantly traumatic for SA. Starvation and dehydration proved even more traumatic, but as these methods took the most time, they had the least number of attempts. The subject had the most severe reaction to termination when he was delivered to and consumed by the local 'monsters,' specifically the creatures referred to as gibber-kin.

But ironically, attempting to perform research on captured natives in SA's presence yielded the most shocking research. In every instance of SA observing harm on the native test subjects, he always chose to terminate himself. The choice was not immediate, as SA would usually (and in the beginning, successfully) attempt to free himself from restraints and assist the natives, harming the staff on one or two occasions. Damage was deemed minimal and the tests were able to resume in less than a month's time on every occasion. Whenever SA deemed himself unable to assist the natives, the result was always immediate self-termination, using whatever unrestrained part of his body possible to administer lethal blunt trauma to himself. SA would even go as far as to asphyxiate himself by severing his tongue while attempting to communicate threatening messages to the staff using his eyes. Such actions reflect a serious dependency on pleasing others and serve as one more example to demonstrate why Challenger-related power is ultimately self-destructive.

The greatest find was that the subject's ability to resurrect is exhaustible. The nature of the death had no bearing, but after a certain threshold of terminations was reached, the subject began to resurrect more slowly, and in an increasingly damaged state, no matter which method of termination was used. After approximately one hundred terminations, the subject was unable to create a projected body at all, even after waiting a significant period of time.

To remove eventual evidence, SA's original body was moved through our portal network into Avalon. For reasons unknown, SA found the use of our portals to be more traumatic than any of his earlier terminations, eventually placing the subject into a coma for a period of time that lasted longer than his final resurrection. It is believed his original body will be unable to return to Earth; however, as SA's original body is now due for final termination, that information is now irrelevant.

SA has awoken from his coma and is currently displaying a low level of awareness for his surroundings. He appears to have resumed his earlier disabilities to their full extent, suggesting Primary Containment's protocol has finally achieved success. As staff has gained all relevant data from the subject, we recommend a final termination for the subject's original body.

This report concludes both our study and our obligations to said project. All staff are now switching to other roles in their new respective worlds.

He's all yours, Rhodes. Just be sure and clean up afterwards.

End of Final Log.

* * *

Chris's Perspective

"Come on, Chris," my father said to me as we walked back through the portal.

"What?" I asked my father. "You want me to take my original body this time?"

"Yes, Chris. I assume my son would feel safe enough to take his original body into our original headquarters, like everyone else in the company is doing."

I bit down my father's latest insult. After eighteen years, I had finally figured out that this was his way of controlling me, of pushing me to develop while always feeling inferior to him, so that I would also feel dependent on him. But telling him I had figured it out wouldn't do me any favors, so I just shrugged and tried to figure out why he wanted the most vulnerable part of me in their newly discovered little wonderland.

"Just wondering," I said. "Every other time, you've only let me project over there. Was just curious to see if I was going to take over a new role," I lied.

I had no interest in their magical fairyland. Daily bullshit notwithstanding, I had been perfectly happy with my life on Earth. Getting assigned to Avalon or Camelot or whatever the hell that place was would have been the second-worst scenario I could think of.

"Did anyone say that you had a new job?" Rhodes Sr. growled.

"No, Father," I said formally. "Just exercising my brain."

"Apparently not hard enough," my dad growled. "Now shut up and do what I say."

"Got it," I replied neutrally.

There was a thin line here, and even after eighteen years, I was still learning how to walk it. On the one hand, my father didn't want a weak son, so I couldn't be as submissive to him as the rest of the staff. His six-and-a-half foot tall combat staff could grovel at him, and that was fine. But I had to show I had a spine. But not too much of one, because if I disrespected him, in public or otherwise, he would take it as an attack on his position, and he'd be forced to retaliate.

The hardest and most important rule about being the firstborn son was this: never make Dad look weak.

But apparently I had pulled it off this time, because Dad just snorted and we made our way to the glowing, spinning, purple disk-thing located deep underground in Dad's special building that most people thought was just a power plant. I kept my eyes forward and paid no attention to either the nearby computer terminals or the people chanting nearby in black robes.

Sights like this were just part of growing up for me, and the minute I started having a problem with them was the minute Dad found another way to make my life worse.

The portal, however, was going to be a bigger problem. But I couldn't afford to let Dad see it, so I just squared my shoulders and stepped through the swirling purple energy at the same time he did.

Everything disappeared for a moment, and then a bunch of half-formed images I'll never be able to describe appeared. They only lasted for a split-second each, not even long enough to leave a memory. But the words they spoke were easy enough to hear and let linger.

"Traitor-prince!" mouth-less voices chanted. *"Traitor-prince! Give us back the traitor-prince!"*

This was a new development, I had heard someone tell my father. These voices started back when we dragged Wes' body through the portal. Maybe that was the reason for his coma.

"Traitor-prince! Traitor-prince! Maim his flesh and damn his soul and give us back the traitor-prince!"

This was another reason I hated Wes Malcolm. Because no matter how bad your day was, he was always, always having a worse one, and the cock-blocking prick made everyone else look bad by almost never complaining about it.

But I got the feeling that wouldn't matter after today. In fact, if either of the two scenarios I was thinking of happened, both my problems and Wes' would be largely over very soon.

The portal and creepy voices ended the very next moment. Concrete bunker-type walls were replaced with underground dirt and stone, like some kind of medieval mining tunnel. Light still came from the oily black torches and the purple glowing stones Dad's freaky alien friend had somehow taught us how to build. I had to suppress a shudder whenever I thought of that thing. I was not looking forward to dealing with it ever again, but as soon as my father noticed that fact he was going to make me deal with it every chance he could. We walked down the halls and saw Dr. Dalfrey leaning against the stone wall. She was still wearing her chic business suit, because down here, modern clothing was a cheaper form of keeping uniforms and made it easy to tell who worked here from who was a native trying to spy on us or escape.

"Morning, Rhodes," she said with a smile. She seemed very happy today.

"Morning," we both replied at the same time, which earned me another scowl from my dad. Her eyes twinkled at our reaction.

"Why aren't you boys happier?" she asked with another smile.

Dad didn't answer her. I just shrugged.

"It's been a long day, and it's still not over yet. Why are you so happy?" I replied. I didn't add that I was wondering why I was here in my original body instead of my projected one. Seeing my father work over the years had given me a healthy respect for what other people called paranoia.

She seemed even more pleased that I had chosen to answer her.

"Can I tell him, Warren?"

My father gave an indifferent nod, not even reacting to her use of his first name. She almost pranced with happiness.

"Well I'm happy for the same reason you should be. The last and worst piece of my old job goes away for good after today."

"Is that what I think it is?" I asked carefully.

"Only if you're smart enough to think that the worst part of my old job was listening to a sad little virgin brood and mope about his problems for the last two years."

For a half-second I almost pointed out that Wes never really moped, no matter what we threw at him. Then I hated myself because I had inadvertently taken his side again.

God damn it.

"Ah," I said instead. "We're done with him then."

"Yes," she replied with a smirk. "Finally."

"Are we really the only ones watching?" I asked. "Didn't Barnes want to tear into him for out-Bibling him that one time?"

"We're getting rid of him tomorrow," Dad grunted. "Consider this his farewell party. And we're not the only ones. Just the first in line."

"Really?" I asked. Then I kept my mind as blank as I could.

Because this just might be the most perfect opportunity I could get.

"The three of us all have the biggest grudge with him," my father growled. "We're first. And anything goes, as long as he doesn't die."

"You're serious?" I repeated.

"It's not like he needs to be in top shape for his last day tomorrow. This is mostly just a morale exercise for the company."

Company. He still called our freaky, magic-using, world-ending organization a company. As if the people being cursed by our magic or eaten by our monsters could buy our publicly traded stocks. That was cute.

But that wasn't the important point.

"I want to go last," I said firmly.

My father slowed in his steps and looked at me.

"Last?"

"Yeah, last," I risked affirming.

"You want to be last in line, in the opportunity to hurt your most hated enemy?" His gaze was considering me. I reminded myself that I was used to it and didn't flinch.

"Exactly. I want to show that even after everything has been taken away, even after he finally lost everything he thought possible, that I can still hurt him. I want permission to finally hurt him as much I want, without restraint. Without worrying about letting him escape because we still need him for something. So that by the time he dies, he knows for a fact that he's finally been broken."

"He's already broken," Dad replied. I shook my head.

"I finally figured out there's one more thing that can be done to him. And I'm not telling, because I want to be the one who does it."

My father looked at me carefully for a moment.

"You're finally learning," he said, nodding after a minute. "Good."

My father's approval washed over me the way a half-inch of rain washes over a long-dead landscape.

Too little, and far too late.

"We're here," Dalfrey said as we came by a reinforced door. "This is his new cell."

She opened it, and we stepped inside.

Wide space and a high ceiling greeted us. Apparently my father had intended to use this room as a kind of conference space, or for 'company'-wide events. Or possibly for training troops or doing mass rituals. It was hard to tell at this point.

But today, we were apparently using it to beat the hell out of Wes Malcolm one last time.

A morale exercise, my father called it.

In the direct center of the room was what was left of my high-school nemesis, wearing some uncomfortable sackcloth rags we made him wear, because fuck him. Wes' red hair had grown long and ragged, and it draped all over his face, sometimes plastered against it and blending with the bloody wounds all over him. He seemed almost motionless until we got closer. Then I could see his limbs twitch, making the familiar spasms his condition had made back when it was at its worst.

I suppressed a frown when I thought of the day we did that to him. I even remembered calling the play that was designed for nothing but making him a broken wreck. We gave up a touchdown on that play and had lost our most dependable tight end for good. But I was just following orders, I told myself at the time. Not that it would have mattered. With the new laws, I would have been found to be an accessory in juvenile court at the very least. I remember the time I'd told my father that, and how hard he had laughed at me.

That was the only way I knew how to make Dad laugh these days. Mutter words like "jail," "court," "indictment," or "consequences." I'd get a humored snort at the very least, every time, guaranteed.

"Well, look at that, Chris," Dad said, and judging by his tone, he was in the best mood he'd been in all month. "You finally get to see the result of your handiwork."

"Yeah, finally," I admitted. Because the truth was, I didn't owe Wes any favors. Had the little shit made one, just *one*, decision differently, it would never have come to this. Dad's ego would have been appeased, and I could have had another purpose in high school other than "spy on, control, and destroy Wes Malcolm." But the prick had refused to take the hint and play ball, so that was how I had spent the last four years.

"Alright, normally I'd go first, but the idiots I'm meeting with are running late. Since Chris wants to go last, we have time for you to go first, Dalfrey."

"Really?" The blonde woman's eyes twinkled.

"Just be done in ten minutes," my father answered with another grunt.

"I won't need anywhere near that long," she answered brightly. Her heels clopped as she walked toward the limp figure lying in the middle of the room.

I looked at him again, watching carefully. After being his nemesis for this many years, there were signs I had learned to look for. Subtle cues that told me I wasn't getting to him today, but he wanted me to think I was, so that I could just fuck off for once and we could both get back to having our own lives for a bit. I made a point to never share these signs with anyone, because that would just make my job harder, and give me less time for things I actually enjoyed.

I found those signs again.

His whole body was having spasms, but they always happened on the same count. But you had to count a long time to notice, and I think only I did that. His breathing tore out of his mouth in ragged gasps, but if I counted to thirty I would always hear the exact same gasp tear out of his mouth. Then he'd go through the same pattern of tormented breathing, of carefully rehearsed spasms.

Son of a bitch, I swore in my skull. But secretly I was relieved. *See?* I wanted to say. *He doesn't ever crack! It's not just me! You all couldn't do it to him either!*

I would have been vindicated. But it would have ruined my plans.

"Careful, Doc," I called out. "Remember how strong he had gotten last time. He could still be dangerous."

The blonde doctor just chuckled at me and tossed her hair.

"That's cute of you to worry, Chris. Rhodes, you should have told your boy about his best friend. Our little Wes is back to normal now." She made long, arrogant strides around the rasping form on the ground. "No magic powers. No freakish strength. No special trick that lets him resist and recover from wounds. Just back to being a sad little boy," she snickered, stepping closer to his head. "A sad boy with a broken brain, once again. How does it feel, Wes?" she taunted. "To take a dozen steps forward, and then a thousand steps back?" She walked even closer. Very carefully, her foot kicked the long, unkempt hair out of his eyes. "But then again, you're probably relieved. You were never good at being strong. I could tell that, just after three meetings." She bent her leg, so that her skirt would slide up, mocking him with a better view of her limb. "You were never more than a sad little boy in a grown man's body, afraid of his own masculinity. I dared you every session to try and take what a real man would have wanted, but you were always too shy. The sad thing was, if you had been a lot smaller or younger, it would have been attractive on you." She stepped away. She didn't notice that he hadn't looked away from her leg because he hadn't needed to. As soon as she stepped in front of him, he had just looked right through her, as if she was a sack of something dead and offensive. That was Wes' stare when he wanted you to think you were getting to him, the fake, glazed stare, that was actually focusing on something else. Something that wasn't in the room, but he had still set his eyes on it, some goal he was still after for that particular day.

"It's a pity your parents never taught you about girls," she continued obliviously. "Women like two things, Wes: a cute boy that's pitiful, harmless, and non-threatening, or a big strong man that's useful and brave enough to get what he wants. You were the wrong mix of both of those things. So you died," she added simply, then she turned on her hip and swayed away from his face.

"If it makes you feel any better, Wes," she added, turning her head to look at him as she walked away from him. "I've been writing down that you actually were brave enough to try for me, every session, but I always resisted you. On our final session, I actually got scared enough to call for help, and you escaped, stumbling out of the door, to our total shock. This way, you get to die looking stronger than you actually were. Just like your dad did," she couldn't help adding, and I sneered inside. Her last comment was like a player taking a cheap shot that didn't help the game. Wes had been hearing lines about his dad the whole time he'd been tortured and killed down here. Even I knew that. If there was one thing he had almost three years to get hardened against, it was the shit he had taken from people about his father.

Especially now, when he'd probably figured out what really happened with his dad.

"I'm done!" she said brightly, looking like a cat that had gotten the last of the cream.

She kept swaying as she walked past me, flashing me a wink before she walked out of the door. I watched her go and shook my head in disgust.

"Don't even think about it," Dad growled. He must have misread my gesture. "She would tear you apart before you ever got into her bed."

"No kidding," I said with a snort. "You didn't think I was..."

"I think you need to remember what I've taught you about sex," he interrupted. "Say it for me."

I sighed.

"Everything is about sex," I began the quote he had stolen from someone else. "Except sex. Sex is about power. Which means everything is really about power."

"And if your time with a woman doesn't get you more power, especially over her," my father continued. "What you had wasn't sex. Just assisted masturbation. You were half-assed with your first girlfriend, and let this little shit," my father pointed over to our special friend, "stop you, even though you had back-up and no one else there would have said anything. Then you were half-assed again with his little blonde friend, and let her stop you by herself, even let her leave the party when she was supposed to need you to get home. You let the family down on both occasions, Chris. And Dalfrey would use it to have you wrapped around her fingers. And then she'd try to use you against me, which would mean I'd have to act against both of you. For good."

I turned to look at him incredulously. Explicit death threats from Dad were rare.

"Yes, for good, Chris," my father said levelly. "Now that things are changing, I want to make one thing entirely clear to you, son. You are no longer needed to continue on my legacy. Disobedient children are useless to the immortal. So be useful to me, Chris. Don't make me waste eighteen years of investment. Because that's all I'd waste. Stay away from Dalfrey. That's an order."

"Yes, sir," I said calmly, doing my best to submit without appearing too weak. Because it was Dad's bluntness that had been surprising, not his attitude.

I had always known I was expendable.

In fact, deep down, I was grateful.

Every comment that made me look like the lesser of two evils to Wes right now helped my goals.

The only goals I could have now.

"Now, speaking of this little shit," my father growled, as he stepped forward. "Before he dies, I want to know one thing." He walked right next to Wes. "How does it feel," he asked softly. "To have all your magical fairy-tale worlds taken from you, someone they were supposedly made for, and see them put to better use by real men. By people who actually don't want to save somebody else's world, and then go back home with nothing gained. By people who don't want to apologize all the time for being strong, who won't help others for free, who aren't satisfied with the two-bit gratitude the maidens around here normally offer to the virgin boys that save them. How does it feel?" my father asked, sending a kick into Wes' side. As if Wes wasn't completely immune to being kicked at this point. "How does it feel to know that even your freaky half-cougar, half-loli, nerd girlfriend is spoken for at this point, that the monster you failed to kill gets to keep her after all? Tell me, cripple-head! Tell me what happened when you gave up guaranteed survival just to try and be like your dad!" Flecks of spittle flew out of my father's mouth as he kicked my classmate again.

I had been ignoring my father's instinctive display of dominance, watching my enemy's eyes instead. At the mention of his 'girlfriend,' they flashed briefly, almost too briefly to notice. His next gasp had a growl hidden in it.

My dad was closer. He should have noticed. But he was too busy celebrating his victory over his real enemy.

"Are you watching, John Malcolm?" my father roared, sending another heavy kick into Wes. "Are you watching down there in Hell? You staked everything on your little retard, your cripple-headed manling, and he still failed! Just!" *Kick.* "Like!" *Kick.* "You!"

A final kick slammed into Wes' ribs, hard enough to actually lift him into the air. Then he took a deep breath, and calmed himself down. "Alright, that's done," he said, straightening his business suit. "I feel pretty good. This was an even better idea than I thought. Wes," Dad said as he turned. "When you get to hell, do me a favor, and ask your dad if he was watching me. Repeat my questions for him if he wasn't."

Without a word to me, my father turned and walked out the door. He didn't need to say anything. I knew he'd be expecting me in the portal room when I was done. That was good news. It meant I had even more time to myself. Maybe after I finished with Wes, I could work on that new alloy I was designing. Just to calm myself down, since it was basically finished. How finished was a question that would be answered when I finally showed another person what it could do.

I watched some dozen or so people come by to taunt Wes with their goodbyes. Barnes. The medical team in charge of the device in his head, and a few more locals that had made the cut, ones that Wes had grown up with his whole life.

I sighed.

This was the reason I hated watching conspiracy movies now. They sounded too much like work.

I waited until the last idiot left, then I closed the door, locked it, and counted to two hundred. I heard no more footsteps. Then I walked close to Wes and knelt down next to his head. I kept a sneer on my face as I whispered. And don't give me that look. Of course I whispered to him. I'm not an idiot. I was taking a risk talking to him at all. I had to, though. I could read the signs, see just how immortality was changing Dad's long-term plans. Especially those regarding me. I had to bank on the fact that everyone would stay stupid just a little longer, because as soon as Dad felt fully comfortable here, I was going to be disposed of as well.

"Alright, cock-blocker," I said quietly. "I should be the last one for today. Unless someone lied. Then we're both screwed."

No response except for the disguised, steady breathing.

"I'm not going to convince you this isn't a trick. I'm gonna figure honesty stopped working after the first dozen murders. So here's what I'm going to do. I'm going to call them favors, and if you disagree, that's okay. Most of what I want is already in your best interest and won't change any of your plans. So here's what I'm going to do. I'm going to start by saying I am your last visit for today. Tomorrow morning is when they're coming to incinerate you." I had caught that little bit of information from Wes' fifth guest. "I don't know if they're going to burn you alive or terminate you in here first. Probably the second one, given how you thrashed around the last time they burned you to death. There will be only one executioner. The rest of the people here, about a dozen people total, will be spending time with the other native prisoners. And managing the 'indentureds.'"

I caught a flash of curiosity from one of his eyes.

"I'll get to them in a second," I replied. "In fact, I'm going to save them for last, because if I don't, you might kill me first. And yes," I added. "I am the only one here who figured out you're still faking. Everyone else has bought the act, and figured they've beaten you. I don't know how you're still able to fake being broken, instead of actually breaking. If I had known that, things would have been different all these years." I took a breath. "And I don't know how much you're holding back. But I hate you, Wes," I couldn't help spitting. Not on him, I wasn't stupid. "I hate how much Dad obsessed over your father, and wanted me to break you, his son, so badly that was my main job all these years. I hate how you both made me do it until I was sick and tired of it, but still wasn't allowed to stop. And because I hate you, I know you better than all of the other idiots, including my dad. Dad hated your dad, so he just hated you by proxy. Dalfrey hated her job, hated how boring you were, and how you made her move down here from New York, but that was it. You've taken years away from me, Wes. Years that I could have spent doing what I really wanted, figuring out all the things I wanted. Seeing how far I could really go in science. Focusing on taking the football team to the next level. Figuring out a modeling career. Getting far enough away from Dad to where I could find a consenting girl to explore something with. But all of that came second to breaking you. And if you had just backed down *once*, not gotten in my way one single time, Dad would have counted it as my win, and we both could have moved on. He wouldn't have made me escalate and escalate and..." I took a breath. Wes hadn't interrupted me. He had just laid there, staring at me, maintaining his pattern of heavy breathing and fake gasps.

Just exactly what he needed to do to make me look like a little bitch.

"But forget that," I hissed, trying to whisper again. "My point is, I hate you for you, so I know you. You're not going to back down a single time. Not just because we took your dad and your future and whatever else we could think of away. You're not going to give up even one time, no matter how much easier it makes everybody else's life. Including your own. Why, I don't know. There's something wrong with you. That's why even here, even after all of those deaths and torture, every time they tried to hurt someone else in front of you, you got up and resisted. Even though it didn't make a difference. Even though all you did was get yourself killed faster every single time. I don't know what you were trying to accomplish, if a quicker death wasn't it. And if everyone wasn't so excited about the fact that they can come here and be strong and fast and throw fireballs or whatever, they probably would have noticed too. Or maybe not. Maybe Dad just hired a bunch of idiots again—fuck, I'm rambling again. Anyway, Wes, back to the subject. Fuck you, and here's my help."

I took another breath.

"I told you who's coming next. You've got six, maybe twelve, hours to prepare any way you can. And remember: whoever is coming is going to kill you for good. They've done their version of at least one Rise, and no, we don't really have a better name for it yet. I think they're gonna go with 'Descent'. Even though it sounds stupid. Anyway, Wes, they can kill you for good, and if you can, you should try and kill them. Even though you didn't kill anyone in the fight earlier, and even with my dad you still made a half-assed attempt. But unlike you, Wes, they won't stay dead. They'll just go back to Earth. They'll be gone for as short as a day and as long as a month. Unless you take down our portal network. You'll find that if you head left from this door and turn right at the fifth hallway. I have no idea how to destroy it, but using it almost killed you and probably will the next time. Whoever you pissed off is hiding, Wes. I don't know what you did, but every monster we work with here has this massive hate-boner for you. Go figure. But anyway, we can only come back through the portal, so if you destroy our gate, that will set us back until we can build another one. And building those things cost a lot of money, and even more time.

"About what you're fighting," I continued. He was tracking me. I could tell because his breathing was quieter and because his eyes were watching me now and not just staring straight ahead. He still hadn't said anything yet. "Dad's one of the key people in charge of the organization dedicated to some kind of dragon or demon-thing. I'm still not clear about it, because I haven't impressed anyone enough to be initiated into their special mysteries. That was why Dad and the others could use magic on you. It's about the only magic on Earth and even that was barely stronger than the magic we saw you using on Avalon. Anyway, this organization is just the sort of thing they'd use in those crappy movies. Actually, I think they've been hiding behind those crappy movies so that no one would believe they actually existed. They're not completely all-powerful, but they have contacts just about everywhere, and they can call on anyone ranging from the Mafia to the Illuminati to most of Congress. They're the scariest thing you can make an enemy of, and that's exactly what your family has been doing for generations. I don't fully understand it. But a long, long time ago, your family was given something by the thing that powers all of our magic, and it gets passed down to every firstborn male. I don't know why it's only males, or why it's only the firstborn. But your family did something to make everyone mad, and as far as our monster is concerned, you've never really lived up to your potential. Maybe that's why they call you traitor-prince.

"And because what you received is so important, one of the higher-ups in our organization has to keep an eye on you at all times. And even though they hate you, no one's allowed to take your life, especially not before the next firstborn male is born. This is all true even though they don't even want your power to activate, because it would upend everyone's influence and plans. That's how special your gift or whatever is, at least according to their secret devil-dragon-thing.

"Dad was chosen to be the higher-up to watch your family, and he's hated it ever since. But apparently, your dad discovered Avalon. I think he was a Challenger and just never told anyone. I don't know how my own dad found out. Maybe that creepy giant thing that's after your friend told him. And I don't know how they met or where, but that thing was the reason Dad has been so confident we'd find Avalon if we studied you long enough. And that thing hasn't found your friend yet, by the way."

I wasn't sure, but I think I saw the first flash of gratitude fly through Wes' eyes. "It's stopped helping us, both to look for her and to look for whatever you knocked out of it that last fight."

I shook my head at that. Nobody knew it, but I had seen the reports. Wes had managed to get that weirdly cute nerd girl and that tall MILF both to safety somehow, to bear the wrath of our own special demon ambassador all by himself. Then, after that thing killed him in a horrifically violent way that it had no problem bragging about, Wes had come charging back to fight it again, still alone and with fewer weapons then he had fighting my dad's goons.

The second time around the monster had run screaming away from *him*.

But did we learn from that? Of course not. That victory was a fluke, everyone had said. Just a case of mistaken identity. Our 'honored ambassador' hadn't *really* been scared shitless over an eighteen-year-old boy. Because he was just an eighteen-year-old boy. How scary could he be? And even if he did have a few tricks, we had captured both of his bodies. And killed him over and over again, a horrific event that surely no one can recover from. We had won, right?

Besides, we were obviously in control of the entire situation now. Because we could run fast and shoot lightning and crap. Something a lot of the other natives can apparently do too, but that was irrelevant.

I had to stop thinking about all of that. It would just give me another rage-headache. I reminded myself that I didn't care about these people, and that I was going to get away from it all myself soon anyway.

"So your friend's safe for now. For how long, I don't know, but I do know that Jeepers McKrueger or whoever has been frustrated with his lack of success in finding her. I don't even know where that thing is right now either. But apparently it told Dad that it wouldn't bother to check back with us until at least three years had passed." I narrowed my eyes at Wes. "You've got that long to figure out how to save your magical candyland."

He was still breathing normally, but I thought I saw suspicion in his eyes. *Why was I telling him this?* his eyes asked.

"Because I hate you less than Dad, okay?" I answered. "I'm telling you this because even though I hate you, you and I probably wouldn't be in this if Dad hadn't insisted I try and break you. Now, yes," I added. "There was Regina. I..."

I sighed. "I have no excuse."

Instantly, something inside me dropped. And I regretted admitting that. I desperately wanted excuses back to hide behind again. "I mean, you heard about what Dad wanted me to do and..." It didn't work. The excuses wouldn't cover me anymore. "And I regret it. I liked Regina. I liked her a lot. I hate what I did, I hate what I almost did even more, and I don't want to admit that I owe you for stopping me. It doesn't change my hatred for you, it doesn't mean I accept all your bullshit morality, and it definitely doesn't mean you and I will ever be right. But thank you. For not letting me hurt her even worse than I did."

I didn't speak for a moment, and neither did his eyes. After a while, I tried to continue. I failed, but in another moment I tried again.

"That's most of what I got, so I'll go ahead and say what I want out of this. I want you to kill my dad."

There. I had said it.

Now I can be judged for being the worst son ever.

"He keeps his permanent body here, in one of the kingdoms he's been building up. I don't know which, he hasn't bothered to tell me, but since he's on top of the ladder here, it's probably located in your fairy-tale's richest world. You won't be able to kill him right away, but when you've got the best opportunity, I need you to take your best shot. He'll get one last projected body back on Earth. I'll take care of that one."

I watched my enemy's eyes to see how he'd react. I wanted to see if he was judging me, give me an opportunity to explain, to put things in perspective so that the one guy my age that had me figured out first could understand why I wanted to do this, why we both needed to do this.

Nothing. The bastard didn't even blink. It was infuriating.

"God damn it, Wes," I hissed. "Look, we both need this, okay? You know what he did to you. In a minute, you're going to even know more what he's like, but I have to make sure you know to go after him instead of me. At least at first. If I get enough of a head start, I won't care when you go after me, because I'll make sure you never see or hear from me again. But if he doesn't die, Wes, then you and I are never done. And if he kills you, he's just going to make me go after someone else related to your dad, I don't know, your mother or sister maybe."

There.

His nostrils flared.

"Because he can't get over the fact that your dad stood up to him and ruined his plans. Don't make me get into that. That story's complicated. And if he doesn't do that, Wes, then he's probably just going to get rid of me. You heard him. He's found immortality, so he doesn't need a son to carry his legacy anymore. Eventually he's going to think of me as competition, and a liability, and I'm going to wake up one night with a sack over my head and taken off to some place I'll never leave alive.

"And if he does get rid of me, Wes," I continued. "Then this crap still isn't over for you, because, as my dear father has told me over and over even before he found Avalon, I'm replaceable. Not just expendable, Wes, replaceable. Here."

I pulled out a piece of the new alloy I had been working on. It didn't look that impressive, just a small metal box. Dad had looked at it and been unable to figure out what it did, along with any of his vaunted scientists. He had called the whole project a waste of time and smashed my prototype. This one was the second box I made with it.

Watching Wes' face, I pulled open the box, and took my cell phone out of it. As far as I knew, this was the only phone that had survived our portal's technology-scrambling feature. That was the real victory of my alloy and had my father or his friends figured it out when they looked at it, then they would have been ecstatic, and probably already conquered Narnia or whatever by now.

But since pleasing my Dad had been proven to be a giant waste of time, I was never going to let them find out.

I turned on my cell phone. I got zero reception, as expected, but since it powered on I could still access the files I had downloaded on it. I flipped to an audio file with Dad's voice:

"You're replaceable, you understand that, you little worm? If you ever disappear, all I have to do is find a new woman, wave my wallet or grab her by the throat, and in fifteen minutes I've made another you! No one's gonna care what I did, and no one's gonna care how I chose to do it! So think about that the next time you give me lip, you little..."

I turned off the recording to let Wes take in what he heard. I watched for his expressions again, but this time I couldn't be sure if he reacted.

The fact that I could still have trouble reading him right now put a chill behind my neck.

"You understand now, right?" I asked. I was practically begging right now, and I hated myself for it. "You have to want to be done with this as much as I do, right? You..."

"Chris."

My name croaked out of my enemy's mouth. I could hear every single time he had died in that one croak.

"Chris," he repeated. "Deal."

I waited for a second. I was afraid we had gotten too loud, and that someone had heard us. Maybe. I'm not sure what I was afraid of then.

"You'll do it?" I whispered, realizing that I hadn't been as quiet as I should have been for most of our conversation. "You'll do it, so I can do my part too?"

"Yes."

One word sentences, that I could barely hear right next to him.

But it was all I needed from him.

"Good," I sighed in relief. "Then we can..."

"No," Wes' half-dead voice interrupted. "Favor."

"You want something in return?" I hissed back. "What? Compensation for doing what I need? As payback for everything that happened to you? Or because you think I'm that desperate?"

"Yes," Wes summed up in one flatly spoken word.

I chuckled darkly.

He was more aware than I had even dared to hope. He was aware enough to think a dozen moves ahead.

"Fair enough. I'll tell you what, Wes. I'll do what I was going to do anyway, give you everything I can, because I don't want to owe you over Regina. And because I've finally learned it's better to motivate people than to trick or belittle them. Here's payment up front, Wes. I'll make three deposits. The first one is the knowledge that you're going to eventually get your second body back. It might take years, but eventually you'll be able to recreate a projection back on Earth. It's going to only last seconds, at first, but after that, you'll be able to make it last longer and longer. You might even be able to visit Earth every night like you were probably visiting Avalon. I don't think you can ever go back permanently, but that at least gives you the options for visits. Since that might not be a big deal, I went ahead and led with it. Because the other two are going to make you froth at me."

My phone had not been the only thing in the little alloy case. Wes' weird sword-handle thing was underneath it. That was another trick about the alloy, I thought smugly. Its dimensions were always greater than they looked.

It wasn't until I had started getting non-football, non-modeling scholarship offers from universities that I realized I was much smarter than my father had wanted me to believe. The fact that he had failed to clamp down on those offers had also enraged him.

But back to the point.

"Dad's people couldn't figure out what this thing really does," I told him, seeing his eyes flare in recognition of the strange tool he had earlier pulled a blade out of and set on fire. "We've actually had it ever since our people murdered John Malcolm and took it off his corpse. How you got it back from us we have no idea. But to try and keep me in check, he had me look at it last, and when I told him I couldn't figure it out, he called me a dumbass and said his people figured it out in their first fifteen minutes. But it's a storage device, Wes. Beyond the blade we saw you use, it can store other things. Even information from our world. It can somehow download audio and video. And it can share that video with other devices. I've tested it. Just hold it here, Wes. Like this."

I demonstrated, then handed the weapon back to Wes. One of his suspiciously trembling hands opened to take it, then turned it in the direction I demonstrated.

I still didn't really understand the device. I knew how to make it do that recording he was about to see, and I was able to make it work every time. But I had no idea why what I did worked, and I had no idea where that handle-thing had gotten the recording. Dad would have killed a lot of people if he ever learned about the recording.

When Wes suddenly hissed in a breath, I knew exactly what he was seeing.

He was seeing a little girl of Vietnamese descent, about twelve years old, crying and cringing away from a man that wore a ski mask and holding a large claw hammer. Wes was recognizing the little girl as a former family friend, and one of the three girls that had accused his father of sexual assault.

The large man in the ski mask was explaining to her that some men in police uniforms were coming to interview her and ask about what had happened. She was going to say that "the thing" had definitely happened to her and that John Malcolm was the man that had done it to her.

When the man had finished speaking, the little black-haired girl was going to start shaking her head. Mister John was her friend, she said. He had never hurt her, she said.

Then the man in the ski mask interrupted her by slamming the claw hammer next to her head. John Malcolm was dead, the man growled. He wasn't coming to save her. No one was coming to save her now. And it was all her fault, because everyone could tell that she had a crush on him, so of course they were going to believe that he had done "the thing" to her. And if she wasn't going to be a good girl and do her job, the man in the mask said, then "the thing" was going to happen to her every night, and that everyone was going to find out what a bad girl she was.

The little girl cried even harder, but she still said Mr. John had been her friend and had kept her safe whenever he was around. She even started calling out to him for help.

The man in the ski mask had started shouting when she did that. He slammed the claw hammer down inches away from her head over and over, screaming that the whole thing was her fault, and that she was going to die too and get John Malcolm's whole family killed. She was making things worse for the other two girls by being such a wretched thing. They had already confessed, and "the thing" was going to happen to them too, if she didn't cooperate.

The little black-haired girl finally nodded. There was more on that video, but I don't think Wes saw it. He went from having periodic spasms to trembling all over. His long, labored breaths turned into hissing, frothing sounds. The knuckles holding the handle turned bone-white. His head turned slowly, shaking all over, and he looked at me.

"You," he hissed. "Knew?"

"Hell, no," I spat. "I didn't find this until Avalon. If I had found this sooner, I wouldn't have approached you with it because Dad would have too many chances to find out and kill me, or you would have killed me when you found out I was sitting on it." I pointed at the handle in his hands. "There's a time-date stamp on the video and a few clues in the footage to suggest this happened around the time they staged your dad's suicide. And there's more recordings in there. More than I had time to look through. But if you ever get back to Earth with this, the files can transfer onto other media. If I could risk carrying something around with the file on it, I'd show you, but I couldn't. It's too risky to even keep this on my phone. But you'll see for yourself if you ever get back to Earth."

More hissing breaths from Wes. The blood vessels near his pupils were starting to get prominent.

"Trust... you? How?" he finally spat, and he was right. This was a lot to take in, and it could have been staged. Which was why I had saved my final carrot for just now.

"She's here, Wes. I just found out. They call her one of their 'Indentureds', and they keep her in the back with the others. They have the other two girls too. I think they're not done using them. And this way, they can't come back to Earth in their main bodies, just like you. But they haven't died as many times, because they can still be forced to make projections back to Earth. I heard them talking about it. They've got clients for them, Wes. To keep revenue streams going, they said. They said it's a perfect plan because it doesn't leave evidence and keeps the original merchandise preserved, unless they somehow die as many times as you did."

"Where?" Wes growled out, with a lot more force than he had used yet. It made me even more optimistic about his chances, while scaring the hell out of me at the exact time. Because even when he was standing up to me, I had never seen him like this.

"Opposite end of where the portal is," I said quickly. I was starting to lose him and I knew it. "They keep the native prisoners nearby too. Just go right instead of left, but you still turn right at the fifth hallway. The blueprint planning really was that bad. Now if you need, I can try and get Dad to put fewer guards here tomorrow..."

"No," Wes growled. "Want them all here. Especially him. The one I saw with Val."

He nodded at the sword handle, where he had seen that video of the claw hammer guy terrorizing his former family friend. "He do anything else to her?"

"Fuck," I swore. "I swear to God I don't know, Wes. I've had that video for less than a month. But probably," I admitted. "Him and the others. And if not Val, or the other two girls, then they've definitely hurt some of the natives. This is me guessing though, Wes. Because Dad doesn't hire a lot of people who are right in the head."

I took a quick glance at the two of us.

Even counting us, was there anyone left who really was right in the head?

Or were sane people just another fairy-tale?

I shook my head. Those were the wrong questions to ask in this place.

"Alright, that's all I got," I said, moving to get up. "Kill everyone I hate, especially Dad, and don't die until you finish. Do whatever the hell you want after that, and leave me alone if you can. I'm going to do the same, and maybe see if I can get a portal to take me even further away from all of this. Hopefully a place not as shitty as Earth, or as Never-Never-land-ish as this place is. Goodbye, Wes."

I heard him again just before I made it to the door.

"Chris," he somehow hissed from across the room.

I turned to look at him and found I could just barely read his eyes this time.

"Thank you," he spat out. "And... I understand." Another heaving breath. "Because I... hate you too."

I nodded and walked out of the door.

I felt relieved. And angry. Because there had been more balm for my soul in Wes's single declaration of hatred to me than there had been in every word of approval Dad had ever spoken of me.

30

RISE UP AND RAGE. ROUND TWO

B*eat,* my heart said for the thirty-fifth-thousandth time today. *Beat...Beat...Beat...*

Stop counting, a twinge of pain said through my right arm. *It's annoying.*

Shut up, I said back to it. *It's your fault I'm in this mess. Every time I've ever given you the slightest bit of attention, I've suffered for i—*

Crap. I had done it again. Get back on track.

Beat...Beat...

By my guess, I had less than a thousand beats to go.

Chris had told me I had six to twelve hours.

And after our little heart-to-heart, or at least our little hate-to-hate, I believed him.

Six to twelve hours.

Six hours made too little sense. They had gotten up early in the beginning. It was brand new, then, making me die. Then, after I kept coming back, it got predictable. But predictable is still interesting. Based on how I took being stabbed, how would I take being drowned? How would I take being eaten?

It wasn't exciting enough to start at the beginning of the day, but they only came in an hour later. Then they had stopped getting what they needed out of my deaths. My reactions had standardized, they said. I could no longer distinguish how I was dying. The trauma was too much.

Then they decided I couldn't tell even when I was alive anymore, that I was all but brain-dead from the trauma. I was finished. And they were tired of me.

In other words, it had worked.

Beat... Beat... Beat...

They would come for me in twelve hours, I decided. Everyone had looked like they were at the final end of the day when they went to come see me. So that meant they were going to bed. They would wake up late today, I knew, because other than killing me one last time, today was going to be a light day for them.

That was another thing being 'finished' had let me do. Nobody worries about operational security if the only audience is a corpse. I learned all kinds of things about these men. Combined with what Chris had told me, I had a pretty good picture of this place. I mean, dungeon. Let's just call this place a dungeon.

So that I can feel better when I rip it apart.

But from what I understood, this place was a waypoint—their safest, most secure waypoint. But one they didn't like using for some reason. The Order of Malus—that's their name, until I can think of something more insulting—didn't keep any leadership here. Just the least dangerous prisoners. And me. Because this was the most convenient portal to and from Earth. How they got to other places, I don't know. But this is the one location that they believed was completely, absolutely secure from attack from the people in the other worlds. I had to assume this was where they kept a number of prisoners that they didn't mind being out of the way.

I had no idea how many prisoners they had total. But my understanding was that the number was decreasing more quickly than they had wanted. I also didn't know what they were doing with the prisoners, but after what they had done to me, I had only dark guesses.

But after today, that changes, the part of my mind that hadn't broken yet said. I had stuffed most of myself away to the hidden corners of my mind back when all the deaths and tortures started. It was a last-ditch effort to get through what they were doing to me, and the deeper the torture went, the farther away in my mind I retreated. On the one hand, it worked. They hurt me, but they didn't get all of me.

On the other hand though, I wasn't sure I could get all of me back either.

I had no idea where I had stuffed parts of myself, and I may never find those parts again.

But today, that wasn't my focus.

The little piece of me that still peeked out had made Val my focus. Her, and Sam, and Kayla, and anyone else they had down here.

I wanted them back.

I wanted them all back.

And no one had better tell me they weren't mine. Everyone else lost that right to them when they failed to protect them. They were mine. The next person who wanted to hurt them would get to fight me for them.

Now, then. Freedom. I went back to counting how long I had until one of them camc for me.

Beat...Beat...Beat...

Should be right about...now.

"Ugh," a voice came down from the hall. "I can't believe they want me to shred this brat so early on a Friday."

"Why are they doing it at all?" another man's voice whined. "It's not like he's really a loose end. Just leave him down there to starve."

Two of them. Crap.

Was Chris wrong? Did these people finally grow a brain, at the worst time possible?

"Mr. Rhodes' boogeyman said we won't get any new toys until he's dead. And it wants the kid's head in a way that it can preserve it."

"Why the head?"

"Present for the thing's runaway girlfriend. At least that's what people heard it say."

"Hah!" the second voice laughed. "Now *that* is twisted."

There was approval in the second man's voice.

Because of course there was.

"Do me a favor," the second man continued. "Swing by with the head before you drop it off. Shepherd wants me to train the kids for a new confession."

"All three at once?" the first voice continued. "Don't they break easier if you do it one by one?"

"Not at this point," the second voice snorted. "That only mattered back when they thought someone would come to save them. This way, it's just faster."

"What are you going to do if they don't confess, that you weren't going to do anyway?"

"Leave the head with them for an hour."

"Ha!"

The conversation continued for another five minutes. I stopped paying attention to what they were saying because I didn't need any more incentive to kick their asses, and I didn't want my vision to get any redder. Then the second maggot finally said what I was hoping he'd say:

"Well I'm going to go get the tools. Swing by when you're done. The natives are taking a while to break, and I don't have time to go through them all on my own."

"Have you figured out how they keep healing?"

"Hell if I know. Even we're not supposed to heal that fast."

"Either way, we've gotta figure out how to break them, or management will have our asses. I'll see you in a bit." The second voice walked off.

I heard the first man sigh by the door. I stopped counting my heartbeats and got ready.

I had recognized the first voice too. He had been there for a couple of my deaths. Maybe more, because most of me had gone to my quiet place by the end. But I had retained enough awareness to loosely measure how powerful he was.

Rhodes' people had grown powerful quickly here. By now, they could have probably competed with my strength back when I fought them earlier. And I could tell it hadn't taken them nearly as much effort and focus. But there was an... off-ness to them. Like they weren't fully confident in the bodies they had here. I didn't know why.

But as soon as the man opening the door came close enough, I was going to use the one shot I had to take full advantage of it.

The door opened loudly.

"Rise and shine, princess," the man laughed as he walked in.

It was hard not to hold my breath, but I kept my pattern going until I heard the door close behind him. Then I fought the urge to sigh in relief.

He was still talking, but I ignored him.

I had gotten everything I wanted. Now I needed him to keep coming closer.

If he did that, I had him.

One footstep. Two footsteps. Three footsteps.

"Hey! I'm talking to you cripple-head!"

Sigh. *Of course you are.*

"I had to get up an hour early today just to haul your crippled ass to the incinerator! You got anything to say about that?"

Maybe he's drunk, I decided. Not entirely stupid. Just drunk.

Could we even get drunk on Avalon? Or does it depend on which body comes here?

Save it, I told myself. *He's walking again.*

Four footsteps. Five footsteps. Six footsteps.

"Alright, whatever. It's your last death. If you want to just curl up in a ball, that's your choice."

Seven steps. Eight steps.

"But I'll make you a deal. If you can be aware enough to beg, one last time, I'll make it quick. It'll take ten seconds tops for you to bleed out. Then you're gone for good. Promise."

I shifted slightly at that. Just enough to where he could wonder if I understood him. I heard him grunt in curiosity, then I heard him walk closer again.

Nine footsteps. Ten footsteps.

I was facing away from him. Since he needed to remove my head anyway, I knew he had to lean over me to reach it.

I heard him shift. I counted two more heartbeats.

Beat...Beat...

Then...

Push.

I felt my pain scream at me one last time, and then it winked out. Power and memory rushed through all of my limbs, shaking me greater than it had during my first Rise.

Something in my previous deaths had stripped my powers away from me. Or maybe it was one of the tests they had done to me. I didn't know. But they took it to be the final nail in my coffin. I even remembered that some of them taunted me with it, reminding me that I was a cripple again, and that I'd stay that way.

I had nearly lost it then and there. Because I had wanted to laugh.

Outside of Earth, people grow by overcoming Challenges. Big ones, little ones, it doesn't matter. Every little triumph throughout the day helps, even if it's only a little bit.

That might have been the thing that kept me sane. The knowledge that the one thing they were constantly piling on me wasn't deaths, wasn't torture, wasn't pain, wasn't humiliations.

It was Challenges to overcome.

They didn't realize that they were trying to maim me by smothering me in opportunities for more power.

They had piled on so much that if I took it all in at once I might explode.

So I tried to control my inhalation of that power, and perform something called a half-Rise.

Bringing myself to the state I was when Stell had done her first assessment of me.

I wasn't sure what the results would be. But I knew it would at the very least bring me back to my beginning capabilities.

I was wrong.

I felt myself lift up into the air as I pushed off the ground, exerting at least twice the amount of force I had intended to. For a half second, I was an awkward, flailing mess off the ground, nearly colliding into my executioner, but then I recovered enough to get my bearings.

My sudden power had surprised me briefly. It had surprised my would-be murderer for far longer.

I got my bearings enough to whirl and face him. He was a tall man, built much like the ones I had fought at the beginning, large and overly muscular. Scars and tattoos covered most of his face and forearms, and he had black eyes and a shock of black hair. He had the silvery short sword I had gotten from the Horde Pit in his right hand, apparently to kill me with my own weapon.

That was all I needed to know. I launched a kick into his stomach, pulling most of the power as I hit him. I didn't know what would happen if I hit him too hard. Either he'd die on the spot, slam into the wall hard enough to make a loud noise and raise the alarm, or survive the hit, recognize I was dangerous and raise the alarm on his own. But if he thought I just got a lucky hit that barely hurt him, he would take care of me personally. Because he was already ticked off and didn't want to be seen needing help to kill the famously weak cripple-head.

My leg hit his stomach and knocked the air out with a *whoosh.* My foe was lifted off the ground and fell down on his hand and knees, barely holding onto his weapon. As he staggered on the ground for a second, I got my bearings again and became aware of the prompts in my brain.

The Expanse has detected a new inhabitant of the seven worlds. Welcome to life, child of Avalon—ERROR.

Recognizing the newly formed awareness of Earthborn Challenger Wes Malcolm. Welcome to Avalon, Challenger—ERROR.

Inhabitant is displaying characteristics of both having an original body and being from Earth at the same time. Records also show that the inhabitant has Risen in the past, and therefore should have already attained awareness.

Falling back on Starsown-configured protocols for error-detection...

Resolution accepted. Earthborn Challenger has somehow managed to bring their primary body to Avalon.

Challenger should be aware that gains will be different with Rising in their original body.

Challenger's Saga is developing.

I trembled. Data and knowledge were still flowing into my mind faster than I could take in.

Focus, I told myself. *Dangerous guy in front of me. Make him bloody and harmless.*

"How the hell?" the man wheezed as he tried to rise from the ground.

I answered with another kick.

This time I didn't hold back.

My foot slammed into his head with a loud *crack,* and he went prone again. I felt his version of the vital guard trigger, diminishing the damage my blow would have done to him. A moment later, I felt most of his vital guard give way, letting some of the trauma pass to his body. He let out a moan and tried to get up again.

"Did you kill him?" I asked quietly.

It was a mistake. I knew it was a mistake. If I didn't finish him off soon, he'd call for help. I had no idea how strong I was right now, and I didn't know how I compared to the rest of the guards here.

But I needed to know who had killed Dad.

"Huh? What? Who? Where?"

The would-be murdering idiot was being ungratefully uncooperative and was using his recent head injury as an excuse. I was not sympathetic. Especially since I knew just how much a kick to the head did and didn't limit a person.

"Did you," I enunciated. "Kill John Malcolm? Did you pull the trigger? Did you help hold him down?" I kept speaking slowly, walking closer to get ready to launch another kick. "Did you make his wife a widow? Did you make his daughter a half-orphan? Did you kill," my voice rose, "John Malcolm?"

"What? No," I heard him stammer.

He was getting off of his knees now. Fear had moved into his eyes and was beginning to evict all the murderous arrogance right out of them.

"Explain, 'no,'" I raised my voice again. "No, you didn't pull the trigger? No, you didn't make my mother a widow? No, you didn't murder the man who would give my sister away on her wedding? No, you didn't beat him a bunch like you did with me? No, you didn't stab him many times like you did with me? Tell me what your 'no' means! *Tell me!*"

He fell on his back and began to scoot away from me. He had dropped my short sword at some point. Neither of us saw when.

"I didn't pull the trigger! I didn't pull the trigger! It was a big team! I didn't even see who did!"

"That's good to know," I whispered, still walking towards him. "You just 'helped' kill him. Just like you probably 'helped' kill some of the locals here. Just like you probably 'helped' torture Val and Sam and Kayla. But now you're going to stop 'helping' everyone..."

His hand went for his short sword. My foot went for his neck. It was a critical blow that completely overpowered his vital guard. I heard him gurgle as something in his throat stopped working. But it didn't change any of my short-term plans.

I kicked him again. And again. Then I kept kicking him and decided that I would stop doing it just past the point where his vital guard fully expended and he died, or my anger abated enough to where something other than kicking him to death made sense.

The former happened all too fast. He stopped breathing or moving, and his body became slightly translucent. Maybe that was how I had looked all those times where I died.

But I was still angry. He was dead, Dad was still dead, and I didn't feel any different. Maybe that was because I hadn't killed him permanently. But I don't think so.

Something inside of me was saying this was not the way back to myself and was begging me to listen to it.

Maybe someday I would listen.

But not today.

Today was not about me.

I knelt down and picked up my old short sword. Then I looked at the handle Chris had given me. I had forgotten I had been holding it in my other hand. I stared at it for a moment longer, then I pressed down on its grip and touched it to the short sword in my other hand. Something flashed, and I felt my short sword disappear into the strange handle. I moved the item to my primary hand and focused in a way I couldn't explain. The strange handle shimmered, and my short sword was back in my primary hand, super-imposing somehow over the strange grip.

Challenger's signature weapon discovered. Primary function (storage) discovered.

The Order of Malus' Invasion has been resisted by another world-traveler, who has slain a projected body of their faction.

The Stellar Council has witnessed the slaying, and hereby declares that Stellar War has begun once again.

Challenger has enlisted in Stellar War by being the first of his faction to wage it.

Challenger has embarked upon the Path of War.

I shook my head at the number of prompts my mind-screen sent at me.

"Avalon," I whispered. "Can you hear me?"

No answer. I looked around and realized that there wasn't any mist around me. I tried to remember that I was deep underground, and there could be a number of reasons why the planetary super-computer wasn't answering me. Next, I tried to look at my Traits and skills:

Wes Malcolm
Race: Human. Origin: Earth (Challenger)
Growth Level: Half-Rise (Glint)
Path: War (First Step)
Saga: Forming
Profession: Unknown
Vital Pool: 250 points
Stamina Pool: 250 points.
Mana Pool: 220 points

Strength: 17
Dexterity: 17
Constitution: 20

Intelligence: 17
Wisdom: 34
Charisma: 15

Speed: 21
Deftness: 20
Wits: 21
Will: 42

Rise Points Remaining: 12 (can increase the six primary traits at a 1:1 ratio, or the four secondary traits at a 1:2 ratio.

Insight into the Following Ideals
Earth: lvl 5
Air: lvl 5
Lightning: lvl 5

Skill List truncated (New Skills still listed)
Pain Tolerance Rank 5
Mental Preservation Rank 6 (Initiate) (New Resistances Gained)

Spell list truncated

4 skill points available.
Signature Spells have improved since last viewing.
Spark Bolt's mana cost has decreased.
Outer Circuit's activation time has decreased to instant.
Earth Bones' activation time has decreased to instant.
Stoneskin's activation time has decreased to instant.
Quick Step's activation time has decreased to instant.
Wind Armor's activation time has decreased to instant.
Further changes observed, but unidentified.

For a second, I didn't believe the information, until I tried to match it with what I felt. I did feel more powerful than when I first came here. That shouldn't have been the case, I thought. I had died over and over. All of my muscles should have probably suffered some form of long-term damage, but then again, that was in my projected body.

I had wanted to laugh when I realized that. Of course. That was part of the deal Stell talked about. I got to keep part of what I *gained*, not lost, here in Avalon and the other worlds. That was by design, because Stell, or whoever had designed the system, wanted the Challengers to be rewarded, not punished, for facing all sorts of desperate scenarios on other worlds.

This wasn't Earth.

This wasn't a place that aimed to break a person every time they tried to do the right thing.

So I still had working legs and arms. In fact, since this was my original body, they were finally working better than they ever had. I could hear Pain whining in the background, but it could no longer jump up and grab my limbs or brains.

For a brief moment, it felt like I hadn't lost anything at all.

Then I nearly kicked myself. I had lost a lot of things for good. I was just now learning exactly what I'd lost in these past three years. What had been stolen from me. *Who* had been stolen from me. My future on Earth. My ability to think of being stabbed and kicked and torn and burnt as anything but a normal experience.

My dad. And probably my mom and sister. And Davelon and Christina and my other friends.

I had to shut it off right there because, well, sanity. But in retrospect, my magical powers and traits were probably the easiest thing I could have gotten back.

And if I was reading this right, I had kept at least half of everything I had before. Even more so with my Constitution. And I had either kept all of my Wisdom and Will or already gained it back while going through the torture. Not that I felt particularly wise or strong-willed at the moment.

I did know one thing. Whatever I had lost, however I had been damaged, the trauma hadn't destroyed me. Not here. Not yet.

So as long as I still had the opportunity, I would fight and I would claw, and I would not stop until I had gained something back.

And right now, that something was the rest of the people they had kept here.

A quick glance told me my executioner didn't have anything else on him that I could use. I don't know why the people here weren't more heavily armed. Sure, they had clubs and short blades from what I had seen, but I was expecting them to take advantage of swords and plate and chainmail. Maybe they just felt that secure, to where they didn't think they'd need heavy gear. Or maybe they just weren't familiar with this world's equipment yet, and didn't feel like learning whatever they thought they didn't need.

That sounded stupid, but maybe they weren't used to clawing for every single scrap they could gain, like I was.

I walked to the door to listen for anyone else out in the hallway. Nothing. Sound didn't travel that much.

I thought about how easily I had dispatched my first foe here, and wondered if I should Rise again or just wait. The longer I waited, the easier it would be to increase my traits and skills through use. But if I didn't summon power I wound up needing, I'd be killed for good. And everything would be lost. For everyone. Stell. Guineve. Val. The other natives here.

Thinking of Stell reminded me that I could summon Breena back to me.

I focused on the familiar summoning spell I had been granted, and went through the procedure to call forth my tiny pink-haired friend.

When the spell completed, a tiny portal briefly opened, then closed again.

That cold sinking feeling I was all too familiar with crawled right back into my stomach.

"Wes?" a tiny voice whispered in my mind. *"Wes?"*

"Breena," I sighed in relief, sending back to her in my mind. *"Thank God. Where are you?"*

"Hiding." A one-word answer. As if her breath was now precious and rare.

"Hiding?" I asked with a frown. *"From what?"*

"Bad thing," she whispered in short sentences. *"Wants us. Stell knows it."*

"Cavus?"

"Shhh. No names. He'll hear you."

"Is he near you right now?"

"No. Not close. Not anymore."

"Where is he?"

"Gone now. Wants Stell."

"Did he find her?" I asked desperately. *"Is she safe?"*

"Don't know."

"What about you?" I asked. *"Are you hurt?*

"No."

"Are you safe?"

"No."

"Why?"

"Bad men. Have magic. Have Horde. New kinds. Never seen either before."

For all of her child-like nature, my little friend had seen nearly every type of magic and almost certainly every type of Hordebeast. The news she gave was troubling at the very least.

"Are you still on Avalon?" I asked.

"Shh. No names."

I had to growl away my impatience. My friend was in danger, and her tone was scaring the hell out of me. Which should have been impossible after what I'd already been through.

"Breena, help me know where you are."

"Near shelter. Almost made it."

"Shelter?" I asked. *"There is a shelter on—there is a shelter here?"*

"Old shelter. Never needed. Needed now." A pause. *"Didn't make it."*

"Are the bad things in your way?" I asked.

"Yes."

"Can they get in the shelter?" I asked carefully.

"No," she whispered back. *"Safe place."*

"Can you make it around them?"

I suppressed another growl. This was like pulling teeth, in the middle of the night, out in the woods where wolves were howling.

"No. Too late. Guarding."

"Well, can you get away from there without being seen?"

"No. Too late. Hunting me."

She paused, then whispered again in my mind.

"Too strong to fight. Have to stay still. Stay silent."

She was saying that much to herself, I realized. And those were two things I had never noticed Breena do very well.

"Okay, new plan," I sent back. *"Just stay where you are, and when I'm done here, I'll find the place and come get you."*

"No. Too late. Bad thing hunts us. Go home, Wes. Stay safe. Live long. Be well."

Ha.

She didn't know.

"I can't do that, Breena," I said back quietly.

"Wes," the whispering became more urgent. Pleading, even. *"Go home. Can't help. Bad thing hunts us. Hates boys. Will hurt you."*

"I know." And this time I didn't hide any of my irritation with her. *"We've already met. Twice,"* I added with a growl.

"What? Wes...no." There was pain in that voice. Old pain.

Breena knew this thing too.

"Focus, Breena, and listen," I was speaking harshly to her. And even as twisted as I felt I'd become, I still hated doing that to her. *"Things have changed for me. I'll explain when I find you. But that shelter is probably going to be my home now. And there are other people here I need to bring to it.*

"I'll ask you more questions later, because I'm probably not safe right now either. There are people here I've promised to help, and when I get everyone secure, I'm coming for you. Tell me if you move or if anything happens. Otherwise I'll just find you. And don't tell me to stay away," I growled. *"It doesn't work."*

"Wes... thank you...sorry...love you."

Her empathy was fixed.

I don't know why I thought that. But in that awful moment, I suddenly realized Breena was finally expressing herself without anything else getting in the way.

"Love you too," I sent back. We didn't talk about what kind of love she was offering. I just took it and returned it, hoping it would help us both survive. *"Stay safe. I'm coming either way."*

I didn't know what 'sorry' meant either, and it scared me a whole lot more than 'love you.'

Alright, I decided that was enough teen angst. I still needed to decide if I wanted to undergo a full Rise, and how many.

It was a stupid question. There was too much at stake here. Breena was in danger. Stell was probably in danger. Val and the other girls were definitely in danger, and my family had made them a promise a long time ago to take care of them if they ever needed help.

I had let the lies about Dad, and about how they supposedly didn't want to talk to us anymore, keep me away.

That was on me. Time to fix it.

I *pushed.* Then I did it again. Then one more time.

Then something locked up inside of me, like some automatic latch designed to keep something from overloading. I still felt the pressure that compelled me to lift it off of me, but I couldn't do so anymore. Which was good because right now my body felt like it was breaking in half anyway.

The changes made from the Ideals alone increased most of my Traits by over a third of their original total. Furthermore, not only did I have the left-over points I never spent, now I received seven points for Traits and five points for skills, every single Rise. Even after the Ideals were allocated I had 23 points for Traits and 19 points to increase my skill knowledge. Again, this was all I could afford to save, so I went and got to work:

Wes Malcolm
Race: Human. Origin: Earth (Challenger)
Growth Level: Third-Rise (Spark)
Path: War (First Step)
Saga: Forming
Profession: Unknown
Vital Pool: 350 points
Stamina Pool: 350 points.
Mana Pool: 350 points

Strength: 30
Dexterity: 30
Constitution: 30
Intelligence: 30
Wisdom: 38
Charisma: 25

Speed: 37
Deftness: 34
Wits: 39
Will: 46
Rise Points Remaining: 0 (can increase the six primary traits at a 1:1 ratio, or the four secondary traits at a 1:2 ratio.
13 skill points remaining

Insight into the Following Ideals
Earth: lvl 6 Initiate Level Unlocked: Mana Cost decreased
Air: lvl 6 Initiate Level Unlocked: Mana Cost decreased

Lightning: lvl 6 Initiate Level Unlocked: Mana Cost decreased

Skill List truncated (New Skill levels listed)
Unarmed fighting 6 (Initiate) (Expand for Details)
Light Blades 6 (Initiate) (Expand for Details)
Dodge 6 (Initiate) (Expand for Details)
Pain Tolerance Rank 6 (Initiate) (New Resistances Gained)
Mental Preservation Rank 6 (Initiate) (New Resistances Gained)

Spell list truncated

I shuddered through another explosion of change within my body and mind. I felt new changes unlock through my Ideals, but they would take more time than I had to fully understand. At any rate, though, I tried to increase all of my traits to just above the maximum potential of a human being on Earth. I finally pushed some of my skills to level 6, mainly my Ideals and the combat skills I was likely to use, but increasing the skill level above my Risen level made me feel like each empowered skill was its own special migraine.

But once again, no time. *Move.*

I reached for my enhancement spells. My signature ones were all instantaneous now, but there was no reason not to test them here instead of in the heat of the moment. I felt my bones become stronger, yet still flexible, like some powerful alloy. Minerals crawled over the very tip of my skin, creating thick layers in some places that were, oddly, more comfortable than they had felt in the past. The air very close to me whipped about, and smelled like ozone whenever a crackle of current ran along my limbs. I felt a similar current travel down my sword.

Still taking too long, I told myself. *Back to the playbook.*

Kick the door down, disarm the traps, kill the monsters, save the princess, get the treasure.

The door opened with a creak. I walked out into the hall. I tried to remember how many people I had seen here. Then I asked myself why Chris thought I could fight my way out of here on my own, after being captured for so long. I had caught my last opponent unaware with every attack, and while that gave me an idea of his intelligence, I still could only guess as to how strong these guys were...

"Hey, you!"

Huh, I thought. *Free research. Never mind then.*

I made a show of looking around me, then I looked at the guard while pointing to myself.

"Who, me?" I asked. "Where am I?"

Seeing my dazed look, the guard came closer, looking uncertain as to what to say to me and what to do. Had I turned combative he would have probably raised an alarm, but I didn't think he'd been trained on dealing with an escaped prisoner that was also a head-case.

"You're supposed to be in your cell," he growled, walking forward. This one had brown hair, but otherwise looked similar to the one I had killed earlier. He was holding a club, but the way he was holding it seemed a little off to me.

"Cell?" I asked, realizing he still couldn't see the weapon I was holding behind me. "Which cell? What's a cell? Who are you? Why does everything feel fuzzy?"

He came closer still. I could tell he was still confused.

"You, um, where is Rick? Rick, are you back in there?" he called out to the room I had left.

"Rick?" I asked, noting that he was almost in range. "Who's Rick? Who are you? Am I late for school?"

"Rick is, um, shit." The goon was having a really hard time with this. I reflected that bluffing guards had been way harder in my sister's games. "He's your executioner... I mean, nurse. He's your nurse. He's uh, he's supposed to take you back to your room."

"Room?" I asked. He was almost in range. "What room? Where am I?"

"You're uh, in a hospital. For sick people. We're supposed to be trying to make you better. Come on. Let's, uh, go to your room and find Rick."

He was reaching his hand out to me, now that he was in range. Apparently, it hadn't occurred to him that since I was supposed to die today anyway, he could have just killed me himself.

"Okay," I said, still keeping my confused tone. "But why did you just walk up to me and not sound the alarm?"

His eyebrows narrowed, almost understanding, and almost soon enough.

"Huh? What do you..."

And with a shriek of pain, he interrupted himself.

A red line had followed the path across his arm that my hidden sword had taken. It was his own fault for not taking the time to look behind my back.

Since he wasn't done making mistakes, I dashed forward and stabbed into his chest. I felt his vital guard kick in over his organs, somehow holding them together, and I felt them kick in again when I twisted my blade violently out. He screamed in pain and swung his club at me.

That was why I thought he was holding it wrong, I realized as his weapon scraped against the wall. His grip was wrong for fighting in a hallway this size.

Why didn't he know that?

And what else was wrong with these people?

He wasn't even wearing armor. Just that Kevlar vest and a uniform he probably wore back on Earth. Did he not know swords were a thing here?

Was I fighting the Malus junior varsity squad or something?

He finally got his weapon clear of the wall and swung it at me with something that almost showed practice, and I finally placed my finger on the problem.

He was awkward. In a way he probably wasn't back on Earth. But everything he was doing here, he was only doing with part of himself.

Their projection tech didn't work. He wasn't fully in Avalon, and he probably didn't even realize it until now.

I stepped back to dodge his blow, and then stepped in for another murder stab. This time when I stabbed at him, I felt the air cut around my sword, felt its weight suddenly increase as it impacted him. Then something hummed, and he spasmed on my blade in a way that reminded me of those self-tasering videos I had seen online.

He seemed even more confused as my last attack shredded his vital guard to rags. I ripped my sword across his throat, and as he fell clutching it, I realized the wound was blackened and bloodless.

When I started to ask myself why, my sword crackled in my hand.

Cooperation among Ideals achieved, my mind-screen said. *Challenger has comprehended the preliminary stage of Battleform.*

A second casualty has been lost to Stellar War.

Challenger's infamy has increased.

Current Participation has earned Challenger the rank of conscript.

Challenger may summon a basic weapon from the Cosmic Armory.

Updates flew across my mind and eyes, and a new spell formed in my head. I held out my hand, worked out the mental requirements of my newest spell, and a six-foot spear with a diamond-shaped blade, something resembling the ancient Roman *hasta*, appeared in my other hand. I got the feeling it was a free emergency weapon, granted by my dutiful murder of two (fully deserving) fellow Earthlings, and it was probably something to be used to further that same end. It felt cheap, and replaceable, until I felt my Earth, Air and Lightning magic creep up it, making it sturdier, sharper, and, well, tasery.

I kept it in my other hand for now, then thought better of it. I reached down to remove my recent victim's belt and fastened it over my own rags. Then I thrust my short sword into my belt as safely as I could, and began walking down the left hallway. I had wanted to leave the portal open. And I had wanted to save the girls and other prisoners first. But as long as it was open, I'd have to deal with reinforcements, and I couldn't even guarantee that the enemies I killed would stay down.

I hurried, but I didn't like it. The two earlier idiots hadn't had a chance to raise the alarm while alive, but they had just gone back to Earth. Even if their original bodies were both alone, all it would take was for one of them to remember what cell phones were, and I'd lose the element of surprise.

I ran faster. I felt my stronger bones aid me in propulsion. It felt like my synapses were firing faster. And the wind pushed on my legs with every leap, buffeting me forward to faster speeds.

I had reached the corner Chris mentioned almost before I realized it, and then I turned and charged to where he had mentioned the portal was. Now was a perfect time to find out if he was tricking me.

He wasn't.

I saw the purple-black light flickering ahead. Three men were standing or sitting on crates around the portal. One of them looked like he was trying to smoke an authentic pipe and failing, judging by his coughs. I couldn't hear them talk, because I was moving too fast. And that was great.

I was really tired of hearing these guys talk.

The most important thing I could tell, though, was that they were all relaxed, which meant Stupid and Stupid Jr. hadn't let anyone know I was reenacting one of those ancient prison-break dramas on television.

They weren't even looking at me until I was almost in the room. Then the one standing in the middle, who was actually wearing real armor and had a spear like me, let out a shout and pointed in my direction.

Marking him as the greatest threat, I braced my spear toward him and rushed forward as fast as I could.

My speed surprised the both of us. I heard air whistle past my ears, and it felt like the ground was pushing my feet further forward. The man kept screaming and turning toward the portal when my spear took him in the throat. His vital guard felt like sandpaper as I punched through it. My spear shuddered in my hands, as if it had suddenly gotten stuck in a thin tree limb, and as it bounced out of my grip I realized I had punctured the man's spine as well, something the vital guard couldn't really fix. He fell limply, not even screaming anymore.

I staggered past his new corpse, coming dangerously close to the portal as I did so.

Then I heard it again.

"Traitor-prince! Traitor-prince! Curse and kill the traitor-prince!"

That old thing, right.

The voices were trying to crawl into my head again, and I couldn't have that. I turned to the guy currently dropping his pipe and reaching for his machete. Since my hands were free, I pointed all ten of my fingers at him, and the tiny bolts leaped out and shocked into him. They had vastly progressed in power since the first time I used them, and I saw him go down twitching, opening his mouth without making any sounds. The last guard was running toward me with his combat machete. I darted to the right, far faster than I thought I would, causing him to stumble as he missed me entirely. Barely retaining my own footing, I began to cast another spell. My casting speed had somehow increased as well, because as soon as he got to his feet and turned to charge me, my *Friction Slash* took off his head.

"Traitor-prince! Traitor-prince!"

I staggered away from the portal, the voices diminishing slightly. Then I faced it and felt the small voice speak up again.

Use me.

Who are you? I asked once more.

You know me. And I know you.

Where in the hell have you been? I growled. *Do you know what happened to me?*

Yes. I was there. And I rage.

Use me, the voice begged again. *I rage. And so do you.*

Fine, I growled. I didn't have time for an argument right now anyway. *But this isn't over.*

The familiar burning-melting sensation ran down my knuckles again. And the strange handle was once again in my hands.

Let the lightning beget light and fire. Then let the fire beget more light. Then let the light beget growth. Darkness becomes fuel for light, fear becomes fuel for courage, courage becomes fuel for triumph, triumph becomes fuel for growth. Light your fires, smite your unrighteous fears, expand every joy in your defiant heart.

The words were doing something inside of me that I couldn't put my finger on. It was almost like something new was fluttering around, like paper and furniture was being rearranged. I felt Pain writhe in outrage at being shuffled around, but I couldn't even hear its voice at the moment.

The gray fire was melting something off my hands, and, as before, I felt whole and not harmed. Not even my prior trauma bothered me. Lightning traveled between my two flaming palms until I brought them together. Then a bolt as thick as my forearm shot into the portal.

"Traitor-prince-traitor-prince-noooo!"

The voices shut off as the lightning impacted, and the purple-black hole began to smoke and create silver sparks. The lightning traveled in and out of its center hole, and the whirling disc finally seemed to get knocked off balance. The hole began spinning in an off-center direction, getting smaller and smaller until it finally winked out.

Are you still there? I asked the quiet voice, panting after the expenditure of magic.

No time. Go. Needed. By many.

Swearing under my breath at the unwanted new mystery, I picked up the spear I had killed the first guard with.

The armored guard's body faded completely. His studded leather fell to the ground along with a much more useful belt than what I was wearing.

A third, fourth, and fifth casualty has been lost to Stellar War, my mind-screen suddenly said.

"Gah!" I said out loud. "Time the freak out! Is this going to happen for every instance of constructively solving my problems with a deadly weapon? Are other people getting these messages, because operational security is supposed to be a thing! And what the hell is Stellar War?"

I got even madder, in part because I had just made the hypocritical mistake of loudly complaining about operational security, and also because I had no idea how to adjust the messages in my mind-screen. That was another thing I had never fully worked out with Breena, because these messages were never this distracting, and in early cases, gave important information too late.

Pre-recorded Message:

The Challenger should be aware that mind-screen information is always released personally. Global broadcasts can only come from a planet's core. Furthermore, next time you have a question for your mind-screen, Wes, just think it out instead of screaming loudly or by doing some other roundabout method that Breena's already tired of dealing with. And yes, I programmed this message in advance. I had to start doing that after the last Challenge because Breena was threatening to figure out how labor unions worked and form one of her own. Now save the rest of your questions for Breena after finishing whatever Challenge you're currently on.

-Stell

That answered that. And made me miss her again. And worry about her. And get back to work again.

The Council has been contacted regarding Challenger's exploits in Stellar War. Challenger is being recognized as a notable leader of his faction. Challenger's Infamy has risen given his personal role in the war.

Current rank is private recruit. Challenger can now summon a uniform denoting his rank and affiliation in the current Stellar War. Challenger's status as a noted leader allows him to temporarily conscript other willing sentients to his faction.

I blinked as I tried to process all of that information, and failed. Still had no clue what this Stellar War was, didn't care for the name, frankly, and then I decided that the more important thing was that someone was actually offering me a uniform.

More importantly, someone was offering me a shirt and pants that didn't itch and might very well have pockets I could use. They were apparently going to offer me some kind of aid for every act of murder—no, that's unfair right now. It was self-defense. Let's call it self-defense. Aggravated self-defense, and with a deadly weapon, but still self-defense. That's my story and I'm sticking to it. Anyway, they were going to meet my basic needs for every count of aggravated self-defense with a deadly weapon that I provided them with.

Screw it. I'd take it right now. My suspicion was trumped by my need for pockets to carry more gear, and so that I could actually own a set of non-scratchy clothing.

Because I couldn't exactly go to a retail store anymore.

More twirly, stupid hand motions. Then I felt my already threadbare rags rot off, and something else wrapped around me. I really hadn't pictured anything but something practical, comfortable, and reasonably durable. And with a lot of pockets.

That was just about all I got. And I had no complaints.

Comfortable, fitting underclothes appeared over all the necessary areas. Then some weird, snug-fitting, medieval version of military fatigues and boots covered the rest of me. On one leathery bicep sleeve was a single stripe that probably signified my rank as a private. On the other sleeve was some sort of coat-of-arms-ish picture of two dueling dragons. It felt comfortable enough to move easily in, and durable enough to not shred apart at the first sign of trouble. I also got the impression that I could wear other armor over it. Most importantly, there were pockets all over the thing. Probably more than any medieval tailor ever thought was practical.

My skin hummed for a moment, then I felt the magic on me recognize my new clothes and adjust to them. I knew I didn't have much time but I went around grabbing everything I could. I figured the other prisoners would need any clothing and medicine I could find at the very least. And I grabbed all the weapons, since it wouldn't hurt to have some armed bodies behind me that were actually on my side. Not that any of them were as good as my new spear, let alone my silvery short sword.

I grabbed the pipe and pouch of tobacco too, because why not.

I needed to move fast, but I went ahead and checked the piles of boxes around me. I found what looked like wrapped packets of bread and jerky, a bow and a quiver of arrows—*good quality*, something said in my mind—and packets of herbs that Breena had taught me could be used to treat the more common diseases and injuries.

The last box had a satchel with old books and scrolls in it. The satchel was a good sign because I needed more carrying space. But I'd have to take the books and scrolls out of it, and I had just played too many games to be stupid enough to leave what could easily be a whole bunch of magic behind. Even if it turned out I couldn't use it, Rhodes' people would probably find a way.

Provided that the rest of them were smarter than the bunch I was fighting here.

Carrying space, the back of my mind said. *Container...*

My handle.

My new uniform had come with a sheath, so there was no reason to store my short sword in the handle I was carrying around.

I tried holding out the handle, and when I waved it over the books, the entire satchel disappeared. I grunted, and the hand-grip felt heavier for just a moment. I got the feeling that its capacity was limited, and that it couldn't hold much more weight than what I could carry on my own. I didn't complain though, because that still meant it had doubled what I could lug around. I went back and put everything fragile or heavy in my new magic hand-grip of holding, hoping that nothing broke when it landed in the extra-dimensional pocket. I even put the second spear I found, but I strapped the guy's leather armor over my frame before I finally headed out.

I just hoped I wasn't taking too long.

The black-oil torches fluttered on the wall as I walked past. They seemed to have gotten dimmer after I blew up the portal. I still hadn't seen anyone come out. I figured they didn't hear the earlier battle. Or they had finally smartened up and had picked a rally point to ambush me at.

"Come on, Rick! How long could it take to cut off a little retard's head?"

Nope. Still working with room-temperature IQs. That was fine. Murphy's Law could have the day off if it wanted, and I wouldn't even dock its pay.

I didn't answer the voice, but I walked close to the corner and held my spear. I listened for the footsteps to get close. The man kept calling for his friend, and I had to fight to stay focused. This was the one that said he was going to go torture Val and Sam and Kayla, so I had special plans for him. I just had to make sure those plans didn't cost me anything important.

Val's tormentor kept calling out and swearing until he walked around the corner. I let him make eye contact with me for half of a second before I stabbed my spear above his waist and just below his belly. He was still surprised, and since the vital guard partially depends on awareness, I was able to overcome its ability to protect his spine. I felt it crack, taking away his legs for now, and twisting it to try and keep it in place. He dropped the weapon he was holding, and my eyes narrowed in anger as I saw what it was. It was a medieval warhammer, although the head was blunt, instead of spiked like most of the real ones were. It still had the billed hook on the other end, though. But I quit paying attention to the dropped weapon, because he was about to scream in pain.

I leaped over my weapon and slammed a shale-covered fist into his mouth. It wasn't a perfect idea, but it cut off his scream just enough to be effective. I hit him a few more times, probably a lot more than an anger management counselor would be comfortable recommending, and then I grabbed him by the throat and squeezed enough to keep him from yelling out.

"Be quiet," I said, slowly, clearly, and (probably) calmly. People would debate that last one, but the important thing was that he had gone quiet, and stared at me with wide, shocked eyes.

"I'm going to let go enough for you to talk in a minute. There are some questions you really need to answer as best as you can. You're not going to lie or evade them, and you're not going to call out for help. You're not going to do any of that, because I remember every time you and the others murdered me. Right now, I have the time, knowledge, and inclination to give one of those deaths back. I remember which ones hurt and broke me the most, and if you aggravate me, I'm going to do at least one of them to you, assuming I don't try to combine the worst two. Nod if you understand me."

I shouldn't have been able to intimidate him. He was at least my height and almost half-again my weight. Given his background, he had probably seen all kinds of horrible torture and murder, and probably had a hand in the worst examples.

But he nodded anyway.

Maybe it was because of the spear in his spine. Maybe I had hit him harder than I thought earlier. Maybe it was the wind and earth and lightning magic crackling quietly around me. Maybe something in my eyes said I was the honest type, and that he could trust me to keep my promises.

"First question. Are Val and Sam and Kayla still here?"

I had relaxed my grip, but he still chose to nod.

"Are they still alive?"

Another furious nod.

"Are they okay?"

Silence.

"Let me clarify," I growled. "You should assume I already know very bad things happened to all of them. You should also assume that I'm very, very angry about it, and that the fact that those bad things were done to them just to help disguise my father's murder makes me that much angrier. It's too late to fix either of those things. Actually, I take it back. There's one thing that might help a tiny bit."

With my free hand, I pulled out the handle again.

Use this, the voice that had guided my lightning said. *It will bear witness.*

"Record," I said aloud. "This is a voluntary confession from... what was your name again?"

"Steve," the man under me croaked. "Just Steve."

"Okay, first names are fine for now. And this is a voluntary confession, right, Steve?" I asked levelly.

"Yes! Yes! Completely voluntary!" the man said desperately. "Not, not coerced at all!"

"That's wonderful, Steve. Thank you so much for coming forward. Now I wanted to ask you some questions about the events surrounding John Malcolm's death. You have time for that, right, Steve?"

"Yes, absolutely! Happy to help!"

Sheesh, he's agreeable, I thought. *Am I really that scary right now?*

I didn't think I was. But then again, I had died dozens of times, and these days I was hearing voices and having all kinds of internal conversations with myself.

I was going to have to find a way to fix me. Later, though. Not right now.

"Thank you so much. Alright, Steve, what can you tell me about the letter John Malcolm allegedly wrote concerning the three girls named Valerie Nguyen, Samantha Banks, and Kayla Green?"

"He didn't write it," 'Steve' whispered.

"I'm sorry, Steve, I'm not sure I caught that. Could you repeat your last response in a louder tone?"

"He didn't write it!" the man gasped. "He didn't write it! They staged the whole thing!"

"Staged?" I asked, breaking character for a moment. "Who staged it?"

"I can't say. They'll kill me." Seeing the look in my eyes, he added quickly, "And no one would believe me even if I said their name. I promise!"

"Don't worry, Steve. Your identity is safe right now," I replied slowly. "But maybe you could find a few names to share? Was there more than one person involved?"

"Yes! Yes! Um... Pastor Barnes! We got the girls from Pastor Ronald Barnes!"

"A pastor gave you children? That you abused?" I tried to keep the growl out of my voice. It didn't look like I was successful.

"He's not a real preacher. And I didn't abuse them!" the man said desperately.

"Are you sure?" I asked. "We talked about this earlier, Steve. How important the truth was?"

"I just swung the hammer! I didn't touch them! I didn't touch them!"

"Explain, Steve. What does 'swinging the hammer' mean?"

"We had to scare them into confessing," the man was whispering again, but he was still loud enough to be heard. "It was my job. I had to do it. I just swung the hammer near them so that they'd say what we wanted them to. That's all I did. I wasn't really going to hit them."

"Of course you weren't," I said, staring at him with dead eyes. "Were they really abused though, Steve? Did someone sexually abuse those little girls?"

"It wasn't going to be me," the man begged. "I swear!"

He was desperately meeting my eyes, which convinced me he was telling the truth.

"That's not what I'm asking, Steve," I replied carefully. "And you don't need to act so afraid. This is a voluntary interview, right, Steve?"

"Yes! Yes, absolutely!"

"Alright, Steve. Let's go back to trying to help those little girls. Did John Malcolm ever have inappropriate contact with them?"

"No," the man sucked in a breath. "But we figured people would think that, because he and his wife were with them all the time. We heard they were going to try and adopt them."

That part was true. Mom and Dad had talked about getting those girls out of foster care and being a family for them. But Dad's death and the surrounding scandal had ruined that, so the girls stayed in foster care.

That fact was one more rock atop my mountain of rage.

"Another guy is supposed to be training them," 'Steve' continued. "He said they... they could find a buyer for them. Especially now that we brought them here. The buyer wouldn't need to careful with them if they're just projections."

"Who?" I asked in a flat, dead voice.

"I never got his name. But they said he was one of Val's foster parents. He's about five-ten, brown hair and glasses. He doesn't wear them here. He has blue eyes. That's all I know."

"Is there anything else you're willing to share, Steve?" I asked.

"That's all," he begged.

I decided that was all the time I had for now.

"End recording," I said, feeling in my mind that my hand-grip turned off.

"Now tell me why you were so agreeable. Because I'm not stupid enough to believe that a hardened criminal like you is afraid of every high-school student he runs into."

"My legs," the man gasped. "You broke my legs just like that. I can't even feel them."

"And?" I asked, prompting him to continue. "If you can't feel them, they don't hurt. I know how that works. Next reason. The real one this time. Why did you go along with those questions even though we both know I'm going to kill you anyway?"

"I heard you die," the man said, after a moment. "I've heard and seen others die. Yours was the worst. The top ten worst. Every single one of them was one of yours."

"And?"

"And the victims know our jobs even better than we do," the man said bitterly. There was defeat in his eyes. "You're the only ones that can really pay us back. And you know exactly how to do it the best."

"That's right," I said, reaching for his hammer.

"Wait!" he said. "Not that!"

"Why?" I asked, not even looking back at him as I picked it up.

"I can tell you more!"

"Probably not," I said indifferently. "I'm running out of time anyway."

"They moved the girls!" he said hurriedly. "They moved the girls!"

I held the hammer in front of his face.

"Where?"

"To where we keep the locals! They weren't cooperating!"

"What do you mean?" I asked carefully. "I thought Rick was supposed to give you my head to show them?"

"I was just kidding—no!"

I had raised the hammer as if to strike him.

"Okay! Okay! They still weren't listening! They had brought in a fourth one today and the other girls won't let us near her!"

"What?" I asked. The deadness was crawling back into my eyes.

"I didn't know about it until now. She's a little Mexican girl! Barnes wanted her to say you touched her!"

"Me?" I spat. "Why? I wasn't even going to leave a body when I died."

"Barnes was still mad at you from church. And he was mad at the little girl for giving him lip in front of everyone."

"Gabby," I realized, and something deep in me shook. "No. She's supposed to be with her grandmother. Or her aunt."

"They make her say that. She doesn't have any family there. But we can't just admit she's an orphan, because Barnes got rid of all those programs at his church."

I felt like I was sliding down a dark hole where everything I loved stayed on the top of the pit. I used my rage to distract me from that feeling, and I raised the hammer above the torturer's head.

"We haven't hurt her yet! I swear! We haven't hurt any of them! But if you don't hurry, someone will! They were gonna kill a native in front of them to break her! And to punish the other girls for rebelling!"

"Which room?" I asked, though I figured I probably knew.

"Just one hallway over! On the left."

That was pretty much what I expected.

"Okay," I said. "What were you hoping for in return?"

"Just a clean death," the man begged.

"No," I replied.

He screamed as I swung the hammer down. He flinched when it landed next to his head. Then he screamed again when I slammed the weapon just above his skull. I rapidly swung the hammer down as many times as I had seen him do so with Val, and then I stopped.

"If I ever even think about you again, next time I won't miss," I promised quietly. "I'll just crack little pieces of your skull here and there, until one finally pierces into your brain and slowly kills you. Just like they did with me that time. You'll die knowing you're forgetting things here and there—somebody's name, your favorite television show, maybe how to walk to or to go to the bathroom by yourself. And when, or if, you resurrect, you'll do so with the fear that maybe you didn't get everything back, because no one really knows what they don't remember anymore, until they find they need to, and can't."

Then, before he could reply, I jammed a finger against his chest. Since his vital guard was still expending itself to try and repair his broken spine, the finger bolt I fired went directly into his heart. He shuddered for a moment, then went still. My mind-screen beeped with another message about my kill count and how some council somewhere was watching while eating popcorn or some crap. I'd ask Stell or Breena later, when I could. But the number of people I needed to save was piling up, and I needed to move fast.

I headed to my new destination. My magic was still holding up, and I still felt an earthy covering all over my skin and wind pushing my legs as I walked. It was as if all three Ideals of my magic were all working in tandem to help every part of me, unlike before, where one spell only did one or two things.

I began to hear muffled voices around the corner. The laughs of harsh men. The begging of desperate women. The crying of children. Then I heard another guard call out.

"Hey, Ice! What's taking so long?"

Ice? I thought. *What kind of dumb name was...whatever. He should have just stuck with Steve.*

"Help!" I called out, trying to disguise my voice. "Shit! Ow! It hurts! Help!"

Everything went silent for a moment. Then I heard an older voice, one that sounded familiar, speak.

"Go see what the dumbass has done now."

I ran back behind a corner as quietly as I could. I heard two voices complain loudly as they called out Ice's, or Steve's, name. With one hand, I held my spear in reverse grip; with the other, I cocked Steve's hammer back for a swing. I held my breath as they came around, and I had stood far away enough from the corner that they didn't see me at first. They turned their heads the wrong way, looking to where Steve was supposed to have come from. I acted.

I slammed my spear into the left one's center mass, aiming roughly where Breena had taught me to aim in fighting other humanoids. I felt my spear pierce before most of the enemy's vital guard could engage and the enemy went down wheezing—not dead, but not sounding the alarm either. I think I got his lung.

The other one was wearing some kind of leathery chest armor, so I swung my hammer into the back of his head before he could finish turning around. There was a meaty *thwack,* but his vital guard must have engaged in time because I didn't hear the crunching sound that would have signified his death. I slammed my hammer into his head again, and this time I punched through as he began to turn to me. He went down screaming. I knelt to follow him, swinging again and again until I heard the sound I was searching for and he went completely limp.

The other one's vital guard was still futilely trying to repair his lung, so I flicked my hammer over to the spiked end and slammed it into his temple. It killed him almost instantly, and I reflected that I probably should have done that on the first swing to the other man.

Because he had finally managed to sound the alarm.

"What's going on?" a new voice shouted. When he didn't get an answer, he continued. "You and you, with me. The rest, guard the door and watch the prisoners."

Were they not in chains and behind bars? I wondered. *Why leave anyone to watch them at all?*

I saw the door at the middle of the hallway open, and three more men came out. Two of them were wearing the standard armorless uniforms I had seen, with knives and clubs, but the middle one was wearing a chainmail shirt, the heaviest armor I had seen so far, and was holding a one-handed longsword.

"Morning," I said casually, yanking my spear out of the left corpse. "Anyone know where the coffee room is?"

"Oh my God," the one on the right said. Whether that was directed to me or to the sight of his two dead friends, I couldn't tell.

"I thought he couldn't move," the one on the left said. "What's he doing outside of his cell?"

"Coffee room," I repeated. "I'm out because I got hungry, and wanted a bagel and some caffeine. Or maybe there's a cafeteria you guys could let me use?"

I stuffed the warhammer into a back pocket on my belt. I kept the hand back there and started working gestures for my next spell.

"Don't just gawk like idiots!" the man in the middle said. "Alert!" He then shouted, "Alert! Portal room! We're under attack!"

"By who?" I asked, still crafting a spell one-handed as quietly as I could. "Are we having an alien invasion? Or is this more like one of those zombie apocalypse movies?"

The one on the right still had his mouth open. In fairness, he was probably trying to shake off his surprise, but the more I talked, the further his jaw fell. The middle guy, who seemed like he was in charge of security, slapped him on the back of the head.

"I said quit gawking! Charge him and take him out! Make for the portal room if you can!"

They rushed at me from down the hall, not giving me any more time to talk.

That was fine. I had just finished my spell anyway.

Muddy Earth.

Next to my signature spells, this was probably the one I had the most practice with. The muddy patch of ground formed just as the three men charged into it. The leader almost recognized it in time and began to backpedal out of it, but the other two stumbled to their knees as they slipped. More swearing commenced as they tried to get back to their feet. The pair did a better job of it than all of the monsters I had fought previously, but the result was that they got their heads up just in time to take my *Friction Slash*. By now the spell created a four-foot disc of sharp spinning air, and they both screamed as the attack took big chunks out of them. But their vital guards had engaged and prevented my spell from killing them outright. Sighing at the waste of another spell, I opened both hands just enough to release all ten charges of my finger-bolt spell. Five blazing bolts burned into each skull. They jerked and spasmed for a second before falling limply into the mud.

Their leader swore again.

"Alert to portal room!" he shouted down the hall. "He's got his magic back! And I need more help out here!"

I heard a grunt of acknowledgment, and then shouts, screams, and crashes. I couldn't tell whether that was a good sign or bad. Probably both. But my opponent swore again and backed further away from the mud pit. Then he took a running leap over it, landing on the other side easily and charging me with the point of the sword. I had time to fire off another *Friction Slash,* but to my surprise, he dove under it, rolled back to his feet, and stabbed out at me.

He twisted his blade to catch my spear thrust. I twirled my weapon free, but wasn't able to get more than a glancing blow on his mail-covered arm. Then he knocked my spear almost completely out of my hands and grabbed for me.

I grabbed his arm and found that he was the strongest opponent I had faced so far. For whatever reason he had integrated his projected body into Avalon far more efficiently than any of the other guards. He was probably a few points stronger than me, I reflected, or he would have been without my active Earth Magic.

But then the magic in my new *Battleform* surged, adding air gusts to my movements, and I was able to throw off his grasping hand. His eyes widened in shock, but he quickly leaped back just far enough to swing his longsword at my head. I twisted enough for it to graze my shoulder instead, and then my short sword cleared my belt and I charged forward to stab him with it. He kicked me back a few feet, wincing at how painfully sturdy my enhanced body was.

"How did you get your strength back?" he asked calmly, bringing his sword up to guard. "How did you regain your magic? Why are you still sane?"

"Practice, never really lost it, and I'm probably not anymore," I growled, answering his questions one by one. I feinted a stab, but he didn't take it. Now he was cocking his blade in a way better suited for hallway fighting, making short thrusts that kept me back without making large movements on his part.

"Alert!" he shouted again. "Portal room! Answer me, dammit! The Challenger's escaped!"

"Portal room, answer us!" I shouted with him. "The coffee room's out of bagels!"

"What?" He lost focus for a half-second as he processed what I said.

I charged him again, and when he tried to force me away with his weapon, I parried with one of the looted combat knives I had just drawn. He swore and kicked at me again. My short sword tore into his unarmored leg, and this time, a jolt left my weapon and traveled into his leg. The shock stunned him for another half-second, and I used it to close further in, ripping my blade out of his leg and crossing both weapons across his neck. I shrugged off another grapple from his still-twitching free hand and slashed his jugular with both of my weapons.

He gurgled at me, but still pulled his outstretched weapon close and went for a slash on my back. The angle was wrong, so he didn't manage more than a shallow cut into my armored, spell-worked back. My own attack angles were still fine, so I stabbed at his throat with my short sword and at his healthy leg with my combat dagger. This time, electrical current traveled down both weapons, and he finally went down.

My shoulder and back hurt, but I had still come out far better than he had, and I could feel my vital guard working to repair me. I sheathed the combat dagger and picked up his longsword, watching his corpse fade out.

A sergeant-ranked officer has been lost to Stellar War.

Challenger Wes Malcolm has gained more Infamy. New rank has been recognized as lance corporal and he may now lead a squad of four to conduct further Stellar War.

Oh really? I thought sarcastically. *I needed someone else's permission to do that? Well, thank God I waited to get help until just now! I can't wait until I'm allowed to accept surrenders, or maybe set camp for the night on my own!*

Pre-recorded Message:

Wes, don't snap at your mind-screen so much. It won't change anything, and it could distract you during a Challenge. Just talk to one of us about it afterwards.

-Stell

I sighed and took my lesson. Then I chose to believe that if I was still getting these messages, then she must be okay.

Back to work, I told myself. *Refresh your spells, get the right weapons out, and finish this.*

I marched toward the door, hearing signs of a fight as I grew close. I took a moment to listen carefully, hating the delay, but knowing charging in without knowing anything could get the girls killed just as easily. As soon I could understand the voices, I began to move.

"Just kill them before they get the others free!" the first one said.

I ran faster.

"Shit! Black Gandalf's loose too—" the second voice cut off with a scream and some strange crackling noises.

"I told you that was not my name," the last voice said.

At that point, I had reached the open door.

I saw the girls immediately as I walked in. They were to my left, and my vision reddened a little when I saw the first three huddled in front of Little Gabby. Two men looked like they had been trying to get to them, but they were struggling with a short, stout, hairy man in front of them, that kept throwing one of them off every time they grappled him together. His unkempt beard looked like bloody-brown steel wool, and I saw snapped manacles covering his wrists.

Further down the left wall was a huddled mass of people that had a similar guardian standing in front of them. This man was also short, with dirty unkempt hair hanging over his face. He was much thinner than the man protecting the four girls, but he was armed with a shiv he must have found somewhere, and he would swing it out whenever one of the guards came close. His weapon had the shorter reach, but he still somehow kept them all at bay.

The sight closest to me, however, was the one that took my breath away.

Two men were facing each other. One of them, the one farthest from me was a tall black man whose stern gaze initially took my attention away from his tattered robes and a shaved head. His unwavering visage contrasted with his constantly moving arms, creating symbols around himself out of thin air. Whatever magic he was using was a type Breena hadn't shown me yet.

Facing him was a figure in a black hooded robe that covered everything but his face and hands. Unlike the black man in front of him, he was constantly chanting. Blood-red fire formed around one of his hands, and he somehow managed to laugh maniacally from time to time without disrupting his chant.

"Impressive, wanderer," the robed man intoned, and I recognized the voice. Not Barnes, but another voice from church.

Mr. Shepherd.

One of the foster parents.

"Impressive that your magic works at all without your tools," the robed man cackled in an odd pitch. "I was expecting my little girls to have seen you die by now."

A litany of raging expletives swept over my mind as I looked at yet another man who had betrayed my trust and harmed people I cared about.

"Let these people go," the ebon man spoke as his hands worked. A blue shield manifested in front of his left hand's symbols, washing away a burst of fire from the dark robed man. As the man's right hand flashed about, blue bolts shot toward the foster parent-turned-cultist, which he caught with the ball of fire in his hand.

"Let them go? Let them go?" my robed neighbor cackled again. "Did we not make it clear what happens to men who help little girls? Did you not see the other one die, over and over? Do you think you will fare better? Do you think he was still trying to save anyone in the end?"

"Buddy Wes! Buddy Wes!" Little Gabby called out excitedly, pointing out to me from behind the other girls. "Hi Buddy Wes!"

"Hi, Gabby," I said. "Hi, Val. Hi, Kayla. Hi, Sam... Hi, Mr. Shepherd. How it's going with the whole framing my dad and abusing girls and joining a weird demonic cult?"

Deep inside my head, I was murdering him, over and over again, with my bare hands and teeth. But I couldn't lash out just now. Not yet.

Mr. Shepherd was less than pleased to see me.

"How?" he asked shrilly. "*How?* You're dead! You're supposed to be dead!"

"Yeah, I've been getting that a lot today," I replied calmly, restraining my anger like it was a dog that knew it would get a treat if it behaved. "That and the old 'you're supposed to be crippled' or 'you're supposed to be broken.' Some things just don't keep, Mr. Shepherd."

I looked back over to the girls that had been through hell just so that someone else had a cover for murdering Dad.

"These men are bad, Buddy Wes!" Little Gabby shouted again. "And... and they want to do weird things!"

"I know Gabby, I've heard about that," I said softly. "I'm sorry I wasn't here sooner. I need you girls to all close your eyes so that I can make the bad men go away."

"Okay, Buddy Wes."

Little Gabby reached for the other three girls and pulled at them, closing her eyes as she did so.

"You're going to regret this, cripple-head!" Mr. Shepherd shouted. "They're going to kill you for good when they come back through the portal!"

"He's right," the ebon man said through gritted teeth. "You need to get these people out of here while we still have time."

"One sec," I said, reaching into my weapons belt and turning to the dwarf-like man defending my girls. Heck, he probably *was* a dwarf, but I didn't know how he'd react to being called that.

A third man had come over to try and help hold him down, and between the three of them, they finally got him on his back. The third man was actually armed and stabbing at him with a combat dagger. The stocky man grunted but maintained his hold on the other two men, usually getting them in the way of the third man's swings, and finally knocking the third man away by throwing the second man into him. For a long moment, he had his second hand free. Long enough for me to slide the warhammer I had across the floor and close to his hand. I saw him reach out and grab it and then swing the spiked end into his fellow grappler's head.

Feeling pretty confident about his chances, I turned to look at the long-haired man holding back three other men, each a foot taller than him and with longer weapons. This seemed to be a much closer fight, because the long-haired man's foes were all armed, and because he had more people behind him to protect.

He was also harder to help, because he was much further away from me and I didn't have an easy way of getting him a real weapon.

But I had already refreshed my finger-bolt spell, so I put all ten bolts into the head of the man on his left. The sizzle and pop sounds told me his vital guard was overcome. Then I reached into my belt and began to awkwardly chuck long combat daggers at the other two. They dodged them easily, and curiously, because they both knew those knives weren't balanced for throwing. That was the point, because eventually a knife landed near the shiv-wielding prisoner and he finally had a decent weapon to fight with. In fact, he was agile enough that he actually managed to get a hold of two. Less than half a minute later, another one of his enemies was limp and bleeding on the ground. A quick glance to the left told me my new hammer-wielding friend had his last opponent pinned under him and was about to be on his third kill.

Now that they were finally armed, the ease these two men had at tearing through their foes made me wonder how they had become prisoners in the first place.

I turned to face the last group, my demonic neighbor facing off against the dark-skinned man that didn't look to be much older than me. Shepherd was growling in frustration, and the desperate look in his eyes told me he had also seen his men cut through like cream cheese.

"They're going to kill them all," he growled at us. "As soon as the reinforcements come in, I'm going to tell them to kill every person you just tried to save, cripple-head."

This time his speech had interrupted his chanting, and he stumbled backward under a blast of blue energy from the other magic-user.

"Why do you call him cripple-head?" the black man said calmly as he kept scrawling symbols through the air. There was some sweat on his face, but otherwise he seemed to be holding his own in this duel perfectly.

I sent another look to make sure the four girls were okay. Both of the former prisoners had pinned down their remaining foes and were striking their way through the last of their vital guards.

"A better question would be to ask why the reinforcements he keeps bragging about haven't shown up from the portal room," I said calmly. "Or, where is he supposed get help from if the portal is already destroyed?"

"The portal can't be destroyed!" Shepherd said as he flung another blast of fire at the other mage, who grunted as he created another blue shield out of thin air to take the blast. "Stop bluffing!"

"Sound like you put all of your eggs in that one basket," I noted. "That's a relief." I looked back over at the mage whose name I didn't know. "You guys aren't having some kind of private duel, are you? Because I'd really like to be lethal without being rude here."

"Be my guest," the man said with gritted teeth. I began working my next spell.

"Don't even think about it, cripple-head," Shepherd spat as he created another blast of dirty flame. "I don't care how many of our guards you've killed. You're not a match for my magic and after I kill this little—"

Spark Bolt.

Excluding the spell I cast at Cavus and the portal, my single-bolt lightning spell was my most powerful attack. I hadn't had much of a chance to use it because the casting time was so long, so I hadn't really seen it in action until now. The result was immensely satisfying.

Blood-red force shields immediately appeared and just as immediately winked out under the force of my spell as it struck the cultist. Shepherd flew through the air and landed against the wall in a groaning, smoking heap. He tried to get up, jerked oddly, and then collapsed back onto the floor. The other wizard grunted in wide-eyed surprise, then quickly began writing new symbols into the air. Glowing blue bands began to wrap around the Malus cultist.

My mind-screen beeped at me with more murder-messages. I ignored them for now.

"Everyone okay?" I called out. "Gabby? Val? Other folks?"

I got a lot of excited nods, and Gabby piped up cheerfully:

"I told you he'd come to save us!"

Then I turned to face the three possibly friendly, but definitely dangerous, men.

Reading their wary glances, I realized then and there that the enemy of my enemy is not necessarily my friend after my enemy dies.

"I'm Wes," I said, offering my name.

"Eadric," the short man with the warhammer said.

"Weylin Fellas," the lean, dual-wielding man said, and I finally noticed his slanted ears. I vaguely recognized his race from Breena, and realized he was a type of elf—and yes, they called themselves elves. They're probably owed royalty fees for the use of the name.

"Karim, of the Bright Towers," the dark man said with a nod. "You seem to be from Earth like these other men," Karim said carefully. "May we know your motives for aiding us?"

"Texan," I corrected. "I'm from Texas. I was a prisoner too. And I want to get everyone out."

"Don't listen to him!" Shepherd croaked in a voice full of pain and hate. "He's a pervert and a cripple-head! He'll betray you!"

Karim and I both looked at him for a moment, then resumed our conversation.

"The portal room's destroyed," I continued. "There were three guards there that are down. There were two more in the halls, and three more that left this room that I took care of. Then there is this clown and the six others we all slew in here. Do you know if there are any more?"

The dark-skinned wizard shook his head.

"There have been fewer and fewer people here recently, but we haven't left our cells until today. I would be surprised if there were any more, though."

Eadric was staring at me, working out something in his mind.

"You're him, aren't you?"

"Him who?" I asked.

"You're right," Weylin said. "We'd have to hear him scream to be sure, but he's the only Earth human down here with red hair."

"That's a rather roundabout way of confirming if I'm the guy they've been killing over and over," I said dryly.

"He's broken!" Shepherd snarled from the floor. "You should be broken! Freak!"

I turned down and looked at him.

"You're currently bound on the floor," I began. "Unable to move. Anyone who was going to help you would have shown up by now, with all the shouting, fighting and magic being thrown around. At least one of us, chiefly me, is already angry enough to tear you into tiny pieces, and I'm not being figurative at all when I say that. Close your eyes, take a deep breath, and ask yourself: am I really getting something out of what I'm doing right now?"

He bared his teeth at me again.

"It's the magic," Karim said, his dark eyes examining the cultist as he thrashed against his magic. "Their magic changes them. The stronger they get, the more hateful they become. Some handle it worse than others."

"You don't know anything!" the hooded man said as he thrashed. "You wouldn't have become our prisoner if you did!"

"Huh," I said, looking down at his enchanted restraints. "Irony." I looked back up at the three men. "I'm going to go on a limb and trust you guys because you were protecting people I was trying to save. If you're willing to do the same thing, then we can work together to get everyone out of here. Then we can talk about long-term plans."

Karim shook his head.

"There is no way back home. These people took us using some kind of magic craft that lets them jump between worlds."

"You mean portals?" I asked, confused. We had just finished talking about their portal room. "Are those really that rare?"

"They were far more common fifty years or so ago," Karim continued, giving me a look that said he found my ignorance suspicious. "Back when the Last Challenger was alive."

"Last Challenger?" I asked. "What do you mean 'Last Challenger'? And what do you mean fifty years?"

"He wouldn't know," Eadric said calmly. "He's from Earth, Karim. This is probably all new to him."

"Up until fifty years ago," Weylin began. "It was said that heroes called Challengers once came from the world of mists, Avalon, to aid our worlds in times of trouble. Calamities would befall, the Challengers would appear, and the disaster would be averted in a way that let us all grow in many ways. But in this last century, dark clouds formed in the minds of every mighty dreamer. Signs of famine, plague, storm, strife, and monsters. Across every land, and all at the same time. The Tumults were so severe, and so numerous, that no man or woman of any race would be able to rally to the aid of another. It was also said that these disasters would fall far sooner than the earlier tribulations, and so the Lady of the Mists could not use the ancient laws to call forth a Challenger."

His voice had changed from explanation to recitation, like a storyteller speaking to children. He continued speaking, and it was almost as if he couldn't help it.

"The Lady of the Mists knew these disasters would be the end of us all, and in her grief, she wept great tears, tears made all the greater by knowing no one else would hear or see them, on faraway Avalon. But someone did.

"A young man, battle-bred from the brokenness of Earth and chief among Challengers. It was said that he heard her tears fall all the way from Earth. And because his heart was so great, and so puissant, he came out of the silent planet under his own power, to comfort her and to meet her need for a hero. It was said that she began to train him in the weapons and ways of our lands, but that she could not finish, for our worlds had already began to cry out with need. Yet whenever he strode forth, he still rescued, because he was familiar with victory, though not yet with sword and spell. He made sea-storms halt at the edge of his feet, and turned ravenous monsters into bounties for those who starved. Even the then-rare Horde was powerless to keep him from pulling captives out of their Pits, a feat that had never been done before nor after. His legend was already growing long before his appointed time, for the dark ones found no monster strong enough to make him flee, no task too complex for his mind to mend, no person too small for his mighty heart to ignore. Where there was fear, he was fearless, where there were troubles, he was wise, and where there was need, he was compassionate. Therefore, he was the first of his kind to gain songs and renown before his appointed Trials and Challenges.

"But it is said that such songs were too loud, and too lofty, and that it undid him in the end. The crooked men he had battled on Earth heard his praise, and became wroth. They hunted him in his sleep, and with the dark magic that lurked on that silent world, they bound him and followed him here. They used the curses of demons long damned and summoned one of the old, hungry things that crawl between the stars in the night sky. The Lady of the Mists tried to rescue her hero, but the Old Hungry Thing overcame her magic, and slew her champion, forcing her to flee across the worlds. It is said that she travels from star to star in the night, ever moving, ever hiding from the Old Hungry Thing that would claim her.

"Her hero rose again from death, as Earth's champions are known to do, but the craven ones that followed him here finally bound him for good, using the rarest of curses that have kept Earth silent since ancient times. Once bound, they stole his inheritance and used it to travel to our lands, becoming the first Earth-men to come here for conquest instead of salvation. The magic the strongest of them wielded was enough to battle, and sometimes even throw down, our mightiest of Icons. Kingdoms fell, tribes were enslaved, and the map of every civilized land shrank by portions all too great. And as they went, they proclaimed the last Challenger was dead for good, and that they had spent fifty years ensuring his end. They further proclaimed that Earth was done winning our battles for free and would now take what it was due. Since then, no Earth-man, and no Earth-woman, has gone any place without dyeing the land red with blood and black with fire."

I half-heard all of that. It was too much to absorb without thinking about, so I tried to replay the man's words in my head.

"I must be really tired, because for a minute it almost sounded like you were singing there. And it sounded like you were immortalizing the poor guy every time he gave a tissue when someone sneezed."

The long-haired man's face hardened, but after moment he merely shrugged.

"You are from Earth, and have helped us, so I will excuse you. But know that outside of your planet, those who gain victory for the sake of others' lives are held in the highest of regard. Think of such heroes the way that your own people celebrate those with great wealth, or that run and jump quickly, or that entertain large crowds."

"What's even more ironic," Karim interjected as he spoke to me, "is that the last Challenger was humble enough to share your opinion of him."

"Guys, I'm not humble," I sighed, exasperated. "In fact, whenever I try, I actually suck at it. I remember everything I did and it really was all small-scale. It wasn't even that inconveni—wait," I suddenly said. "You guys keep saying fifty years. We were just talking about that before. There's no way it's been fifty years."

The three didn't answer my question. Instead they were all giving me and each other these weird looks, as if lightbulbs were suddenly sputtering on inside their heads.

"Fifty years?" I demanded, still trying to wrap my head around that part. "How could it have been fifty years?" I turned to look at Shepherd. "Why are they saying fifty years? What have you done? How could you have possibly taken fifty years to kill me all those times? How could Stell be gone for fifty whole years? What have you done with Guineve and Breena and everyone? What have you done? *What have you done?*"

I was still shouting when I stepped forward and lifted Shepherd of the ground. "Tell me how it could have taken fifty years! Tell me!" I slammed him against the wall, and used the wall to punctuate every next word. "What! *(Slam)* You've! *(Slam)* Done!" *Slam!*

His eyes widened and the breath knocked out of him with every impact, but after a moment he laughed. "Young, dumb fool. You really think you can intimidate one of us? With the things we've seen, and the powers we wield?"

"Yes," I said quietly, leaning forward as I spoke. "I do."

"Wait," Karim said slowly, and carefully. "Who did you say you were?"

"He's a failure!" Shepherd said quickly, but he was sweating as he spoke. "Just some dumb, crippled boy! He can't help you!"

The men's eyes continued to widen.

"No," the one named Weylin said. "It's impossible. He's too young."

"It may not be," the dark man in robes muttered. "It is said that time can flow either slower or faster in the land of mists. It could very well have only been a few months for him..."

"He's died, over and over," the short man rumbled. "Before these idiots, there was only one kind of hero who did so. And if he wasn't him, why would they torture him so?"

"You can't scare me," Shepherd spat with a quivering voice. "You couldn't even save your magical fairy-land, Malcolm! You lost years for every month you stayed here, and even more years for every death! It's too late to be a hero for your MILF and your little nerd girlfriend! They're gone!"

The three men hissed at those words, and I could feel them staring at me like they had just realized I had also walked in with two stone tablets. But my eyes were still on the man writhing on the floor.

"What do you mean 'gone?'" I said, still speaking quietly and still holding the other man firmly off the ground. "Tell me where Stell is. Tell me where Guineve is. Tell me where the Ladies of the Mist went. Think very carefully, so that you can answer very completely, and very honestly."

"Hell if I know," Shepherd spat, but his teeth were chattering as he spoke. "The MILF's wherever the hell you've hidden her. The other one's still playing hide and seek with her real boyfriend. You're all lucky he hasn't caught her yet or the whole Expanse would already be ours. Well, you're not going to be lucky. Everyone's really clear about that."

"Bastard idiot," I growled. "Do you know how many catastrophes you've probably guaranteed? Do you realize just how much Stell does for these worlds? How badly they need her? Do you even realize what you've put her through by sending that thing after her? Do you even..."

"Buddy Wes," Little Gabby called out. "Can we open our eyes yet?"

Shit. I had forgotten to be angry about that too.

"Not yet, Gabby, I'm sorry... go ahead and count to three hundred first."

"Counting to three hundred is really hard, buddy Wes."

"You can do it, Gabby," I urged. "You're a really good counter. You used to show me all the time, remember?"

I turned to look at the three other men, who were all looking at me like I was now ten feet tall and glowing gold.

"I need a favor," I said. "Drag any of the bodies that haven't faded yet out of the room. When I come back we can talk about everything."

"Are you him?" Karim asked urgently. "You said your name was Wes. He called you Malcolm. Are you Wes Malcolm, the last Challenger? Tell us the truth, before we agree to anything else."

I sighed.

"Yes, I'm Wes Malcolm. But I have no idea how I can prove that other than my word."

"Think of your Deeds," the dark man insisted. "You are on Avalon. Merely think on your Deeds and they will appear."

I let out another sigh but closed my eyes and did what he said. A moment later the three men quietly sucked in gasps of surprise.

"It is true then," Karim intoned. "We have found the last Challenger, and he is still alive. This act is hereby witnessed in script..."

"Witnessed in song..." Weylin added.

"And witnessed in stone," the dwarf-like man finished.

That whole thing was weird enough for me to pause and give them an inquisitive look. The robed man must have noticed.

"Outside of Earth, there are those who keep records, in different ways, on every corner of the Expanse. We are called the Testifiers. The three of us were charged with finding the old gates between worlds, so that we may learn for certain the fate of Avalon's Challenger." He paused for a moment, looking at the two others with him. "We did not expect to find the Challenger himself. We will discuss this later."

Then, without another word, the three men began grabbing the lingering bodies and dragging them out of the room.

I was curious about what they had just said, but right now I needed to handle other concerns. I looked back at Shepherd. "You hurt those little girls, didn't you? You weren't just in charge. It was you, specifically, wasn't it, Mr. Shepherd?"

My former neighbor bared his teeth at me again, but he didn't answer.

"He did, Mr. Wes!" Gabby spoke up again. "Val and Kayla and Sam! He hit them! And all the people in the other corner! He made a whole bunch of them cry!"

"I thought so. Thank you, Gabby," I said quietly. "I'm sorry I wasn't there to stop it. Just keep your eyes closed for a little longer."

"Do I have to keep counting, Buddy Wes?"

"I really need you to, Gabby. Please do it as a favor for me."

"Okay," she pouted. "But only because you're my friend."

"Thank you, little Gabby." I turned to look at the other men. "I'll be right back."

"With him?" the dark-skinned wizard asked, pointing to the cultist in my hands. "Are you bringing him back?"

"No," I said flatly.

"Good," Karim said with a nod. The dwarf-like man looked at me for a second longer, but then he nodded as well.

"What do you mean?" Shepherd spat. "You can't kill me for good, cripple-head."

Instead of answering, I started dragging him out of the room. He struggled, but not only was he bound, he was weaker than me, so he wasn't able to stop me from just grabbing one of his limbs and pulling him along the floor.

"Where are we going?" the evil idiot demanded. "Let go!"

"Do you know if they've changed out any of the rooms since they've killed me last?" I asked before I left. Karim shook his head.

"We weren't often let out of our cells. But they do not strike me as a very diligent group. I would be surprised if everything wasn't exactly as you remembered it."

"Thanks," I said as I grabbed Shepherd's leg. "Come along, neighbor."

"Ow!" the man said as he bumped his way past the door frame. "You're not going to scare me, Wes. All of us who wield power have seen horrors you can't even imagine!"

I grunted apathetically as I kept dragging him.

"You think I'm scared of fire?" the struggling man said as he scraped along the floor. "You think I'm scared of losing blood, or drowning?"

"Nope," I said, not looking back at him. "Hadn't even bothered to think about it."

"Of course you haven't!" the idiot spat. "The tortures I've seen would break your mind!"

"Good thing I haven't seen them then," I said, keeping the fake calm wrapped around my screaming brain. "Otherwise I'd be broken enough to be dragging a man across the floor right now."

"Exactly! So why don't you just... wait," Shepherd said, as if he was finally paying attention to me.

Idiot.

"Where are you going?" he said. "You passed the fire room!"

"Oh, I know," I replied. "This is the one hallway that I know where everything is."

"And you think you have a better way to kill me?" The idiot spat again. "I'm just going to come back on Earth! Then I'm going to bring every team we have through the portal and finish you off for good!"

"Portal's broken," I said without looking at him. "You're probably going to have to explain that to your boss when you're back on Earth."

"Liar! The portal's indestructible!"

"Sounds like you've got nothing to worry about then. Go ahead and keep talking," I replied casually.

He shut up for all of a blessed minute. Then, when I had turned a certain corner, he started jabbering again.

"Wait," he said. I finally heard him speak without arrogance. "This... this is the wrong hallway! There's nothing down here!"

"Were you always this stupid, Mr. Shepherd?" I asked calmly. "Because I don't remember you being this stupid back on Earth."

"You... you're the stupid one! There's nothing down this hallway!"

"Yes, there is," I said quietly. "This is the one torture room you had to keep separate from the others because it's so dangerous. I remember it, because you guys really liked the reactions I gave when you put me in it."

"No!" Shepherd shouted desperately. "We moved it! We moved it! It's not here anymore!"

I didn't dignify him with a response. He was lying, and he knew I knew it.

"You... you can't do this!" he sputtered. "You can't!"

"Why?" I asked thoughtfully. "Did you get this cause of death trademarked? Are there copyright issues involved? Do I risk getting sued for intellectual property theft?"

"What?" he asked.

"Didn't think so. We're almost there though," I added.

"But you can't do this!" he repeated desperately. "It's... It's not Christian!"

"Christian?" I asked. For a moment I stopped dragging him and actually turned back to look at him. "You, a member of a cult that worships some kind of demonic being who gives you all kinds of unholy magic, a person that has been hiding in my church, helping the other cultists steal and abuse children, is trying to get me, a person you have repeatedly tortured and murdered, a person whose friends and family you have helped target, to be more Christian? Are you trying to be concerned about my immortal soul, Mr. Shepherd? Is that what's happening right now?"

He didn't reply immediately, so I continued answering him.

"Number one," I said, growling a little more than I meant to. "Assume I have developed a crisis of faith alongside of all of the trauma and psychological issues you've helped inflict on me. I am more concerned with getting answers for all the horrible things that were allowed to happen to me and everyone else that I care about."

Grief, the quiet voice said. *I grieve. And weep. And rage.*

I ignored it. I'd start screaming again if I didn't.

"Number two," I continued. "Since we are on the subject of Christianity and the Bible, I've got a fun lesson that you apparently didn't pay attention to back when the old pastor was there. Back when we actually talked about the Bible, instead of all the hatred, fear, and useless political issues that Barnes kept harping about. Did you know that, in the New Testament, arguably the only group of people who Jesus seems to directly threaten are those who target little children?" My brain could remember facts easily now, so I went ahead and called up specific verses. "Matthew 18:6, King James Version: 'But whoso shall offend one of these little ones which believe in me, it were better for him that a millstone'—that's a rock that can weigh over a thousand pounds—'were hanged about his neck, and that he were drowned in the depth of the sea.' There's a similar passage in Mark 9:42," I continued. "Different translations say 'be a stumbling block to' or 'cause them to sin' or even 'bully or take advantage of their trust' but since you both tortured them and forced them to tell lies about my dead dad, you qualify either way."

"You couldn't know the Bible!" Shepherd shouted. "You're too young! It doesn't say that!"

"Believe what you want," I said. "But I'm done arguing with you. And I don't have a millstone, and the room you people drowned me in isn't big enough to count as a sea, so we can't go that route. We're going this route instead."

I kept walking towards the door at the end of the hall, still dragging my burden behind me.

"Y-you can't throw me to the gibber-kin! You can't do that!"

"Yes I can."

"They eat people alive!"

"That's right," I replied. "I remember. It's extremely painful."

"But it's not right! It's an eye for an eye!"

"Not even," I replied. "Because I'm only doing this once, unlike what you people did with me. And don't say you didn't have a hand in it, because I remember you getting excited about your turn to torture me. It doesn't even begin to qualify as retribution. Not after what you all put me through. It's just the closest I can do to justice," I continued. "There's no police here I can turn you over to. There's no judge or jury that can take forever deliberating what should be your fate. There's not even a jail I can keep you in, because you could just send yourself back to Earth as soon as you worked up the courage to commit suicide or use some other magic trick I don't know about. So my only recourse is to kill you in some form, right now, while the portal's down and you can't come back."

"You don't have to use the gibber-kin! You don't have to use them!"

He was screaming at this point.

"No, I don't," I agreed. "But hurting little girls should not be free, should not be easy, should not be painless. So here we are."

We reached the door. And I opened it. The familiar growls and screeches and snarls reached my ears, coming from the pit in the middle of the room. I dragged him in, whirled him through the air once or twice, and then my magic-enhanced strength was enough for me to toss him down into the pit. The magic bindings were still covering him, so all he could do was scream before the monsters were upon him.

It didn't work the way I wanted it to. I had said this wasn't about vengeance, but I still wanted to feel some form of closure, some form of vindication for my own suffering. But instead, when I heard them tear into him, I just felt every bite all over again. The only difference was that he somehow died quicker than I had either time, so I wound up feeling cheated as well.

Then I reminded myself that I had promised to make this about the little girls down in the other halls, and I felt a tiny bit better.

Maybe.

At any rate, he wouldn't get near Kayla and Sam and Val and Gabby again, and maybe the next time he tried to hurt someone, he'd associate the crime with this experience, and it would deter him on some level. Maybe permanently.

I didn't know. This was the best I could come up with, okay? Nobody else was around with a better idea.

Whatever, I finally told myself. I had to get back to the others. I'd figure out what to do with the gibber-kin and the other monsters later.

But as I turned to walk away, I heard a moan. A dirty red mist, the same color as Shepherd's fire, floated out of the pit. It formed the shape of a skull, then wailed, as if in defeat, then finally dissipated.

Challenger Wes Malcolm has slain a lieutenant-ranked enemy in Stellar War.

The Order of Malus has lost their principal stronghold on the world Avalon. The planet's designation has changed to Highly Contested.

Challenger Wes Malcolm has seized a territory from the Order of Malus. The Stellar Council has awarded appropriate merits and resources for his role in the victory.

Great. I was going to get more clothes, basic equipment, and hand-me-downs. Whatever. I'd take them.

Then the ground around me suddenly hummed.

Everything shook very, very slightly, and then I heard a familiar voice boom out.

"Malus taint has diminished sufficiently for primary consciousness to come back online. Avalon is once again operational."

I looked up at the noise.

"Avalon?" I said carefully. "Are you really back?"

"Confirmed," the supercomputer replied. *"Power is restored and emergency protocols are re-engaging. Applying new power toward efforts of contesting and destroying the Order of Malus' local presence."*

"Fantastic," I said. "Finally some good news."

31

FROM DOWNFALL TO RISE

I began walking back down the hall toward the other prisoners.

"Assessing location of Starsown Steward," Avalon's voice sounded from the hallway walls. *"Confirmed Starsown is off-world. Time lapse is sufficient for additional systems to go dormant. New steward is necessary to maintain certain functions."*

"Avalon," I answered. "State the parameters needed for a new steward and identify anyone on Avalon able to meet them."

"Searching..." I waited as the supercomputer went silent. *"No candidates available."*

"What?" I demanded. "Why? Avalon, identify the locations of Lady Guineve of the Mists and Breena of the Fair Folk. Confirm whether they are suitable candidates."

"Confirmed that Lady Guineve of the Mists and Breena of the Fair Folk are alive and located on Avalon. Confirmed that both individuals are suited for their current roles and are unavailable to become a Steward of Avalon. Confirmed that no other candidates are eligible to become Stewards. Searching for alternative measures."

"Avalon," I said patiently, continuing the walk back to the other prisoners. "Explain what will happen if no Steward is appointed."

"If no other alternative measures are discovered, Avalon will cease to be a territory and go into a dormant state. All current measures being taken against the Order of Malus will cease."

"Measures?" I asked. "What measures?"

"Insufficient clearance. Access denied."

I swore again. It was probably a full-on habit by now. Probably long before now, in fact.

"Fine. Keep me posted on all of your efforts to remain functional."

"Command confirmed."

I clamped down on making a harsh and sarcastic response, and focused on the next thing I needed to do. Find the others. Get everyone out of the dungeon. Figure out what the hell to do next.

Hopefully take a nap afterwards, because I was rapidly becoming exhausted in every sense of the word. *No,* I corrected myself. *Find Breena and Guineve. Then maybe take a nap.*

"Search over," the walls boomed next to me. *"Alternative measure found."*

"Fantastic," I replied, coming up to the door to the other prisoners. "Knock yourself out."

"Seeking confirmation that Avalon has permission to activate alternative measures."

"Yes," I said very slowly. "But why would you need confirmation? Stell already lifted all your restrictions a long time ago."

"Confirmation for alternative measure is necessary because protocols demand Avalon respects the impacted individual's free will. Specifically, that of Challenger Wes Malcolm."

"Wait, wait," I said quickly. "You're saying it will directly impact me? How? Go ahead and explain before you do anything."

"Confirmation of permission has already been obtained," Avalon replied. *"Beginning protocol for alternative measures."*

"No, wait!" I demanded. "I didn't know you meant me—"

The air hummed, and mist began to wrap around my feet.

"Confirmed that the following Parameters for Right to Rule exist in Wes Malcolm. Parameter One: Puissance. Sufficient amount detected. Parameter Two: Wisdom. Sufficient amount detected. Standing request that Challenger acquires more. Parameter Three: Compassion: Abundant amount detected. Parameter Four: Item of Authority. Item of Authority detected. Recommend Challenger finishes repairing or constructing said item....

"Parameter Five: Influence. Detecting Challenger Wes Malcolm has sufficient amount of influence with all current inhabitants. Hostile non-sentients disregarded. Order of Malus invaders disregarded.

"Parameter Six: Original Body. Confirmed that the original body of Challenger Wes Malcolm is available for modification. Parameter Seven: Bloodline. Abundant amount detected. Challenger Wes Malcolm is of Earth-born Blood, therefore inheriting his species' natural right of kingship. Secondary Bloodline detected. Bloodline of Primal-class Power confirmed. Foreign Contaminant detected in Bloodline. Further Right to Rule will be gained upon removal of said contaminant. Seven parameters for Right to Rule have been detected. Acknowledging Noble status of Challenger Wes Malcolm.

Awakening dormant Avalonian blood available for further integration. Avalon has detected that Challenger Wes Malcolm has 0.0001% Avalonian DNA, allowing for Avalon to link with him. Challenger's Right to Rule is assisting in activating bloodline, per ruler's responsibility of assimilation."

I quivered all over. Mist tendrils wrapped around my limbs and went in and out of my pores.

"Modifying Challenger to give, share, and receive power from Avalon. Modification complete. Avalon recognizes new Lord Wes Malcolm, first citizen of Avalon. Assigning information about surviving structures to Wes Malcolm. Assigning right to close and open portals to Wes Malcolm. Providing information of all upcoming Trials and Tumults to Wes Malcolm..."

"Wait," I interrupted. "Other than what's been going on here, confirm that the previous Tumults and Trials have or haven't happened yet."

"Negative," Avalon replied. *"No Tumults on other worlds have been failed as of yet. No global Trials or Tumults off Avalon have officially begun. Status of Avalon's current Tumult has been changed from Failed to Overcome, as the Order of Malus has lost direct access to the planet."*

"Wait, wait," I interrupted. "We can fully restrict Rhodes' people from coming back here when they die? Permanently? And failed Tumults can still be salvaged?"

"Confirmed. As of now, Order of Malus has lost the ability to maintain portals on Avalon, due to the destruction of the primary portal and due to Avalon's systems engaging. Avalon can prevent all hostile portals forming on-world for as long it maintains its link with its new Lord.

"Further confirming that Tumults can be overcome after Failed Status. Reasoning: Universal Law. Specific Law: ***Failure is non-permanent. The ability to try again exists wherever life and motivation also exist.***

"Life and motivation have existed in sufficient measure to overcome Avalon's failed Tumult. New Tumult rating: Overcome. Receiving power from Universal

Law. Avalon is returning to pre-apocalyptic state. Habitation ability regained. Avalon's Lord can now modify certain areas to be more suitable for sentient life. Technological ability: regained. Upon certain conditions, Avalon will yield technology previously unavailable to its current Lord. Should the Steward return, more technology will become available, and more opportunities for research will be created.

"Avalon's Lord has been detected as the significant contributor in overcoming Avalon's Tumult. Right to Rule has been increased. New ruler-related powers are forming. A Challenger has been detected as the significant contributor in ending Avalon's Tumult. Challenger is credited with the power due for ending said Tumult and will reap the appropriate benefits. ERROR: Showing both a Challenger and Avalon's Lord as the primary contributor for overcoming Avalon's Tumult. Redefining parameters previously considered impossible.

"Challenger Wes Malcolm has been detected as overcoming mortal Challenge designated Defiant To the Very End. Challenge is designated as Unique, with no previous records of being overcome. As the Challenge is Mortal by nature, results of the victory will be scattered among the cosmos, with focus directed at those the deceased Challenger knew. ERROR: Showing multiple completions of the same Mortal Challenge by the same Mortal individual. Redefining parameters previously considered impossible.

"Avalon's Lord is shown to be a key leader in Stellar War. Avalon's Lord is recognized as acquiring infamy in Stellar War. Avalon's Lord has been recognized as conquering territory in Stellar War. Avalon's Lord has gained resources specifically for his civilization and has acquired the ability to create a base of operations in his territory. Suitable base detected. Designation: defunct shelter. Request if Lord wishes to reactivate shelter. Confirm?"

"Clarify if Shelter will be under attack or discovered by hostile forces if reactivated," I asked calmly. None of this seemed overwhelming in that moment. I didn't know why. But instead, something felt right, that hadn't in a very long time.

"Negative," Avalon informed. *"Shelter was warded upon creation. Hostile forces will suffer severe penalties detecting its existence and even greater penalties attempting to enter its boundaries. Current hostile forces do not have sufficient ability to perceive or enter Avalon's designated shelter. Confirm activation?"*

"Yes," I said. "In that case Avalon's Lord, the Challenger Wes Malcolm, hereby grants permission to reactivate Avalon's shelter."

"Permission granted. Protocol designated In Case Of Trouble activating. Shelter will be online in twelve to forty-eight hours."

"Good," I said. It would probably take me that long to get everyone together anyway, because I knew there were far more prisoners here than the ones in that one room. "Avalon, confirm that Fair Folk Breena is still located near the shelter, and is still safe."

"Confirmation that Fair Folk Lady Breena is alive and unharmed and located near protocol site In Case Of Trouble. Hostile forces detected in the area. Recommended that Avalon's Lord direct assistance to said location."

"Agreed," I said. "That's definitely top priority. So is Lady Guineve. Confirm her location and status."

"Lady Guineve is located in her bonded lake. Status: Damaged, recovering. Currently not under attack. Hostile forces are also in the area but are unable to interact with the Lady of the Mists. Hostile forces are currently greater in power and number than those surrounding Lady Breena."

"Noted. So they're both hiding and need help. I'll make it happen."

"New Cosmic event noted," Avalon continued. *"An undiscovered Challenge has been overcome on Avalon. Redefining parameters previously considered impossible. Parameters include 1: victory over an Umbra Lord in single combat (Contention: records indicate possibility of this being a second occurrence), 2: recovery of a devoured Individual from an Umbra Lord, 3: the revival and existence of a second Starsown. Detecting common thread of all three parameters to be Challenger Wes Malcolm. Event has caused rediscovery of Universal Law, Specification:* ***All is Not Lost****. Previously Dead Races are now considered possible candidates for Resurrection. Previously ruined civilizations are considered possible candidates for Renaissance. Previously doomed individuals are considered as possible recipients for Deliverance. Update: Deliverance already occurring this century in Defunct Horde Pit located in the Woadlands, and in battle with Umbra Lord Cavus at unspecified location. Avalon recognizes Challenger Wes Malcolm as under assistance of rediscovered Universal Law* ***All is Not Lost****. Patron suspected."*

All is not Lost...

Those words whispered over and over, bouncing around my heart and soul and restored mind.

All is not Lost...

Images of me losing control of my body, gaining it back, losing it again, and once more gaining it back.

All is not Lost...

My mother's face flashed in my mind. Along with that of my sister and my friends. Along with Guineve, and Breena, and Stell.

All is not Lost...

Other memories of events hidden until now flashing into my mind, the source behind knowledge I never knew I had, until Stell had pointed it out.

All is not Lost...

Faces other than mine, dreams other than mine, whispering at the corner of my soul, begging for rescue, and a chance to be again.

All is not Lost...

Cities and people scattered among many different worlds, looking up in time to see world-ending disasters, disasters that could be prevented as long as one person—just one—chose to be at the right place at the right time.

All is not Lost...

Little lights that were once people, thrashing inside a hungry tyrant's body, suddenly aware that if deliverance can come to one, it can come to others.

All is not Lost...

An entire planet, one I had never seen before, completely shrouded in world-damning darkness. With a tiny, narrow opening that someone brave enough to storm the gates of hell could use to bring deliverance.

All is not Lost...All is not Lost...

"All is not Lost," I finally said aloud.

Something inside of me moved.

Initial stages of Saga formed, my mind-screen noted. *Challenger is embarking on the Saga of the Unconquered Hero. First stage: Defiant Heart.*

Challenger has also taken a step on the Path of Kings.

Inherent Changes are forming.

My hand was gripping a door-bar. On the other side were former prisoners. On the other side were my new people. My new sons. My new daughters. My new subjects.

And they were not lost.

"*Further information is available,*" Avalon intoned. *"Requesting confirmation to continue sharing logs or to perform other tasks instead."*

"Negative on sharing further information for now," I told Avalon. "Allow me time to process previous information while you handle normal directives. However, as Lord, I have a new directive: maintain control of orbit, because I am about to risk knocking it free."

"Confirmed. Attempting to secure planetary orbit."

"Good," I said.

And with that, I grabbed the mountain that had been sitting on my soul for over two years on Earth, and over fifty years here, and with one inner hand, I lifted.

And *pushed.*

ALSO BY NATHAN THOMPSON

Challenger's Call

Brace For the Wolves

Woad Children

Lighting Distant Shores

False Skies

Knives in the Night

Rival Crowns

Soul Ship

First Orbit

Soul Shelter

Anchor Knight

Corefire

AFTERWORD

Hello everyone! I hope you enjoyed my book and I really appreciate you reading up to this point. This is my first published work, so I would love for you to leave feedback on a review on Amazon, especially if you liked it. Reviews are the lifeblood of indie authors like me, and in my case, I would like to know if my work is good enough to deserve a second book. Please let me know what you think!

You can also join my facebook page for more information on dates for my work and also meet other people who read my stories. It will be my primary method of communication, so that no one gets lots of email spam. Barring that, you can also follow me on Amazon by clicking the button here. I can also be contacted at the email address nathan.thompson.writer.email@gmail.com

Thanks to all the people that helped me edit my book: Stephen Whaley, Jennifer Haviland, Corey Grimes, Patrick Harris, Ege Arikan, Ezben Gerardo, Doyle Williams, Robert Peterson, Jesse and Ruth Campos, Bill and Beth Thompson, Regina Benton, Max Madlaw, Kegan Hall and Jordan Steinberg. I greatly appreciate both your feedback and time spent reading my earliest drafts. Special thanks also to my editor, Celestian Rince, who has worked figurative and probably literal magic on this story.

Special thanks to writers Andy Peloquin (author of the dark fantasy Hero of Darkness Trilogy among other books) and Michael-Scott Earle (author of LitRPG Lion's Quest as well as many other books) for being both generous with their valuable time and gracious with my floundering questions about publishing a book. Both are phenomenal writers in their own right, and if you enjoy their listed genres you will certainly enjoy their works as well. You can find the first book of Andy Peloquin's Hero of Darkness here.

LITRPG is a growing genre, and there are a number of places to find more books like mine. One of those is the facebook group, LITRPG Books. You can find both authors and fellow readers there, who can help you discover this genre. https://www.facebook.com/groups/LitRPG.books/

Gamelit is also a growing genre in fantasy, mixing elements like video or tabletop gaming into literary form, albeit with slightly less mechanics than what LitRPG has. To learn more about Gamelit, talk to authors including myself, and just have an awesome time, you can join the Gamelit facebook Group here: https://www.facebook.com/groups/LitRPGsociety/

www.ingramcontent.com/pod-product-compliance
Lightning Source LLC
Chambersburg PA
CBHW020931310726
48980CB00007B/723/J
* 9 7 8 0 5 7 8 3 4 6 1 6 8 *